THE CHILDREN OF THE GODS SERIES BOOKS 26-28

DARK DREAM TRILOGY

I. T. LUCAS

Copyright © 2021 by I. T. Lucas

All rights reserved.
No part of this book may be reproduced in any form or by any electronic or mechanical means, including information storage and retrieval systems, without written permission from the author, except for the use of brief quotations in a book review.

NOTE FROM THE AUTHOR:
Dark Dream Trilogy is a work of fiction!
Names, characters, places and incidents are products of the author's imagination or are used fictitiously and are not to be construed as real. Any similarity to actual persons, organizations and/or events is purely coincidental.

CONTENTS

DARK DREAM'S TEMPTATION

Prelude	3
1. Julian	9
2. Ella	12
3. Kian	16
4. Ella	19
5. Vivian	24
6. Ella	27
7. Julian	30
8. Ella	34
9. Vivian	37
10. Magnus	41
11. Syssi	44
12. Julian	47
13. Ella	50
14. Kian	53
15. Ella	57
16. Turner	61
17. Vivian	64
18. Ella	67
19. Syssi	70
20. Kian	73
21. Julian	76
22. Losham	79
23. Julian	82
24. Ella	85
25. Tessa	88
26. Ella	91
27. Julian	94
28. Ella	97
29. Vivian	100
30. Ella	103
31. Carol	107

32. Ella	110
33. Losham	113
34. Ella	116
35. Kian	119
36. Ella	122
37. Julian	125
38. Ella	128
39. Julian	131
40. Ella	134
41. Julian	137
42. Ella	140
43. Julian	143
44. Ella	147
45. Ella	151
46. Julian	155
47. Ella	158
48. Julian	161
49. Ella	165
50. Vivian	169
51. Ella	172
52. Amanda	177
53. Ella	179
54. Julian	182
55. Ella	184
56. Kian	187
57. Ella	190

DARK DREAM'S UNRAVELING

1. Ella	195
2. Julian	199
3. Ella	203
4. Julian	207
5. Ella	211
6. Julian	215
7. Kian	218
8. Ella	222
9. Julian	225
10. Ella	228
11. Julian	231
12. Ella	235

13. Kian	239
14. Ella	242
15. Kian	245
16. Julian	247
17. Ella	251
18. Magnus	254
19. Ella	258
20. Kian	261
21. Dalhu	264
22. Julian	268
23. Ella	271
24. Magnus	274
25. Ella	277
26. Julian	281
27. Ella	285
28. Julian	290
29. Ella	293
30. Julian	296
31. Ella	299
32. Kian	302
33. Syssi	305
34. Kian	308
35. Ella	311
36. Carol	315
37. Magnus	318
38. Ella	321
39. Kian	324
40. Ella	327
41. Julian	330
42. Ella	333
43. Julian	336
44. Ella	339
45. Ella	344
46. Ella	347
47. Julian	351
48. Ella	354
49. Julian	357
50. Ella	360
51. Julian	363
52. Ella	366
53. Julian	370

54. Ella — 373
55. Julian — 377
56. Ella — 380

DARK DREAM'S TRAP

1. Julian — 387
2. Ella — 391
3. Bridget — 394
4. Losham — 397
5. Ella — 399
6. Losham — 403
7. Ella — 406
8. Bridget — 410
9. Turner — 412
10. Ella — 415
11. Julian — 418
12. Bridget — 421
13. Ella — 425
14. Julian — 429
15. Ella — 433
16. Ella — 436
17. Kian — 439
18. Julian — 442
19. Ella — 445
20. Vivian — 448
21. Ella — 451
22. Julian — 454
23. Ella — 457
24. Amanda — 461
25. Julian — 465
26. Ella — 467
27. Ella — 470
28. Vivian — 473
29. Ella — 476
30. Julian — 479
31. Ella — 482
32. Kian — 485
33. Julian — 488
34. Ella — 491
35. Julian — 494

36. Ella	497
37. Vivian	499
38. Ella	502
39. Turner	505
40. Ella	508
41. Julian	511
42. Ella	513
43. Magnus	516
44. Ella	518
45. Vivian	521
46. Ella	524
47. Magnus	526
48. Ella	529
49. Turner	532
50. Ella	534
51. Turner	537
52. Ella	539
53. Turner	541
54. Julian	543
55. Ella	546
56. Julian	549
57. Ella	551
58. Julian	554
59. Vivian	557
60. Ella	559
61. Julian	561
62. Ella	563
63. Julian	566
64. Ella	569
65. Julian	571
66. Kian	573
67. Ella	575
Dark Prince Excerpt	581
The Children of the Gods Series	591
The Perfect Match Series	601
Also by I. T. Lucas	603
FOR EXCLUSIVE PEEKS	607

DARK DREAM'S TEMPTATION

PRELUDE

"Ella? Are you even listening?"

Despite how fascinated she was by Julian's story, Ella was drifting off. With the hum of the private jet's engines lulling her to sleep, she was fighting a losing battle with her eyelids. They simply refused to stay up no matter how hard she tried to stay awake and hear more about the mythological gods, their immortal offspring, the immortals' split into two warring factions, and their millennia-long fight over humanity's future.

It was a riveting tale, especially since it pertained to her and finally explained her telepathic ability. According to Julian, she was a descendant of the gods and a carrier of their godly genes.

At any other time, Ella would've hung on Julian's every word. But not today, not after what she'd been through.

"I'm sorry, Julian, but I can't keep my eyes open."

"I understand." He looked disappointed. "It's too much information for you to absorb, especially so soon after all of that excitement. You need to rest."

A wave of guilt washed over Ella.

She owed her freedom to Julian. The least she could do was keep her eyes open and listen to him as he revealed his most guarded secrets to her.

Without his help, Ella would've still belonged to the Russian mafia boss who'd bought her, his wife for the rest of her freaking life and a mother at eighteen.

She'd been spared the first part; however, a pregnancy was still a possibility.

Her period was a week late. She could be carrying Gorchenco's child.

But then, stress had caused delays before, and Ella prayed it was the culprit this time as well.

She had to believe that Fate had arranged the chance meeting between Julian and her mother for a reason. After that, and then all the trouble that went into rescuing Ella, it didn't make sense that Fate would abandon her now.

What also didn't make sense was that one conversation with a woman he'd met at a psychic convention had such a profound effect on Julian, prompting him to mobilize his entire clan to help Vivian rescue her daughter.

He must've done one hell of a sales job convincing them to take on a powerful Russian mafia boss. Especially since Gorchenco was known as paranoid about security and never stayed in one place for more than a couple of days. Planning a rescue around that had been difficult and costly in the extreme.

She owed Julian her life.

If she'd stayed with the Russian, Ella would have died. Either literally or figuratively. Her soul would've shriveled and withered away.

"It's not that I don't find your story interesting. It's fascinating, and I don't want to miss any detail. But I'm just so damn tired." She smiled apologetically. "If I had known that the part of a damsel in distress getting rescued was such an exhausting job, I would've never signed up for that movie."

Julian's expression softened. "You're crashing from the adrenaline high. It's perfectly normal. Getting away from an exploding gas tanker will do that to a person."

"Yeah, I guess." Even though she'd known that the explosion had been staged and perfectly timed, it had still been a terrifying experience.

But it was more than that.

The rescue had been a *Mission Impossible* style operation, and its complexity and perfection of execution had been awe-inspiring, but that was just the last straw, the explosive climax that had come on the heels of a traumatic month.

She wasn't a doctor like Julian, but Ella could figure it out on her own.

Ever since her ordeal had begun, her stress levels had been sky-high, and her body had gotten used to operating on that super-charged fuel. Now that the reasons for her flight-or-fight response were gone, she was deflating like an overblown balloon.

God, she could imagine staying in bed for two weeks straight with her mom coddling her like a little girl.

Yeah, that sounded like a plan.

Despite it all having been her own fault, Ella deserved a little tender loving care after what she'd been through.

Her only crime had been stupidity, and the price she'd paid was too high for that. Nevertheless, it could have been even worse.

If only she hadn't been so gullible.

She should never have fallen for Romeo and gone with him to New York. Except, in her worst nightmares, Ella could not have imagined something like that happening to her. Suburban girls from good homes just didn't get lured into a trap by pretend boyfriends and sold into sexual slavery.

"The seats recline all the way." Julian got up and opened an overhead compartment. "You can take a nap until we land."

He pulled out a folded blanket and a pillow, then waited for her to turn the seat into a flat surface. When she was ready, he handed her the pillow and put the blanket over her. "We should be landing in about two hours."

"Thank you. You're an angel."

"You're welcome."

Gazing at her for a long moment, Julian looked like he wanted to tuck the blanket around her or kiss her, but he did neither.

Instead, he raked his fingers through his hair. "I'll wake you up when we start the descent."

What a sweet guy.

Her guardian angel.

Gorgeous, kind, and a doctor, Julian was too good to be true, but she was too tired to speculate as to his motives. Whatever they were, they couldn't be worse than Romeo's. Most likely, Julian was precisely who he seemed to be.

Except, Ella was never again going to trust anyone implicitly.

Curling up on her side, she tucked the pillow under her cheek and closed her eyes. As Yamanu started humming another tune, a small smile curled her lips. Was he singing for her?

It was nice of him. But she didn't need a lullaby. In no time, Ella was dreaming.

She was in a cemetery?

That was odd. What was she doing there?

Who'd died?

"You did." A man appeared next to her, his face hidden behind a huge bouquet of red roses.

Turning to look at the tombstone that they were both standing in front of, she read the inscription on the granite slab. Most of it was written in the Cyrillic script which she couldn't decipher, but the name of the deceased was written in English.

Ella Gorchenco.

Cool, her subconscious had provided burial for her sham of a marriage.

But who was the guy with the roses?

As if moving in slow motion, he took a step forward, bent to put the bouquet down, and then straightened and turned to her.

The moment she saw his face, Ella sucked in a breath and prepared to scream.

He lifted both hands. "I come in peace. Please don't scream murder."

"What are you doing in my dreams, Logan, or rather nightmares?"

He shrugged. "I'm a figment of your subconscious."

"Right. And my subconscious also conjured the kiss you forced on me the other night?"

Smirking, he leaned forward and got in her face. "But that didn't really happen, did it? The lunch meeting with your former fiancé was the only time we've actually met in person, and we've done nothing but talk. The rest was created by your mind." He waggled his brows. "Maybe you fancy me? Could I be the mysterious and dangerous stranger that you want to explore your dark side with?"

Hmm. There was something to that.

She was both attracted and repulsed by Logan, and it wasn't even about his good looks, although he was one of the most striking men she'd ever met. The other being Julian. But where Julian seemed to be pure light and goodness, Logan was the opposite.

One was her Jedi Knight, and the other the Sith Lord.

The question was, who was she?

The way she was feeling now, Julian's light was almost too bright for her. He belonged to a universe she was no longer a member of. Maybe in time she would feel worthy of someone like him, but not yet.

Logan's pull, on the other hand, was as undeniable as it was disturbing. Something about his darkness resonated with her.

Like recognizing like.

Ella would've never tolerated the presence of the real Logan. He was too scary and too intense. But in her dreams, he posed no threat to her.

After all, if he did something she wasn't happy with, she could always wake up.

Pushing his hands into his pockets, Logan started walking. "By the way, congratulations on your escape. You must have really powerful friends."

Ella followed him, compelled to keep the conversation going. "It seems that I do. Although I've never met any of them before. They are my mother's friends. Not mine."

Logan slowed down, waiting for her to catch up to him. "Gorchenco is probably heartbroken."

"Yeah, I know. And I hate feeling guilty for making him go through the grief. But it's his fault. He should never have bought me."

"He saved you from a much worse fate. Anyone else would've raped you on day one."

Ugh, that was blunt. Dream Logan was just as rough around the edges as the real one.

"That's true. But if not for Gorchenco, Stefano would have never hunted me down. After seeing my picture in a magazine and realizing that I looked exactly like the Russian's long-lost love, Stefano seized the opportunity to make some quick money. He knew Dimitri would pay any price to get her back from beyond the grave, even knowing he was buying only a lookalike."

For some reason, Logan seemed fascinated by her story as if he was hearing it for the first time. The real Logan had probably never heard it, but since he was a figment of her imagination, he should not have looked so surprised.

Except the mind was a strange thing, creating realistic scenarios where she could pretend that she was having a conversation with the real Logan.

In a way, it was liberating.

She could tell him her darkest thoughts and let her subconscious react to them. There was no need to pretend that she was a nice girl with nothing but goodness inside of her. Maybe if she gave that dark energy an outlet, she could get rid of it.

"Gorchenco seemed enamored with you, Ella, not with the ghost of his long-lost love."

She shrugged. "What is it to you? You wanted to buy me from him."

Logan laughed. "I did. I still want you."

Ella stopped and turned to him. "Why? Is it the pretty face?" She waved her hand in front of her.

"That too, but it's not the main reason. I've had plenty of girls who were even prettier than you. But you're special. One of a kind."

Ella rolled her eyes. "Did you also lose a girlfriend who looked exactly like me?"

"No, Ella. You're one of a kind not because of what you look like but because of what you can do." He pointed to her head. "You and your mother are probably the only two in the world with such powerful telepathic ability, and that's what makes you both so special."

Ella was a much more powerful telepath than her mother. Except, she wasn't going to point it out because it wasn't important. Besides, she didn't like to boast.

1

JULIAN

*A*fter the limo with Ella and her family had left, Julian dropped his duffle bag in Turner's trunk and joined Arwel in the back seat. With Yamanu sitting shotgun, it wasn't as if he had much choice, but it was fine. His conversation with Turner could wait for later, and Arwel was good company.

Tagging along with Ella's rescue team had produced two unexpected side benefits. Julian had made friends with several of the Guardians, and he'd even made some progress with Turner.

His mother's mate was a good man with an exceptional mind, but he wasn't easy to befriend and was as warm as a calculator. This mission had brought them closer. Not close enough to start calling the guy by his given name, that was a privilege only Bridget was allowed.

But still, it was progress, and Julian wasn't going to let it fizzle away. "I'm glad you left your car here, Turner. It would've been awkward riding with Ella in the limo and intruding on the family reunion."

Turner glanced at him through the rearview mirror. "How did it go with her? I had my noise-canceling earphones on throughout the flight, but she didn't seem overly distraught to me."

Julian raked his fingers through his hair. "I think Ella was in a state of overload. In the beginning, she asked some questions, but the longer I droned on, the more her eyes glazed over, and finally she just flat out told me that she was too tired and couldn't keep her eyes open."

One thing Julian was sure of. Ella had shown absolutely no interest in him. Hopefully, it was just a side effect of what she'd been through, and not something deeper and more permanent.

He hadn't encountered a problem like that in a while. In fact, the only times he'd been rejected were when the ladies were already in committed relationships, and even then, their refusal was usually accompanied by wistful looks.

It wasn't vanity, it was just the way things were.

Being a single, handsome young doctor put him at the very top of the food chain as far as desirability went.

But maybe he'd overestimated his appeal.

Julian was kind, which he'd been told showed on his face, he was cordial, which was so ingrained in him that he couldn't be any other way, and he wasn't pushy, which just wasn't in his nature. In short, Julian was as far from a bad boy as a guy could get.

He'd never even cheated on a test.

Was Ella one of those girls who preferred jerks?

Why some women liked to be treated poorly was an inexplicable phenomenon, but during his extended stay among humans, Julian had seen it happen time and again. It wasn't just an urban legend.

"I'm sorry," Arwel said.

"What for?"

"That Ella didn't fall in love with you at first sight. I know that it was what you'd been hoping for."

Damn. Was everyone going to give him pitying looks from now on?

Julian shrugged. "That rarely happens in real life, and when it does, it's usually an infatuation or just lust. I much prefer for us to get to know each other first, and then fall in love with the person inside and not the superficial shell."

Except, he'd fallen for even less than that. Ella's damn picture had been enough to turn him into a man obsessed.

Arwel patted his shoulder. "You are right. I wish you luck." The guy didn't even try to mask the sad look in his eyes.

"Give her time." Yamanu turned his head back. "Ella has been to hell and back. You can't expect your pretty face to magically melt all that crap away. Right now, she's probably wary of men."

It would've been easier if she were. But Ella hadn't been wary of him, or Turner, or even Yamanu with his impressive height and creepy eyes. Arwel, with his ever-suffering expression, was not the type anyone felt wary of, so he didn't count.

Ella had been at ease with all of them, even friendly, and it hadn't been only a show of confidence. Her scent had been free of fear.

Being placed in the friend zone by an attractive young woman was a first for Julian, but that was precisely where Ella had put him. She'd followed him to his hotel room, borrowed his clothes, including his underwear, and had even joked about the stink that she had thought he'd left in the bathroom.

She was treating him like a brother, or a close cousin.

If he weren't an immortal with extra sharp senses, Julian might have entertained the hope that Ella was putting on an act while secretly thinking he was hot. Regrettably, though, he hadn't sniffed even a whiff of arousal from her.

But then, that was too much to expect from a girl just rescued from what had been basically sexual slavery.

Fates only knew what Gorchenco had done to her.

Perhaps she'd told her mother some of it, but it wasn't as if Julian could've asked Vivian for details. Besides, Ella probably hadn't told her mother the worst parts.

From the little he'd managed to glean of her personality, Ella believed herself to be strong and didn't like to burden anyone with her troubles.

Both were admirable qualities, but Julian had a feeling that they would be detrimental to her recovery. No one could force Ella to get psychological help if she refused it. But without it, her mental wounds would either fester or heal all wrong.

He couldn't let that happen.

Worst case scenario, he would thrall the nasty memories away, provided she agreed, of course. Julian wasn't a psychologist, but if he were in her shoes, he would never tolerate his choices being taken away from him again, no matter how good the intentions.

"I hope no one is planning a welcome home party for Ella," Arwel said. "She's not going to like it."

Turner lifted his eyes to the rearview mirror. "I know Bridget is going to be there to give her a checkup."

That was news to Julian. "Why? I already did that, and she's fine. There wasn't even a scratch on her."

Turner shook his head. "Ella might want to talk to a female doctor."

"Oh." He should've realized that.

"Kian and Syssi are going to be there too, and I'm guessing Amanda as well. But don't worry. Your mother is going to take charge of the situation and kick them out after the obligatory introductions, and welcome words are done. Bridget takes shit from no one, and that includes Kian."

Turner was right. Bridget was an assertive lady, and not just in her capacity as a doctor. His mother would take care of Ella.

"Do you think I should be there?"

"No," Arwel and Turner said simultaneously.

"You'll just look desperate," Turner said.

Arwel waved a dismissive hand. "It's not about that. Ella needs space to breathe and time to recuperate. You need to be patient, Julian. When she's ready, she'll come to you."

2

ELLA

Squashed in the back seat of the limousine between her mother and her brother, Ella ran her hand over the fabric of her jeans. They were stretchy, comfortable, and probably had cost no more than thirty bucks. They felt wonderful.

Even though there were panties in the paper bag her mother had brought, Ella was still wearing Julian's boxer briefs. They were roomy. That's why. And the panties her mother bought were too skimpy.

The first chance she got, Ella was going to buy a pack of boy shorts that were just as comfy as Julian's.

"Tell me more about the village, Mom," she said, mainly to stop her mother's sniffling. "Where is it?"

They'd had their cry, but enough was enough.

"Somewhere in the Los Angeles area. We are not supposed to know exactly where it is. The limo's windows will turn opaque when we get near it, and the car will switch to autonomous driving."

"It's so cool," Parker said. "Not even Magnus knows where the village is. So, if the bad guys catch anyone, they can't torture the information out of us."

Ella grimaced. "The things you consider cool are weird. Is it really that dangerous to be an immortal?"

"To us, it is," Magnus said. "We need to hide from humans and from our enemies alike. Though for different reasons."

On the plane, Julian had given her an abbreviated history lesson, so she knew about the Devout Order of Mortdh, or Doomers as they were called for short. She also remembered the love story that had started the conflict between the two groups of immortals, but many of the other details were fuzzy, probably because she hadn't let him finish the story and had fallen asleep.

"It's like a real village," her mother said. "In the center of it, there is a nice park with ponds and walkways, and the buildings around it house the offices and the clinic and the like. The residences are not too close together, and there is lots of greenery between them. It's like living in a park. And it's so quiet, nothing but birds chirping and crickets."

"There are no kids," Parker said, looking grim. "Just two babies. All the rest are grownups."

That was weird. "Where are all the kids? In boarding schools?"

Magnus shook his head. "I wish. The price of immortality is a very low fertility rate."

"I see." Ella's gut clenched.

She needed to get that pregnancy test as soon as possible.

Mom, is there any way we can stop at a pharmacy on the way? It was a good thing she didn't need to wait to be alone with her mother to ask.

Why? What do you need? I have tampons if it's that time of the month.

I wish. I need to get a pregnancy test.

Her mother turned to her with a pair of worried eyes. *Are you late?*

One week.

Shit.

Yeah, you could say so. I hope it's only stress. It happened before. Remember the SATs? I was supposed to get my period then but didn't because I was so stressed out before the tests.

Her mother let out a breath. *I hope you're right. But in any case. I'm sure Bridget has some in the clinic.*

Who is Bridget?

Julian's mother. She's a doctor too.

"Mom, are you and Ella talking to each other in your heads? Because if you are, it's rude."

"I'm sorry." Ella wrapped her arm around Parker's shoulders. "It was girl talk." She leaned to whisper in his ear, "I'm sure you didn't want to hear us talking about tampons."

Making a face, Parker shuddered. "No, gross. But next time wait until we get home instead of that weird staring into each other's eyes that you do. It looks creepy. I don't know how come I didn't notice it before."

Because they'd been more circumspect about it and hadn't done it often. Parker had been too young to be told about their telepathic connection. He would've blabbered about it to his friends and endangered their family.

But a lot had changed during the time Ella had been gone. Her little brother had been turned immortal, and her mother had found love with her immortal bodyguard.

Freaking unbelievable.

Now with Magnus in the house, they would have to limit their telepathic communication even more. Keeping it a secret was no longer an issue, but Parker was right, and it was rude to do it in front of other people.

Peeking from under her lashes, Ella glanced at the Guardian. No wonder her mother had fallen for him. Magnus was a handsome man, but it was more than that. He had that aura about him of someone a woman could depend on.

Then again, Ella was a lousy judge of character, so maybe she was wrong.

The Russian had been dependable too, but it came with a price no sane woman would be willing to pay. Besides, he'd bought her and coerced her into having sex with him. That was not dependable, it was despicable. She should hate him, despise him, and not feel sorry for him. He deserved the suffering he was most likely feeling right now.

Ella closed her eyes.

If only there was a way to forget the last month, erase it from her memory as if it had never happened.

She remembered Julian mentioning something about the immortals' thralling ability. It was like hypnosis that they could use on humans, but some were immune to it. Russians in particular, which was one of the reasons her rescue had been so complicated. The Guardians, as the clan's fighters were called, couldn't just assume that they could thrall Gorchenco and his people. They had to use more mundane methods to get her out.

Was that also the reason Parker had volunteered to transition first, or was she confusing the stories?

Ella tightened her arm around her brother's slim shoulders. "So, you're an immortal now, eh?"

"Not yet. But I'm going to be. Doctor Bridget says that my body can heal faster and better already, but it's not at full power yet. I need to grow my fangs and venom glands first, and she says it can take six months or more."

"Was it difficult?"

"The fight?"

Ella frowned. Julian had said that Parker had been brave to volunteer to go first so she and her mother wouldn't have to rush into it. But when she'd asked him what was involved in a Dormant's activation, Julian had started telling her the entire history from the beginning of civilization, and then she'd fallen asleep.

"What do you mean by a fight?" she asked. "Julian didn't explain how it works."

Squaring his shoulders, Parker lifted his chin. "I had to fight an immortal male. But they didn't have anyone my age, so I had to fight Jackson who is nineteen and really strong. But I head-butted him, and he almost fell on his ass, but because he's immortal and has great reflexes, he didn't, and he came after me. I was a little scared, but it was okay. The bite didn't hurt so bad. And after that, when the venom hit, I was so loopy that I saw stars." He chuckled. "I didn't just see them, I flew by them. It was like a hallucinogenic trip."

Ella waved a dismissive hand. "Like you would know how that feels." But then the rest of what he'd said registered. "Hold on one sec. Why did that Jackson guy bite you? Is that some warped part of a coming of age ceremony?"

"It is, but the bite is what induces the transition. The venom is what activates the dormant genes."

Now Julian's comment about Parker's bravery made sense. It must have been really scary.

"But why did you have to fight him first? Couldn't he just bite you and be done with it? Or is that the ceremonial part?"

"In order for the fangs to elongate and the venom glands to produce venom, immortal males need to turn aggressive," Magnus said. "That's what the fight is for."

"It's why I head-butted Jackson. He didn't see it coming." Parker sounded smug. "And that is also why Magnus couldn't induce me. He likes me too much."

3

KIAN

"Do you think Gorchenco will buy it?" Kian asked after Turner was done with his update.

"I wouldn't if it were me, and given his security measures, it seems that we think alike. So no, I don't think he is going to buy it. But proving it isn't true is another thing altogether. He won't find anything no matter how much he digs."

Kian wished he could share Turner's confidence. But then he had no reason to doubt him either. In matters of this kind, he should rely on the guy's expertise and not on his gut.

Except, his gut refused to calm down.

"I don't want Ella leaving the village until we can ascertain it's safe. It will take a long time before Gorchenco concedes defeat and stops looking for her."

"Couldn't agree more." Turner reached into his pocket and pulled out a diamond ring that made the one Kian had gotten Syssi look small and modest.

"This is a donation from Ella. Or rather Gorchenco." He put it on Kian's desk.

"What do you want me to do with it?"

Turner shrugged. "Ella suggested that we use it to cover the cost of her rescue and finance others."

Kian lifted the ring and turned on his desk lamp. "I'm no great expert, but this looks flawless to me. It's worth a fortune, but who are we going to sell it to? It's probably one of a kind and easily traceable."

"I can think of a few potential buyers. My friend Arturo might be interested. Not necessarily to keep it for himself or give to his wife, but to sell it to some rich sheik or one of the new Asian billionaires. Those are the kinds of people we don't have access to, but he does."

"Would he keep the source confidential?"

"Of course. He wouldn't have been in business for so long if he didn't. The rules of conduct are even stricter for the black-market traders than they are for the legit ones."

Kian chuckled. "I bet. Legitimate business people don't kill each other for bending the rules."

"Sometimes they do."

Handing the ring back to Turner, Kian leaned back in his chair and crossed his arms over his chest. "How are you going to get it to him? It's not like you can mail it or entrust someone to deliver it."

Turner put it back in his pocket. "First I need to check if he's interested. Then I'll figure out the logistics."

"Just make sure to tell him not to offer it to any Russians. Imagine Gorchenco buying back his own ring."

"I don't see how that's a problem. Anyone could've taken the ring off Ella and sold it on the black market. If he wants to buy it back for sentimental reasons, so be it."

Kian shook his head. "I'll feel better knowing it's not getting back to him."

"As you wish. But I'm sure you can put the proceeds to good use, and it might be difficult to move."

"No doubt about it. But let's see how it goes first. If it doesn't sell, I'll reconsider."

Since they'd started the new operation, Kian had found himself making business decisions based on costs more than anything else.

Which meant that promising technologies didn't get funding when they required too much capital to get going, and that wasn't good. But as hard as he tried, and as many hours as he worked, Kian couldn't increase profits fast enough to cover the ever-increasing costs of their humanitarian initiative.

"Julian and I had an interesting conversation," Turner said. "Apparently, Vanessa is running out of space in the sanctuary. The idea of a halfway house came up."

Kian shook his head. "Unless we can find a donor to finance it, I'm afraid it will have to wait. We will need to buy a place and hire people to run it. I'm doing my best to keep all the balls up in the air, but I'm not a magician."

"The proceeds from the sale of this ring will cover several buildings. And as for hiring people, you may get away with only two paid staffers, and the rest could be done by volunteers."

"And where do you suggest that I get those?"

Turner waved his hand in an arc. "You have an entire clan of people who are getting paid every month just for breathing. You can demand that in exchange for getting their share of the clan's profits, they volunteer a few days a month at the halfway house."

The idea had merit, but it wasn't going to be an easy sell. Perhaps Bridget could pull off the same kind of miracle convincing the civilians to volunteer as she'd done convincing the Guardians to come back from retirement.

"If I do that, I risk alienating my clan members. There is a limit to what people are willing to do for a cause, no matter how worthy."

Turner nodded. "It's just an idea. What you do with it is your decision."

"Right. Let's run it by Bridget and see what she thinks. Of the three of us, she is probably the only one with a good grasp on what our people are willing or not willing to give up. I never expected her to be so successful with luring back the retired Guardians. She pulled a fucking miracle."

The satisfied grin on Turner's face was a rare sight. "Bridget is the best. You made a good choice putting her in charge of this operation."

"Indeed."

4

ELLA

"Someone pinch me," Ella said when they walked out of the entry pavilion. "This is unreal."

As the glass doors slid open onto the picturesque grounds of the village, a gentle breeze brought with it the smell of freshly-cut grass. To see all that lush greenery was as surreal as what it had taken to get up there.

Parker hadn't been kidding about the clan's use of futuristic technology. He'd warned Ella about the limousine's windows getting opaque, but he hadn't said anything about driving into the belly of a mountain and then taking an elevator ride up to the surface.

It was like a scene from a sci-fi movie.

Men in Black came to mind. Was she going to open a locker door and discover an entire civilization living there too?

"It's beautiful, isn't it?" Vivian wrapped her arm around Ella's waist. "Just listen to how quiet it is. From up here, you can't even hear the cars driving down on the road below. That's what I call true serenity."

"Or *The Twilight Zone*." Ella looked around.

The village was beautiful, but it seemed deserted. Other than the chirping of birds, it was devoid of human or animal sounds.

Even Gorchenco's Russian estate hadn't been this quiet. There had been gardeners with their air blowers and grass mowers, people talking and arguing, dogs barking, horses neighing, and even the occasional sheep bleating. Being isolated and far away from the city didn't mean it was devoid of life.

She turned to Magnus. "Where is everyone?"

"The café is closed at this time, so there is no reason for anyone to be out and about. I just hope they are not in our house preparing a welcome party for you." His grimace didn't bode well.

On the way, Magnus had said that the welcome wagon would only include

Julian's mother, the big boss and his wife, and maybe the boss's sister. Four new people she would have to smile and chitchat with were too many already. All Ella wanted was to take a shower in her own private bathroom, crawl into her own bed, and go to sleep without fear of anyone joining her.

Except, even that was too much to hope for because she might be stuck with the specter of Logan following her around in her dreams.

"I thought that only a few people were going to come."

Magnus rubbed the back of his neck. "That was what I've been told. But as you are about to discover, our clan is full of busybodies. They mean well, but it gets annoying at times."

"Don't worry about it," Parker said. "They are all very nice."

"I'm sure they are, and I'm grateful for everything the clan has done for my family and me, but I would've appreciated a softer landing."

Whatever, she would survive. She'd smile, and shake hands, and thank everyone for their help. It was the least she could do. Eventually, everyone would go home, and she could get that shower she was yearning for.

"This is our house." Her mother pointed. "I don't see a crowd, so that's a good sign."

The door opened, and a short redhead stepped out, smiling and waving. "Welcome to the village, Ella."

"That's Bridget, Julian's mom," Parker said.

She looked like his sister, but Julian had warned Ella that everyone looked about the same age, although they weren't. For some reason, she found it easy to make a mental switch and not assign an age to any of the immortals based on how they looked. What bothered her, though, was that it seemed that the village was like a commune, and people walked into each other's homes even when the owner wasn't there.

"Is it always like this here?"

Her mother frowned. "What do you mean?"

"People going into other people's houses whether they are invited or not?"

Vivian paled and leaned to whisper in her ear. "Didn't Julian tell you about their exceptional hearing? Your comment was very rude."

He had, but she'd forgotten about it. "I didn't mean for it to sound like that. I'm just curious how things work here."

Bridget walked down the steps and offered Ella her hand. "Normally, no. We don't go into each other's houses uninvited. But your mother allowed us to wait for you here." She clapped Ella on the back. "Don't worry, for now it's only me. Kian, Syssi, and Amanda are coming a little later, but none of us is going to stay long. I know you must be tired after all of that excitement and can't wait to get in bed."

Feeling like a jerk, Ella nodded. "Thank you for organizing my rescue. Julian told me that you were in charge of the entire operation."

"I'm the one who coordinates everything. But the actual missions are Turner's department. He plans them, although normally he doesn't join the teams on the ground."

"Come on, Ella." Parker waved her in from the door. "I want you to see my room."

"I'll take Scarlet for a short walk." Magnus patted the dog's head. "She was too shy to do her business with Ella around."

Scarlet adored Parker, but she seemed suspicious of the newcomer joining her family. Or maybe she just didn't like Ella for some reason.

Whatever, the dog liking her was the least of her concerns. Ella had an entire village of immortals to befriend.

Not yet, though. Maybe after two or three weeks of hibernation.

"That's a gorgeous house," she said as she entered. "Did it come like that? No offense, but I know it's not your work."

It was evident that the decor had been done by a professional. Everything was high-quality and perfectly coordinated, but it wasn't ostentatious or over the top like Gorchenco's homes. It felt cozy and homey and nothing like the estates Ella had been living in lately.

Thank God for that.

She wanted no reminders.

No more fancy houses, no more limousine rides, and no more private jets with bedrooms and a staff of servants on hand.

"Thank you for the non-compliment," Vivian said. "But you're right. All the homes in the village are furnished and decorated by the clan's interior designer, and they come ready and supplied with everything. And I mean *everything*. There was even food in the fridge."

"Excuse me," Bridget said when her phone rang. "I'll take this outside."

As Bridget stepped out into the backyard, Vivian beckoned Ella to follow her to the kitchen. "Just look at this cookware. It's almost a shame to use it. I would hate for these beautiful pots and pans to get scorch marks."

"So why cook if we can get takeout?" Parker asked.

Vivian ruffled his hair. "Your brother has developed a taste for restaurant food. He treats what I make like punishment."

"No, I don't. I just like eating tasty food."

Ella rolled her eyes. "I love you, but you're such a dweeb."

As the door opened and Magnus entered with Scarlet, the dog rushed in and headed straight for Ella, then stopped a couple of feet away from her and sat back on her haunches.

It seemed that Scarlet had changed her mind and was ready to be friends.

"She wants you to pat her," Parker said.

Scarlet tilted her head as if saying, "What are you waiting for? I'm ready to be friends with you."

Crouching in front of her, Ella reached with her hand, letting Scarlet sniff it first. She knew the ice had been broken when the dog licked her hand and started wagging her tail.

"You're such a good girl." Ella patted her solid head. "How old is she?"

"A little over five months. But she's big for her age." Magnus sounded like a proud father.

As Bridget opened the living room's sliding glass doors, Scarlet bounded outside, and a moment later returned with a rubber ball between her teeth.

"That thing doesn't belong in the house, and you know it!" Vivian pointed to the backyard.

Tail tucked between her legs, Scarlet trotted out.

It was such a homey scene that it was almost surreal.

Ella felt as if she'd crossed into an alternate reality. Even though she was in a secret village whose occupants were immortals, everything seemed so normal here, so familiar.

After having everything taken away from her, she had her mother and brother back, and even a dog, and a future stepfather who seemed like an awesome guy.

So why the hell did she feel like an intruder in someone else's life?

"Do you want to meet Merlin?" Parker asked. "He's our only neighbor, and he's the coolest guy ever. He's teaching me magic tricks."

Ella pushed up to her feet. "Maybe some other time."

"Come see your room," Vivian threaded her arm through hers, and then glanced at Bridget. "Do you want to see what I've done with it?"

Ella didn't need to communicate with her mother telepathically to know what this was about, and apparently neither did Bridget.

"Sure. Lead the way." The doctor waved her hand.

The room was much bigger than the one she had in her old house, and it was better furnished and decorated, but Ella missed her old room and the innocence she'd left behind there.

Bridget closed the door and motioned for Ella to sit on the bed. "Julian said that you weren't injured during the rescue. Is there anything else you'd like me to check on?"

Ella nodded. "I need a pregnancy test," she whispered. "I'm late."

"You're not pregnant."

That was as unexpected as it was welcome. Except, Julian hadn't said anything about immortals' ability to sense early pregnancies. Then again, he had no reason to. The subject hadn't come up.

"How could you know that?"

Bridget tapped her nose. "Immortal sense of smell. The hormonal changes start right away, and I've trained myself to detect them in humans. But if you want to make sure, I can give you a kit. But since I need to take blood samples anyway, we might as well test for that too."

"Why?"

Bridget cast a quick glance at Vivian, who shook her head, saying no to Bridget's implied question.

Ella wondered what that was all about.

"Every newcomer to our village gets thorough blood work done as well as other tests."

That sounded ominous. "What tests?"

Bridget waved a dismissive hand. "Nothing to get all worked up about. Mostly it's bloodwork and measurements. Naturally, I'll also check your lungs and your heart, just to make sure everything is running like it should."

"So, it's like a physical?"

"Precisely."

"So why didn't you say so from the start? You had me scared for a moment."

"My apologies." Bridget cast her a pitying look.

Here it goes.

Up until now, no one had looked at her like that. Ella had been wondering when that would come, and she'd just gotten her answer.

As long as she acted as if she was fine, people treated her like everyone else, but the moment she showed fear, it was a reminder of what she'd been through and a catalyst for the sad faces.

The take-home lesson was clear. Fake it till you make it, or in her case, show no fear and hold your chin up.

5

VIVIAN

*B*ridget's confident assertion that Ella wasn't pregnant had done a lot to improve the girl's mood. Still, it was obvious that Ella didn't consider the doctor's nose a reliable test.

Except, Ella didn't know Bridget as well as Vivian did. Not that she and the doctor were close, but Vivian was convinced that Bridget would've never made a claim she wasn't absolutely sure of.

Bottom line, a huge weight had been lifted off her chest, and if Bridget weren't such an intimidating woman, Vivian would've hugged her and kissed her on both cheeks to express her gratitude.

There was so much to be thankful for, and the doctor had been instrumental in bringing most of it about.

Ella was back, and she seemed in better emotional shape than Vivian had expected. Not only that, her daughter and Magnus had hit it off from the first moment. There hadn't been any awkwardness between them, and they seemed to genuinely like each other.

But if everything was going so well, why was Vivian's gut still churning?

Perhaps because she was predisposed not to believe in happy endings, and when things seemed too good to be true, it was because they probably were.

Or, maybe she just didn't know how to be any other way.

Her life up till now had been one disaster after another, and her natural state was to expect the next one in line.

"I can swing by tomorrow and take the blood tests and measurements," Bridget said as she opened the door.

In the living room, Magnus and Parker were setting up the table for the late dinner Vivian had planned to have with her family. Hopefully, there was enough food to share with their guests.

"Kian and Syssi are on their way, and so is Amanda," Magnus said. "It's good that Callie prepared a welcome feast big enough to feed a unit of Guardians."

"Who is Callie?" Ella asked.

"She's the fiancée of one of the Guardians and an amateur chef." Vivian cast an apologetic glance at Bridget. "I wanted to prepare the dinner myself, but she wouldn't hear of it. She said that an occasion like this called for a celebration feast."

"And thank goodness for that," Parker said. "Callie is an awesome cook."

A loud knock preceded Amanda, who didn't wait for anyone to open the door for her. "Hello, Ella." Entering with her usual dramatic flair, she sauntered in with a smile and wide open arms. "Come give your Auntie Amanda a hug."

Ella cast Vivian a sidelong glance and mouthed, "Auntie?"

"It's a figure of speech, darling." She pulled Ella into a crushing hug. "Aren't you a beauty." She pushed her away but kept her close with a hand on her shoulder. "Let me get a good look at you." She gave Ella a thorough appraisal. "You rock the sweet girl-next-door look. Just so you know, though, if you're sick of that and desire a makeover, I'm the one to turn to."

"Thank you. In fact, I would love one. What do you think I should do to change my appearance as much as possible?"

Vivian didn't like where this was going, but Amanda seemed to side with her daughter. "We can change your hair color." She reached behind Ella, pulled the rubber band off her ponytail, and fluffed her shoulder-length hair out. "What do you think about going short? Like me."

"No," Vivian said.

"Sure," was Ella's enthusiastic response. "That's different for sure. I also like your hair color. Do you think black will look good on me?"

"No way." Vivian put her hands on her hips. "Your hair is beautiful. Why would you want to change it?"

Ella pinned her with a pair of hard eyes. "Because I want to change everything about me."

That was new. Vivian had seen Ella upset, angry, and even furious, but her eyes had always remained soft.

As she imagined what had put that hard expression on her baby's angelic face, a lump formed in her throat.

Amanda wrapped an arm around her shoulders. "Relax. We are not going to do anything today." She leaned closer and whispered in her ear, "There are all kinds of methods to exorcize demons. Some of them involve dancing naked in the woods, and some involve a pair of scissors and a box of hair dye."

"Someone is at the door," Parker said.

Vivian hadn't heard anything, but a moment later there was a knock. Undoubtedly, Parker's hearing was improving by the day.

That must be the big boss and his wife, she sent to Ella. *Kian and Syssi.*

As Magnus opened the door for the couple, Ella sucked in a breath.

"Wow, you look so much like Julian," she exclaimed.

Kian smiled. "Hello, Ella, and you look a lot like your mother."

She and Ella exchanged looks.

"I don't see it," Ella said.

Behave, Vivian sent.

Do I need to agree to everything he says?

No, but try to be polite.

I am.

"Mom," Parker said. "You're doing that thing again."

An awkward silence followed, which Syssi broke by walking up to Ella and pulling her into a quick hug. "Welcome to the clan. We are overjoyed to have you here, free at last."

"Thank you. I'm forever grateful to you and everyone who took part in getting me out. I don't know how I'll ever be able to repay you."

"You already did," Kian said.

Vivian arched a brow. What was he talking about? Was it a figure of speech? Maybe he'd meant that the joy of rescuing Ella was worth the huge effort and all the resources that had gone into it?

Somehow that didn't fit what she knew about Kian. The guy was too pragmatic to say something nice like that.

"That ring you gave Turner will finance a halfway house for the girls that are ready to graduate from the sanctuary and transition into semi-independence."

"What ring?" Parker asked.

Ella shifted from foot to foot. "The engagement ring from the Russian. I thought it was the least I could do to repay the clan for what it has done for us."

That was news to Vivian. "You didn't tell me that he gave you a ring."

"Yeah, well. It wasn't important." She shrugged. "I wasn't going to keep it anyway."

Vivian knew her daughter well enough to tell when she was being evasive. But this wasn't the time for a frank conversation. It was up to Ella to decide when she was ready to share more of what had happened to her.

Until then, Vivian would have to wait patiently.

6

ELLA

"The guy in booth four is looking at you," Maddie whispered in Ella's ear as she passed by her on the way to the kitchen. "He's cute. Do you want to take his order?"

Casting a quick glance in the guy's direction, Ella wondered if she was experiencing a *Groundhog Day* phenomenon and reliving that pivotal day.

Except, in the movie, it had happened right away and not a month later. Which meant that she was probably dreaming.

Since the guy's face and most of his body were hidden behind the diner's tall menu, all she could see were his hands holding it up. They were long-fingered and olive-toned.

If that was Romeo, and it most likely was him, she was going to empty the carafe of hot coffee on his head. After all, this was a dream, so she wouldn't get fired for it, or arrested for assaulting a customer.

It would be so satisfying.

She wondered what had happened to him and Stefano in real life. But to find that out, she would have to ask questions and bring up things she preferred to forget. Thankfully, no one had volunteered any information, and other than her mother, no one had tried to coax it out of her either.

Not yet, anyway.

The full coffee carafe heavy in her hand and an evil smirk on her lips, Ella strode toward booth four and its olive-skinned occupant.

He sensed her approach and lowered the menu. "Hello, Ella."

"Logan." The smirk dissipated and was replaced by a frown. "What are you doing in my dream again?"

He looked around as if surprised. "This is a dream? It feels so real." He smiled up at her. "You have a very vivid imagination."

"Not really." Ella sat down across from him. "I used to work in this diner, and

I remember every little detail about it. The only thing different is you. What are you doing here?"

He shrugged. "How should I know? I'm a figment of your imagination. You brought me here."

Yeah, she probably did. But why?

Was it a warning that Logan wasn't who he seemed to be, the same as Romeo? Was that why she was replaying the scene, just with a different actor?

But then Ella had no illusions as to who and what Logan was. The guy bought weapons from Gorchenco, so he was probably some sort of a mercenary or a warlord. He was dangerous and reeked of evil. Well, not literally, but figuratively.

"I don't know why I would do that. But since you are created by my subconscious, you must have an idea why we are meeting here of all places. It's not like I miss this diner."

He looked around. "Yeah, I see what you mean. It's quite drab. Where would you like to go? Is there a place you miss?"

"The beach."

Pushing up to his feet, Logan offered her a hand up. "Then let's go."

Even though she didn't like the real Logan and feared him, she took it. The moment his hand closed around hers, they were both transported to the boardwalk.

Dreams were fun that way.

"That's so cool." She pulled her hand out of his clasp. "One moment we were at the diner, and the next we are on the beach."

He smirked. "That's one of the many reasons I love dreaming. Unfortunately, I can't spend all my days sleeping."

"Yeah. You are too busy buying weapons from the Russian mafia. What do you do with them?"

"I supply my army. Technology keeps improving, and if we want to stay on top of things, we need the latest weapons."

She arched a brow. "You have an army? Are you a mercenary?"

"Not the way I see it. It depends on how you define a mercenary."

Ella thought it was self-explanatory. Mercenaries were soldiers for hire. They fought for whomever paid them.

"What's your definition?"

"A mercenary fights for money. But although I do that too, it's only to finance my people's cause. Fighters for a cause are either rebels, defenders, or conquerors. Not mercenaries."

"Which one are you? Rebel, defender, or conqueror?"

"Conqueror, of course."

Rolling her eyes, she waved a hand. "Why am I not surprised? And who or what do you intend to conquer?"

"The world."

"Naturally." She shook her head.

In books and movies, all evil masterminds wanted to rule the world. No wonder her imagination came up with that answer.

He smiled, looking actually friendly and not terrifying. "What about you? Is there anything you want to conquer?"

"My fears, mainly. And my disgust with myself."

The second part of her answer surprised her. She hadn't felt disgusted with herself when awake, not consciously anyway.

Logan seemed surprised too. "Why would you feel like that?"

"I should've resisted the Russian. I should have been braver and at least put up a fight, but I was too scared, too weak."

"To resist him would have been stupid, and you're too smart for that. You did precisely what you needed to do to survive and to eventually escape." Logan stopped walking and turned to her. "The truth is that you impress the hell out of me. Gorchenco is a smart and cautious guy, and yet you managed to fool him, lulling him into a false sense of security. Quite an achievement for an eighteen-year-old girl from the suburbs."

Well, that made her feel a little better. "Thank you. I thought so too, logically." She put a hand over her heart. "But in here, I feel icky, and nothing I do makes it better."

He tilted his head. "And what is it that you do? You've just gotten free this morning, and you expect to feel better right away?"

"Yeah, you're right. I need to give it time. It's just that I'm afraid the taint is going to stay."

Reaching for her cheek, he cupped it gently and smiled down at her. "Sweet, innocent Ella. There is nothing more boring than squeaky clean. The taint you're imagining makes you stronger and more interesting. It also makes you less fearful, not more. Once you've experienced the dark side and dealt with it, you know that you can survive it."

"Spoken like a real Sith Lord." Ella laughed and then continued in a deepened voice. "Welcome to the dark side, my young apprentice."

7

JULIAN

It was a quiet morning in the clinic, and Julian had nothing to do. In moments like this, he found it difficult to resist his obsession. Not that he'd put much effort into it.

His addiction was harmless.

Pulling out his phone, he gazed at his screensaver.

How ironic was it that he was seeing as much of Ella now as he had prior to her rescue ten days ago? Which amounted to staring at her picture longingly and trying to convince himself that all she needed was time.

Like a lovesick human teenager, he'd altered his evening running route so he could pass by her house and get a glimpse of her through the windows before the nighttime shutters came down. He'd managed to steal a few, which had only made his torment worse.

It seemed that Ella never left the house.

In case he was mistaken, Julian had asked Magnus, who'd confirmed that she was spending her days in her room, reading, or surfing the net, or just vegging in front of the television.

Had she given up on life?

Not that ten days was a long time, not even by human standards, but Julian had hoped for some interaction with Ella.

Nothing major, just a hello-how-are-you sort of thing. Heck, he would've been happy to watch her from afar.

But knowing she was so near and yet unapproachable was pure torture.

The pitying glances he was getting from everyone didn't help make him feel any better.

His life officially sucked.

Except, feeling sorry for himself because of such minor things made him feel even worse. Ella had been to hell and back, and here he was, acting as if it was all about him.

Instead of moping around, he should get busy and actually do something, like sinking his teeth into the halfway house project.

With Merlin taking over the clinic, Julian had been relegated to the role of an intern, and the truth was that even with the miscellaneous tasks Merlin was assigning to him, he didn't have much to do.

It was ten o'clock on Monday morning, and other than rearranging the medicine cabinet and checking expiration dates, Julian hadn't done one useful thing.

Staring at Ella's picture didn't count.

"Do you need me for anything today?" he asked Merlin.

As he waved Julian away, the guy didn't even lift his head from whatever he was reading. "You can take the rest of the day off. Tomorrow too. I'll have a load of things for you to do Wednesday, so don't make plans for that day."

Julian arched a brow. "Are we brewing potions again?"

On more than one occasion, he'd had the passing thought that Merlin might be nuts, believing that he was indeed a wizard who could wield magic.

Or the guy could be a genius who was really creating new natural remedies.

Merlin was trying to come up with natural ways to enhance immortals' fertility, males and females alike, but to Julian, it seemed like the guy was delving in witchcraft. Especially since he was poring over a bunch of archaic pseudo-medical books that he'd brought with him from Scotland and then brewing stinky potions from Gertrude's herbs.

He'd overheard Merlin and the nurse having long-winded discussions about the different plants she was growing in her garden and their medicinal use.

It was possible that Gertrude was just as crazy as Merlin, but if she was as sane as she appeared and was supplying ingredients for Merlin's creations, then maybe the two were onto something.

"No potions, my dear boy. I'm compiling a list of research papers that I want you to read and summarize for me. If we tackle them together, we can cover twice as much material in the same time."

"No problem. I'm all yours on Wednesday."

As he left the clinic, Julian headed to his mother's office.

Her door was open, and he walked right in. "Do you have a moment?"

She put her tablet down and smiled at him. "For you, always. What's on your mind?"

A lot, but he wasn't going to bother his mother with his unrequited love.

"I want to talk to you about the halfway house project. I would like to get it going."

She sighed. "I gave Turner's mandatory volunteering idea a lot of thought, and I believe that it's not the right approach. It will create resentment toward the entire project. With the right presentation, I'm sure I can get people to volunteer their time without conditioning their share in the clan profits on it."

"You won't get many."

Smirking, she crossed her arms over her chest. "That's what Kian said about bringing back the retired Guardians. I think I've proved that my methods work."

"They worked once. It doesn't mean they would work again. You've played your ace. Every clan member has seen your presentation. What else can you show them?"

Leaning forward, Bridget smiled. "I can show them progress. I can prepare one hell of a presentation showing them success stories, and then tell them how many more of those we could be having with their help."

That was good. His mother was a natural at manipulating people's emotions and getting them to do what she wanted.

"You missed your calling, Mom. You should've gone into politics or fundraising."

"Nah, I just know our people and what works on them."

He nodded. "Assuming that you're right and that you can rope them into volunteering, we still need an actual house."

Uncrossing her arms, she put her hands on the table. "That's Kian's department. You should talk to him."

"I'll do it right now." He got up.

"Good luck."

"Thanks."

Pausing in front of Kian's door, Julian took a deep breath before knocking and braced for a refusal.

"Come in." The boss sounded impatient.

"Do you have a moment?"

"No. But take a seat anyway. What can I help you with?"

"Did Turner talk to you about the halfway house?"

"He did." Kian put down his pen and leaned back in his chair. "Right now we don't have the funds to purchase a property. I've recently made several investments in new promising startups, which I believe will begin bringing in nice profits in a year or two. But at the moment we are at the red line. I'm not willing to dip below it."

"What about Ella's ring? Turner said that it could finance several projects."

Kian nodded. "But he hasn't sold it yet, and I'm not sure when he'll find a buyer. So, until that happens, you'll need to find some other solution."

Julian arched a brow. "Me?"

"Yes, you. It seems to me that you're passionate about this project. Make it your baby. I certainly don't have the time for it, and neither does Bridget."

Taken aback, Julian swallowed. He was a doctor, not a businessman. What did he know about raising money and purchasing properties?

"I'm not sure I'm qualified."

"You're a smart man. You'll figure it out." Kian picked his pen up, indicating that Julian's time was up.

"Thank you for the vote of confidence. I'll see what I can do."

Lifting his head, Kian cast him an amused glance. "I'm sure you'll come up with something."

I'm not sure at all.

Maybe Turner could be of help. The guy's mental gears worked at triple the average speed, if not more.

Outside of Kian's office, Julian leaned against the wall and pulled out his phone. He shot Turner a quick text. *Any idea when the ring will be sold? We need that halfway house and Kian wants me to come up with the financing.*

He didn't have to wait long for the response.

Kian is overthinking this. All you need is a down payment on a property. The rest can be financed. I can provide the down payment from my personal funds, and once the ring is sold, the clan can pay me back and pay off the mortgage.

Julian read the text twice. Could it be as simple as that?

He fired off another text. *How come Kian didn't think of that?*

Habit. He's not accustomed to the use of financing for purchasing clan properties.

That still left the remodeling and furnishing and other necessities, but that wasn't where the big money went.

Pocketing his phone, Julian smiled. This was doable. But first, he needed to find a suitable property. How did one go about that?

Kian should know. With the number of properties he was purchasing, he must have people who found them for him. Turning on his heel, Julian headed back to the boss's office.

8

ELLA

There were several advantages to having a private bathroom, Ella thought as she submerged herself in the tub's warm water. Aside from the obvious one of not having to share it with Parker so she could soak for as long as she wished, it was also a good place to hide from her well-meaning family and their expectant looks.

"Would you like to join me at the café?" Her mother.

"I can take you to the gym and show you around." Magnus.

"Do you want to take Scarlet for a walk?" Parker.

"Would you like to go to a cooking class with me?" Her mother.

And other variations on the same theme of trying to get her out of the house, or at least to interact more with her family.

With a sigh, Ella scooped two handfuls of frothy bubbles and combined them into a small mountain over her chest. Another scoop went on top, looking like a castle on top of a cliff.

If she were a princess, and her home were a castle, she wouldn't need the wicked witch to lock her up in the tower. She would choose to live there and allow no visitors. Sitting on the windowsill, she would gaze at her people living their lives down below. And when she got bored with that, she could read a book and live between its pages.

"Ella!" Parker knocked on the door.

Annoying kid.

Apparently, having his own bathroom didn't mean he was going to stop bothering her during her relaxing soak. "What do you want?"

"Do you know where the pain meds that Dr. Bridget left for me are?"

Ella pushed up to a sitting position, her mountain together with the castle on top sliding down into the water. "I put them on top of the fridge. Why? Are your fangs finally coming out?"

"I think so. I have the worst toothache ever."

Poor kid.

"I'll be out in a minute."

"I can get the meds myself."

"I know you can." In the month she'd been gone, her little brother must've grown an inch. "I just want to take a look at your gums." She got out of the tub and grabbed a towel.

'I'll be in the kitchen."

"Take two pills," she called after him before heading into her closet.

Bridget had warned them that once the fangs started coming out, the pain was going to be intense.

She'd also confirmed that Ella wasn't pregnant.

It had been such a huge relief to know that for sure. Now she could really forget about the Russian. Except, it was easier said than done. Every time someone mentioned his name, bile rose in Ella's throat.

Which was a weird reaction.

Was she suffering from a post-traumatic stress disorder?

While it had been happening, she'd dealt with it and hadn't thought it was horrible, so why such a strong reaction now when it was over?

Normally, Ella would've talked about whatever bothered her with her mom, but Vivian was already worried sick about her and didn't need more fuel thrown on top of that.

Logan would have been a better choice as someone to figure things out with. Somehow, he'd managed to lift her spirits when no one else could, maybe because he'd said that she had impressed the hell out of him.

He didn't think of her as a victim.

Logan thought of her as a fighter, a survivor, and that gave her strength, while pity made her weak.

But Logan wasn't real, and she was basically talking to herself.

Then again, self-talk was a powerful tool for shaping one's opinion about oneself, so she shouldn't feel guilty about hoping to see him in her dreams again.

Talking to her subconscious while sleeping seemed to have a therapeutic effect on her, and it didn't matter who her weird brain had chosen for the role. Although selecting Logan, of all people, must say something about her and who her psyche gravitated toward.

Except, Ella hadn't dreamt about Logan since her first night in the village, and it seemed that her subconscious had entered the same sloth mode that her conscious self had.

The therapist her mother kept harping on about could probably shed light on what was going on in her head, but Ella wasn't going to see her. Her current issues would resolve with time, the same way her grief over her father's death had.

No therapist could talk the pain away, and Ella wasn't willing to take antidepressants either.

It was like putting a bandage over a bullet wound but leaving the bullet in. From the outside, everything would seem just peachy, which would make everyone happy, but the insides would fester, eventually killing the patient.

Ella chuckled. That analogy would no longer work when she was an immortal, but there was plenty of time before she attempted that.

Instinctively, she felt she had to get better first.

With a sigh, Ella pushed her feet into a pair of flip-flops and opened the bedroom's door.

The mental break she'd taken from life had to end, even though ten days were not nearly enough for the brain reboot she needed.

It was back to putting on a smile and acting as if everything was fine.

She was a pro at that. Pretending had become second nature to her, so much so that she'd even believed in the lies she'd told herself.

She'd done it twice already—once after her father's death, and the second time with the Russian.

She could do it again.

The first two times had been necessary for her survival. This time she was going to do it for the sake of her family.

And who knew?

Maybe pretending to be okay would actually help her feel that way?

9

VIVIAN

The sun was setting, and it was getting cold, but Vivian dreaded going home. The evening walks with Magnus were a much-needed respite from the dark mood permeating their house, and as guilty as it made her feel to think like that, she wasn't ready to get back yet.

"You seem chilly." Magnus shrugged his jacket off and draped it over her shoulders.

The warmth that was trapped inside enveloped her like a cozy blanket, and when she pushed her arms into the sleeves, Vivian let out a contented sigh.

"What gave me away? The goosebumps on my arms, or the chattering teeth?"

"The goosebumps. I would've never allowed you to get so cold that your teeth chattered." He rubbed his hands over her arms.

Stretching on her tiptoes, she kissed his cheek. "My knight in a fancy suit."

"I think it's time to go back."

"Yeah, we should. It's going to be dark soon."

As they neared their house and Magnus unhooked the leash from Scarlet's collar, she loped toward the front door. The dog seemed equally excited about going out for walks as she was about coming back.

"Mom!" Parker opened the door. "My fangs are finally coming out." He fended off Scarlet, who lifted up on her hind legs and was trying to climb up his thighs. "Come take a look!"

From behind him, Ella grinned.

It was the first genuine smile Vivian had seen on her daughter's face since the day she'd been rescued.

Ella put her hand on Parker's shoulder. "The very tips are out, and they are pointy. So cute. He looks like a baby vampire."

"Let me see." Vivian hooked a finger under Parker's chin and lifted his head up to the setting sun. "Yep. I can see them."

"This calls for a celebration," Magnus said. "How about we go to a restaurant tonight?"

Vivian shook her head. "I already cooked dinner."

Ella looked relieved. Apparently, the grin didn't mean she was ready to go out yet.

Parker, on the other hand, was disappointed. "We can eat yours tomorrow."

Vivian wrapped her arms around him and kissed his soft cheek. "You don't have the teeth to eat a steak with, so what's the point? That's the only thing you order when we go out."

His old canines had fallen out on Friday, and it would be a long time before his fangs were long enough to bite into a steak again. "But even if you did, it would've hurt too much. Your gums are swollen. Did you take the pain meds Bridget gave you?"

"Yes."

"Good. I think you should stick to the mashed potatoes tonight."

"Blah. I don't like them. Why didn't you make fries?"

She patted his back. "You'll thank me once you start eating."

"I'll set the table." Ella flip-flopped to the kitchen.

Was it her imagination, or did Ella look a little more upbeat?

Perhaps she was caught up in the excitement over Parker's fangs finally coming out.

Vivian shook her head.

Her sweet baby boy was growing fangs. Reality was indeed stranger than fiction.

When the table was set, Vivian opened the warming drawer and pulled out the meatloaf and mashed potatoes she'd made before going out on a walk with Magnus.

"It's Monday," Parker said.

Ella lifted a brow. "So?"

"Mondays and Wednesdays are supposed to be steak days." He sounded so despondent that it was almost funny.

"Says who?"

"We made a deal. Each of us got to choose what we eat two days of the week, and Sundays we eat out. I guess now that you're back we need to redo the schedule. But Mondays are still steak days." He cast Vivian an accusing look. "Meatloaf is for Fridays."

"I know, sweetie. But as I explained before, you can't eat meat without canines, and your gums will hurt even when chewing something softer. I made these easy to chew dishes especially for you."

With a long-suffering sigh, Parker put a small chunk of meatloaf on his fork. "The fangs are worth it." He closed his eyes and pushed the chunk into his mouth.

"I can make you an awesome ravioli with mushrooms dish," Ella said. "It will melt in your mouth."

"I don't like mushrooms."

"Since when are you so picky?"

Vivian put her fork down and wiped her mouth with a napkin. "When we stayed at the other location, Magnus spoiled him with restaurant food takeout. Now he doesn't want to eat anything home cooked."

"I'm still good with steaks and anything else barbecued."

Ella eyed him with an evil smirk. "Oh, yeah? I can barbecue some zucchini and eggplant for you. Comes out delicious."

The banter between her kids that had used to annoy Vivian was now the best table conversation she could hope for.

It was familiar and reassuring.

"I almost forgot," Magnus said. "Roni asks what name do you want to put on your fake papers?" He reached behind him to the suit jacket he'd hung over the back of the chair. "I have a list of possible names." He pulled out a folded piece of paper and handed it to Ella.

"Can't I just make up my own?" She took the note and opened it.

"Good fake documents use the names of real people who've passed away, and in your case, it is doubly important to have the best possible. Gorchenco might be still looking for you."

Ignoring his comment about the Russian, Ella asked, "So Magnus is not your real name?"

"It is. The MacBain isn't."

"What is it then?"

"I don't have one. It's just Magnus."

"And what's Mom's fake name?"

"Victoria MacBain."

Ella glanced at the note and frowned. "I don't see MacBain on the list." She seemed disappointed.

"It's better for you and your mom not to share the same fake last name."

"Yeah, makes sense." Ella looked at the note for a long time. "I like Kelly Rubinstein, age twenty-one." She smirked. "It opens all kinds of possibilities."

As long as it got her out of the house, Vivian didn't mind Ella going to a bar and getting herself a drink or two. Anything was better than rotting away in her room for days on end.

"Indeed," Magnus said. "I'll tell Roni. Now, all we need is to get your picture."

Since the drinking age in Scotland was sixteen when accompanied by an adult and eighteen to order their own, Magnus probably hadn't suspected Ella's motive for choosing the name of a twenty-one-year-old.

"Can he wait with it for a few days? Amanda offered to give me a makeover, and I would like to take her up on that. I want the picture to look nothing like I look now."

Magnus took the note and put it back in his suit jacket's pocket. "There's no rush. For now, we can take you wherever you need to go, but if you want to get a car and drive yourself places, you'll need a driver's license."

Ella waved a dismissive hand. "I'm not in a hurry. Even with the wig and glasses, I'm still scared to leave the safety of the village."

"Even when you're with us?" Magnus asked.

"Even with you. I know he's still looking for me."

Leaning back in his chair, Magnus nodded. "Right now, Gorchenco is back in Russia, and rumors are that he's mourning the death of his young wife. But that doesn't mean that his people are not looking for you."

Vivian's eyes widened. Did Magnus say wife?

"But don't worry," he said. "We've covered our tracks well and the staging was impeccable. His people will snoop around and double-check every piece of information, and eventually, they will have to give up and accept that you are really dead."

Closing her eyes, Ella put a hand over her heart and slumped in her chair. "That would be the best news ever. I'm afraid he'll never stop looking for me."

"Because you are his wife?" Vivian bit out.

It rankled that Ella hadn't shared that information with her. Had Gorchenco forced her to marry him?

"No, not because I'm his damn wife, or was. But because he knows he'll never find another lookalike of his lost love." Ella opened her eyes and leveled them at Vivian. "Can we please never talk about this again? I'm about to barf out the meatloaf, and it's not going to be pretty."

10

MAGNUS

"Why didn't you tell me he married her?" Vivian asked when Ella excused herself and went back to her room.

"I thought you knew." Magnus rose to his feet and started collecting the dishes.

She handed him her plate. "If I did, I would've told you."

"It's not a big deal. Ella is dead to the world. That marriage is null and void. I don't know why you're so upset about it." He carried the plates to the sink.

Following him, Vivian sighed. "I don't like to put Ella and dead in the same sentence. And I'm upset that she didn't tell me about marrying Gorchenco. The only reason she wouldn't was that my daughter didn't think I could handle it."

"Don't take it too hard. It was her way of protecting her family, and it probably made her feel like she had at least some control over what was happening to her. She couldn't refuse Gorchenco, but she could choose whether to tell you or not."

His explanation seemed to mollify Vivian. Leaning against the counter, she crossed her arms over her chest. "I need to find a way to get her out of the house. Sitting in her room all day and cooking in her own juices is not doing her any good. She needs to meet people."

Magnus put the last plate in the dishwasher and closed it. "The obvious solution is to invite people over here. But you said she didn't want you to do that."

"She said she didn't want pity visits and threatened to go to her room if I invited girls I thought could become her friends. Like Tessa and Wonder. They are not much older than Ella. Sylvia too, even though she's in her mid-twenties. She's mated to Roni who's not even twenty yet."

Magnus chuckled. "Technically, Wonder is ancient." He'd told Vivian Wonder's story, but she must've forgotten.

Vivian waved a dismissive hand. "She didn't actually live for all those years, so they don't count."

As Parker walked into the kitchen and reached for his pain meds, Vivian put a hand on his shoulder. "When was the last time you took them? Bridget said no more than two every four hours."

He grimaced. "Are three and a half hours okay? My gums are killing me."

She nodded. "Maybe we should get you some topical numbing."

"Like for babies?"

"Yeah." She ruffled his hair. "You're my baby, and you're always going to be even when you're six feet tall and have a beard on that beautiful face."

He pretended to grimace, but it was more of a crooked smile. Despite protests to the contrary, the boy loved being babied by his mother.

Magnus handed him a glass of water. "Here you go, buddy. If you want, we can go over to Merlin's and ask him for that stinky stuff he makes to numb pain. If you don't mind the smell and taste of it, the paste is effective."

"I'm willing to give it a try. Do you want to go now?"

"Let me check with Merlin."

Magnus fired off a quick text to which Merlin replied with a thumbs up.

"Grab a jacket, Parker. It's getting cold outside."

The kid rolled his eyes. "It's less than a hundred feet to Merlin's house, and I can't catch a cold anymore."

"As you wish. Don't complain to me when you're shivering." Magnus turned to Vivian. "I'm going to leave Scarlet with you. Merlin has too much breakable stuff for her to get into."

The guy's house was a mess. Stacks of books were tucked into every corner, and the lab equipment was strewn over every surface. Not to mention the smell. For some reason, all of Merlin's creations stank.

Vivian kissed his cheek. "Don't take long. I'm making coffee."

When they got there, Merlin's door was open, which Magnus took to mean they were invited to just walk in.

"Wow, it stinks in here." He pinched his nose closed.

Parker looked up at him with a raised brow. "It's not so bad. I like the smell of cooking potions."

"You're a weird kid. This is okay, but your mother's meatloaf is not?"

"Smell and taste are not the same. It's like the cologne you put on. It smells good, but you wouldn't drink it, right?"

"You have a point."

"Hello, neighbors." Merlin walked into his living room, wearing purple pajamas with little white stars and moons printed on them, a long, gray house robe, and a pair of fluffy orange slippers. "I have just the thing for you, my young friend." He pulled a tube out of his robe's pocket. "Smear it all over your gums whenever they bother you."

Magnus eyed the thing suspiciously. "What's in it?"

"Just some medicinal herbs. Organically grown without the use of harmful pesticides. It's perfectly safe."

Taking a quick sniff, Magnus crinkled his nose. As a boy, he hadn't given much thought to what was in the paste. As long as it helped with the pain, he'd been willing to smear cockroach juice on his gums. But as an adult, he now knew of several herbs that although safe were not something a kid should ingest. "You sure about it?"

Merlin waved a dismissive hand. "Positive." Removing a stack of newspapers from the couch, he put them on the coffee table. "Now come sit with me and tell me how Ella is doing."

The couch, which had been brand new just a few short weeks ago, was covered in stains and burn marks.

"I would love to stay and chat, but Vivian is expecting me back home for coffee." Feeling uncomfortable about leaving right after getting what he'd come for, Magnus added, "You're more than welcome to come and join us."

Merlin grinned. "I would love to. It gets a bit lonely here in the evenings." He walked toward the door, and then glanced at them over his shoulder. "Are you coming?"

"Don't you want to change first?" Parker asked.

"No. I'm very comfortable." Merlin tightened the belt around his waist. "This will do."

Magnus shrugged. As long as the guy wasn't naked, he could wear whatever he wanted. "Let's go."

"Is Ella still staying in the house all day?" Merlin asked as they stepped out the door.

"I'm afraid so."

"It's so sad." Merlin shook his head. "Maybe I can prepare a potion for her. Something to lift her mood."

"Ella will never take anything like that," Parker said. "What we need to do is invite Julian for dinner at our house."

"Ella doesn't want anyone visiting her."

"He won't. Julian will come because you and Mom want to thank him for organizing the rescue. And then he can stay and play computer games with me."

"I don't know if he plays."

"Come on. Julian is a young dude. Of course, he plays. He can come every evening to keep me company." Parker rolled his eyes and made air quotes. "If he hangs around the house enough, Ella will get used to having him there, and maybe they'll start talking, and then maybe he'll ask her out on a date."

"The kid is a genius." Merlin patted Parker's back.

Parker shrugged. "I just know my sister. Ella is stubborn, and she wants to do things her way, but she is a nice person. She will not be rude to Julian and go hide in her room when he comes. And when she gets to know him better, she'll see that he is a really cool guy."

It sounded like a good plan, but Ella might see right through it.

Then again, it didn't matter whether she did or not. The excuse for Julian's invitation was valid, and so was him staying after dinner, especially if he and Parker seemed to hit it off, which they already had.

11

SYSSI

"Welcome to my humble abode." Merlin made an exaggerated bow, waving Syssi and Kian inside.

As usual, he was dressed in a ridiculously colorful outfit. Red skinny pants that made his slim legs look even scrawnier, and a blue sweater with little white stars that was at least three sizes too big for him. Somehow, though, it all worked for Merlin. It was his signature look.

"I still don't understand why we couldn't meet at the clinic," Kian grumbled.

Syssi smiled and gave Merlin a quick hug. "Thank you for inviting us."

It was hard to believe that the house had been brand new when Merlin moved in. Aside from the clutter, which was just staggering, the place looked like it hadn't been cleaned even once. No wonder Merlin didn't want roommates. No one would've tolerated living like that.

"Please, take a seat. I cleaned up the couch." Merlin winked. "Nothing is going to jump at you from between the cushions."

Kian wasn't amused. His lips pressed tightly together, he sat on the sofa and glared at the doctor. "This is not a social call, Merlin. I don't have time for that."

"Right."

Merlin removed a stack of books from a dining room chair, dusted it with his hand, and brought it over to face the couch. Crossing one long leg over the other, he smoothed his hand over his nearly white beard.

Syssi wondered how he could work with that thing on his face. It looked clean, but it was long and messy and, in general, beards weren't sanitary, which should have been a concern for a doctor. And since it seemed that Merlin was brewing potions in his house, that beard was also dangerous.

It could catch fire.

"You're probably wondering why I invited both of you here."

"Indeed." Kian crossed his arms over his chest.

Syssi was waiting for an explanation as well. Kian's presence wasn't really necessary, and she could've come alone.

He had promised to be there for her throughout the fertility treatments, except, knowing her husband, in addition to wanting to be supportive he wanted to make sure that she wasn't submitting herself to anything dangerous.

Kian had admitted as much, saying that she was desperate for a baby and not thinking clearly, and that Merlin was loony.

"As you can see," Merlin waved his hand around the room, "I've been doing a lot of research. My approach to the problem of immortals' infertility is somewhat unorthodox." He chuckled. "Or maybe I should rephrase that since my sources are ancient. But anyway, I believe in holistic medicine. Which means taking into consideration both the physical and mental states of my patients."

Kian groaned. "I don't have the patience for this New Age crap."

"Oh, but it's not New Age. If anything, it's old age." Merlin scratched his head. "Since you've interrupted my well-prepared speech, I have to start at the beginning."

The low growl vibrating in Kian's throat would've scared anyone except for Merlin, who either pretended not to hear or was too distracted to notice.

"As I was saying, my approach is holistic." He made an air circle with his hand. "That's why both of you should start treatment at the same time. Our low fertility is not only a female issue, immortal males are not fruitful either."

Kian shrugged. "Fine with me. What do I need to do?"

Merlin smirked. "First of all, you need to relax. You're a stress ball, and in turn, you're stressing out your lovely mate. Excess stress hormones create an environment that is far from optimal for conception."

Syssi's heart sank. If in order for her to get pregnant Kian needed to relax, they would never have a child.

"And how do you suggest that I do that?" Kian asked. "Do you have a relaxing potion?" he scoffed.

"Indeed, I do, but because you need a clear head for what you do, you can't take it. I'm talking about daily meditation sessions and romantic vacations."

"I don't have the time or the patience for those either."

"Type A personalities are the most difficult to deal with." Merlin sighed. "Very well. I can put you on a bio-feedback program. You can teach yourself how to calm down."

"How long does it take?"

"At least an hour a day. You may still wish to consider meditation, which in my experience is more effective."

Kian shook his head. "I tried it once. It's a catch-22. Meditation is supposed to be conducive to relaxation, but in order to meditate, I need to calm down first. I don't see how it can work."

"Bio-feedback it is, then," Merlin said and pushed to his feet. "The other part of the treatment is the natural fertility enhancers I've prepared."

He walked over to the dining table and lifted two small decanters. One had a blue ribbon tied around its neck and the other pink.

"So you don't get confused." He handed the pink one to Syssi and the other one to Kian. "Drink one ounce twice a day. When these are finished, come to me for more."

Lifting the decanter, Kian pulled out the stopper. "Phew, this stinks." He turned his face away from the fumes. "And you expect us to drink it?"

Bracing for hers to smell just as bad, Syssi unplugged the pink-bowed decanter. The smell was different but just as repulsive.

"It's a good idea to have a piece of chocolate at the ready," Merlin suggested.

Braving another sniff, Kian asked, "What's in it?"

Merlin waved a hand. "A little bit of this, and a little bit of that, with a touch of magic." He winked at Syssi. "I want to start with this and see if it works before we attempt the human-made commercial medicines."

"Are there any side effects?" Kian asked.

"Enhanced libido is one." Merlin smirked. "I know that you don't need any enhancers in that department, but it was unavoidable. I'm afraid that throughout the treatment the two of you will be frolicking like bunnies."

Syssi felt her face turn red.

"You're embarrassing my wife." Kian wrapped a protective arm around her shoulders.

Merlin dipped his head. "My apologies. I meant no disrespect, but as a doctor, I have to be direct." He cast Syssi an apologetic glance. "In this line of treatment, I expect many more embarrassing moments. You should prepare yourself for it."

She had. But if the potion worked, there would be no need for the more invasive methods she'd read about.

Syssi crossed her fingers.

Lifting the decanter to the light, Kian gave it a little shake, stirring the sediment. "Do you have other test subjects, or are Syssi and I the only ones?" He glared at Merlin. "I want others to try it, so my intense personality won't be blamed for your potions' failure."

"Naturally," Merlin said. "Right now, other than the two of you I have Hildegard and Gertrude on board. Bridget wants to try it too, but she needs to sweet-talk her mate into it first."

Kian chuckled. "Good luck with that. You'll have to offer him the same advice you offered to me. Turner is not exactly a chill kind of guy either."

Crossing his arms over his chest, Merlin nodded. "I have a feeling Magnus and Vivian would want to join the program too. But first, Vivian needs to transition."

"It's going to be easier for her to conceive as a human," Syssi pointed out.

"Yes, this is true. But then she will have to wait for the transition until after her baby is born, and she's not getting any younger."

Syssi nodded. "I still remember how difficult it was for Nathalie and Andrew. He was going insane because he couldn't bite her. Bridget was afraid that it would trigger Nathalie's transition, which might have endangered the baby."

"I don't think she would've gone into transition while pregnant." Merlin smoothed his hand over his beard. "But I would hesitate to test that hypothesis."

1 2

JULIAN

In the bathroom, Julian brushed his teeth and his hair, checked his shoes for scuffs, and then adjusted the collar of his button-down. It was blue with thin stripes, not overly dressy but well made. Together with a pair of dark blue jeans and trendy shoes that were a cross between sporty and fancy, the look was precisely what he'd been going for. Casual and yet elegant enough for a Friday night dinner.

For the past two weeks, people had been inviting him over nearly every evening, and since he was too polite to decline, he'd accepted and had to suffer through hours of pitying looks and forced smiles.

Julian had cracked jokes and tried to look as cheerful as can be, but no one was buying it. Regrettably, he wasn't a good actor, and the truth was written all over his face.

This time, though, he was invited to Ella's house for a Friday night family dinner. Not as Ella's anything, just as a family friend. Magnus had mumbled something about Parker having no friends in the village and looking for a partner to play computer games with.

Magnus's intentions, although good, were quite transparent, and the excuse he'd used for the invitation was lame. The guy probably didn't know that those games were played online, and that there was no need for gamers to be in the same room.

Nevertheless, Julian was grateful. It was an opportunity to spend time with Ella without putting any pressure on her. At this stage of the game, even the friend zone seemed appealing. It was better than being on the outside without the ability of even looking in.

Besides, perhaps the friend zone was exactly where he should be.

Ella needed time. This wasn't just another hookup he was going to charm the pants off. She was the real deal, and Julian was in unfamiliar territory.

He knew very little about the intricacies of the wooing and dating game.

He'd seen it in movies and had read about it in books, but even though he'd spent a long time among young humans, he hadn't seen much dating or romancing on campus.

It was all about hookups and booty calls, which had suited him perfectly. Romance hadn't been on his horizon, and he'd felt no need to prepare for it.

Perhaps some old romantic films would help him get the gist of it. Going to see a girl in her parents' house was like a trip into a fifties movie. But unlike in the old movies, Julian was on much friendlier terms with the parents than with the girl.

Magnus wasn't officially Ella's father yet, but he was mated to her mother, and he seemed to care about Ella as if she was already his daughter.

Was that how Turner felt about him?

They weren't close, but then Turner had dropped everything to rescue Ella only because Julian was infatuated with her picture.

He doubted a real parent would've done that for him, so there was that.

As he reached Ella's house, the shutters were just coming down for the night, but he managed to catch a glimpse of her helping her mother set the table.

Ella was so lovely that she was almost painful to behold.

Parker opened the door before Julian had a chance to knock. "Hey, Julian. Long time no see." He offered him his hand. "Do you want to see my fangs?"

"Sure. But maybe I should come in first. The light is spilling out through the open door."

"Oh, yeah. I keep forgetting about the blackout rules." Parker opened the door even wider to let him in.

"Good evening, Vivian, Ella," he said as he walked toward them. "Thank you for inviting me to dinner."

"I'll tell Magnus you're here," Parker said. "He's in the backyard with Scarlet."

"Hello, Julian." Vivian pulled him into her arms. "I'm so glad you could make it."

"Hi." Ella forced a little smile and looked away.

"Come, sit at the table." Vivian turned to her daughter. "Ella, can you get the wine? It's in the cabinet over the fridge."

"I can't reach it. I'm too short."

"You can climb on a chair."

Julian jumped to his feet. "I'll get it."

As he followed Ella into the kitchen, he wondered whether Vivian had done it on purpose so he and her daughter would have to do something together.

Ella let him in front of her and leaned against the counter as he opened the cabinet's doors.

"Which one does your mom want, do you know?"

"Mom, is there a specific wine you prefer?"

"Could you get one red and one white? I don't care which brand."

"Okay." He pulled out two bottles and handed them to Ella. "Anything else I can get for you?"

For a moment, she just looked into his eyes as if seeing him for the first time, then shook her head. "Thank you, but that will be all."

Strange girl. What thoughts had crossed her mind during that long moment when their eyes had been locked together?

Typically, his nose could supply the missing clues, but not with the strong cooking smells masking the more subtle ones.

"I didn't know what you liked to eat, so I made several dishes to choose from," Vivian said. "There is baked salmon, grilled chicken, and a vegetable curry dish in case you don't eat meat. I know that your mother is a vegetarian."

"I'm an omnivore." Julian spread the napkin over his knees. "And I'm very easy to please. Food wise, at least."

Ella cast him another one of her penetrating gazes. "What are you picky about?"

"Movies, books, music."

"What's your favorite movie?" Parker asked.

"Of all time, or recent?"

"Recent."

"*Avengers: Infinity War.*"

Parker put his fork down. "No way! That's my favorite too!"

Ella rolled her eyes. "Why am I not surprised." She lifted the glass of wine to her lips, but then put it down without drinking any of it.

Julian arched a brow. "You don't like it?"

"It was a horrible movie. Everyone died."

He'd meant the wine, but discussing the movie would keep the conversation going.

"I guess you're right. I'm just expecting a trip back in time or something like that to fix everything. It's a Marvel movie. The good guys have to win."

"I hope so. I love the characters, and Thor is just to die for, but I didn't like how dark that one was."

Thor was to die for?

Was it the muscles?

Julian was going to hit the gym starting tomorrow.

He took a long sip from his wine. "What's your favorite music?"

She shrugged. "I don't have a favorite band or anything like that. I just like what I like. It has to be catchy, though, something I would like to sing along with. What's your favorite?"

"A couple of months ago, I would've said progressive and psychedelic rock, mainly Pink Floyd, but since I moved in with my new roommate, it's classical music. He's a pianist and a very talented one. Listening to him play just soothes my soul. Except for when he plays Debussy."

"Why? What's wrong with the French dude?" Parker asked.

"Nothing. I'm sure many people love him. It certainly takes skill to play his stuff. But I just happen to prefer more melodic, romantic music."

13

ELLA

*J*ulian was a romantic.
Figures.
Just one more thing to make a perfect guy even more perfect. If only she'd met him before Romeo had burst her naïve little bubble and ruined her life.

Sitting next to Julian, Ella fought the irrational urge to go to the bathroom and scrub herself clean. Only, no amount of soap could do that. The taint was on the inside, and she had no business indulging in what-ifs about a pure soul like Julian.

If only he were a little wicked, she could've felt more comfortable with him. Couldn't he be a compulsive shoplifter, or a gambler, or a pothead?

As ridiculous as the thought was, Ella would've loved for Julian to have a vice or two. But she had a feeling that he had never stolen anything, and that he wouldn't know what a joint was even if it hit him in the face.

"I've heard talk about Kian assigning you to the halfway house project," Magnus said.

"You did? I'd only talked to him about it yesterday. But yeah." Julian raked his fingers through his chin-length hair. "He expects me to organize everything, but I don't know where to start. I'm a doctor, not a businessman."

"Who wants coffee?" Her mother came back from the kitchen with a full carafe in hand.

"I would love some. Thank you." Julian lifted his cup.

He had such good manners. Too good. According to her mother he was twenty-six, but he acted much older.

Magnus took the carafe from Vivian and poured coffee into the rest of the cups. "Every big project seems overwhelming until you break it down into a step-by-step action plan. What's the first thing you need to do?"

"Find a suitable place. Not only that, though. Kian expects me to arrange financing for it as well. Turner offered to provide the down payment and suggested we take out a mortgage for the rest. I guess I'll need his help to do that as well because I don't have a clue how to go about it."

"Isn't the clan rich?" Ella asked. "How come he can't just buy the building?"

Julian put his cup down. "I think it's a cash flow problem. Kian tries to keep all the balls in the air. Building this village cost a shitload of money, which severely depleted the clan's cash reserves. Then we've undertaken the huge humanitarian project of fighting trafficking, and with all this going on, Kian still invests in promising technologies whenever the opportunity presents itself."

"What about my ring? That should cover the cost of several halfway houses."

"It hasn't been sold yet, but once it is, we will pay Turner back for the down payment and close the mortgage."

Ella didn't know much about buying real estate and getting loans, but what she did know was that the bank would want to see where the mortgage payments would come from.

"Are you going to charge the girls rent?"

Julian chuckled. "Of course not. Once they have jobs that can pay rent, they should graduate into full independence."

"So how are you going to get a mortgage? The loan officer will want to see where the monthly payments will come from."

And he was raking his fingers through his hair again.

Apparently it was a nervous tick.

"I'm sure the rules are different for a charity." He shook his head. "I'm so out of my element with this. Kian should dump this task on someone who knows a thing or two about running charities."

Not pretending to be a know-it-all was another point in Julian's favor. She liked that he had no problem admitting being lost and confused. It made him seem a bit more human.

Well, the term human didn't apply. Fallible was better.

Ella scrunched her nose. "Have you ever heard of GoFundMe?"

"No, what is it?"

"It's a fundraising platform. When my teacher's house burned down, the school organized a fundraiser, and they collected a lot of money to help her out. I think a lot of people will donate to an important cause like this."

Magnus frowned. "But that's small money. How much would people give? Five bucks?"

"Some will give five, and some will give more, but this can reach millions of people around the globe. I think it would be awesome if a project like this was to be financed by regular people and not some deep-pocketed donors."

"A double-whammy," Julian said. "Raising money and awareness at the same time."

As a plan started forming in Ella's head, tingles of excitement rushed up her spine. "We can make a video of a girl telling her personal horror story. We won't show her face, of course, only a silhouette, and we can even change her voice in the recording. But think what a powerful motivator it would be. I can already imagine the money pouring in."

"You can make several videos," Vivian suggested. "You can even create a fundraiser for each girl featured. It's much more powerful when people see and listen to the person they are helping out."

Ella's excitement was growing by the minute. There were so many possibilities to explore, and the beauty of it was that it was so simple she could do it all on her own.

Not only would she be helping girls who'd gone through hell and deserved every bit of support possible, but she would be repaying the clan for what they had done for her and her family.

"I can shoot videos with the camera on my phone. And I can also post them on YouTube. This can be huge."

Julian shook his head. "I think we should get a professional camera crew to do that. Brandon can help with that."

"Your uncle in Hollywood?" Vivian asked.

"Well, he's not really my uncle, more like a distant cousin, but he is a clan member. He's the one responsible for spreading our message to the world."

Ella frowned. "What message? Vampire and shapeshifter movies?"

Julian chuckled. "Not exclusively. I'm talking about the message of freedom from oppression, equal opportunity, and quality of life for everyone. In order to strive for something better, people need to first know that it exists. For example, a female starship captain in a sci-fi movie demonstrates that women can hold the highest military positions. After seeing enough movies like that, people wouldn't think twice about nominating a woman for a position that was previously thought of as exclusively male. Like the chief of police."

Ella crossed her arms over her chest. "We're not there yet, but I get what you're trying to say. I'm just wondering what is the best way to showcase our girls without causing them too much grief. I know how hard it is to talk about that stuff."

Crap, she shouldn't have said that. Suddenly, the mood around the dinner table switched from enthusiastic to sorrowful, with everyone but her looking into their coffee cups.

That wouldn't do.

"Don't look so glum, people." Ella lifted her cup and took a sip. "I think this is going to be a very uplifting experience for the girls. The humanity that has turned a blind eye and a deaf ear to their suffering is going to rise up to support them. Personally, I like the idea of millions of individuals acknowledging their silent part in the crimes committed against those girls and trying to buy redemption with their contributions."

14

KIAN

"I know one way that is sure to help me relax," Kian said as they left Merlin's house. "You can come work with me. We will take breaks every couple of hours to make out." He pulled her close against his side. "It's a double whammy. I'll be less stressed, and because we will be having so much sex, we'll have a baby on the way in no time."

It had been fun having her with him in the office. The problem was that neither had managed to get much work done. That was why Syssi had decided to work for Amanda instead.

"Sounds lovely. But we are already making love several times a day, and you know what happened the last time we tried to work together." She chuckled. "All we did was fool around. I don't want to be responsible for single-handedly ruining the clan's business empire."

He leaned to kiss the top of her head. "But we weren't trying to make a baby back then. This would be fooling around with a purpose."

Syssi lifted her eyes to him. "You aren't serious, are you?"

"I kind of am. You have a calming effect on me, and I know that having you around would help me relax. But I also know that this is wishful thinking on my part. You love what you do at the university lab, and office work can't compete with that."

With a sigh, Syssi leaned her head on his chest. "Life is full of compromises, my love."

And wasn't that the truth. At first, right after Syssi had gone back to the lab, they'd been meeting for lunch at Gino's, which was more or less midway between the university and the keep. But pretty soon it became clear that he couldn't take an hour and a half break from his work day, and the daily lunches turned into once a week lunches. After the move to the village, it was more like once a month. They still called each other several times a day, but hearing Syssi's voice over the phone didn't have the same calming effect as having her near him.

He wondered whether the effect was caused by something chemical or was it all in his head? It was a question he might have an answer for pretty soon.

"Did I ever tell you about the virtual reality startup I invested in a while back?"

"I don't think so. Is it a new gaming platform?"

He chuckled. "In a way. In crude terms it's a platform for virtual hookups. People fill out a very extensive questionnaire, listing their ideal partner's attributes and creating a fantasy that they would like to enact. After the software pairs them with the best match in the company's database, a virtual meeting is arranged. Each of the partners is hooked up to a machine, which can be on different continents or in the next room for all they know, and they get to experience a fantasy in cyber world that feels as authentic as any real one."

"Sounds fascinating. Is it up and running already?"

"Not yet. They got stuck with a problem they couldn't solve. I didn't want to lose my investment money, so I sent William to help them with the code. With him on board, I believe they will be ready to start beta-testing soon."

Syssi cast him a seductive smile. "Can we take part in that testing? I can think of several interesting adventures for us to try out." She batted her eyelashes and lowered her voice. "You know I have a wild imagination."

Minx.

He cocked a brow. "Am I not fulfilling all of your sexual fantasies?"

"I meant we should test it together. A joint fantasy. You can be a pirate captain who kidnapped me and is holding me captive, or even better, a space pirate. Or I can be a rich lady on some distant planet who buys you on the slave market and orders you to pleasure her. I'm sure you can see the possibilities."

He'd meant it as a tease, but his imagination hadn't gone that far. Since time moved differently in the virtual world, and a week of experiences could be crammed into a three-hour session, his original idea had been to spend a cyber vacation with Syssi and see if it had the same calming effect on him as being with her physically.

But whatever the scenario, he was going to wait until the beta-testing was done and all the glitches were cleared. Syssi's brain was too dear to him to risk on an experiment.

"We can try it when the company is officially open for business."

"How long until then?"

"It depends on William and on funding. Their original estimated budget was depleted a long time ago. I kept pouring money into it because I believed it was going to be a huge success, but at some point I had to say enough was enough. Now they have no choice but to scrabble for more investors."

"Is it because of the financial squeeze the clan is in?"

"In part. But if that were the only obstacle, I would have sold another company to keep financing the development. The main problem is that the service is going to be expensive. Not only because of the enormous initial investment, but because it's costly to operate. This means that only the wealthy would be able to afford it, and that's a limited market."

"Hmm." Syssi didn't continue, and for a long moment, they walked in silence.

"Does the clan have a controlling interest in it?"

"The founders were not willing to give it up. We have thirty-four percent, and the founders retain sixty-six. Any additional funds they need will be in the form of a loan and not shares."

Syssi stopped and turned to face him. "If the founders are struggling financially, they might reconsider, especially if you promise them creative freedom or whatever else they are afraid to lose."

"They might. But as I said, that's not the only problem. I'm not sure how profitable they will be, and if it's smart for us to keep pouring funds into what seems to be a money pit."

"I have a good feeling about it."

He put his hands on her waist and pulled her closer. "Is it because you're impatient to experience it? I can pretend to be a pirate right now." He waggled his brows. "I'll throw you over my shoulder and take you somewhere I can ravish you. Harrr…"

Laughing, she slapped his chest. "No, silly. Well, yes, that too. But mainly because I have a feeling about it." She lowered her eyes. "Remember Starship Enterprise's holodeck?"

"What about it?"

Star Trek, the old one and the new generation, had been two of the few television series he'd watched. His current guilty pleasure was *Game of Thrones*.

"I kept fantasizing about it. It was a way to experience things I was terrified to do in real life, like skydiving or mountain climbing, or even an open-Jeep safari."

"And sexy pirates?"

"Yeah, that too. But anyway, I would've loved a service like that. I'm sure there are many people like me, men and women, who would love to have a unique experience at least once. A special occasion kind of thing."

"Like a couple's twentieth anniversary."

"Exactly. A way to be young again in a dream world, or rather cyber world. And since everyone is so busy, and time is the most precious commodity, a cyber vacation, even a costly one, might seem like a very attractive alternative to a real one."

"Okay, I understand why you think the company will succeed. But why should I go after a controlling interest?"

"Because a technology like that is a breakthrough, and I believe we should be in a position to defend it and to expand it. Besides, when all the bugs are fixed, we can get a machine or two for the clan's use."

Kian laughed. "It might work for the females, but not the males. Mental biting would not release the pressure from the venom glands."

In addition, because of their unique situation, there was a possibility of being paired with a cousin. Even though it was only virtual, the idea was so abhorrent to them that it would be enough to deter clan members from trying it out. Then again, if they had control over the database, they could ensure that no clan members were paired.

"You don't know that for a fact. It might. If men can ejaculate while dreaming, why not this?"

"Because most men do not, at least not after puberty. But I guess we will find out when we try it."

"You keep calling the startup 'it.' Don't they have a name for the company?"

Kian grimaced. "For now it's called Dream Encounters, but it's only a working title, and I don't like it. It sounds like an advertisement for mattresses."

"Yeah, you're right. That's a sucky name. How about Perfect Match? After all, they are promising to pair people with the best possible partners."

"That sounds like a matchmaking service."

"It does. But in a way it is. People can go on virtual dates, and if they enjoy it, they can request a real life meeting."

Kian chuckled. "I doubt it's a good idea. Imagine finding out that the handsome dude from the fantasy is a middle-aged bald guy with a potbelly. Or that the beautiful young woman who was a tigress in bed is a seventy-year-old grandmother."

Syssi nodded. "That is true. Although it's kind of sad. In their minds they are young and beautiful. But then that's the beauty of a service like that. The mind is free from the body's constraints. The possibilities are endless, and the benefits can be tremendous for people with mobility and other issues. Besides, they can always deny the request for a meeting."

Syssi's enthusiasm was contagious.

Kian wasn't as imaginative as her and therefore hadn't considered all the possibilities. In addition to generating profits, a service like this could improve people's lives, which fell under the overriding umbrella of new technologies the clan wanted to encourage.

"I'll suggest it to the founders when I meet with them."

Kian seldom met with the heads of enterprises he either purchased or invested in. But since this was important to Syssi, and the company was faltering, his personal involvement was needed. He was going to make sure it succeeded.

"And the name too," she added.

"Perfect Match. It has a nice sound to it. It's definitely less cheesy than the Perfect Hookup, although that would be more truthful."

"Don't worry. People will get it." She smiled and put her hands on his chest. "Even though I've already found my perfect match, I can't wait to try out a virtual adventure with you."

"You don't have to." He lifted her up, threw her over his shoulder, and smacked her bottom. "Off to my cabin, lassie. Harrr...."

15

ELLA

*L*ong after Julian had left, Ella was still thinking about him. When dinner was over he hadn't gone home right away, but had stayed to play computer games with Parker.

She'd enjoyed listening to them together, shouting, laughing, poking fun at each other, and teasing like a couple of old friends. Julian had a gift for putting people at ease. He hadn't acted below his age just so Parker would like him. It seemed that he'd been genuinely having fun with a kid half his age.

No wonder Parker liked him so much.

Heck, everyone did, and that included her.

The problem was that right now all Ella could offer Julian was her friendship, while it was quite obvious that he wanted more.

He'd done an admirable job trying to hide his attraction to her, but she'd caught the quick glances he was stealing when he'd thought she hadn't been looking.

It was kind of sweet.

And if Ella were okay in the head, she would have signaled him that she was interested. But she wasn't okay, not by a long shot, and if Julian wanted her, he would have to wait for time to heal her wounds.

When there was a knock on the door, Ella's heart skipped a bit, thinking that Julian had come back, but when she opened the door, she found Okidu's twin brother standing on her doorsteps with a mannequin grin spread over his face and a Saks shopping bag in his hand.

"Good evening, Mademoiselle." He dipped his head and lifted the bag. "Compliments of Mistress Amanda, who sends her best regards along with these items."

"Thank you." Ella took the bag. "And thank Mistress Amanda for me."

It was awkward to say mistress, but Ella was afraid the butler would feel scandalized if she just called his mistress by her name.

"I shall." He bowed. "Good night, Mademoiselle." He turned on his heel and walked down the steps.

"Who was it?" Vivian asked.

"Amanda's butler. Or at least I think that's who he is. He looks like Okidu's twin."

"That's Onidu, and he is indeed Amanda's butler." Her mother pointed at the bag. "What's in it?"

Reaching inside, Ella pulled out a short, dark wig. "Oh, how cool. It's just like her hairdo." She pulled it on her head, tucking her braid under the back. "How do I look?"

Her mom shook her head and grimaced. "Go take a look. If I say something, you're not going to believe me anyway."

Ella peeked into the bag to see what other goodies Amanda had sent. "There is also a ginger-colored wig. I'm going to try both." She glanced at her mother. "Do you want to come with me to my room?"

That brought a smile to Vivian's lips. It wasn't an invitation Ella extended often. After letting her mom tuck her in for the first two days, she'd gone back to her usual 'my room is my castle' attitude.

Standing in front of the vanity mirror, Ella had to agree with Vivian that black wasn't her color. She was too pale to pull it off without putting on a darker foundation, and she had no intention of doing that.

"Try the red. It should suit you better," Vivian suggested.

"Yeah. I like the short style, but I don't like the color." Ella took the black wig off and pulled on the red.

It was a bob with bangs, and it looked cute on her. But since her natural color was light brown with reddish undertones, it didn't change her appearance that much.

The idea wasn't to make her look better, but to disguise her.

"Maybe I should go for bleached blond." She took the wig off. "Or purple."

Vivian followed her out of the bathroom. "You can use the black in the meantime, because it's a better disguise, but you should take Amanda up on her offer for a makeover. I think this was her way of reminding you about that."

"I should, shouldn't I?" Ella sat on her bed. "I need to have my picture taken for my fake driver's license, and I can't do that until I decide on the look I want. And without a license, I can't go anywhere."

Vivian sat next to her on the bed and wrapped her arm around Ella's shoulders. "I'm glad that you want to get out of here, but I don't think you're ready to get behind the wheel and go driving around. I think that you should get out of the house first and mingle with the people in the village. It's so liberating not to have to hide who you are and what you can do."

"Is it? Do you really feel more comfortable here than you did in our old home?"

"There is no comparison. When you start spending time with the immortals, you'll get what I mean. You'll feel at home like you never have before. These are our people."

Ella smirked. "So that's why I liked Julian so much. Because he's an immortal."

"Oh, I think that in his case, it's more than that."

"He is very handsome, and charming, and kind, and he played with Parker, and he's a doctor." Ella winked. "That last one was for you, since that seems important to you."

Vivian narrowed her eyes at her. "I hear a *but* coming up."

"He's too good for me, Mom, too pure."

"What the heck are you talking about? I'm sure that boy has bedded hordes of women, while you've been with only one man."

"I'm not talking about that, Mom." Ella put a hand over her heart. "I feel like there is darkness in me now. Maybe it was always there, and I just haven't acknowledged it." She lifted a pillow and hugged it to her. "I'm not naïve anymore. I'm constantly on the lookout for ulterior motives, and I no longer believe that people are essentially good. They might think that they are, but they are not."

"That's part of growing up, Ella, not some mysterious darkness lurking inside of you. Heck, I don't trust people either. When Julian came to see me at the dental office with Turner and Magnus, I thought that he'd organized your kidnapping so he and his buddies could swindle me out of every penny I owned."

That was news to her.

"You thought that they were running a scam?"

Vivian nodded. "It was easier to believe in that than the alternative. But when I asked Turner how much your rescue was going to cost me, and he answered nothing, I knew that the situation was much worse than I thought. Compared to what they were telling me, dealing with a bunch of scammers would've been a walk in the park."

Ella could just imagine how devastated and hopeless her mother must have felt. "Oh, Mommy." She leaned her head on Vivian's shoulder. "I'm so sorry for causing you so much grief."

"Don't. It wasn't your fault any more than it was mine. We were both fooled."

"Only Parker wasn't."

Vivian smirked. "Parker likes Julian."

"I like Julian too."

"So what's the problem? Don't you find him attractive?"

She snorted. "I would need to be blind or dead not to realize how gorgeous he is."

"So?" Vivian made a rolling motion with her hand.

This was hard to let out, but her mother deserved the truth even when it was painful. "I can think of him as an attractive guy, and I can see it with my eyes, but I can't feel it on the inside."

"Why not?"

"Because I'm dead in here." Ella patted her belly. "Because I can't feel anything physical for anyone right now. Put a nude Thor in this room with me, and he would stir nothing. I could appreciate his beauty, but there would be no arousal."

Her mother looked so sad that Ella regretted fessing up to the truth. She should have come up with another excuse.

"I wish I could help you, but I don't know how. You should really talk to

Vanessa. That's what she does day in and day out. She helps girls get over their traumas."

Ella shook her head. "No shrinks."

"If you want to video the girls under her care, you will have to talk to her."

"Not as a patient."

Her shoulders slumping, Vivian sighed. "Why are you being so stubborn about it? You must realize that you need help."

"I don't. Grief takes its time, and there is no rushing it. Ten shrinks with Nobel prizes can't make it go away, or ease it, or shorten it. I know that from experience, and so do you. And if you're wondering why I'm bringing grief up, it's because I'm mourning my old self. That carefree, naïve girl is gone, and I'm damn sorry to lose her because I liked her."

16

TURNER

As Turner opened the door, the appetizing smells had him lifting a brow. Bridget was cooking?

Or was she just heating up leftovers from yesterday's takeout?

Dropping his briefcase on the counter, he walked into the kitchen and kissed her cheek. "What are you making? Or better yet, why?"

"We haven't had a home cooked meal in a while. I thought I'd throw something together. I'm making curry."

He was surprised she even had the necessary ingredients. It wasn't as if they'd done any grocery shopping lately. With both of them working twelve-hour days, going out to dinner or bringing home takeout made much more sense.

Still, it was a nice change of pace.

Pulling out a barstool, he sat at the counter. "I talked with Sandoval today."

She glanced at him over her shoulder. "About the ring?"

"I didn't bring it up right away, of course. First I hit him up for a donation."

"Did he agree?"

Turner shifted on the stool. "Two hundred and fifty thousand. That's chump change for him, but it will help with the down payment on the halfway house."

"Nice."

"Thank you, I thought so too. After I got him to make the pledge, we talked about his nephew and how things were working out. I let him go on and on about how grateful he was for what I've done for the brat, and I only brought the ring up after half an hour or so of chitchat."

"As a casual aside."

"Precisely. I told him I'm looking for a buyer for it as a favor for a friend who has fallen upon hard times. I added that my friend doesn't want anyone to know that he's selling his dear departed wife's engagement ring, and therefore is asking not to offer it to anyone in Russia."

"Did he buy the story?"

Turner shrugged. "It doesn't matter whether he did or not. It's a matter of appearances. Arturo would never admit to dealing with contraband on the black market. That way he only agrees to help a friend who is helping another friend, and we both come out smelling like roses."

"So he agreed?" Bridget pulled out a bottle of ready-made curry sauce from the fridge and dumped it on top of the vegetables in the wok.

"He said that he might know someone who'd be interested. I need to bring the ring to him, though."

"Is it safe to take something like this to South America?"

"He invited me to his house in Miami. I told him that I need to check with my fiancé."

"When?"

"Next weekend."

Bridget loaded the curry onto two plates and brought them over to the counter. "I'm curious to meet the infamous Arturo Sandoval, but I don't know if I can take the entire weekend off."

Turner spread his thighs and pulled her between them. "Yes, you can. All the missions for the coming month are scheduled, and thankfully there are no crises to deal with. We haven't gone on a vacation together in a long time."

She leaned into him and wrapped her arms around his neck. "You're right. A weekend in Miami sounds fun. Is it safe?"

"I wouldn't offer to take you if I thought it wasn't."

"Then it's settled." She pushed away from him and sat on the next stool over. "We should schedule time for dates."

He arched a brow. "We go out to dinner at least three times a week."

"Those are not dates. A date is when you dress up and go to a fancy place like By Invitation Only. Or a concert, or a play."

"Don't tell me that you bought a membership in your cousin's snooty restaurant."

"I didn't, but I can have Kian make a reservation for us. I thought that you liked it there."

"I did, but this is not the time for frivolous spending. I could probably afford to get it for us, but I think it would be in bad taste considering the budget cuts."

"No, you're right. That's why I decided not to purchase a membership for us and mooch off Kian instead."

Turner scooped some curry on his fork and put it in his mouth. It wasn't bad, considering that it was made with store-bought sauce, but it wasn't great either.

"It would've been nice to have a gourmet restaurant in the village."

"Maybe one day we will. Callie is thinking about it. But first, she wants to get her degree."

"That's more important than having a restaurant. If Merlin's research is successful and he finds a way to increase fertility, the village might have a bunch of kids who'll need a school and a teacher."

Bridget nodded. "I agree."

She pushed a piece of carrot around her plate. "Speaking of Merlin and his research, how would you feel about joining his program?"

Turner was a smart man, but it took him a moment to process what Bridget had meant.

"You want to have a baby with me?"

"Yes, I do."

"Shouldn't we get married first?"

She eyed him as if he wasn't making any sense. "That's it? I wasn't sure what to expect, but it wasn't a proposal."

Yeah, as usual, his emotional intelligence rivaled that of a brick.

"What do you want me to say?"

She waved her hand. "Tell me how you feel about it. Do you want to be a father? Are you scared? Are you worried that our lives would get messy?"

Taking a deep breath, Turner smoothed his hand over his hair. "I would love to have a child with you, and I would love to actually be there for my child, and not only financially."

"But?"

"First of all, Merlin is only starting out, and we don't know if and when his fertility treatments will work. Secondly, we both work very long hours, not because we need the money, but because what we do is important. I don't see how we can fit a baby into this schedule."

She sighed. "Don't you think I know that? But as you said, it will probably take a long time until Merlin refines his treatments, and there is always a possibility that nothing he does will work. But on the remote chance that the treatments are successful, it takes over nine months for the baby to be born. That's plenty of time to find a solution. I can train a replacement, and you can downsize a little. Isn't our child worth the effort?"

It seemed that his pragmatic and logical Bridget was taking a leap of faith, and assuming a child was a certainty.

Turner didn't have the heart to burst her bubble. If going to Merlin for treatment would make her happy, he would support her in any way he could.

"I have no problem with giving it a try."

"Remember that you said that." She grinned. "Syssi told me that Merlin's potions are absolutely vile."

He lifted a brow. Was she concerned that her mouth would taste bad when they kissed?

"How much of the potion does she need to drink?"

"She and Kian both have to drink an ounce of it twice a day. Not the same potion, obviously, but she says that they are both terrible."

17

VIVIAN

*A*s Vivian turned into the Sanctuary's parking lot, Ella pulled down the shade and glanced at the mirror. "Do you think I should put on some lipstick? I look like a chemo patient with this black wig."

Vivian parked and reached to get her purse from the back seat. "Here." She handed Ella a red lip pencil. "Dab a little on the outline and then smack your lips. The color is very strong."

Once she was done, Ella examined her reflection again. "Now the shadows under my eyes look even worse. Do you have an eyeliner pencil in there?"

"Yes, I do." She handed Ella a blue one. "Go easy with that too."

The sudden fussing with her appearance belied Ella's nonchalant attitude about meeting with Vanessa.

She'd agreed to come on the condition that all they were going to discuss was her idea for the fundraising project, and she had threatened to walk out if Vanessa tried to psychoanalyze her.

"How do I look now?"

"Gorgeous and barely recognizable."

"Perfect." She smiled. "Let's do it."

Her head held high, Ella walked into Vanessa's office with an impressive show of confidence. It was fake, but Vivian was impressed nonetheless. Her daughter was a fighter.

"Hello, Dr. Vanessa." Ella glanced at the desk as she offered the therapist her hand. "I'm sorry, but I don't know your last name."

"Everyone just calls me Vanessa. No doctor and no last name. Nice to meet you, Ella." She shook the hand she was offered. "Please, take a seat."

"Thank you."

"Your mother told me that you have an interesting idea that you would like to run by me." Vanessa smiled. "She insisted that I should see you as soon as possible because I was going to love it."

Not wanting to steal Ella's thunder, Vivian hadn't told Vanessa what it was about. It was Ella's baby, and if she was allowed to run with it, her sense of accomplishment would do wonders for her self-esteem.

"Are you familiar with the GoFundMe fundraising platform?" Ella asked.

Vanessa nodded. "I am. It's a way to raise money for a friend or a relative. The platform takes care of collecting the donations, but the fundraising is done by the individual setting it up."

"It can be much bigger than that. My idea is to make short videos of the rescued girls telling their stories in their own words. Each video will be about one girl, and we will only show her silhouette. We can even change her voice if you think that's necessary. Then we post it on YouTube, and on Facebook, and ask people to fund the halfway houses for the girls, or share the video, or both."

Vanessa leaned back and crossed her arms over her chest. "The idea is worth exploring, but I foresee a couple of problems. First of all, I don't know how many girls would be willing to talk on camera, even in silhouette. Secondly, for this to succeed, these videos would need to go viral, and I sincerely doubt that it would happen. People don't like sad stories. Show them pictures of puppies and kittens, and they will share that, but not depressing stuff."

Ella lifted her hand and made air quotes. "Beware. This can happen to your daughter. Save a life. Watch and share."

Raising a brow, Vanessa asked, "And you think a heading like that will motivate people to share a horror-story video?"

"It would motivate me," Vivian said. "If I saw this heading, even before what happened to Ella, I would click on it, watch it, and share it. It could have prevented her ordeal. I might have been more vigilant and investigated Romeo right from the start."

"Yeah, me too," Ella said. "In my gut, I knew that something was off about him. I even told my best friend Maddie, and she agreed with me. But I wanted to believe that he was for real." She shook her head. "I was so naïve."

Vanessa leaned forward. "It wasn't your fault, Ella. He was so convincing that he even fooled your mother, who has much more life experience than you. Good people don't expect others to be bad. They are under the illusion that most people are just as good as they are."

"I guess." Shifting in her chair, Ella tugged on her wig to readjust it. "But back to my fundraising idea. I get what you're saying about people not wanting to listen to harrowing stories. The videos will have to be edited, and the production will have to be done at least semi-professionally. Not too polished, but not too crude either."

Vivian stifled a sigh. Ella had smoothly sidestepped Vanessa's attempt to redirect the discussion toward what had happened to her.

"If you're thinking about bringing in a camera crew, that's not going to work, not even if it's all female. A girl might be willing to talk to you, someone who's gone through a similar experience, but not to strangers, and especially not in front of a group of people."

Ella shrugged. "Originally, I thought to just shoot them with my phone's camera and then do some editing to make sure the girls were not recognizable, but I think I'll need better equipment."

"Do you know how to use a professional recording camera?"

"No, but I can learn. The videos don't have to be movie quality. In fact, it's better if they aren't. People are going to be moved by their authenticity, not their high production value."

"Are *you* willing to tell your story on camera?" Vanessa pinned Ella with a hard look.

As evidenced by Ella's audible gulp, she hadn't considered the possibility.

A long moment passed until she nodded. "I'll hate doing it, but I will. It's important for people to realize that this can happen to any girl anywhere. I don't know how the other girls got lured into a trap, or what their circumstances were before, but I guess some of them were just like me. Middle-class girls from good homes that were tricked by pros."

Vanessa sighed. "There are as many versions of this as there are girls who've been deceived. Every girl's story is different. The common factors are naïveté, wishful thinking, and romantic notions. A new boyfriend who's too good to be true comes with a fantastic offer that's impossible to refuse."

"Hook, line, and sinker," Ella murmured.

18

ELLA

*V*anessa leaned forward and steepled her fingers. "At some point, you'll have to deal with what you've been through, Ella. Rape is not easy to recover from on your own. I just want you to know that when you're ready to talk, I'm here to listen."

Crap, she'd walked right into the shrink's trap. "I wasn't raped."

Next to her, Vivian shifted in her chair and started fussing with the hem of her blouse.

The traitor.

"Then what would you call what happened to you?"

"I was coerced."

"Isn't it the same?"

"No, it's not. That's like saying that a punch to the face is the same as a slap with a glove."

"Is that how you feel about it? That it was a slap with a glove?"

God, she hated shrinks and the way they turned everything into a question. She'd just said it.

"Yes." Here, that should be the end of it. Unless Vanessa could turn even a yes answer into a question.

"Was it a playful slap with a glove? Or an invitation to a duel?"

Ella snorted. "It was an invitation to a duel alright. Except, I wasn't given any weapons, and my opponent was armed to the teeth."

A victorious smile bloomed on Vanessa's face. "You've just proven my point."

"Well, whatever. I had no choice, and I did what I had to in order to survive. I just want to forget about it."

"When you think back, is there anything you could have done differently?"

Ella rolled her eyes. "Isn't that obvious? I would've never gone with Romeo to New York."

"And other than that?"

"As I said before, I did what I had to do to survive and eventually to escape. I had to make the Russian believe that I wanted to be with him, so he would lower his guard and not keep me in the dark about where we were going and when."

"So you don't regret succumbing to his coercion?"

Ugh, this woman, or immortal, was making her so angry. As a shrink, she sucked even worse than that other one. Was she suggesting that Ella should've fought?

To what end?

Pinning Vanessa with a hard glare, Ella bit out, "Not even for a moment. If I'd done anything differently, I wouldn't be here, talking with you about making videos. I would be married to a mafia boss and pregnant."

The therapist smiled. "That's very good. Many of the girls blame themselves for not fighting harder, but after talking with those who did, they change their minds. He could've starved you, drugged you, even beaten you or forced you physically. The end result would've been the same. I'm glad you realize this and don't blame yourself."

Would Gorchenco have done any of those things?

Ella didn't think he would've starved or beaten her, but he could've drugged her. It would've been so easy for him to slip a date-rape drug into her drink.

But the worst he could've done was to lock her up and not tell her anything. If he hadn't shared his travel plans with her, the rescue operation would not have been possible.

Crossing her arms over her chest, Ella lifted her chin. "Now that we've had our little chat, I'm sure you can see that I don't need therapy."

"You're doing better than expected. Self-blame and a diminished sense of self-worth are usually the first hurdles to overcome. The second is fear, and the third is mistrust. After such a traumatic experience, it's difficult to interact with people who haven't suffered anything like you have, and even more difficult to have a relationship."

Damn. Vanessa had hit all three nails on the head.

But Ella wasn't going to admit it and give the shrink and her mother more ammunition against her. Hopefully, this had been as close to a therapy session as she was going to get.

It was time for a smooth redirect. "My mother mentioned something about a sewing class she was going to teach. Do you have any other arts and crafts classes here?"

"Yes, we do. Are you interested in joining? It's a great way to meet the girls in an informal setting and get to know them a little. They will be more willing to talk to a classmate."

That sounded like Vanessa's way to trick her into participating, but what she'd said made sense.

"Wouldn't they get suspicious about an outsider joining the class?"

It was Vanessa's turn to pin Ella with a hard stare. "But you're not really an outsider, are you? You just don't live in the sanctuary. If you want to gain their trust, you can't lie to them."

Sneaky shrink. Did Vanessa think Ella was that gullible?

"I have no intention of lying to them. I'm going to tell them the truth of why I'm here, which is making videos for a fundraiser that will help them transition into independent life."

19

SYSSI

"I missed you all day." Kian put his hands on her waist and pulled her into his body. "The reason I hate Mondays is not work. It's not having you around."

Even though Kian often worked on the weekends, he did it from his home office, and she could be there with him, reading a book on the couch. Or making out on it when he wanted a break, which was quite often. After two days of all that wonderful togetherness, separating on Monday was hard on both of them.

"I can put a couch in your official office, quit my job at the university, and read books all week long. With the occasional interruptions, of course." She waggled her brows.

But even if Syssi were willing to quit her job, which she wasn't, the problem with Kian's official office was that unlike the one at home, Kian was rarely alone in there. People were coming in and out all day long, and the phone didn't stop ringing.

It wasn't the same.

Besides, even though they hadn't been successful in identifying any new Dormants, she loved working at the lab with Amanda.

Eventually they'd have a breakthrough, she just knew that in her gut. And in the meantime, they were collecting important data on paranormal abilities. As far as she knew, no other lab was doing it, probably because there was no funding for paranormal research.

In the past, when the army had been interested in exploring the possibilities of remote viewing and other special abilities, funds had been plentiful. But the subject had fallen out of vogue and was considered pseudoscience rather than science.

Except, proving that paranormal abilities existed wasn't even all that difficult. Most people had at least some extrasensory perception. Like knowing who was calling them before picking up the phone or sensing when someone was looking at them even when their backs were turned. Still, few were willing to explore their abilities, and only when they were strong. Most tried to explain away the inexplicable.

"Sounds like a plan to me." Kian took her lips in a soft kiss. "It would do wonders for my stress level."

"I'm not sure about that. Once your business starts failing because of your neglect, your stress level will skyrocket."

He sighed. "It was a nice fantasy while it lasted."

"Speaking of fantasy. You know what time it is, right?"

"Time to make love to your pirate?"

"First, it's potion time. Then making love."

The concoctions were supposed to make them hornier than usual, but Syssi hadn't noticed any difference. Keeping their hands off each other had always been a struggle, even before they'd started Merlin's dubious fertility program.

Kian grimaced. "Let's get it over with."

In the kitchen, she pulled the two decanters out of the fridge together with two Godiva chocolates.

"Cheers." Kian lifted the shot glass she'd used for measuring the ounce of potion.

"Cheers." Syssi quickly swallowed the vile concoction, and then immediately stuck the chocolate in her mouth. "I really hope Merlin knows what he's doing. I would hate to keep drinking this stuff for nothing."

As he finished chewing his piece of Godiva, Kian pulled a bandana out of his back pocket and tied it around his head.

"Harrr, lassie. It's time for ravishing." He picked her up and carried her to the bedroom, thankfully not throwing her over his shoulder this time.

Her sweet guy was smart enough to know that she would've barfed all over him if he had. It warmed her heart, though, that he'd remembered her fantasy and had even prepared a prop to act it out.

"Oh, no, please don't ravish me!" she pretended to plead.

Taking her seriously, Kian immediately put her down.

"Oh, no, please do!" She laughed so hard that her belly was heaving.

"Make up your mind, lass." Kian picked her back up and kept striding to their bedroom. "I don't have all day." He pulled her shirt off even before they got there.

Gently lowering her to the bed, he kissed her quickly before continuing the act. "What do we have here? A lass dressed as a lad? What kind of a garment is this?" He pulled down her stretchy jeans.

Eyeing her white cotton panties, he put his hands on his hips and leaned forward to inspect them. "That's much better. I was half expecting to find boy briefs." He pulled those down too. "And that's even better than before." Smacking his lips, he dove between her legs. "I need to have me some of that honey to wash the bad taste from my mouth."

"Is that what ravishing is?" Syssi asked innocently.

"That's just the prelude, lass." He flicked his tongue over her sensitive nub.

"Ooh, I like this. Do it again."

"Like this?" He repeated what he'd done before.

"Yes. More."

"Before I do that, there is the little matter of your impudence." He grabbed her by the hips, turned her around, and smacked her bottom. "I don't take orders from my prisoners, is that clear?"

Syssi giggled. "Yes."

His hand landed on her other cheek. "No giggling either."

"Okay."

"And you answer me with a yes, captain." Another smack.

"Yes, captain." Syssi smiled into the mattress.

"And take off your bra. I want to play with those succulent nipples of yours."

This was fun. It had been a long time since they'd played their naughty games, and never like this. She didn't even know Kian could get this playful. Maybe the biofeedback was working, helping him to loosen up and have some fun.

Lifting her bottom up, he licked into her, and all thoughts of biofeedback and anything else flew off. As he alternated licks with light swats, supercharging her arousal, Syssi's hips started gyrating of their own accord.

Her hands fisting the duvet, she buried her face in the soft fabric to stifle her moans, which earned her a couple of harder swats.

"I want to hear every sound you make, lass. Your moans belong to me."

"Yes, captain."

He massaged the small sting away, and then kissed each globe. "Lovely ass you have, lassie. And it's mine too. Mine to spank, and mine to kiss."

Enfolding her with his body, he thrust into her wet folds, eliciting a throaty groan from her. "And that's the ravishing part." He pulled back and surged inside her again.

His arm reaching under her, he found her swollen little nub and rubbed it gently as he kept up a steady rhythm that was enough to have her climbing higher and higher, but not enough to push her over the edge.

He knew her body so well, knew how to bring her to the very precipice and hold her there until she was ready to scream in frustration, but she knew this game just as well. When he finally released her, she was going to fly up to the stratosphere.

As his strokes gained momentum, he grabbed her hip, holding her in place with one hand while the fingers of his other kept massaging, faster and faster until she threw her head back and screamed out his name.

20

KIAN

*A*s Syssi erupted, Kian clamped his lips on her neck and sank his fangs into her soft skin. As always, the double release was so powerful, it felt like he was dying and being resurrected at the same time.

Nothing compared to this, and as impossible as it seemed, the experience not only hadn't diminished with time, but had grown even more earth-shattering.

Kian felt blessed.

He hadn't known that he'd been lacking a vital part of himself until Syssi had entered his life. But now that he was sharing it with her, it was so painfully clear to him that up until he'd met her, he'd been running on empty.

Would the same be true for the child they would hopefully create together? Would he feel the same wonder?

Still buried deep inside his mate, Kian wrapped his arms around her middle and toppled them both sideways. Spooning behind her, he nuzzled her neck, but she was out.

It didn't happen as often as it had in the beginning, but from time to time Syssi still blacked out for several moments after a venom bite.

Knowing how much she loved the sensation of soaring on the clouds of euphoria, he loved giving it to her, which meant waiting patiently for her to come back down to earth.

Sometime later Syssi sighed contentedly. "We should go to sleep like this. I like the feel of you inside of me."

He kissed her shoulder. "I'm not nearly done with you yet, sweet girl."

"Oh, I know." She chuckled. "I can feel you charging up already. I'm just saying later, when we actually go to sleep."

He pulled out a little and then pushed back in, lazy, shallow thrusts that were more about the connection than ramping things up again.

A moment later, he pulled out all the way and pushed Syssi onto her back. "I want to see your face when I make slow love to you." What he really wanted to say was, *when I put a baby inside of you*, but he could make no such claim.

Straddling her, he feasted his eyes on her beautiful face, her gorgeous, smart eyes, and those lush lips that were curved in a coy little smile that was reserved just for him.

He could never get enough of kissing them. Hell, he couldn't get enough of kissing every part of her perfect body.

"Are you just going to stare?" Syssi cupped the undersides of her breasts. "Or are you going to take care of me?"

As his eyes zeroed in on her nipples, the scent of her arousal flared, and the little pink peaks tightened under his gaze. His mate loved it when he paid attention to her breasts, and no lovemaking session would be complete without him pleasuring them thoroughly.

Leaning down, he licked one, sucking it into his mouth, and then took care of the other with his fingers, pinching it lightly and tugging on it in sync with his suckling on its twin.

When both nipples had been properly pleasured, he smoothed his hand down her inner thigh. And as he cupped her between her legs, Syssi moaned and arched up, grinding her core on his palm.

"Come up and kiss me," she breathed.

That was an offer Kian couldn't refuse. Pushing up, he braced on his forearms and cradled her head in his hands.

For a moment, he just gazed into her luminous eyes, still marveling after all this time that she was an immortal like him.

"I love you," he whispered before taking her mouth in a kiss that was all about possession.

Her nails digging into his shoulders, Syssi kissed him back with just as much fervor. Owning him as surely as he owned her.

She was his everything, but even though she was well aware of it, mainly because he told her as much almost every day, she never tried to use her power over him to gain any kind of advantage.

She just loved him back.

"Do you know that I'm the luckiest guy on the planet?"

With a sweet smile, she lifted her head and kissed his lips. "I know. And I'm the luckiest woman." She swiveled her hips under him. "But I'm getting a little impatient."

"Are you now?" He gripped her wrists in one hand and brought them over her head. "What are you impatient for?"

"For you to get inside me and put a baby there."

"Oh, love." He dipped his head and kissed her lightly. "There is nothing I would like to do more, but it's not up to me. Not entirely."

Her eyes hooded with desire, she smirked. "We just need to keep working on it tirelessly."

"Tirelessly, eh?" He pushed just the tip into her.

"Yes, like this, but a little more."

He pushed a little deeper. "Is this good?"

"Almost. But it's still not enough."

He withdrew and pushed in again, going all the way in until he was fully seated inside her. "You meant like this?"

"Yes, please don't stop." Syssi lifted her legs and linked them behind his ass, spurring him on with her heels.

In no time, he was pounding into her, taking her as roughly as she loved being taken while thanking the Fates for giving him the perfect mate.

When Syssi's core tightened around him, and she cried out, Kian's climax was ripped out of him. Throwing his head back, he released a roar that would've been heard by every occupant of the village if not for the topnotch soundproofing of their house.

Panting, he had the presence of mind not to collapse on top of her but to drop sideways.

"Wow," Syssi breathed. "That was baby-making sex."

"Fates willing."

21

JULIAN

"What do you think?" Julian asked.

He'd done his damnedest to sell Ella's idea to the boss. Mostly because he thought it was a good one, but also because it would give her something to do and get her out of the house.

What did she do all day? Think about what she'd been through?

It couldn't be healthy for her to cook in her own juices like that.

And if she needed an assistant, he would jump on the opportunity to be with her in any capacity she was willing to have him.

"I like the idea," Kian said. "Anything that brings donation money and eases our financial burden is welcome."

Bridget pulled out her tablet and opened a page. "After Julian told me about it, I did some research on these kinds of fundraising platforms. There are several of them, with one being the clear leader, but I expect many to pop up in the near future because they are getting so popular. It's a new and fascinating phenomenon. People donate straight from their phones, supporting either someone they know who needs a helping hand or a cause they believe in. I was surprised to find how successful a fundraiser for fertility research was. Apparently, we are not the only ones struggling with the issue. Many humans are as well."

Kian snorted. "Who knows. Maybe Merlin's potions are the answer to our financial difficulties. If they work on us, they should work even better on humans. But that depends on how many would be willing to tolerate the foul taste."

Bridget cast him an amused glance. "I'm not sure about it working at all. But since Merlin tailored it for us, it might not be suitable for humans. In any case, I just wanted you to know that Turner and I are going to start the treatments too, so at least you and Syssi won't be alone in your suffering."

Shifting in his chair, Turner tightened his lips into a thin line. He was either uncomfortable with Bridget talking openly about their conception attempts, or perhaps he wasn't enthusiastic about becoming a father and was only agreeing to it to please her.

Julian wished them luck.

Having a little brother or sister was something he'd never even wished for because it was like wishing for the moon. Now that it seemed possible, he was rooting for his mother and her mate's success.

Hopefully, Merlin wasn't as loony as he appeared, and his potions were not just snake oil.

"We need to discuss logistics and security," Turner said. "For this to succeed, the videos need to be done professionally, but on the other hand, bringing in a professional camera crew and a director to run the show is out of the question."

"What if they are all female?" Bridget asked.

"I wasn't even thinking about the girls' reaction to a bunch of strangers with cameras showing up in their sanctuary. I'm concerned about word getting out. For their safety, we need to keep the location secret. It's next to impossible to get civilians to keep a secret, especially if selling the story can bring them a nice cash reward."

Kian drummed his fingers on the conference table. "What if we have everyone sign non-disclosure agreements with steep penalties for violations?"

Turner shook his head. "Not tight enough as far as safety is concerned. There is too much at risk. My recommendation is to keep the recording in-house. You can get Ella a professional camera and an assistant to handle the lighting."

He glanced at Julian and winked. "I think Julian could do that."

To see Turner wink was so shocking that for a moment Julian just gaped.

"As much as I adore my son, and as sweet as he is, I think a female assistant is a better choice." Bridget cast Julian an apologetic glance. "You can help with the editing, though. It's very labor intensive. I've seen a documentary about film-making, and I was astounded that a five-minute end product required hours of work in the editing room. Sometimes even days. I expect you and Ella will be spending a lot of time on that." His mother waggled her red brows.

They meant well, but they made him feel so damn pathetic.

"Do you have a particular female in mind?" Kian asked. "Because if you're thinking about Sylvia, don't. She's just started on another master's degree."

With all due respect to education, Sylvia was taking it too far. The woman was a perpetual student. It was a perfect example of why Turner's suggestion to demand volunteering from clan members had merit.

"I was actually thinking about Tessa," Bridget said.

There were rumors about Tessa having been through some rough times as a teenager, but Julian didn't know the details. Did his mother know? Had it been something similar to what Ella and the girls in the sanctuary had been through?

"Tessa is a good choice," Kian said. "But she works full time for Eva."

Bridget waved a dismissive hand. "Eva's detective agency is now running less than half the jobs it used to when Eva was active. She is only offering its services to old clients who she doesn't want to lose during her maternity leave. Sharon is too inexperienced for the more complicated field jobs. Nick is only a tech guy, not a detective, and Tessa is an office person. Eva just doesn't have the personnel needed to run more jobs. With the diminished workload, I'm sure she can spare Tessa for a few days."

Turner perked up. "If Eva doesn't need Nick full time either, I can certainly use him."

"I'll ask her," Bridget said.

"Good." Kian tapped his palm on the conference table. "Bridget, you are in charge of talking to Eva. If she can spare Tessa, talk to the girl and see if she's game." He turned to Julian. "If that goes well, explain the arrangement to Ella and coordinate a meeting between her and Tessa."

Julian nodded. "I'll do that. But what about the camera and other equipment as well as training on how to use them?"

"I'll call Brandon and see what he can get us. The equipment can be rented, or we can buy used stuff. We don't need the latest and best for this. I hope he can hook us up with someone to train our new filming crew."

22

LOSHAM

*A*s Losham was escorted into his father's reception chamber, he was unpleasantly surprised to find the brothel's manager sitting across from Navuh and sucking on one of his expensive cigars.

That was a privilege that only Losham had been granted up until now. How the hell had the sniveling Herpon gained such favor in their leader's eyes?

"Greetings, my lord." Losham bowed low. "You wanted to see me?"

He wasn't used to sharing his father's time with another, not even his halfbrothers. Losham wasn't a military man, so there was no need for him to attend the mundane field-operation decisions his brothers dealt with.

Usually, the issues Navuh wished to discuss with him were confidential.

Besides, the leader liked to take credit for all of Losham's good ideas, which would have been difficult to do with witnesses. He would have been forced to eliminate them, and that was wasteful.

"Yes. Take a seat, Losham. Herpon came to me with a problem that I think you can solve for him. I will let him explain."

Even though the man was good at what he did, Losham detested Herpon. He was an underhanded and cunning bastard who had somehow managed to rise in the ranks despite his lowly parentage. He was a crude and offensive fellow, who pretended to be refined in front of Navuh.

Not successfully, though.

Losham doubted his father was fooled by the fake mannerisms, but then Navuh cared about results and not the means to get them.

"The customers are tired of the Eastern Bloc stock we have," Herpon said. "Most of the girls can't speak any English, and those that know a few words would do better using their mouths for something else."

Raising a brow, Losham crossed his legs and leaned forward. "Since when do customers care about the whores' conversational skills? They come here to fuck, not to talk."

Herpon shook his head. "Things are always changing and shifting, and what was good a decade ago is no good now. The more sophisticated customers, those who are willing to pay the most, want to do both. They want a girl they can take out for a drink or to dinner, have a pleasant conversation with, and after that take her to their bungalow and fuck her all night long."

Losham shrugged. "I don't see how I can help with that. You need to discuss this with our suppliers and demand that they bring in a higher caliber stock."

"I did. The answer I got was that girls like that were difficult to obtain, and the cost I've been quoted per specimen was too high."

"I still do not see where I can be of help."

Navuh lifted his hand. "We need college girls, not the runaways and junkies that we usually get, preferably from English-speaking countries, but other Western Bloc countries will do as well. As long as they are fairly educated and intelligent, we can teach them English in some form of an accelerated program."

Losham smoothed his hand over his beard. "I'm sure we can get educated Russian and Ukrainian girls and teach them English. They are not going to be as costly as those from English-speaking countries because it's not as dangerous to obtain them on the Eastern Bloc and then ship them over here."

Navuh's brows drew tight. "I did not bring you here to hear suggestions and excuses. I want solutions. You are a smart man. I'm sure you can come up with a way to supply the island with the kind of stock our top customers require." He leaned toward Losham and pinned him with a hard glare. "The law of supply and demand states that where there is unmet demand, someone will figure out a way to meet it. If we cannot satisfy these customers, someone else will, and we will lose them."

That was not what the law of supply and demand stated, but in principle Navuh was right.

"Perhaps I can pull warriors away from the drug trade and have them visit local colleges. Most of the men are not big charmers, but they can thrall well enough to have girls come with them. The question is what to do after that."

Navuh waved a dismissive hand. "Even if we have each girl escorted by a warrior and pay for plane tickets for both, we are still going to save a lot of money compared to what we are paying the suppliers now. And the one thing we have no shortage of is men. You can have your pick of the most handsome and charming ones."

That was doable. While posing as a couple on vacation, the soldier could keep thralling the girl through several plane rides and airports. Naturally, Losham would have to come up with a number of different routes and use international airports that didn't employ facial recognition software. Another option was cruise ships. People disappeared from those all the time.

With their natural ability to learn new languages as well as the local vernacular, the men could pretend to be American or British or Australian. It would be easier to lure a girl away from her college friends if the man didn't appear foreign.

"When I'm back in San Francisco, I'll organize several test runs. One way or another, I'm going to get you what you need."

Navuh smiled. "I knew you'd find a solution, my son."

To call Losham 'son' in front of Herpon, getting quality stock for the brothel must have been of utmost importance to Navuh.

Losham pushed to his feet and bowed. "I will keep you updated, my lord."

"Very well. You may take your leave."

23

JULIAN

By the time the meeting was over, Carol's café was closed, but the vending machines still had a selection left over.

Choosing a Danish, Julian inserted his card into the slot, pressed the right number combination, and then watched the wrapped pastry getting grabbed by the mechanical arm and dropped into the receptacle.

"Julian, how are things going for you?" Jackson parked his loaded cart next to the sandwich machine.

Great, he was about to get dating advice from the kid.

No thank you.

"I'm just getting a Danish and coffee and then heading home. Since when are you doing deliveries in the evenings?"

Jackson opened the back of the machine and started refilling the empty rows with new sandwiches. "I've gotten complaints about the machines emptying by seven in the evening. People get hungry, and there is nothing to eat. They have to drive half an hour to the nearest fast-food joint or to a supermarket. So I hired another part-timer to prepare an evening batch."

"At Ruth's?"

Jackson peeked at him from behind the machine. "So it's Ruth's now, eh? Don't let Nathalie hear you say it. It's called Fernando's Café, and technically it's half mine and half Nathalie's. We are equal partners now."

Julian didn't know what business arrangement Jackson had with Nathalie, and frankly, he didn't care. "That's nice."

"How is Parker doing?" Jackson asked. "I haven't seen him since the transition ceremony, and I feel bad about not checking up on him. I'm supposed to be his mentor and all that. But I'm so fucking busy all the time."

"He's doing great. His fangs finally came out, and he would be very happy to show them to you." Julian leaned on the machine's side and crossed his arms over his chest. "Do you play War of the Dragons?"

Jackson lifted his head and looked at him. "Does it look like I have time to play computer games?"

"I meant do you know how to play it? It's an old game, but it's one of Parker's favorites. He'd love it if you played with him."

Pushing his long bangs away from his forehead, Jackson let out an old man's sigh. "In my previous life as a carefree bachelor, I played it."

Julian frowned. "You sound like you're not happy to be mated."

"Are you kidding me? No way! Tessa is the best thing that has ever happened to me, and I thank the merciful Fates every day for her. I just wish I had more free time. I miss hanging out with my buddies, and I miss kicking it with a good video game and a box of lousy pizza."

"I have an idea. How about you and I both go to play with Parker? But instead of lousy pizza, we can munch on your sandwiches and pastries."

Jackson rose to his feet and closed the back of the machine. "Let me check with Tessa. She's babysitting little Ethan so Eva can take a breather. I told her I'd join her there, but maybe she can do without me for the next hour."

As Jackson exchanged texts with his mate, Julian wondered whether Bridget had already spoken with Eva and Tessa about the video project. His mother was a pragmatic lady who didn't postpone until later what could be done right now, so chances were that she had.

"I'm good to go," Jackson said. "Tessa is taking Ethan to Nathalie's and is going to hang out with her until Eva and Bhathian are back."

"Did she tell you anything about the video project Ella came up with?"

"No." Jackson pushed the empty cart behind the café's counter and handed a box filled with sandwiches and pastries to Julian. "What is it about?"

As they made their way to Ella's house, Julian told Jackson about the fundraiser, the videos Ella wanted to shoot, and about Bridget suggesting Tessa as Ella's production assistant.

When he was done, Jackson shook his head. "I'm not sure Tessa would want to do that."

"Why not?" He had his suspicions, but he didn't want to assume anything.

"She likes working for Eva."

"I understand that at the moment things are slow at the agency."

"They are, which means that Tessa can take it easy. She's working on reorganizing files and transcribing the old ones into the computer. When Eva first started her agency, she kept handwritten files."

Julian chuckled. "Turner still does, even though he's several decades younger than Eva. But that's because he's paranoid and doesn't trust cyber encryption. I'm trying to convince him that for the right amount of money he can have an impenetrable system, but he insists that any system can eventually get hacked, and that some information is too crucial to keep anywhere other than in his notes."

"What if someone breaks into his place and steals them?"

"I think he has some form of personal encoding he uses."

Jackson nodded. "So does Eva. She has a shorthand script that she invented, and no one other than her and her crew can decipher it."

"Don't you just love all this cloak and dagger stuff?"

"I love hearing about it, but not living it. I'm not a big risk taker." Jackson chuckled. "I get my thrills from making money."

"Different strokes for different folks."

Jackson was working his ass off, and even though none of it was glamorous or overly exciting, it seemed like he was loving every moment of it.

Julian, on the other hand, didn't feel passionate about anything. Except for Ella, of course, but that was an obsession, not an occupation.

He loved being a doctor, but he wasn't as passionate about it as he'd been at the start of medical school. Money didn't thrill him either, and what Turner did for a living required nerves of steel he didn't have. Besides, strategizing wasn't Julian's thing either.

"When I was a kid, I wanted to be a rock star," Jackson said. "I had fun. Gordon and Vlad and I even got some gigs of the non-paid variety. It didn't take long for me to realize that performing wasn't a good way to make money, and that I needed to find something else. Still, if not for Bhathian introducing me to Nathalie, I might not have discovered my entrepreneurial streak so early in the game."

"I'm glad that you found your groove. I'm still looking for mine."

Jackson frowned. "You're a doctor, dude. There is nothing nobler than that. You can save lives, or at least improve them."

"That's why I chose to be one. But reality kind of slapped me in the face. I'm too empathetic to work with humans because it's torture for me to absorb all that suffering and worrying and grief. And with Merlin here, I'm not really needed in the village. Kian dropped an assignment on me that I'm unqualified for, mainly because I have the time to do it."

"What's the assignment?"

"He wants me to find a place that can be turned into a halfway house for the rescued girls, and also to come up with the financing for it."

Jackson cast him a sidelong glance. "So that's what the fundraising is for?"

"Among other things. If it succeeds, we can have more than one halfway house and help many more girls get back on their feet."

"I'll talk with Tessa. If all she needs is a little nudge in the right direction, I'll encourage her to do it. But if she's really reluctant, you'll need to find another assistant for Ella. Carol would've been fantastic, but she already has too much on her plate."

Jackson thinking of Carol as a suitable replacement for Tessa made it clear to Julian that Tessa's past involved something similar to what Carol and Ella had gone through.

Not that the experiences were comparable.

Carol had been abducted by Doomers and tortured by a sadist. In comparison, Ella's ordeal had been much less traumatic. Except, Carol was a resilient immortal and as far from naïve as it got, while Ella was a very young human girl, who hadn't been exposed to evil until that scumbag Romeo had trapped her, luring her away from home and delivering her into the clutches of a sex trafficker.

24

ELLA

*A*s Ella strolled along one of the many trails meandering through the sanctuary's grounds, she was surprised at how eerily quiet everything was. Usually, nature was full of sounds, leaves rustling in the wind, bugs buzzing, birds calling, crickets chirping, but the landscape around her was static and quiet as if it was a backdrop in an indoor filming studio.

"That's because you're dreaming." Logan appeared at her side. "But I can fix that for you." He snapped his fingers, and suddenly, they were surrounded by all the sounds that had been missing before.

"How did you do that?"

He tapped her temple with his finger. "I just activated your imagination. You weren't working hard enough on your scenery." He looked around. "Although I have to admit that it is pleasant enough, I would make it greener, and maybe add a brook. More trees would be nice too."

As he was about to snap his fingers again, Ella lifted her hand to stop him. "You've got a hell of a lot of nerve to give me crap about my landscape after not showing up for nearly two weeks. Besides, this is as green as it gets here. This place is a memory, not something I created in my imagination."

Logan took a quick look around before returning his eyes to her. "My apologies." He bowed with exaggerated flair. "Did you miss me?"

Ella shrugged. "Not really. I've been busy."

His dark eyes widened almost imperceptibly. "Doing what?"

"Oh, this and that. But I'm going to be very busy soon enough."

He waved a hand. "Don't keep me in suspense. Tell me what you're planning. Perhaps I can be of help."

"I doubt it. I'm organizing a fundraiser to help girls who were rescued from situations similar to mine." She pinned the specter with a hard gaze. "Unless you want to make a donation, that is. I'm sure a rich mercenary warlord like you can afford to spare a few thousand for a good cause."

It was silly to scold a specter, but on the other hand, it was fun to act as if she could be so brave and outspoken facing the real Logan, telling him what she thought of him straight to his face.

"As you can imagine, I'm not a philanthropist, but I would do it for you." His eyes went to her mouth. "You could auction your lips, and I'd bid for a kiss from you."

"Dream on, perv. I'm not kissing you, no matter how much money you pledge to the cause."

He pouted, pretending offense. "Why not? I'm handsome, and I know for a fact that you're attracted to me because I'm in your head."

There was no point in lying to herself, which talking to Logan essentially was. Her subconscious probably needed to sort this out.

"I don't know why I am. It must be some chemical reaction. Did you put on a pheromone imbued cologne the one time we met?"

"I did no such thing. It's just my natural magnetism." He waggled his brows.

"It's not working on me, so you may as well stop it."

He didn't like her answer, and with his smile and fake charm momentarily gone, Logan looked just as scary as he had in her first and second dream encounter with him.

"You're such a hypocrite, Ella. Are you telling me that you wouldn't sacrifice one little kiss to get thousands for a cause that's so dear to you?"

Well, when put like that, he had a point.

Except, giving even one kiss to Logan was dangerous. To raise money for the halfway house, Ella was willing to auction her kisses to complete strangers, but not to Logan.

"That's because I don't like you, and I don't trust you. You're really bad, and I doubt you'd be satisfied with one kiss."

He laughed. "True on both counts, but oftentimes naughty girls like bad boys to take charge and steal more than one kiss."

"I'm not naughty, and I'm too smart to fall for a bad boy again. I was stupid once, and I paid dearly for that. I'm not going to repeat that mistake with you."

Logan rolled his eyes. "You had sex with Gorchenco, who loved you and cherished you, and you're making a big deal out of it. Only a spoiled American girl would make such a huge fuss about such a trivial matter."

Ella frowned. No way was this her own thought.

"Are you in my head, Logan? Because that wasn't me talking."

He smiled. "Are you sure?"

She was about to answer that yes, she was absolutely sure, when Logan started fading into mist, and then with a hand wave and a wink he disappeared.

Jerking awake in bed, Ella sucked in a breath. Had the actual Logan been invading her dreams?

She shivered at the thought.

It didn't make sense, though. Even if Logan was a telepath and could communicate with other telepaths from afar, Ella had put up extremely strong mental walls, and she knew they held up while she slept because her mother couldn't penetrate them no matter how hard she tried.

The simpler explanation was that the words she'd put in dream Logan's mouth were probably what she thought the real Logan would say, and not her own subconscious thoughts. That was why what he'd said had sounded so foreign and offensive to her.

Her mind had just reminded her why she'd found the real Logan so repulsive in the first place. This was precisely the kind of reasoning he would use.

Shaking the bad feeling away, she decided not to let the dream ruin what was going to be a great day.

Later this morning she was meeting with Brandon, the clan's media specialist, and Tessa, Jackson's fiancée, for a crash course in operating professional recording equipment.

If Tessa was half as nice as Jackson, the two of them were going to get along great.

What a charmer that guy was. He'd won over everyone in the family, including her brother, her mother, and the dog. Ella was so glad he'd been chosen as Parker's initiator. According to the clan's tradition, that meant they were honorary brothers, which was so cool.

Not for the first time, Ella wondered how her mother was going to be initiated. It didn't make sense for her to fight an immortal male, and as far as Ella knew, immortal females' tiny fangs were only for show.

But every time she tried to steer the conversation in that direction, either Magnus or Vivian would change the topic.

It must be something really bad for them to act so evasively.

Which was another reason to finally start leaving the house and mingling with other immortals. Jackson had told her that Tessa used to be a human, so maybe she could ask the girl what was involved in a female Dormant's activation.

25

TESSA

As Ella walked into Kian's office, Tessa smiled and got up. "Hi, I'm Tessa." She offered the girl her hand.

Ella was just as ethereally beautiful as Jackson had described her. Looking away from that angelic face was hard. No wonder Julian had fallen for a mere picture of her. She was short, but not as short as Tessa, and Ella was more full-figured—not fat, and not skinny, kind of average.

But then, with that face, Ella didn't need anything else to call attention to herself.

That beautiful face, however, was probably what had gotten her in trouble in the first place. People didn't realize that sometimes beauty could be more of a liability than an asset for a girl. Especially when it was as striking as Ella's.

Shaking Tessa's hand, Ella smiled. "It's nice to meet you and thank you for agreeing to do this."

She seemed nice, friendly, but also reserved.

Sadly, Tessa was well familiar with that guarded look—the one worn by those who'd been hurt and had lost their naïveté and innocence. For many years, the same expression had been staring at her from the mirror. And if not for Jackson, it still would be.

She smiled back, trying to look as friendly and as welcoming as she could. "My pleasure. When Jackson came home last night, he was so excited about your idea that I had no choice but to get swept away by his enthusiasm. When my guy gets like that, he can convince Eskimos to buy ice from him."

"I've noticed. Your Jackson is so charming and charismatic."

Tessa was about to say something nice about Julian when the door banged open, and Brandon walked in with a stack of boxes tall enough to hide his face.

"Let me help you with that." She took two from the top.

Ella took two more.

"Thank you." He dropped the rest of them on the conference table and handed Kian an invoice. "That's all the equipment Ella and Tessa are going to need, except for the background paper roll. I ordered it online, and it should be arriving tomorrow."

Tessa cast Ella a puzzled glance, but apparently Ella didn't know what he was talking about either.

"Hello, Ella." He shook her hand. "Welcome to the clan. I'm glad your story had a happy ending."

"Thank you."

He shook Tessa's hand next. "How are Eva and the baby doing? I haven't seen them since little Ethan's party."

"They are both doing great. And Ethan is not so little anymore. He's such a cute, chubby baby."

"Give Eva my regards, would you?"

"I will."

Brandon was one of a small group of immortals not residing in the village. He kept his penthouse in Hollywood and was apparently too busy to come and visit more than once in a blue moon. The only reason Tessa even knew him was that Eva had introduced them at Ethan's party.

Kian looked at the invoice and shook his head. "Professional equipment used to be expensive. You're telling me that you bought everything for under a thousand bucks?"

The media specialist chuckled. "When was the last time you purchased a camera, Kian? The eighties?"

"More or less. I didn't have much use for one."

"A lot has changed since then, and with the explosion of blogging, the market became much less niche. Mass production always lowers costs."

"That's good. So other than the paper roll you've mentioned, this is everything they will need?"

"Yes. The white background paper is for the silhouette shoots, but the girls can learn all they need to know about filming that from YouTube."

He pulled out his phone and turned to them. "Give me your phone numbers, and I'll text you a list of links I've prepared. Watch the videos, and if after that you still have questions, you can call me. But I doubt it will be necessary. All you need to know is on YouTube."

With that done, Brandon put his phone back in his pocket and pushed to his feet. "It was a pleasure to see you, ladies, but now I have to run."

And off he went.

Ella looked at the door closing on Brandon's back and shook her head. "If he wasn't going to show us anything, he could've just ordered the stuff online and sent it here."

"YouTube," Kian bit out. "He wants you to learn everything from YouTube? I don't understand why he even bothered to come."

Tessa had a feeling she knew the answer to that. Brandon had been curious about Ella and wanted to see her in person. Maybe he thought that he could steal her away from Julian?

The rumors claimed that Ella was not showing any romantic interest in the handsome doctor, which meant that pretty soon all the sharks would start circling around the unattached Dormant, and Brandon had probably decided to beat them to it.

Except, if that was his intention, teaching Ella in person would have better served his agenda.

Maybe he didn't like what he saw?

But that didn't make sense either, and not only because Ella was so beautiful. She was a Dormant. That was enough to make her a coveted prize.

"Brandon seems like a busy guy," Ella said. "It would've been a waste of his time to show us something that we can learn from YouTube. And he was nice enough to compile a list of videos for us. We should be fine, right, Tessa?"

"I hope so. I don't know anything about cameras. Do you?"

Ella shook her head. "I only ever used my phone. But I've learned to do many things from YouTube videos. I even fixed a problem with my computer after watching a guy explain what to do step by step. And trust me, other than turning it on and typing on the keyboard, I know nothing about it." She eyed the pile of boxes. "Let's each grab a few and take them to my house. We will have to come back for the rest."

"You don't need to carry anything," Kian said. "I'll have Okidu bring all the boxes to Ella's house. You can go ahead and start on those videos."

26

ELLA

"Do you like it here?" Tessa asked as they left the office building.

Ella waved a hand at the greenery. "What's not to like? It's like a little piece of heaven here."

In her previous life, she might have found the village boring, especially since it seemed like the only place to hang out was the café. But the new Ella appreciated the reclusiveness and serenity.

Tessa pushed a strand of her straight bleached-blond hair behind her ear. "It's safe. I've never felt as safe as I feel here. If not for Jackson dragging me out of here from time to time, I would never leave. But he likes to go out to clubs, and bars, and movies, and I don't want to be the drag that keeps him from having a life."

It sounded like Tessa was a lot like Ella. The new one. Not the old one. The old Ella would have loved to hang out with Jackson at all the places Tessa had mentioned. Not as his girlfriend or anything, but perhaps with a larger group of friends. Even though the guy was gorgeous and charming, she wasn't attracted to him.

Besides, Jackson and Tessa were practically married.

Except, Ella would not have been interested in him even if he were available. He was a pretty boy, but a boy nonetheless. And anyway, dating was the furthest thing from her mind. If she ever felt like going out with anyone again, it would be with Julian.

The question was whether she would ever be ready for that.

Maybe things would change after her transition, and the transformation would be more than physical. Perhaps a third version of Ella would emerge, one that was better and stronger than the first two.

"Can I ask you something?"

Tessa cast her an amused glance. "Depends on what it is."

"It's okay if you don't want to answer, but I can't get anyone to tell me how female Dormants transition. I know that Dormant guys have to fight an immortal male, but I can't imagine a woman fighting one of them, and as far as I know, female immortals don't have venom in their tiny fangs."

Eyes widening in surprise, Tessa nearly stumbled over a crack in the paving stones. "You've been here for two whole weeks, and no one has told you what's involved in transitioning yet?"

Ella shook her head. "Every time I bring the subject up, someone manages to steer the conversation to another topic. Is this a taboo subject?"

Hands on her hips, Tessa looked up and sighed. "No, it's not. But I know why no one wants to tell you."

"Does it have anything to do with what happened to me?" Ella asked in a hushed voice as they resumed walking.

"Yeah, it does. But they are making a mistake by hiding it from you. You may not like it, but you should know." Tessa stopped again and faced Ella. "To produce venom, immortal males have to either get aggressive or aroused. They bite during fights with other males and during sex with females."

Ella's hand flew to her neck. "Ouch. That's nasty."

"Not really. The venom is a powerful euphoric and aphrodisiac. It hurts for about two seconds when the fangs break your skin, but after that, it's unimaginable bliss and the best orgasms of your life. Not a bad trade-off."

"Isn't it dangerous, though? If it's used for fighting, it must be potentially lethal."

"It's not. Because the venom production in each situation is triggered by different hormones, its composition is different."

"Do they always bite, or only sometimes?"

"Biting is the same as ejaculating for immortal males. They can refrain if they must, but it's difficult."

Now it was Ella's turn to stop in her tracks. "So, if Magnus is biting my mom, which I must assume that he does, how come she didn't transition yet?"

"They must be using condoms. To induce transition, the venom bite must be combined with insemination."

Great, so if she wanted to transition, Ella would have to have sex with an immortal male and also chance getting pregnant.

It seemed like she wasn't transitioning anytime soon.

"I see. Thank you for telling it to me straight. I don't know why my mom thought that I couldn't handle it. It's not like I'm a blushing virgin and can't talk about sex."

Come to think of it, when Julian had told her the truth about himself, the clan, and her being a Dormant, he'd evaded her questions on the subject too. But then he might have been embarrassed to talk about it with a girl he hardly knew.

Her mother had no such excuse. Before, they used to talk freely about sex.

Tessa smiled, but it was a sad smile. "Don't be angry at her. Her intentions are good. She and Magnus probably assume that because you were violated, any mention of sex will bring you grief, and they don't want to hurt you. What they don't realize is that it's even more hurtful to be treated like a victim."

It seemed like Tessa had more in common with her than Ella had initially suspected. "You sound as if you're talking from experience."

"Unfortunately, I am. Not many people know that about me, so don't tell anyone. I hate to be regarded with pity. I'm telling you only because you understand how I feel."

"I do. And your secret is safe with me. I wish no one knew about what happened to me either. Pretending to be normal would have been so much easier."

"I'm glad we see eye to eye."

The question was how come Tessa got to keep her ordeal a secret, while everyone in the clan knew about Ella's. "I'm guessing that the clan didn't rescue you. Otherwise, everyone would've known about you like they know about me."

Tessa shook her head. "Eva, my boss, saved me. I owe her my life. She killed the scumbag who'd bought and abused me, she took me in, and she gave me a home and a job. But as I said before, this is between you and me. Don't tell anyone."

It sounded as if Tessa's ordeal had been much worse than Ella's. At least Gorchenco had not abused her.

"Your boss must be a kickass lady."

"Oh, she is." Tessa perked up. "You have to meet her. But it's not like she's doing any ass-kicking recently or planning to return to it anytime soon. Eva has a cute baby boy, and she is wholly dedicated to being a mother."

"I'm happy for her. I'm sure it's more fun taking care of a baby than killing scumbags."

Tessa chuckled. "For you and for me, almost anything would be better than going after scum, but I'm not sure about Eva. I think she's secretly itching to get back to work."

"What exactly is her work? I was told that she can hook me up with prosthetics to change my features. I need to have my picture taken for my fake documents."

"Eva is a detective. Mainly, she's done corporate espionage, but she's also gone after cheating spouses. Elaborate disguises are her specialty. That's why she has taken it upon herself to provide movie-quality makeup to clan members, including prosthetics, for their licenses and other documents. My friend Sharon has taken over the detective work, but she's still a rookie, so Eva doesn't send her out on anything too dangerous or difficult."

The more Tessa told her about Eva, the more fascinating the woman sounded. "I'd love to meet her. Can you check with her when is a good time for her to hook me up with prosthetics?"

Tessa pulled out her phone. "It would be best to go see her when Bhathian is there, that's her husband, so he can take care of the baby while she's busy. This evening work for you?"

"Sure. But first, we need to unpack the equipment, watch a few YouTube videos, and familiarize ourselves with how everything works."

Tessa waved a dismissive hand. "That shouldn't take us more than a couple of hours."

27

JULIAN

"Is this it?" Yamanu poked his head out the window and regarded the building Julian had parked in front of. "Not much to look at. It's a dump."

"That's because you have no imagination." Julian killed the ignition. "A new coat of paint, some more trees in the front, and it will look great."

Yamanu got out of the car and waited for Julian to join him. "It's like putting makeup on a pig. It's not going to make it pretty."

"If we are using animal analogies, then the one about not looking a gift horse in the mouth is more appropriate."

Yamanu slapped his back. "Can't argue with that, mate. How come Kian is being so generous, though? I thought money was tight."

"He bought this old hotel a while back and was planning on erecting a new one in its place. But the city dropped an unexpected obstacle in his path, and they did it after the plans for the new hotel were almost done. The pencil-pushers came up with some crap about it being a historic building because someone no one has ever heard about had stayed there once in the late thirties, and therefore it had to be preserved."

"Kian should have sold it as is."

"No one would've bought it after it was declared a historic building. And instead of waging battle with the city bureaucrats, Kian decided to donate it and take a tax write-off."

Yamanu looked at the broken windows and shook his head. "Lucky us."

It was ironic that after all of his posturing about the halfway house project being Julian's baby, and expecting him to find a location and the financing for purchasing it, Kian had ended up taking care of it.

Now it was up to Julian to make it work.

Inside the building, the situation was even worse. Between the peeling paint, rotted through carpet, and broken windows, the structure seemed suitable for only one thing. Demolition.

Yamanu opened the gate of the ancient elevator. "Just to bring it up to code will require massive work. I don't think one elevator is enough for a building this size."

"There are two staircases. One interior and a fire escape in the back. That's good enough."

"Are you sure?"

"I checked."

A grimace on his handsome face, Yamanu turned in a circle. "At least the neighborhood is decent."

"And it's close to the village."

"Twenty-five-minute drive, and it's not a heavy traffic route, which is the biggest plus." He rubbed his huge hands together. "Let's see the rooms. If they are okay, then the rest can be worked on."

Julian eyed the ancient elevator. "I suggest we take the stairs."

Hesitantly, he put his foot on the first stair, and the next, and the one after that, but the staircase ended up being surprisingly sturdy.

The carpet covering the corridor was in better shape than the one in the lobby, but not good enough to stay.

As Julian opened the door to the first room, he was surprised that it was still furnished. Given the broken windows on the lobby level, he'd been sure that vandals had either stolen or destroyed everything.

Yamanu went over to the narrow four-poster bed and gave it a shake. "Sturdy. We can use it." Next, he checked the nightstands and the writing desk. "I'll be damned. We can use all of it. The mattress needs to be replaced, but other than that the furniture is good quality."

"Let's check the bathroom." Julian opened the door.

It was tiny, with a pedestal sink, an old-fashioned toilet, and a charming claw-foot bathtub.

"What do you think?" He turned to Yamanu.

"Looks good. The question is whether the stuff works. Do you know if the water is connected?"

"I think so." Julian twisted the faucet knobs. "Water pressure is fine. The heaters are not on, so it's cold. We will have to check those too."

The toilet flushed, the faucet in the bathtub worked, and the tub drained adequately.

Yamanu lifted his eyes to the ceiling. "No leaks either."

"How much do you think we will need for remodeling?"

Yamanu shrugged. "No clue, buddy. This is not my area of expertise. Dealing with idiot bureaucrats, however, is. I'm surprised Kian didn't ask me to take care of this problem for him."

"Does he usually?"

"When it's something ridiculous like this, then yeah."

Interesting. It seemed that Kian had changed his mind about financing the halfway house and had donated the building even though he could've salvaged the situation with Yamanu's help.

Why hadn't he just come out and said it?

There had been no need for him to make it look as if he had no choice and was forced to donate the building.

"We need a name," Yamanu said. "A halfway house has a negative connotation. How about Chateau Clarice?"

"Who's Clarice?"

Yamanu shrugged. "No one I know. It just sounds nice."

"If it's going to be Chateau anything, it should be Chateau Bridget."

"I like it. But both are a mouthful. It needs to be something simple and generic, like The Grove or The Orchards."

"Or The Palms. Because of the two palms up front."

"That's good. The Palms it is."

28

ELLA

*E*va was awesome.

A fierce, unapologetic, master of disguise, defender of the weak, and a killer of scumbags.

This was who Ella wanted to be when she grew up.

Maybe not the killer part, she didn't know if she had it in her, but a kickass woman who inspired respect and a healthy amount of fear.

And according to Tessa, this was Eva at her mellowest.

Sitting in Eva's living room and sipping on virgin margaritas, the three of them had let go of all pretenses and laid it all out, but only after swearing to take the secrets to their graves, of course.

Tessa shook her head. "I can't believe you were an active vigilante during the years I worked for you. I thought that Martin was the only scumbag you killed."

Eva smirked over the top of her margarita glass. "If I got caught, I didn't want my kids to get in trouble."

Tessa cast Ella an amused glance. "She's talking about Sharon, Nick, and me. She's always treated us like we were her kids. We loved it but thought that she was a little nuts. We didn't know that she was old enough to be our grandma."

"It must've been so hard for you to keep your immortality a secret." Ella put her glass on the coffee table. "Always on the run. You're so brave."

Eva shrugged. "I did what I had to, but it was also in my nature. When I joined the DEA, I didn't know I was immortal. I just wanted to fight the bad guys. At the time, I believed drugs were the worst problem, so that's what I wanted to fight. If I'd known about human trafficking back then, I might have chosen a different path. Except, there is no agency that deals with that. And that's a shame. After rescuing Tessa, I started looking into it, and that's how my vigilante days started."

After hearing Tessa's story, which she was sure was a highly diluted version of what had really happened to her, Ella could totally sympathize with Eva's motives for assassinating traffickers.

It made Ella feel guilty for the self-pity she'd allowed herself to indulge in. Poor Tessa had been to real hell, but she didn't pity herself. She counted herself lucky for getting out alive, and she'd even managed to fall in love.

"You are both so brave, each one in her own way. I feel humbled."

Eva waved a dismissive hand. "You're brave too. The way you handled the Russian was perfect, and you did it without any prior training, relying only on your instincts. But still, if it makes you feel safer, I can kill him for you. Not right now, but in a couple of years when I'm back to work."

Ella almost choked on her virgin margarita. "Thank you," she croaked after the coughing fit had subsided. "That's a very generous offer, but if I wanted Gorchenco dead, I would've let Turner's team do it. I specifically asked that they spare him, which complicated my rescue."

"I understand," Eva said. "You're young and soft. But if I hear that he bought another girl, he's dead."

"He won't. That's not how he is. I was a special case."

Eva shook her head. "He took what wasn't his for the taking. That's bad. But it's your choice to forgive him. However, if he does it again to someone else, I'll deal with him when I'm ready. But if he comes searching for you, the Guardians should take him out, and you shouldn't try to stop them. You shouldn't live in fear."

Ella loved Eva's bluntness, and she loved even more that the woman didn't regard her or Tessa as victims.

On the contrary, it seemed as if Eva felt closer to the two of them than she did to others. It was kind of a weird symbiosis. They were kindred spirits, with Eva on one end as the savior, and Tessa and Ella on the other end as the saved.

"I need to change the way I look. When you say prosthetics, what exactly are we talking about?"

"Movie makeup." Eva emptied the rest of her margarita and took the glass to the sink. "But that takes a lot of time and skill. It's not something you can just slap on in the morning." She came back with a box of cookies. "A makeover will work better. When Tessa had hers, it gave her confidence a nice boost, am I right?" She glanced at Tessa.

"Yeah, it did. Before that, I had mousy hair, and I wore kids' clothes. Subconsciously, I wanted to look like a kid and not a woman, so no one would approach me. I don't think anyone seeing me now would recognize me as that girl. Which also boosted my confidence and made me less fearful. Before the makeover, what I was most afraid of was Martin's brother coming after me."

Ella reached for a cookie. "I don't have a confidence problem, and I'm not particularly fearful either. I just made one really big stupid mistake."

"Stop beating yourself up over that," Eva said. "You're eighteen, that's still a baby. Your mother should've been smarter, though."

"But I tricked her. I told her that I was staying at my friend Maddie's."

Eva smirked. "You see, that's the difference between your mother and me. I would not have bought that story and would've been immediately suspicious. Vivian needs coaching."

"Not really. I'm not going to do anything stupid like that ever again. She has nothing to worry about."

"But she does worry, and that's why she's not going for the transition, which she should do sooner rather than later."

"Why? What's the rush?"

"Your mother is not getting any younger, and the transition is more difficult the older the Dormant."

"I'll talk to her." About this and about keeping important details from her.

Her mother should've told her about how Dormants were turned, and that age was a factor. Ella shouldn't have learned it from Tessa and Eva, whom she'd just met that day.

"Anyway, back to the makeover," Eva said. "Since gaining confidence is not important to you, we should go for the most drastic transformation possible. Are you okay with it making you look worse rather than better than you do now?"

"A hundred percent." Ella pointed to her face. "This is what has gotten me in trouble. I'm sick of people gawking at me, and I don't want to be a target."

Eva smirked. "What I have in mind will not solve the gawking problem. How do you feel about going Goth?"

"Ugh, black hair looks really fake on me. It's not going to work."

"I was thinking more along the lines of pink, or maybe purple."

"Then we should wait for my mother to transition because when she sees me with pink hair, she's going to have a stroke."

Tessa frowned. "But you need to change your appearance to get your picture taken for your fake documents."

"I was just joking. My mom will have to deal with it. When can we do it?"

"Let me check with Amanda." Eva reached for her phone. "She'd never forgive me if we do it without her."

"Right. She told me the first day I got here that she's the one I should turn to."

The answer to Eva's text came right away.

"She says that she's free on Saturday, and that we should meet up either in her house or yours."

29

VIVIAN

"Mom, I need to talk to you," Ella said as she entered the house. "In my room, if you don't mind."

Vivian put her book down. "Did something happen at Eva's?"

"Nothing happened, I just want to talk to you in private." She motioned with her head toward Parker. "Girl talk."

"Oh, okay." Vivian pushed to her feet and followed Ella to her room.

"What is it, sweetie?" she asked after closing the door.

"When were you going to tell me about how female Dormants are turned?"

With a sigh, Vivian sat on the bed. "Did Eva tell you?"

"No, Tessa did."

"What did she tell you?"

"That it involves sex with an immortal male and getting bitten." Ella threw her hands in the air. "Did you think I couldn't handle it? We used to talk about everything, Mom. Nothing was taboo. I don't want to lose this together with everything else I've lost because of one stupid mistake."

As Ella's chin started quivering, Vivian felt like crying herself. "Come here, baby. Sit with me." She patted the spot next to her on the bed.

Sitting down, Ella leaned her head on Vivian's shoulder. "Talk to me, Mom. Like we used to."

Her arm around her daughter's shoulders, Vivian kissed the top of her head. "It's more than just sex for the immortal guys. And I didn't think you were ready to hear that yet."

"I might not be ready for sex, but I'm ready to listen and learn."

She was right, and Vivian felt stupid for keeping this from her. "When an immortal male induces a female Dormant, it's a big deal for him. For her too. He's not supposed to do that unless he is sure that she's the one for him, and he is the one for her. If the connection isn't there, he's supposed to step aside and let another immortal take his place."

"So, let me get it straight. In order to transition, I'm supposed to fall in love with an immortal male before we have sex, and he has to fall in love with me?"

"You can have sex. In fact, you should do it before you decide if he's the one, just with protection."

"Yeah, Tessa told me that the venom works together with semen to induce transition."

"The romantic involvement was the reason I didn't tell you. I knew you weren't ready for that. Or for the sex."

"I'm not."

"You know that Julian is completely infatuated with you and thinks that you're his one, right?"

Ella's eyes widened. "Why? He doesn't even know me. I know he likes me, and I like him back, but we talked for what, one hour, two?" She rose to her feet and started pacing. "That's not enough for anyone to fall in love. It's this." She circled her hand around her face. "That's all he and everyone else sees. Not what's inside." She pointed to her chest.

"Perhaps you should allow him to get to know you, and you get to know him. Physical attraction is what brings a couple together in the first place, not some intellectual or metaphysical connection. But if they are lucky and discover that they also like the person inside the attractive cover, then love can bloom. It's not going to happen without spending time together, though. That's why I think you should give Julian a chance and go out with him. He's a very nice guy, and thanks to him you're free. Not that it's a reason to date him, but maybe it's just another reason to give him a chance."

Plopping down on the bed, Ella covered her eyes with her arm. "Maybe I should. I don't know. Julian is so handsome, and he seems so sweet, but what the heck can he see in me other than my face? He's eight years older than me, and he is a doctor. We have nothing in common. I wouldn't even know what to talk to him about."

"You did fine over dinner. And you've started this whole thing with the fundraiser idea. You can talk to him about that. Don't sell yourself short, Ella. You have a lot more to offer than your pretty face."

As Ella lifted her arm off her eyes, there was a cunning look in them. "If I go out with Julian, would you start your transition?"

"What does that have to do with anything we've talked about?"

"Eva said that you're waiting for me to get better before you attempt it, and that the longer you wait, the more difficult it will be. I don't want you to endanger yourself because of me."

"Oh, sweetie. That's not the only reason I'm dragging my feet about it. The truth is that I'm scared."

"You're scared because you think that you'll be leaving Parker and me alone."

"Well, that too. But I also don't want to die just when I've found happiness again."

Bracing on her forearms, Ella pinned her with a hard stare. "You're not going to die, Mom. Stop being such a pessimist. Fate didn't bring you and Magnus together just so you could break his heart."

Vivian grimaced. "As much as I would like to believe that, I don't put much faith in fate."

"At least promise me that you'll give it some thought."
"I will."
"For real?"
"Yes, for real."

30

ELLA

"Mom, can I do the dishes tomorrow? I'm going to be late for archery practice with Carol."

Ella rolled her eyes. Parker and his excuses. He'd probably eaten dinner slowly on purpose so he could get out of doing the dishes.

"Sure, sweetie. Say hi to Carol for me."

As usual, her mother had fallen for it. Or maybe not. Poor kid was braving growing fangs, which Magnus had confirmed hurt like hell, so he deserved a little slack.

"Ella, do you want to come and see me shoot arrows?" Parker asked. "Last time, I hit the bullseye eight times out of ten."

He'd asked her to come with him to the gym several times already, but the place was teeming with immortals, and Ella hadn't been ready to interact with them yet, so she had declined.

Except, it had been a good day so far, and meeting Tessa and Eva had been not only fun but uplifting and encouraging as well. Even Brandon, the clan's media specialist who she'd expected to be intimidating, hadn't made her feel uncomfortable. He hadn't looked at her with pity in his eyes, and he hadn't leered either. At most, he'd shown mild curiosity.

If everyone reacted to her like Brandon had, she could handle new introductions.

"Okay. I guess it's time I met the famous Carol."

"You could've met her at the café on day two," Vivian said. "But you didn't want to come."

"I will, the next time you go. I think I'm ready to meet people."

Her declaration was met by three happy faces and a thumbs up from Magnus.

Ella's heart swelled a little.

Her family.

As long as they didn't push her too hard, thinking that they were doing it for her own good, it was nice to have her own cheering squad. It was on the tip of her tongue to tell them that she loved them, but that would've led to a mushy moment with hugs and tears, and Parker was running late.

Besides, it would've weakened her just when she was finally feeling strong.

"Come on, Parker. We need to get moving if you want to make it on time."

On the way to the pavilion they didn't encounter anyone, and as they exited the elevator on the gym level, Ella braced for some awkward hellos and fake smiles. Not everyone was as cool as Brandon.

But there was no one in the corridor either.

"Where is everyone?" she asked.

Parker pointed to one of the doors. "Most people are in the classrooms, taking self-defense lessons, and some are in the gym and in the shooting range. But don't expect them to stop their exercise routine and come say hi to you."

"I would appreciate it if they didn't," she murmured under her breath.

"Back home, you used to be friendlier."

Crap. She'd forgotten about his super hearing. "That's because I knew all of our neighbors, and I worked in a diner, where I had to be friendly, or I didn't get tips."

"Maybe you should get a job at the café? Wonder told me that it was the best and quickest way to get to know everyone."

Ella ruffled his hair. "I don't think they are hiring."

"You can ask Carol. Or I can ask Wonder tomorrow. I'm going to her house to study."

Ella smirked. Wonder was pretty and sweet, and Parker had a crush on her, which the girl was utterly oblivious to despite it being obvious to everyone else.

Upon entering the shooting range they kept walking past the firearms booths and continued to another hall, where a lone figure was shooting arrows from a very cool-looking bow and hitting the bullseye every time.

"Wow. She's good," Ella whispered, so as not to break the shooter's concentration.

"That's Carol, and she has noise-canceling headphones on, so you don't need to whisper."

The woman released one arrow after another, hitting the target's center every time without fail and making it look so easy and effortless that Ella was tempted to try archery herself. Except, she was sure that it wasn't as easy as it seemed. Unlike a firearm, a bow required muscle power.

Parker waited to approach Carol until the target retracted and the electronic scoreboard flashed her impressive results.

Taking the headphones off, Carol shook out her curly hair and turned around with a big smile on her face. "Ella, finally I get to meet you."

She handed the bow and headphones to Parker, then walked over and offered her hand to Ella. "I'm Carol." Tugging on Ella's hand, she pulled her into a tight embrace.

For a small, curvy woman, Carol was incredibly strong, and as the air was squeezed out of Ella's lungs, she tapped the immortal on her back. "I can't breathe."

"Oh, I'm sorry." Carol let go. "I forgot that you're still a fragile human."

Pursing her lips, she gave Ella a thorough once over that thankfully didn't hold even the tiniest trace of pity. "A situation which should be rectified as soon as possible."

Ella tilted her head in Parker's direction. "I'm not in a rush."

"Right." Carol smiled and turned to him. "Ready to start your practice?"

He lifted the bow up in the air, already assuming victory. "Can't wait."

"Let me program the target sequence for you." She walked over to the control screen and typed a series of instructions. "Put the headphones on."

Parker arched a brow. "Why? It's not noisy in here."

"As I've told you before, it helps with concentration, which is the most important component in your skill set." She turned to Ella, including her in the explanation. "When you shoot, you need to be in the zone, and that means the outside world has to disappear while you're at it. Once it becomes second nature to you, you'll be able to slip into that state even with distractions. But until then, use headphones during practice."

"Yeah, I get it." Parker put the bulky things on and reached into the arrow bag, pulling the first one out.

For several moments they watched him shoot, and as he finished the first round, Ella gave him the thumbs up. "I thought he was boasting, but he's really good," she told Carol.

"I know, right? He has a natural talent for it." She turned and motioned to the row of chairs lined up against the wall. "We can be more comfortable watching him from over there."

She waited for Ella to sit down. "I'm here mostly as a supervising adult. It's rare that I need to adjust his form. At the rate Parker is going, Brundar will have to take over his training soon."

"Who's Brundar?"

Carol arched a brow as if Ella should've known that. "He's one of the head Guardians and the clan's weapon master, which probably makes him the best in the world."

"If he's so good, why would he want to waste time on my kid brother?"

"Training a new prodigy is a privilege. Besides, everyone likes Parker. I'm sure that even stoic Brundar won't be able to resist his charm."

That was good to hear. Apparently, her little brother was becoming the darling of the clan. She just hoped it wouldn't go to his head. It would be a shame if Parker turned into a self-entitled brat.

"Are you also training to become a Guardian?" she asked. "I know that you're running the café and that you're teaching a self-defense class. That's already a lot."

Carol chuckled. "I'm a busy, busy girl. Doesn't leave much energy for hunting. But perhaps it's a good thing."

Despite her mastery with the bow, Carol looked so delicate and sweet that Ella couldn't imagine her shooting arrows at living things.

"Hunting? Like in animals?"

Laughter bubbled out of the immortal's chest. "Some claim that all men are animals. So yeah."

With that angelic face, there was no way Carol was a killer. Not of animals and not of people.

Ella shook her head. "I don't get it. I'm sure you don't mean that you're an assassin."

Snorting, Carol slapped her thighs. "Aren't you just precious. When immortals talk about hunting, we usually refer to hookups. I don't know whether you've noticed, but we are a highly sexed bunch, and since most of us don't have mates, we have no choice but to seduce humans for casual sex. That's why we call it hunting."

Ella glanced at Parker, making sure he still had the noise-canceling headphones on. "Julian told me about the mates problem. I hope more Dormants can be found for all of you."

He hadn't told her, however, about the highly sexed part, and since she hadn't interacted with clan members much, Ella didn't know whether Carol was exaggerating or not.

"I hope so too. But until then, a girl has to do what a girl has to do, and this girl likes to hunt—men, that is. Animals, not so much. But I'm starting to realize that I'll have no choice if I ever want to go on the mission I've been training for."

"Now you've lost me completely. You said you're not a Guardian and not training to become one, right?"

This time it was Carol who glanced Parker's way before answering. "I have a special set of skills that makes me perfect for a particular secret mission, but my trainers are not going to clear me for it unless I prove that I can be ruthless. And the way they expect me to prove it is by killing an animal and then cutting out its heart."

Ella grimaced. "That's awful. Are you actually considering doing it?"

"I want to go on that mission. I figured that I can kill something nasty, like a coyote. Sometimes at night, I can hear a pack of them howling as they attack some poor animal and its horrible squeals as it's torn apart. At those moments, I don't have any qualms about getting a rifle and taking them out."

"It's just nature. If they don't hunt, they don't eat."

"I know. Still, I think they are horrible, and I have no problem killing at least one to prove that I can be a badass." She narrowed her eyes at Ella. "Which I totally am."

There was a determination in that beautiful cherubic face, and even though Carol was teasing, Ella could sense the steel in those blue eyes that on first impression had looked so guileless.

"Oh, I believe you. You don't have to prove anything to me."

A sweet smile replaced the hard stare. "You're smart. Most people just look at the exterior and think that I'm soft, which is actually one of my biggest assets. No one expects me to be dangerous."

"Are you?"

Carol shrugged. "I'm not a soldier or an assassin, if that's what you mean, but I can make one hell of a spy."

Ella arched a brow. "Is that what your mission is about, spying?"

"Yeah. But other than providing proof of my ruthlessness, some technical issues are preventing it from getting approved."

"Can you tell me about it, or is it a secret?"

31

CAROL

To buy herself a moment, Carol tucked an errant lock behind her ear. Her mission wasn't general knowledge, and the fewer people who knew about it, the better. But no one had told her it was a secret either, probably because it was self-explanatory.

The head Guardians knew about it, as did Turner and Bridget, and obviously Kian. But so did Robert. And if it was okay to tell an ex-Doomer about the plan then why not Ella?

Except, maybe it hadn't been okay to tell Robert?

But what the heck. Something about the girl tempted Carol to share her secrets. Could it be the eyes?

Looking into them, Carol could understand Julian's obsession with Ella's picture. Ella's gaze reminded her of Edna's, just without the age-old wisdom and without the judgment.

With that accepting and understanding expression on her angel face, she must have people pouring their hearts out to her all the time.

But there was more to why her gaze was so compelling. Ella's eyes were intense, penetrating, soul searching. Either that, or the girl was just very short-sighted and in need of corrective lenses.

"Do you wear glasses or contacts, Ella?"

"No. Why? Do I squint?"

"Not at all. In fact, now that I think about it, you don't blink much at all. Did anyone else ever notice that about you?"

Shaking her head, Ella blinked twice in quick succession as if to prove Carol wrong. "Sometimes, when I concentrate really hard, I forget to blink. It's kind of like holding my breath. But it doesn't happen often. I guess I was so excited to hear about your secret mission that I forgot to blink. Can you tell me anything at all about it?"

"I can tell you some of it, but it has to stay between the two of us. I'm starting to think that too many people know about it already."

"Like who?"

"Kian, naturally, some of the Guardians, Eva, Turner, probably Bridget too. My ex-boyfriend, who happens to be an ex-Doomer."

Ella's eyes widened. "I thought the Doomers were the clan's enemies."

"They are. But there are exceptions. Dalhu, Amanda's mate, is one, and Robert, who is now happily mated to Sharon, is the other."

"Eva's Sharon?"

"That's the one."

"If you don't mind me asking, how did two Doomers become part of the clan?"

"Dalhu left the Brotherhood because he fell in love with Amanda. Robert did it to save me from his sadistic commander."

Ella recoiled. "Do I want to hear this story? Or more to the point, do you want to tell it?"

Shrugging, Carol glanced at Parker who seemed to be getting tired. "What happened to me isn't a secret. The entire clan was mobilized when I was kidnapped. It was just a dumb misfortune. I happened to be in a club's parking lot when a bunch of Doomers showed up. They grabbed me and brought me to their sadistic commander who tortured me for information."

She smiled sadly. "I played the ditsy blond part so well that he believed I had no idea where the clan's headquarters were. But then he tortured me just for fun."

Looking paler than a ghost, Ella put a hand on Carol's arm. "I'm so sorry."

Carol released a shuddering breath. "It was a dream come true for the sadist —an indestructible fuck-toy he could whip and rape as much as he pleased because by the next morning she was as good as new."

Why the hell was she telling this young and impressionable girl all of this?

People knew the dry facts about her abduction and about Robert helping her escape, and they also knew that she had been tortured for information that she hadn't revealed. But Carol hadn't talked with anyone about what had actually happened to her. Not like she was doing now.

Perhaps enough time had passed and talking about it didn't bring the memories to the surface as it had in the beginning, or perhaps it was the special something about Ella that was pulling the words out of her throat.

Now that she'd started, though, Carol felt compelled to keep going. "No matter what he did to me, my body would heal by morning, but my mind would've eventually snapped if not for Robert. At first, he brought me powerful painkillers to help with the suffering, and eventually he helped me escape just before the clan attacked the place and freed the other girls that had been imprisoned with me."

Carol closed her eyes. "I was afraid that with me gone, the sadist would go for the human girls. None of them would've survived that level of cruelty. But the attack went well, Dalhu killed the sadist, and all the girls were freed."

"Dalhu? The ex-Doomer?"

"Yeah. By then, Kian was over his initial mistrust of Dalhu and took him along because he was an insider and therefore could be helpful in anticipating his former comrades' moves. Dalhu, who held a grudge against the sadist, was delighted to be the one to cut off his head."

Ella nodded. "Remind me to thank him personally for that. What happened with Robert, though? How come you two broke up?"

"For a while, I tried to repay Robert's kindness by being his girlfriend, but at some point, I realized that letting him go so he could find his true love would be kinder."

"Sharon."

"Right. It didn't happen right away, and it required some matchmaking on Amanda's part, but they found each other and the rest is history." She smiled. "I was so happy. You can't imagine the guilt I felt for kicking him out. Everyone thought I was such a colossal bitch for doing that."

32

ELLA

"You did the right thing. I can imagine how much courage it took to break things off with Robert and face everyone's scorn, and I'm sure it wasn't easy either. People are stupid. They should've realized that you were doing it for his own good, and you should be proud of yourself for having the guts to do it."

"I am. Screw what everyone else thinks."

"Amen to that." Ella raised her hand for a high five, which Carol returned, thankfully moderating the force of her slap.

The woman was so incredibly brave. Ella couldn't imagine what Carol had been through, and the truth was that she didn't want to. The images Carol had painted in her head were enough to cause nightmares.

Twice in one day, Ella had heard stories so much worse than hers. First Tessa's, and now Carol's. Which made three things abundantly clear to her.

First and foremost, this kind of shit happened a lot, and it claimed numerous victims. The village was a small community, and if three out of its female residents had fallen victim to despicable evildoers, then it was a widespread phenomenon. There could be even more women who'd been wronged but who hadn't told anyone about it.

Secondly, both Tessa and Carol were such bad asses. Carol even more than Tessa. If the entire clan had been mobilized to rescue Carol, then everyone in the village knew she'd been violated, and yet no one thought of her as a victim. On the contrary, they were considering her for some super-duper secret spy mission that she was uniquely qualified for.

And thirdly, Ella was done feeling sorry for herself and hiding in her room. She was going to be like Tessa and Carol. She would hold her head high, look everyone in the eye, and be a badass like those two.

How did the saying go? That which doesn't kill you makes you stronger?

Tessa and Carol were proof of that, and so was Ella.

Since she wasn't dead, not for real anyway, it meant that she was stronger now than before what had happened to her.

As the buzzer announced the end of the session, and Parker's last target retracted, he took off his headphones and looked at the scoreboard. "Awesome. I improved on my last score." Turning around, he grinned from ear to ear.

Ella clapped her hands. "I'm impressed."

"Do you want to go another round?" Carol asked.

His eyes widened in delighted surprise. "Could I?"

She got up and walked over to the control screen. "You're on a winning streak. I'll give you another short session. Four targets."

"Thank you."

Ella hoped that Carol was giving Parker extra practice time because she wanted to talk about her mysterious mission. That was how their talk had started, but it had veered off in other directions that had been no less illuminating.

When Parker put his headphones back on and lifted his bow, Carol sat down next to Ella. "We have fifteen minutes."

"Are you going to tell me about the mission?"

Carol tucked a lock of hair behind her ear. "So, you know who the Doomers are, right?" When Ella nodded, she continued. "Their base is on some uncharted island in the middle of the Indian Ocean. Not even Dalhu and Robert can tell us where it is because they fly people in and out of there on planes with no windows and everyone is searched for tracking devices. Anyway, other than serving as their home base and training grounds, the island is also a high-class resort for the rich and the perverted."

She smiled at Ella. "It's trafficking taken to the next level. As far as we know, they buy girls from suppliers rather than carry out the abductions themselves. The place is a giant brothel that serves the Doomer army as well as some discriminating clients. My idea is to get in there as one of their victims and do two things."

She lifted one finger. "One is to collect information for the clan." She lifted another one. "And the second is to sow the seeds of rebellion. If I can seduce a high-ranking Doomer and have him fall for me, I'll have a good start."

That was the craziest idea Ella had ever heard, and she couldn't understand how anyone was even considering it.

"Are you nuts? Do you know what they will do to you? And how in hell are you going to start a rebellion even if you get some top-level Doomer to fall for you?"

Carol smirked. "I may not look it, but I'm a pro. I love sex, and I have no problem with multiple partners. And as far as having someone fall in love with me and do everything he can to please me?" She rolled her eyes. "I've done it so many times. Men are incredibly easy to manipulate, and I'm an expert at it. I know I can start something."

Ella swallowed hard. What had Carol meant by that? Was she a pro at sex? Or was it more than that? And what did any of it have to do with killing animals and cutting out their hearts?

Then it hit her. Carol had to be capable of killing, and the animals were just the test.

She leaned closer and whispered in Carol's ear. "Does Kian want you to assassinate their leader?"

"Navuh?" Carol pursed her lips. "That's actually not a bad idea. He is the glue that holds the Brotherhood together. I doubt any of his sons would be able to do that with him gone. But no, Kian doesn't want me to kill Navuh. He wants me to incite someone else to do it." She sighed. "But unless we find a way to sneak some form of communicator into the island, Kian won't approve the mission. That's one obstacle. The other one is an extraction plan in case things go wrong. Unless he has solid solutions for these two problems, it's a no-go. And of course, there is the little detail of me proving that I'm capable of killing if the need arises."

"Can you? I mean when it's not a coyote?"

Carol nodded. "I'll kill in self-defense and to defend others. I only have a problem with killing for no reason."

Ella pinched her brows between her thumb and forefinger. "If the island is a resort, then I'm sure they need staff for cleaning and cooking, right?"

"Yeah. They do. The girls they bring over there are given a choice. They can work in the brothel and enjoy lavish accommodations and lots of perks, or they can do the menial jobs, sleep four to a room, work sixteen-hour shifts, seven days a week, and get no perks."

"So, if you want, you can work in housekeeping, right?"

Carol waved a dismissive hand. "I'm a trained courtesan. And anyway, how am I supposed to seduce a high-ranking Doomer while working in the kitchen?"

Well, that answered the question about what Carol's specialty was.

"Actually, I was thinking about myself. I can't do the courtesan stuff, but I can clean and cook."

Carol regarded her with a puzzled expression. "What on earth are you talking about?"

"I'm offering a solution to your communication problem. My mother and I can communicate telepathically from anywhere in the world. If I'm on the island and she's here, your problem is solved."

Leaning, Carol hooked a finger under Ella's chin. "That's so sweet of you to offer, but hell would freeze over before anyone would allow an innocent like you on the Doomers' island. You think that with a face like that you'll be given a choice? And besides, I'm quite sure that pretty kitchen maids and room attendants are not given the option to say no on that island."

"What if I'm not pretty? What if I make myself look ugly?"

Carol laughed. "You can try, but even if you succeed, there is no way you're going. Forget I ever told you anything about it."

"Why? Why is it okay for you and not for me?"

"Because, my sweet Ella, you're an eighteen-year-old human girl who's slept with maybe two or three guys. I'm an immortal who is nearly three hundred years old, and I can fill a couple of phone directories with the names of men I've bedded."

33

LOSHAM

"I have the list of properties you asked for, sir." His laptop tucked under his arm, Rami stepped out into the backyard. "Would you like me to print them out for you?"

Losham put down the shot of whiskey he'd been sipping on and sat up. "First, let's see what you've found."

"Very well." Rami put the laptop on the table, opened it, and then sat down on the chair across from Losham. "Here you go, sir." He turned it around. "I made a page for each property, including pictures and prices."

"Excellent. Thank you, Rami."

Scrolling through the list, Losham smirked. Navuh might have lowered his position (from the mastermind of global intrigue, Losham had been reduced to a pimp and a drug lord), but by doing so, Navuh had lost his best advisor's loyalty.

Not that he'd been overly loyal before.

The simple truth was that Losham was well aware of his limitations. He might be brilliant, but he lacked Navuh's charisma to inspire and lead. That was why he'd never entertained leadership aspirations or wasted his time on plotting a revolt against his father.

Losham had been satisfied with being Navuh's right-hand man and charting the Brotherhood's course in the background. The game—the planning and scheming and seeing it all come to fruition—was the part he enjoyed.

Navuh's global agenda was less interesting to him.

Come to think of it, it wasn't all that important to Navuh either.

Or maybe it was.

Navuh was a complicated man. Sometimes it seemed as if he was indeed striving for world domination, and sometimes it seemed as if he was using this far-fetched goal as propaganda aimed at solidifying the Brotherhood and ensuring the warriors' loyalty and dedication.

It was the classic 'us versus them' motivator that never failed to work on groups of people large and small.

Losham, however, had left that train and boarded his own.

He was still going to supply the island with the high-quality female stock Navuh had tasked him with acquiring, and he was still going to run the drug trade to provide funds for Navuh's ambitious plans.

But in addition to all that, he was going to accelerate the accumulation of his independent wealth.

The house he'd bought for himself in the hills overlooking San Francisco Bay had appreciated more than twenty percent in less than a year. That was a staggering rate of return.

It seemed that in the United States, and especially in the Bay Area, the best way to build wealth was through real estate.

The funds he'd been allotted to provide accommodations for the new stock of warriors arriving shortly were not going toward renting apartments for them. He was going to use the money to buy a multi-unit property instead, and house them there.

But investing in real estate didn't mean that Losham had given up on reclaiming his previous position. While the properties he bought were making him money, he was going to search for hot spots around the globe and make strategic plans that would appeal to Navuh.

After all, instigating wars was always a profitable business for the Brotherhood, and if Navuh's top priority was filling its coffers, then he would be open to suggestions.

Providing the idea was good enough, Navuh might even reassign Losham to a more lucrative spot, like Lokan's post in Washington, and put Lokan in charge of the drug and prostitution operations.

Except, it seemed that his much younger half-brother had gained Navuh's trust, leapfrogging over Losham to the position of Navuh's favorite. To get booted out, Lokan would have to incur Navuh's displeasure, but that wasn't likely to happen.

The cunning son of a bitch had always managed to avoid shit sticking to him.

Losham, on the other hand, had been responsible for several recent blunders, and even though he'd covered them up flawlessly, Navuh must have found out somehow. That was probably why Losham was elbows-deep in human refuse, while Lokan was hobnobbing with Washington's movers and shakers.

But perhaps getting assigned Lokan's post wasn't all that desirable.

Moving to Washington would mean leaving the comfortable arrangement Losham had in San Francisco, specifically the lovely house overlooking the bay and his relative independence. Politicking in Washington would also mean more frequent meetings with his father back on the island, which would ruin Losham's illusion of autonomy.

Even dealing with muck was preferable to that.

"I like this one." He turned the laptop around to show Rami. "I want to see it. Please arrange for a viewing with the realtor."

His assistant swallowed. "I know you've told me to ignore asking prices, sir, but we don't have the money to purchase it. Where are we going to get ten million dollars to pay for it?"

"Mortgage, Rami. The building has twenty-two units. We only need eight to house the thirty warriors I've chosen. We rent out the rest and pay the mortgage with the proceeds."

The story Losham had sold Navuh was that the warriors would need good-quality accommodations, and because they had to pose as humans or even students, they had to reside in a building near the university where other students rented apartments. Those were costly.

Navuh hadn't even batted an eyelid. He'd let Losham have his pick of the best-looking warriors, and then from that selection to narrow it down to those possessing a good command of the English language and reasonable charm.

To capture top-quality females, Navuh had agreed that they needed the most attractive males the island had to offer.

Nevertheless, the bunch would need coaching. Used to either paying for sex or thralling for it, the men were not skilled in seduction. Losham might have to hire someone to teach them.

"The warriors will be pleasantly surprised to be assigned such luxurious accommodations," Rami said.

Compared to what they were used to, the apartments in the building he planned to put them in were indeed luxurious, even if four men shared a two-bedroom two-bathroom apartment.

It was no less than what he'd promised them.

To ensure the best selection, Losham had to whet their appetites, and the accommodations were the least of it. Instead of grueling training in the tropical island's unbearable heat and humidity, the men would be seducing women and traveling with them around the globe on so-called romantic vacations.

After he'd dangled that bait, Losham had no shortage of volunteers. The men had fought each other to be chosen for the "Acquisition Squad."

34

ELLA

Breakfast is ready, Vivian sent.

Ella replied, *I'll be out in a minute.*

Usually, she and her mother made an effort to limit their telepathic conversations when around other people, but with the excellent soundproofing of the house, the only two ways to communicate through closed doors were phone to phone or mind to mind.

These houses should've come with an intercom system.

Shuffling her feet and yawning, Ella got to the kitchen. "Good morning." She sat at the counter next to her mother.

Vivian cupped her cheek. "You have dark circles under your eyes, sweetheart. What happened? Did you have bad dreams?"

Leaning into her mother's hand, Ella sighed. "I did, but not about what you think. I talked with Carol yesterday, and she told me some things from her past. It was very disturbing."

That wasn't the only reason Ella hadn't slept much, though. After waking up with Carol's screams of agony still echoing in her head, she'd spent the rest of the night thinking about the island and the hundreds or maybe even thousands of girls who would never leave it alive.

She kept agonizing over how terrible it was for them—spending their lives in servitude of one kind or another with no possibility of ever having a family of their own or fulfilling any of their dreams.

Slavery should not be tolerated.

It was irrational, but Ella couldn't help feeling guilty. She was free, while they had no chance to ever be. Those girls' only hope was Carol, provided that she could somehow infiltrate the island and cause a revolution before it was too late for them.

The plan was so crazy that even Ella, who didn't know much about anything, realized that it was more a fantasy than an actionable mission. She'd spent hours trying to come up with something better, but none of her ideas were good.

Well, what did she expect? Smarter people than she had pondered the problem, and she thought to outdo them?

"Do you want to talk about it?" Vivian whispered while casting a quick look at Parker's open door. "After breakfast, we can go for a walk."

Ella shook her head. "Carol asked me not to." She looked at the coffeemaker. "I'm not hungry, but I'd love some coffee."

Vivian poured what was left in the carafe into two mugs and handed one to Ella. "I know that she was rescued too. But I don't know any of the particulars. I have a feeling that it was nasty, though. Carol is usually so upbeat and easygoing, but the moment that subject comes up, her expression turns deadly." Vivian chuckled. "In a blink of an eye, the sweet angel turns into a cold-blooded killer. It's scary."

"Yeah, I don't blame her. And by the way, she wasn't rescued by the clan. One of the Doomers couldn't stand her torment and helped her escape before the clan had a chance to organize a rescue. But she wasn't the only prisoner held there, and they ended up saving a bunch of human girls. So, it wasn't a waste."

Vivian put her coffee mug down. "I know that part of the story. But did she tell you where she was held?"

"No."

"The sanctuary. I just love the poetic justice of it. When the clan freed the girls and eliminated the Doomers, they burned the old monastery that had served as the Doomers' base to the ground. Later on, Kian bought the property, and the clan built the sanctuary for rescued girls in the same spot where others were imprisoned."

Ella wasn't sure how she felt about that.

The place must have absorbed tons of dark energy, and even though the building was new, that darkness might still linger there. If it did, the sanctuary wasn't a good place for healing.

"What are you frowning about?" Her mother pressed a finger between Ella's eyebrows. "You'll have wrinkles."

"I don't think either of us needs to worry about those. Immortality comes with many perks."

Avoiding Ella's eyes, Vivian lifted her mug and took a long sip before answering. "I hope it will take care of the wrinkles I already have. And the freckles. I would love to get rid of those too."

It seemed her mother had given transitioning some thought. "Did you decide when you're going to start working on your transition?"

A smirk lifting the right side of her lips, Vivian cast Ella a challenging look. "We had an agreement. You and Julian have to start dating first, and then I'll wait a couple of weeks to see how it's going."

"This is blackmail, Mom. What if we start dating and it's a disaster? Once Julian gets to know me, he's going to realize that we have nothing in common and that he's way out of my league."

Vivian lifted two fingers. "Two weeks, Ella, no less. And at least three dates each week. Total of six."

"Fine." Ella took her mug to the sink and rinsed it out before putting it into the dishwasher. "But he has to ask me first."

"Oh, he will."

Pointing a finger at her mother, Ella glared. "Don't you dare tell him to do that. And tell Magnus not to say anything either. It has to come from him without any prompting."

"He's not going to ask if you don't signal him that you're interested."

"I will smile and bat my eyelashes." Pursing her lips and crossing her eyes, Ella demonstrated how she was going to do that, making Vivian laugh.

"I guess I'm going to stay human." Vivian shook her head. "Magnus is going to be so disappointed."

"Blackmailer." Ella wagged her finger. "I'm going out for a walk."

"Do you want company?"

Ella wanted to do some more thinking, but she didn't want to insult her mother. "Maybe some other time. I want to give running a try."

Any mention of running would dissuade her mother from joining. Vivian liked to stroll, not even fast walk.

"Have fun."

Out on the pathway, Ella started with a couple of minutes of brisk walking, then jogged for a couple of minutes before slowing down to a fast walk again.

Carol had said that the two main obstacles preventing her from executing the plan were communication and a means of escape.

The communication part would be a non-issue if Ella could convince Kian to let her accompany Carol, and extraction shouldn't be that hard if humans visited the resort part of the freaking island all the time.

All the clan needed to do was to find those humans and either bribe them or thrall them to take Carol with them when they left. It wouldn't be easy, but it didn't seem impossible.

As that line of thought brought up a forgotten memory, Ella stopped in her tracks. Gorchenco and Logan had talked about an island. Logan had asked the Russian whether he would be visiting it again, and Gorchenco had answered that he wasn't going anywhere without Ella. Then Logan had said something about Ella's beauty being appreciated over there, and that had gotten the Russian pissed.

Could they have been talking about the Doomers' island?

Gorchenco was definitely rich enough to afford it, and he liked exclusive, high-end things, which no doubt included the paid company he sought.

If the clan followed Gorchenco around, he might just lead them to the damn island.

Her first instinct was to turn around and tell her mother, but that was something the old Ella would have done. The new Ella headed in the opposite direction.

35

KIAN

As someone knocked hesitantly on his door, Kian frowned. Usually, he could tell who it was by the signature mix of their emotional makeup, but not this time.

Except, strangers didn't just come knocking on his door.

It took him a moment to realize that the slight anxious scent was human and not immortal, which meant that the knocker could be only one of two people, Vivian or Ella.

"Come in," he called out.

The door opened slowly, and Ella poked her head inside. "I hope I'm not interrupting anything, but there is no receptionist up front, so I had no one I could ask. Do you have a moment?"

"Sure." He didn't. But if the girl had braved seeking him out it must be important. "Please, take a seat." He motioned for the chair in front of his desk.

"Thank you." She sat on the very edge. "There were no signs on the doors either, but I figured the corner office would be yours." She smiled. "And I was right."

"It seems so. How can I help you, Ella?"

"I spoke to Carol yesterday, and she told me about the Doomers' island." Ella lifted a pair of worried eyes to him. "She told me about the mission she's training for. I hope she won't get in trouble for telling me because it's not her fault. Sometimes I have this weird influence on people. They feel compelled to tell me their secrets. I thought I was imagining it, or that I was just easy to talk to, but I'm starting to think that there is more to it."

The girl was rambling on, probably because she was nervous. But if what she was saying was true, it was good to know that he had an asset like her at his disposal.

She kept going. "I don't know. It still might be nonsense." She waved a dismissive hand. "Anyway, after Carol told me about the mission and the problems with it, I figured that the communication one could be easily solved if I joined her on the island. The telepathic connection between my mother and me is not location bound. I can transmit any information Carol needs me to."

Kian was shaking his head vehemently, but Ella ignored him and kept on going.

"So, then I thought about the extraction problem. It shouldn't be too difficult to find some of the men who visit the island regularly, and either bribe them or thrall them to get Carol out if needed."

"Even if that was on the table, which it is not because you are never setting foot on that island, the clients don't arrive on their own planes. They are flown there in windowless aircraft, and every piece of luggage is carefully checked. No one can smuggle Carol out."

"Are you sure that they check the luggage upon departure? Because it would make more sense if they checked it upon arrival to make sure that there were no trackers. They have no reason to check on the way out. The visitors are all filthy rich, so it's not like they are going to pilfer anything. And Carol is small. She can fit in a suitcase."

The image of Carol folded into a suitcase brought a smile to his face. "You're very imaginative, and I'll take what you've said under consideration. But I'm afraid we are not anywhere near an acceptable risk margin."

Syssi should have heard this. She would've been proud of how politely he'd phrased his refusal. Normally, he would have just said that the idea was ridiculous and that no way in hell was he going to allow Ella on the island. This was progress.

Except, it didn't work.

Ella narrowed her eyes at him. "I'm so sick of everyone treating me like a breakable doll. I'm a survivor, and I have a special skill no one else has. Are you just going to waste it because you think of me as this fragile girl who needs to be protected?"

The girl had guts. He had to give her that. Not many people dared glare at him or challenge him to a verbal duel.

Should he take her down a peg?

Nah. Let her keep her spunk. Right now, it was probably what was keeping her from falling apart.

"I know that you are strong and brave, but you're still a very young human, Ella. Compared to us, to Carol, you are extremely fragile."

Slumping in her chair, Ella nodded. "I get it. As long as I'm human, all of you are going to keep me in bubble wrap." She looked up at him, the spark of defiance burning in her eyes. "I want to help those poor girls. But since you're not going to let me do the most helpful thing I have to offer, I can at least help out with some information. I'm pretty sure Gorchenco visits that island. I heard him talking about it with someone. If you can track him or maybe even thrall him to assist you, he can lead you to its location."

That was indeed a good piece of information, but not as useful as Ella thought it was. Finding men who visited the island wasn't all that difficult. The problem was that just like Dalhu and Robert, they were clueless about its location.

Not wanting to disappoint Ella, he nodded. "Gorchenco isn't easy to follow, but we will give it a try." He raked his fingers through his hair. "To tell you the truth, I've given up on that plan. I just don't have the heart to tell Carol. It's too risky, and the benefits are iffy at best. With all due respect to Carol, it was a crazy idea to think that she could start a revolt. And we are not strong enough to launch an attack, nor do we want to. For better or worse, the Doomers and we are all that's left of our people. Even though they are my enemies, I'm not going to seek their annihilation."

Fuck, why had he told her that when he hadn't told anyone else?

Maybe there was something to Ella's claim about people feeling compelled to tell her their secrets.

"What about all those girls?"

"My heart goes out to them, but there isn't much I can do about it. Their suffering was what prompted me to even contemplate the insane idea of planting Carol on the fucking Doomers' island."

Pinning him with those big soulful eyes of hers, Ella asked, "Isn't there another way?"

"The only way to end the Brotherhood's reign of terror and free the girls they enslave is to start a change from inside the organization. That's still the best approach. The big question is how to do that. I've been wracking my brain trying to come up with a more viable idea. Unfortunately, I don't see how it can be done. My hope is that unrest will eventually start naturally."

Surprising him, Ella snorted. "Yeah, right. Their leader has managed to stay in power for the past five thousand years. He must know every trick in the book to subdue rebellion before it even starts. Either that or he has complete mind control over his people."

"I can't argue with that."

"So, what do we do, nothing?"

Reaching across the desk, he patted her hand. "You seem to be the kind of person who thinks outside the box. Maybe you can come up with a fresh idea?"

Taking his teasing seriously, she nodded. "I will come up with something. I know that Gorchenco is the key to unlocking this puzzle. I just don't know how yet."

"Why do you think he is the key?"

She put her hand over her heart. "Even though he wronged me, I knew Gorchenco shouldn't die because there was some important task he still needed to do. I have a strong feeling that this is it."

"Feelings are subjective, Ella. You can't trust them."

"Sometimes that is all you can trust. I'm not a normal person, that's quite obvious given the telepathy, and when I have a strong feeling about something, I shouldn't ignore it. I've learned that the hard way."

36

ELLA

The polite goodbye Ella had forced as she'd left Kian's office had taken a monumental effort.

Glad that there was no one around to see her stomping along the pathway, she decided to take the long way home to cool off.

Kian had basically blown smoke up her ass with all that crap about never really intending to send Carol to the island. He'd treated her like a child. Had he thought she'd fallen for his fake assignment?

Right, as if he was ever going to listen to any of her ideas even if she managed to come up with something brilliant.

Not that she had a freaking clue.

For that, she needed much more information about the island and its safety protocol, as well as any other information that could be useful. Which meant picking the two resident Doomers' brains. Dalhu and Robert.

Hopefully, Carol maintained a good relationship with her ex and could introduce them. Dalhu might be easier, though. Ella could visit Amanda, using the makeover she'd been promised as an excuse, and try to get Dalhu to talk.

Eh, who was she kidding?

Why waste time on it?

An ancient and powerful immortal like Kian was not going to take the advice of an insignificant young human. The only thing she had going for her was the telepathic connection to her mother.

A two-way radio of apparently limited usefulness.

Because if Kian wouldn't allow her anywhere near danger, he sure as hell wouldn't allow her mother either, which meant that gossiping and talking through closed doors was all their telepathy was good for.

Well, that and communicating while being held captive by a Russian mobster, but that wasn't going to happen ever again.

Except, would Kian still refuse their help if both Ella and Vivian were immortal?

After all, he'd been willing to use Carol, so why not them?

One thing was clear. As long as they were weak and breakable, there was no chance of anyone being willing to even consider using their unique ability. Bottom line, they both needed to transition.

Not a problem for Vivian, but a big problem for Ella.

She didn't want to think about anything sexual, let alone do it. But maybe that was because sex equaled the Russian in her head. Perhaps the way to get rid of those nasty memories was to replace them with good ones?

How had Tessa done it?

She'd been even younger than Ella when she'd been violated, and she had been treated much worse. How had she managed to let Jackson touch her?

The guy was gorgeous and charming, a real prince, but so was Julian, and still Ella couldn't think about getting intimate with him without a major freak out. Time was supposed to take care of that, but Ella didn't have the patience to wait.

Pulling out her phone, she texted Tessa. *Are you busy?*

I'm at work, but I can take a break. What's up?

I need to talk to you. Can you meet me at the playground?

I can be there in fifteen minutes.

Awesome. See you here.

Asking Tessa to drag up a past which she obviously preferred to remain buried wasn't fair, but Ella desperately needed advice.

She would start with a few gentle questions and see if Tessa was willing to talk. If not, she'd drop the subject and pretend that she wanted to talk about the practice video they were going to shoot later that evening.

With no one using the playground, Ella sat on one of the swings and pushed back with her legs. It had been ages since she'd been on one. Starting a slow rhythm, she closed her eyes.

"Having fun?" Tessa sat on the other swing.

"In fact, I am. I had forgotten how much fun swings were."

"Yeah, me too."

"I'm sorry for dragging you out of work."

Tessa waved a dismissive hand. "There isn't much to do. I'm transcribing old files into the computer. There is no rush on that. What did you want to talk about?"

Ella decided to start with what she thought was an easier topic. "Did you know right away that Jackson was the one for you?"

"Not at all. First of all, he is several years younger than me. Secondly, he's a god, and I'm a plain Jane. I couldn't see us together. Never mind that I was emotionally and physically closed off. I have no idea what he saw in me. I was dressed in kids' clothes, on purpose, and I did my damnedest to impersonate a mouse."

"Did Jackson know right away that you were the one for him?"

Tessa nodded. "He was so sweet and so patient with me. At first, I couldn't stand being touched at all." She chuckled. "Jackson must've had the worst case of blue balls in the history of men. But he suffered through it for me."

"How did you manage to get over it?"

"Slowly and with a lot of patience on his part, and sheer determination on mine. I wasn't willing to let the scumbags who'd hurt me win. I was sick of feeling weak and scared all the time. So, I joined a Krav Maga class and really got into it. It gave me confidence, and some of it spilled over into my relationship with Jackson."

Tessa sighed and let her head drop back. "I remember being afraid that he'd lose patience and leave me. Then I was worried that maybe I would never be ready and thought that I should leave him because it wasn't fair to him. Jackson is such a sensual guy. It's not just about sex with him. He likes to touch me all of the time." She smiled. "Now I love it. I could not imagine life without him."

By the time Tessa was done, Ella had tears in her eyes. The love that girl shared with her fiancé was epic.

Ella wanted it too.

Could Julian be her Jackson?

Although her situation was vastly different than Tessa's had been, there were a lot of similarities between their stories too.

Tessa had thought that she wasn't good enough for Jackson, and Ella thought the same about Julian, but for different reasons. It wasn't about her not being pretty enough, it was about being less in every other area. She wasn't as smart, and she wasn't as good, and she wasn't as pure.

She was contaminated by darkness.

"Did you ever feel tainted?" Ella blurted out before thinking better of it. It was such an intrusive question.

"Of course. How could I not have? I think every victim feels that way."

"Do you still feel it?"

Tessa nodded. "I was touched by evil. I've seen it, I've tasted it, I've been immersed in it. I don't think I'll ever feel clean again. I envy those who have never been touched by it. Not because of the suffering that they've been spared, but because they can't really internalize the evil that's out there. I wish I never knew it existed."

37

JULIAN

*J*ulian buttoned up his dress shirt and straightened the collar, which refused to stay put. Should he button the shirt all the way up?

Nah, it made him look like a dork. It would've been okay with a tie, but that was too dressy for a family-style Friday night dinner. Magnus, who was a fancy dresser, hadn't worn one the other Friday.

Maybe two open buttons were better than one?

He popped another button, but that revealed too much chest. Would Ella find it hot? Or would she think he was a slob?

Probably the second one.

It was back to where he'd started, with one button open and a collar that flopped on the right side.

He could get another shirt or pull out the iron. If he could find it. Did he even own one? His dress shirts were the kind that supposedly didn't need ironing because who had time for that?

Right. He was obsessing over nothing. The shirt was fine. His beard was neatly trimmed, his hair was combed back but not slicked, and he was wearing his best-fitting pair of jeans.

His looks had never been a problem. If Ella didn't find him attractive, a straight collar was not going to change that.

What did she find attractive?

Grabbing a wine bottle, he headed out the door. He could think while walking to her house.

Should he try to be more amusing? Maybe she appreciated humor?

Or maybe the opposite was true, and she was attracted to the silent, brooding types?

Except, Julian didn't want to pretend to be someone he was not. She either liked him the way he was, or she didn't.

Perhaps the simple answer was that she found him too old for her, and he couldn't really fault her for that. The eight-year difference would become a non-issue when they both got older, but at this time in their lives, it was huge. Especially since he'd spent most of those eight years furthering his education.

That gap was probably bothering her too.

In fact, he should be bothered by it as well, but he wasn't. On the plane after her rescue, he'd done all the talking while Ella had tried to keep her eyes open, and the only time he'd actually had a conversation with her had been last Friday over dinner.

He'd found her just as engaging if not more so than any of his fellow students at medical school. She was smart and eloquent, and her idea for the fundraiser demonstrated that she had the capacity to think outside the box.

Fates, he wanted her.

He wanted those beautiful big eyes of hers looking at him with more than just gratitude and friendship. He wanted her to gaze at him with adoration. Lust too, but that was too much to expect after what she'd been through.

Stifling a sigh, he knocked on her front door.

"Julian." Vivian opened the way with a smile and pulled him into a quick one-armed hug. "Come on in. Dinner will be ready in a minute."

"Thank you for inviting me." He handed her the wine bottle.

"It's our pleasure."

"Hi, Julian," Parker said. "Do you want to play a bit before dinner?"

"No time, buddy." Magnus got up from the armchair. "Go wash up." He offered Julian his hand. "I heard that you've found a place for the halfway house."

Shaking Magnus's hand, Julian chuckled. "Not me. Kian. It was an old hotel that he bought with the intention of demolishing it and building a new one, but the city declared it as a historical building, so all he could do was remodel it, which wouldn't have been profitable. Instead, he decided to donate it to the charity and take a tax write-off."

"Whatever works." Magnus clapped him on the back. "Is it habitable?"

"It needs some work."

As a door down the hallway opened, Julian turned his head in that direction. With the rest of the family all in the living room, it could only be Ella.

His heart skipped a beat or two when she entered.

"Hello, Julian." She walked over to where he was standing next to Magnus and offered him a sweet smile. "I heard that you've been busy."

For a moment, he was too stunned to answer.

Could it be that she'd dressed up and put makeup on for him?

It was nothing fancy, just a long, curve-hugging skirt and a loose sweater that exposed one bare shoulder, but it was enough to cause his tongue to stick to the roof of his mouth.

When he finally found his voice, it was to blurt, "Busy?"

"Yeah, with the new place for the rescued girls."

"Oh, that." He raked his fingers through his hair. "It needs a lot of work. Yamanu and I named it The Palms because we didn't want to keep calling it the halfway house, and there were palm trees up front."

He was rambling like an idiot.

She tilted her head. "Is the name still negotiable?"

"It is. Until we officially open."

"I'll think of something more original. By the way, I would love to see it. Is there a chance you can take me there?"

Julian wasn't the only one surprised.

Parker gaped, Vivian grinned and nodded enthusiastically, and Magnus regarded Ella with narrowed eyes.

"I would love to."

She put a hand on his arm and smiled. "Thank you. When can we go?"

Up close, Ella's feminine scent was doing all kinds of things to him, none of which were okay given present company. And that was without her emitting even a whiff of arousal.

"Whenever you want." He forced a smile. "If you'll excuse me, I should wash my hands before dinner."

Ducking into the powder room, Julian closed the door behind him and ran a frustrated hand over his face as he leaned against the wall.

He hadn't imagined it. Ella had been coming on to him. She was subtle, but he had enough experience with girls wanting to start something to recognize it for what it was.

Usually, though, he was much better at controlling his reactions. A hand on the arm shouldn't have given his dick and fangs ideas.

Yeah, he'd been as smooth as a porcupine in a balloon shop.

Lifting his head, he glanced at the mirror. Not surprisingly, his eyes were glowing.

The long abstinence must have been the culprit. Julian wasn't as sexually driven as some of the older immortals, and he could go for prolonged periods without, but this had been a really long stretch.

In fact, he hadn't been with anyone ever since he'd met Vivian and had gotten obsessed with Ella's picture. It hadn't even been a conscious decision on his part. He just hadn't been in the mood for hunting, which was understandable given how worried he'd been for her.

Still was.

Nothing in his life could've prepared him for handling that kind of stress. Up until Ella, the only times Julian had felt anxious were during finals. Unlike Kian or Turner or even his mother, Julian hadn't accumulated the set of tools necessary to deal with catastrophes.

But now that it was all over, and Ella was safely home, Julian's sex drive had not only returned, but it was demanding compensation for missed time.

38

ELLA

*A*t the dinner table, Ella had chosen to sit next to Julian, which had turned out to be a smart decision. If she were sitting across from him, she would have to keep up the façade of confidence, which was really tough to maintain since he was not responding the way she'd thought he would.

And besides, looking at his gorgeous face throughout the evening would have been too distracting for her to carry on an intelligent conversation.

Tessa's words were playing on a loop in her head. So much of it had been a mirror reflection of her own feelings, but Tessa had added a new dimension that Ella hadn't thought of before.

What if Julian lost interest?

What if he decided that she was a lost cause?

What if he wasn't as patient as Jackson?

What if he found another Dormant and decided that she was the one for him?

Losing her chance with him, probably forever, because she was a scaredy-cat would be a big-time win for the dark side, and she wasn't going to allow it to happen.

Romeo, Stefano, and Gorchenco had cost her her innocence and her positive outlook on life. Ella wasn't going to let them rob her of her future as well.

Having time to heal was an illusion.

A wounded soldier wouldn't opt to stay in the trenches to regain his strength if the chopper that could take him home was only a few feet away. He would crawl, dragging his mangled body by his fingertips over shrapnel, if that was what it took. Because if he didn't, that chopper would lift off, never to return, and he would die in that trench.

Ella's wounds would have to heal on that helicopter because missing the ride could mean that her only chance of recovery was gone.

The problem was that her chopper was missing all the signals she was sending his way. Or at least it seemed like it.

It should not come as a big surprise, though. Ella's flirting skills were nonexistent. She knew how to fend off over-eager guys, but not how to lure them to her.

Not them.

Him.

The only one she wanted to lure was Julian, and he was supposed to be an easy target. According to her mother, he believed that Ella was the one for him.

Had her mother misinterpreted Julian's interest?

He seemed more interested in her little brother than in her.

Apparently, Parker had much more in common with Julian than she had. The two were fascinated by aliens and UFOs and conspiracy theories.

"There are rumors that the government is hiding alien bodies and crashed aircraft in a secret military base called Area 51. Some claim that there is also something going on in a hidden complex built under the decommissioned Montauk Air Force Station."

Parker's eyes were sparkling with excitement. "I heard about Area 51. Everyone did. But not the air force station."

"Did you ever watch *Ancient Aliens* on the History Channel?" Julian asked.

"Dude, I love that show. In our old house, I had all the episodes recorded."

"It's obviously overdramatized, and some of the claims they make are absurd, but among all the rubbish there are kernels of truth. Before going to medical school, I took several months off and went exploring. Those sites are just as fascinating and inexplicable as they claim on the show."

"I don't know about inexplicable," Magnus said. "Our people could've been behind those building projects."

Julian shook his head. "As far as I know, the gods didn't have settlements on the American continent."

"They didn't have to if they had air travel capabilities. Some could've visited and left building instructions for the primitive locals. That would explain the level of complexity and precision of those ancient masons' work. You said that the technology to duplicate it didn't exist until recently."

Vivian smiled. "You didn't tell me that you're into that stuff too."

Magnus shrugged. "I'm not. It just makes sense."

"I love the part about alien bases hidden under the oceans," Parker said. "I think Atlantis was such a base, and that it was submerged to hide it from humans." He looked at Julian hopefully, waiting for him to acknowledge the possibility.

"That's a question to address to the goddess. But frankly, I don't think so. From the little information I was able to gather, the gods brought with them technology from wherever they'd originally come, but something happened, and contact with their home world was severed. After that, their equipment slowly fell apart, and they didn't have the means to repair it. A floating city is not mentioned anywhere."

"Eva talks about Atlantis in her book," Vivian said. "But that's fiction. She's writing a romance. I don't think she has any secret information about it."

That was news to Ella. "Eva wrote a book? I didn't know that."

Vivian waved a dismissive hand. "She is in the process of writing it. I've read several chapters."

"Is it any good?" Julian asked.

"Let's say it's a work in progress."

Parker snorted. "That's Mom's polite way to say that it sucks."

"No, it doesn't suck, Parker. But this is something new for Eva, and like every new skill, it requires endless hours of practice to get good at. Her ideas are great, though, very imaginative, but there's too much blood and gore for my taste. It's supposed to be a romance geared towards attracting Dormants, and not a murder mystery with horror elements. Eventually, I hope she'll get it done."

Ella frowned. "How is a book going to attract Dormants?"

"The idea was to write a story of a Dormant's life and how she felt different than other people. In Eva's story, she's a lie-detector like Andrew and works as a police detective. During a murder investigation, she meets an immortal who suspects what she is, and the adventure starts from there. Eva's idea was to create a social media group for people who loved the book and who felt different themselves. She hopes it will attract real Dormants."

Ella crossed her arms over her chest. "It's not the craziest idea I've heard lately. It may actually work if she ever gets to finish that book."

Her comment must've intrigued Julian. Turning toward her, he arched a brow. "What other crazy ideas are you referring to?"

Crap. She'd been thinking about Carol infiltrating the Doomers' island and starting a revolution, but she wasn't supposed to talk about it. Julian might know because he was Bridget's son, and maybe even Magnus knew because he was a Guardian, but her mom and Parker didn't and shouldn't.

Waving a dismissive hand, Ella snorted. "Where do I start? The government hiding debris from alien spaceships and alien bodies in Area 51. Hidden alien bases under the ocean floor. Atlantis submerged but still functioning. Should I go on?"

39

JULIAN

Once coffee had been served and dessert eaten, there was no more reason for Julian to stay.

He was about to thank his hosts and leave, when Parker asked, "How about a game now?"

"Sure."

Thank you, Parker.

The good news was that he'd gotten to talk some more with Ella. The bad news was that he'd either misunderstood her friendliness as flirtation or had blown his chances by not responding to it right away.

After those initial coy smiles and resting her hand on his arm, Ella hadn't done anything to indicate her interest. But maybe if he stayed a little longer, he'd have a chance to correct his mistake.

If he'd made one.

Julian still wasn't sure that he hadn't imagined Ella's subtle come-on.

"After I'm done with the dishes, I'll come to watch you." Ella got up and started clearing the table.

Damn it, he should've offered to do that.

"Let me help." Julian picked up the largest serving platter and followed Ella to the kitchen.

She waved him away. "Go play with Parker. I'll be done in a few minutes."

"Can't do that." He winked. "My mother would box my ears if I don't help."

That got a laugh out of her. "I don't think Bridget can reach your ears, let alone box them." She looked him up and down. "Your father must've been tall."

The compliment combined with the appreciative once over had Julian's ears heat up for the first time in forever.

He cleared his throat. "I've never met him, but my mom used to have a thing for tall guys." He chuckled. "And then she fell for Turner. Go figure."

A thoughtful look in her eyes, Ella nodded. "Turner is very handsome. And he has those incredible pale blue eyes that make him look so intense. I can totally understand what she sees in him. He's a born leader."

Why the hell had her appreciation of Turner made him so jealous?

Maybe Ella was into short, intense guys?

The leader types.

Was he a leader?

Julian wasn't sure. He was competitive, and excelling at school had been important to him, but he'd never felt the need to lead anyone.

Deciding it was best not to respond with something that would make him sound defensive or worse, arrogant, Julian opted to make a quick exit. "I'll get the rest of the dishes while you load the dishwasher."

"Thanks."

Magnus stopped him. "I'll help Ella finish up. Parker has been waiting all day to play with you."

"He has? Then I guess I should go."

It would give him time to calm down from the unexpected jealousy spike over Turner of all people.

"Ready to play?" He sat on the bed since Parker occupied the only chair in the room.

"Here." The kid thrust a controller into his hands. "It's the same game we played with Jackson."

"You played with Jackson and then with me. Jackson and I never played against each other."

Parker closed one eye as if that was going to help him remember. "Yeah, you're right. But you know what I mean." He smirked. "Get ready to lose again."

"Not going to happen, kid. I've been practicing."

"Since Wednesday?"

"Aha."

"We will see about that." Parker started the game.

After each of them had decided on an avatar and a weapon of his choice, it was time to battle it out.

Julian had been joking about practicing, but once he'd gotten the gist of the game, his competitive streak kicked in, and he forgot all about wanting to let Parker win.

His lead in the game didn't last long, though. As soon as Ella joined them and sat next to him on the bed, his concentration was blown, and he barely managed to keep going without dying in the game, which would've ended that round.

Her nearness, her scent, it was scrambling his brain, and sitting on the bed wasn't helping either. He had the insane impulse to drop the controller, push her back on the mattress, and kiss her like she'd never been kissed before.

It was good that the girl was still human and couldn't hear his heart racing. To his ears, it sounded like a locomotive was accelerating inside his ribcage.

Parker, however, didn't suffer from his sister's limitations. The moment the game ended, with him the winner, of course, he turned off the console.

"Hey, aren't you going to give me a chance to win the next round?"

"Next time you come over I might let you win." Parker put his controller on the charging station. "I promised Magnus that I'd go swimming with him after dinner. See you later, guys."

The kid couldn't hide the smirk as he grabbed his swimming trunks and left the room, closing the door behind him.

Ella frowned. "I didn't hear them making plans to go to the pool."

Not knowing what to say, Julian shrugged. "Maybe it was a last minute thing." He lifted the controller and offered it to her. "Do you want to play?"

"I'm not big on blood and gore. Out of all the games Parker plays, I only like *Minecraft*." She smiled. "I guess boys are more into the shooting and killing games."

He lifted a brow. "That's a sexist remark."

"But it's true. I bet you also like watching war movies. I can't stand them. They make me so sad."

"But you like Marvel movies. Those are pretty violent."

"It's different. I know there is nothing real about them. But I hated *Infinity War* because it was so dark. Movies about real wars always make me think about the poor soldiers, and how scared they must've been, and then I think about the families grieving for those who didn't make it back."

As Ella's eyes misted with tears, Julian was taken aback. It took him a moment to realize why such a mundane conversation had made her so sad.

Her father had died in the line of duty.

Fighting the impulse to pull Ella into his arms and kiss her pain away, Julian pushed to his feet and offered her a hand up. "Would you like to go for a walk with me?"

"I would love to." She smiled and took his hand.

As an electric bolt zapped his hand, and from there traveled to his groin, Julian quickly pulled Ella up so her eyes wouldn't be level with the erection straining his jeans.

"Perhaps you should put on something warmer. It's chilly outside." A big puffy coat that covered her from head to toe would be great.

She chuckled. "It's not that cold, and I'm already wearing a sweater." She threaded her arm through his and leaned against him, causing the locomotive in his chest to go into hyper speed. "And if I get a little chilly, you can warm me up."

Damn.

40

ELLA

You can warm me up?

Had those words actually left her mouth? Where had they come from? Some cheesy movie or romance novel?

Ella didn't know who was more shocked by them, she or Julian.

While the guy almost stumbled over his own feet, her cheeks flamed with embarrassment.

"Just kidding. I should get a warmer sweater." She pulled her arm out of his.

"Don't." He caught her elbow. "If you get cold, I'll wrap my arm around you. If that's okay with you."

Lifting her head, she braved a look at his eyes and took a step back. "Your eyes are glowing."

"Don't mind them. It's an immortal thing. When you transition, yours will glow on occasion too."

Way to throw gasoline on her already flaming cheeks. There was only one way she could transition, and it would probably involve the tall and handsome guy holding on to her elbow.

She wondered what shone brighter, her cheeks or Julian's eyes.

Covering her embarrassment with a chuckle, she pulled her elbow out of his grasp. "That's a useful trick. I was afraid we'd get lost walking in the dark, but your eyes can illuminate the trail."

Out in the living room, she found her mother sitting on the couch with a book.

"Julian and I are going out for a walk. Are you going to be okay here by yourself?"

Vivian grinned. "Of course, sweetheart. Have fun."

"Thank you for dinner," Julian said. "Everything was delicious."

"I'm glad you liked it. Goodnight, Julian."

"Goodnight, Vivian."

It was weird to hear him call her mother by her first name, but then the age difference between them wasn't that great. Julian was only ten years younger than Vivian.

"I can't believe that all of this started with you hitting on my mom," she said as they took the stairs down to the walkway.

Julian pushed his hands into his pockets. "Vivian is a knockout, and she looks a lot like my childhood idol, Kim Basinger. But if she told you the rest of the story, you know how she responded to my clever come-on lines."

"By showing you my picture. I'm so sorry about that. I don't know what possessed her to do that. Usually, she's a chill mother who doesn't pull embarrassing stunts like that."

In the dark, Julian's eyes seemed to be glowing even brighter as he looked at her. "I'm grateful beyond words that she did that. If not for that picture and my promise to try and get you an audition, there would've been no rescue. The only reason I called your mother was because Brandon found a part for you."

She'd heard the story, but with a different spin. Her mother was positive that Julian had fallen in love with that picture, and that was why he'd mobilized his clan to save her.

Could Vivian have been wrong?

Maybe Julian had done it just because he was a nice guy?

If that was the case, then she was wasting her clumsy flirting efforts on him. Perhaps she should seek another immortal for her transition?

The idea was enough to make her gag.

Julian was the only one she could envision herself getting intimate with. Not right away, she wasn't ready for that yet, but maybe she could follow Tessa's advice and start with something easy. Like a kiss.

He seemed like the kind of guy who could be patient and would not assume that she was ready to hop into bed with him after one little kiss.

On the one hand, she wanted to have with Julian what Tessa had with Jackson—a slow build-up of trust and passion that would erase the taste of her bad experience and replace it with something wonderful. On the other hand, though, she wanted to turn immortal as soon as possible, so dragging things out was not going to be helpful in that regard.

Still, she had to start somewhere, and she was pretty sure she could handle a kiss. The question was how to let Julian know what she wanted.

Maybe flattery would work?

If she let him know that she found him attractive, maybe that would be enough?

Threading her arm through his, she leaned her cheek on his bicep and sighed. "You are so handsome, Julian. I bet you have many girls chasing you."

Had that sounded as lame as she thought?

Given the puzzled expression on his face, it had. "Thank you for the compliment, but I'm a little confused. Until today, you've shown no interest in me."

"I wasn't ready."

He arched a brow. "And now you are?"

"I'm trying to figure it out. I thought..." She couldn't look into his eyes and shifted her gaze to a spot on his shirt. "I thought that maybe we could start with a kiss," she whispered.

Hooking a finger under her chin, Julian lifted her face, so she was forced to look at him. "There is no rush, Ella. Don't get me wrong. I would love to kiss you, but I don't want you to do anything before you're ready. Take all the time you need." He chuckled. "And don't worry about all the other girls who are supposedly chasing me. They can't catch me because I don't want anyone but you. I will wait for as long as it takes."

Was he the sweetest guy, or what?

Except, he'd misunderstood her clumsy attempt at complimenting him as her worrying about losing him to someone else if she didn't hurry. It was a concern, but she hadn't thought of it at that moment.

"It's not that. Well, not only that. You're a gorgeous, sweet guy, and to top it off you are also a doctor. It doesn't get any better than that, and I'm not sure for how long you can fight off the temptation my competitors are no doubt throwing at you. I would be a fool to ignore that. But that's not the main thing I'm concerned about."

Crap, if she admitted why she was rushing, Julian might feel that she only wanted to use him as a catalyst for her transition. She did, but that wasn't the only thing she needed him for.

Ella wanted to have with Julian what Tessa had with Jackson, but she didn't know how to get from here to there.

"What are you concerned about?"

"I need to transition, Julian. I will feel so much safer once I do, and maybe all of you will stop treating me like I'm made from glass. I have a special talent the clan can use, but Kian won't let me do anything that even smells of danger because I'm human and breakable."

She should've stopped talking the moment his expression soured, but she'd been on a roll, and her mouth had just kept on flapping.

No longer mellow, the softness gone from his eyes, Julian looked scary when angry.

Suddenly, she was very aware of how much bigger than her he was, and how much stronger. Except, she didn't really fear him. Even when angry, Julian would never do anything to hurt her.

The worst he could do was walk away from her.

"Don't be angry with me," she whispered.

41

JULIAN

Fates, he was a fool.

He should have known better than to fall for Ella's coy smiles and her compliments. If her sudden interest in him had sounded too good to be true, it was because it was.

Like a stupid teenager, he'd gotten all excited about the prospect of a kiss from her. She wanted to transition. That was the only reason for her flirting. He was a means to an end.

"Don't be angry with me," she whispered, her eyes pleading for him to understand.

And just like that Julian's anger went up in smoke.

How could he be mad at her?

Ella wasn't a sophisticated temptress who was out to get him. She was a young girl with limited experience, who was scared and hurting and sought to get over both by becoming an immortal.

It was true that she needed him to transition, and right now she might not realize that she needed him for much more than that, but with a lot of patience, guidance, and persistence, he could prove it to her.

"I'm not angry." He smoothed a finger over her cheek.

Her eyelids drooped a little as she leaned into his touch. "A moment ago you looked mad."

"I was a little disappointed, that's all."

"Why disappointed?"

There was no guile in her eyes as she looked up at him. She really didn't know.

"I think it's natural to want to be desired for who I am and not for what I can do for you."

"Oh." A pink hue colored her pale cheeks. "I just let my mouth flap without thinking. The way I said it made you think that I came on to you only because of the transition."

He shrugged. "It's okay. I understand. If I were in your shoes, I might have done the same thing."

"You don't understand anything, Julian." She shook her head and started walking again.

He followed, afraid that she'd gotten offended and was leaving him without even saying goodnight.

Except, Ella found a bench and sat down with an exasperated sigh. "It's my fault. I didn't explain myself right."

Relieved that she was still talking to him, he sat next to her. "Do you want to give it another try?"

"I don't know." Lifting her feet, she tucked them under her long skirt and hugged her knees. "I'm all over the place. One moment all I want to do is hide in my room and never come out, and the next one I feel like I'm ready to take on the world."

Without thinking, he wrapped his arm around her shoulders and kissed the top of her head. "How about finding a middle ground between the two? Hiding in your room is obviously not a solution to anything, but instead of taking on the whole world all at once, how about taking one step at a time?"

She looked up at him and waved her hand. "But that's exactly what I've been doing. The fundraising idea was the first step. It got me out of the house. I met Tessa, and Eva, and Carol, and I even went to talk to Kian about another idea I had."

That was a surprise. Ella was showing more spunk than he'd expected from her. Kian was an intimidating guy, and to approach him with an idea took guts.

"Care to share your idea with me?"

She shook her head. "It's not important. Kian would never allow a human girl to do what I proposed."

Now he was really curious. "I would like to hear it anyway."

"I can't tell you."

"Can't or won't?"

"Can't. It involves information I was asked to keep a secret. I can check if it's okay to tell you, but until I get permission, I can't."

"Understandable."

It also explained her sudden rush to secure an immortal male for her transition.

He rubbed her arm. "Is that why you flirted with me? Because Kian wouldn't allow you to do that thing you wanted unless you were immortal?"

As she lowered her head onto her upturned knees, the pink color in her cheeks deepened into a peachy red. "That was part of it."

He waited for her to continue, but when she didn't, he asked, "What's the other part?"

A long moment passed until Ella answered with a question of her own, "Do you like me, Julian?"

"Of course, I do. Isn't it obvious?"

Without lifting her head off her knees, she shook it lightly. "My mother is convinced that you have feelings for me that are more than just friendly. But I think she just wants it to be true because you're such an awesome guy. How can you have feelings for me if you don't know me?"

She was right and explaining it without sounding like a romantic fool was going to be tough. But maybe he should just swallow his ego and tell her the truth?

"It started with the picture. You're very beautiful, but I don't think that was why I reacted so strongly." He put his hand over his heart. "I felt as if the eyes gazing at me from that picture were trying to tell me something. I could almost hear you calling me, asking me to find you, to help you. I know it doesn't make sense."

He chuckled. "Even though I believe that aliens and UFOs are real, I'm not prone to flights of fancy. I thought I was going nuts. But when I called your mother to tell her about the audition Brandon arranged for you, and she told me that you were missing, everything suddenly made sense. I was meant to meet your mom. I was meant to help save you. And I was meant to be your mate."

42

ELLA

Ella shook her head. "I asked if you liked me, and you didn't really answer that. You talked about fate and meaning, but that could all be a coincidence. It's quite a leap to jump from that to being my mate. I would think that love should come first. But how can there be love if we don't know each other?"

Raking his fingers through his hair, Julian released a puff of air. "I realize how it must sound to you. Coming from the human world with human attitudes and expectations about what brings two people together, you probably find me irrationally romantic, or just foolish. But immortals, and by that I mean Annani's clan, believe in fated true-love mates—two people who are meant to be together and bond for eternity. It's what every immortal, male or female, yearns for, but only a few get lucky enough to be blessed with a true-love mate. I believe you are mine. Now all I have to do is convince you that I am yours."

As if she needed convincing. The guy was perfect.

Her cheek still resting on her upturned knees, she looked up at him and smiled. "It's not going to be a hard sell, Julian."

"You're not in love with me."

"And neither are you with me. With all that talk about fated true-love mates, I'm still waiting for you to tell me that you like me."

"Of course, I do."

"Why? Is it this face?"

He smoothed a finger over her heated skin.

She'd been blushing so much that her face was warm even when she wasn't embarrassed.

"Yes, you have a beautiful face, but that's not the only reason."

She waved a hand. "Do tell. I'm eager to hear what you can possibly know about me after spending about eight hours together, half of which I was asleep for."

Lifting his arm off her shoulders, he leaned back and crossed his ankles.

"You're a fighter. Right after your rescue, when I expected you to be wary of all males, you followed me to my hotel room and asked to borrow my clothes. I was flabbergasted. Then when I told you about who and what your rescuers were, you listened calmly and accepted my explanations without going into panic mode or denial. I like that you're not impulsive and that you are logical and think with your head and not your heart."

So far so good. Everything he'd said was not only true, but things she prided herself on. The only time she'd failed to think before acting was with Romeo, and it was never going to happen again.

"There is more," he said. "Your fundraising idea is absolutely brilliant. You're a creative thinker. I also think you're a wonderful sister and daughter, which speaks volumes about your character."

It was embarrassing to hear him say all those nice things about her, and Ella's knee-jerk reaction was to make fun of it. "Hey, you make me sound so good that I want to marry me."

He waved a hand. "There you go. Now you know how I feel about you."

"Just so you won't get disappointed when you find out, I'm also argumentative, opinionated, and I don't do well with authority. On the positive side, I try to be polite, I don't cuss much, and I'm not a big spender."

Grinning, Julian returned his arm around her shoulders. "Sold. I'm ready for the altar."

Yeah, the question was whether she'd be able to tolerate more than his arm around her shoulders and a kiss to the top of her head. As good-looking and charming as Julian was, Ella was attracted to him in her head, but her body remained on neutral.

If she had never felt the stirrings of desire before, she would've thought nothing of it, but she had.

For freaking Romeo of all people, and then for Logan, who might have been even worse.

What was wrong with her?

Did her body respond only to dangerous, evil men?

Julian hooked a finger under her chin. "I was expecting a smile, not a frown. What's the matter, did I make a bad joke?"

As if she was going to tell him that he didn't excite her or share her suspicions with him as to why her body's response to him was so lackluster.

Except, it might have nothing to do with him and everything to do with what she'd been through. It was as if a comfortable numbness had settled upon her, blocking any sexual yearnings she might have normally felt. It was safe inside that numb blanket, but it was also unsettling.

This wasn't her.

It wasn't normal.

It was the same as hiding in her room, only instead of getting her sense of security from walls made from wood and plaster, she was deriving it from walls made of emotional and physical indifference.

"Ella? Can you answer me?" He sounded impatient.

She hadn't realized how long she'd been lost in thought while staring blankly at his handsome face. "Who's rushing things now, Julian? All I wanted was a kiss, and you've taken it all the way to the altar."

"You think you're ready for a kiss?" He arched a brow.

"Only one way to find out."

Crossing her fingers, Ella hoped that Julian's kiss would awaken some of her dormant arousal, but she was willing to settle for none provided that it didn't evoke repulsion.

If it did, she was going to swallow her pride and take Vanessa up on her counseling offer because it would mean that there was something very wrong with her.

The glow in his eyes intensifying by the second, several expressions passed over Julian's face, but his hesitation didn't last long.

Moving faster than she'd thought possible, he lifted her onto his lap and tucked her close to his hard body.

She was trapped, his arms feeling like iron bands around her, and yet there was no fear, only breathless anticipation.

43

JULIAN

It felt incredible to have Ella's body nestled against his chest, his arms wrapped around her and holding her tight. But she was tense and knowing that she wasn't aroused even in the slightest dampened Julian's excitement.

Up close, there was no way he was missing it, and given the plethora of other scents Ella was emitting, he knew she wasn't an anomaly like Turner who didn't produce any emotional scents at all.

Julian's nose and his empathic ability made it easy for him to read her emotions. She was a little anxious, a little worried, and more than a little sad, but she was also determined.

But what was she determined about?

Getting the kiss she'd asked for?

If she wasn't attracted to him, why did she want him to kiss her?

Maybe she hoped the kiss would awaken her desire?

The situation was entirely unfamiliar to him, and therefore utterly confusing, not to mention disappointing.

Usually, the women Julian hooked up with were eager for him, their arousal unmistakable. And as long as he found them even moderately attractive, that unique feminine scent was enough to turn him on. In its absence, his initial arousal dissipated.

It seemed like he was a different kind of animal than most of his immortal brethren and even his human counterparts. His first response to an attractive female was the same as any other heterosexual male's, but unless she responded with clear sexual interest, his arousal would fade away.

Perhaps it was good that he was wired like that. Exercising patience was not going to be a problem for him.

His palm gently cradling the back of Ella's head, he brushed his lips over hers. That tiny contact was enough to send a zap of electricity straight to his deflated arousal, awakening it and shattering his theory of only a moment ago.

Leaning away, he gazed at her face.

Her eyes closed, she parted her lips and darted her tongue out to moisten them.

Experimentally, he took a long sniff and there it was—a faint scent of feminine arousal. It seemed like his body had sensed it before his nose could confirm that it was there.

"My beautiful, sweet Ella."

She smiled without opening her eyes and relaxed in his hold, her body losing some of the rigidness. He should remember to use terms of endearment with her.

Apparently, Ella liked it.

"I've wanted to kiss those lush lips of yours for so long." He smoothed a finger over the bottom one. "Your cheeks." He smoothed a finger over one and then the next. "Your eyes." He dipped his head and kissed one eyelid and then the other.

With each little touch, Ella seemed to loosen up some more, and he debated whether to keep going with what appeared to be working so well or to give her the kiss she wanted.

"Your skin is so soft," he murmured.

Wrapping her arms around his neck and pulling him down, she solved his dilemma. "Kiss me, Julian. I'm not going to break."

The next time he touched his lips to hers, Julian was bolder, flicking his tongue over the seam and coaxing her to open for him.

As she parted her lips, the scent of her arousal flared, and that was all the encouragement he needed.

His hand tightening its hold on the back of her head, he took her mouth, sliding his tongue inside and tangling it with hers in a slow and deliberate dance of discovery.

It wasn't the way he normally kissed. But being attuned to Ella's every response, he realized that the urgency his other partners had responded so well to needed to be tempered for her.

As he drew back, Ella pulled him back down and kissed him, thrusting her little tongue into his mouth.

Julian's first instinct was to deny her access, but then he remembered that there was no need to hide what he was. She knew about his fangs. The question was whether she remembered to be careful around them.

"Watch out for the sharp tips," he murmured against her mouth.

In response, she cupped his cheek and twirled her tongue around one fang, and then around the other, sending shivers up his spine. But more than the intense pleasure of his fangs being licked, he was turned on by Ella taking the initiative and the growing scent of arousal she was emitting.

When she let go of his neck and slumped in his arms, he resisted the impulse to kiss her again.

He needed to take cues from her.

Until she felt completely safe in his arms, he was going to stifle his need for dominance and let her dictate the pace.

"Oh, wow," she said after a long moment. "Talk about butterflies. That was a kiss for the memory book."

Julian would've been puffing his chest out and strutting like a peacock if not for his empathetic and olfactory extrasensory perception. The kiss had aroused Ella, but for some reason, the strongest emotion she was experiencing at the moment was relief.

What was she relieved about?

That he had finally kissed her?

That he hadn't pushed for more?

Or maybe for being able to get excited over a kiss?

Should he ask her?

Normally, revealing his superhuman abilities was not an option, which had provided an excellent excuse for using them to his advantage with his partners none the wiser. But that loophole didn't apply to Ella.

Other than exercising patience, Jackson's advice had been to build up trust first, which meant that Julian couldn't keep his extrasensory perception a secret from Ella because it gave him an unfair advantage.

"I sense your relief," he said.

"I am relieved. But how did you know? Am I that obvious?"

He tapped his nose. "Immortals can smell emotions. When you're this close, the scents that you emit tell me a lot about what you're feeling. I'm also slightly empathic."

She narrowed her eyes at him. "Does it mean that I can't keep any secrets from you?"

"I can't read your mind." He chuckled. "And frankly, being able to read your emotions confuses me more than it educates me. Like right now. I don't know what's the connection between a hot kiss and feeling relieved. I would expect arousal, elation, appreciation for my incredible kissing skills, maybe even a little bit of adoration, but relief?"

Shaking her head, Ella laughed. "You're honest, I'll give you that." She cupped his cheek and looked into his eyes. "I like that."

His gamble had worked. Ella seemed to appreciate his humorous self-aggrandizing that was actually meant to be self-deprecating. "I'm glad. But you're evading my questions. Why relief? Were you afraid my breath was going to stink?"

She took him seriously. "Of course not."

Averting her gaze, she sighed. "Ever since my rescue, I've felt numb. I would look at you and think how gorgeous and attractive you are, but my body didn't follow my brain. There were no tingles, and I was afraid that the numbness was permanent, and that I'd never feel normal again. Or even worse, that I'd feel repulsed by any kind of intimacy."

She lifted her gaze to him. "I bet your sense of smell has already told you that my fears were baseless. It felt wonderful to be kissed by you and to kiss you back." Lowering her eyes again, she whispered, "I'm relieved because now I know that I can make new memories to replace the old ones. Maybe plenty of the good kind will erase the bad."

Julian frowned. Ella sounded as if all of her prior sexual encounters had been terrible. Had there been others who'd mistreated her before Gorchenco?

"I'm sure not all of your memories are bad. Before that scumbag lured you into a trap, you must've had some good experiences."

She shrugged. "Romeo was my first serious boyfriend, and I enjoyed kissing him, but now that I know it was all fake, the memory of those kisses disgusts me."

Julian was starting to get a really uncomfortable feeling.

If Romeo had been Ella's first boyfriend, and kissing had been all that she'd done with him, then she'd been a virgin when Gorchenco had taken her.

Fates, it was bad enough to be coerced into having sex with a man she hadn't wanted. It was ten times worse to have had her virginity taken in such a despicable way.

"Julian? Why are your fangs getting longer?" She pointed at his mouth. "And they are dripping something."

Damn, his venom glands had been activated, but not by arousal.

"I'm going to kill that son of a bitch with my bare hands, and I'm going to do it slowly."

Stiffening in his arms, Ella tried to back away. "Uhm, Julian? Didn't anyone tell you that Romeo is dead? I think Turner beat you to it."

Using his hand, he wiped the venom drops away. "I meant Gorchenco. He deserves to die for what he did to you."

44

ELLA

Julian's fangs were so long by now that he looked like a saber-toothed tiger. And the venom dripping from them was gross. Getting all worked up over a dead issue, he was ruining the memory of that wonderful kiss.

"That's a bit overdramatic, don't you think?"

"The bastard took your virginity."

She stifled the need to roll her eyes. It was her virginity, not his, that had been taken. He had no right to get so angry.

"I know, and I think I have the right to be more pissed about it than you. But he doesn't deserve to die over it. If you get the chance and it makes you feel better, you can beat him up for me."

Heck, if Julian were gay, she would have suggested that he coerce the mafioso into unwanted sex with him. That would be very sweet revenge.

An eye for an eye kind of thing.

But thankfully, Julian was into girls, or rather one girl. Ella.

A small smile lifted one corner of Julian's lips, making him look comical. A smiling tiger. "If I can beat him up within an inch of his life then I accept your offer."

"Nah-ah." She shook her head. "He's too old for that and might die from heart failure. We still need him."

"What?" Julian hissed.

"He used to vacation on the Doomers' island. Now that he's a widower, I'm sure he's going to visit it again. I told Kian about it. Gorchenco can lead them to the island, provided they can find a way to track him."

"How do you know that?"

"I heard him talking with someone about it. When Carol mentioned the kind of resort the Doomers run on their island, I made the connection."

"Finding rich bastards who fulfill their perverted desires on that island is not difficult. Placing any sort of tracker on them, that's the hard part."

"Oh."

Kian hadn't mentioned that, letting her believe that she was being helpful.

The jerk.

He was treating her like a kid.

"So, do I have permission to pound him to the ground?" Julian smiled his grotesque fanged smile that did nothing to detract from how gorgeous he was.

"No. I have a gut feeling that the Russian is going to be instrumental in something. If not in finding the island, then in something else. He needs to live a while longer."

"I don't understand, but it's your call."

"It is." She pushed off his lap, and he let her go. "I should be getting back. My mom is probably worried about me."

They both knew that wasn't true, but it was a polite way to say that she wanted to go home.

The kiss Julian had given her was incredible, but his later angry outburst was tiring her. It didn't matter that it wasn't directed at her. It was negative energy she was still too frazzled to handle.

"I'm sorry," he said at the door to her house. "I'm usually a much mellower guy." He took her hand. "I care about you, Ella. Your pain is my pain."

No, it wasn't.

Julian was an immortal male who was not only stronger than most human males but who could also get out of sticky situations by thralling his assailants. He didn't know how it felt to be small and defenseless with only her wits to aid her, or having to make terrible compromises in order to survive or protect his loved ones.

Still, it was nice of him to say that.

Stretching up to her toes, she kissed his cheek. "I had a lovely time, Julian."

"Me too. How about I take you out sometime? Like on a proper date?"

"I'd love to, but unless you invite me to the village café, I can't. Not until I'm given a makeover. I don't feel safe going out as me."

He nodded. "I'll wait then. Because we will have no privacy in the village café. You have no idea how quickly rumors spread through here."

"Okay." She smiled. "Goodnight, Julian."

"Goodnight, Ella." He lifted her hand to his lips and kissed the back of it.

Crap. That brought back bad memories.

Yanking it out of his clasp, she blurted, "Don't do that."

"Kiss your hand? Why?"

"I'll tell you some other time. I'm tired, and I want to get in bed."

He looked so hurt. "Okay. Goodnight, Ella."

"Goodnight."

Forcing a smile, she opened the door and went inside, letting the smile drop as soon as she closed it behind her.

Thankfully, there was no one in the living room. Tiptoeing to her bedroom, she opened the door as soundlessly as she could and closed it just as gently.

Letting out a whooshed breath, she plopped down on the bed and closed her eyes.

The evening had been a success, but it had been exhausting as well. She'd pushed her boundaries, which was good, and it hadn't backfired, but she'd also overestimated her resiliency.

A lot of residual crap still lingered inside of her. It was sticky and disgusting, and she wished she could just cough it up like phlegm and flush the toilet.

Except, mental discomfort wasn't as easy to alleviate as a physical one. She had a trick for that, though. If she closed her eyes and imagined a pleasant scene, the emotional phlegm would feel less suffocating.

What should she imagine though?

The stroll with Julian had been very pleasant, she could start with that, but instead of it being under the evening sky, she could change the scenery and make it a sunny day on the beach.

Smiling, she imagined the sun kissing Julian's light brown hair, highlighting the blond and gold strands interwoven in between the browns. His eyes would look so blue because his pupils would be pinprick-sized and not overtake his irises like they did at night. He would be smiling, but his fangs would be fully retracted.

With a contented sigh, she let herself drift off into the fantasy, letting the dream unfold on its own.

The scene was so real that she could actually feel the warm sand under her feet, and as a bigger than usual wave broke onto the shore, the cold water lapped at her toes.

It was a glorious day, made even better by walking hand in hand with a gorgeous guy.

She leaned on his arm and sighed. "I love walks on the beach, Julian."

"Who's Julian?" Logan asked.

Gasping, she yanked her hand out of his. "None of your business."

"A new boyfriend?"

For some inexplicable reason, she didn't want to share Julian with Logan even though he wasn't another entity and was just part of her psyche. For the sake of sanity, it was easier to think of him as separate from herself.

"I said that it was none of your business. Can you go away? You're intruding on my dream."

He arched a brow. "Isn't this our beach?"

They were walking along the boardwalk, the same one he'd transported her to before. But it was her beach, not theirs. The same one she used to hang out at with Romeo.

Maybe she should find a new dream beach. This one had too much bad juju.

"It's not our beach, and it's not even mine. Go away. I was enjoying someone else's company until you popped in and replaced him."

Why the heck had it happened, though?

Ella had no idea. She hadn't thought about Logan in days.

"That Julian fellow?"

She shrugged.

His dark features darkened even more, and the sun that had been shining bright a moment ago was suddenly obscured by rain clouds. Scary Logan was back, and apparently his mood was affecting their dream environment.

"Are you having sex with him, Ella?"

Even though he terrified her, she regarded him with a sneer. "Really? You think I'm going to answer that?"

With a snakelike hiss, he grabbed her by the back of her neck. His fingers digging painfully into the soft flesh, he smiled with a pair of fangs very similar to Julian's. "You don't let anyone other than me touch you, Ella. You'll be very sorry if you do."

"Let me go!"

Surprisingly, he released her. "We are meant for each other, Ella. No one can give you what I can."

"And what's that? A missile launcher? I don't need anything from you, Logan."

As he smiled, his fangs were almost back to normal. "We will see about that."

Ella jerked awake and bolted upright.

What a creepy dream. Julian must have scared her with his venom-dripping fangs and his anger more than she'd realized because now she'd given Logan his fangs.

Except, hadn't Logan had fangs and glowing eyes in the first dream she'd had about him?

Ella scrubbed a hand over her face.

This was bad.

She hadn't known about immortals back then. Could it have been a prophetic dream?

Or was Logan an immortal just like Julian? Except, unlike Julian, he was an evil one.

"No fucking way!"

Suddenly it all made sense. Logan was a Doomer. That was why he had fangs in her dreams, and why he and Gorchenco had been talking about the Doomers' freaking island.

Since she hadn't known about fanged immortals before her rescue, she couldn't have given fangs and glowing eyes to dream Logan. Which meant that somehow he was getting inside her head while she slept.

Could thralling be done long distance?

That wasn't likely.

Even Yamanu, the clan's secret weapon, had distance limits. He could cover a large area, but he needed to be there. That's why they'd flown him to New York for her rescue mission. If he could've done it from the village, he wouldn't have gone.

But then none of the clan members could communicate telepathically like her and her mother either, so different and unknown abilities existed. Logan could have the special ability to penetrate dreams.

What was she going to do?

Could he see the village through her eyes?

Was she endangering everyone by being there?

Should she tell someone?

45

ELLA

After spending half the night freaking out over Logan's possible identity, Ella had managed to pass the second half in dreamless sleep.

By morning, the entire episode seemed silly.

Fangs and glowing eyes were a trope used in every book and movie about vampires and demons, and she'd watched and read quite a few of those. The *Twilight* saga alone, which she'd watched twice, once with Maddie and another time with her mother, could explain dream Logan's appearance.

The island with its secret resort coming up in a conversation between two powerful, rich, and dangerous men shouldn't be taken as proof that Logan was a Doomer either.

Probably every mafia boss, arms dealer, warlord, and drug lord had visited the exclusive brothel at one time or another, and she wouldn't be surprised if some of the high-ranking politicians were its clients as well.

She'd learned a thing or two from Gorchenco.

Power was corruptive, and politics, although legitimate, was a nasty business in which only the most brutal and unscrupulous reached the top, regardless of their so-called ideological leanings. Corruption and the thirst for power didn't care about party lines.

Still, it was possible that Logan was indeed a Doomer, but Ella wasn't going to run into Kian's office and tell him about her dream encounters. She could only imagine his response.

He would probably suggest that she visit with Vanessa and get her head checked.

Before she did anything rash, she was going to wait for the next dream visit and test Logan. If she asked him a question to which she couldn't possibly know the answer, and what he said checked out, then she'd have proof that he wasn't a product of her mind but a separate entity.

But even that wouldn't prove or disprove that he was a Doomer.

Logan could be a human with special abilities, and maybe even a Dormant.

One thing she was going to make sure of, though. Every dream encounter from now on was going to happen on "their" beach. Just in case he was a Doomer, she wasn't going to show him her real surroundings and give him clues as to the village's location. Also, she was going to be very careful not to mention anything about Doomers or immortals because that would give her away too.

Luckily, up until now, nothing about immortals had been mentioned in their dream encounters. To make sure, she'd gone over every word they'd ever exchanged.

When her phone buzzed, she snatched it off the charging station, hoping it was a text from Julian, but it was from Amanda, reminding her that today was the big day.

Ella was finally getting her makeover.

The good news was that her mother together with Magnus and Parker were going shopping and would be gone most of the day.

Vivian wasn't going to be happy about the changes Ella intended to make, and it was best she didn't see the work in progress, but was presented with the completed project. Other than lamenting Ella's pretty hair, there wouldn't be much her mother could do after the fact.

When the doorbell rang two hours later, Ella was alone in the house, with only Scarlet for company.

"Hello, darling." Amanda sauntered in with a big duffle bag slung over her shoulder. "I hope you don't mind, but I decided to make it a girls' get together."

Ella had been expecting Carol and Eva to join, but not Tessa and another woman she didn't know.

"This is Sharon," Eva introduced her assistant. "Sharon, this is Ella."

"Hi." Sharon offered her hand. "I couldn't resist seeing Eva's magic in action."

Eva shook her head. "I told you that you were going to be disappointed. This is Amanda's show. I'm here only as an advisor."

"Where do you want to do it, Ella?"

Good question. Hair coloring was messy, and Ella didn't want to chance staining any of the nice furniture or the rug in the living room.

"Can we all squeeze into my room?"

"Sure." Amanda waved a hand. "Girls, grab a couple of chairs and let's go."

"You go ahead," Carol said. "I'm going to make us virgin margaritas."

Amanda grimaced. "Why virgin?"

"Because Eva is breastfeeding, and Ella is only eighteen."

"That doesn't mean we all have to suffer."

Sharon patted her shoulder. "It's only ten-thirty in the morning. It's too early for alcohol."

"Oh, well. I guess virgin it is."

Carol headed to the kitchen, Sharon and Tessa each grabbed a chair, and the five of them filed into Ella's room, with Scarlet closing the procession and promptly jumping on the bed.

Amanda patted the dog's head. "Since you're a girl too, you're allowed. But you need to behave."

Scarlet wagged her tail.

"I see that we have an understanding."

Putting her duffle bag down on Ella's desk, Amanda started taking stuff out. Several boxes of hair color, four different brushes, two pairs of scissors, a hair dryer and a hair curler. Next came up a bottle of shampoo, a conditioner, and miscellaneous other hair treatments Ella could only guess the use of.

"I also brought several outfits for you to try out once we are done with the hair and makeup."

Eva lifted a rectangular box. "I brought several colored contact lenses. You can change your eye color every day of the week if you want."

"I've never worn contact lenses."

Eva waved a hand. "You'll get used to them. And anyway, you only need to put them in when you go out."

One hour later, Ella looked into the mirror and could hardly recognize herself. "My own mother could pass me on the street and not know it was me."

Amanda had bleached her hair, colored it pink, cut it short, and then spiked it using tons of hair glue. Smokey-eyes heavy makeup framed her new amber colored eyes, and her brows grew to twice their size thanks to some specialty brow product that mimicked real hairs. Her face had been primed and contoured, giving her a hollow-cheeked appearance.

"What do you think?" Amanda looked at Eva.

"Couldn't have done it better myself."

"I have some fake piercings for you to try on," Carol said. "They look so real I'm tempted to play with them myself."

"Why fake?" Tessa asked. "Ella can have fun with real piercings as long as she is still human. When she transitions, the holes will close."

"I prefer the fake ones." Ella reached for the box. "They don't hurt."

First, she put in big hoop earrings, then she added a removable nose ring, and lastly she stuck a glue-on fake diamond on top of her new bushy brow. "I look like a pink goth."

"That was the idea," Amanda said. "Now let's move to the wardrobe." She pulled a pair of shredded black jeans out of her duffle bag.

"Be careful when you put them on. There are more holes in them than fabric."

She hadn't been kidding. And they were really tight too.

Next was a black T-shirt with some band name printed in pink lettering on the front.

"That's so awesome." Ella turned this way and that in front of the mirror. "I look like such a badass."

"You do, darling. But I'm not done." Amanda pulled out a pair of monster boots from her bag. "Put them on."

They were six inches high, but since they were basically chunky platforms, Ella had no trouble walking in them. They must've been expensive. The leather was soft, and they weighed very little considering how bulky they looked.

"I love it."

"Now the bangles." Amanda handed her a bunch of bracelets made from various materials.

"Anything else?" Ella asked after putting several on each wrist.

Amanda shook her head and smiled. "I think my work here is done. What do you think, girls?"

"Unbelievable," Tessa said. "That's even more drastic than my makeover."

Eva nodded. "I agree. No one is going to recognize you, Ella."

Looking in the mirror, Ella liked what she saw. The question was whether Julian would too.

"What do you think will happen if I go out into the village looking like this? Am I going to trigger the intruder alert?"

"You might." Tessa chuckled. "You'll have to reintroduce yourself to every person you meet."

Sharon shook her head. "I'm worried about your mother. She's going to faint seeing you like that."

"I can handle my mom. After the initial shock, she'll get used to it, especially since this makeover is supposedly for my safety."

"Supposedly?" Eva asked. "I thought that was the entire purpose of this."

"It was. But I like the new look. It's so drastically different from the good-girl-next-door one I was ready to get rid of. It makes me feel cool, like an individualistic badass who is not scared of anything. The only thing I'm missing is a tattoo." She arched a brow at Amanda. "Any chance you do those too?"

Amanda laughed. "No, darling. Tattoos don't hold on immortals."

"Bummer."

"You can have a fake henna one," Carol offered. "It will hold for a couple of months. Where do you want it?"

"On my face." Ella smoothed her hand over her left cheek. "A vine that will start around the eye and continue down to my neck."

"That's going too far," Eva said. "You don't want to encourage close inspection of your features, and a facial tattoo will make people want to take a closer look."

There was some logic to that, although she already looked weird enough to attract attention, but at least it would be for a different reason than before.

She was no longer as pretty, which was precisely what she'd wanted to achieve with the makeover. Her beauty had brought her nothing but trouble.

The only thing she was worried about was Julian's reaction.

"Any of you know where Julian's house is? I want to surprise him with my new look."

Tessa cleared her throat. "Maybe you should text him first and let him know that you're coming."

"Yeah, that's a good idea," Sharon said. "And include a selfie with your text."

Amanda, on the other hand, smirked like a she-devil and wrapped her arm around Ella's shoulders. "Let me show you how to get there."

46

JULIAN

As the piano playing abruptly stopped, Julian lifted his head from the article he was reading and glanced at his roommate.

"Are you expecting a visitor, Julian?" From his bench, Ray had a good view of the path leading to their house. "Because someone is walking this way."

"Who is it?"

"No one I know, but she's hot."

Ray didn't hang out much with other immortals, but he could probably recognize each of the village's residents. The only newcomers were Vivian and Ella, whom he might've not met yet.

Hot could apply to both mother and daughter. Except, neither had a reason to come visit him.

Suddenly worried, Julian got up and rushed to the door, yanking it open and leaving his visitor with her hand up in the air ready to knock.

"Hi, Julian."

He gaped. "Ella?"

The voice was the same, the body shape was the same, but that was it. The disguise must've been Eva's work. The transformation was so complete that he would not have recognized Ella on the street. Even her unique personal scent was barely accessible under the heavy perfume she had on.

Brown contact lenses with a tint of amber covered her blue eyes, and her hair had been cut short, colored bright pink, and spiked. Two large hoops pierced her ears, a much smaller one was threaded through her nostril, and a fourth one through her brow.

The tight black jeans, black punk-rock T-shirt, and monster shoes made her look much thinner and taller.

Despite the godawful getup, she was still beautiful, but he'd loved her old, softer look and hated the new, edgy one.

Smirking, she turned in a circle. "Do you like?"

He rubbed a hand over his face. "It will take some getting used to."

Her smile faded, but then she shrugged. "It's good to know that you're honest. May I come in?"

Damn, he'd kept her on the front porch instead of inviting her in.

"Of course." He threw the door open.

"Hello," she said to his roommate. "I'm Ella."

"Ray." He got up and offered her his hand. "I don't know what you looked like before, but this is hot."

She beamed at him. "Thank you."

Barely managing to stifle the growl that had started deep in his throat, Julian coughed.

Ella pulled her hand out of Ray's and turned to Julian, handing him the plastic bag she'd brought with her. "Your clothes. I totally forgot to return them. I'm sorry it took so long. But better late than never, right? They are washed and ironed, so you can put them right back in your closet."

Apparently, when embarrassed, Ella talked a lot.

"You ironed my socks and boxer shorts?"

That wrested a smile out of her. "Just the T-shirt and the sweatshirt."

"Do you iron all of your T-shirts?"

She scrunched her nose. "I do. Is it weird?"

"Not at all. I do that too," Ray said.

Liar.

The dude was supposed to be his friend, or at least stick to the bro code. It wasn't cool to flirt with his roommate's girlfriend.

Glaring at him, Julian motioned to the couch. "Would you like to sit down, Ella?"

She shifted from foot to foot. "In fact, I came here to take you up on your offer to go out. I've been cooped up in this lovely village for far too long, and I need to do some shopping. But I don't have my fake driver's license yet, and I'm also afraid to go out by myself, so I thought you could take me."

Probably feeling awkward about initiating their date, Ella was rambling on, the scent of her embarrassment overpowering the stinky perfume.

Shopping was a great idea.

He was going to buy her a lineup of good smells and ask her to throw out the hippie patchouli or give it back to whoever had thought it was a good scent on her.

"Let's go." He grabbed his phone, his wallet, and his car keys off the kitchen counter.

She glanced at his feet. "Don't you want to put shoes on first? And maybe exchange your sweatpants for jeans?"

"Yeah." He raked his fingers through his hair. "I should, shouldn't I?"

Smiling, she nodded.

"Do you want to wait here? It will only take me a minute."

"If you don't mind, I would like to see your room." She stuck her hands in the back pockets of her torn jeans. "I want to see if you are really as tidy as you claimed to be."

For a moment, he had no idea what she was talking about, but then he remembered the hotel in New York. When he'd hesitated to invite her to his room, she'd assumed he was embarrassed about it being messy.

"By all means." He motioned for her to go ahead of him.

Later, he should thank his mother for insisting that he always make his bed. The habit was so ingrained in him that he couldn't leave his room in the morning unless everything was in its place.

"Very masculine," she said as he opened the door for her. "And tidy. I'm impressed."

He noticed her looking at his motorized reclining armchair. "Take a seat." He motioned to it. "I'll be out in a moment." He ducked into the walk-in closet and closed the door.

Changing into one of his nicer pairs of jeans, he heard Ella engage the recliner's motor, and a moment later her contented sigh.

Julian smiled. Ray could laugh all he wanted about his old-man chair. The thing was the most comfortable seat in the house.

As if sensing that someone was thinking of him, Ray resumed his playing, no doubt in an effort to impress Ella.

It worked.

A moment later Julian heard the chair's motor engage again and then his bedroom door open. Ella's chunky boots clanked on the hardwood floor as she walked toward the grand piano in the living room.

Grabbing a button-down off the hanger, Julian pushed his feet into a pair of loafers, saving the time it would have taken him to put on socks, and tackled the buttons on his way to the living room.

He found Ella leaning with her elbows on the side of the piano and gazing at Ray with open admiration.

"Ready to go?" Julian asked.

She nodded and waved at Ray. "See you later."

His roommate stopped playing. "Pop in anytime. I'm home most days, practicing. Maybe next time you could stay a little longer and listen to one piece from start to finish."

"I would love that. You play beautifully."

47

ELLA

The first ten minutes of the drive were unnerving. As soon as the self-driving mechanism engaged and the windows turned opaque, Julian sat back and crossed his arms over his chest.

He was brooding, and the compliments she'd paid Ray could be the only reason for it. Julian seemed to have a jealous streak and Ella wasn't sure how to feel about that.

With her limited dating experience, she didn't know if that was true of most guys, or just the possessive and controlling types. Julian didn't seem like one, but she'd been wrong before.

Well, that was why they were going on an actual date. They were going to talk and get to know each other, and she was going to pay close attention to any telltale signs of character flaws that were unacceptable to her. She didn't expect perfection and was willing to overlook one or two annoying habits, maybe even more, but some things were not negotiable.

A little jealousy was fine, she wouldn't want a girl to flirt with Julian either, and so was a little possessiveness, but not control. The moment he started to demand that she do or not do things, she was going to walk away from him no matter how attractive Julian's total package was.

Heck, she was willing to settle for a much more modest package deal in exchange for a respectful and easy-going attitude.

Like Magnus's.

Observing him interact with her mother and her brother was warming Ella's heart. The guy somehow managed to balance everything perfectly. He was easy-going and accommodating, helpful and respectful, but he wasn't a pushover.

He had what she thought of as a good alpha vibe.

Magnus often took charge, but it was seldom about him. His primary concern was taking care of the people he loved and being the pillar of strength they could lean on.

That was what Ella wanted from a partner, or mate, as the immortals called it. Hopefully, Julian could be that person for her.

But that was putting the cart in front of the horse, or as Amanda would say the eyeshadow before the foundation.

He cast her a sidelong glance. "You know that those piercings will close once you transition."

Chuckling, she removed the hook from her nostril. "These are fake piercings. The one on my brow is glued on."

"Why use them at all? They don't help to obscure your features."

"It's for the total effect. Like the nails." She wiggled her fingers. "Metallic blue nail polish just goes with the Goth look."

He cast her another glance just as the windows started to clear. "I'm getting used to the pink hair. It's actually not so bad."

"I've heard better compliments, but as I said before, I appreciate the honesty."

As the computerized voice announced that self-driving was going to disengage in thirty seconds, Julian put his hands on the steering wheel. "That's good because I'm a terrible liar."

"Tell me what you hate the most about my new look."

"Easy. The contact lenses and the eyeshadow because I love your eyes so much. But that's also the best part of the disguise. Your eyes are very distinctive." He reached with his fingers and smoothed them over her cheek. "I also don't like those dark smudges on your face. They make your cheeks look hollow. I like your softness."

"So, you're okay with the hair?"

He glanced at her again. "Yeah. It's cute."

Cute wasn't what she was going for, but she could live with that. "I'm only going to put in the colored contact lenses and heavy makeup when I go outside the village. The only thing you're going to see is the hair, which you're okay with."

Tapping his fingers on the steering wheel, Julian shook his head. "If you enjoy the new look, you shouldn't change it on my account. I'll get used to it. You're beautiful even when you impersonate a Goth fairy."

That was so sweet of him to say. "Thank you. But I don't like makeup, and I really don't like contacts. They irritate my eyes."

"What did your mom say about all that?"

"She didn't see me yet. The three of them went shopping."

"I hope you called her and told her that I'm taking you to the mall. She'll be worried if she comes home and you're not there."

Arching the brow with the fake piercing in it, Ella tapped her temple. "Did you forget about this? I don't need to call or text my mom. I sent her a mental message." She chuckled. "It will be so funny if we bump into them at the mall and my mom doesn't recognize me. She'll get mad at you for going out with some other girl."

"Then we should go to a different mall. I don't want to be there for the showdown."

"Chicken."

"You bet I am."

Cute. She liked that he didn't mind belittling himself, even if only teasingly.

With his many attributes, Julian could've been a pompous ass, but he wasn't, not even a little.

She wondered how it was possible. Bridget probably had a lot to do with it, raising Julian to be modest and not boastful.

"You keep surprising me," she said.

He glanced at her with a cocked brow. "Me? I'm the most boring and predictable guy."

"You've just proven me right. Those are precisely the kinds of things I would not have expected a guy like you to say."

"What do you mean by a guy like me?"

"You know what I mean. Your good looks alone would make any human guy strut around like a peacock and expect girls to drop their panties as soon as they saw him. But you're also a doctor, and most of them are the most pompous people I've met. They think that they know everything."

Pushing his fingers through his hair, Julian grimaced. "The panty-dropping thing I've been guilty of, I admit that, but it just happened whether I expected it or not. And as to knowing everything, I'm well aware of my limited knowledge. Even in my own profession I still have a lot to learn, and I certainly don't know much about other disciplines."

He waved a hand. "For example, if this car broke down, I wouldn't know how to fix it. On the other hand, I know that I can learn almost anything I put my mind to."

"Almost? What can't you learn?"

"Quantum physics. I just can't wrap my mind around it. And believe me, I've tried."

"Perhaps you just need a good teacher. Did you try learning about it from books?"

"Books and recorded university lectures. I still don't get it."

Fiddling with the frayed edges of her jeans, Ella was reminded of something the Russian had told her. "I hate to bring him up, but Gorchenco told me that you should always hire professionals to do what they are trained for. You need to find a good teacher and pay him. That will be the fastest way to learn a difficult subject."

Julian's hands tightened on the steering wheel. "I don't want to take anything from a morally corrupt, evil man. Even if it's good advice."

That wasn't smart. Julian was letting his emotions cloud his judgment. As much as she resented the Russian and detested what he'd done to her, Ella wasn't going to ignore the things she'd learned from him.

48

JULIAN

"I'm sorry." Ella gave him a lopsided grin. "I know that shopping for clothes is torture for guys."

She wasn't sorry at all, and she hadn't bought that much either, but she sure as hell had spent hours going from store to store and trying things on.

Julian took the latest shopping bag from her hand. "Ready to call it a day?"

"Yeah, my feet hurt and my eyes are burning. I can't wait to take the contacts out. But I had fun. Thank you." She looped her arm around his neck and pulled him down for a quick kiss. "You're a prince for letting me drag you around all day long."

Transferring all the shopping bags to one hand, he wrapped his arm around her waist and kissed her back. Just a quick peck on the lips because they were in a crowded shopping mall and getting aroused was out of the question. "I had fun too."

They'd eaten an early dinner in one of the mall's restaurants, and after that Ella hadn't made too much of a fuss when he'd insisted on buying her perfumes, especially when he'd told her how much he hated the patchouli smell she had on.

It had been a good day.

Hell, it had been great.

Nothing had been said, but they were officially a couple. Ella's acceptance of his gift had been the final proof of that.

She'd been relaxed with him, comfortable as if they'd been dating for a year and not just one day, and the longer they were together, the better it got.

Was that what being fated for each other felt like?

Or maybe it was just his inexperience with actual dating, and that was how everyone felt? Or at least those who found someone they really liked?

He was trying hard to keep some emotional distance and not let his obsession with Ella cloud his judgment, but what he was discovering was better than the fantasy, and the very real and down-to-earth Ella was much more than what he'd built up in his head.

Like her crusty sense of humor, which was increasingly surfacing the more comfortable she got with him. Julian hadn't expected to like it so much, but it was refreshing being with a girl who wasn't afraid to express herself without worrying about making a guy think that she was sweeter than cotton candy.

She also liked to touch and be touched, which suited him perfectly because he craved the closeness and implied familiarity. They'd been holding hands or having their arms wrapped around each other throughout the day. He especially loved the way she'd leaned her head on his arm or thanked him for doing that or this with a smile or a peck on his cheek.

The truth was that he was looking forward to many more days like that, shopping with her, carrying her bags, and giving his opinion about the things she wanted to buy. Being a couple was so much better than prowling for hookups and spending his days alone.

"You're just saying that." Ella's eyes smiled as she threaded her arm through his. "Admit it. You've been suffering valiantly."

"How about I prove it to you? I'll take you shopping tomorrow too."

She laughed. "I think I spent enough money today. I need to find a job before I go on another shopping spree."

"Guardians are paid very well. I'm sure Magnus can afford it." They exited the mall and headed for his car.

"It's not a question of whether he can afford it or not. I don't want to spend his money. I want to have my own."

He opened the passenger door for her and dropped the bags on the back seat. "Magnus thinks of you as his daughter," he said as he turned the ignition on.

"That's very sweet of him, but I am not. And even if I were his daughter, I would've felt bad about mooching off my parents instead of working for my spending money."

"What about when you go to college? The clan will pay for your tuition, but you'll need spending money."

She shrugged. "I can work part-time."

Julian frowned. He hadn't considered it before, but there was a very real possibility that Ella would choose an out-of-state college.

If she did, he would have to follow her there because there was no way he was letting her out of his sight.

Just thinking about it felt like a vice was closing around his heart.

"What's the matter, Julian? It suddenly feels as if the temperature in this car has dropped ten degrees. Did I say something to upset you?"

He reached for her hand, remembering at the last moment that she didn't like it kissed. Was it something that reminded her of Gorchenco?

Instead, he threaded his fingers through hers and just held it, resting their conjoined hands on her thigh. "I hope you're going to choose a local college. Now that I found you, I can't fathom being without you."

"Oh, crap." She pulled her hand out of his and reached for her eye. "Why did you have to make me emotional? Now my eyes sting, and I have to take the freaking contacts out, and I don't know how to do that. Eva didn't show me how."

"I'll pull over and help you."

Searching for a place to park, he spotted the vacant lot of a closed-for-business mattress store.

He parked, killed the engine, and turned to Ella. "Let me see." He cupped her chin and lifted it. "Your eyes are red."

"They feel as if I polished them with sandpaper. Can you take the contacts out?"

"Ouch." His own eyes teared as his empathy kicked in. "Look up and open your eyes wide."

"Yes, doctor."

Since Ella didn't expect him to move so fast, the first contact was easy. She didn't even have time to blink before he got it out.

"Oh, wow. It's such a relief."

He caught her hand, stopping her from rubbing the eye. "It's going to itch much worse if you get makeup in it."

"Right. Can you get the other one too?"

"Look up again."

"Yes, sir."

This time, she blinked before he could pinch the contact out. "I'll either have to hold your eye open or show you how to do it yourself."

"You do it. I'm scared to do it myself."

Her trust melted his heart.

Holding her eye open, Julian quickly pinched the contact, got it out, and let go. "All done." He kissed her lips. "Should I kiss the boo-boos away?"

"Yes, please."

He gently kissed one eyelid, and then the other, not caring about the shadow he was getting on his lips. If it made her feel better, he would lick the makeup off them, but he doubted she was willing to go that far.

"You don't happen to have tissues in here, do you?"

He shook his head. "I don't get sick. But I can drive to the nearest pharmacy and get you some."

"No, that's okay." She bent down and lifted the bottom of her T-shirt to her eyes, exposing a very tempting midriff.

It wasn't flat, and Ella didn't have the muscles of someone who exercised regularly, but her skin looked so soft and creamy, and her slightly rounded belly was cute and feminine.

Once she was done wiping the makeup off, she glanced up at him. "I probably look like a raccoon."

He couldn't lie. "A raccoon that got punched in both eyes, or an escapee from a zombie movie."

"Great." She covered her eyes with her palms. "I will have to spend the rest of the drive like this."

"Don't be silly." He pulled her hands away from her face. "No one is going to notice."

A slight scent of fear wafted off her. "There are traffic cameras on the way. Without the contacts, I'm exposed to facial recognition software."

"Would sunglasses help? I have a pair in the glove compartment."

"I don't know if regular sunglasses would do the trick."

As she looked at him, Ella's worried blue eyes stood in stark relief against the backdrop of the dark makeup smeared all around them.

"I have an idea. You can lie down on the back seat and cover your face with the sweatshirt you bought."

"What if the police stop you?"

"I'll thrall the cop to think you're a dog."

"That's nasty, but I like it."

49

ELLA

Awake even though it was after midnight, Ella rubbed a finger over her lips, the phantom memory of Julian's goodnight kiss still lingering despite the long hot shower she'd taken after he'd walked her home.

Her mother had been so ecstatic over their date that she hadn't made a big fuss about the pink hair, or the raccoon eyes, or the Goth clothing and monster boots.

Vivian was okay with whatever got Ella out of the house, especially with Julian.

She should've gotten a tattoo at the mall. It had been a missed opportunity to do something wild and not get an earful from her mom about it.

Turning to her back, Ella stared at the ceiling.

Even though they hadn't done anything special, the date with Julian had been magical. Other than her mother, she'd never felt as close to anyone, not even Parker.

She could see herself spending her life with Julian, and it would be a good one.

Except, she couldn't help the feeling that it was all too good to be true. Life had taught her that shit happened often and for no good reason, and when everything seemed to be going her way, she should brace for a disaster to ruin it.

Ella still remembered how elated she'd felt when Parker was born. Being a big sister had been a wish come true, and for one wonderful year their family was as happy as could be.

But then her father was killed, and nothing was the same again. From the height of happiness, their family had descended into the pits of despair.

It had taken years for the pain of his loss to recede. The wound had crusted over, but the part of her heart that had died with her father remained numb.

Then things started to look up when Romeo showed up in her life. She'd thought she was falling in love, but that had been another disaster in the making.

Every time Ella had allowed herself to be happy, the universe decided that she didn't deserve it.

What was it going to throw at her now?

Gorchenco's goons sniffing out her trail?

Would Logan turn out to be a Doomer and storm the village because she somehow revealed its location even though she didn't know where it was?

What if he ended up hurting Julian?

A shiver running down her spine, Ella curled up on her side and tucked her hands under the pillow. She needed to fall asleep and dream of him.

Hours passed as she tried to deep breathe herself to sleep, and when that didn't help, to count sheep. Eventually, though, exhaustion did the trick. Once again, Ella found herself walking along the shoreline, but Logan wasn't there.

Should she try and call him? Would it work?

"Logan, where are you?"

The good thing about dreamland was that there were no other people on the beach unless she willed them to be there. Maybe she should try to do the same with Logan?

Closing her eyes, Ella willed him to appear at her side.

When a couple of minutes passed and nothing happened, she was ready to call it quits, but then the air in front of her shimmered, and Logan stepped out through what looked like an arched doorway. It blinked out of existence as soon as he was entirely on Ella's side.

"You called?" He arched a brow.

"Yes, I did. I want to talk to you."

Suspicion clouded his dark eyes. "About?"

"Gorchenco."

Hopefully, Logan would buy the excuse. She knew he would get suspicious if she claimed to just want his company.

"What do you want to know?"

"Is he okay? I worry about him."

As much as she wished it was just an excuse, it wasn't. Gorchenco was too smart to buy her staged death. Something must've happened for him to concede defeat so quickly. It wasn't like him to give up so soon.

"You must have a sixth sense, Ella. Gorchenco had a heart attack."

When she gasped, he lifted his hand to quickly qualify. "He's not dead. He's recuperating on his Russian estate."

"How do you know that?"

"Did you forget? I do business with him."

"Right. He supplies you with weapons."

"Indeed. No one can get the stuff he does. He must have excellent connections in the Russian military. Maybe even to Putin."

"Perhaps they are related. Did you notice how much alike they look?"

He chuckled. "I don't think they are, but maybe. Who knows? They might be distant cousins."

If only she had a way to verify Gorchenco really had had a heart attack, she would know whether Logan was a separate entity from her or not.

"I don't know if I believe you. He seemed very healthy to me. He didn't overeat, or over drink, and he didn't smoke." Except for the one time he'd lit up a joint for her.

Logan shrugged. "You don't have to take my word for it. Who knows? Maybe your guilty conscience is making it up."

"Right. As if I would feel guilty for escaping from the guy who bought me and wanted to keep me against my will."

Logan shrugged again.

Tomorrow, she could look for information about Gorchenco on the internet. Perhaps his supposed heart attack would be mentioned somewhere. But if it was, it would probably be in Russian. Unfortunately, she hadn't learned it and would have to find someone who could read it.

Except, that would take time, and the need to know the truth couldn't wait that long.

"I need to ask you something."

"I figured you didn't call for me to talk about your husband."

"He is not my anything," she bristled. "That wedding was a sham. But that's neither here nor there. I need to know whether you're really a figment of my imagination or are you real?"

"Why? Do you want me, Ella?" He smirked. "Do you crave what only I can give you?"

"And what's that?"

He cupped the back of her head and leaned, so his lips hovered a fraction of an inch away from hers. "Passion, Ella," he murmured. "Like you've never experienced before."

For reasons she refused to examine, he was affecting her, and she hated it. Why was he making her feel things she wanted to feel for Julian and no other?

Pushing on his chest, she took a step back and was surprised that he didn't try to stop her.

"Tell me the truth, Logan. Are you real? Or am I making you up?"

He caressed her cheek with the tips of two fingers, much in the same way Julian had done, but Logan's touch felt more erotic in nature than loving.

"If I tell you, my sweet Ella, you have to promise not to tell anyone."

Seeing no other choice, she nodded.

"I need to hear you say it."

"I promise not to tell anyone about you."

He smiled with too much satisfaction over her small concession. "Very good. Just so you know, your promise is binding."

"What does it mean?"

"It means that you really can't tell anyone."

"Well, I promised."

Not that she had any intention of keeping the promise if he admitted to being a Doomer. Except, she couldn't ask him if he was without giving herself away.

"I'm real. I'm a telepath like you, and that's why I find you so fascinating. I've never met a woman who could do what I can."

"If you were a telepath like me, you could've contacted me while I'm awake and not only in my dreams. Although that would've been one hell of an achievement since I have very strong protective walls up. Even my mother can't communicate with me unless I allow it."

"There is no fooling you, is there?" He sighed as if resigned to revealing his big secret, but it looked fake. "I don't know anyone else who can do what I can, and the name I invented for my ability is dream-walker."

"So, you can enter my mind while I dream but not while I'm awake?"

"It's more complicated than that. The best way I can explain it is that when you dream you create another dimension, a non-physical one, and we can meet there if I happen to be dreaming at the same time."

"Can you do it with anyone?"

He shook his head. "Only with people whom I've met in person, and only those who have at least some telepathic ability. I think the telepathy is the conduit for the dream encounters."

For a change, he sounded sincere, and Ella believed him.

"So other than me, who else have you shared dreams with?"

"Very few people." He caressed her cheek again. "I told you, my sweet Ella. You're a rare treasure, and I intend to find you. And when I do, you're not going to escape me as easily as you did the Russian. I'm going to keep you forever."

50

VIVIAN

As the door to Ella's room opened, Vivian reminded herself to stay calm and say nothing about the pink spikes on her daughter's head.

It had been quite a shock to see her return from her date with Julian looking nothing like her sweet little girl. Between the horrendous eye makeup that had been smeared all over her face and the dark shading under her cheekbones, she'd looked like a character from the zombie apocalypse.

But the smile on Ella's face and the dreamy look in her eyes had been worth every splash of paint Amanda had applied to her face and hair.

Evidently, the date had gone very well. Vivian couldn't wait to hear the details.

"Good morning." Ella shuffled into the kitchen in her bunny slippers.

Her eyes seemed blurry, and at first glance, the dark circles under them looked like smeared makeup that she hadn't done a good job washing off last night. On closer inspection, however, that wasn't the case.

"Good morning. Did you have trouble sleeping again?"

"Uh-hum." Ella lifted the coffee carafe and poured herself a cup.

"Good dreams or bad ones?"

"A little bit of both."

When Ella didn't elaborate, Vivian decided to drop the subject and move to the one she was more curious about.

"How did it go with Julian?"

A smile brightened Ella's tired face. "Great. I dragged the poor guy all over the mall, and he didn't complain even once."

"That's your proof that he's a keeper. I was right."

Ella rolled her eyes. "As if it was needed. Julian is every mother's dream son-in-law. The question I keep asking myself is what the heck does he see in me?"

She took another sip of coffee. "If it was about my pretty face then the makeover should've turned him off." She chuckled. "You should have seen his expression when he opened the door to let me in. He looked horrified."

"You went to his house?"

Ella shrugged. "I returned the clothes I borrowed from him and used it as an excuse to ask him out."

Ella had asked Julian out? Not the other way around?

If it weren't early in the morning, Vivian would have opened a bottle of champagne to celebrate. There was no doubt Ella was getting better.

"I'm so happy that you initiated it."

Cradling the cup in her hands, Ella leaned forward. "It was a test. I wanted to see his response. If he was willing to be seen with me in public when I looked like a cross between a fairy and a zombie, it would prove that he liked me for me and not just for my pretty face."

"Given the way you were soaring on a cloud last night, I assume that he passed your test with flying colors."

Ella raked her fingers through her short hair that thankfully wasn't spiky anymore. With the glue washed out, there was nothing to hold it up. It was kind of cute, making Ella look like a pink-haired pixie.

"He exceeded my expectations. First of all, he admitted to hating the new look, which was really brave of him. And he was so much fun to be with. I wasn't stressed, and I wasn't anxious. I was as comfortable as if that was our hundredth date and not the first."

Vivian wasn't sure that was a good thing.

There should have been at least some sexual tension between them. A new couple that hadn't been intimate yet shouldn't feel so comfortable with each other on their first date or even the fifth or the seventh.

"Good morning, Mom, Tinker Bell," Parker said as he entered the kitchen. "Is there anything to eat?"

"For you." Ella rubbed her fingers over his head. "Fairy dust should do."

"I'll make French toast for everyone." Vivian got up.

He blew at the imaginary dust. "I shall destroy your magic with my telekinetic power."

Ella ruffled his hair. "Any luck discovering what your special talent is?"

He grimaced. "It's not telekinesis, that's for sure. And it's not telepathy."

"Did you try remote viewing?"

"I don't know how."

"Simple. You close your eyes and imagine some place you've never been to, and then look for it on the Internet to see if you were right."

His eyes brightened. "I'm going to do it right now."

Vivian waved her spatula. "Can it wait until after breakfast?"

"Sure. What else can I try?" he asked Ella.

"Precognition, but I guess that's trickier. You can try to guess the lottery numbers and then check if you were close."

That got Parker even more excited. "Why didn't you tell me about it before? I could've asked Mom to buy me a ticket when we went shopping yesterday."

Ella chuckled. "Don't you want to test it first before spending your allowance money on it?"

"I was only going to spend one dollar." Parker pouted.

Letting out a big yawn, Ella got up and stretched. "I need to get dressed."

"Any plans for today?" Vivian asked.

"I thought about hanging out with Carol. She's such a fascinating woman."

"Has she invited you?"

Ella waved a hand. "She said I can come over whenever I want. But I'll text her and ask if today is good for her."

"Don't forget that later today we are going to Dalhu's art exhibition. You need to come home and change clothes." Vivian glanced at the pink hair. "Maybe wear a wig too. We still have the short black one Amanda gave you."

"It's fine, Mom. I just need to put the gel on to spike it."

"Please don't. Maybe I can blow dry it for you, slick it back and away from your face?"

"Can we talk about it when I come back?"

Which in Ella speak meant forget it.

Vivian sighed. "Did you at least buy something nice to wear yesterday?"

"I got everyday stuff. I'll borrow something from you."

With Vivian's closet getting frequent new updates courtesy of Magnus, Ella had plenty to choose from.

"Okay. Just be back on time. The exhibition is at six-thirty, and I want us to have dinner before we go. You need to be here no later than five."

"I'll be back long before that."

51

ELLA

As Ella walked down the pathway leading to Carol's house, she was still asking herself the same question that had been bothering her since she'd woken up that morning.

How could she find out whether Logan was a Doomer without asking him point blank if he was? Which she couldn't do because she was pretending not to know anything about immortals.

Besides, after he'd threatened to find her and keep her, it was better if she didn't engage with him at all. The chances of Logan ever finding her were slim, so she wasn't scared, but it creeped her out.

Next time he showed up in her dream, she was going to ignore him and pretend he wasn't there. And she was certainly never voluntarily inviting him again.

Eventually, he would get tired of that and leave her alone.

But then she would have to find some other way to determine if he was a Doomer. Regrettably, it seemed like she had no choice but to dream share with him at least one more time.

Because if he was, she needed to tell Kian or Turner. Not that either of them could do anything about it, but maybe she should go away from the village for a while and hide somewhere until Logan stopped popping up in her dreams.

She should describe him to Dalhu and Robert, the two ex-Doomers who'd left the Brotherhood and joined the clan. Carol had access to one of them, and maybe she could arrange a meeting with the other.

During the makeover, Ella had planned to ask Amanda about a meeting with Dalhu, but even though the goddess's daughter was nice and friendly, she was also as intimidating as her brother. Maybe even more so because she couldn't be manipulated like a man.

Even without realizing it, men were more inclined to listen to a pretty, young girl, as well as help her. Ella had no doubt that if a guy came to Kian with the same ambitious plan as she had, Kian would've thrown him out much less politely than he had her. The end result was the same, but at least she'd gotten to say what she'd come for.

When the path she was walking on intersected with another, Ella checked the village's map on her phone and continued straight.

If she'd followed the directions Carol had given her, she would've gotten lost for sure. Luckily, Magnus had overheard them talking and gave Ella a map, but only after she'd refused his offer to walk her there. It was time she got familiar with her new home.

"There you are." Carol waved at her from the doorway. "I was afraid you got lost."

"I almost did. It's good that Magnus gave me a map."

"There is a map?" Carol threw the door open. "I didn't know that."

Inside, a guy Ella didn't know was sitting on the couch and watching a football game.

"This is Ben, my roommate."

"Hi." The guy waved his hand without turning his eyes away from the television.

"Ben, pause that stupid game for a moment and come say a proper hello to Ella."

"That's okay. Let him watch. Parker and Magnus are also glued to the screen. I don't know what it is with guys and football. I think it's boring."

"Sacrilege," Ben gasped dramatically and offered his hand. "I love the hair."

"Thank you." She fluffed it with one hand while shaking his with the other.

"You're welcome. Well, nice meeting you and all that, but I'm going back to my game."

"Sure. And nice to meet you too."

Threading her arm through Ella's, Carol led her outside to the back yard. "What happened to the spikes?"

"Too much hassle." She sat on the double chaise lounge next to Carol. "I'll spike it when I go out."

"It looks good like this too. It's soft." Carol smoothed her hand over Ella's short hair. "You look cute."

"My brother calls me Tinker Bell."

Carol shrugged. "That's cute too. He could have come up with something much nastier."

"That's true."

Leaning sideways, Carol lifted a ginger ale soda can from the side table and handed it to Ella. "I was in the mood for a beer, but given your tender age, I decided against it."

"Isn't it too early for that? It's only eleven in the morning."

Carol smirked. "I don't care for conventions. I do pretty much as I please."

Yeah, she did, and that was why Carol was Ella's new role model. Eva was a bit too extreme to emulate. Or a lot.

"I wanted to ask you for a favor. Can you get your ex-boyfriend to talk to me? Or is it against the rules because he's Sharon's now? Do I have to ask her?"

Carol narrowed her eyes at her. "Why do you want to talk to Robert?"

"I want to ask him questions about the island. Kian challenged me to come up with a better plan, but I can't do that without having more information about it."

"You went to Kian with your crazy idea?" Carol shook her head. "You have guts, girl, I'll give you that. But he was just teasing. Kian doesn't expect you to come up with a plan."

"I know that. But I want to prove to him that I can."

That had been her original plan, but now she needed information for a different purpose.

"I see." Carol leaned back on the lounger and crossed her arms over her chest. "I can probably answer any questions you might have. I've already talked with both Dalhu and Robert extensively, picking their brains about the security measures, possible access points, and anything else I could think of."

Crap. What should she ask?

Perhaps she should just go for it and have Carol think what she would.

"How can you tell if a guy is an immortal if he's not showing fangs or glowing eyes?"

Logan had both in some of her dreams, but she could've given them to him. Dream Logan hadn't looked exactly like the real one, with his appearance changing according to how she was feeling about him that night.

Carol tapped her nose. "I can smell the difference between a human and an immortal."

Great, not so useful in dreams. Besides, until she transitioned, Ella wouldn't be able to smell the difference anyway.

"Do Doomers smell different than clan males?"

"No."

"So how do you know if an immortal guy is a Doomer?"

"Easy. I know all of my relatives. I might not remember everyone's name, but I know their faces. If I meet an immortal guy that I don't know, then he must be a Doomer."

"What if he is neither?"

Carol shook her head. "There are no other immortals. It's either them or us. But what does any of this have to do with the island? Everyone there is either a Doomer or a human."

There was another possibility Ella hadn't considered before. What if Logan was a clansman? Maybe he belonged to the Scottish branch?

She shouldn't assume that they were all decent people just because their ideology and leadership were good.

In the same way that there could be decent Doomers, there could be rotten clansmen.

"It's all new to me." Ella waved a dismissive hand. "I was just curious. But now I feel like I should learn the face of every male clansman, so if I ever meet a Doomer, I would know what he is. Do you have something like a yearbook or a directory?"

"No, but with all the newcomers, that's a good idea. We should have one and post it on the clan's virtual board. Although if you're worried about randomly encountering a Doomer, don't. The chances of that are very slim."

"I'm not worried." Hopefully, Carol couldn't smell the lie. "I just wanted to know if there was a way to differentiate between the good guys and the bad."

Carol chuckled. "Their attitudes. Doomers still think women are good only for breeding. They also think that humans are too dumb to govern themselves and should be enslaved."

Hmm, that was a clue. Maybe she could get Logan engaged in an ideological debate and see where he stood on those. Not that it would be proof positive. Entire human societies still believed that women were inferior. On the other hand, very few thought that slavery was a good idea, except for the traffickers, of course, but that was mostly about women as well.

Regrettably, it seemed like she had to arrange for another dream meeting with Logan and find out what his position on male slavery was.

It wasn't much, but it was better than nothing.

"Anything else you wish to know about Doomers?"

"Yeah. I want to know as much as possible about the island and what's going on there. How are the visitors screened, and how is it possible to hide its location so well, and who's in charge…"

Over the next hour or so, Carol provided her with so much information that Ella was afraid she'd forget half of it if she didn't write it all down.

"I think that's enough for today. Next time I'll bring a notepad."

"You could've recorded me on your phone."

"Shit, I should've thought of that. I'll go home and write down what you've told me. But next time I'm going to record it. If that's okay with you."

"Sure. Just make sure to keep your phone away from your little brother. Some of the things I've told you are not for his young ears."

Just thinking about it Ella felt herself blush. Carol was very open about her sexual promiscuity, and very blunt in her descriptions too.

It was cool that she'd confided in Ella so openly, not treating her like the young, inexperienced human she was. If Ella ever needed advice on sex, she now knew who to turn to.

"Maybe I should write it down and lock the notepad somewhere he can't get into. He's a nosy little guy, and way too good with technology. He probably knows my lock code."

"Not so little anymore." Carol winked. "I give him a year or two before he starts chasing immortal females around the village. Not that they'll be running away all that fast. An immortal male who is not a cousin is a rare find."

"Ugh, gross. I can't think of my little brother as some gigolo."

Carol stifled a snort, turning it into a cough. "Of course not. Now tell me, are you coming to Dalhu's art exhibition this evening?"

"Yes. My mother is a fan of his work."

"What are you going to wear?"

"I don't know yet. I'll borrow something from my mom. I don't have any fancy stuff. Why are you asking?"

"I ordered this really sexy dress online, and it's a bit snug on my butt. We are about the same height, and I thought you'd look great in it." She pushed to her feet. "Let's go to my room. I want you to try it on."

"I thought we were done with the makeover." Ella followed her inside.

Carol patted her arm. "This is a different kind of makeover." She winked. "I'm going to make you look so sexy, Julian is going to salivate."

"Oh. I don't know if that's a good idea."

"Trust me. It is."

52

AMANDA

Amanda followed Dalhu as he walked from one room to another, regarding his work critically, the muscles of his shoulders getting tighter instead of looser.

There was a reason she hadn't allowed him anywhere near the office building while her team of helpers had worked on transforming the place into an art gallery.

Dalhu had agreed to do the exhibition grudgingly and only because she'd convinced him that selling his art and donating half of the proceeds to the clan's humanitarian effort would erase the last doubts some of the clan members still harbored about him.

Showing him the completed project ensured that he couldn't change his mind at the last moment and cancel the entire thing.

"What's the matter? You don't look happy."

Stopping in front of a landscape, he rubbed his jaw. "It's not good enough, Amanda. I should have waited until I'd gotten it right."

She wrapped her arm around his middle. "You are a perfectionist. If I wait until you deem your work worthy of display, no one will get to see it, and it would be a shame. People love your landscapes, there is so much feeling in them."

He turned to look at her with an arched brow. "What are you talking about? Those are depictions of nature. They have no feelings."

Leaning her head against his shoulder, Amanda sighed. "It's the feeling they evoke, which is probably how they make you feel, and it shows in your work."

Her guy was so incredibly talented and yet so unaware of his own process, perhaps because he'd never taken classes and had never been taught how to reach down into his soul and transfer what he found to his art.

He did that on pure instinct.

"I think you are either imagining things or trying to boost my confidence."

He turned her toward him and kissed her lips. "You're amazing, do you know that?"

"Of course, I do."

Dalhu chuckled. "Thank you for organizing this. I've never been to an art gallery, but I'm sure you topped them all. Everything looks beautiful."

"You're welcome, my love." She kissed him back. "I had a lot of help, which just shows how many people love your work."

"Not necessarily. You're one hell of a bossy lady, and people are afraid to say no to you."

She slapped his bicep. "Not true."

"Oh, yeah? I bet most of the Guardians you've roped into moving furniture out of the offices have never even seen my work."

"Yes, they did because they helped hang it on the walls. You should have heard them oohing and aahing."

A soft growl started deep in his throat. "I'm sure it wasn't over the landscapes. Did you let them hang the nudes I did of you?"

"I did no such thing. You asked me not to." Which was a shame. Amanda wasn't bashful about her body, and those were some of Dalhu's best works. "They are still at home, hidden under the bed."

She shook her head. "You should at least let me hang them in the bedroom. No one goes in there but us and Onidu, but he doesn't count."

"You've invited people in there before."

"Only ladies."

"Not true. Kian was there, and so was Anandur."

Amanda waved a dismissive hand. "First of all, they are my relatives. And secondly, it was a one-time thing because Wonder fainted after seeing Annani's portrait and we had to take her somewhere private. Speaking of that portrait, you haven't seen what I've done with it yet. Come on."

She took Dalhu's hand and pulled him behind her to the next room. "What do you think?"

As befitting the work and its subject, Annani's portrait was the only painting in the room. Amanda had had several chairs brought in for people to sit down and ponder its many layers of meaning. A casual look just wouldn't do. It was a piece of art worth spending time admiring.

53

ELLA

*A*fter styling her short hair as best she could, Ella pulled on the little black dress Carol had loaned her.

It was short and tight, but the round neckline wasn't too deep, and it didn't show much cleavage, which made it passable for the occasion.

Ella liked it.

It was sexy, young, and nothing like the wardrobe the Russian had commissioned for her.

No bad memories there.

The problem was that she didn't have shoes to match. The black monster boots could go with it if she wanted to look edgy, but that would mean spiking her hair and applying tons of makeup, which she wasn't in the mood for.

After all, Dalhu's art exhibition was in the village, so she didn't need to disguise her appearance.

Well, that was what she told herself. The truth was that she wanted to look nice for Julian, and he didn't like the Goth getup.

Talking with Carol had been educational on many levels.

Apparently, sex with an immortal male was an entirely different experience. Carol had compared it to eating at a Michelin four-star restaurant, qualifying that statement by emphasizing that currently the most stars a restaurant could get were three. In contrast, she'd said, sex with a human was like eating a stale, gas-station sandwich.

Yuk.

Carol's detailed descriptions of the differences had started a low burn. And when Ella had gotten home and allowed herself to imagine Julian doing some of those things to her, that burn intensified tenfold.

Could he be so dominant in the bedroom?

According to Carol, all immortal males were dominant. It was how they were designed. It was the rare exception to find one without a dominant streak, which had been the case with Robert, and one of the main reasons things hadn't worked out between him and Carol.

Ella was starting to suspect that Carol actually wanted to go to the Doomers' island because of all the great sex she'd be expected to have with immortal males.

Strange female.

But whatever, to each her own.

Ella couldn't fathom having a lover she didn't have feelings for, let alone several a night.

Yuck, and yuck again.

There was just one guy she could envision being with, and that was Julian.

Liar.

She could almost hear Logan whisper the word in her ear. Maybe in addition to being a dream-walker he was also a warlock?

Had he put a spell on her the one time they'd actually met in person, and was he now tempting her in her dreams?

Last night, when he'd told her that he intended to find her and keep her for himself, Ella had experienced two conflicting emotions.

One had been fear, the other arousal.

It was very disconcerting.

Her attraction to Logan didn't make any sense. So yeah, he was handsome and mysterious, and Ella had no doubt that he was dominant as hell in bed, but he was also scary, and most likely human, which meant that he couldn't be all that great.

Ella shook her head. As if that was even a consideration. Maybe for Carol, but not for her.

Sex wasn't nearly as important to her as having a good, loving relationship, and in that respect, Logan wasn't in the same league as Julian.

Heck, he wasn't even in the same galaxy.

She should remember that every time thoughts of Logan drifted through her head. Even magic couldn't help him become a decent man.

Releasing a relieved breath, Ella applied a little eyeliner, some lip-gloss, and then brushed her hair one last time before leaving her bedroom.

"Mom, do you have a pair of black pumps I can borrow?"

"I do. But they have very tall heels. I don't know if you'll be able to walk in them."

Ella grimaced. "I had practice."

"I'll go get them." Vivian looked her up and down. "You look lovely. Where did you get the dress?"

"Carol loaned it to me."

"It looks great on you. With the heels, you're going to look like a fashion model."

"Yeah, a very short and padded one."

Ella wasn't fat, but the models she'd seen in magazines looked like they hadn't eaten anything other than lettuce in months.

Her mother waved a dismissive hand and headed to her room. A moment later she returned with a pair of gorgeous pumps.

"Here you go, sweetie. Try them on."

They weren't the same make as the ones Pavel had gotten her, but they looked just as pricey.

"Oh, wow, Mom. Fancy, fancy. You've never worn shoes like these before."

Her mother nodded. "They are not practical, and they cost way too much for collecting dust in my closet, but Magnus insisted I had to have them. You know how he is with clothes."

"He sure is stylish." Ella braced a hand on the kitchen counter as she slipped her feet into the shoes. "Suddenly I feel so tall."

As the front door opened, Scarlet bounded in first, with Parker and Magnus walking in behind her. Luckily, she skidded to a stop as Ella lifted her hand instead of jumping on her.

Parker whistled. "Nice dress." He looked down at her feet. "And shoes. You look like a runway model."

Vivian waved a hand. "Told you. But do you ever listen to your mother?"

"Do the walk," Parker said. "The one with a hand on your hip and swaying from side to side like models do."

"I don't want to." She would feel silly strutting like that in the middle of her kitchen, especially with Magnus watching.

"Why not? In the old house, you used to do it all the time." Parker moved a chair to make a clear path for her. "Just do it!"

Bossy dweeb.

Ella still didn't want to do it, but surprisingly, she found herself putting her hand on her hip and doing the runway walk like she used to.

Parker whistled.

Vivian clapped her hands.

Magnus smiled.

Ella felt strange.

She hadn't wanted to do that, and yet here she was, putting on a show for her family because Parker had told her to do it.

Unless she felt like it, Ella wasn't in the habit of obeying her little brother's commands.

Something wasn't right about this scenario.

54

JULIAN

Halfway to the village square, Julian bumped into Jackson and Tessa who were heading the same way.

"Hi, Julian," Tessa said. "Where is Ella? Isn't she going to the exhibition?"

"She's going with her family."

Jackson shook his head. "It's a missed opportunity, my man. You should've asked to accompany her."

Smiling, Tessa patted Julian's arm. "It's not too late yet. Go get her."

Raking his fingers through his hair, he hesitated for about a second. "Yeah, you're right. I should." He turned around. "Thanks for the advice."

"Any time," Jackson called after him.

This dating thing was turning out to be much more complicated than it seemed at first glance. It wasn't the same as prowling for hookups and making booty calls. There were rules to follow of when and how and where, and the embarrassing truth was that Ella, an eighteen-year-old high school graduate, probably knew more about it than he did.

As Julian knocked on her front door, he hoped the last moment change of plans wasn't going to get him in trouble with her. He hadn't even texted her to let her know that he was coming.

Parker opened the door and grinned. "Hi, Julian. Are you going with us to see Dalhu's paintings?"

"If you don't mind me tagging along." He wanted to take Ella and go, but that would be rude.

"Of course, we don't. We would love for you to join us," Vivian said from behind Parker. "Don't just stand there. Come inside."

"Thank you."

Talk about awkward.

Standing by the entry door, he didn't know whether he should come in and shake hands, or just wait for everyone to be ready to leave.

"Ella!" Parker yelled. "Come out already. Julian is here!"

That solved the dilemma.

"She can't hear you, Parker," Vivian said. "I'll tell her."

Julian heard her bedroom door open, and then the clicking of heels as she walked down the short corridor. And yet, when she entered the living room, he hadn't been prepared for the punch to the gut impact her appearance delivered.

His jaw going slack, Julian gaped.

Even the Goth getup and pink hair hadn't been as startling.

When he'd first seen Ella in the ambulance, she'd worn a shell-shocked expression and an elegant cream-colored pantsuit, looking confused and just a little disheveled. Later, when she'd put on his clothes, she'd looked young and fragile.

Since then, he'd seen her mostly in jeans and T-shirts, looking like a typical teenager, and that included yesterday's disguise.

"You look amazing," he finally managed to say.

Her pink hair was slicked back and held away from her gorgeous face with a pin. Long earrings dangled from her ears, nearly reaching her bare shoulders, and the short black dress she had on was lovingly hugging every curve of her delectable body.

Then there were the shoes. They made her shapely legs seem to go on forever.

Damn, he might develop a shoe fetish because all he could think about was her wearing nothing but those damn heels as she wrapped her long legs around his waist.

"Thank you." She turned in a circle, letting him see her from all angles. "Do you like the dress?"

His Ella wasn't a shy girl, that was for sure. And she wasn't even trying to hide the satisfied smirk on her lush lips. The girl had seduction on her mind, and if he needed proof, the sweet scent of her nascent arousal confirmed it.

"I love it. But you should wear something over it." Like a long coat and a scarf. "It's getting cold outside."

"I've got just the thing," Vivian said. "I'll get it for you."

Ella smiled. "Thanks, Mom."

Julian could only imagine the looks she was going to get from all the single guys, which was nearly every male in the village. He had a feeling the bro code was not going to cut it tonight. The men were going to go after her like a pack of hungry hyenas and try to take her away from him.

He hadn't claimed Ella as his yet, and she hadn't claimed him either, which in their eyes would mean that she was up for grabs.

Except, luck seemed to be on his side.

If he hadn't bumped into Jackson and Tessa, Ella would have arrived at Dalhu's art exhibition with her family, and the situation would've been difficult to salvage.

Now everyone was going to see them arriving together, and Julian was going to do his damnedest to demonstrate that Ella belonged to him.

He should remember to thank Jackson and Tessa again for their excellent advice.

55

ELLA

"This is the goddess?" Ella arched a brow as she and Julian entered a room with only one large portrait hanging on the wall.

The girl in the painting looked younger than Ella, but as she looked closer, she realized how wrong her first impression had been.

The eyes staring at her from the picture were smiling as if the goddess was hiding a secret or planning some mischief, but they were also ancient and full of wisdom.

It was astounding how Dalhu had managed to capture both in one painting. Even without knowing much about art, it was apparent to Ella that the guy was extremely talented.

"Larger than life, and I mean it literally." Julian chuckled. "This canvas is probably taller than her. Annani is tiny. She's shorter than you." He glanced at Ella's high heels. "Even without the shoes."

"A big wonder in a small package." Ella giggled. "I guess you have two wonders. A small one and a big one."

"Funny that you should say that. Wonder is Annani's best friend. They've known each other since they were both young girls."

"No way. Wonder looks my age. Well, so does Annani, even younger, but Annani has smart old eyes. Wonder doesn't."

"It's a long story. But Wonder was buried in the ground, surviving in stasis for thousands of years. She was awakened only recently. So, you are right about her being young. She hasn't really lived for all those years."

"What do you mean by stasis?"

"When deprived of air and nutrients, immortals go into stasis. They can survive like that for thousands of years. Maybe even more. Although Wonder's is the longest anyone has heard of."

"Fascinating." Ella took a few steps back and looked at the portrait again. "I can't wait to meet the goddess in person. Is there a chance she might visit anytime soon?"

"I don't know. Annani is impulsive. She doesn't plan ahead." He furrowed his brows. "Actually, that's not true. She has charted a course for the clan thousands of years in the making. I guess she acts impulsively only on a personal level."

"I totally believe it. Her eyes are ancient and smart but also full of humor and life."

Julian wrapped his arm around her shoulders. "Ready to move to the next room?"

"Sure. What's in there?"

"I don't know. Let's find out."

They stepped out into the corridor and entered a room across from the one they'd just left.

Ella glanced at the printed sign propped on a tripod. "Early works in charcoal."

Julian walked over to the wall. "I wonder who those dudes are. I don't recognize any of them."

"Maybe he drew pictures of his old buddies." Ella joined him in front of the portrait he was looking at and threaded her arm through his. "Handsome, but foreboding. He doesn't look like a nice guy."

"That's because he isn't," Amanda said as she entered the room. "This is one of Navuh's sons." She pointed at a larger portrait of a stunning man with a severe expression and hair that was so dark it looked pure black. "And that's Navuh. The bane of our clan's existence."

"Funny, he doesn't look evil," Ella said. "And his son doesn't look much like him either."

"You think?" Amanda put a hand on her hip and looked at one portrait and then the other. "I think there is a familial resemblance."

"They are both dark and wear twin severe expressions, but they don't look much alike. The son probably looks more like his mother."

"Perhaps." Amanda moved to the next charcoal drawing that was hanging on the opposite wall. "What about this one?"

Since the tripod with the sign on it was in the way, obscuring both Amanda and the portrait she was pointing to, Ella couldn't offer her opinion without getting around it.

But as she cleared the contraption and the portrait came into view, her throat clogged up and her heart started racing.

Logan's eyes were mocking her from the picture, just as dark and intense as she'd remembered them. His lips were curled on one side in a smirk.

Pointing, she tried to say his name, but nothing came out.

"What's the matter?" Julian asked.

She kept pointing like an idiot and then wagging her finger at the picture, but she was still unable to speak his name.

"What are you pointing at, darling? Is there a scary spider on the wall?"

Ella shook her head. "No spider." Encouraged by finally being able to speak, she tried to say Logan's name again, but her throat contracted once more, and a splitting headache assailed her out of nowhere. It was so bad that she whimpered and her hands flew to squeeze her temples.

"Let's get you out of here." Julian wrapped his arm around her waist and turned her around. "Maybe fresh air will help."

Outside, the headache eased enough for her to be able to draw in a breath.

"Better?" Julian asked.

"Yes, thank you."

"What happened in there?" Amanda asked.

Ella opened her mouth, but nothing came out. Afraid of the pain coming back, she shook her head.

Amanda regarded her with worried eyes. "Okay, let's try something else. When I ask you a question either nod for yes or shake your head for no. Can you do that?"

Ella nodded.

"Did something in that room scare you?"

She nodded.

"Was it the picture?"

She nodded again.

"Was it because the guy looked scary?"

Ella shook her head.

Amanda's frown deepened. "Was it because you recognized him?"

Ella nodded.

"Did you see his picture somewhere?"

Ella shook her head.

Her expression incredulous, Amanda asked her next question. "Did you meet him in person?"

Ella nodded.

"Damn." Julian's arm tightened around her middle. "Was it in the auction house?"

She shook her head.

"After?"

She nodded.

"With Gorchenco?"

She nodded again.

"We should go talk to Dalhu," Amanda said. "And Kian."

56

KIAN

Kian watched Amanda enter the room and saunter toward him and Syssi while smiling at the people admiring her mate's work. But he knew his sister well, and there was worry in her eyes.

When she reached him, she put a hand on his shoulder and whispered, "Something is wrong with Ella. You should come with me."

Syssi leaned closer to Amanda. "Is she sick? Should I go find Bridget?"

Despite her worry, Amanda chuckled. "Julian is glued to her side. I think one doctor will do. I don't want to talk here. I took them to your office."

Kian didn't like having people there while he was away, but with most of the offices converted to an art gallery for one day, Amanda didn't have much choice.

"Did you call her parents? I mean Vivian and Magnus."

It hadn't been done officially yet, but everyone in the village already thought of Magnus as Ella's and Parker's father.

"Parker is with them. I don't think he should see Ella like that."

Now Kian got really worried. "Let's go." He took the stairs two at a time, rushing into his office ahead of his wife and sister.

As he saw Ella sitting at the conference table, he let out a relieved breath. She looked pale and scared, but other than that she seemed fine.

Julian looked worse.

Amanda and Syssi entered right behind him, and a moment later Dalhu came in holding one of his charcoals.

"That's what started it." Amanda waved her hand at the portrait. "Ella pointed at it and tried to tell us something, but couldn't. It was like a blockage of some sort was preventing her from speaking. I asked her several yes and no questions, and basically, we ascertained that during her time with Gorchenco, she met one of Navuh's sons."

"His name is Lokan," Dalhu said. "And Ella is most likely under compulsion not to talk about him. He has the ability to compel humans. One of the other brothers can compel immortals as well."

Kian looked at Ella. "Is that so? Did this man compel you not to talk about him?"

She lifted her hands in the air as if to say that she didn't know.

"Is this the guy you told me about? The one who talked with Gorchenco about the island?

She nodded, but then grimaced and pressed the heels of her palms to her temples.

Dalhu put the portrait on the floor, bracing it against the wall. "She'll get a headache every time she tries to override the compulsion. You should keep your questions to a bare minimum."

"Understood."

As Dalhu pulled out a chair for Amanda, Kian pulled one out for Syssi and another for himself.

"Okay. So, what we know so far is this," he said as he sat down. "Gorchenco has dealings with the Doomers, supplying them with weapons. Ella also told me that he visits the island. He took her with him when he met with Lokan, and during that meeting, Lokan must have put her under compulsion not to talk about him. The question is why?"

"While we ponder that, I'll get us drinks." Amanda got up and walked over to the buffet.

"Who wants what?" She opened the fridge. "We have coke, sprite, water, and beer."

"I'll take a beer," Julian said.

Ella cleared her throat. "Water for me."

It seemed she could talk as long as it wasn't about Lokan.

"I'll take water too," Syssi said. "Is there any Perrier?"

Pulling out the bottles and cans, Amanda brought them to the table and handed them out.

"I assumed you'd like a beer." She handed Kian a Snake's Venom.

"Is there a way to break compulsion?" Syssi asked.

Kian shook his head. "Not that I know of. Only the one who put it on can remove it."

"Crap," Ella said. "So, I'm trapped."

Syssi crossed her arms over her chest. "Maybe Annani can do that. She compelled my parents to keep us a secret. Perhaps if she can compel people, she might be able to also remove a compulsion even though she wasn't the one to do it."

"Perhaps." Kian nodded. "But I doubt she'll hop over to help us out unless it's an emergency."

"It might be," Ella murmured and then grimaced.

"Don't force it," Julian said. "It might be dangerous to you. If you get a terrible headache every time you try to talk about him, you might suffer neurological damage."

Ella nodded and lifted the water bottle to her lips, drinking half of it in one go.

"That's good. Drink up." Julian massaged her shoulders.

"What about Merlin?" Syssi asked. "He has a potion for everything. Maybe he has one for that too?"

"I doubt it, but it won't hurt to ask." Kian pulled out his phone.

57

ELLA

"I can cook up something, a kind of a tongue relaxer," Merlin said. "But I've never tried to use that to release someone from compulsion."

At this point, Ella was willing to try anything. It was so incredibly frustrating not being able to speak up and say what she wanted. Not that there was much more she could add to what everyone in Kian's office already knew.

Except maybe for the unimportant detail of Lokan using Logan as his fake name, which was very unimaginative on his part.

She was sure to tell him that the next time he invaded her dreams, along with a few other choice words.

Except, she couldn't do that because it would give her away. Logan aka Lokan didn't know where she was and with whom. Otherwise, he would've said something to that effect, or asked her questions about the people she was with.

And it wasn't because he was so cautious.

In his wildest dreams, Logan couldn't have anticipated her finding out who he was, so there was no reason for him to be overly careful about what he asked her or what he told her.

She was pretty sure that he was only interested in her because of her telepathic ability and her pretty face.

Still, it seemed that Dalhu didn't know about Lokan's dream-walking ability, and perhaps that was information that could be potentially helpful.

"How long is it going to take you to prepare the potion?" Kian asked.

"I need to get the ingredients first. I can have it ready by late morning tomorrow." He gave her a pitying look. "Come to my house at around ten."

"Okay," Ella said in a small voice.

Merlin was cool, and she liked him, but the idea of drinking some concoction he made was a bit scary. Sometimes, she wasn't sure how sane the guy was.

"I'll come with you," Julian said.

That was a relief. At least she would have a real doctor with her in case something went wrong. "Thanks, I appreciate it."

"Well." Kian tapped his fingers on the table. "There isn't much more we can do today. I suggest you go home and get some rest, Ella. Try not to think too much about this and give your brain time to recuperate."

"I will."

"I'll take you." Julian rose to his feet and gave her a hand up.

"Thanks." She turned to Kian. "Sorry for giving everyone a scare."

"Take care of yourself, darling." Amanda gave her a peck on the cheek.

As they headed outside, Ella wondered if she should find her mother and tell her what had happened or wait with it until they got home.

The problem was that in order to tell her mom, she would have to fight the compulsion again, and according to Julian, it was dangerous to her brain.

"Julian." She looked up at his worried face. "Can I ask you a favor?"

"Anything."

"Can you tell my mom and Magnus what happened? I don't want to talk about it because of what you said it can do to my head."

"Sure, no problem."

"Thanks." She leaned into him.

"You're cold." He tightened his arm around her.

The shawl she'd borrowed from her mom wasn't doing much to block the night's chill. Or maybe she was cold because of the exhaustion that followed the excruciating headache attacks when she'd fought the compulsion.

She was cold all over, her feet hurt from the shoes, and her home was another fifteen-minute hike through the village.

What had been supposed to be a fabulous day had turned into a miserable one.

The story of my life.

When another uncontrollable shiver shook her body, Julian swung her into his arms and held her tightly against his chest. "Better?"

"Yes. Thank you." She was too tired to object, and he was too warm and solid to resist. "The moment I get too heavy for you, put me down. I should be fine in a minute or two."

Dipping his head, he planted a kiss on her forehead. "Silly girl. You'll never get too heavy for me. Even if you gain a hundred pounds."

"God forbid." She put her hand over his mouth. "Don't speak such blasphemy."

Julian chuckled. "Now I know that you're okay. You didn't lose your sense of humor."

"You think I'm joking? You really don't know anything about girls, do you?"

His confused expression was just adorable. Teasing Julian was so much fun.

"Apparently, I don't."

She cupped his cheek. "Never ever mention weight to a girl. It's a touchy subject."

"Noted. What else?"

"That's it. I'm not going to teach you how to charm other girls. That wouldn't be in my best interest."

"You don't have to worry about that. There is only one girl I'm interested in, and if you're wondering who she is, it's the one I'm holding in my arms right now. I just regret having to take you home. I would much rather bring you to mine and never let you leave."

She would like that too, and not only because she was scared of Logan invading her dreams again. Tonight, she didn't want to sleep alone.

Would her mom mind?

Ella wasn't a little girl anymore. She was an adult, and if she wanted to spend the night at Julian's, she could.

"Take me to your house. I'll let my mom know that I'm staying with you."

He stopped walking. "Are you sure it's okay with her?"

"I'm an adult, Julian. And my mom adores you. So yes, I'm sure."

"What about telling her and Magnus about what happened earlier?"

She cupped his cheek. "Tomorrow, my dear, is another day."

DARK DREAM'S
UNRAVELING

1

ELLA

*E*lla woke up to complete darkness. Disoriented, she tried to move, but the strong male arms banded around her were holding her imprisoned.
No, no, no! It can't be. She was no longer the captive of the Russian.
Had her rescue been only a dream?
"Let me go!" She pushed on the hard chest she was plastered against. "Let me go, damn it!"
Her efforts were futile, but she couldn't just give up.
Ella shoved harder.
Unexpectedly, the arms fell away, releasing her, the force of the push sending her tumbling down the other side of the bed and all the way down to the carpet.
She landed on her butt with a thud. "Oof!" That hurt.
"Ella! Oh, dear Fates, I'm so sorry." He was on the floor beside her before finishing the sentence. "Did you have a bad dream?"
Getting all banged up had at least one positive outcome—Ella's brain fog was gone.
Those arms that had held her so tight hadn't belonged to Gorchenco, they were Julian's, as were the glowing blue eyes regarding her with so much concern. Last night, she'd fallen asleep cradled in the comfort of his embrace, and he must have held her all night long.
And how had she repaid his kindness? By waking him up with a blood-curdling scream.
Twice.
Poor guy.
"I'm so sorry. It was completely dark, and I couldn't see anything. I thought I was still with the Russian and that the rescue was just a dream."
"Oh, sweetheart."
He hugged her gently, giving her every opportunity to pull away, but when

she wrapped her arms around his neck and kissed him, he tightened his hold, lifted her off the floor, and sat on the bed with her cradled in his arms.

"You should've left a light on. There are too many scary ghosts in my closet for me to be okay with total darkness."

He hugged her closer. "Next time, I'll remember that." Reaching out with his long arm, he turned the bedside lamp on.

Now she could see the room, but since the shutters were closed, it was impossible to tell whether it was still night outside or if day had begun.

"What time is it? I'm supposed to be at the clinic at ten, and I still need to go home to get dressed."

Sleeping over at Julian's had been a last-minute decision, so naturally she didn't have a change of clothes at hand, and going to the clinic in the little black dress and high heels that she'd worn to Dalhu's exhibition was a no go.

"Why?" He chuckled. "Can't you go in my shirt? I can also lend you my briefs and socks again."

She'd done it once, right after her rescue, but that was because she hadn't wanted to take anything the Russian had gotten for her to her new home. Concern about appearances had been the last thing on her mind.

Things had changed since then. She'd embraced life in the village and the clan of immortals who'd become her new extended family. People here knew her, and parading around in the T-shirt she'd borrowed from Julian to sleep in was not an option. Even though it was long enough to serve as a mini-dress, she wasn't leaving his house like that.

"Very cute, Julian. Talk about a walk of shame to shame all others."

"But you have nothing to be ashamed of."

That would have been true even if they'd had sex, but doubly so since they hadn't done a thing. The headache that had assailed Ella every time she'd tried to talk about Logan had exhausted her, and after taking three Motrins and changing into Julian's well-worn T-shirt, she'd fallen asleep in his arms.

Which had been very nice.

Sleeping in the same bed with a man she actually cared about and wasn't afraid of was a new and pleasant experience. Julian made her feel safe, or at least he did when she was fully awake and knew it was him and not a dream walker, aka Logan, or a dream specter, aka Gorchenco.

"Do you have a new toothbrush I can borrow? My mouth probably smells like a garbage can."

Julian shook his head. "No, it doesn't. But yes, I have a toothbrush."

"Why are you shaking your head like that?"

"Because I've never met a girl who would mention a stinky garbage can in the same sentence as her mouth. Most try to appear delicate and refined."

Great.

Way to go, Ella.

Talking to Julian wasn't the same as talking to her younger brother. Now that she was an adult, she should try to act more ladylike.

He hooked a finger under her chin and looked into her eyes. "Did I say something to offend you?"

Crap.

She also kept forgetting his super senses. Not that she could've done anything about it. Her body broadcast her emotions by emitting scents that only immortals could smell, probably dogs as well. She had no control over that, which meant that there was no hiding her feelings from Julian or any of the other immortals.

Her only consolation was that the others probably couldn't sniff her from afar, and she had no intention of sitting on any other immortal's lap.

Ella shrugged. "It's not important."

Holding on to her chin, he smiled. "Come on. Sharing socks and underwear means that we are close enough to tell each other everything."

That was a weird leap of logic. One had nothing to do with the other. But whatever. He probably thought it was something worse than what it actually was.

"I'm not refined and delicate enough for you?"

Julian's eyes widened, and then he laughed. "I love that you are such a tomboy. Beautiful girls are usually full of themselves and act entitled. You're nothing like that."

The tension left Ella's shoulders. It was a relief to know that she didn't have to put on a special act for Julian to like her. He accepted her the way she was.

His nice compliment deserved one in return, though. "Neither are you." She cupped his cheek. "You are every girl's dream guy, and yet you are not a jerk. I wonder why?"

He frowned. "Why would that make me a jerk? It's not a bad thing to be wanted."

She was proof that his statement was not true. "It can be bad, but I digress. It's just that most successful, good-looking guys are exactly like the girls you were talking about. Too full of themselves and self-entitled. When guys get a lot of female attention, they think that they don't need to be nice."

Julian looked away. "I'm not successful. In fact, I feel like quite a failure."

This time it was Ella's turn to stare at him with wide eyes. "Are you nuts? What are you talking about?"

Raking his fingers through his hair, Julian sighed. "I spent seven years studying to become a doctor, and now I'm not sure that this is what I want to do. I can't work with humans because I can't handle the barrage of their intense emotions, and with Merlin here, the village immortals don't need my medical services."

Ella could understand that. Grief was a frequent visitor in hospitals, and feeling it day in and day out must have been draining for someone like Julian who absorbed it all as if it was his own.

Not a fun way to spend his days.

"You could become a plastic surgeon and have a private practice. Not much angst there."

"Are you kidding me? What about all those who are unhappy with their results, which I'm sure would be the case with my patients. I don't have any artistic talent, which I think is a necessary tool for a plastic surgeon. I would be doing people a disservice."

That was true. What else was there? "How about optometry?"

"That's a possibility. It's a bit boring, though."

"Psychiatry? That's not boring for sure, and it could be potentially beneficial to the clan. I bet that some people with special abilities think that they are crazy. It could be another way to identify Dormants."

He arched a brow. "Did you ever feel like that?"

"That I'm crazy? No." Ella pushed out of his arms. "I was born with my ability, and I thought that everyone could talk with their moms in their heads. Later, when I was older and realized that my mother and I were unique, I already had years of proof that our telepathic connection was real."

"It must have been difficult nonetheless. Being different, I mean. And hiding what you can do."

"Yeah, it was. The hardest part was hiding the truth from Parker. But he was too young to be entrusted with our secret. Besides, my mom thought that he would feel left out because he couldn't do what we could."

"I wonder what his special ability will be."

Ella shrugged. "He might have none, and then he's going to be very disappointed. I understand that not all Dormants exhibit special abilities, and that transitioning into immortality only enhances what is already there."

"Every Dormant is unique." Julian stood up and took her hand. "I have a feeling Parker is going to surprise us all. You and Vivian have such a powerful telepathic connection that it doesn't make sense for him to have no paranormal talent at all."

"Our telepathic connection may be strong, but it's quite useless because we can only communicate with each other. I hope Parker gets something better." She smiled up at him. "We can talk about all this later. I really need to get going."

"Let me give you a new toothbrush and a clean towel."

2

JULIAN

As Ella emerged from the bathroom wearing the tight black dress and high heels she had worn last night, Julian rubbed his hand over his mouth and commanded his elongating fangs to behave.

Having a basically platonic relationship with her was pure torture, but it was a pain he was willing to endure for as long as it took. Hopefully, that wouldn't be too long.

"Ready to go?" he asked in the most nonchalant tone he could muster.

She wasn't fooled though. A light blush coloring her cheeks, she smoothed her hand over the side of the dress. "Yeah."

"Come on." He took her hand.

As they entered the living room, Ray looked Ella up and down. "Good morning." He didn't even try to hide his leering. "You look stunning in that dress. That look is so much better on you than the jeans with holes and Frankenstein boots from the other day."

The guy needed a serious attitude adjustment. Leering at a woman was rude and leering at a man's girlfriend was an invitation to trouble, but leering at an immortal male's mate was suicidal.

Taking a moment to indulge in imagining the various methods of showing Ray the error of his ways, Julian decided that a punch to the guy's smug face would be the most satisfying.

"Good morning, Ray." Ella smiled at his obnoxious roommate, but her smile was much less friendly than it had been the first time she'd met him. Evidently, she didn't like his attitude either.

She waved at him on her way out. "And goodbye."

As Julian followed Ella out, Ray nodded at him and lifted both hands with his thumbs up. "Congratulations, man."

Julian pinned him with a hard glare. "If you value your precious thumbs, which I know you do, I suggest that you keep them either in your pockets or on the piano keys. And I don't want to hear any comments about Ella from you either."

The smile evaporated off Ray's face. "Peace, roomie. I meant no disrespect."

His anger over Ray's behavior was disproportionate, Julian was aware of that, and if Ray's rudeness had been directed at him, he would have ignored it or made a joke out of it. But his roommate's behavior had been offensive to Ella, which was unforgivable.

Casting the guy another glare, Julian closed the door and schooled his expression for Ella's sake. "I'm sorry about that." He wrapped his arm around her waist. "I don't know what has gotten into him. Usually, he's a decent fellow."

Ella shrugged. "I told you. The walk of shame." She threaded her arm through his and pushed her hand inside his back pocket. "But I don't care. Let them think whatever they want."

It was such an intimate thing to do. Her hand on his ass made his jeans feel way too tight, and not because she was pulling on them from behind. Nevertheless, he wanted it exactly where it was.

"It's not what you think it is. He wasn't trying to shame you," he said. "Immortals' attitude toward sexuality is different. The inappropriate smiles and leering was Ray's way of congratulating us. Not that it makes it right, and he was being rude, but in no way was it meant to shame you."

She shrugged. "I don't care about what Ray thinks. What I do care about, though, is the circus we are about to encounter in my house."

"Circus?"

"Yeah. My mom is going to be ecstatic, thinking that we've finally sealed the deal. And I don't even want to think what Parker is going to say. Hopefully, Magnus has left for work already, so at least I'll be spared his response. Although I can't even begin to guess what it would've been. I don't know him that well."

"Probably none." Julian chuckled. "It's funny how everyone is going to assume that we had sex last night when the truth is that we didn't even kiss."

"Sorry about that." She cast him an apologetic sidelong glance. "And thank you for being so patient and understanding. You're a true gentleman."

Julian wasn't sure what she was thanking him for.

For not kissing her?

Or for not having sex with her?

He'd known it hadn't been on the table when she'd asked him to take her to his house. The only reason Ella had gone home with him and had spent the night was that she'd been so shaken up over Dalhu's depiction of Navuh's son and her inability to say anything about it.

It must have felt awful to be controlled from afar by a puppet master, unable to use her own mouth and say what she wanted to say.

If Julian ever got his hands on that Doomer, he was going to exact payment from his hide for every little bit of discomfort he'd caused Ella.

She'd recognized Lokan as someone she'd met during her captivity, but she couldn't tell anyone how and where because he'd compelled her silence. Dalhu had filled in some of the information, like the bastard's name, and that he had the extremely rare ability to compel humans. Kian had added another piece of

DARK DREAM'S UNRAVELING

the puzzle. Apparently, Ella had told him about a lunch meeting she'd attended with a shady character the Russian was selling weapons to.

Come to think of it, there must've been more to it than the one business meeting Ella had told Kian about. Otherwise, her panicked response to Lokan's portrait didn't make sense.

He frowned. "Did Lokan ever touch you?"

Ella opened her mouth to answer, but then grimaced and shook her head.

"Damn. I'm such an idiot. I shouldn't have asked you about him. I'm sorry. Did I give you a new headache?"

"Yeah, but it was only for a moment."

He should have been more careful and avoided mentioning Lokan at all. Every time Ella tried to say something about the Doomer, she suffered severe headaches.

Julian gave her hand a light squeeze. "I'm sorry for causing you unnecessary pain."

She squeezed his hand back. "We are apologizing too much to each other. I don't like it."

"Right. It's not a good way to start a relationship."

Ella didn't respond to that, but the expression on her face bothered him.

What was going through her head?

Hopefully, she wasn't reconsidering being in a relationship with him. Was she?

"Well, we're here," Ella said as they climbed the steps to her front porch. "Brace yourself." She opened the door.

Maybe that was what her troubled expression had been about. She'd been bracing for facing her mother.

"Oh, good," Ella whispered. "There is no one in the living room." She took off her high-heeled shoes, motioned for him to follow her, and tiptoed to her room.

"Ella? Is that you?" Vivian called out.

"Damn. Busted," Ella whispered. "Yes, Mom. I'm just going to change before going to the clinic."

Vivian's footsteps got faster, her house slippers flapping a rapid tempo on the living room floor. "The clinic? Why? What's wrong?"

Ella turned a pair of pleading eyes at him. "Julian?"

"Go, I'll take care of this."

"Thanks." She gave him a quick peck on the cheek before ducking into her room.

"What's going on?" Vivian asked.

"Let's go back to the living room."

Vivian shivered. "You're scaring me, Julian."

He took her elbow and turned her around. "Ella asked me to tell you what happened yesterday at Dalhu's exhibition."

"Should I call Magnus in?"

"Is he home?"

"He's out in the backyard with Scarlet."

"I thought he went back to work."

"He did, but he has the morning off. This evening he's going out on a mission." She grimaced. "I hate it, but I knew what I was signing up for when I allowed myself to fall for him."

"Magnus is a good man."

"The best."

"I'm sure he will want to hear this too. But if possible, I don't think Parker should be here. Not that any of this is age-inappropriate, it's just that you should decide what he needs or doesn't need to know. Not me."

Vivian nodded. "Parker is in his room, studying. I'll get Magnus." She walked over to the sliding door and opened it. "Can you come in for a moment? Julian needs to tell us something."

The Guardian stepped in with Scarlet trotting behind him. Sensing the tension, the dog tucked her tail between her legs and plopped down on her doggie bed.

When the couple sat on the couch, Julian took the armchair across from it and debated where to start. Ella hadn't told him whether Vivian and Magnus knew about her meeting with Lokan, but he shouldn't assume that she had.

"While still with Gorchenco, Ella attended a meeting he had with a business associate. She heard them talking about the Russian supplying the other one with weapons and about an island, which later on she figured out must've been the Doomers' island. She told Kian all of that, but without mentioning the guy's name. Yesterday, at the exhibition, she recognized him from one of Dalhu's charcoal portraits. According to Dalhu, his name is Lokan, and he is one of Navuh's sons. Lokan has the unique ability to compel humans."

Vivian frowned. "Is there a difference between a thrall and a compulsion?"

"A compulsion is much stronger than a thrall and lasts longer. Sometimes it can last indefinitely. It depends on the strength of the compeller and the susceptibility of the compelled."

"What does it have to do with Ella?"

"Apparently, and for unclear reasons, Lokan compelled Ella not to mention him. When she recognized him and wanted to say his name, nothing came out. When she tried harder, she got a bad headache. Bottom line, Ella can't tell us anything about him."

Magnus smoothed his hand over his goatee. "I don't understand. You said that she told Kian about meeting him. So, mentioning him was okay but saying his name wasn't? That doesn't make sense."

"I agree. That's why I think there is more to it than that one meeting. Unfortunately, Ella can't tell us what it is. That's why she's going to the clinic. Merlin is preparing what he calls a tongue relaxer for her. Hopefully, it will help her tell us a little more."

3

ELLA

"Fates, Merlin. Do all your potions have to be this stinky?" Julian held out the small decanter to Ella. "I know that we've decided we shouldn't apologize to each other so much, but I have to apologize in advance for this."

She took the bottle and held it away from her. "If this helps with my problem, I don't care how vile it smells or tastes."

"Hold on. I'll get you a Godiva chocolate." Merlin rushed out of his office.

Her favorite, but one was not going to cut it. She was like an addict with those. Once Ella got a taste of one, she craved more.

"Do you know where he hides them?" she whispered.

"The chocolates?"

She nodded enthusiastically.

"No clue."

"Then follow him." She waved her hand, shooing him on. "We can raid his stash later."

Merlin was such a scatterbrain that he wouldn't notice some of it missing. Or most of it. Besides, he was a chill guy, and she knew he liked her. He wouldn't mind if she pilfered some of his chocolates.

Julian crossed his arms over his chest and affected a stern expression. "I'm not raiding anyone's stash. I'll buy you as many chocolates as you can possibly eat." He leaned to whisper in her ear. "But then you'll run the risk of gaining those extra hundred pounds you've mentioned."

For a moment, she wasn't sure what he was talking about. Was it something she'd said? It sounded like it.

The headache had done a number on her last night, and everything was kind of fuzzy. But then she remembered Julian picking her up and carrying her to his home. He'd said something about her weighing nothing, and then they'd joked about it.

Gasping dramatically, Ella put a hand over her heart. "God forbid. Don't say such things when I'm about to risk my life, drinking this stuff." She lifted the decanter. "Nasty things are floating near the bottom. Do you think Merlin used spider webs to make it? Or was this just a very dirty container?"

"No spider anything." Merlin returned with a small box of chocolates. "I brought you four, so you'll have enough to share with lover boy."

Crap. Was everyone assuming she and Julian got it on last night?

And how did Merlin even know where she'd spent the night?

Apparently, Julian had been right about gossip in the village. These immortals needed to get a life, which apparently they didn't have because they couldn't find anyone, immortal or Dormant, to have a relationship with. That would also explain their excessive fascination with any new couple and their sex life.

"Okay, young lady. I suggest that you pinch your nose, drink up, and follow with a chocolate."

"Do I have to finish the whole thing?"

Merlin nodded. "As much as you can stomach. The more, the better."

Ella eyed the floating unidentifiable objects, hoping they were just residue from the herbs or whatever else Merlin used to cook his potions from.

Once she removed the stopper, the smell almost knocked her over, but she was determined to do whatever it took to remove the freaking compulsion. Pinching her nose with one hand, she lifted the decanter with the other, gulped down its contents, and then snatched the chocolate from Julian's palm.

Popping it into her mouth, she chewed it up and then reached out her hand. "Quickly. Give me another one."

She ended up eating all four and not leaving any for Julian. "I'm sorry. It's just that it tasted really awful, and I can't control myself with these small pieces of divine goodness."

He shook his head. "No apologies. I'm not a great lover of chocolates."

It was on the tip of her tongue to ask him what he was a great lover of, but that would have been cruel considering that she wasn't ready to let him demonstrate.

Instead, she asked, "What now? How long before we know if it worked or not?"

"Twenty minutes or so." Merlin pulled a fob watch out of his pocket. "You can sit in the waiting room if you want. Or you can take a walk and come back by eleven o'clock."

"I'd rather take a walk."

"Let's go." Julian tossed the empty chocolate box into the wastebasket.

A few minutes into the walk, Ella started feeling the potion's effects. It reminded her of the time she drank too much wine at Gorchenco's prompting.

"I don't feel so hot." She leaned on Julian.

Without heels, she was so much shorter than him that her head barely reached his armpit. If he wanted to, he could have tucked her head under his arm.

"Do you want to sit down?" He eyed her worriedly.

"Yeah. I'm getting dizzy."

As they found a bench, Ella motioned for Julian to sit down first and then sat in his lap. "I hope you don't mind. But I want you to hold me."

"Mind?" He wrapped his arms around her, propping up her back so she could get comfortable. "I love it."

"Good. Because I'm planning on doing it a lot." She cupped his cheek and smirked. "I'm so evil."

Julian frowned. "Why would you say that?"

"Because I know what it does to you. I can feel you getting hard under me, and I know it must be torturous."

What had possessed her to say that?

Tongue relaxer.

Well, now she knew what it meant.

"I'm sorry. Crap. I keep saying it. It's the freaking potion's fault. I mean, about what I've said before. And about apologizing. Damn. This is hard. I didn't realize how compelling it is to say sorry."

Julian rubbed her back. "It's okay. No need to feel bad about pointing out the obvious." He kissed the top of her head. "I have a beautiful girl sitting in my lap. It's a natural response."

"Right? That's so true. I should feel good. If you didn't get hard, I would've felt way worse."

He laughed. "I think the potion has done what it was supposed to. We can head back to the clinic."

"We should." She tried to lift her head, but then let it plop back on his chest. "I can't. You'll have to carry me."

"No problem. I love doing that too."

Merlin opened the door for them. "Back so soon?"

"I can't lift my head," Ella complained.

"You must be very sensitive." He followed them inside into his office, then pulled out a chair for Julian and one for himself.

"Let's give it a try, shall we?"

Ella nodded.

"What can you tell us about Lokan?"

She opened her mouth, tried to speak, but nothing came out. Shaking her head, she tried again. "I can't."

"Headache?"

"No. I just can't talk."

Merlin smoothed his hand over his long beard. "At least there is that. But that's a temporary effect. Once the potion is out of your system, I'm afraid the headaches will come back every time you try to talk about him."

"What I don't understand," Julian said, "is how come Ella could tell Kian about the meeting and what was discussed, but not anything else. Did Lokan just compel her not to say his name?"

Ella shook her head, but that was all she could do.

She'd wondered the same thing. It occurred to her that the trouble had begun after Logan had made her promise not to tell anyone about his dream visits. The first and second dream encounter had happened while she'd still been with the Russian, and she'd told him about them. The compulsion hadn't been there yet.

Damn, how she hated this.

Even here, in the hidden village, he was controlling her from God knew where. He could be on the other side of the planet for all she knew.

The big question was what Lokan aka Logan wanted.

Why was he doing this?

Was it his way of amusing himself?

Or did he really plan on coming after her?

And if he did, how?

She had to find a way to keep him out of her dreams. Sleeping in Julian's arms might have helped, but on the other hand, Logan's visits hadn't been nightly. He might have just happened to skip last night.

There was no guarantee that Julian's presence was helpful. She'd dreamt about Logan while sleeping with Gorchenco. If his presence hadn't deterred Logan, Julian's probably wouldn't either. Ella doubted that her feelings toward her bed partner made a difference.

The thing was, she couldn't even ask anyone's advice on keeping her dreams private because she couldn't talk about it.

Or maybe she could if she didn't mention anything specific?

It was worth a try.

She turned to Merlin, who seemed to know a lot about many things. "Is there a way to guard dreams against intruders?"

Once the question had left her mouth, Ella clapped her hands in glee. It worked. She'd voiced it, and her head didn't feel as if it was going to explode.

Merlin shook his head. "There isn't. If you have disturbing memories or thoughts, they might manifest in your dreams. Even thralling you to forget them won't help. The subconscious is very difficult to control."

Ella's smile melted away. Merlin hadn't understood the meaning behind her general question, and neither had Julian.

Damn. There must be a way around the stupid compulsion, and she was going to keep trying until she found it.

4

JULIAN

"I think I can walk by myself," Ella said as Julian pushed to his feet, still holding her in his arms.

He could understand her embarrassment about being carried around the village in broad daylight, but she was still a little woozy. Merlin had brought coffee for the three of them, and it had seemed to help with Ella's dizziness, but she was still slurring her words, and her eyes were unfocused.

"Let's give it a try. Lean against me, and I'll prop you up."

Merlin shook his head. "We should have a golf cart here for cases like this."

"There is one for deliveries. I'll go get it." Julian was about to put Ella down on the chair when she clutched his sleeve.

"Don't go. Please, just help me up. I'll walk home."

When she looked up at him with those big blue eyes of hers, pleading for him not to leave her, he was helpless to refuse even though getting the golf cart was the smart thing to do.

"Okay."

Lifting Ella off the chair, he tucked her against his side and wrapped his arm around her middle. "On one."

For several steps, he had to hold her up, but the movement combined with the fresh air seemed to be helping, and Ella tried to walk on her own. That lasted for about ten steps, and then she leaned against him again.

"Are you sure Merlin's potions are safe? The only other time I felt like this was when I got drunk on too much wine. My bodyguard had to carry me up to the bedroom."

"The one who tried to save you from the fake explosion?"

She nodded. "Misha. I hope he's okay, and that Gorchenco hasn't killed him for letting me die in that explosion. I liked him."

As the jealous bug gripped him with its poisonous pinchers, Julian forgot all about being a gentleman and took unfair advantage of Ella's drunk-like state. "How much exactly did you like this Misha guy?"

"A lot. He was huge." She lifted her hand as high as it would go. "Tall, almost like Yamanu, but twice as wide, and he had a crooked nose that looked like it had been broken once or twice, and scars. And the back of his head was flat." She chuckled and patted the back of her own head. "Like Frankenstein's monster. But he was nice to me. I know he was only following Gorchenco's orders, but he could've been grumpy about it, or mean. He wasn't. Misha always had a smile for me."

As a tear slid down her cheek, she wiped it away with the sleeve of her hoodie. "I hate not knowing what happened to him and having no way of finding out."

It dawned on Julian then that Ella was holding in a lot, and not all of it was about enduring Gorchenco. What he wondered, though, was whether she was putting on a brave face just for others or for herself as well.

At some point, the dam was going to break, and all those suppressed emotions were going to burst out to the surface. It wasn't a question of if, but of when.

Poor girl.

And her ordeal wasn't over yet.

What did that fucking Doomer want with her?

Had he suspected that she was a Dormant and was planning on getting his hands on her?

Did he want to use her to find the village?

What if there was more to this compulsion, and he'd planted a command in her head to contact him with information about her location?

But that didn't make sense.

When Lokan had met Ella, she had known nothing about the clan or who the people organizing her rescue were. So even if that Doomer had thralled her and scanned her memories, he would've found nothing of interest there.

Nothing other than her telepathic ability. But that could only make him suspect that Ella was a Dormant, not her connection to the clan.

Unless Vivian hadn't followed their instructions and had revealed something to Ella that had given Lokan a clue.

When Ella's step faltered once more, Julian lifted her into his arms. "We are almost at your house, and there is no one around."

"Thank you. I was about to ask you to carry me." She chuckled. "No matter what, I'm never drinking one of Merlin's potions again."

Unexpectedly, his heart sank a little when she said that. What if they wanted a child sometime in the future? Without help, that future might be very distant.

But that was a silly thought and way too premature. They hadn't even had sex yet, and Merlin's fertility potions might not work. In fact, Julian was pretty sure they wouldn't. He had more faith in the human fertility treatments that had been proven to work. Those, if adapted to immortals, might actually be successful.

As Julian took the steps up to the front porch, the door opened and Vivian came out.

"What happened?"

"It's the potion. Apparently, Ella is very sensitive to it."

"Hi, Mom." Ella waved a hand. "Don't worry. I just feel like I'm drunk. It will pass."

Vivian kissed her cheek. "Will coffee help?"

"I already had some. I think that it's best for me to sleep it off."

"As you wish, sweetie." Vivian led the way to Ella's bedroom and opened the door. "Let me know if you need anything."

"I will, Mom. I love you."

"Love you too." Vivian closed the door, leaving them alone.

Since Ella was dressed in street clothes, he put her down on top of the comforter. "Do you want to get undressed before I tuck you in?"

"No. I'll just take a short nap. My clothes are clean."

"As you wish. Let me take your shoes off."

She toed her sneakers off before he had a chance to get to them. "All done."

Leaning, he kissed her forehead. "Are you going to be okay here by yourself?"

"Yes." Closing her eyes, she tucked her hands under the pillow, and a moment later her breathing became deep and even.

Adorable.

When he left Ella's room, Julian closed the door quietly behind him and then strode to the living room where her family was waiting for him.

"Did it work?" Magnus asked.

Julian shook his head. "She still couldn't tell us anything."

Magnus's eyes began glowing. "I hope that son of a bitch is not planning anything."

In the corner, Scarlet whimpered.

Julian lowered his voice so as not to scare the dog. "I was thinking about it on the way here. Lokan had no way of knowing that Ella would end up with the clan. When she met him, she didn't know about us, so he couldn't have thralled the information out of her. The only thing I can think of is that he guessed she was a Dormant and wanted her for himself. The question is how he's planning to do it. Did he plant a secret command in her head to contact him?"

"If he did, she would've done it already," Vivian said. "Why wait so long?"

It wasn't long at all, but still.

"We have to assume that he pulled the rescue plan out of her head. So he knew there was a chance she'd get free. Planting a command like that would've made sense. There is one more possibility, though." Julian pinned Vivian with a hard stare. "If he knew who the people rescuing her were, he might have planted a different command in her head. To disclose the village's location to him."

Vivian's eyes widened. "But how? Ella didn't know anything about the clan until you told her the story after the rescue when she was already on the plane."

"Are you sure? Maybe you let something slip during your telepathic conversations?"

"I did not. I was very careful not to reveal anything about the clan. Turner warned me not to."

"Yes, I know he did. But sometimes people blurt things out accidentally."

Even without the immortal glow, Vivian's eyes blazed with anger. "You can ask me the same question in a hundred different ways, Julian, but my answer will still be the same. I didn't tell Ella anything about the clan or about immortals, and I didn't let anything slip either."

5

ELLA

After Julian had left, Ella tried to nap, breathing slow and steady and counting sheep floating on fluffy clouds, but it was no use. She felt too nauseous to fall asleep.

It was like having a hangover combined with an upset stomach.

Merlin's potion was vile, and it went beyond the taste. Maybe she was having a reaction to it?

It wasn't like over the counter medications that she could get in the supermarket. Those had been tested and approved, while the things Merlin was cooking in his kitchen hadn't been checked by anyone other than the loony doctor, and he'd probably tested them only on other immortals.

Hopefully, the effects would dissipate soon because she had things to do. Like figuring out how to circumvent Logan's compulsion so she could tell Kian and the others about his dream intrusions.

Just thinking about it made her head hurt, but it was probably the concoction's fault and not the compulsion's. Propping herself up on a pile of pillows, Ella closed her eyes and once again tried to deep-breathe the headache away. Sometimes it worked, though that was when the headache was stress related, which could have been the case now, but she had a feeling that this one had been caused by the potion.

When deep breathing didn't help, she got up, padded to the bathroom, and pulled out a container of Motrin. Popping three capsules into her mouth, she washed them down with tap water.

The next weapon in her arsenal of natural remedies was a shower. There was something rejuvenating and relaxing about the heat and the moisture, and it was very effective for headaches.

On second thought, though, a bath would be better. It was more conducive to thinking.

It took a good five minutes for the tub to get full, and when it did, Ella got in and sighed with pleasure. This was such a nice, big tub. She could actually lie flat in it and submerge her body completely. The bathroom she used to share with Parker in the old house had only a basic tub that doubled as a shower, and even though Ella was small, she couldn't get comfortable in it. Even worse, it hadn't had a working lock, and her mother had refused to fix it, claiming it wasn't safe.

Not safe from a little brother, that was for sure. Ella had had to prop a chair against the door to prevent him from *accidentally* barging in.

Her mom was such a worrywart. Vivian would go into a full panic mode if she entered the room and didn't find Ella right away, and only then think of checking the bathroom.

Opening the channel, Ella sent her mother a quick message. *In case you're looking for me, I'm soaking in the tub.*

Are you okay? How are you feeling?

I'm fine. A headache started, so I took three pills.

Can you keep the channel open? I worry about you being in the tub when you don't feel well. I've heard of people drowning in shallow bath water because they fainted.

Ella rolled her eyes. *I can't keep it open because it's draining my energy. But I can talk to you every five minutes. Okay?*

Don't forget, or I'll have to come in.

The door is locked.

As if I can't open those locks. I don't know why you even bother. Parker knows how to do it too.

Which means that I need a better lock.

Ella closed the channel before a new argument started. She loved her mother, and she even tried to be understanding about the super-charged protective streak Vivian had developed, but it was annoying.

Thank God for her mental barriers. If her mother could enter her mind whenever she wanted, it would be awful.

Hey, maybe telling her mother about Logan via their private channel would work? What if only speaking about him out loud was a problem?

Mom. And that was it. She couldn't send anything about Logan or her dreams.

What is it, sweetheart? It hasn't even been five minutes yet.

Oh, then never mind. I love you.

Love you too, sweetie.

Well, that was a bust.

Perhaps she could try to write it down and then let Kian read it.

No, she shouldn't think about showing it, just about writing it down. Logan had said not to tell anyone about him, and the command was literal. As long as she tried to communicate information about him to others, she was going to get blocked. But what if she wrote it in her personal journal?

Not that she had one. But it was never too late to start.

Excited about her new idea, Ella got out of the tub, pulled her bathrobe on, and padded back to her room.

I'm out of the tub, so you can stop worrying, she sent to her mom.

Do you want me to bring you something to eat or drink?

Just thinking about food makes me want to barf, but I'd appreciate some black coffee.

Coming up.
You're the best, Mom.
Pulling out a notepad and a pencil, Ella started writing. To get herself going and forget about the purpose of it, she decided to start by making a list of things worth putting in a journal.

What was her first memory of telepathic communication with her mom?

There had been so many of them.

She would think of it later. For now, she was just jotting down major turning points in her life, like Parker's birth and her father's death. Again, she didn't want to start writing about it because once she did, she would never stop. Almost twelve years later, she still missed her dad and thought about him nearly every day.

Wiping away a tear, she continued to her graduation from high school, the prom that had been such an underwhelming event, her job at the diner...

Meeting freaking Romeo. Stupidly falling for his fake charm and false declarations of love. She'd been such a painfully naive idiot.

Damn, it was hard to keep writing with a hand that shook, and once again she decided to only put down bullet points. Falling for Romeo, lying to her mother and going with him to New York for what she'd thought would be a fun weekend, meeting the scumbag's uncle and realizing that she'd been lured into a trap. The auction house, getting bought by the Russian and what that had entailed, and then she got to meeting Logan.

Now it was time for putting down details.

Ella wrote about going to lunch with the Russian, his handsome lunch guest, hearing them talk about weapons and then about some island Gorchenco used to vacation at.

So far so good.

Dreaming about...

And that was it.

She couldn't continue, and the headache that assaulted her was so bad that Ella felt like vomiting.

Crap, crap, and triple crap...

Throwing the pencil across the room, she got up and rushed into the bathroom. Leaning over the sink, she cranked the faucet open and splashed cold water on her face.

It helped with the nausea, but not the headache.

Except, the headache was what had caused the nausea, so she needed to eradicate it too.

Simple, everyday thoughts, that was what she needed. Like planning to go shopping for shoes online. She needed a pair of pumps that weren't as high-heeled as the ones she'd borrowed from her mother.

The longer Ella distracted herself with mundane, unfocused thoughts, the more the headache subsided, until she felt safe to return to her room and not barf all over the carpet.

Her mother entered with a coffee mug. "Are you okay? You look pale."

"I'll be fine. Thanks for the coffee." Ella took the mug.

Thankfully, her mother had gotten the hint. "I'll be in the kitchen if you need me. I know you're nauseous, but if you feel better, I'm making soup and salad for lunch."

Ella shook her head. "Maybe later."

When Vivian left, Ella started pacing. What else could she try?

Her laptop caught her eye.

It was probably a stupid idea, but it wouldn't hurt to try. Snatching it off her desk, she sat on her bed and opened a new note.

This time she skipped the preamble and went straight to the point, but decided not to mention the name. She typed: *Dreaming about Mr. D.*

D for Doomer and for dream-walker.

Without letting herself get carried away by the small success, she wrote: *Mr. D can enter my dreams. He calls his ability dream walking.*

Ella's relief was so monumental that she felt dizzy, but for a good reason this time. Her first instinct was to run out and show Vivian her laptop, but her mother could miss the reference and start asking questions that would bring the headache back.

Having Julian around, filling in the missing pieces, would work better.

Instead of texting like she would normally do, she called him. "Are you very busy?"

"Not at all. What's up?"

"I need you to come over. There is something I want to show you."

"What is it?"

"I can't tell you. You need to see it."

"I'll be there in five minutes."

"Thanks."

To make it in such a short time, Julian would have to jog, not walk...

Crap. She was still in her bathrobe.

Rushing into her closet, she pulled on a pair of panties, skipped the bra and grabbed a sweatshirt off the shelf. A pair of leggings and her house slippers went on next.

She looked like a hobo, with mismatched clothes and wet pink hair that was sticking out in all directions because she hadn't brushed it after getting out of the bathtub.

Finger combing would have to do.

6

JULIAN

*E*lla hadn't sounded scared. She'd sounded excited. Still, Julian dropped the stack of estimates he'd gotten for the remodeling of the halfway house and then ran all the way to her place as if his tail was on fire.

"Hi, Vivian," he said as she opened the door. "Ella called me. She wants to show me something."

"Come on in." Vivian threw the door open. "She's in her room."

"Thanks." He headed down the corridor.

"Can you stay for lunch?" Vivian called after him. "It's nothing fancy. I made soup and salad, but we would love for you to join us."

"Thank you. I would be happy to."

"I'll tell Ella to open the door."

He stopped with his knuckles an inch away from it. With Ella's human hearing, she might not hear him knocking on the soundproof door.

As she opened it, looking like she'd gotten dressed in the dark and with her pink hair in disarray, he wanted to pick her up and kiss her.

Adorable.

But it was apparent that Ella was pumped about something that she couldn't wait to share with him.

"That was fast. Come in. You have to see this." She pointed at the laptop propped on a cushion on her bed.

Sitting down, Julian lifted it and put it on his knees. There were only two lines of text on the screen.

Dreaming about Mr. D.

Mr. D can enter my dreams. He calls his ability dream walking.

"Who is Mr. D?"

Rolling her eyes, Ella affected a stern and haughty expression, lifted her chin, and turned her face slightly to the side as if posing for a portrait.

Did she mean Lokan? But why Mr. D and not Mr. L?

"Is the D for Doomer?"

She nodded enthusiastically and pointed to the word dream.

"And for dream walker?"

Jumping up and down, Ella squealed and clapped her hands.

"You found a way around the compulsion?"

She nodded again, then snatched the laptop from his hands, put it on her desk, and started typing.

It seemed like Ella was afraid to say anything out loud. Even a yes.

When she was done, she handed him the laptop. The third line said: *I need to know how to block Mr. D from visiting my dreams.*

"This is big. We should tell Kian. I've never heard of an ability like that."

He reached for her hand and pulled her into his lap. "I'm so glad you found a way to let us know what's going on. I knew it had to be more than just one lunch meeting. Now it all makes sense. He didn't want you to talk about his dream visits. What does he want from you?"

Ella took the laptop and typed: *I'm special because I can communicate telepathically. Mr. D wants to find me and take me.*

Julian felt his fangs elongate and his venom glands swell. "Over my dead body. But that's an empty threat because he can't find you. You're safe here. Just don't give him any clues."

She rolled her eyes again and pointed to the previous line she'd typed.

"I get it. That's why you want to block him."

She nodded.

"Let me text Kian. Maybe he knows of a clan member who can help with that."

His text was short and to the point. *Ella found a way around the silencing compulsion. She can type what she can't say. Lokan is invading her dreams, and she wants to know how to stop him.*

Kian's answer came back a moment later. *Bring Ella to my office at five in the afternoon. I'll get Turner and Bridget.*

"Five o'clock at Kian's office. Turner and Bridget are going to be there too."

"Good. Can you explain this to my family?"

"Sure. Your mom invited me to stay for lunch."

As he and Ella entered the living room, Parker and Magnus were setting up the table.

"Right on time," Magnus said. "Take a seat."

Julian glanced at Ella. "Should I wait with this for after lunch?"

"What is it?" Vivian put a large salad bowl on the table.

"Ella found a way around the compulsion. She can type what she wants to say, but without mentioning his real name. She calls him Mr. D."

Vivian grinned. "My clever girl. I knew you'd find a way."

"I wasn't sure at all," Ella said. "It was a last-ditch effort after I tried communicating it to you telepathically and then writing it by hand."

Parker came in with a plate piled up with toast. "What is everyone talking about?"

"Remember what I told you about the clan's enemies?" Magnus said.

"The Doomers."

"Ella has met one, but she didn't know that he was a Doomer."

"There is more to it," Julian said. "Apparently, this guy has the ability to intrude on people's dreams."

Magnus lifted his hand. "Let's serve the soup before it gets cold. You can tell us the rest while we eat."

"Need any help?" Julian got up.

"Vivian and I got it." Magnus clapped him on the back.

When everyone was seated, Julian waited for Magnus's signal to continue. Perhaps the Guardian didn't want Parker to hear the rest?

Feeling Julian's gaze on him, Magnus lifted his spoon. "Eat your soup first, Julian. The story isn't going to get cold. The soup is."

For the next several minutes, no one talked. When Julian was done, he wiped his mouth with the napkin and glanced at the Guardian again.

"Go ahead," Magnus said.

Thank the merciful Fates. Sitting on exciting news like this wasn't good for digestion.

"What Ella typed on her laptop was that Mr. D has been invading her dreams. What I think happened was that he discovered her telepathic ability during that one face-to-face meeting they had, and he decided that he wanted her for himself. I'm guessing that he didn't act on it because he needed Gorchenco for the weapons, so he couldn't antagonize him by taking Ella by force, and he couldn't thrall the Russian to give Ella up either. Somehow, though, he must have established a connection with her that has allowed him access to her dreams."

Julian turned to Ella. "Is this a correct assessment so far?"

She nodded.

Vivian groaned. "Is this nightmare ever going to end?"

"I'm so sick of guys coming after Ella," Parker said. "Maybe if she gets married, has ten kids, and gets really fat, it will stop."

Ella threw a crumb of toast at him. "Oh, gee. Thanks, Parker. That's exactly what I want from my life."

"What?" The kid threw his hands in the air. "Isn't having ten kids better than being chased by every evil guy who sees your face?"

Chuckling, Vivian looked pointedly at Julian. "Why jump all the way to ten? One child might do."

Uncomfortable, more for Ella than for himself, Julian raked his fingers through his hair. "Ella is only eighteen, so this conversation is pointless. Besides, I don't think it would stop someone like Lokan. He'd probably want to get his hands on Ella's child as well."

7

KIAN

"I've never heard of a dream walking talent," Kian said. "Have you, Bridget?"

She shook her head. "Nope. I can ask Merlin. The guy is a fount of knowledge. We could also ask Dalhu and Robert."

Kian waved a dismissive hand. "I doubt they know anything. But go ahead."

"What about the goddess?" Turner asked. "Maybe there were dream walkers among the gods or the early immortals?"

"I'll do it right now." Kian pulled out his phone, at the last minute deciding to call instead of texting.

He hadn't called her in a while, and Annani would be on his case for being a neglectful son, contacting her only when he needed something. Which regrettably was true, and there was no excuse for it.

After all, he wasn't only her son but also her regent, and it was his duty to call her with regular updates, which he failed to do. She had every right to be upset with him.

"Kian, my beloved son. How good it is to hear from you."

"Hello, Mother. How have you been?"

"Excellent, my dear. But I know you are not calling to inquire after my well-being. How can I assist you?"

There was no point in denying the truth, especially not with the audience listening in.

"Have you ever heard of a dream walker? A god or an immortal who could enter another person's dream from afar?"

She took a long moment before answering. "It should be possible for someone like Yamanu to thrall people from afar while they are asleep. But I do not think he can pinpoint a specific person."

"I'm not talking about thralling. I'm talking about interacting with a person in his or her dream, conducting an actual face-to-face conversation."

"I do not see how it is possible. Again, an elaborate thrall can mimic a dream. But it would be like planting an entire scene in the person's head. They would not be really interacting. Do you understand what I am trying to say?"

"I do. Except, it seems that one of Navuh's sons has the ability."

"Are you sure? It could be trickery. I would not put it past Navuh and his subordinates to pretend to have powers they do not."

The thought had crossed Kian's mind. But to determine that, he needed to ask Ella some more questions. "Thank you. I need to investigate this more in depth. I'll let you know what I find out."

"Please do. It is very troubling. We could be vulnerable to dream attacks."

"Indeed. I'll talk to you later. Goodbye, Mother."

"Goodbye, my son."

Ella, who was the only one who hadn't heard the other side of the phone conversation, was looking at him expectantly. "What did the goddess say?"

"Annani has never heard of a god or immortal who could interact with another person in his or her dream." Kian tapped his fingers on the conference table. "I need to ask you more questions. Are you going to type your answers?"

She opened her laptop. "I'll do my best."

"In those dreams, did Lokan try to get information out of you?"

Julian cleared his throat. "We should call him Mr. D from now on. It makes things easier for Ella."

"No problem."

In the meantime, Ella finished typing and handed the laptop to Julian. "You can read it out loud for everyone."

He nodded. "Ella says that he didn't ask her anything. Sometimes she felt as if he was leading her into revealing things, but she was always careful not to."

"How much in control of the dream are you, though?" Bridget asked. "Can he glimpse your thoughts while sharing your dream?"

When Julian handed the laptop back to Ella, she typed up a quick response and handed it back.

"Ella says that she's in full control. It's the same as if she were awake. Because of the telepathic connection with her mother, she has practiced blocking from a young age, and her shields are always up. She has to lower them to communicate with her mother. Mr. D can't see what she doesn't want him to."

Frowning, Ella took the laptop and typed some more before handing it back to Julian.

"The only exception was the sanctuary. In one of the dreams she was walking the grounds when Mr. D joined her, and as he commented on the landscape, she said that it was typical of the region. That could've given him a clue as to where the sanctuary was located. In another dream, he joined her at the diner where she used to work, so that's not a problem, and then he met her at her favorite San Diego beach. Ella is afraid that he might enter a dream while she's dreaming about the village and see it through her eyes."

"The village is not a problem," Turner said. "Seeing it through Ella's eyes will not tell him anything about its location. The sanctuary is another story, though. The Brotherhood might have records of the place from when it served as their base. He can recognize the landscape from pictures if they kept them, and if he suspects what and where it is, he can find old newspaper articles about the sanctuary from its monastery days."

Kian leaned back in his chair. "I don't think we should be overly concerned, but just as a precaution, it's a good idea to beef up the sanctuary's security."

"I agree." Turner flipped his notepad open. "I'm on it."

"The question is how to protect Ella from his visits," Bridget said. "This must be really hard on you." She cast Ella an empathic look. "Going to sleep is probably stressful instead of relaxing."

Ella grimaced. "It is."

"Killing Mr. D or putting him in stasis would solve the problem," Julian hissed through slightly elongated fangs.

Kian snorted. "For that, we would need to find him first."

Ella took the laptop from Julian and spent a couple of minutes typing away.

"Ella says she can do some snooping around and ask him questions. Maybe he'll tell her where he is. We know what he looks like. So, if we know where he is, we can catch him."

"That would require Ella to pretend she enjoys his company," Bridget said. "Can you do that?"

Ella snorted. "I fooled a paranoid mafia boss into believing that I liked him."

"That's true." Bridget looked at Kian. "Gorchenco had a reason to be suspicious of Ella's motives. Mr. D has none. He'd be much easier to fool."

Perhaps. An old and experienced Doomer would not be so easy for Ella to wrap around her little finger. Was Lokan old? Kian had forgotten what Dalhu had written in the dossier he'd prepared on the guy.

Besides, Lokan was likely spending most of his time on the island where they couldn't get to him anyway.

On the other hand, Lokan wanted Ella and was probably planning to lure her somewhere he could snatch her. He knew she was in California, so that meant that he knew he'd have to be in the States to get her.

Which would make catching him much easier.

It could be an incredible step forward for the clan. As Navuh's son, Lokan would know the location of the island. Not only that, they could hold him as a negotiating chip. Navuh didn't care much for his rank and file, but he must care for his sons, if not emotionally, then for their usefulness.

The question was whether they would manage to get Lokan to talk.

The Doomers the clan had captured in the past hadn't been privy to the information, and on top of that, they'd been under compulsion not to reveal any of the Brotherhood's secrets. Even Dalhu suspected that he'd been compelled before leaving for his mission in the States.

Kian wasn't sure he was right, though.

Dalhu had claimed that the compulsion had eased the longer he'd stayed away from the island. But that sounded more like a thrall than a compulsion. Then again, immortals could only get thralled by gods, and Navuh was no god.

Kian had the passing thought that maybe Annani's half-sister Areana had something to do with it, but he then dismissed it out of hand.

First of all, they had no proof that Areana was alive. Neither Dalhu nor Robert had ever heard of her. And secondly, Areana was a weak goddess.

According to Annani, her sister had been weaker than some of the more powerful immortals.

"I want you to keep me updated," he told Ella. "Every time you dream about him, text me the details. Or you can type it in your laptop and text me the page. Whatever works for you."

She nodded. "I'll do that."

8

ELLA

"I'm hungry," Ella said as she and Julian climbed the steps to her front porch. "I hope my mother saved dinner for us."

With all the excitement, she hadn't eaten much at lunch, and the meeting had taken longer than expected.

He rubbed his stomach. "We should've gotten something from the vending machines. I'm hungry too, and I don't want to impose."

"Don't be silly." She cast him an incredulous glance. "Even if there are no leftovers, I can whip us up a couple of sandwiches, or we can heat up a frozen pizza." Other than salads, which she had several good recipes for, that was the extent of her culinary expertise.

As she opened the door, Ella scanned the living room for her mother, but no one was there. It still felt strange to her that the front door remained unlocked at all times, even when no one was home, and stranger still that she had no need for a key.

Heck, she didn't even have one. Maybe there was no key?

She wasn't sure. On the one hand, it was nice to know that the village was so safe that no one locked their doors, but on the other hand, having no key to open the door with made her feel as if this wasn't her house.

It was just a passing feeling, a niggling in the back of her head, or maybe just an uncomfortable sensation in her stomach, not a conscious thought. Logically she knew that this was home, even more so than their old house.

Her family didn't belong in the human world. They belonged right here, in this village, and in this brand new, gorgeous house that was theirs to keep.

"Mom? Where are you?"

"I'm right here." Vivian entered through the glass doors with Scarlet trotting behind her. "I was reading outside. How did it go?"

"Good. Is there anything left over to eat? I'm starving."

Vivian waved them over to the table. "I would have waited for you, but

Magnus had to leave. I have your plates in the warming drawer. You can tell me everything after your bellies are full."

Once they were done with the main course, Julian summed up the meeting for her mother.

"I don't like it," Vivian said. "Encouraging those dream visits is asking for trouble."

Ella couldn't argue with that assessment. Her mother was right, but she was going to do it anyway.

Finally, Kian was taking her seriously and seeing her as a valuable asset, and not the pesky human girl with grandiose ideas.

Ella hadn't missed the sparkle in his eyes when he'd realized that she had access to one of Navuh's sons and could get information for the clan that they couldn't obtain in any other way.

Julian put down the bread roll he was munching on. "Kian doesn't think it's dangerous. Even if Mr. D can see the village through Ella's eyes, it's going to be meaningless to him. Ella doesn't know the location, and there are no landmarks visible from here."

"The ocean is a big one," Vivian said.

He waved a dismissive hand. "It's only visible from the very edge of the village."

"And I never saw it," Ella added. "I'll just avoid that spot."

Vivian sighed. "Well, I guess that everyone other than me is in favor of this." She pushed away from the table and snagged an envelope from the counter. "While you were gone, Magnus brought your fake papers." She handed it to Ella.

"Oh, good. Now I can go to a club." Ella opened the envelope and pulled everything out. "A driver's license with an awesome picture, a passport, a social security card, and a birth certificate." She glanced at Julian. "You guys are thorough."

Popping the lid off a Snake Venom bottle, he smiled. "I'm only the doctor. I know as much about the production of fake papers as you do."

"This is freedom." Ella lifted the driver's license and waved it in the air. "Now I only need a car."

Her mother flinched. "It's not safe for you to go out by yourself yet. The danger from the Russian is not over."

"I can take you out," Julian offered. "We've just eaten, so a restaurant is not an option, but I can take you to a nightclub."

Across the table, Vivian sucked in a breath.

It's okay, Mom, Ella sent. *I'm not ready for a club.*

Relieved, her mother slumped in her chair.

"How about a movie?" Ella turned to Julian. "I haven't been to a movie theater in ages."

He put his beer down. "You know that we have one in the underground complex, right?"

"I do. But you probably don't have any of the new movies that are now playing in theaters."

He snorted. "Are you kidding me? Have you forgotten about Brandon? We get new movies before they are released to the public. He gets us the early screening copies."

"Do you have *Vampires in Paris*? It's supposed to come out next month."

"I've never heard of it, but I can check." He pulled out his phone. "We have a list of available movies on the clan's virtual board."

"Let me see." She leaned closer and peered over his arm at the phone. "Anything else interesting on that board?"

He handed it to her. "Take a look."

"Class schedules, a list of movies, and some items for sale. That's uninspiring."

He took his phone back. "What do you think should be there?"

"A horoscope." She lifted a finger. "An advice column." She lifted another one. "Recipes. Short stories." She lifted two more. "Cleaning hacks. There is so much that can go there."

Julian lifted a brow. "Cleaning hacks?"

"Yeah, like shortcuts, or ways to remove stains. Things like that."

"All of the things you've mentioned can be found on the internet. They are not clan specific."

"True." Her excitement dimmed.

For a moment, Ella imagined having her own column on the board. "I'll talk with Carol and Eva. See if there is anything they would like to have there. Carol suggested that you should put up pictures of all clan members so the newcomers could familiarize themselves with their faces. I for one wouldn't want to run into a Doomer and mistake him for a clan member."

"There is a very slim chance of that."

She arched a brow. "Really?"

Not that she would've known what Logan was when she met him, but still. Out of the billions of people on the planet she'd gotten to have lunch with a Doomer.

"Yeah, you're right." Julian glanced back at his phone. "We have *Vampires in Paris*, but it looks like a horror movie. Are you sure you want to see it?"

"Pfft. It's a parody on the vampire lore. You're going to have fun watching it."

9

JULIAN

"Let's hope no one is watching a movie already." Julian held the elevator door open for Ella.

"Is it a popular hangout spot?"

"I don't know. If I watch movies at all, it's usually in my room on my tablet."

"Netflix?"

"Yeah."

"I used them extensively during my hibernation period." She chuckled. "Mostly Christmas movies. They are sweet and romantic, and I know nothing bad is going to happen. A guaranteed happy ending."

"It seems that we have the place all to ourselves." Julian pushed the theater's doors open. "Do you want popcorn?"

"Sure." She followed him to the enclave with the antique-looking popcorn machine. "It's just a replica, right? It's not a real antique."

"It's as modern as it gets. Makes awesome popcorn." Julian turned the thing on. "Three minutes."

"That's so cool. Where do you keep the movies?"

"Stored on a server." He picked up the controller and wrapped his arm around her waist. "Front row or back?"

"Back, of course."

As they sat down, he leaned and whispered in her ear, "This is the making-out row."

She laughed and waved her hand at the empty seats in front of them. "Obviously. So, all the people watching the movie won't see us kissing."

"We can pretend that the place is packed."

She cast him an amused glance. "Let's not. I like having the entire theater to ourselves." Sniffing, she turned in the direction of the popcorn machine. "I think it's ready."

"I'll get it."

Ella was so hard to read.

It was driving Julian nuts. His sense of smell and even his empathy were useless with her. She seemed to like him, was acting as if they were best friends, had worn his clothes, and had even slept in his bed, but that was it.

Here and there her arousal would flare for a brief moment, and then it would get snuffed out as if there wasn't enough kindling to keep it going.

Was it the result of what she'd been through, or was it him?

He'd never had a problem like that before. Throughout the ten years that he'd been sexually active, Julian hadn't encountered even one woman who hadn't responded to him right from the very first kiss.

Returning to his seat with an overflowing bucket of popcorn, he handed it to Ella. "Taste it. I bet it's better than any you had before."

And so am I, he wanted to add.

She popped a piece into her mouth. "It is. What makes it so good?"

"You'll have to ask Okidu. He's the one who buys the supplies for the machine and keeps it clean."

"I will. Now let's watch some bloodsuckers terrorize Paris."

Wrapping his arm around her shoulders, he pressed play and braced for an hour and a half of boredom. Parodies were usually too stupid to watch.

He ended up laughing his ass off.

When the credits rolled in, he clicked the movie off and the lights on. "I have to admit that it was fun." Despite the fact that no making out had been going on.

But he'd had his arm around her for the entire time, and when she hadn't been doubled over with laughter, Ella had been resting her head against his bicep.

"It's a sequel to *Vampires in London*. That's how I knew it was going to be hilarious. Maddie and I watched it together, and Maddie laughed so hard she almost choked on a piece of popcorn. I had to use the Heimlich maneuver on her." Ella sighed. "I miss her. That's my only regret about being here."

He offered her a hand up. "When you are an immortal, you can visit her and then thrall the memory away."

Her eyes peeled wide. "I'll be able to thrall?"

"You'll have to practice doing it, but yeah."

"Awesome. I can't wait. There are so many perks to being an immortal."

It was on the tip of his tongue to remind her what she had to do in order to become one, but he didn't want to push her. Ella already knew that.

When they passed the village square, Julian stopped. "Where do you want to sleep tonight? The way to my house is straight ahead, and yours is to the left."

Despite how hard it was to have her so near and not touch her like he wanted to, Julian hoped Ella would sleep in his bed again. Holding her throughout the night had forever changed how he wanted to spend his nights. It was going to be so lonely without her. So empty. So cold.

"I need to sleep at home." She put a hand on his chest. "You know why."

He nodded. She was anticipating a dream visit. But that didn't mean she had to be alone while it was happening.

"I can keep you safe."

"It's sweet of you to offer, but I can't. Having you in my mind is not a good idea. I need to put other people in there. People from my old life."

"I get it."

It was smart of her to plan ahead and fill her head with old memories, but that didn't help with his sense of disappointment.

As they reached her front porch, he turned her to him. "Can I at least get a kiss goodnight?"

Ella smiled and took his hand. "Let's do it like in the old movies from the fifties, sitting on the steps in front of my house and being very quiet so my mom won't hear us moaning into each other's mouths." She pulled him down as she sat down. "Except, in my case, instead of coming out with a shotgun, my mother would clap her hands in glee."

"We wouldn't want that." He lifted her and put her in his lap. "That's better."

As she wrapped her arms around his neck, the slight scent of her arousal reached his nose. "I agree. Kiss me, Julian."

He did, pouring all his feelings into that kiss, but at the same time making sure not to overwhelm her.

If she needed more, she would let him know.

Ella's comment from before had given him an inkling as to what she wanted. In those old movies, the girl was a virgin, and her parents wanted to make sure she remained intact until her wedding night.

He needed to treat Ella as if she were a virgin.

Because basically, she was. She'd never had sex with a male of her choosing and had missed out on the wonder of joining for the first time with someone she cared about.

It had been stolen from her. She'd been taken against her will by someone she could barely stand.

The rage that bubbled up to the surface every time he thought of that was difficult to stifle, but Julian didn't want to add insult to injury by allowing himself to vent it in Ella's presence. Perhaps after they said goodnight, he should hit the gym and obliterate a punching bag.

"Julian? Your eyes are glowing. Is it because you're turned on?" She sounded like she knew it wasn't the case.

"I'm sorry. Every time I think about what was taken from you I get angry."

She cupped his cheek. "Forget about it. Let's focus on the future, not the past."

He rested his forehead on hers. "I want to make you happy, Ella. I want to erase every bad experience you ever had and replace it with a good one. But I know that you are not ready, and I'm not going to pressure you into anything. All the power is yours. I will never try to take it away from you."

10

ELLA

In her room, Ella plopped down on the bed and draped an arm over her eyes.

This was hard.

To fool Mr. D, she had to distance herself emotionally from Julian, but by doing so, she was bound to hurt him. For her plan to work, she shouldn't have even kissed him goodnight, but he'd looked so disappointed, and a kiss was the least she could do to cheer him up.

He was such a sweetheart, so considerate, and hopefully patient.

Until the situation with Mr. D got resolved, she couldn't open up to Julian. Keeping her emotions suppressed was what had allowed her to put on such a convincing act for the Russian. She needed to use the same tactic on the Doomer.

It was like creating a blank canvas to paint a fake staging backdrop for her act.

Heck, maybe she should pursue an acting career. Except, more than a makeover would be needed to change her appearance enough for Gorchenco not to recognize her. Besides, once she turned immortal, she would have to avoid notice, like the rest of them.

For Mr. D, however, she needed to look like she had before. Which meant thinking and imagining her old self and not looking into the mirror, or at least as little as possible.

Perhaps she should tape a picture of her old self over the bathroom mirror? Eva had taken some before the makeover and had shared them with Ella. All she needed to do was to print one out.

She ended up printing her face on twelve pages and taping them on the mirror like a collage.

Changing into her pajamas, Ella got in bed and closed her eyes. If Logan showed up, should she treat him exactly like she had the Russian?

The situation wasn't the same, so she needed a different approach. Logan hadn't bought her, and except for that first dream, he hadn't tried to force her into anything.

Well, he was popping uninvited into her dreams, but that wasn't even close to what the Russian had done. And Mr. D was handsome.

Heck, he was gorgeous. A true Lucifer if she'd ever seen one. Perhaps it painted her shallow, but it was much easier to pretend attraction to a guy who looked like that. And if she cared to be frank with herself, not much pretending was needed.

But what if Mr. D remembered her saying Julian's name?

If he asked about Julian, should she lie that he was a nobody, or tell him a semi-truth?

When sleep finally came, Logan didn't take long to appear.

"I've been waiting for you," he said. "What time is it where you are?"

They were once again on her favorite beach, walking along the water line. She didn't know whether it was her imagination supplying the details or Logan's, but the setting was perfect for an evening stroll on the shore. The sun was setting, and the sky was gray with a light cloud cover.

There were no other people on the boardwalk that was normally pretty crowded, but there were plenty of sounds and smells to make the setting feel real. Waves crashing to shore, seagulls' cries, and even the smell of hot dogs coming from a nearby stand.

She smiled. "I have no idea. It was a little before midnight when I got in bed, but it took me a long time to fall asleep."

And how was that for an evasive answer? She was quite proud of herself for coming up with that.

"Is there something troubling you?"

As if he cared. She saw right through his fake concern. "Do you have to ask? I have a shitload of bad memories that haunt me at night. I'm afraid to fall asleep."

He stopped and faced her. "Am I one of those bad dreams you dread?"

She could've said yes. Especially after his dark promise from the other night. But when not trying to intimidate her with a harsh expression, his face was so handsome that it was hard to look away from it.

The term 'handsome devil' had never suited anyone better.

A beautiful, dangerous predator.

Waving a dismissive hand, she kept on walking. "I got used to you. Or maybe you are nicer now than you were before."

Logan followed, arching one perfectly shaped dark brow. "How so?"

"You're no longer acting like a brute, and when you're not trying to look scary, you're quite handsome."

"What about that Julian guy? Is he behaving?"

It was good that she was ready for that question and had prepared an answer. "Yeah, he is. He's a nice guy, but it's not serious." Not at the moment, so she wasn't lying.

"On his part, or yours?"

Ella sighed. "Mine. I would like to blame Gorchenco for that, but the truth is that there is something missing. Julian doesn't have the *it* factor."

Logan's nearly black eyes sparkled red, which she now knew was the color of his inner glow. "And may I ask what that mysterious ingredient is?"

Hesitating, Ella went with the closest thing to the truth. "He's sweet, mellow, and way too nice. Apparently, you were right about me, and I do have a thing for bad boys."

Taking her hand, Logan turned her around to face him. "I am a very bad boy, Ella."

As he hooked a finger under her chin and tilted her head up, his lean body was so close to hers that she could feel the heat rolling off him. Was he putting that sensation in her head, or was she supplying the extrasensory input?

Dipping his head, he didn't attack her mouth like he'd done in their first shared dream. Instead, his lips hovered a fraction of an inch away from hers, giving her the option to back away.

Ella closed her eyes and forced a small smile, bracing for the kiss.

As his lips touched hers, Logan wrapped his arm around her waist and pulled her against his hard body. Gently, his tongue flicked against the seam of her lips, coaxing her to open for him instead of invading her forcefully.

Nevertheless, she reacted to his subdued dominance, her arousal flaring hot and quick, so different to her reaction to Julian.

The hand on the small of her back slid down, cupping her bottom and lifting her a little, so her mound was pressed against his hard shaft.

Again, Logan wasn't forcing anything. If she wanted to back away, she could. But she didn't.

Instead, she moaned into his mouth and wrapped her arms around his neck. Suspecting Logan had fangs even in his dream version, she submitted to his kiss instead of kissing him back.

It felt so right even though it definitely wasn't.

Crap. Why did she have to be attracted to the wrong guy?

Way to go, Ella.

She had the best man possible fawning over her, and instead of falling head over heels in love with him, she had the hots for the worst man possible.

Except, for now she wasn't going to fight her inappropriate reaction to Logan, she was going to embrace it.

It was, after all, for a good cause. Any information she could get out of him would greatly benefit the clan.

She was a spy, which should allow her some moral wiggle room, right?

11

JULIAN

After the kiss last night, a heavy weight took residence in Julian's gut and refused to move out no matter what excuses he threw at it.

Logically, he understood that Ella was still traumatized even though she wasn't admitting it. Not only that, she was dealing with Lokan's compulsion and his dream visits, which must be extremely upsetting to her.

Was it a wonder that romance was the furthest thing from her mind?

But the annoying voice in the back of his head was whispering that none of that would have mattered if she was his true-love match, and that the force of that should've overcome everything else.

But those nasty whispers were lies. Had Kian and Syssi fallen into each other's arms right away, declaring their love?

Or why go that far? Had Magnus and Vivian?

They'd all struggled with some kinds of issues that had prevented the bond from snapping into place immediately.

What about Carol and Robert? the annoying voice whispered.

They'd tried to make it work, but it hadn't, and they'd separated. Robert had found his true-love match with Sharon, but Carol was still alone.

"Why the long face, my young friend?" Yamanu wrapped his arm around Julian's shoulders, his frying-pan-size hand hanging loosely over Julian's chest.

"Just thinking where we can cut costs. The glazing contractor has been measuring these windows for over an hour and shaking his head. I have a feeling we are not going to like his bid."

This was just the first of a long lineup of contractors Julian had arranged meetings with for today. The last one was scheduled for seven in the evening, so basically, he and Yamanu were going to spend the entire day there.

At least he wasn't missing out on time with Ella.

She'd gone to the sanctuary with Vivian, using her mother's sewing class as a pretext to be there. The real reason behind it was getting to know the girls and gaining their trust.

It was good thinking on her part. She couldn't just drop the filming on them without preamble. A lot of preparation work was needed.

"It is what it is, my friend. This is an old building, and those windows are not standard sizes. They will have to be custom ordered."

Julian cast the Guardian a questioning glance. "How do you know so much about construction?"

Yamanu shrugged. "A long time ago, I decided that I needed a break from the clan. I found a job as a construction worker. The human contractor was a swell fellow who loved what he was doing. He would go into a dump like this one and see potential no one else did. I learned a lot from him."

"I don't get it. You hate leaving the village and interacting with humans. How come you decided to live and work with them?"

The big guy sighed. "It's a long story."

After that evasive answer, Julian didn't expect him to continue, but Yamanu surprised him.

"I thought that since we were safe here in Los Angeles, the clan could do without me. There is no worse feeling than not being needed. Naturally, Onegus and Kian tried to convince me to stay, but I was itching to do something different."

"How long did it last?"

"Not long. I was back after five months."

"What happened?"

"Nothing major. I didn't like the stares. Even when I put sunglasses on, people still stared because I'm so tall and beautiful." He flipped his long hair back.

"I get stared at too. But so what? Why do you care?"

"Because I'm not just a pretty boy like you. I'm strange looking. When among humans, it's never good to be too different."

That was true, but Yamanu was strange looking in a good way.

"So that's why you offered to help? You miss your construction days?"

"Yeah, I do. I like working with my hands. Creating nice things. But I'm no good with the paint brushes like Dalhu."

"Did you know that he donated half of the proceeds from the exhibition to this project? That's where the money to start the remodeling came from."

"That ex-Doomer is a decent guy. Full of surprises."

Julian shook his head. "I don't think he likes being referred to as an ex-Doomer."

"You might be right. What should we call him then? Amanda's mate?"

"I'm sure he wouldn't mind that."

"It's a shame he didn't join the Guardian force. The guy is even better with the sword than he is with the brushes."

Julian had heard all about Dalhu's epic battle with the Doomers' commander. Rumor said that he'd had an old grudge against the guy, but it wasn't clear about what. As much as people liked to gossip in the village, some things still remained a mystery.

Like Yamanu. There was more to the story about his construction stint, but the guy was as elusive as ever. Seemingly open and charming, but keeping everything about himself close to his chest.

That didn't mean, though, that Julian couldn't poke around some more. "Dalhu got a second chance and took full advantage of it. He doesn't miss his fighting days. Lately, I've been thinking of changing direction as well. Doing something different. How about you? The village could use an in-house contractor."

Yamanu laughed. "I don't know enough to be the boss. And besides, who will join my crew? I don't see any clan members jumping at construction jobs."

"I see your point. It's a shame, though. You should do what brings you joy."

The smile that was almost a permanent feature on Yamanu's face melted away. "Being needed is no less important. And it is fulfilling, just in a different way. Besides, I'm stuck in what I'm doing because I'm irreplaceable."

That was an unexpected revelation, and Julian was starting to get an inkling about what made the Guardian tick. He was one of a kind, and his talent was essential. The problem was that there was limited use for it, and most of the time Yamanu had nothing to do.

Then again, it was his choice. He didn't go on missions unless his special talent was needed or there was a shortage of Guardians, and he had to help. He could've easily joined the ranks and done some good with his regular fighting skills.

Perhaps he didn't like to fight. Being capable of it didn't mean he enjoyed it. But the man had to fill his days with something. Julian would hate sitting around and doing nothing. It would drive him insane.

As far as he was aware, the halfway house was the only project Yamanu had actually volunteered to help out with.

"You are irreplaceable, that's true. But you have plenty of spare time to dedicate to whatever you want. Like this project. I really appreciate your help, and I'm glad you have some construction background because I don't know what I'm doing here. These contractors could've robbed me blind, and I would have thanked them for it."

That brought the smile back to Yamanu's face. "I like hanging out with you. And I want to help these girls in any way I can."

"That's good." Julian clapped the guy's wide back. "I can't wait for your first karaoke night."

He wondered if that was what Yamanu was doing with all his spare time.

"Do you practice singing in your house?"

Yamanu lifted a brow. "I sing when I'm in the mood. Why do you ask?"

Not wanting to offend the guy, Julian scratched his short beard as he thought of a plausible answer. "No reason. It's just that it takes practice to sing as well as you do."

"I'm a natural."

As the glazing contractor waved them over, Yamanu headed his way, and Julian followed behind, pondering the Yamanu mystery.

The Guardian was rooming with Arwel, who was a powerful telepath. He should have more insight than anyone else.

Perhaps chatting with Arwel could provide more clues to the mystery. Provided that the guy was willing to talk.

Damn, he was turning into a busybody like the rest of the village occupants. Julian had never thought it would happen to him. Except, anything that could take his mind off Ella was a welcome distraction.

Obsessing about her twenty-four-seven was not good for him.

"Tell me, Yamanu. Do you and Arwel have a karaoke machine in your house?"

"Naturally."

"Would it be okay if I came over and gave it a try?"

A wide grin spread over Yamanu's face. "Not only okay, it would be fantastic. You can come over any time you want, but check with me at least two hours in advance. I might be busy."

Doing what?

Could it be that Yamanu spent his days in the gym? He wasn't big like a weightlifter, but his lean physique was perfectly sculpted. Perhaps that was his gig?

12

ELLA

The first thing Ella did as she got comfortable in her mother's car was to text Kian an update about her dream. She'd tested her phone this morning, and apparently texting was the same as typing on her laptop, which made life much easier. She could text what she wanted to say instead of passing her laptop to Julian or whoever else was going to read her messages out loud.

Mr. D visited me last night. I made him think that I'm into him and it looked like he bought the act. The only thing he tried to get out of me was my time zone, but I managed to avoid answering him.

She didn't mention the kiss. First of all, because it was embarrassing, and secondly because it was nobody's business how she went about her new spying job.

Kian's return text came a few moments later. *Next dream visit try to find out his time zone.*

Will do.

When they got to the sanctuary, Ella spotted the tall redheaded Guardian doing a walkabout.

"Mom, what's the name of Wonder's fiancé? I forgot."

"Anandur."

"Right. Anyway, I'm going to ask him to help us carry the supplies inside."

"Good idea. It will save us from having to make multiple trips."

It had taken Vivian over a week just to collect everything she needed for her sewing class. That included two sewing machines, two big trash bags filled with donated old clothes that she'd laundered and folded, two boxes full of miscellaneous craft and sewing supplies, one two-pound box of rhinestones, and twelve new Bedazzlers.

She should change the class name from 'sewing with Vivian' to 'rhinestone mania.'

It was going to be fun.

Ella still remembered bedazzling with her mom and the many pleasant evenings they'd spent embellishing old shirts, refreshing old dirty sneakers, backpacks, hats, and jeans pockets. Among other things, it was the perfect way to cover stains that wouldn't come out. Saved them from having to throw away clothes that were otherwise still serviceable. Money had always been tight, but she and Parker had never felt like they were missing out on anything.

So yeah, they hadn't worn the most fashionable labels, and eating out had been reserved for special occasions, but that hadn't been much different from what their friends had. Her mother had worked so hard to provide for them and take care of them, never taking time off for herself or splurging on anything that hadn't been an absolute necessity. Ella was so glad that she could finally take it easy. Her mother definitely deserved a break.

For some reason, the nostalgic memories brought with them a sense of tranquility Ella hadn't felt in a long time. Mother and daughter doing fun things together while the rest of the world was forgotten.

Despite the tragedy of losing their father, which had always loomed heavily in the background, and despite their modest means, those had been the good times.

Before her innocence had been lost.

With a sigh, Ella got out of the car and walked over to the tall Guardian. "Hi, Anandur. My mom and I could use your help. We have tons of things that need to go inside."

"I'll gladly carry everything up to the front door for you, but I'm forbidden from entering." He grimaced. "Vanessa thinks my hulking size will scare the girls."

As Ella looked up at his smiling eyes, she couldn't imagine any woman thinking of him as threatening. He had 'protector' written all over him. In a way, he reminded her of Misha. Anandur was much better-looking, and his smile showed a row of perfectly straight white teeth, not yellowing ones with gold crowns thrown in for embellishment. But he had that aura of a man that a woman could feel safe with, protected, and it was priceless, especially for someone who'd experienced the opposite.

Misha's company had made Ella's stay with Gorchenco tolerable.

Then again, she wasn't the best judge of character, and even if she was, traumatized girls might not see anything beyond his height and bulging muscles.

Stretching up on the very tips of her toes, she put a hand on his shoulder for balance and whispered in his ear, "I don't think you are scary at all. And to prove it, I'm going to have girls peeking at you from the second-floor window. So, if you hear giggling, smile and wave. I'm willing to bet that after seeing you, most will have no problem with you coming inside."

He scratched his red curls and smirked. "I hope Wonder won't mind. I love having girls peek at me, especially when they giggle because they think I'm such an irresistible hunk, but my mate might get jealous."

Ella patted his massive shoulder. "It's for a good cause."

Following her to the car, the Guardian hefted most of what they'd brought. "Make sure to tell her that. She's in there with Kri, helping out with the self-defense class."

He walked over to the front door and deposited the packages there. "That's why I'm here. I'm usually assigned to Kian, but since he's not leaving the village today, he okayed for me to accompany my girl here."

Ella chuckled. "I know your girl, and I doubt she needs you to hover over her. She can take care of herself."

His bushy brows drew tightly together. "Why, what have you heard?"

"Should I have heard something?"

"Never mind. Let me get the rest of the stuff."

There was a story there that Ella intended to pry out of Wonder the next time she came to study with Parker.

"Thank you so much, Anandur," Vivian said when all their packages were stacked by the front door.

"It was my pleasure, ladies." He bowed his head and walked over to his station at the building's corner.

"Do you think he is here because of you know who?" Ella asked. "Increased security?"

Vivian lifted one of the trash bags. "I didn't see any guards the other times I've been here. But that doesn't mean there weren't any."

Ella took the other bag and followed her mother inside. "Where to now?"

Vivian glanced around, but the receptionist wasn't there. "I don't know where Linda is. I'll get Vanessa to show us where to set up shop."

"I'm coming!" Vanessa called out from her office.

A moment later, she and the missing receptionist rushed out. "Let me help you." She grabbed one of the two boxes. "Follow me."

It didn't escape Ella's notice that Vanessa was hiding her superior strength. She could've easily taken a heavier load.

Linda, the receptionist, who like the rest of the sanctuary's staff was human, lifted four Bedazzlers and trailed behind them.

"This is our crafts room," Vanessa said. "We don't have enough classrooms to dedicate one to just sewing. After your class is over, you will have to store your things in the closet to make room for the next one."

"No problem." Vivian put the trash bag on the floor. "Ella will help me organize it so everything will fit."

Doubtful.

The closet barely had any shelf space left, but then her mother was an expert at stuffing as much as possible into closets and refrigerators alike. She didn't really need Ella's help.

"I was hoping to take a look at Kri and Wonder's class."

"Then go." Her mother shooed her away. "I can set up everything by myself."

Ella felt guilty about leaving. "I'll be back in time for the class."

"Don't worry about it, sweetie. Go have fun with the girls."

Vanessa smiled. "Let me take you there."

"Thanks."

When they were out in the corridor, the therapist gave her a once over. "I love your new look. It's edgy."

Ella had the torn jeans and monster boots on, but she had gone easier on the makeup.

"You should've seen me with the fake piercings and the brown contact lenses. They look awesome, but they irritate my eyes, and I figured sunglasses would do for this trip."

"Indeed. The sanctuary is safe."

"About that. I met Anandur outside. Is this something new, or did you always have Guardians patrolling the sanctuary?"

"We have two stationed here during the night and one during the day. Security was beefed up, but Anandur is here because of Wonder. Usually, we don't get the senior Guardians."

"He told me that you didn't allow him inside because you thought he would scare the girls."

Vanessa arched a brow. "Do you question my assessment?"

"I do. And I'm going to prove it to you."

"How?"

"You'll see. I bet you five bucks that at lunch at least half of the girls are going to take their plates outside to keep Anandur company."

Chuckling, Vanessa wrapped her arm around Ella's shoulders. "You are a rebel at heart, aren't you? You like to challenge authority."

"A very astute observation, madam therapist."

13

KIAN

*E*lla's text from earlier that morning kept bugging Kian throughout the day.

She was playing a dangerous game with Lokan, one a young girl like her was ill-suited for. This was a job for Carol, who could have run circles around the Doomer, ensnaring him without breaking a sweat.

Except, Lokan wasn't dream sharing with Carol.

Fuck. Kian threw his pen on his desk. As the Montblanc bounced off the surface and landed on the floor without falling apart, he released a relieved breath. The pen was a present from Syssi, engraved with a sweet love message. He would've hated to have broken it.

His volatile temper was hard to control on a good day, and this wasn't one of those. Sometimes doing the right thing wasn't as clear cut as he would like it to be.

On the one hand, it was low of him to use Ella for what he had in mind, but not to do so was just plain stupid.

This was most likely the only opportunity he would ever get to capture a high-ranking Doomer. And Lokan was nearly as high as they got. Navuh's sons ran the entire Doomer operation.

Kian wasn't sure about their hierarchy. According to Dalhu, Navuh kept it fluid, promoting one son over the other and ensuring that none of them gained too much power.

At this moment in time, Lokan could be the least important or the most, but it didn't really matter. Capturing him and getting him to reveal the island's location would be invaluable. Any other information they could get out of him would just be a bonus.

He needed to brainstorm this with Turner.

Funny how the guy had become so indispensable to him in such a short time. It was becoming a knee jerk reflex to call Turner up and get his advice on anything having to do with security. But the truth was that he trusted Turner's instincts and his insight more than he trusted his own.

Over the years, Kian had become more of a businessman than a commander. Turner, on the other hand, was an expert in modern warfare in general, and special ops in particular.

Then there was his famous temper. Kian was well aware of his shortcomings. He was impatient, and often too emotionally involved. Sometimes it was hard to shove all that aside and think clearly. That was where Turner came in. His cold, calculated and logical brain was the antidote to Kian's hotheadedness.

Picking up his desk phone, he punched in Turner's number and counted three rings. The guy never broke protocol and picked up the phone before that.

On the fourth, Turner answered. "What can I do for you, Kian?"

"I have an idea I want to run by you."

"Shoot."

"Lokan wants to get his hands on Ella. What if she can lure him into a trap?"

"The thought has crossed my mind once or twice. The problem is that she's not sophisticated enough to pull it off. What does an eighteen-year-old know about playing a game like this?"

"Not much, I agree. But she can get coaching from a pro. What if we get Carol to instruct her every step of the way?"

"Carol can't help Ella while she's dream-sharing with Lokan."

"That is true. But she can instruct her before and after."

"I think you've already made up your mind."

"Catching Lokan could be the biggest breakthrough we've had since this has started. If we know where the island is, we can revisit the idea of planting Carol there and letting her do her thing because we can get her out. I'm asking your opinion because right now I can't think of a downside. Lokan can't learn anything from Ella, and if we set a trap for him, we will make sure that she is not in any danger. I'll get the entire Guardian force to watch over her if needed. This is that important."

"What if after all this he doesn't talk?"

"Then we will hold him as a bargaining chip."

"In stasis?"

Kian hadn't thought that far. "We can decide what to do when we get there. But I'm inclined to keep him prisoner. The anticipation of torture can be worse than the torture itself, and we are in no hurry. We can wait long years for him to talk."

For a long moment, Turner remained quiet, and Kian imagined him staring into the distance while the cogs in his brain moved faster and faster, running through different scenarios and calculating the probabilities of success or failure for each.

"I agree. We need to seize this opportunity. If Lokan is the one doing the compulsion, then chances are that he is not under compulsion himself, which means that we can get him to talk one way or another."

Kian leaned back in his chair and swiveled it around to look out his window to the village square. "I'm not sure about that. Lokan can compel only humans. One of the other sons is rumored to be able to compel immortals as well. He might have done it to Lokan."

There was another long moment of silence. "What if it's Navuh himself who does the compelling?"

Kian frowned. It was possible, but it didn't make sense for the leader to bother with things like that. "I don't think Navuh would deal with such mundane matters. He is above that. But even if it is him, does it make a difference?"

"That depends on how he does it. I've given it some thought, and I suspect that he can do with compulsion what Yamanu can do with thralling. Think about it. He has an army of tens of thousands of warriors, loyal to him despite being treated like disposable trash. He is a demagogue, using propaganda to unite his people, but with a twist. How else is he keeping such tight control over his troops?"

"Fear can be a very effective motivator for loyalty. Any unrest is dealt with quickly and brutally." Kian swiveled back to face his desk. "With all due respect to your brilliant mind, Turner, I think you are jumping to conclusions. The propaganda and the iron-fist rule are the most logical explanations for his control. We don't need to look further than that."

"Perhaps. But you know me. I like solving mysteries, and things don't add up as neatly as you think."

Kian chuckled. "Then by all means, try to solve this one. But while you do that, can you come up with a plan for us to catch Lokan?"

"Shouldn't be too difficult."

"Maybe for you it isn't. I've already thought about and discarded several ideas."

"Let me hear them. Maybe I can use one and improve on it."

"I'd rather not. I don't want to contaminate your thinking process with my lousy suggestions."

14

ELLA

"I'm glad we don't have to schlep anything back home," Ella said as her mother parked the car in the village's underground.
"Did you have fun?"
"Yeah, I did. The best part was getting the girls to come out and eat lunch with Anandur on the front lawn." Ella smirked. "I proved the hoity-toity therapist wrong."
Tucking her new bedazzled T-shirt under her arm, she closed the door and headed for the elevators. Vivian had left hers as a sample for the girls to copy, which was a shame because it came out beautifully.
The purple T-shirt had been donated by Amanda, so of course it was top quality and as good as new, and the huge butterfly her mother had added to the front had turned it into something that could've been displayed proudly in a boutique.
"I wondered about that," her mother said. "I saw the lunch exodus, but I thought you'd convinced them it would be fun to eat out in the sun. I didn't know they were going to hang out with Anandur. How did you manage that?"
Ella shrugged. "Easy. I convinced the two queen bees to come with me to the second floor and peek at him from a window. He did his thing, winking and waving and looking charming. Then I told them that he was Wonder's fiancé and that was it. They were convinced he was a harmless teddy bear. When the other girls saw them picking up their plates and going outside, many followed."
"Queen bees, eh? Even in the sanctuary?"
"Of course. They have cliques like any other bunch of girls stuck in the same place. High schools, women's prisons, sanctuaries, it doesn't matter. I figured that if I got the queens to tell their stories first, it would be easier to convince the others."
"Did you ask them?"
"Not yet. I'm building up a rapport first."

Ella was starting to realize that it was going to be harder than she'd imagined. The girls were suspicious and skittish, and she braced for weeks of coaxing instead of days.

Her mother smiled. "Do you have a plan?"

"The stunt with Anandur was great for that, and also joining your bedazzling class and the self-defense training that Kri is teaching. I'm making friends. But this is going to take much longer than I anticipated. Those girls have been through a lot, and asking them to do something as emotionally draining as telling their story in front of a camera is not going to be easy."

Vivian leaned and kissed her cheek. "I'm so proud of you."

"It's nothing. It's just common sense."

"Still. You've taken on this difficult project, and you're pushing hard to make it happen."

By the time they reached the house, it was starting to get dark, and Ella's stomach was rumbling. "I'm hungry. Do we have any leftovers from yesterday?"

Vivian chuckled. "The guys probably finished them off. But we can make some sandwiches and a salad for dinner."

"Sounds like a plan." Ella opened the door and was hit by aromas that made her salivate. "What smells so good?"

"Barbecue," Parker said. "Magnus has ribs and steaks on the grill."

"And how are you going to eat them?" Vivian asked.

"I took four Motrin's, and I'm going to chew even if my gums bleed."

Shaking her head, Ella patted his shoulder. "Good luck with that."

"Your timing is impeccable." Magnus walked in with a loaded platter. "You are just in time for dinner."

Vivian smiled and gave him a quick peck on his cheek. "You are the best."

Ella eyed the table. "Should I cut up some veggies for a salad?" Other than meat and more meat, the only side dish was corn on the cob.

"Why spoil the taste?" Parker said. "Forget the salad, Ella. Sit down and let's eat before all of this amazing beef gets cold."

As she pulled out a chair and sat down, Ella had that same weird feeling she'd experienced when Parker had told her to do the model walk. She'd really wanted some fresh veggies, and yet she'd done what the little dweeb had told her to do.

"Anything wrong, Ella?" Her mother looked at her with concern in her eyes. "Suddenly, you seem troubled."

She smiled and waved a dismissive hand. "It's nothing. I'm just hungry."

Magnus forked a juicy steak and dropped it on her plate. "Do you want some ribs too?"

"Sure. And also corn."

How was Parker doing that? Was he doing anything? Or was it her?

The thing was, the sensation was familiar, just in reverse. Logan's compulsion prevented her from talking about him, and Parker's commands were making her do things she didn't want.

Could Logan messing with her head have opened her up for manipulation by others?

Or just by Parker?

"You're not eating, sweetie." Her mother pointed at her full plate. "Is it not well done enough for you?"

"I can put it back on the grill," Magnus offered.

Ella shook her head. "Mom, tell me that I have to eat."

Vivian looked at her with worry written all over her face. "Why?"

"Just do it."

"Okay. You have to eat, Ella."

Perhaps a direct command was needed? Or maybe it had to be issued by an immortal?

"Magnus, please tell me to cut a piece of steak and put it in my mouth. Just humor me."

Thankfully, Magnus just did what she'd asked without demanding an explanation. "Ella, cut a piece of the steak, put it in your mouth, and tell me if you like it."

Nothing.

"Parker, ask me to pass the salt."

Her brother rolled his eyes. "Is it a game?"

'Yes. Now say it."

"Please, pass the salt, Ella."

Nothing again.

But then Parker didn't care whether she did as he asked. Maybe he had to put some conviction behind it?

Rising to her feet, Ella lifted the platter. "There is too much meat on the table. I'm taking this back to the kitchen."

As she'd expected, Parker responded. "Put it down! I'm not done yet."

The moment he said to put it down, she almost dropped the platter, barely managing to hold on to it in order to lower it to the table without incident.

Letting out a breath, Ella slumped back in her chair. "I guess we've just found out what Parker's talent is. He can compel."

15

KIAN

As Kian hung up the phone with Magnus, he lifted his eyes to the ceiling and offered a prayer of thanks to the Fates. The last time he'd felt so grateful and so elated was when Syssi had come into his life.

The stars seemed to be aligning in his favor.

It had started with the very tangible possibility of capturing Navuh's son and finally discovering where the Doomers' fucking island was.

That in itself was a cause for celebration.

But if what Magnus had reported was true, then they finally had a compeller in the clan. Having an asset like that opened up a host of possibilities, and that was true even if the kid could only compel humans. But since Parker was exhibiting this talent so soon after his transition, he might grow up into a powerhouse.

Heck, the boy hadn't even transitioned fully yet, and already he could compel his sister without even meaning to do it.

"Is Amanda coming?" Syssi came out of the closet, dressed and ready to go.

The only downside of that phone call had been interrupting their making out session in the Jacuzzi that he'd planned on continuing in bed. But the news he'd gotten from Magnus was well worth the sacrifice. Besides, they could continue when they came back home.

After all, they were on a mission. Almost as much as Kian wanted to give Syssi the baby she craved, he wanted to be done with drinking Merlin's foul-tasting potion.

"Amanda is just as excited as I am. Probably more. So, of course, she is coming. I wouldn't be surprised if she's already there. Do you know how long we've been waiting for this?" She had no way of knowing, so he told her. "Since we discovered that someone in Navuh's camp could compel. If they have an immortal who can do it, then we should too. And here he is."

Kian shook his head. "Little Parker. Who would have thought."

Stretching up on her toes, Syssi wrapped her arms around his neck and kissed his lips. "We don't know that for sure yet. Ella might be imagining it. I don't want you to get your hopes up and then get disappointed."

"I won't. The girl knows what compulsion feels like. If anyone would know, it's her."

Syssi smiled sadly. "Parker could be inadvertently pushing a thrall on her. I don't think she can tell the difference. Heck, I don't know if I can tell a thrall from a compulsion."

She was right, of course. As always, Syssi was the voice of reason.

He stroked her cheek. "I know. And I have some doubts too. But on the other hand, I have a good feeling about this. Things are going our way for a change. First with Ella and Lokan, and now this. I sense a shift coming up in this conflict. We are finally getting a break."

"Did we switch places? Are you the seer now?"

Kian laughed. "I don't know about that. First, you will have to start barking orders at everyone and cussing up a storm. Then I'll consider us switched."

"Oh, no." She pretended horror. "I can't do that. If I start cussing, you're going to spank me."

Chuckling, he cupped her butt cheeks and lifted her up. "That should be an incentive, not a deterrent." He pressed his erection against her mound.

"Indeed." Syssi's cheeks pinked as they usually did when she was thinking naughty thoughts. "People are waiting for us. We'd better get moving."

He nuzzled her neck and then let her slide down his body. "I want you to think up some creative cuss words for later tonight."

Syssi was funny that way. Even though cussing was their agreed-upon invitation to playtime, she had a hard time saying anything harsher than shit or crap. Instead, she invented cusses that were often too cute or just plain hilarious. Like Wooly Wanker, or Jerkemaia Johnson. That one had another variation —Jerkorama Douchensky.

Her blush deepened. "It's a deal."

16

JULIAN

$\mathcal{B}$y the time Julian was done with the last contractor, the sun had set, and he was more than ready to call it a day. Or rather call Ella and ask her how her day at the sanctuary had gone and see if she wasn't too tired to see him.

Even though it was torture to hold her in his arms and wait for her to make each move, it was a sweet torment.

Yeah, he must be a closet masochist. No one should look forward to a case of blue balls. But he did.

Perhaps it was the novelty of it. After years of having girls practically dropping their panties for him without him having to even ask, the old-fashioned courtship dance was refreshing.

"Do you mind driving?" he asked Yamanu. "I want to make a phone call."

"No problem, buddy." He smirked. "I know you're missing your girl."

As Yamanu got in the driver's seat, Julian got in on the other side and pulled out his phone.

Ella answered right away. "Julian, I'm so glad you called. Are you back home?"

"I'm on my way. What's up?"

"Come straight to my house."

He frowned. "Why? Not that I need a second invitation. But did something happen?"

"Maybe. We are not sure yet. But you will want to be here. Heck, I want you here."

"Can you give me a clue?"

She hesitated for a moment. "It has to do with Parker and his special talent. But that's all I'm going to say."

Julian let out a relieved breath. As long as it wasn't more bad news about Ella, he was good. "I can be there in about twenty-five minutes."

"Perfect. Kian and Syssi are coming too. And so is Amanda."

"Now you've really got me curious."

She laughed. "See you here, Julian." The call ended.

"Little Parker has discovered his special talent?" Yamanu asked.

"It sounds like it's a big deal. Otherwise, Kian wouldn't have bothered coming over there to check it out."

Yamanu rubbed his hand over his clean-shaven jaw. "I wonder what it is. Probably telepathy, like his mother and sister."

"Not necessarily. Talents are kind of random. I'm surprised that Vivian and Ella share the same one. The commonality is usually in how powerful it is."

"Makes sense." Yamanu chuckled. "My mother can't thrall for shit. But she can do other things."

Julian's ears perked up. Any nugget of information about Yamanu could shed some light on the mystery he was. "What's her talent?"

"Nagging."

"Seriously."

"I am serious. She has everyone doing exactly what she wants just to stop the nagging. That's one hell of a power."

Julian sighed. Yamanu was pulling his chain. This mystery wasn't going to get solved anytime soon, but at least he was going to find out what Parker could do.

The rest of the drive was spent with Yamanu telling him one anecdote after another about his mother's nagging and what she'd managed to achieve with it, and by the time the Guardian parked the car, Julian was inclined to believe him that it was a special talent.

"Is she very charming? Because I can't see people cooperating with a horrible nag unless she has some redeeming qualities."

Yamanu smiled wistfully. "My mother is one hell of a woman. She's always ready to help in any way she can, and she can do a lot. Many owe her favors, and she is not shy about collecting."

They parted at the village square, with Yamanu heading to his house and Julian turning toward Ella's.

He got there at the same time as Kian and Syssi did.

"Hello, Julian." Syssi gave him a quick one-armed hug.

Kian nodded in his direction and knocked on the door.

Amanda opened it. "Good, you are all here, so we can finally begin with the testing."

Given Amanda's excitement, Parker's talent must really be a big deal.

As soon as he entered, Ella ran up to him and took his hand. "Come sit with me. We are about to begin."

He let her pull him to an armchair. "Both of us can squeeze in here."

"Or you can sit on my lap."

She smiled. "I can do that."

"Okay, Master Parker. Let's start," Amanda said. "You've demonstrated that you can compel Ella to do what you want, now let's try your mother."

Julian's eyes widened. "Compulsion? That's his talent? It's impossible."

Ella patted his arm. "We will find out soon enough."

"Mom, give me ten dollars," Parker said.

DARK DREAM'S UNRAVELING

Vivian shook her head. "I don't feel anything."

"You need to really want it," Ella said. "Ask for a steak dinner every night for the rest of the week."

Parker grimaced. "Right now I don't want any. My gums are hurting."

"So think about something else that you really want, and that Mom wouldn't normally agree to."

Parker scratched his head, crossed his legs, looked up at the ceiling, and then smirked. "I know the perfect thing." He looked at Vivian. "Sing me that lullaby you used to sing when I was little. The one about me being your sunshine."

Ella snorted. "That's a good one, Mom. I know how much you hate singing in public."

Vivian's cheeks turned red, and she shook her head, but she started singing. Very, very quietly.

"Louder, Mom. I can't hear you."

It was evident that Vivian was struggling against the compulsion. Nevertheless, her voice got louder.

She really was a lousy singer. Not tone deaf, she was on key, but her voice was cracking like a teenage boy's.

"Okay, Mom. That's enough. You can stop."

Vivian let out a breath and then looked at Ella. "Now I know how you feel. It's terrible."

Amanda clapped her hands. "Amazing demonstration, Master Parker. Now we need to try it on an immortal."

Sitting on a bar stool and facing a room full of adults, Parker was grinning from ear to ear. The kid was eating up the attention.

"Julian, come play video games with me."

Julian wasn't sure whether he felt something or not, but he found it easy to refuse. "Sorry, kid, I'd rather take your sister out for a walk."

"Try me," Magnus offered.

Parker smirked. "No problem. Just remember that I have a good excuse."

"Go ahead."

"Magnus, give me your beer. I want to taste that Snake Venom you guys keep chugging."

Magnus held out the bottle as if handing it to Parker, but then shook his head and laughed. "Not working, buddy."

"Bummer."

"Did you really want to taste that beer?" Ella asked.

"I did. And I tried really hard. But I guess it doesn't work on immortals."

Amanda walked up to him and kissed his cheek. "You did very well. Your powers are just starting to develop. I have no doubt that you'll become formidable."

Parker looked at her with hopeful eyes. "You really think so?"

"I'm positive. You just keep practicing and flexing those mental muscles of yours. Just make sure you don't do that on unsuspecting victims. You need to tell people before you try it on them. Compulsion is a very serious matter and doing it without getting permission is considered a crime. The only exceptions are the same as for thralling. If it's in self-defense or to defend others and to keep the secret of our immortality."

He nodded. "I get it."

"Good. Now I want you to try something that is most likely not going to work, but it's worth a try. Command Ella to talk about Mr. D."

Julian sucked in a breath, and so did Ella.

"I've got my fingers crossed." She lifted both hands to show everyone. "Go for it, Parker. Give it all you got."

The kid swallowed and nodded. "Ella, tell me who Mr. D is. Now!"

"Logan," Ella blurted out and then clapped her hands. "It worked! I can't believe that it did!"

She jumped off Julian's lap and ran up to her brother. "I love you." She wrapped her arms around him and tried to lift him off the stool, but he was too heavy for her. "Crap, you're getting big." She wiped her eyes.

"He calls himself Logan?" Kian asked.

Ella turned to him and nodded. "Not very imaginative, right?"

"Tell us a little more," Amanda prompted. "I want to make sure it worked."

"I met Logan when I was with Gorchenco. Then he started popping up in my dreams. At first, he was really creepy and scared the hell out of me, but then he learned to behave, and now he's okay. He even helped me out right after the rescue. When I was feeling down, he complimented me at a time when I really needed it."

Julian felt his fangs starting to elongate. The way Ella was talking about the Doomer, it sounded as if she was fond of him. He knew she was supposed to pretend when Lokan invaded her dreams, but there was no reason for her to pretend now.

Kian got up, walked over to Parker, and clapped him on the back. "Parker, my boy. You have no idea what a great asset you are to the clan. You're the first clan member with the power to compel, which in itself is a miracle. But that you can remove a compulsion, or rather overpower someone else's, is an even bigger one."

Embarrassed, Parker lowered his eyes. "Thank you." But his momentary shyness didn't last long. "So, does that mean that I can be a Guardian? You need me, right?"

Kian chuckled. "The clan needs you, Parker. And yes, you're welcome to join the Guardian training program once you reach majority. Which is seventeen in our culture."

Parker waved a dismissive hand. "That's silly. Why wait so long? I can be helpful right now."

Kian shook his head. "I know. But you're still a kid. We will see. The clan's needs will have to be balanced with yours. And naturally, your mother will need to approve every time we ask for your help." He glanced at Magnus. "And once the adoption is complete, your stepfather will have to approve too."

Parker squared his shoulders. "My mom and Magnus are both cool. You have nothing to worry about, Boss man. They will approve."

17

ELLA

"It's such a relief to be out from under his control," Ella said, just to say something.

Walking hand in hand through the lush village grounds could've been pleasant if not for the big fat elephant lodged between her and Julian.

It used to be easy to talk to him, about anything, but that was when Ella hadn't felt like a cheater.

"I can imagine. Parker saved the day."

She chuckled. "Yeah, he did. From now on, it's going to be a nightmare living with him and his overblown ego. It's not good for a kid his age to have such power."

"Magnus should have the talk with him."

She lifted a brow. "About girls? I don't think it's necessary. Mom already did that, and I'm pretty sure Parker watches porn."

"Not that kind of talk." Julian spotted a bench and headed in its direction. Sitting down, he pulled Ella onto his lap. "It's the talk every newly turned boy gets. Mostly it is done by the mothers, but sometimes one of the male immortals gets involved. Especially if the boy gets in trouble."

Ella wished he hadn't done it. Sitting in such an intimate way after dream-kissing another guy felt wrong. Then again, refusing to sit in his lap would hurt Julian's feelings. Good thing that she'd become such an adept actress. If she played it right, Julian might not notice the change in her. And if he did, she could come up with plenty of excuses.

"What kind of trouble?"

"Let me put it this way. Being able to thrall and refraining from using it requires a strong moral code that many teenage boys don't have. You think being good-looking leads to feelings of entitlement? Imagine what being a powerful immortal among humans leads to."

"Dropped panties?"

He nodded. "But not for the right reason, and not voluntarily. That's why the talk is necessary. The penalty for abusing the thralling power is severe. I'm sure the same applies to compulsion."

It reminded her of Logan's behavior in the first dream they'd shared. Apparently, Doomers didn't get the same talk as the clan boys, and thralling an unsuspecting human female into having sex with them was the norm. That's why Logan had just gone for it and had forced a kiss on her without bothering to check if she was interested.

Entitlement.

He was the son of a powerful leader, which probably made him much worse than the average Doomer in that respect. Heck, the human sons of politicians and rich people weren't much better.

She'd read about that. The son of a well-known CEO had raped a girl in his Ivy League college, and it had been covered up.

Power and money were morally corrupting. Or maybe it was simply that some people were naturally moral or amoral, and the amoral ones acted upon their urges when they were guaranteed immunity.

What she wondered, though, was whether Logan's behavior had improved because of her influence, or just because he knew he needed to do better in order to entrap her.

Most likely, it was the second one. But then again, maybe not. People could change, right?

"What are you thinking about that makes you frown like this?" Using his forefinger, Julian massaged the crease between her eyebrows.

Crap. She didn't want to talk to him about Logan.

What she was doing was already bad enough. She didn't need to hurt his feelings too. But what about honesty?

Looking at her hands instead of his face, she shrugged. "I was thinking about my dream encounters. Doomers don't get the talk you mentioned. They think that they can take what they want either by physical or mental force."

Julian's entire body stiffened. "Did he force you to do anything in the dreams?"

She nodded. "The first time he invaded my dreams, he kissed me against my will. But, later on, he mellowed down. I don't know if it's because he wants me to like him, or because he's realized the error of his ways."

His eyes blazing blue fire, Julian snorted. "He's trying to play you. Don't fall for that."

"Yeah, that was what I thought too. But the joke is on him, since I'm playing him back." With that admission, Ella looked away once more.

She hadn't disclosed any details, but Julian was a smart enough guy to figure it out.

When a long moment passed, and he didn't respond, Ella chanced a glance at his face and wished she hadn't.

Not because of the glowing eyes or the pointy fangs that had punched out over his lower lip, she was no longer scared of those, but because of the inner emotional battle that was raging on his handsome face.

"I don't want you to do that."

Ella sighed. "I know. And I don't want to do it either. Even though it's happening in dreamland, it feels real, and it's like a replay of what I had to do with the Russian. But this is too important an opportunity." She looked up at him. "You must realize that."

"Did Kian ask you to do it?"

She shrugged. "You were there with me, so you know what he asked for. But I have a feeling he is going to ask for more. Kian doesn't want to involve me in this either, but guess what? I'm in it whether I want to be or not, so I'd better make the best of it and get something valuable for the clan."

Julian nodded. "Logically, I get it. Emotionally, every cell in my body rebels against it. I can't stand the thought of you smiling at the Doomer, let alone doing more than that."

Ella tilted her head. "Is it because you are jealous, or because you are afraid for me?"

"Both. But mostly I'm jealous."

She liked that he was honest with her. Two points for Julian.

"Don't be. I only pretend to like him, but you I like for real." It was the truth, just not the whole truth. She wasn't going to fess up to her annoying attraction to the bad boy.

Letting out a breath, Julian rubbed a hand over his jaw. "Perhaps it would not be so bad if you weren't distancing yourself from me. I can feel you pulling away."

She was, so there was no denying it.

"I'm afraid my feelings for you will seep through into the dreams. He can't know that I'm serious about you."

Julian arched a brow. "You are?"

"Of course, I am, you silly."

"Then prove it. Kiss me."

Ella preferred for Julian to do the kissing. "Why don't you kiss me?"

He shook his head. "I told you. All the power is yours. I'm not going to pressure you into anything."

"You are not pressuring me if I'm asking you to kiss me."

Letting out an exasperated sigh, Julian cupped the back of her head. "But I did. I've already broken my own rules. I asked you to prove that you like me by kissing me."

"Semantics. Just kiss me, Julian."

His lips were soft on hers, gentle. Julian wasn't demanding anything, he was coaxing.

It wasn't what she wanted, and for some reason she felt annoyed, which made her feel like a jerk. But even though Julian was pouring his heart into his gentle kiss, it wasn't doing anything for her, and Ella hated the lukewarm response his kiss was eliciting.

Why wasn't this enough to ignite her passion?

Frustrated, she threaded her fingers through his hair and pulled him down to her, kissing him the way she wanted to be kissed.

With a tortured groan, Julian's hand tightened on her nape, his fingers digging into her flesh for a brief moment before he loosened his grip.

"I'm sorry," he murmured into her mouth. "I got carried away."

18

MAGNUS

As Magnus collected the empty coffee mugs and carried them to the sink, he thought about the talk he had to have with Parker.

The one every immortal boy got.

The difference was that Parker was much younger than the average age that it was usually done at, and if not for his newly discovered talent, it could have waited for at least a couple of years.

By then Vivian would have been familiar with clan laws and could have done it herself.

Unfortunately, though, the task fell to him, and it was not going to be easy to explain to both mother and son the consequences of using compulsion or thralling on unsuspecting victims to one's advantage.

Cleaning the mugs by hand, Magnus took his time at the sink while planning his speech.

If only he didn't suck at things like that. Maybe it would be better to send Parker to Kian for the talk? If anyone was going to instill fear in the kid, it was him.

But that was a cowardly move.

If he hoped to be a father to Parker in more than just name, Magnus had no choice but to step up to the plate and give the kid the talk himself.

Wiping his hands on a dishrag, he glanced at the living room. Parker was already gone, probably in his room gaming, and Vivian was wiping the dining table clean.

When she was done, he walked up to her and pulled her into his arms. "One hell of a night, eh?"

"Yeah, you could say so. I'm still trying to wrap my head around it. How come my kids' talents are so powerful? My mother, who we obviously inherited the genes from, never exhibited anything out of the ordinary."

"How about her family? Any weird aunts or uncles? Eccentric grandparents?"

Vivian shook her head. "I was a miracle baby who came when my parents were in their mid-forties. I had one grandmother who lived in Florida and died when I was ten, and she had no siblings."

"It's a shame." He leaned and kissed her lips. "Now you have an entire clan of relatives."

She smiled. "I love it. It's so nice to have a big family."

"I agree." He leaned his forehead against hers. "I have to talk to Parker about his new powers, and I need you to be there when I do it."

"Why?"

"Clan law is very specific about the use of thralling, and the same rules apply to compulsion even though it's not specified. But since both can be used to gain an unfair advantage over humans, I'm sure the punishment for using either in an unlawful way is the same."

She frowned. "What's the punishment?"

"It'd be better if I explained it to Parker and you at the same time. You know how bad I am at things like that."

"You'll do fine."

He definitely hoped so. "Do you want to call him out here, or should we go to his room? I don't know what the protocol is for having a talk with a kid."

"I'll get him."

"Thank you."

Without thinking, Magnus headed back to the kitchen, opened the fridge, and pulled out another bottle of Snake Venom.

Like that was a good example to give the kid.

Was that the message he wanted to impart on an impressionable boy? That when a tough talk was coming the way to go was to reach for liquid courage?

Vivian expected him to be a positive role model for her kids.

Magnus put the beer back and pulled out a water bottle instead.

"You wanted to talk to me?" Parker asked as he sat on one of the barstools.

"Yes. But let's take it to the living room couch."

When Parker and Vivian were seated, Magnus sat on the coffee table facing them. "Remember what Amanda told you about asking permission before practicing your talent?"

"What about it?"

"I want to explain what she meant so there will be no misunderstandings."

"I got it. She said not to do it without asking permission first. What else?"

"You shouldn't use it on humans either. At times, you'll be tempted to, and other times you might not even realize that you're pushing compulsion on them. You need to pay attention and make sure that you don't do it unintentionally."

Parker nodded. "I didn't know I was compelling Ella to do the model walk. I just asked her to do it, and she did."

"Do you remember how you felt when you asked her? What tone of voice you used?"

"I didn't feel anything different, if that's what you mean. I wanted her to do it and thought that she was being stubborn, or shy."

"Did you get angry?"

"Maybe a little bit."

"When you practice on Ella and your mom, pay attention to how it feels."

"I will."

"You can also practice on me. But every time you do, you need to give us a warning."

"Okay."

Magnus smoothed his hand over his goatee. "Right now it's not a problem yet, but when you get a little older, you might get tempted to use your power on girls."

Parker's eyes widened. "What do you mean? Like to get a kiss or something?"

It was endearing that he was still so innocent despite his secret forays into anime porn.

"Yeah, like that. Always ask permission first. You might think that the girl wants a kiss, but don't kiss her unless you're sure she does."

Parker frowned. "Should I just ask, can I kiss you?"

"That's one way, and it's a very good one. But if you're embarrassed about asking, you can also stop a moment before your lips touch and let her close the distance."

Blushing all shades of red, Parker shrugged, pretending nonchalance. "I'm not going to kiss anyone for years. And besides, what does it have to do with my talent? This is basic stuff every guy should know."

Magnus felt his chest swell with pride even though Parker's attitude wasn't his doing. It was Vivian's.

"You are absolutely right. But when you can thrall or compel, it is easy to get consent that otherwise would not have been granted."

"I will never do that."

"I believe you. Nevertheless, I have to tell you what the consequences of breaking this most important law are." He took a deep breath. "It might seem barbaric to you, but you have to remember that teenage boys are usually not as mature and level-headed as you are, and when they have supernatural powers, it's even worse."

"You're scaring me with all this pep talk, Magnus. Just say it."

"Whipping. The penalty is whipping."

Vivian sucked in a breath. "That really is barbaric. Tell me that it hasn't been done in ages."

Magnus grimaced. "Unfortunately, I can't. It wasn't a boy, though. The offender knew what he was doing and was willing to suffer the consequences. I don't want to say too much, but he had a good reason for what he did. The judge wanted to reduce his sentence to a short prison stay, but he preferred to get it over with."

She shook her head. "Is he a masochist?"

"I don't think so. You forget how quickly we heal. He was fine the next day and could go back to work."

Parker hadn't said a word and was still staring wide-eyed at Magnus.

"Are you okay, buddy?"

Parker shook his head. "I'm just not going to do it. At all. I'm going to always ask nicely and say please, so no one can accuse me of compelling anyone."

"Don't be scared. As long as you ask permission, it'll be okay. And anyway, you are only going to practice on your family. We are not going to judge you too harshly if you slip up here and there."

19

ELLA

With thoughts of Julian filling her mind, Ella was afraid to go to sleep. If Logan entered her dream, she couldn't afford to be consumed by thoughts about another man.

Except, things were not working between them, and even though she'd told herself to wait until the thing with Logan was over, it bothered her.

Julian was the one for her. Ella knew it like she knew her own face in the mirror, before and after the makeover. They were destined to be together, and she had to fix what was broken.

Was it her?

Yeah, it definitely was. How could she be falling in love with one man while feeling attracted to another?

Julian was the one she wanted to spend her nights with, sleeping in the safety of his arms, listening to his heart beating against her chest, looking into his eyes first thing when she opened hers in the morning.

This was her future, the one that gave her hope and made her heavy heart feel lighter.

Until she remembered the dark one, with his semi-evil smirk, his condescending attitude, and the dark eyes that emitted a red demonic glow whenever he got excited.

Then her heart would get heavy again, and the hope for a better future would seem distant and unachievable.

If only the clan didn't need her help, and if she could find a way to banish Logan from her dreams, she might be able to forget him and concentrate on building her relationship with Julian.

Except, indulging in what ifs was not going to solve those problems for her. The clan needed her, and she had no way of getting rid of Logan.

With an exasperated sigh, Ella opened her laptop and searched the internet for her old high school's site. If her login credentials still worked, she could download pictures from the recent yearbooks which, thankfully, had all been digital to save on printing costs.

It was a small security breach, but she was sure Gorchenco's people wouldn't go as far as checking that. Entering her user name and password, she had little hope of getting in, but apparently her school hadn't revoked her user credentials yet.

First, she copied and pasted Maddie's picture, then enlarged it until it filled an entire page. Next, went Mr. Panties Fetish, Jim. A best friend and a pretend boyfriend would be enough to fill her head.

After printing out both, she taped them to the bathroom mirror next to hers.

Jim even had the same coloring as Julian, though his hair was short, his face was clean-shaven, and he wasn't nearly as handsome. But he would do. As far as Logan was concerned, that was the guy she was dating.

Lying in bed, Ella closed her eyes and replayed old memories in her head. Hanging out with Maddie, Jim's smiling face, sleeping over at Maddie's, laughing her ass off as she'd told her best friend about Jim's panties obsession.

She hadn't realized it back then, but those were the good times. That Ella no longer existed, but the new Ella could still enjoy those memories and fall asleep smiling.

"Come on, Ella, what's the big deal? I'll pay you for the fucking panties. How much did they cost? Five bucks?" Bracing his beefy arm on the lockers, Jim smirked and leaned over her. "Or are you hiding something sexy under those jeans?"

Laughing, she pushed on his chest. "Give it up, Jim. You're not adding mine to your collection."

He didn't resist, letting her push him off. "To be included in my collection is an honor, Ella."

Walking away, she flipped him the bird. He was such an asshole, but she liked him anyway. The good thing about Jim was that he didn't take himself too seriously.

"Is that the guy you're seeing?" Logan asked.

Suddenly, she was not walking down the wide corridor of her high school, but a fancy shopping mall's.

"Where are we?"

"Paris. I got sick of your beach. I hope you don't mind the change in scenery."

Wow, that was progress for Logan. He was actually interested in her opinion.

To reward him, Ella threaded her arm through his. "Not at all. I've always wanted to see Paris. Although the inside of a mall doesn't count as sightseeing."

He grinned at her. "Where would you like to go?"

"The Champs-Élysées."

He snapped his fingers. "Voilà."

"Awesome." She leaned her head against his bicep. "You're learning. Taking a girl to Paris is so romantic."

He chuckled. "No one has ever accused me of being romantic. I've never even taken a woman on a date."

Ella faked surprise. "A handsome guy like you? You must be joking. I'm sure it was not for lack of candidates."

"No, of course not. I just don't date." He winked. "I take them straight to my bed."

Ella huffed. "Well, I'm not that sort of girl. If you want a chance with me, you'll have to behave like a gentleman and take me all over the world." She waved a hand at the street. "Or just to Paris. It's such a beautiful city."

"I can take you wherever you want to go. The one caveat is that it has to be a place I've been to before. Otherwise, I can't create it in my mind."

"Have you been to many places?"

"I've traveled all over the world." He looked down at her. "But most of it is not as pretty as this."

"Then take me only to the nice parts. Which city is your favorite?"

"St. Petersburg is beautiful."

That reminded Ella of the Russian. "How is Gorchenco doing?"

"Recuperating. He's a stubborn human. He'll be fine. Physically."

Ella ignored the 'human' slip up, pretending not to notice. "Maybe you should suggest a visit to that vacation spot you guys were talking about at that lunch meeting. Something to take his mind off his loss. In fact, I'm curious about that place. Can you take me there?"

Logan laughed. "It's beautiful, but I don't think you're going to like it there. It's where rich men go to indulge, if you catch my drift."

"Wow, Logan, you've changed so much since our first meeting. Back then you would've just said that it was a sex resort."

Wrapping his arm around her shoulders, he tucked her closer against his side. "I want you, Ella, you know that, and it gives you power over me. In the past, I would've resented you for it, but I find myself enjoying being different with you. It's a new experience for me, and I didn't think there were any left for me to try."

She smiled at him sweetly. "That's nonsense, Logan, you are talking like an old man. There is plenty you haven't experienced yet. And if you play your cards right, and by that I mean keep being nice and not acting like a jerk, you might enjoy those experiences with me."

20

KIAN

"Have a great day at work." Kian pulled Syssi into his arms for one last kiss before they had to part for the day.

He hated letting her go and kept on kissing her until she pushed on his chest. "I'm already late, my love. I have to go."

He nodded, handing her the coffee thermos Okidu had prepared for her. "Don't drink and drive." He winked.

She popped the lid and took a sip. "Only when I'm waiting for the lights to change. Don't work too hard."

"I'll try." Kian closed her door and then watched her drive away.

On his way to the office, he stopped by the row of vending machines and bought a pastry, popping it into his mouth as he moved over to the coffee machine and ordered a double cappuccino.

Usually he and Syssi had breakfast together, and that included at least two cups of her unrivaled cappuccinos, but this morning's romp had taken a little longer, and they'd had to rush out without eating.

Cappuccino cup in hand and his laptop tucked under his arm, Kian took the stairs to his office two at a time. With as little time as he was spending in the gym lately, he needed to take every opportunity to do at least something.

Regrettably, frequent sex with his wife didn't count as exercise.

Kian smiled. If it did, his quota would have been covered.

Ah, the good life.

As he reached the top of the stairs and turned into the corridor, he found Turner waiting for him outside his office.

If it were anyone else, Kian would have sensed his presence as he was coming up, but with Turner's lack of emotional scents, he had no forewarning. It was disconcerting to an immortal who relied on his sense of smell to detect unexpected visitors.

The guy should at least put some cologne on to announce his presence, but he was probably avoiding it purposely so he could sneak up on people.

"Good morning, Turner. What brings you here so early?"

"I wanted to talk to you before I left for the office. I have an idea I want to run by you."

"You could've waited inside. My door isn't locked." Kian opened the way.

Following, Turner closed the door and then pulled out one of the visitors' chairs. "After our talk yesterday, I spent some time thinking about a safe way for Ella to lure Lokan into a trap."

Putting his coffee cup and laptop down, Kian sat behind his desk. "Go on."

"Ella is eighteen and a recent graduate from high school. Before she was taken, she had plans to go to college. I think she should start looking into that again."

"That is a good excuse to get her out in the open. But if she lives on campus, it's going to be difficult to guard her."

Turner shook his head. "That's not what I'm suggesting. All she needs to do for now is start thinking about colleges and talk about it with Lokan. Let him suggest one. If he takes the bait, he will probably choose one that's near him, and reveal his general location. Not that it's necessary for my plan to work. But if she schedules a visit to the college he suggested, he's not going to be overly suspicious about her decision to check it out."

"We lure him during her visit."

"Precisely. And that also solves another variable that kept bothering me. What if Lokan is interested in Ella because of the telepathy, and he uses seduction as a way to lure her to him?"

"That's a possibility, but I don't see how it affects our plans for capturing him."

Turner smirked. "Since Ella and Vivian can only communicate with each other, their talents are useless unless he has both of them. If Lokan wants to use Ella's telepathy, he would need Vivian too. We have to assume that he probed Ella's mind during their one face-to-face meeting and that he knows that."

Although by now Kian shouldn't have been surprised by Turner's smarts, he was nevertheless impressed. The idea that Lokan might be more interested in Ella for her ability than her looks hadn't even crossed Kian's mind. He'd been so focused on her uncommon beauty and what had happened to her before that he hadn't taken into consideration the most unique thing about her.

Unlike Kian, Turner was logical and methodical. Now that he'd brought it up, it seemed so obvious, but it had taken someone who thought with his brain and not his heart to consider all the variables.

"Brilliant as always, my friend. An eighteen-year-old girl wouldn't travel alone to tour a college. Her mother would go with her."

Turner nodded. "We can have Guardians stationed in the same hotel Ella and Vivian are going to stay in, other Guardians posing as the taxi drivers taking them places, and we can have some posing as students who are giving them the college tour. They won't be without protection even for a moment."

Kian smirked. "I like it."

"I can see only one problem with my plan, but it's a major one. If Lokan can compel immortals, then this is out because we won't be able to keep Ella and Vivian safe. Not if he can compel a Guardian to let them go."

Kian rapped his fingers on the desk. "Dalhu doesn't think so. As far as he knows, Lokan can only compel humans."

"But he is not certain. I won't risk Ella and Vivian's safety unless I'm sure we can protect them and overpower Lokan."

Kian pulled out his phone. "Instead of speculating, we should talk to the man himself." He looked at Turner before pressing the call button. "Do you have time now, or should I tell Dalhu to come over this evening?"

Turner leaned back in the chair and crossed his arms over his chest. "I'll wait. Otherwise, the uncertainty is going to bug me all day long."

21

DALHU

*A*bsorbed in sketching the outline for a new painting, Dalhu ignored the phone ringing.

Whoever was calling was most likely looking for Amanda, not him, but she had left for the university already. The caller would either leave a message or try her cellphone number.

But when the ringing stopped and immediately started again, Dalhu got worried.

What if it was Amanda trying to reach him?

What if she had car trouble? Like a blown tire she needed him to change?

But why would she call the house phone instead of his cell?

In his rush to pick up, Dalhu didn't wipe his hands clean and cursed as his charcoal-covered fingers stained the white receiver.

"What?" he barked into the phone.

"Am I calling at a bad time?" Kian asked.

Fuck.

"No, it's nothing. I answered the phone with dirty hands. If you're looking for Amanda, call her cellphone. She already left."

"For a change, I don't need Amanda. I need you. How quickly can you get to my office?"

Dalhu tensed. "What's going on?"

"Relax. Everything is fine. I have Turner here, and we need to ask you a few questions about Navuh and his sons."

"I'll be there in ten minutes."

"We are waiting."

Dalhu would rather not talk about the fucking island and its leaders. The less he thought about it, the more he could forget. He would much rather focus on the blissful life he led with Amanda and his canvases.

But Kian needed his help, and he owed the guy.

Kian hadn't welcomed him into the clan with open arms, far from it, but he had been man enough to change his mind and accept a former enemy not only as his sister's mate, but as a full-fledged, trusted clan member.

In a hurry, he washed his hands and put on clean clothes that he double-checked for paint splashes. If he was being called in as a consultant, he'd better look the part.

When Dalhu knocked on Kian's door, it was precisely ten minutes after he hung up the phone.

"Come in!"

He walked in and pulled out a chair next to Turner. "Morning."

The guy nodded.

"How can I help you?" Dalhu asked Kian.

Turner answered, "Tell us everything you know about compulsion on the island. Who was doing it, when was it done, what were the effects, how long did it take you to shake it off, and how did you manage to do it?"

Dalhu rubbed a hand over the back of his neck. "That's a lot of questions, and the truth is that what I know is no more than speculation. It's not like we got lined up for compulsion before leaving the island. I didn't even know I was under one until over time it started to fade, and I realized that I could think more clearly."

The rage had subsided too. But that might have had nothing to do with the compulsion. He'd had a lot of baggage stored deep inside him, and it had simmered and festered for centuries. If not for Amanda and his love for her, that rage might have still ruled his life.

Kian waved a dismissive hand. "I told Turner that. Just tell us what you can. Figuring out Lokan's powers is most important to us. The more information you can provide, the more clues we will have to piece together and maybe get a better understanding as to who is doing what and how."

Dalhu nodded. "Two of Navuh's sons are rumored to have compulsion powers. One is Lokan, and I know for a fact that he is the one who's compelling the human pilots to never reveal the island's location. In his case, there is little or no doubt that he can do that. I don't think he can compel immortals because he is not in charge of debriefing the units going out. Although things could've changed since I left."

"Who is the other son?"

"Kolhud. But the thing is that he wasn't there to brief my team either. I never interacted with him. We got briefed by Hocken, who as far as I know has no special powers."

"Interesting." Turner rubbed his chin. "Are you sure you've been compelled at all?"

"I'm sure. The more time I was away from the island, the saner I got. It felt like a fog was lifting from my brain." He shook his head. "Not a fog, since fog is benign. It was more like a suffocating haze."

Kian and Turner exchanged glances. Did they doubt him? Were they thinking that he wasn't right in the head?

Pinning Dalhu with his pale blue eyes, Turner leaned closer. "What you've felt could have been psychosomatic. You weren't happy in the Brotherhood, and you were conflicted about what you were doing."

"I don't think so."

He hadn't been. Back then he hadn't cared one way or another. Not about the Brotherhood, and not about the clan, and certainly not about the humans.

He'd been filled with hate and loathing for everything and everyone.

Amanda had changed that. His love for her burned away all the sludge that had taken residence in his soul, or at least most of it. Her people had become his people, and that was why he cared. It was as simple as that.

"What about the others?" Kian asked. "Were you the only one under compulsion, or was the rest of your unit as well? It seems like a waste of resources to compel each soldier before sending him on a mission. If it were me, I would've bothered only with the commanders and left it up to them to control their men."

Dalhu shrugged. "Doomers never stay away from the island for more than a couple of months. Even those who are stationed abroad have to come back once a month and give a report in person. Two at the most. They usually stay for a few days and attend Navuh's propaganda sermons. And then there are the five daily mandatory adulations to reinforce the soldiers' devotion. Navuh personally leads the evening one. He is a very powerful demagogue."

Turner rubbed his chin again. "Maybe he is more than that. What if he is capable of mass compulsion? That would explain his tight hold on his people, and why there has been no rebellion against him yet. In fact, he must be controlling the sons too, since they are the most likely usurpers."

Kian shook his head. "It doesn't make sense. Navuh is vain. Why would he hide having such power and pretend that one of his sons has it instead?"

"Actually, it makes perfect sense," Dalhu said. "Compulsion is like thralling. A cheat. A hack. An ability that is inherited. What would gain Navuh more respect? This, or a belief that his success is the result of his charisma and unparalleled leadership skills?"

Kian still didn't look convinced. "So let me get this straight. What you and Turner are saying is that through his propaganda sermons, Navuh compels his entire force to believe in his lies and stay loyal to him and the cause, and then reinforces it every evening through the mandatory devotions?"

Turner nodded. "We are speculating here. But it is the only logical conclusion I can make. If Dalhu and his team didn't get briefed by either of the two sons suspected of having the ability, then who could've put the compulsion on Dalhu? On the other hand, they all attended the sermons and the devotions on a regular basis. If Navuh's compulsion works the way we think, then there is no need to do anything special before sending the soldiers on a mission."

Staring at Turner, Kian rapped his fingers on his desk. "None of the Doomers we captured in the past talked. Most because they didn't know anything, but some must have known something but were under compulsion not to talk. How was that command delivered?" He turned to Dalhu. "Does Navuh repeat a silencing order in each of his sermons?"

Dalhu shook his head. "Not directly, but he repeated the word secret a lot. He would talk about our secret mission to one day rule the world, and that it would no longer be a secret once the clan was obliterated and all of humanity trembled before us. Or he would talk about the secret island paradise he'd created for the Brotherhood and how grateful we all needed to be to him for that. I've never thought much of it, regarding it as propaganda and self-aggrandizing, but maybe there was more to it."

22

JULIAN

His eyes getting blurry from all the reading he had done, Julian closed his laptop and glanced at Merlin. "Can you make love potions?"

"Maybe." Merlin arched one white eyebrow. "Why would a handsome guy like you require a love potion?"

"Who said it was for me? You left a book about love potions in the bathroom, so I flipped through it."

It was a bunch of nonsense, but Julian was tired of the dense research material he'd been reading all day, and discussing love potions seemed like a topic that didn't require a lot of brain bandwidth.

Merlin swiveled his chair around, turning his back on the open monitor and the paper he'd been reading. "I can make it. But using it would be unethical. There is not much difference between this and compulsion."

Julian's interest was piqued. "How so?"

"Pheromones, my boy. Consumption of certain compounds can increase their production, and these can be found in nature as well as chemically produced. The thing is, when you emit an unnaturally high concentration of pheromones, the females around you can't resist the spike in desire. So, in a way it's the same as compulsion. Just instead of brain waves, you'd be using chemicals."

Julian pretended disappointment. "So, it's not like you can give a girl a potion and make her fall in love with you. It's like broadcasting to every female in the area."

"You got it. And it's not about love. It's about sex."

"Did you find the recipe for this in that old book?"

"Not everything in these ancient scripts is a fable or a myth. In fact, a lot of it isn't. These books are the result of centuries of experiments, of trial and error. When something finally worked, it was recorded in a book."

"Good to know. Next time I try to find a cure for cancer, I'll consult your ancient books."

Merlin wagged a finger at him. "You can mock it all you want, but you'll be ignoring a fount of information."

"Is that where the idea for the fertility potion came from?"

"In part. Gertrude and I have been working on improving it and adapting it for immortals." He turned back to the monitor.

"I have another question."

"Yes?" Merlin looked at him over his shoulder.

"Why do all your potions taste so horrible? It shouldn't be too difficult to add strong syrup to sweeten them."

"I don't want to. If the potion tastes bad, there is less chance of overzealous patients overdosing on it."

There was some convoluted logic to that. But then the flip side was often the more problematic one. Making sure patients actually took the medicines prescribed to them was difficult enough when all they had to do was swallow pills.

"I need coffee to go back to those research papers." Julian pushed to his feet. "Do you want me to get you some?"

"I'll make it." Merlin got up.

Looking at the sink full of dishes, Julian doubted there was a clean cup left in Merlin's house. "I was thinking of jogging to the café and bringing coffee from there. Maybe a couple of Danishes?"

Merlin shuffled to the kitchen. "That would take too long. I can have coffee ready in five minutes." He pointed at the sink. "And in the meantime, you can wash a couple of mugs."

With a sigh, Julian pushed his sleeves up and got to work on the pile of dishes. "You should have a housekeeper, Merlin."

"I know. And I had one in Scotland. But over there I lived among humans, and it wasn't a problem to find domestic help." He sighed. "I miss Maggie. She kept my house clean and cooked my meals, and sometimes she even stayed to eat dinner with me." He chuckled. "Her husband got so jealous. I think she did it just to get a rise out of him."

"Was she pretty?"

"Beautiful, for a sixty-four-year-old grandmother, that is. But you know how love is. Her husband saw her with the same eyes as when he'd fallen in love with her forty-some years earlier. To him, she was still a bonnie lass."

"How long did she work for you?"

"About five years. She lasted longer than most. Dealing with me and my mess isn't easy."

"William should invent a housecleaning robot."

"I have the one for floors. But using it requires lifting stuff, so I don't. But maybe now that we have a compeller in our midst, we can hire some human help out here."

The plate Julian had been washing slipped from his hands, but he caught it before it hit the sink.

"What are you talking about?"

Merlin shrugged. "Do you have two clean mugs over there?"

"Here." He put them next to the coffee maker. "Now explain what Parker has to do with bringing humans to the village."

"When the kid gets good, we can hire a cleaning crew and have him compel them not to reveal our location or even that they work here. We can have one of the Odus pick the crew up with the bus and bring them here, then at the end of the workday drive them back. And the same goes for all the other projects we need to be done here. Like gardening and remodeling." He waved a hand around his messy kitchen. "Not everything can be solved with automation."

Well, that wasn't exactly true, and the Odus were proof of that. The technology that had created them had been lost, but new advances in artificial intelligence were promising thinking machines in the not so distant future.

23

ELLA

"I love bedazzling." Tessa tucked her new and improved wallet into her back pocket. "Thanks for inviting me, Vivian."

After the success of the day before, Ella had thought it would be a good idea for her future production assistant to mingle with the girls as well, and what better way to start than in her mother's sewing class. Not that any sewing had been done.

It really should be renamed the bedazzling workshop.

"You're welcome to join every class. It's become so popular that Vanessa asked me to come every day this week." Vivian closed the closet with her craft supplies.

"I wish I could, but I also need to work sometimes." Tessa followed them out into the corridor. "By the way, Eva sent me a message that she's coming to visit during lunch today, and she's bringing Ethan with her."

"Did she check with Vanessa if it's okay? I'm sure it's not a problem, but still."

"I assume she did."

As they headed toward the dining room, Ella told Tessa about organizing the little riot the day before. "You have no idea how good it felt to prove Vanessa wrong. I knew the girls weren't going to be afraid of Anandur."

Tessa nodded. "He is such a nice guy. One look at him and anyone can see that."

"Not everyone," Vivian said. "Magnus told me that Anandur and his brother are called the undefeated duo because they are so deadly together."

Tessa giggled and then lifted her hand to cover her mouth. "I'm sorry."

"What's so funny?" Ella asked.

"I'm not one to gossip, but this is a story everyone in the village knows, so it's not fair to keep it from you. The undefeated duo got their asses handed to them by Wonder."

Ella's eyes widened. "Get out of here. She is a big girl, and I can see her overpowering a guy, but two Guardians? And why?"

Tessa leaned closer to whisper in her ear. "The why is a story for another time. But the how is easier to explain. Wonder's special talent is physical strength. And she has killer fighting instincts too. Unfortunately for the rest of us, she doesn't want to be a Guardian. Wonder likes being a girly girl."

"Good for her," Vivian said. "The fact that she is capable of fighting doesn't mean that she is obligated to do it."

Ella wasn't so sure. Weren't people supposed to utilize their God-given gifts, or Fate-given as the immortals liked to say, for the greater good?

At least Wonder had been given a choice, though. Ella hadn't. No one believed she could be a badass, but she was going to prove them wrong. When they entered the dining hall, Eva was already surrounded by a bunch of girls fawning over Ethan and pleading with her to let them hold him.

"Okay, girls. One at a time. Ethan is a friendly baby, but you need to give him some space. Back off, you all." Eva pointed to one of the girls. "What's your name?"

"Sarah."

"Did you ever hold a baby before?"

"Yes, I did, ma'am."

"Sit down next to me."

"Yes, ma'am."

"Here." Eva handed her the baby. "You can hold him for five minutes."

Ella stifled a chuckle. Eva sounded like a drill sergeant, and the girls were responding to her commanding attitude with the right mixture of respect and fear.

"Thank you!" Sarah cradled Ethan close to her chest. "Aren't you a cutie?"

Eva lifted her head and winked at the three of them. "Come and sit with me." She waved them over, while at the same time shooing the girls sitting at her table away. "Make room. Everyone except for Sarah move to the next table."

No one argued.

"I see that you are making friends." Vanessa joined them at the table.

Eva arched a brow. "Do you have a problem with how I go about it?"

"I wouldn't dare. What brings you here? You said that you wanted to check out the place, but knowing you, this visit wasn't born of just curiosity. You're too pragmatic for that."

"True. I want to help out."

Vanessa smiled. "That's wonderful. We always need more help around here. Do you have something specific in mind?"

"I can do makeovers. It's a great way to boost a girl's morale. It did wonders for Tessa, am I right?"

Tessa nodded. "I felt like a different person. From a mouse who looked like a twelve-year-old, Eva turned me into a sophisticated, confident woman. At first, it was just skin deep, but some of it got internalized. Naturally, Jackson helped too, and so did the Krav Maga training." She lifted her arm and flexed her muscle. "Strong and confident."

Stretching, Eva sighed. "I'm bored. And I need something to do besides being a full-time mom. Makeovers are fun, and they will generate positive energy rather than the negative one I deal with in my regular line of work."

"I bet." Ella snorted.

A kick under the table reminded her that what Eva had shared with her and Tessa was a secret between the three of them.

Except, killing scumbags hadn't been all that Eva had been doing before taking a break to be a full-time mom, and Ella knew how to fix her slip up.

"It must be difficult to spy on cheating spouses and not bring it home with you." Ella sighed. "Witnessing it must leave a bad taste and make you doubt your own husband. I know it would have affected me."

Eva waved a dismissive hand. "I don't doubt Bhathian. But you are right about the taste. And the same goes for the industrial espionage. Getting exposed to the rotten underside of things is contaminating, and I don't want it anywhere near my baby. That's why I stopped writing the book too. I got carried away and made it into a thriller, and the more I wrote, the darker it became. I had to stop."

"That's a shame," Vivian said. "It was very interesting."

"Maybe I'll pick it up again when Ethan is older. For now, I'm only engaging in positive activities." She glanced at Vanessa. "Like makeovers."

"I think it's a wonderful idea," Vivian said. "As one very smart woman once told me, some demons can be exorcized with a witchy ritual, while others can be exorcized with a box of hair-dye and makeup."

Ella pointed to her pink, spiky hair. "Exhibit two."

"How soon can you start?" Vanessa asked.

"Today." Eva bent down and lifted a case from the bottom compartment of Ethan's stroller. "I brought my equipment. I can come twice a week and do two or three makeovers at a time."

"What about clothes?" Tessa asked. "Those are an important part of a makeover."

Vanessa chuckled. "If everyone was tall and skinny, we could've done it with Amanda's discards alone. The woman doesn't wear anything more than twice, and she buys new stuff all of the time."

That gave Ella an idea. "We can post a request for female clothing donations on our bulletin board." She glanced at Sarah.

The girl was listening intently but not taking part in the conversation.

Nothing Ella had said sounded out of the ordinary, so she continued. "I'll put a big box for the donated clothing in the mail center."

"What do you think, Sarah?" Vanessa asked. "Does that sound like a good idea to you?"

The girl nodded enthusiastically. "I volunteer to babysit the baby while Ms. Eva is doing the makeovers."

Ella smiled. Eva's visits were going to be popular not just because of the makeovers. There would be a line of girls waiting to entertain Ethan while she was at it.

24

MAGNUS

"I'm going to Merlin's." Ella wiped her hands on the dish towel. "Julian is there, and he said I can come over."

"Merlin or Julian?" Vivian asked.

"Julian. But Merlin said it's okay. They are having a marathon of reading research papers about fertility. I offered to help."

"Doing what?"

"I don't know. Maybe Merlin can tell me what they are looking for and I can read some too."

Vivian huffed. "Good luck with that. All that medical jargon is going to be like reading Chinese."

Ella shrugged. "Then I'll just sit next to Julian and read something on my phone. See you later." She headed for the door.

"I'm going out too," Parker said. "Wonder invited me to her house to study math." He sounded smug.

Magnus wondered how Anandur was taking that. Parker was just a kid, and his infatuation was harmless, but it probably didn't escape the Guardian's notice that Wonder's study buddy was drooling all over her.

"Have fun, kids." Vivian waved.

As soon as the door closed behind Parker, she sighed and plopped on the couch. "It was a long and tiring day, especially because of the drive. But I'm really enjoying helping out in the sanctuary. Who knew that my bedazzling skills could bring so much joy to a bunch of traumatized girls?"

Sitting next to her, Magnus wrapped his arm around her shoulders. "You bring bling into their lives."

She laughed. "Almost as good as the real thing."

"We have the house to ourselves for the evening. That doesn't happen often." He nuzzled her neck.

"For the next couple of hours. Any ideas for how we should fill those?" She waggled her brows.

"Several, and all of them involve you getting naked. We can grab a bottle of wine and get into the Jacuzzi. Or I can give you a massage first and then we can shower together."

"After the sex, or before?"

"Maybe after. So we don't have to shower twice."

"Hmm. Let me think. We have two hours, which is enough to do all three. We can make out in the Jacuzzi, after that you can give me a massage, and after that, we can hop into the shower."

"You forgot the sex."

She laughed. "I didn't. We can have sex in the Jacuzzi, then again after the massage, and again in the shower."

Pulling her closer against him, Magnus hooked a finger under her chin and planted a soft kiss on her lush lips. "I like the way you think. But two hours are not enough for all that."

"We don't have to come out of the bedroom. The kids will think that we are sleeping."

"True." He rose to his feet and offered her a hand up. "To the Jacuzzi."

As the big tub filled up, Magnus went back to the kitchen and grabbed a wine bottle and two glasses.

Wearing her fluffy white bathrobe, Vivian sat on the tub's lip and checked the water's temperature. "This thing is so big that it takes forever to fill up."

"That's plenty for me." He put down the wine and the glasses on the ledge, and then took his clothes off.

"I'm getting in." He liked the way Vivian's eyes followed his nude body.

Lying in the half-full tub, he patted his chest. "Come on, love. Get in here. I'll keep you warm."

"You seem in a hurry." Vivian reached for the robe's belt. "How about I add another feature to tonight's entertainment." She waggled her brows. "A striptease."

"A lovely suggestion." He waved a hand. "Please proceed. But don't take too long. As much as I like watching, I like touching more."

Turning around so her back was to him, she shrugged the sleeve off one shoulder, then peeked at him over it with a sultry smile. Satisfied with the effect her teasing had on him, she repeated the same with the other shoulder. Not letting the robe drop all the way down, she tempted him with just the top part of her rounded bottom exposed.

Focused on her slow reveal, Magnus didn't notice that the tub was full until water splashed over the rim. "Now, look what you made me do, lass." He opened the drain to let some of it out.

Laughing, Vivian tossed the robe on the vanity counter. "Can I come in? Or is the water too high still?"

He reached for her hand, pulled her closer, put his hands on her waist and lifted her off the floor. "Come here, you minx." He lowered her down to lie between his outstretched legs, her back to his chest. Some water splashed out, but as long as it wasn't a flood, Magnus didn't care.

Vivian sighed contentedly and let her head drop back against his shoulder.

"This could have been very comfortable if not for that thing poking me in the butt."

"What thing?" He swiveled his hips, grinding his shaft into her soft ass cheeks. "I don't know what you're talking about."

She giggled. "I just hope the kids are not going to come back early and look for us. Did you lock the bedroom door?"

"I forgot. But don't worry, they are not going to come in without knocking first. They know I can hear it."

"Yeah, but I don't want to go into a mad scramble. Parker sometimes knocks and then just walks in."

"When they get back, I'm going to hear them coming in."

She turned around in his arms, her hard nipples poking at his chest. "How? There are two soundproof doors between us and the living room."

He motioned with his head toward the slightly open window. "If anyone comes up the walkway, I'll hear it."

"I'm at such a disadvantage here. It's like being hard of hearing in the outside world. Perhaps I should get a hearing aid."

"A simpler solution would be for you to transition. I think it's time."

She shook her head. "I can't. Not until this latest crisis with Ella is over."

"There will always be something, Viv."

"After this situation is resolved, I promise no more stalling."

Cupping her cheek, Magnus kissed her softly. "I'm going to remind you that you said that when you come up with the next excuse."

"No more excuses. A promise is a promise."

25

ELLA

"I'm sorry." Exasperated, Ella closed her laptop. "I can't understand any of it."

When her mother had told her that it would be like reading Chinese, Ella had thought she was exaggerating. But it seemed these research papers were purposely written so that no layman could understand them.

It just confirmed her opinion about most doctors being pompous asses.

Present company excluded, of course. Julian was the most unassuming guy ever, and Merlin was eccentric, but in a nice way.

"It's not as difficult as it seems at first glance," Merlin said. "You're just not familiar with the jargon yet."

She waved a hand. "I'm not going to keep on trying. I give up. You guys will have to do without me."

Glancing at Merlin's cluttered and dirty living area, Ella decided she could be useful in a different way. "How about I clean up and organize a little while you two finish up with those papers?"

Merlin smoothed his hand over his long beard. "You are my guest, Ella. I don't feel right about you cleaning up my mess."

"Don't be silly. First of all, I'm not a guest, I'm a neighbor. And neighbors help each other out. You made that paste for Parker to ease his fangs-growing pains, and you also made that tongue relaxer for me. The least I can do is help you with something you're apparently not good at, but I am. I'm the queen of cleaning hacks."

Merlin cast Julian an amused glance. "You're going to have your hands full with this one. When Ella sets her mind to something, she doesn't let anyone or anything stand in her way."

"That is one of the many things I like about her." Julian winked. "My girl is a fighter."

She rolled her eyes. "Come on, guys. I'm only going to clean up, not solve world hunger. Now, enough with the chitchat. You have work to do, and so do I."

Less than an hour later, the place was unrecognizable. The stacks of books were dust free and piled high against one wall, the lab equipment was stowed in the kitchen cabinets, the floor was vacuumed, and the tables and counters wiped. The fridge still needed cleaning. The moldy leftovers were not going to get up and walk out on their own. But she would do it next time.

"Do you want a cup of coffee?" Ella asked, mainly to get their attention so they would notice how nice everything looked.

They'd been so focused on reading and taking notes.

Merlin looked up. "You're a miracle worker, but I feel bad about you doing this for me. Let me at least treat you to some coffee and Godiva."

As Ella's mouth watered, she put her hand over her chest. "You know the way to a girl's heart."

"Just don't show her where you hide them." Julian leaned back against the couch cushions and stretched his arms over his head. "She'll sneak in here in the middle of the night and raid your stash."

"You're welcome to raid it anytime." Merlin pushed to his feet and headed for the kitchen.

He stopped by the dining room table that was now clear of equipment. "Where is my stuff?"

"In the kitchen cabinets. You should order some bookcases. If you have a place for everything, it's not going to get as messy in here."

He pulled out a coffee can from the fridge. "I was just telling Julian before you came in that Parker opens up new possibilities for us. When he gets the hang of his ability, we can hire human crews to do cleaning and maintenance, or even put up bookcases. He can compel them to keep this place a secret."

Ella took the carafe and filled it up with water. "It's something to think about, but I'm afraid the village will lose its charm if we bring outsiders here. I like it that it's isolated from the world. It feels safe."

Merlin eyed her as she measured out the coffee for the machine. "What about when you go to the sanctuary? Do you feel unsafe?"

"No. Well, maybe a little. I look at it as going to work, and at the end of the day, I come home. But home is not just my house where my family lives, it's the entire village. And just as I don't want strangers hanging around my house, I don't want them hanging around the village. Does that make sense?"

"It does." Julian walked up behind Ella and wrapped his arm around her middle, pulling her against him. "We are like one big family who lives together."

Merlin opened a cabinet, pulled out a box of chocolates, and offered it first to Ella and then to Julian. "And just like with any family, little birdies need to spread their wings and fly away. At least for a little while. Don't you want to go to college, Ella?"

With everything that had been going on lately, she hadn't thought about her education, but it didn't mean that she'd given up on going to college. She just hadn't decided what she wanted to do with the rest of her life.

"I always wanted to be a nurse, but now I need to rethink it. There are already two nurses in the village, and there is no need for a third one."

Merlin arched a brow. "How about a doctor? Nowadays it takes almost as long to get a nursing degree. So why not take the extra step?"

Behind her, Julian groaned. "As if we need any more doctors in the village."

As the coffee maker was done spewing, Merlin lifted the carafe off and filled the three lined-up cups. "If we continue with the humanitarian effort, we will need more therapists. Vanessa is already stretched to the max."

Ella added cream and sugar to her mug. "But she can use humans. Why doesn't she hire a couple of full-time assistants?"

Merlin shrugged. "I guess part of it is monetary constraints, and part of it not wanting non-clan people in the thick of things. People are nosey."

Taking a sip, Ella tried to imagine herself as a therapist and cringed. "I can't be a psychologist. It's too emotional. Especially what Vanessa deals with. I don't want to hear stories like mine all day long. I want to forget."

Julian kissed the top of her head. "I can help with that. If you want, I can thrall you to suppress those memories."

She shook her head. "No offense, Julian, but that sounds creepy. I don't want to forget it completely. What happened to me didn't destroy me, it made me stronger. I just don't want to swim in that emotional cesspool on a regular basis. Do you get what I'm trying to say?"

"I guess so." He leaned his chin on her head. "Besides, it's not over yet. Even if you wanted to forget, you can't because of your dream visitor."

"Yeah, talk about creepy. But I'm dealing with him too." She chuckled. "It amazes me how easy to manipulate men are. I got a badass mafia boss wrapped around my finger, and now I'm doing the same to a big-shot Doomer. If I'm not careful, it will go to my head."

"By the way, Ella," Merlin said. "I was wondering about something. From what I understand, you could talk about Lokan with Kian and then suddenly you could no longer do that. Am I right?"

"Yeah. When he confessed to being a dream walker, Mr. D made me promise that I wouldn't talk about him. I thought nothing of it, and I had no intention of keeping that promise, but that was when he must have compelled me."

Merlin nodded. "That's what I've been afraid of. If the Doomer can compel you in the dreams, he is much more dangerous to you than you think. He can make you do things you don't want to."

"Then I guess Parker will have to release me. Just as a precaution, I'll have him do it every day."

"That's a very good solution. And also make sure to report everything to Kian."

"I will."

As Ella reached for another chocolate, a hopeful thought flitted through her mind. What if Logan was compelling her to be attracted to him, and not feel attracted to anyone else?

He'd said something to that effect several times. She'd dismissed it, thinking of it as nothing more than harmless flirting and boasting, but it might have been more sinister than that.

If that was true, it was a huge relief.

There was a logical explanation for why she craved a man she shouldn't want, while being indifferent to the man she should. The problem was that even if that was the case, Parker couldn't help her get rid of that particular compulsion. First of all, because she wasn't going to explain what was going on to her twelve-year-old kid brother, and secondly, if he commanded her to want Julian, that would be a compulsion too.

But what if that wasn't the reason after all, and there was something wrong with her?

That made sense too. She was damaged goods, with hidden emotional scars that she was trying to ignore. Julian was like a pristine-white glove she wouldn't put over dirty hands, but Logan was already dirty, so her soiled hands fit right in.

Crap, she needed to talk to someone, and it wasn't Vanessa. Perhaps Carol would have some words of wisdom to help her sort it out.

26

JULIAN

"Well, I think that's enough." Merlin turned his computer off. "Let's call it a day."

Julian offered a quick thanks to the Fates. "You mean call it a night." He pushed to his feet and offered Ella a hand up. "Are we meeting up in the clinic tomorrow, or here?"

"I like working in my pajamas." Merlin smirked. "Come here when you're up."

"I'll see you tomorrow morning."

"Good night, Merlin." Ella kissed their host on the cheek. "Are you going to monopolize Julian's entire day tomorrow too?"

"I'm afraid so. I want us to be done with those papers, making sure that I'm not missing out on any new developments. Sometimes a small detail that no one thinks much of is a pointer in the right direction and leads to a new breakthrough. Especially anomalies." He smirked. "If not for those pesky discrepancies that kept popping up, we wouldn't have discovered quantum physics."

"In that case, I'll come over when I'm back from the sanctuary."

He wagged his finger at her face. "Just don't think about cleaning anything else!"

"We will see about that. That fridge of yours needs cleaning. You have leftovers there that are ready to walk out on their own."

"Now you're forcing my hand. I'll have to clean it, so you don't."

She shrugged. "Whatever works. Good night, Merlin."

Once outside, Julian wrapped his arm around Ella's waist, and as soon as they were a few feet away from Merlin's front door, he turned her around and pulled her against his chest.

"I've been wanting to kiss you for hours." He took her lips, trying to be gentle but failing miserably.

The entire time she'd been bending to lift books off the floor or stretching on her toes to reach the top kitchen cabinets, Julian had been struggling to keep his focus on the reading material.

That curvy, compact body of hers had been very distracting.

He threaded his fingers into her hair, gripping fistfuls of the pink tufts as his tongue teased her lips, urging them to open for him.

When he delved into her mouth, her long lashes fluttered down and her soft body melted against him.

Surprisingly, Ella didn't seem overwhelmed or frightened by his sudden attack. The scent of her arousal flaring, she clung to him instead of pulling away, her fingers digging into his shoulders as she kissed him back with just as much urgency.

Well, almost as much. He was damn sure she didn't have the urge to bite him.

The need to claim her, to have his shaft deep inside her while his fangs sank into the creamy skin of her neck, was overpowering.

He should disengage before doing something he was going to regret.

Ella wasn't ready for an immortal male's intensity. She needed patience and gentle coaxing, neither of which he was capable of at the moment. Except his arms refused to obey, and instead of pushing her away he clutched her to him even harder.

Slanting his mouth over hers, he lifted her up and deepened the kiss, devouring her. But that wasn't going to cut it. There no way he was going to sate his hunger like that.

With a monumental effort, he let go of her mouth and put her down.

Looking dazed, Ella touched a trembling finger to her swollen lower lip.

"I'm sorry. Did I scare you?"

She lifted a pair of confused eyes to him. "What?"

Damn. She was in shock, and it was his fault.

"I got carried away, I should've been more gentle."

Shaking her head, Ella patted her lip again. "You didn't scare me. I was surprised, that's all." She put a hand on her hip and struck a pose. "Tell me the truth, Julian. Were you just pretending to read fertility research papers and were watching porn instead? Because you seemed awfully excited all of a sudden."

For a moment, he thought she was serious, but then her lip started twitching. "Or maybe you're just weird this way, and research papers make you horny."

Grabbing her arm, he pulled her against him, his erection prodding her belly through his jeans and her shirt. "It was you. Watching you from the corner of my eye was very distracting."

Ella chuckled. "I didn't know cleaning could be sexy." As she wrapped her arms around his neck, her eyes were hooded with desire. "Kiss me again, and don't hold back. I loved the kiss."

He was tempted, but in his current state, it was too dangerous. "I'd better not. I promised you that I would let you dictate the pace, but I'm barely in control right now, and I don't want to push you to do things you're not ready for."

As a long moment of indecision passed, he could see several emotions drift through Ella's eyes. Because of the strong mental blocks that she'd erected to guard against telepathic intrusions, she wasn't broadcasting her feelings as loudly as most humans, and even with his empathic sensitivity, Julian had to rely on other clues to guess her moods.

The good thing was that Ella's face was very expressive. The bad news was that she'd proven to be an excellent actress. To fool someone like Gorchenco, she had to be.

Finally, she nodded and pushed away from him. "Can we still go for a walk, or do you have to rush home and take care of business?"

Damn, she was blunt. Or was it sarcasm?

Again, it was hard to tell with Ella.

"Let's talk about something else." He took her hand and started walking.

"Like what?"

"College. I think you should rethink medical school. Merlin is right about nursing taking almost as long and being nearly as difficult. Why limit yourself? And you don't have to work in the village once you get your license. You can work in a human hospital or open your own practice."

"Same goes for you."

He waved a dismissive hand. "Ignore me. I'm suffering a midlife crisis at twenty-six."

Resting her head against his arm, Ella looked up at the sky. "During my hibernation period, I looked into some schools. Columbia seems awesome, but it's very hard to get into. I have a high GPA, and I've done some extracurriculars, but that's not enough to get me in."

"You know that it doesn't matter, right? You can't use your real transcripts anyway. We will have to supply fake ones for you. Might as well give you amazing grades."

She cast him a sidelong glance. "People go to jail for stunts like that, Julian. I hope that's not how you got into medical school."

"I worked my ass off. That's how I got in. And we don't falsify records for clan members just because they want to get into good universities. This is reserved only for extreme cases. Like you needing a new identity after faking your death, or a clan member who finished high school fifty years ago and now wants to go to college."

"Do you fix their grades as well?"

"We use professionals to do those things, so I wouldn't know, but it makes sense that we can make your application look a little better. I would not have suggested it if you were a lousy student, but you said that your grades were good."

For some reason, Ella seemed disappointed. What did she want to hear? That he would cheat for her? Because he would.

"I'll think about it." She threaded her arm through his. "Right now I'm not ready to make any more big changes. I've had enough for a while. But I do need a job that pays. What I do at the sanctuary keeps me busy, and I love the chance to make a difference, but I need money too."

Hmm, that was a problem.

Ella didn't have a share in the clan's profits, and even after Magnus officially adopted her, she wouldn't qualify for one until she was twenty-five or went to college, whichever came first.

"I have an idea. It won't get you money right away, but once the charity starts bringing in donations, it will. Kian can nominate you as the charity director, and you'll get paid a salary from the proceeds. Every non-profit organization has paid employees, and the director is usually paid well."

Smiling, she lifted her chin. "Ella Takala, Director of Save the Girls. Sounds important. Maybe I should go study charitable organization management."

"Sounds like a plan, but then who is going to run it while you're away at college?"

"Good point. And I forgot that Ella Takala is supposedly dead. The director's name is going to be Kelly Rubinstein."

"That's a shame." He chuckled. "I think another makeover is needed. Somehow I can't picture Kelly Rubinstein, director of Save the Girls, with spiky pink hair and fake piercings. I like the name you gave it, though. We should keep it."

27

ELLA

"I wish the sanctuary was closer to the village," Ella said as the car switched to self-driving, which meant that they were almost home.

Her mother nodded. "I hate driving so long. It's the most exhausting part of this volunteering gig."

As the windows turned opaque, Ella removed her sunglasses and put them in her purse. They were such a convenient solution to the whole contact lenses and eye makeup routine. As long as she wasn't going out shopping or on a date, Ella wasn't going to bother. The sanctuary was safe enough, and the glasses were specially designed to fool facial recognition software.

The car entered the tunnel, and several minutes later parked itself in the underground garage.

"Did you make any progress in regard to the videos?" Vivian asked as they headed for the elevators.

"I didn't bring it up yet. I'm rethinking my approach."

Her mother cast her a sidelong glance. "Care to elaborate, or is it still in the thinking stage?"

"I haven't made up my mind yet. The thing is, even though I'm making friends, it will take weeks or even months until the girls are comfortable enough with me to entrust me with their stories."

"There is no rush, you know." Vivian threaded her arm through Ella's. "Kian donated the building for the halfway house, and your engagement ring will provide the money to run it."

Leaning against her mother's shoulder, Ella sighed. "I don't have the patience to wait. I want it up and running, and then I want Kian to nominate me as the charity's director so I can get paid for running it. I need money, Mom, and don't tell me that all I need to do is ask. I don't want to ask. I want to earn my own."

Vivian laughed. "I stopped listening after I heard the word director. Are you serious?"

"It was Julian's idea, but yeah. Why not?"

"Indeed. Don't you need to go to school for that, though?"

"That's what I said. But then Julian pointed out that if I go to school someone else is going to have to run the charity. I doubt anyone would volunteer for that, and besides, it's my baby. I'm not willing to give it up."

Narrowing her eyes, Vivian attempted a stern look. "You are going to college, Ella. I don't care if your charity is successful or not. I want you to get an education."

"Yeah, yeah. I know. But before I go to college, you have to transition. I'm not going to leave Parker and Magnus with no emotional support."

"Blackmailer."

"No, I'm not." Ella lifted a brow. "You made me a promise that if I started dating Julian, you'd do it."

"It hasn't been two weeks yet. Heck, it hasn't been even one. And anyway, that was before I knew about your dream visitor. I can't check out while this is going on."

Ella had no answer for that. Especially after what she'd said before. If she wasn't willing to leave Parker and Magnus to deal with her mother's transition without her, she could understand Vivian not wanting to leave her while she was dealing with Logan.

"That's a problem, Mom. I don't know how to get rid of him. Thank God for Parker, though. With his help, I can at least manage it."

It reminded her that she wanted to speak to Carol about what was going on with Julian.

"I'm heading to Carol's," she said when they reached a fork in the pathway.

"Don't you want to come home first and eat dinner?"

"I can't. I promised her I'd come to see her as soon as I was back. And then I'm going to Merlin's."

"What about food?"

"I'll grab something from the vending machines."

Vivian didn't look happy about it, but her mother was cool, and she wasn't going to make a big deal out of a missed meal.

"Have fun, sweetie." She kissed Ella's cheek. "And say hi to Carol and the guys from me."

"I will." Ella gave her a quick hug. "You're the best, Mom. Thanks for schlepping me to and from the sanctuary every day."

The drive took over an hour in each direction, and Vivian wouldn't have done it more than once or twice a week if not for Ella. Instead, she'd agreed to do the class every day that week.

"It's my pleasure. Seeing the girls' smiling faces as they bedazzle their outfits and their accessories gives me great satisfaction, and so does helping you with your project."

Ella kissed her cheek. "As I said, you're the best."

Heading toward Carol's house, Ella regretted not wearing something warmer. As usually happened at that hour of the evening, the temperature was dropping fast. Hopefully, the immortal would offer her some nosh because Ella didn't feel like making a detour to the café for a sandwich.

By the time she knocked on Carol's door, her arms were prickling with goosebumps.

"Oh, dear," Carol said as she opened the door. "I don't know what was louder, your knock or your chattering teeth." She pulled her into her arms. "Come on. I'll lend you a sweater."

Passing through the living room on the way to Carol's bedroom, Ella glanced at the vacant couch. "Where is Ben?"

"Went out. We have the house to ourselves." Carol walked into her closet and a moment later came out with a pink sweater. "Here, it matches your hair."

"Thanks." Ella pulled it over her head. "I'm glad that Ben isn't here, so we don't need to go outside to have a private conversation. What's the deal with this weather? Hot during the day and freezing at night."

"This is normal for here. I guess San Diego is more temperate?" Carol headed back to the living room.

"It is." Ella sat on the couch. "The differences in temperatures between day and night are not as crazy."

"Did you have dinner already?"

Ella shook her head. "I came here straight from the sanctuary."

"Good, then you can join me." Carol motioned to a barstool. "I love cooking, and I don't like eating alone. Usually, I have Ben to feed, but since he's not here, I'm glad that you haven't eaten so I can feed you instead."

She pulled out two plates and ladled a pile of spaghetti on each. "My spaghetti bolognese is to die for, if I may say so myself."

"It smells amazing." Ella wanted to attack the thing like a hungry wolf, but she was wearing a pink angora sweater that wasn't hers. "Do you have a napkin I can stick in the collar? I don't want to put stains on your sweater."

"Good thinking." Carol got up and pulled out two aprons from the broom closet. "I'm a messy eater too." She handed one to Ella.

"Thanks."

For several moments, Ella just chewed, pausing only to utter the occasional moan. "This is so good."

Carol chuckled. "If you're making so much noise when enjoying food, I can only imagine what you sound like during sex."

"You mean good sex, the kind I haven't had yet."

Momentarily embarrassed, Carol pushed a lock of hair behind her tiny ear. That probably didn't happen often. The woman could talk about the most intimate of subjects without breaking a sweat.

"Yeah, I forgot. Sorry about that. Except, if you're here, that's probably what you want to talk to me about." She narrowed her eyes at Ella. "I hope you are not still thinking about the island."

"I can't," Ella said over a mouthful of spaghetti. "Mr. D will recognize me."

"Mr. D?"

Ella had been sure that by now the entire village knew about her dream visitor and her compulsion problem.

Finishing chewing, she put the fork down and wiped her mouth with a napkin. "Did you hear about what happened to me at the exhibition?"

"Someone said something about Julian carrying you home. I assumed you either didn't feel well or were swept off your feet." She winked.

"I had a bad headache."

When Ella was done telling her story, Carol frowned. "You think that he's compelling your attraction to him?"

"How else can you explain it? Navuh's son is handsome, and he can even be charming when he wants to, but he is so bad it practically radiates from him. I don't want him. He is not the one for me. Julian is."

"But you said that you're not attracted to Julian. That's not a good sign."

"I didn't say that. Julian is gorgeous, and smart, and kind, and everything a girl could ever want in a guy. He just doesn't excite me as much as Mr. D does. So, it's either because the Doomer is messing with my head or because of what I've been through."

"Meaning?"

Ella sighed. "To put it in the simplest terms, Julian is pure, and I'm not. I don't feel worthy of him, but before you give me a speech about how wonderful I am, it has nothing to do with me as a person not being good enough, well, maybe a little. But the main problem is that I feel kind of dirty."

Carol took her hand and clasped it between hers. "It's all in your head, Ella. You have this scratchy recording playing on a loop in there. Get rid of it and put on some good music. Imagine that you are made of a special kind of Teflon. Nothing bad can ever stick to it. It will just wash off. Good things, on the other hand, stick to you like paperclips to a magnet."

"Is that what you do?"

"I don't need to. I've never felt dirtied by sex. I could not have been a courtesan if I did. For me, sex was always a game, one that I was very good at, could use to my advantage, and enjoyed immensely at the same time."

"What about when you were captured?"

Carol's expression darkened. "That's complicated. The cruelty was much worse than the sex. For me, anyway. But I got over it. My tormentor paying for it with his head helped."

"Yay for Dalhu!" Ella pumped her fist. "I forgot to thank him for it."

Carol chuckled. "You were kind of busy trying to break through a compulsion."

"Yeah. About that. So, what do you think? What should I do about my wayward hormones misfiring? Or is it firing in the wrong direction?"

"You need to figure out what excites you and why. I'm not discounting the possibility that the Doomer is compelling your attraction to him and at the same time blocking you from being attracted to anyone else, but there might be a simpler explanation. Women are complicated creatures, and we each have our preferences and triggers and so on." She smiled. "Sometimes I feel sorry for the men. Figuring out what makes a woman tick is not easy. They have to work hard at it."

Running her fingers through her spiky hair, Ella scrunched her nose. "I have to be honest with you. If Mr. D was blocking me, it would make sense for me to feel nothing at all. But that's not the case. Last night, Julian and I kissed, and it was exhilarating, but then Julian pulled away because he was afraid of pushing me into doing things that I was not ready for."

"Was he right?"

Ella nodded. "We both got carried away by the intensity of the kiss, and for a moment there I wished he would do more, but then I got scared. Not of Julian, because it would be insane to be afraid of a sweet guy like him, but of my own response. What if he touched me intimately and it brought back bad memories? I don't want to associate any of that with him."

Carol smiled sadly. "At some point, you'll have to take a risk and try. Don't let fear stop you from having the life that you deserve."

"I want a clean start with Julian. I don't want any contaminants from before crossing over to my relationship with him."

"I can't tell you what to do, but I can share a little secret with you." Carol took her hand and gave it a squeeze. "Life is full of compromises, and we don't always get what we want. Still, it's better to get some of it than none at all."

28

JULIAN

"Okay, kids. Time to go home." Merlin got up and stretched his long limbs. "We've made good progress."

Regrettably, they weren't done, but it was time to call it a night. Ella had been yawning for the past hour, and Julian felt guilty for keeping her up. But when he'd suggested taking her home, she'd refused to leave unless he was ready to head home as well.

"Did you find anything useful?" Ella asked.

"I hope so. We will see. Thank you for cleaning up my fridge." He lifted a finger. "Wait here."

Rushing into the kitchen with his purple bathrobe flying behind him like a cape, Merlin pulled out a big box of Godiva chocolates from the pantry cabinet and then rushed back.

"A small token of my gratitude." He bowed and offered her the box with both hands.

For a split second, Ella looked at the box as if she wasn't sure whether to accept the gift or not, but Julian had a feeling she couldn't say no to the chocolates any more than she could say no to Merlin. Besides, the guy would be offended if she refused.

Instead, she curtsied. "Thank you. Your gift is much appreciated and will be consumed promptly."

Julian groaned. "Please don't tell me you're going to finish it all tonight. You'll be sick."

Eyeing the box wistfully, she handed it to him. "Save it for me and don't let me have any more than four at a time." She eyed it again. "Maybe six."

Laughing, Merlin patted her back. "Another benefit of turning immortal will be eating as many chocolates as you want and not getting a tummy ache."

"What about gaining weight? Are immortals immune to that?"

"Unfortunately, we are not. But it takes a lot of overindulgence for us to gain excess weight." He glanced down at his thin frame. "Although in my case, it seems like I can eat and eat and not gain an ounce even though I would like to."

Julian chuckled. "You only think that you eat a lot. I think you often forget to eat because your head is somewhere else."

"You might be right, my boy. I get distracted by my work, and I don't have Maggie here to remind me to eat."

"Who is Maggie?" Ella asked.

"His old housekeeper." Julian took her hand and led her toward the front door. "Good night, Merlin."

Hopefully, it would be the last day of that. He had a project to run, which in his absence had fallen on Yamanu's capable shoulders.

He was curious to see what progress had been made. Not that much could've been accomplished over three days, but this was his baby, and he didn't like not being on top of that.

"Would you like to go see the halfway house?" he asked Ella as they took the steps down to the walkway.

"When?"

"Right now."

"It's after ten at night."

"Are you tired?"

"A little. But what the heck. Let's go. Do you have your car keys with you?"

He patted his pocket. "I do."

"Then we have all we need." Ella took his hand. "I didn't go home yet, so I have my purse and my sunglasses with me."

"I've been meaning to ask you about it. I've noticed that you no longer wear the contact lenses or eye makeup. Are you sure the glasses are enough?"

"I'm only going to the sanctuary and back. It's not like I'm going out." She looked up at him. "Do you realize that we haven't gone out on a date since the one time I asked you to take me to the mall?"

Damn. Way to make him feel like an ass.

Then again, he really was an ass. Instead of having her come see him at Merlin's, he should've taken her out to a nice restaurant, or to a club. The poor girl had kept herself from getting bored by cleaning the guy's house.

"I'm sorry. Let me make it up to you. How about tomorrow night we do something nice together? Would you like to go dancing? Or maybe to the movies?"

"What's the point? You have all the new releases right here. We can watch a movie in your theater again. And you have the best popcorn too."

Ella was confusing him. "One moment you're complaining about us not going out, and the next you want to spend Friday night in the village?"

"I wasn't complaining. I was just stating a fact."

"Are you sure? Because if I'm supposed to get some hidden messages, I can admit right now that I'm clueless."

Threading her arm through his, she put her hand in his back pocket. "You are so cute, Julian."

Cute was not a term he wanted her associating with him. Women were not attracted to cute. Hot, sexy, manly, brave, those were heat inspiring, not cute.

As they reached his car, he opened the passenger door for her, but she didn't get in. "Can I ask you a favor? Can I drive? I haven't driven a car in so long that I'm afraid that I've forgotten how."

It was going to be nerve-wracking to let a human drive his car. Ella's responses were nowhere near as fast as his, and Julian was not looking forward to the trip. But saying no was out of the question.

His track record as her boyfriend couldn't count even as decent. This was the least he could do.

"No problem." He walked to the driver side and opened the door for her. "I'll put the address into the GPS, but it will not engage until after the self-driving mechanism disengages."

"That's fine. Until it does, all I have to do is just keep my hands on the steering wheel, right?"

"That's correct."

29

ELLA

"It's so dark in here," Ella whispered. "Can you see anything?"

The old hotel reminded her of every creepy horror movie she'd seen, and she'd only watched parodies of them because real horror was too scary.

She and Julian were like the stupid teenagers who on a dare enter a deserted building at night.

"Perfectly." He held her to him tightly. "Let me find the light switch."

Clinging to Julian, Ella was very glad that he was a big guy. Potential attackers wouldn't know that he was the gentlest soul. All they would see was a tall, muscular guy and, hopefully, it would be enough of a deterrent.

Did he even know how to fight?

Ella doubted it was included in his medical training, but he had to work out to look so good.

When Julian found the light switch, Ella let out a relieved breath. All the scary shadows that had looked like crouching monsters or potential robbers were nothing more than piles of either construction material or debris.

"That's the lobby, right?"

He nodded as they walked deeper inside. "We are going to build a wall right there." He pointed. "That will create a separate entry, where a guard station can be put, or a receptionist's desk. The area behind the wall is going to be the communal living room where people can hang out together and where the different activities are going to take place."

"Like what?"

He chuckled. "Right now we have only one idea. Yamanu wants to organize a karaoke night."

"Sounds like fun. And my mom can have a bedazzling evening. The girls are loving it."

He arched a brow. "Is that some make-believe magic?"

That was funny, and not entirely out of left field. Bedazzling sounded like something similar to thralling.

"It's make-believe alright, just not magic. It's about decorating clothes and accessories with rhinestones. Fake bling. My mother's original idea was to have an arts and crafts sewing class about refreshing old things in all kinds of creative ways. She started with the rhinestones and got stuck there. That's all the girls want to do."

"Fascinating. I would've never guessed that would be a popular activity."

She patted his bicep. "That's because you are a guy."

Suddenly, the muscle under her hand tensed, and Julian's head tilted up.

"What's the matter?"

He put his finger to his lips and then pointed up. "Someone is upstairs," he whispered. "I'm taking you back to the car." He started to back away with her clutched tightly against his side.

Ella had no idea what he'd heard, but she trusted his superior hearing. Except, the place was probably infested with rats and that was what he'd heard.

"Maybe you heard a rat?" She whispered so quietly that no one other than an immortal could've heard her.

"Yeah, rats who walk on two."

They were almost back to the front door when the sound of several footfalls running down the stairs confirmed Julian's assessment.

It seemed like there was more than one two-legged rat in the building.

As one of those rats jumped down from the half-story landing, Julian pushed her behind his back.

"What do we have here?" one of them said.

Hiding behind Julian, she couldn't see the guy, but he sounded either drunk or high.

There was another thud, which she guessed was one more junkie jumping off the landing.

"A pretty boy." This was a different voice than the first. "What are you hiding there, pretty boy? A pretty girl?"

"I'll take either. I don't care which," the first one said.

The low growl that started deep in Julian's stomach didn't sound human, and if those guys weren't so shit-faced, they would have scurried away.

"Look, Vince. Pretty boy is baring his teeth at us. Do you think he'll bite?"

"Not if one of us holds a knife to his girlfriend's throat while the other shoves his cock deep down pretty boy's."

As the guy talked, the growl intensified until there was no way the idiots didn't hear it.

"Stay back," was the only warning she got before Julian turned into a blur.

If Ella had any doubts about his ability to fight, they were gone now.

Closing the distance in one giant leap, Julian caught both guys by their throats and lifted them up, each dangling from a hand.

One of them had a knife, and Ella screamed as he jabbed at Julian with it, but Julian saw it coming and flung the guy away before he had a chance to stab him.

Sailing through the air, the guy landed at least thirty feet away in a pile of debris, the impact sending it flying every which way.

He didn't get up.

And the one still dangling from Julian's hand wasn't moving either.

"Are they dead?" Ella whispered.

Her hands were shaking, and she was cold despite Carol's warm sweater, but she couldn't fall apart yet. Julian had enough to deal with without a panicky girl making a scene.

"Not yet," he hissed.

His fangs were fully descended and dripping venom.

"Don't kill them."

"Why not?"

She came up to him and put a hand on his back. "Because you're a doctor. You save lives, not take them."

Releasing his grip, he let the one he'd been choking drop down to the floor.

Julian was in a weird state, looking dazed as if shocked by the violence that had exploded out of him. He needed her help.

Letting out a breath, Ella collected her wits about her and forced her hands to stop shaking. There was a situation she needed to defuse, and a boyfriend who looked as if he was suffering from a post-traumatic stress disorder.

"Can you thrall them to forget what happened here?"

He nodded.

"Then do that, and then call the police."

"I'm still not sure I want to let them live."

She wasn't sure either. If left alive, those two would attack someone else. But Julian wasn't a killer, and this wasn't the Wild West. The police should handle it.

First, though, she had to talk Julian down from his murderous rage.

"Have you ever killed anyone before, Julian?"

He shook his head.

"Then you don't want to start tonight with these rats. They are not worth the stain it will leave on your soul. Let the police deal with the trash collection."

30

JULIAN

With the haze of rage receding, Julian looked at what he'd done and prepared to feel contempt for himself and the violence he'd committed, but all he felt was satisfaction.

Up until tonight, he'd believed himself to be a nonviolent man, but apparently his inner beast had just lain dormant, waiting to emerge when it was needed.

At first, Julian had been ready to deal with the vagabonds rationally and defuse the situation, but they'd made the mistake of threatening Ella. The thought of one of those junkies holding a knife to her throat had flipped a switch inside his head. It had brought out the savage he hadn't known existed inside him, shutting off everything else.

Julian the scholar had turned into Julian the barbarian, and the worst part was that it had felt damn good to annihilate the threat.

If not for Ella's gentle touch and calm voice, he would've finished what he'd started and killed the scum, ridding the world of the two maggots. With their ugly words still reverberating in his head, Julian wasn't sure he'd done the right thing by not finishing them off.

Except, he was dimly aware that he wasn't thinking straight because his rage was still at a near-boiling point.

"Come on, Julian. You need to thrall them before they wake up and start screaming murder, or worse, pull out a phone and send a picture of you with your fangs showing to all of their friends."

He shook his head to clear the haze. "Yeah, you're right."

First, though, he had to arrange them in a way that would make his thrall plausible. He was going to make them think that they'd knocked each other out, and that wouldn't make sense if they were thirty feet apart when they woke up.

Grabbing the leg of the one he'd choked, Julian started dragging him closer to the other one.

"What are you doing?" Ella asked.

"I'm staging them to look like they've gotten into a fight and knocked each other out."

"Don't. Drop him where he is."

"Why?"

"Because we want them to get arrested and locked up."

He arched a brow. "Trespassing is an offense, but I don't think it's serious enough to serve time for."

"Exactly. But rape is. Put it in their heads that they raped me. After all, if you weren't who you are, they would have done it, so it's not as if they're innocent and we are framing them for a crime they didn't commit. In this case, the line between their intentions and what actually happened is very thin."

That was a crazy idea, but he was curious to hear the rest. "And in this scenario, who knocked them out?"

"A bunch of my friends showed up and beat them up. I'm going to call the police, crying hysterically, but refuse to give my name or give a statement in person. But that won't be necessary because you will thrall them to confess to the rape."

Ella didn't understand what she was asking of him. But what he found amazing was how calmly she was approaching this after the scare she'd had. The poor girl had grown accustomed to dealing with intense situations.

"I can't do that."

She grimaced. "The thrall is too complicated?"

"It's not that. In order to put these images in their heads, I need to create them in mine first. I can't do that without killing them." He rubbed a hand over his jaw. "And going crazy while I'm at it."

She nodded. "Okay, I get it. What about drugs? I'm sure they were high, and we can probably find their stash upstairs. We'll call in the trespassing, and when the police find the drugs, they will arrest them."

"That's better."

He picked up the leg he'd dropped and dragged the junkie over to join his friend. Thralling them to forget what had happened required much less effort than planting new memories in their ugly brains. He also added a command to keep sleeping.

"All done. Let's see what's going on upstairs." He took her hand. "Stay close to me. There might be more of them."

"I don't think so. With all the ruckus, they would have either showed up or run away."

"Normally yes, but what if whoever is up there is stoned out of his mind?"

She got closer to him. "That's possible."

They found where the scumbags had been staying after opening the first door.

Ella pinched her nose with her fingers. "You'll have to burn everything in this room."

"I just hope that it's the only one they infested. Let's check."

They went from room to room, but fortunately found the rest of them intact.

When they went back to the contaminated room, Ella glanced at the contents. "Do you think these drugs are enough to get them arrested?"

"I hope so."

"Should we drop a few syringes next to them? Just to make sure the police search for the rest?"

"Good idea. Do you have tissues in your purse? I don't want to touch anything with my hands."

"I have a fabric swatch." She pulled out a folded piece of blue fabric. "Here you go."

It had a small flower design made from rhinestones.

"Are you sure you don't need it?"

She waved a dismissive hand. "There are plenty more where that one came from."

When they were done staging the scene, Julian regarded it for a moment. Would a cop buy that?

He didn't know, but Turner would.

Pulling out his phone, Julian shook his head. "I'm an idiot. I should've called Turner right away. He would know what to do."

Turner listened to the story with his usual stoic detachment. "I'll take care of it, Julian. You and Ella can go home."

Julian raked his fingers through his hair. "Did I mess things up? I shouldn't have staged anything."

"Don't worry about it. As far as you and Ella are concerned this is over. Go home."

"Thanks."

"Anytime."

Julian returned the phone to his back pocket. "We can go. He's going to take care of everything." He took Ella's hand and headed toward the front door.

"How?"

"He didn't elaborate."

Leaning against him, Ella sighed. "It was cool what you did in there." She lifted up on her toes and kissed his cheek. "My hero."

31

ELLA

Julian was a badass.
Was it wrong to think even more highly of him because he'd almost killed two druggies?

Maybe the old Ella would've thought so, but the new Ella, the one who'd been touched by evil, appreciated having a strong protector at her side.

But that wasn't the only reason she was feeling a weird happy feeling deep down in her stomach. To do what he had done, Julian couldn't be as pure as she'd built him up to be.

She'd seen the savage hiding just under the surface of the civilized, well-mannered doctor, and he'd excited her.

Not that she wanted him to be like that all the time. Cavemen were not her style, but Guardians and warriors were. Men who fought not for the sake of fighting, but to protect what they held dear. She had a feeling that Julian could have made an excellent Guardian.

Perhaps it was the career change he should look into?

Should she suggest it?

He had been deep in thought throughout the short drive from the hotel to the village. Figuring he needed time to process what had happened, Ella hadn't interrupted, but now that they were walking toward her house, the silence stretching between them felt awkward despite the closeness of having their arms wrapped around each other.

Especially since Julian hadn't calmed down yet. He was doing his best, and if not for his immortal tells she would have assumed he was fine. But his eyes were still glowing, and his back muscles were tight where she was touching them.

Maybe a little diversion was needed and talking about a career change might just be the thing.

"Have you ever considered becoming a Guardian?"

Julian chuckled. "When I was a kid, I hero-worshiped Kian. He was everything I wanted to be. A warrior who was also a great businessman and a respected leader. But then, I also worshiped my mother. It was a hard choice, but she convinced me that my talents were better suited to medicine than battle."

"Well, I think you could be an awesome Guardian. So, if you're still contemplating a career change, that's something you might want to consider."

"Thank you. That's a very nice compliment, but being a Guardian is not as glamorous as it seems. Most of the time what they do is kind of boring, which is good because no one can function at high levels of stress indefinitely."

Ella smiled. Her diversion tactic had worked. Julian's eyes were no longer glowing, and he was back to his old, calm and civilized self.

Now the question was how to get him to kiss her before they got to her house.

Strangely, the unpleasant incident had brought them closer. On top of everything else, now they were also partners in crime, and that new closeness had brought about an unexpected side effect.

A craving for more physical closeness.

Ella didn't want to go home. She wanted to spend the night in Julian's arms and keep him safe from the bad dreams that were inevitably going to assail him after the violence he'd done.

The aggression had been so out of character for him, and it obviously bothered him.

Except, that would be unfair to Julian on several levels. As long as she wasn't ready to have sex with him, she shouldn't torment him like that. Maybe she should listen to Carol and just go for it?

What was the big deal? It wasn't as if it was going to be her first time. And she wanted Julian.

But then there was the issue of freaking Logan.

"What are you thinking about?" he asked. "I can feel your agitation rising by the minute."

She cast him a sidelong glance. "I thought you couldn't read my mind."

"I don't need to. It's enough that I look at your face. You're very expressive when your guard is lowered."

"That's your doing. You make me feel safe."

"That's a good thing, right?"

"Yeah, I guess so. I didn't do it consciously, though. I'm usually hyper-aware and careful about what I reveal with my facial expressions and body language."

"So, what's troubling you?"

She shrugged. "I want things that I cannot have."

"Like what?"

"Like going to sleep with you in your bed and holding you throughout the night because I know you're going to have bad dreams. But that's unfair to you because I'm not ready for more than kissing."

And then there was Logan and the game she was playing with him. She couldn't tell Julian about that.

Talk about hurting a guy.

Blue balls were easier to deal with than a blue mood. At least in her opinion. A guy might have a different perspective on that.

"I don't want to go to sleep alone either. I won't lie to you, it's going to be hard to have you in my arms and not do anything, but I'd rather have that than not having you there at all. And don't worry about me starting something. You are in the driver's seat, Ella. Nothing happens unless you initiate it."

That shouldn't have brought tears to her eyes, but Julian's kindness and thoughtfulness were just too much. Even the old, naive Ella hadn't thought guys like that existed.

And yet, she couldn't help but feel a little disappointed too.

Damn, she was confusing herself. On the one hand were the cravings, and on the other were the fears, and she was continually teetering between them.

Hiding her little emotional meltdown, she looked away. "I need to tell my mom that I'm not coming home tonight."

32

KIAN

Usually, when the alarm went off at five in the morning, Kian was already awake. His body knew the rhythms of his days.

Not this morning, though.

When the annoying music started, he reached for his phone, turned it off, and went back to spooning his wife. Her naked body was so warm and soft, molding perfectly into his and robbing him of the willpower to get himself out of bed.

"Good morning," Syssi mumbled sleepily.

He nuzzled her neck. "I'm feeling lazy today. I think I'm going to skip the workout."

She turned in his arms and kissed his chin. "What's the matter, couldn't sleep?"

After they'd made love last night, twice, once in his home office and the second in the shower, Syssi had fallen asleep as soon as she'd gotten in bed.

He, on the other hand, couldn't fall asleep for hours. It wasn't often that he felt so conflicted about a decision, but using Ella to entrap Lokan made him uneasy. Not only that, both Ella and Vivian were still human and, therefore, more at risk of getting hurt.

And pushing Ella into having sex just so she could transition was even worse. Vivian could go for it, but then she might be out for a long time.

In short, Kian was stuck with using two fragile human females to entrap a very powerful and dangerous immortal.

He wasn't going to back away, though. The upside of capturing Lokan outweighed any misgivings he might have, but that didn't ease his conscience.

"I have a bad gut feeling about using Ella and Vivian to entrap Lokan, but at the same time, I can't afford not to use them. And the thing is, I don't know why I'm so worried. On the face of it, the plan seems foolproof."

Syssi sighed. "There is no such thing as guaranteed success. But Turner knows what he's doing. He proved that and then some with the rescue he orchestrated, and how well everything turned out. You can trust him to keep mother and daughter safe."

"That's what I've been telling myself last night. But it didn't help. It's just unconscionable to send Ella into danger so soon after what she's been through. She is just a kid. And sending her mother with her isn't making it any easier."

Cupping his cheek, Syssi gave him a closed-mouth kiss. "I know what will make you feel better. Let's get up and have breakfast together, and then go back to bed for a morning delight."

"Why get up?"

She chuckled. "Because your wife needs to brush her teeth and pee. And you should know by now that she can't make love in the morning before drinking at least two cups of coffee first. The other day was a one-time exception."

That was true, and the reason for a five o'clock wake up.

Syssi didn't want him leaving the bed while she was still asleep, and she wanted them to have breakfast together before they left for work, which meant that his workout had gotten squeezed into a twenty-minute routine with free weights that he kept in their master closet.

A far cry from the full hour he used to spend at the gym, but it was a sacrifice well worth making.

"Then up with you, Mrs. Morning Coffee." Reaching down, he playfully smacked her bottom.

"I'm up!" She scooted off the bed and rushed into the bathroom.

He watched her cute little bottom swaying from side to side. Knowing that she wasn't doing it on purpose made it even sexier.

Kian's bathroom routine was much shorter than Syssi's, and when he was done, he put on a robe and went out to the kitchen where a tray was waiting for him.

"Good morning, Okidu. Thank you for breakfast."

His butler smiled and bowed. "It is my pleasure to serve, master."

Taking the tray back to the bedroom, Kian put it down on the table. He was pouring coffee into the two porcelain cups when Syssi came out of the bathroom wearing a silk kimono robe.

After watching an old rerun of *Shogun*, she'd decided that Kian would look even better than Richard Chamberlain in a kimono and had bought them a matching pair.

"Thank you," she said as she lifted her cup.

He watched her face as she took the first sip, waiting for the look of pure bliss that always followed.

Syssi didn't disappoint.

Sitting on the couch next to him, she leaned back with the cup in hand and kept on sipping slowly until it was all gone, and then handed it to him for a refill.

Other than lovemaking, their morning routine was the favorite part of his day.

He wondered how it would change when they had a child. Perhaps Syssi wouldn't mind handing the baby to Okidu so they could keep enjoying their mornings.

Yeah, he was a selfish bastard, already jealous of a child that hadn't even been conceived yet.

"I think the bad feeling in your gut has nothing to do with premonition. You just feel bad about using Ella and her mom. But you shouldn't."

"And why is that? I would love to hear a good excuse for exploiting a traumatized eighteen-year-old for my selfish needs."

Syssi waved a hand. "You see? You've just proved my point. It's that kind of thinking that keeps you up at night and gives you stomach aches. Eighteen is the age young men and women are drafted into the army, given machine guns, and asked to defend their country. It's not too young."

She handed him the cup for another refill. "Besides, I think it will be therapeutic for Ella. She hates feeling like a victim. She wants to feel like she can make a difference, and she wants to feel strong."

Kian added cream and sugar to the cup, stirred them in, and handed it back to Syssi. "She is already making a huge difference with the charity that she's organizing."

"It's not the same."

He arched a brow. "Did you talk with her? How do you know all that?"

"Observational skills." Syssi winked. "And Carol. Apparently, Ella, Carol, Eva, and Tessa have all become good friends. Do you see the pattern?"

"Not really."

She rolled her eyes. "It's so obvious. Carol and Tessa have both gone through similar experiences and managed to overcome them. Carol was always a badass, and Tessa learned how to be one. Eva, as we all know, is the baddest badass of them all. They are Ella's role models. That's who she wants to be."

"She's only eighteen, Syssi. I'm old, but I still remember myself at that age and how reckless I was. I can understand her wanting to prove herself, but I can't use it as an excuse to ease my conscience. Besides, what about Vivian? The poor woman might suffer a heart attack from stress."

"Vivian is only thirty-six, Kian. And if her heart survived the stress before, it's going to survive it now. Besides, can you afford not to use them?"

"Not really."

"Then stop tormenting yourself and just make sure that they have the necessary protection."

33

SYSSI

*K*ian nodded. "As a leader, I'm often forced to make hard decisions. I accept it, but it doesn't make me sleep any better."

Syssi put her cup down and lifted a piece of toast. "Speaking about hard decisions. What's going on with Perfect Match?"

"We are still negotiating. I did what you suggested and offered them full control over the development and design. That made them much more agreeable to selling me more shares and giving me a majority holding. They weren't cowed by me, though, which I respect."

"I'm so excited about this company. I wish it were mine." She regretted the words as soon as they left her mouth.

Thinking out loud about things she wished for usually meant Kian getting them for her right away.

She waved a dismissive hand. "I meant the clan's. It's not like I want to run a company."

Leaning, Kian whispered in her ear, "Liar. And you know what happens when you lie to me."

As a wave of intense heat washed over her, her nipples tightened, and her core flushed with moisture in preparation for what his words had promised. Usually, games were reserved for the night, but the dice had been cast, and Syssi was more than ready to play.

As his hand snaked under the lapel of her robe, she sucked in a breath, then moaned when he pinched her nipple. Lightly, but the message was clear.

The game was on.

Letting out a whooshed breath, she closed her eyes and whispered, "Yes, sir."

Pushing the coffee table further away, Kian spread his thighs. "Stand right here and take your robe off."

His commanding voice alone was nearly enough for her to climax. Merlin's potion was indeed making her hornier, and it manifested in her arousal going from zero to one hundred in a nanosecond.

Releasing the tie, Syssi let the kimono slide down her arms and then fall to the floor.

The bright glow in Kian's eyes was a reminder that her husband was not human, and neither was she. Still, the games they played, although not mainstream, were not all that unusual.

Taking her hand, he guided her to lie down over his thighs.

As four smacks landed on her behind in quick succession, they weren't gentle.

"What did I say about you lying to me?"

"That you're going to spank me if I do."

"You're damn right. And especially when you want something and then deny it."

The next ten were none too gentle either, and Syssi bit on her lower lip to stifle a whimper. But even though he was harsher with her than usual, her arousal flared just as hot if not hotter.

Syssi wished she could blame it on Merlin's potion, but the truth was that she craved Kian's dominance, and from time to time she needed more than his playful warmup type of play.

When he stopped, she thought the punishment part was over and tried to push up, but he held her down with his hand on the small of her back.

"I'm not done."

She didn't know how much more she could take, not because it hurt too much, but because she needed him inside her like she needed to take her next breath.

"Do you want to own Perfect Match?"

"I want us to own it. But it's the same as the clan owning it. I don't know why I said that I wanted it to be mine."

"Tsk, tsk, sweet girl. I'm afraid you're going to have a very sore bottom if you keep lying to me like this."

"I didn't..."

"Ow! That hurt!"

It did, but instead of trying to get away or pleading with Kian to stop, which he would've immediately, she found herself pushing her bottom up for more.

It was true. She was certifiable, and it was time to embrace it and stop berating herself for it.

With another ten done, he rested his hot palm over her even hotter butt cheek. "Would you like to rethink your answer?"

For a long moment, she didn't respond.

"I'm waiting." He slid his finger down her wet folds but didn't push it inside her or touch her where she needed it most.

"You're playing unfairly. I can't think when you're doing that."

He chuckled. "I'm just giving you an incentive to hurry up and tell me the truth. What do you really want, my sweet girl?"

"The truth?"

"Yes, and nothing but the truth."

"Let me up."

Lifting her, he turned her around and seated her in his lap. "I'm listening."

She would have preferred to get on with the sex and talk later, but Kian wouldn't have it.

"I don't know why, but I have this silly wish to own that company. I want it to be mine, but it doesn't make any sense. I don't have time to get involved with it, and whatever is mine is yours anyway. And what belongs to the clan belongs to us too. It's not a dress or a pair of shoes, or even a crazy expensive diamond ring. Although to be frank, I would have rather owned that company than the ring."

He regarded her with a frown. "You are serious, aren't you? If you were free to sell your engagement ring, would you have done it to buy Perfect Match?"

Did he have to remind her that it was his engagement present to her?

"Ugh, now you're making me feel guilty. If it didn't have a sentimental value attached to it, then yes. I would have. But since it's my engagement ring from you, I can't part with it."

Her answer seemed to satisfy him, and his frown turned into a smile.

"I'll make you a deal."

She shook her head. "You and your deals. But okay, let's hear it."

"I'll buy Perfect Match's shares from the clan, and any further investment will come from our private funds. Not the clan's."

To her great embarrassment, Syssi hadn't been paying attention to their finances. "Do we have any left? I know you were funneling your own money into the clan."

"First of all, it's our money, not mine. Secondly, it was a loan, and the clan owes us the funds. I can sell one of the clan's holdings and pay us back."

She lifted her hand. "Deal accepted."

With a broad grin, he shook it. "Well, now that this is settled, let's move to the next item on our agenda."

34

KIAN

"I hope it's not more spanking."

Given Syssi's breathy voice, Kian wasn't sure that she'd meant it, but even if she hadn't, he had something else in mind. Now that she'd confessed her desire and agreed to the deal he'd proposed, she deserved a reward.

Lifting her off his lap, he set her on the couch and then kneeled in front of her. "Spread those lovely thighs, sweet girl, and show me what you've got for me."

Blushing crimson, Syssi inched her legs apart.

"I'll need a little more." He put his hands on her knees and spread them wider, until she was completely exposed to his hungry gaze. "That's better."

As he inhaled her aroma, filling his lungs with it, the effect was euphoric. He was like a drug addict who needed his daily dose to keep going, but he had no wish to ever get over his addiction.

Reaching his hands under Syssi's bottom, he pulled her closer to the edge of the couch, his nose almost touching her moist petals.

At first, Kian just blew a soft breath, cooling her a bit before extending his tongue and licking gently at her opening. Syssi moaned, involuntarily jerking in his hold. Clamping his hands on her thighs, he held her right where he wanted her and licked upward towards the top of her slit.

For a long moment, he just applied pressure, flattening his tongue over that most sensitive part of her and letting her get used to the sensation.

Syssi panted in anticipation, looking down at him with hooded eyes, then groaning when he flicked her clit with the tip, once, twice, thrice.

"Kian." She threaded her fingers through his hair. "More, please."

He nuzzled her opening, then murmured against it, "How can I not oblige you when you ask so nicely?"

Spearing his tongue inside her, he groaned in pleasure as her nectar leaked into his mouth.

"Oh, God." Her hips lifted off the couch.

For several moments, he pumped his tongue in and out of her while his hands kneaded her ass cheeks.

She was ready for more, though, and so was he.

Pulling his hand from under her, he withdrew his tongue and replaced it with a finger. As he screwed it inside her, he parted her petals with two others and flicked her swollen clit with the tip of his tongue.

Syssi's hips bucked up as he added a second finger, and as he curled them inside her, finding that sweet spot that drove her up the wall, she uttered that keening moan that was a prelude to her orgasm.

If they weren't in a time crunch, he would've slowed down and prolonged her buildup, but slow was reserved for the nights. Mornings were for quickies.

Closing his lips around her nub, he curled his fingers inside her and rubbed that inner patch of nerves that was sure to push her over the edge.

As her sheath convulsed, squeezing his fingers, Syssi threw her head back and called out his name. He kept pumping, prolonging her orgasm until her shudders subsided.

His sweet girl.

There was nothing Kian loved more than bringing her orgasmic pleasure and then watching her blissed-out expression. Knowing that he had put it there was more satisfying than closing the best business deal, and even more than his own climax.

After pressing a soft kiss to her lower lips, he lifted up and kissed her mouth.

She was still panting, her eyes glazed over, her eyelids heavy.

"Turn this way, baby." He motioned to the couch's arm.

There was a reason they'd ordered this particular model. It had tall, curving armrests, perfect for draping his lovely Syssi over one or the other, usually with her well-spanked bottom up in the air.

Unable to help himself, he slapped it lightly, first one cheek, then the other, and then pushed inside her, feeding his shaft into her wet heaven an inch at a time until he was seated all the way in.

They both groaned as the joining was complete. More than sex, it was a coming together, and despite the countless times they'd connected this way, that first moment always felt magical.

As Syssi arched up, offering him the perfect angle to capture her breasts, he pinched her nipples, adding to the volley of sensations assailing her.

His wife loved her pleasure spiced up with a bit of pain.

The harder he pinched, the higher she climbed, but even though they were pressed for time, he was not ready to let her orgasm yet. Releasing her stiff nubs, he cupped her breasts, keeping his touch gentle as he rammed into her from behind. Going faster and harder, the couch groaning and screeching in protest at his relentless pounding, Kian felt his own climax bearing down on him.

Once again, he closed his fingers around Syssi's nipples, twisting and tugging. Her tortured moans made holding off his bite nearly impossible, but he didn't have to wait long.

As another orgasm exploded out of his mate, he released her breasts, clamped one arm around her torso, and grabbed a fistful of her hair. Tilting her head to the side, he forced himself to slow down and lick the spot before sinking his fangs deep inside her soft flesh.

Immediately, Syssi's body convulsed with another orgasm. Only then did Kian let his own climax erupt out of him.

35

ELLA

Ella woke up with a start.

Hand over her racing heart, she took several calming breaths. Her throat felt dry and itchy as if she'd been screaming for real and not just inside her head.

Maybe she had?

With the excellent soundproofing of the houses in the village, no one would have heard her, and judging by the pounding headache, she'd also been crying.

But where the hell was Julian? The one she'd been crying over so miserably in her dream?

Glancing at the nightstand, she picked up her phone to check if he'd left her a message.

There was one from ten minutes ago. *Gone to the café to get us breakfast.*

The question was whether Julian had sent her the text as soon as he'd left home or later when he'd arrived at the café.

In either case, he must have been with her in bed when she'd been gripped in the clutches of the nightmare because the freaking dream had lasted for hours. Which meant that she'd been screaming and crying inside her head and not out loud.

Unless only mere minutes had passed in the real world while hours passed in dreamland. She could've done all her yelling and sobbing after Julian had left.

"Wow, talk about messed up." Ella shook her head as she got out of bed and headed to the bathroom. "Thank God it wasn't real."

As she brushed her teeth, scenes from the nightmare replayed in her head.

Logan and Julian had been fighting over her, but it hadn't been one of the dream walker's visits. Those felt eerily realistic. It had been an ordinary dream, with hazy details and a scenario that didn't make sense.

Not that it felt any better. It had been more disturbing than Logan's dream intrusions, which in comparison were much less traumatic. During those, they walked on a beautiful beach and talked.

Or kissed.

But besides feeling like she was being unfaithful to Julian, it was peaceful. There was none of the heart-wrenching agony that she'd just experienced.

If she were a film producer, Ella would've named it *Clash of the Titans in King Arthur's Court*.

In her dream, Logan and Julian were both Knights of the Round Table, and she was Princess Guinevere. King Arthur was Magnus, but he was her father, not her husband, and thank God for that. Otherwise, it would have been super weird.

Her heart lodged in her throat, Ella, or rather Princess Guinevere, sat in the royal booth and watched the knights fighting for her hand.

The rules of engagement were that their battle wasn't going to end until one of them was dead.

Julian was holding his own against Logan, but Logan wasn't fighting fair, and Julian was bleeding profusely from several deep cuts.

Fearing for her beloved's life, she screamed every time Julian suffered another cut, and when it seemed like he was going to lose, those screams turned into sobs.

She'd cried so hard in the dream that her head was still pounding. Going on autopilot, Ella reached for the bottle of Motrin that had lately become a permanent feature on her bathroom counter.

Except, forcing herself to wake up could've been the culprit as well. Ella just couldn't stay and watch Logan deliver the death blow.

What the hell was that about, though? Was her intuition telling her that Julian was in danger from Logan?

Or maybe her mind had been sorting out her confused feelings and showing her who she really loved?

Not that it had ever been a question.

It also could have been triggered by what had happened last night, but Ella doubted it. If that was the impetus for the dream, Julian would have been the victor and Logan the loser. His impressive performance had proven to her that he could be a badass when the situation called for it.

Ella rubbed a hand over her face. It was so confusing. She needed to talk to Carol.

Snatching her phone off the nightstand, she texted Julian. *Are you still in the café?*

There is a long line. I'll be back as soon as I can.

Don't. I'm coming to you. We can have breakfast over there.

And after the morning rush was over, she could have a talk with Carol.

I'll try to get us a table.

At eleven, Tessa was picking her up, and they were going to the sanctuary together, but that was four hours away. Plenty of time to have breakfast with Julian, a talk with Carol, and go home to shower and change clothes.

Taking off Julian's T-shirt, Ella pulled on her own and immediately followed with Carol's pink sweater. Mornings were cold in the village, and besides, she liked it. It made her boobs look larger than they actually were, and it matched the color of her hair.

Naturally, Carol would realize right away that Ella hadn't slept at home last night, but it didn't matter. After all, she was supposed to be Ella's confidant and privy to more embarrassing things than where Ella had spent the night.

Actually, sleeping over at Julian's wasn't embarrassing. The fact that once again they hadn't done anything was.

Rushing out, she waved hello at Ray without giving him a chance to leer or make annoying comments.

Ella didn't jog, but she walked fast, crossing the distance in less than ten minutes. And she didn't get lost, which she congratulated herself on.

Small victories counted for something, right?

At the café, Julian waved her over to where he was sitting. "I didn't pick up our order because I was afraid to lose the table." He rose to his feet. "Guard it with your life."

"Yes, sir." She saluted.

It was indeed crazy, with Carol and Wonder shouting orders to each other, and customers forming two long lines at the counter. On one side were those waiting for their order to be taken, and on the other those waiting to pick them up.

The girls definitely needed help. Perhaps she could convince Carol to hire her for two or three hours to help with the morning rush? And then again with the lunch one?

At least until her charity took off and Kian nominated her as its director.

Yeah, it sounded like a pipe dream and probably was. A girl with no education could only hope for waitressing jobs, not heading charities, even those she helped organize.

Julian came back with a tray and put it down on the table. "I got you a cappuccino, a sandwich, and a muffin. I hope that's okay."

"Perfect."

"Sugar?" He offered her a packet.

"Two, please."

He handed her his sugar packet as well. "I'll get another one."

"Thank you."

Ella waited for him to return before taking a sip. "What got you out of bed so early in the morning?"

Casting a nervous glance around, Julian leaned closer. "You need to keep your voice down here." He tapped his ear. "Immortal hearing, remember?"

She shrugged. "I don't care if people know. I have nothing to hide."

That brought a smile to his handsome face. "Does it mean I can start calling you my girlfriend in public?"

"Of course." She leaned too, almost touching her nose to his. "You can start referring to me as your mate if you like. Everyone assumes it anyway."

He didn't deny it. "I don't care what others assume or not. The only opinion I care about is yours."

"I would like that too."

Julian didn't seem as happy as she thought he would.

Raising a brow, he asked, "What brought that about?"

She didn't want to tell him about the dream because there was too much he could deduce from it. But that had been what had convinced her that she loved him, and that the obstacles she still had to overcome before they could have a real relationship were not insurmountable.

"It was a process. Why?"

"Does it have anything to do with what happened last night?"

She chuckled. "Maybe. You are my hero, Julian. And all girls want to marry a hero."

He eyed her from below lowered lashes. "You're joking, right? Because sometimes I'm not sure with you."

Glancing around, Ella took a fortifying breath and reached for his hand. "This is not the time or place for grand declarations, and even if it were, I wouldn't make any. But it is clear to me now that you were right and that we were fated for each other. The road to a happily ever after for us is still long, but I can see the neon sign flashing in the distance."

36

CAROL

When the morning rush was over, Carol poured herself a cup of coffee and took it to where Ella was sitting alone at a table.

The girl hadn't said anything about wanting to talk, probably because it had been so busy up until now, but it was quite obvious that she was waiting for her.

Julian had left more than half an hour ago, and the girl was still wearing the sweater that Carol had loaned her yesterday, which meant that she hadn't spent the night at home.

No more clues were needed.

"I see that you like my sweater," Carol said as she sat down, giving Ella an opening to talk about her nightly escapades.

Ella smirked but didn't take the bait. "It's cozy. Where did you get it?"

"Online. Where I get all my stuff. It's so convenient, especially now that I'm running around like a headless chicken." She sighed. "Life used to be so much more peaceful when I was a bimbette."

"I never understood that expression. A chicken with no head can't run, and the visuals it brings are just gross." Ella shivered.

"You must have a very vivid imagination."

"I do. I immediately translate everything into pictures."

That was probably enough preamble before they got to the real reason that Ella had been waiting so patiently for her to come over and talk to her.

"So, what brings you here so early in the morning?"

Ella shifted in her chair and took a quick glance around. With everyone gone to work or back to their houses, the only ones left in the café were Wonder, who was in a cleaning frenzy behind the counter, and the two of them.

Satisfied that there were no eavesdroppers, Ella asked, "Remember our conversation from yesterday?"

"You weren't sure whether your lack of response to Julian was caused by Mr.

D compelling you not to feel attracted to anyone but him, or by your unpleasant experience and your fear of it contaminating what you have with Julian."

"Yeah, that sums it up. But I've thought about one more possibility."

"Shoot."

Ella leaned closer and whispered, "I might be a thrill seeker. Danger excites me."

Carol arched a brow. "And you figured that out how?"

"Last night, Julian and I went to see the hotel he is turning into a halfway house for the rescued girls. We encountered two druggies who'd broken in and were using one of the bedrooms. They threatened to do nasty things to us, and Julian snapped. I've never seen him like that. The guy can fight like a freaking Guardian."

Carol had a feeling she knew where this was going. "You got excited."

"Well, not right away. While we were dealing with the situation, I had to somehow calm an immortal male's murderous rage, but after that, when we went home..."

Now it was getting interesting, and Carol leaned closer. "What?"

"I'm trying to articulate it, and it's not simple. So normally, or rather normal for the new me, my emotions are subdued. I try not to feel too much because I'm afraid that if I do, I'm going to break down into a thousand pieces. So, I numb myself."

Carol understood the need to seek emotional disassociation all too well. What surprised her, however, was that Ella was aware of doing that. The instinct to protect the fragile inner self was not readily apparent, and it took a lot of introspection to realize what was happening.

Pushing her fingers through her short hair, Ella continued, "When Julian seemed so shaken by what he had done, I felt an overwhelming need to protect him, to soothe him, and it loosened some of the emotional barriers I've kept up. Or at least I think that's what happened. Anyway, I felt closer to him than I ever did before, and with that came the desire to also get physically closer. But I chickened out. All I could offer Julian was to hold him while he slept because it seemed like he didn't want to be alone."

"And nothing happened? No smooching and no touching?"

Ella shook her head. "Julian decided that it was best if I was in the driver's seat. If I want to move to second base, I'll have to initiate."

"But you are too scared to do that."

"Exactly. And it's not only because of what happened to me. I have zero experience at initiating anything. I wouldn't know what to do."

"I think I know what's going on."

Ella arched a brow. "You do?"

"I might be wrong, but it makes sense given the fact that you're so inexperienced. You are reacting to Mr. D because he's unapologetically dominant. Julian, on the other hand, is walking on eggshells around you, afraid to spook you with the tiniest show of assertiveness. That's why you're not reacting to him. He's not giving you what you need."

"But Julian isn't wrong. I am easily spooked. His restraint makes me feel safe. Otherwise, I don't think I could've slept in the same bed with him."

Carol leaned forward and took Ella's hand. "Poor baby. You are in a Catch

22. What excites you also scares you, so you can't have any. And poor Julian doesn't know what to do with you."

"Do you know?"

Ella looked at her with so much hope in her eyes that Carol felt terrible about having to disappoint her.

"I'm not the right person to give you advice. What's right for me is not necessarily right for you. But maybe it would help if you talked about it with Julian and explained your dilemma. You could start slow and go from there."

"I can't. What if I offend him?"

"Why would he be offended? The problem is mainly yours. In order to get excited, you need to let go and have him drive the show, but you are too scared to do it."

"Yeah, but what if he is not assertive by nature?"

Carol waved a dismissive hand. "Almost all immortal males are dominant. I'm sure Julian is too, despite how sweet he seems."

"Almost is not all. What if he is like Robert?"

"Robert is a great guy. He just needed to find the right woman."

"Right, and apparently Sharon is that woman. But if you are right about me, and Julian happens to be an anomaly like your ex, he and I could end up like you and Robert. Incompatible."

Carol crossed her arms over her chest. "I don't think it's likely, but I can't entirely discount it either. You won't know until you try."

Releasing an exasperated sigh, Ella slumped in her chair. "I'm no closer to a solution than I was before coming here." She lifted a hand. "I'm not blaming you. You did the best you could. It's just that this is so complicated, and it shouldn't be. I know that Julian and I are fated for each other." Ella patted her belly. "I know it in here, as well as in my heart. The only thing standing between us is all the crap that I'm carrying around with me. I wish I could just dump it down the toilet and flush the water."

Carol laughed. "I love your analogies. They are very visual."

Ella waved a hand. "I told you. That's how I think. Everything is a movie. You've said I have a broken record playing in my head, but it's more like a GIF."

37

MAGNUS

"Do you know what Kian wants to see us about?" Vivian closed the fridge. "We were supposed to go grocery shopping."

Magnus had been hoping to spend his day off alone with Vivian. Hopefully whatever Kian wanted wasn't going to take long.

Magnus put his hands on her waist and pulled her closer to him. "He didn't say. But we can still make it to the supermarket after the meeting. I also want to take you out for a nice dinner. We haven't been on a date in too long."

They'd settled into a routine of work and volunteering and taking care of two kids and a dog, and it was all great. Magnus was thanking the Fates every day for the family they'd given him. But a couple needed time for romance too.

Especially an immortal couple.

"In that case, I should put something nice on."

He waggled his brows. "Do you need help choosing?"

"If you 'help' me," she made air quotes, "we will never make it to Kian's on time."

Magnus glanced at his watch. "Regrettably, you're right."

"Give me five minutes." She kissed his cheek.

"While you're getting dressed, I'm going to check the pantry and make a list of what needs restocking."

"I already did that, but you can check the cleaning supplies. I think we are running low on laundry detergent."

When he was done, Magnus added to the list dryer sheets, glass-cleaning liquid, and toilet paper. Perhaps they should stop at the superstore and buy in bulk. It would save them some money.

He was about to suggest it but changed his mind when Vivian returned wearing a black wig, a silk blouse, a pair of tight pants, and spiky high heels.

Whistling, he walked up to her and pulled her into his arms. "Did I tell you lately how beautiful you are?"

She smirked. "This morning, when you groped my ass while I was brushing my teeth, and then after breakfast while I was loading the dishwasher and you were nuzzling my neck."

"Because you are always beautiful to me."

Pushing on his chest, she stepped out of her high heels, suddenly looking so much shorter. "I only put them on to make an entrance."

She pulled a pair of flats out of her satchel. "I'm going to leave the heels in the car and put them on when we are done shopping. They are good only for sitting in a restaurant, not for running around on errands."

"Smart. Walking through the village and then shopping in high heels would've hurt your feet. But then I would've massaged them." He winked.

Vivian loved his foot massages, and they usually ended in him massaging much more than her feet.

"We should go." She headed for the door.

When they arrived at Kian's office, his door was wide open, and he got up to greet them.

"Please, take a seat." He closed the door and motioned to the two guest chairs.

Magnus waited for Kian to sit behind his desk before asking, "What is this about?"

"Ella's dream visitor."

Next to Magnus, Vivian tensed. "Did something happen?"

Ella had left with Tessa for the sanctuary more than an hour ago. She should've arrived already.

Kian lifted his hand. "Nothing happened. You don't need to contact her."

"Thank God." Vivian slumped in her chair.

"I called you in here to tell you about my plan. I didn't discuss it with Ella yet. I thought that as her mother and future adoptive father, you should be informed first. Besides, it involves you too, Vivian."

Magnus had an inkling where this was going, and he didn't like it.

Kian hadn't invited them to his office to ask their permission to use Ella in whatever scheme he had in mind. He was informing them of it, mainly because he needed Vivian's cooperation with sending and receiving covert messages to and from Ella.

"Go on," Vivian said.

"Lokan's dream visits provide us with a unique opportunity. If we can lure him into a trap and capture him, we will finally have the island's location as well as a host of other information that Navuh's son no doubt has knowledge of."

As Magnus opened his mouth to protest, Kian lifted his palm. "Hear me out first. It wasn't an easy decision to involve an eighteen-year-old girl who has just been to hell and back, but I just can't let this opportunity slip away. Besides, if we don't capture him, she will never be safe from him. He can get to her no matter where she is. This is as much for her as it is for us. Once Lokan is in stasis, he will no longer have access to her."

Presented like that, Magnus couldn't argue with Kian's logic.

Vivian shook her head. "What if he can dream-walk even from there?"

"Stasis is a deeper state than a coma. He's not going to dream, let alone do any dream-walking."

"I hope you're right. So, what's the plan, Ella agrees to a date with him?"

Kian smiled. "Nothing that simple. First of all, he might get suspicious, and secondly, we don't want him to know where Ella is. Not even the general geographical area. So far, she's been very smart about it, not revealing even her time zone. The plan is for Ella to start looking into colleges."

That perked Vivian up. "I'm all for that. I told her she needed an education."

"Whether she actually chooses to go is up to her. My plan is for her to share her deliberations with Lokan and have him suggest a college. That will give us an idea where he is. Then she'll apply and schedule an appointment, which we will, of course, expedite, and tell Lokan about it."

Magnus smoothed his hand over his beard. "You think he'll try to capture her during the visit?"

Kian nodded. "She will tell him the date and time of the appointment. Not as a statement, that would make him suspicious too, but as an absentminded slip-up."

"I'll go with her," Vivian said.

Kian nodded. "Of course, and it's part of the plan. Turner suspects that Lokan might be more interested in capturing Ella's ability than her romantic interest, and if that's true, then she would be useless to him without you. The bait will be the two of you together, for which a campus visit is the perfect setting. Naturally, we will have you surrounded by Guardians posing as students, teachers, and taxi drivers, so there will be no single moment when you are unprotected."

Magnus shook his head. "I still don't like it. What if he can compel the Guardians to step aside?"

"According to Dalhu, Lokan can only compel humans. And don't forget that we know what he looks like. We can probably grab him before he gets anywhere near Ella and Vivian."

Magnus kept pressing. "As Navuh's son, he probably goes everywhere with a heavy guard of his own."

"I don't think so, but even if he does, there will be enough Guardians there to take care of him and his entourage. I'm not going to skimp on warriors. If needed, I'll have the entire fucking force guarding Ella and Vivian."

"I want to be there," Magnus said. "I assume Turner is planning this?"

Kian nodded. "He is."

"Then have him write me into the script. I want to be where I can see and hear Ella and Vivian at all times, and by that, I don't mean the surveillance van. If someone manages to grab either of them, I want to be close enough to intervene."

"I understand. It will be done."

38

ELLA

"Are you sure about this?" Tessa looked even paler than usual.
Ella sat in the interview chair. "No, I'm not. Record one minute. I want to make sure that only a silhouette is visible."

It was one of the hardest decisions Ella had to make, but it was necessary. If she wanted to convince the girls to record their stories, she had to walk the walk and not just talk the talk.

"Okay, go."

Ella cleared her throat. "You can call me Heather, but that's not my real name. I don't want you to know who I am, and most importantly, I don't want those who took me from my home and sold me to know that I'm doing this. My story is not the most terrible there is, but it is bad enough, and I'm telling it as a warning to girls everywhere." She motioned to Tessa to stop the recording.

"This will do for now." Getting up, she walked over to the camera and lifted it off the tripod.

"Crap, I need to wear a headscarf. My spikes are showing."

"So what? Many girls spike their hair."

"I don't want there to be any identifiable features."

Tessa waved a hand. "Where are you going to get a scarf from?"

"My mom's supplies. All I need is a long piece of fabric. Wait here."

She ran into the room where Vivian held her sewing class and rummaged through the box of swatches. Nothing was long enough to tie around her head, so she grabbed several safety-pins to hold three swatches together.

Tying it around her head, she took a peek in the window that reflected her blurry image. "Good enough."

It wasn't as if she was going on a date.

"Okay. Let's do it again. Ten seconds should do."

This time, Ella didn't say anything as Tessa shot the video. "Let's see." She rushed to the camera and checked the recording. "Good. That will do."

"How do you want to do it? Do you want to record it first and then show the recording to the girls, or do you want to record it with a live audience?"

That was a good question.

The upside of recording live was that they would see how it was done, and that Ella was for real, and not an actress reading from a script. The downside was that if they made any noise, the recording was going to be useless, and Ella doubted she could bring herself to do it again.

She still wasn't sure she had it in her to confess the entire ugly story on camera. Well, she actually wasn't going to reveal all the details, that would be stupid because those who knew her story would realize that it was her. She needed to change things around to obscure her identity in more than appearance.

"I still don't think you should do it," Tessa said. "I wouldn't want Jackson to see mine." She quickly lifted both hands. "Not that I'm going to make one. I'm not that brave."

"But if you and I are not willing to record our stories, how can we expect the others to do it?"

"It's not the same. Theirs will be truly anonymous. Ours will not. The entire village will watch them and know who we are, and that includes Julian."

"What if we camouflage our voices?"

"Jackson will recognize my story, and most clan members will recognize yours. So, unless you want to change the details so completely that it barely has any resemblance to what happened, or invent a whole new story, they will know it was you."

Ella shrugged. "If they know so much already, then what I say in that video is not going to be news to anyone."

Tessa shook her head. "You are a brave soul. I salute you."

She wasn't brave at all, but she was faking it well. This was going to be hell, and Ella wasn't even sure whether she was doing the right thing.

What if her story was too vanilla compared to what the other girls had gone through?

They might scoff at her, thinking that it was easy for her since there had been nothing truly horrific in what had happened to her.

From what Vanessa had told her, Ella had a clue as to how bad it had been for the others.

Compared to them, she'd been incredibly lucky.

But then Tessa's story was truly horrific, and if she thought that Ella was brave for telling hers, then maybe the others would think so too.

"I have a question for you, and I want you to answer me frankly."

Tessa's expression was guarded when she nodded.

"I need your perspective. I know that what happened to me is nothing compared to what you went through. Do you think the other girls will think that it was easier for me to go on video because of that?"

"Perhaps some will think that, but I don't. I admire your guts for doing it."

"Okay, good. Do you want to come with me to Vanessa? I need to run this by her if I want all the girls gathered for the recording."

Tessa pushed to her feet. "That's the least I can do."

As they headed to the therapist's office, Ella wrapped her arm around Tessa's slim shoulders. "I don't want you to feel bad. You have very legitimate reasons not to go on tape. First of all, because you want to forget, and I totally understand that, and secondly because you don't want Jackson to hear all the gory details, and I understand that too. I think you're incredibly brave for even being here. I'm sure it's no picnic for you to be surrounded by reminders."

"It's not. But again, that's the least I can do."

As usual, Vanessa's door was open, and she waved them in. "How is it going? Ready to start filming?"

"I am," Ella said. "But I decided to go first, and I want to do it with all the girls watching. I think this is the best way to present the idea to them, and to lead by example."

Vanessa looked impressed. "That's very brave of you. When do you want to do that and where?"

"The only place big enough for everyone to fit in is the dining hall. We will have to take the tables out and bring chairs from the classrooms. Tessa and I can set up the stage in the front of the room."

"The only problem I see with your plan is recording live. Are you going to prepare and rehearse what you're going to say?"

Ella had thought about it on the way and decided not to. If her delivery was too smooth, it might intimidate the other girls. She had to stumble and stutter and convince them that they could do a better job than her.

"Nope. Before I start, I'll explain that the video is going to get edited, so it's okay to stumble and repeat things or even tell the story out of order. I shouldn't even try to make it sound good. I don't want to add any unnecessary barriers like performance anxiety to what is already a tough gig."

Vanessa nodded. "You have good instincts."

"Thank you. What do you think about Monday after dinner?"

"Perfect. I'll put it on the schedule as a lecture."

Ella grimaced. No one wanted to listen to a lecture after dinner. "Instead of calling it a lecture, call it a presentation and add my name, so they will know who's doing it. Tessa's too. Several of the girls already know what we are planning, and they can spread the rumor, so it isn't going to be a complete surprise."

"No problem. Again, good instincts, Ella. You keep impressing me."

"Thank you."

Out in the corridor, Tessa let out a breath. "That went well. Things are moving along."

"Yes, they are."

"Are you nervous?"

"I'm shaking in my boots."

Ella was wearing the monster ones that added six inches to her height. Maybe that was why faking confidence had been so easy. They made her feel like a badass.

When her phone buzzed in her back pocket, Ella smiled and pulled it out, but the message wasn't from Julian. It was from Kian.

Come to my office as soon as you're back from the sanctuary. We have things to discuss.

"What is it?" Tessa asked. "You are frowning. Did anything happen?"

"Kian wants to see me this evening. I wonder what he wants."

39

KIAN

"Good evening, Kian." Turner walked into the office and put his briefcase on the conference table. "Other than Ella, did you invite anyone else?"

"Just you. I spoke with Vivian and Magnus earlier today. Naturally, they are not happy about the plan, but they understand that for Ella to be free of Lokan, we need to capture and neutralize him."

Turner pulled his laptop and yellow pad out of the briefcase. "By neutralizing you mean put in stasis."

"I'm not going to kill him, if that's what you're asking. That would be a waste."

"You shouldn't put him in stasis either. Just keep him locked up and well-guarded. There is a lot we can learn from him, and it will take time."

Kian waved a hand. "I'm not going to put him away until we learn all there is to learn from him."

"Even after we are done with the initial interrogation, I prefer to have him available for further questioning whenever needed. As I understand it, stasis is not a state one can go in and out of with ease."

"No, it is not. But as long as he is conscious, Lokan can enter Ella's dreams."

Turner chuckled. "You can tell the story to her parents, but we both know that once she transitions, Lokan's access to her mind will most likely end."

"We can't be sure of that. No one knows anything about dream-walking. It might not be limited to humans."

"But we can be quite sure that he won't be able to compel her."

Rapping his fingers on the conference table, Kian shook his head. "We don't have him yet, and once we do, we will decide what's the best way to handle him."

"Agreed. Now to the next item of concern. I think Julian needs to be here when we present the plan to Ella."

Kian had contemplated inviting the guy, but had decided against it. Just as with Vivian and Magnus, he wasn't looking for anyone's approval.

"He's not her mate. Not yet, anyway. And he has no say in this."

Pinning him with a hard stare, Turner lifted a brow. "Semantics, Kian. He is her mate, and we both know it. Besides, not having him here will just put the problem on Ella's shoulders. She is going to want to do this, and Julian is going to object. If he learns of it with us present, we can deal with him, making it easier for her."

"I can't argue with your logic. It is sound as usual."

After shooting a text to Julian, Kian got up and walked over to the bar. "Can I offer you something to drink?"

"What are you having?"

"Black Label."

"I'll take a shot."

After pouring the scotch, he handed Turner his glass and put his own down on the table, then walked back to the fridge and pulled out two water bottles and one of Snake Venom.

Perhaps Julian would want something to take the edge off, and as far as he remembered the young doctor hadn't developed a taste for whiskey yet.

When a few minutes later Julian walked in looking concerned, Kian motioned for him to join them.

"What's going on?" Julian asked as he took a seat across from Turner.

"Ella should be here any moment, and Turner thought you should be here when we tell her our plan."

"What plan?"

"Let's wait until she gets here, so I don't have to repeat myself."

The guy didn't look happy, but he knew better than to argue.

"How is the halfway house coming along?" Kian asked to pass the time.

For some reason, Julian exchanged looks with Turner before answering. "The work has started, and it's going well. I didn't know Yamanu had construction experience. He claims it's minimal, but at least he understands the contractors' jargon and sounds like he knows what he's talking about. If it had been left up to me, they would've known right away that they could tell me any story they want and I would buy it because I'm clueless."

"I'm glad Yamanu's found something to sink his teeth into. He spends too much time alone in his house."

Julian frowned. "I thought he lived with Arwel."

"He does, but Arwel is a busy guy. Most of the time Yamanu is alone."

As a light knock on the door announced Ella, Julian jumped to his feet and rushed to open it for her.

"Oh, hi, Julian. I didn't know you'd be here too." She glanced at Turner and then at Kian. "It seems like I'm playing with the big boys now."

Julian laughed, making Kian suspect that there was a double meaning to what she'd said, but the only one who'd gotten it was the young doctor.

"It's something from an animated movie," Julian said.

So, it was a generational thing. He really needed to brush up on the latest references. Syssi would probably know what it had meant. Remembering their morning fun time, he smiled. Perhaps he would find an excuse to play with her again tonight.

Pulling out a chair for Ella next to his, Julian waited for her to sit down and then took his seat and wrapped a protective arm around her shoulders.

Turner had been right about having him participate in the meeting.

No big surprise there.

By now, Turner probably knew Julian better than Kian knew the young man. In part because he was mated to Bridget, and in part because of the time the two had spent together in New York, preparing and executing Ella's rescue.

"I'm guessing that we are here to talk about Mr. D, right?" Ella said. "Or is it about the fundraiser?"

"Your first guess was right. What do you think about turning the tables on Lokan and setting a trap for him?"

Ella grinned from ear to ear. "I think it's a fabulous idea, and one I've been toying with ever since I discovered who he was."

40

ELLA

Talk about butterflies.

The swirling frenzy in Ella's belly should have made her float. They were actually going to let her do it, and she hadn't even suggested it.

Maybe that was the reason why. If she had offered to entrap Mr. D, Kian probably would have dismissed her idea and told her that she was a weak human that he wouldn't dare send into danger.

What had changed his mind though?

It hadn't been Julian, that was for sure. The guy's brooding expression made it clear that he didn't want Ella to do it.

"So here is what we propose you do," Kian said. "During his next visit, start talking about colleges and what you would like to study. Don't mention any specific institutions because I hope he will suggest one that is close to where he is staying in the States. Once he does, you will fill out an application and schedule a visit to the campus and perhaps a personal interview with the admissions person. The next dream visit, you're going to blurt the date and time of your interview excitedly, and that you and your mother are going to be there."

"Okay…but why make it so complicated? I can tell him that I want to meet him in a restaurant or something."

"He will get suspicious if you suddenly want to meet him."

"Probably, but he won't be able to help himself. He'd show up."

Julian's hand on her shoulder tightened. "Why?"

Crap, she'd almost said too much. "Because he wants me. Mostly for my telepathic ability."

"I'm glad you are aware of that. Turner brought up the possibility that Lokan is not interested in you romantically but thinks of you as an asset. He might be using seduction as a way to lure you to him."

Damn, she hadn't thought about that. Ella considered her telepathy as another attribute Mr. D desired, and not the only one he was after. If that was true, he was a better actor than she'd given him credit for.

Or maybe he regarded sex with her as a bonus.

In either case, it made perfect sense for him to compel her to want him and not want anyone else. Out of all the possibilities she and Carol had discussed, this one was emerging as the most likely.

Except, what about the times she'd gotten excited with Julian?

It was like the small discrepancies Merlin had talked about that had led to the discovery of quantum physics.

Ella stifled a chuckle.

Sometimes her reactions were just as impossible to understand, at least for her. But maybe the explanation was simple after all, and Logan's compulsion weakened in certain circumstances. Like the adrenaline rush that she'd experienced in the hotel. Perhaps it had burned through the compulsion, allowing her to feel attraction to Julian for a short time before snapping back into place.

The thing was, even the immortals didn't know much about compulsion and how it worked. They were all speculating.

As she thought about her little brother being the only one who could actually shed light on the subject, another chuckle almost escaped her throat.

What a shame that Parker wasn't a bit older. If he were at least sixteen, she would've explained the situation to him and asked him to override Logan's compulsion and order her not to feel attraction for the Doomer.

The way she understood it, Parker hadn't removed Logan's compulsion, he'd just given her a new one that had overridden the Doomer's. Which meant that the little guy was more powerful than Navuh's son, and that was beyond cool.

What was even cooler was that he was going to get stronger the older he got.

Next to her, Julian was sitting stiff as a broom, probably imagining what went on during those dream visits.

She had to say something to reassure him. "Well, Mr. D's not doing a very good job of it. If I didn't want to lure him so you could catch him, I would never agree to meet him face to face."

That wasn't entirely true. Logan was doing a great job with that freaking compulsion of his. If Julian weren't as perfect as he was, her lukewarm response to him might have convinced her that he wasn't the one for her, and that the Doomer was. In fact, the thought had crossed her mind, and if Logan weren't as dangerous and as scary as he was, she might have been tempted to meet him.

"Never is a strong word, and immortals have time," Kian said. "Eventually he would chip away at your defenses. All he needs is for you to accidentally reveal where he can find you, and most likely your mother too. If he is after your ability, you alone are useless to him. He needs you both. Unless he doesn't know that you can only communicate with your mother and no one else."

A chill ran down Ella's spine as she scanned her memory of their conversations. "I've never told him, but he knows. When he said that my mother and I are the only ones in the world with such a powerful ability, I didn't stop to think how he knew that."

"He probably got into your head during that one time you were face to face with him," Turner said. "And then he thralled you to forget it. Fortunately, you didn't know about us back then."

"Can he do that in my dreams?"

Kian shook his head. "Not likely. Thralling works differently than compulsion. He would need to be near you. Yamanu can thrall from a distance, but only when it's a blanket thrall. Everyone is affected. He cannot pick a specific person and thrall only him or her."

Ella raked her fingers through her short hair. "He said something about being able to dream share only with people who he'd met in person. Do you think he planted some kind of a mental tracker in my head?"

"He established a connection," Julian said. "But a tracker is an excellent idea. You and your mother should definitely wear one when you go."

Kian waved a hand. "They will be surrounded by Guardians at all times. I'll even send Kri with them so they will have a female Guardian to follow them into the bathroom."

"That's good. Nevertheless, it will make me feel better if they have another layer of protection."

"He is right," Turner said. "I can get tiny trackers they can easily hide. They can be hidden in a hairpin, or in a pair of sunglasses, or even sewn into underwear."

The idea of trackers helped with Ella's anxiety, lowering it to tolerable levels. As exciting as the prospect of entrapping Logan was, going against him scared the crap out of her.

Hopefully, the three immortals sitting at the conference table couldn't smell her fear. It was good that the whiskey Kian and Turner were sipping on had a potent aroma. Hopefully, it was masking whatever she was emitting.

"I didn't know they made them so small. It's so cool. It will make me feel safer knowing that in case something goes wrong, my mother and I can be located."

Pushing his chair even closer to her, Julian leaned and kissed her shoulder. "I'm coming with you too. Think of it as a third layer of protection."

"Thank you." She took his hand. "I want you to come."

Then again, maybe he shouldn't. What if her dream about him fighting with Logan and losing was prophetic?

She grimaced. "On second thought, maybe it's not such a great idea."

"Why? I'm sure Magnus will insist on going once he hears about this."

Kian cleared his throat. "I've already spoken to both Magnus and Vivian this morning, and you are right. Magnus demanded to go."

Thinking quickly, Ella waved a hand. "But Magnus is a Guardian." She turned to Julian. "I don't want you to be in danger."

He arched a brow. "You know that I'm not exactly helpless. Besides, I don't want you in danger either, and I'm not telling you not to go."

"You can't tell me anything. This is Kian and Turner's call."

Removing his arm from her shoulders, Julian looked down his nose at her. "And the same goes for you. It is not your call, it's Kian and Turner's."

Crap. They wouldn't tell him no.

41

JULIAN

Julian was silently seething when he and Ella left Kian's office.

Why had she changed her mind about him accompanying her? He wasn't a weakling who was going to get himself in trouble.

He knew Turner would clear him to go, and Kian wouldn't oppose Turner, who he deferred to in these kinds of decisions. But Ella's lack of confidence in him was irritating.

Hell, it was offensive.

"Did Turner tell you what he did with the druggies?" Ella asked.

Shaking his head, Julian schooled his tone so she wouldn't detect his anger. "I haven't had the chance to talk to him yet. He went straight to Kian's office when he got back to the village, and Kian called me to join the meeting."

At least Kian and Turner thought that he had a say in what happened to Ella. Apparently, everyone was thinking of them as a mated couple except for her.

"Did he tell Kian?"

Julian shrugged. "Kian didn't comment on it, so I guess Turner didn't share. Which is true to form for him. Everything is on a need to know basis."

"And he didn't think Kian should know? I would think that as the leader of this community, he needs to be told about anything important that happens to one of its members."

"But it wasn't important, and it was irrelevant to the clan."

He was well aware of what Ella was doing. She was very good at changing subjects and redirecting conversations. But it wasn't going to work with him.

"I don't get why one moment you wanted me to come, and then the next you changed your mind."

Scrunching her nose as she glanced up at him, Ella looked so cute that he had a hard time keeping up his anger. With her pink, spiked hair and innocent round eyes, she really looked like a life-sized Tinkerbell.

"Don't be mad at me. There was a good reason for why I changed my mind about you coming along."

He snorted. "There can be only one. You don't think I've got what it takes to defend you, and that I will get in the Guardians' way."

Letting out a breath, she shook her head. "I had a bad dream this morning. You and Mr. D were fighting over me in an Arthurian style tournament, and he was winning. What if it was a premonition?"

Casting her a sidelong glance, Julian frowned. "It could've been one of Lokan's tricks. He might have generated the scenario to scare you. Or maybe to check who you'd be rooting for?"

Hell, he would have loved to be a fly on the wall in that dream and see for himself.

Lokan was a handsome bastard, his looks reflecting how close to the godly source he was. The Doomer was a second generation immortal and the grandson of one of the most powerful gods. Mortdh might have been insane and delusional, but his power had rivaled that of Annani's father.

Perhaps Lokan had inherited his dream-walking ability from Mortdh, or from Mortdh's father, Ekin?

No one knew for sure what those gods could do. Some of them had kept their special abilities a secret.

So yeah, the Doomer was nearly as impressive as Kian, and a young girl like Ella could easily fall for his fake charm even without Lokan compelling her to want him.

Ella might naively think that she was toying with the Doomer, when, in fact, he was toying with her.

Even so, Julian couldn't imagine Ella rooting for the enemy.

She waved a dismissive hand. "It wasn't that kind of dream. It was just an ordinary one. Well, calling it ordinary is not right either. I was Princess Guinevere, and Arthur, who in the dream looked like Magnus, was my father."

He chuckled. "Did you tell Magnus about it?"

"I didn't see him today. When I got back to the house to get a change of clothes, he and my mom were out on a walk with Scarlet. He gets Fridays off."

"Magnus is going to love it. It will prove to him that you've accepted him as your stepdad."

Ella scrunched her nose again. "I accepted him as my mother's fiancé, and even as a stepdad to Parker, but the guy looks so young that I have trouble thinking of him as a father figure."

"Apparently not."

"Yeah, you're right. I guess dreams reveal deeper truths. It seems my subconscious is smarter than my mind, which is deceived by appearances. After all, Magnus is old enough to be my great-great-grandfather."

"I wonder how old Lokan is." Julian cast the bait, hoping Ella would reveal what she thought about the Doomer.

She shrugged. "I have no idea. He looks like all the other immortals. Late twenties or early thirties. I remember the Russian commenting that Mr. D must have made a deal with the devil because he hadn't aged a bit in all the time Gorchenco had known him."

It seemed that a bigger bait was needed to loosen Ella's tongue. "In Dalhu's portrait of him, Lokan looks quite devilish. Does he look like that in real life?"

"Oh, he does. He has those intense dark eyes that are almost black, and when they glow, there is a reddish undertone in the light they emit. When he smiles, he looks charming, and he is a really good-looking guy. But when he is not happy about something, he looks a lot like what I imagine the devil would look like. If he were an actor, he would have been a shoo-in for the part of Lucifer. An evil fallen angel."

Nothing in what Ella had said indicated that she had feelings for the Doomer, but the excitement in her voice and the slight flare in her feminine aroma had told Julian a different story.

Ella was not only impressed with Lokan, but she was also attracted to him.

Julian felt like a boulder had settled in his gut.

If Ella was indeed his fated mate, she wouldn't have felt attraction toward another male.

Could he have been wrong about her? Had he convinced himself that she was the one for him only because he wanted her to be?

Since he'd seen her picture, Julian hadn't looked at or thought about another female. That was one of the best indicators that Ella was the one for him. And maybe she was, but he wasn't for her.

Was the fucking Doomer her fated mate?

That would explain her lack of arousal when they'd kissed.

It wasn't because of her traumatic experience, but because Julian wasn't the one for her.

42

ELLA

For some reason, Julian looked pissed.

Ella had tried to tone down her description of Logan. Calling him good-looking was a huge understatement. The guy was stunningly handsome. And most of what she'd said was her first impression when she'd still been scared of him.

What had gotten up Julian's ass? For sure it couldn't have been her calling Logan good-looking or charming.

Had he expected her to say that the guy was ugly? Anyone who'd seen Logan's portrait would have known that was a lie.

As she reached for Julian's hand, he didn't pull away, but he didn't give it the little squeeze he usually did. It felt like she was holding hands with a stranger.

He cast her an impassive glance. "You look tired. Let me take you home."

It had been a long day, and an emotionally draining one, but Ella didn't want to go home without fixing whatever had gone wrong between Julian and her.

She wouldn't be able to sleep, and thoughts of him and what had caused the change in his mood would permeate her mind.

And if Logan dream-shared with her, he was going to encounter Julian's manifestation because her head would be filled with him.

"I am tired. But I'm not going anywhere until you tell me what has gotten your panties in a twist." She pulled on Julian's hand and led him toward a bench. "Sit." She pointed at it.

That wrested a small smile out of him. "Yes, ma'am."

When Julian did as she'd asked, Ella climbed onto his lap and wrapped her arms around his neck. "Now tell me what's wrong."

"I'm worried. That's all. Lokan isn't stupid, and he is very powerful. I don't remember if I explained it to you, but the closer genetically an immortal is to the godly source, the more powerful he is. Lokan is a god's grandson. Not a great many generations removed grandson like most of us, but a direct one. And not just any god but one of the most powerful. You are no match for him."

She rolled her eyes. "Thanks a lot, Julian. Now I will be so scared of him that he'll know something is up. And since I can't stop him from entering my dreams, I'm screwed."

If she'd wanted Julian to feel guilty, she'd succeeded.

Raking his fingers through his gorgeous multi-colored hair, he sighed. "I'm sorry, but you should know who you're up against. You might think that Gorchenco was the big bad wolf, and that if you outsmarted him, you could outsmart Lokan. That's not the case. It's like with Magnus. Because he looks young, you regard him as you would a human that age. You're aware that he's intelligent and cunning, so you take it into account, but you think that your youth and beauty are enough to blindside him. They are not."

Ella shook her head. "I'm not that vain, Julian, and Mr. D was quite frank about what he sees in me. He told me point blank that it wasn't about my looks. He even said that he has had many girls who were prettier than me. He wants me for my ability, but I'm not sure Turner is right about him wanting to use my mom and me for what we can do. What would he do with us that he can't do with a satellite phone?"

"So why do you think he wants you?"

"Maybe he suspects that we are Dormants? Or maybe he wants me because I'm special. You know, like in rare. Because of my telepathy." She looked away.

Touting her own attributes wasn't something Ella was comfortable with. Heck, she had spent her life trying to act as modest as can be because people took one look at her and assumed that because she had a pretty face, she must be full of herself.

Hooking a finger under her chin, Julian turned her head, so she had to look at him. "You are special, Ella. And not just because of the telepathy. Why do you think I want you?"

"The face. It's always the face. I know you're going to deny it and list all the things you supposedly admire about me, but that is just the frosting on the cake. Maybe you're not even aware of doing it, but you're looking for justification."

"I don't need to justify myself to anyone. Besides, no one questions my reasons except for you."

"I wasn't talking about justifying it to others. I'm talking about justifying it to yourself."

He arched a brow. "Oh, really? And how do you know what's going on inside my head?"

Crap. They had been doing really well up until now, and then she had to go and ruin it because Julian's pissy mood had infected her.

Ella waved a dismissive hand. "People do it all the time, and especially guys. A man meets a beautiful woman who is up to no good, and he finds excuses for why she is marriage material. Women are a little better at this, but they do it too."

Julian's eyes softened, and he wrapped his arms around her, coaxing her to relax against him and put her head on his chest. "I'm no expert, and I might be wrong, but I think everyone does it to some extent."

He kept rubbing his hand over her back in slow, soothing circles. "Falling in love with someone is not a logical process. I don't know if it's a chemical reaction, or if it's our subconscious collecting information lightning-speed fast and making an instantaneous decision for us, but the result is the same. We fall, and then we try to justify the why to ourselves."

Letting out a breath, Ella closed her eyes. "That's probably why it's called falling and not soaring or floating."

He chuckled. "That's such a clever observation. It had never crossed my mind, although it should have. Soaring in love sounds so much better than falling in love."

He was buttering her up, attempting to make up for his lousy attitude from before. "You're just trying to find ways to make me look smart."

43

JULIAN

Julian stroked Ella's hair. "I don't have to. You are smart." It was spiked with a lot of gel and not pleasant to touch.

He wished she didn't have to do that, but on the other hand, he didn't want some random camera picking up her image and then someone running it through facial recognition software. Not that the different hairstyle could fool it, but it was part of her disguise, and an extra layer of security on top of the special glasses she wore every time she went out of the village.

"Sorry about the hair," Ella said. "I put in so much gel that it could qualify as a lethal weapon."

He chuckled, relieved that her sense of humor was back. His anger from before had made her anxious, and he didn't like seeing that look on her face. He'd much rather see the mischievous spark in her eyes and the sly smirk whenever she said something funny or sarcastic.

That was one of the reasons he hadn't answered her questions truthfully. The other was his stupid pride.

Admitting that he was jealous of her dream visitor would have made him seem petty and immature.

Besides, he hadn't lied.

Every word he'd said was true. Lokan was dangerous, Ella was no match for him, and Julian worried that this new plan Turner and Kian had hatched was going to misfire big time.

They'd put too much trust in Ella's ability to wrap Lokan around her little finger. Julian had a feeling Lokan was toying with Ella, letting her believe that she had him fooled, when, in fact, he was fooling her.

The thing was, while this was going on, Ella had to pretend that she was attracted to the Doomer, and it seemed to him that she didn't have to pretend too hard. Still, he had to remember that she was only doing what she thought was right for the clan, and what Kian and Turner wanted her to do.

Besides, it could very well be that Lokan was compelling her attraction to him while at the same time compelling her not to respond to any other male.

If the Doomer was playing a game of seduction to make a naive young girl believe that he was falling for her, it made perfect sense for the unscrupulous bastard to use every tool in his arsenal. And that included compulsion.

Julian let out a relieved breath.

Thinking of it that way made it much easier for him to deal with the situation. The attraction Ella felt for Lokan wasn't natural.

She was forced to feel it.

And the same argument held true for why his fated mate, his one and only, didn't find him irresistible.

"Speaking of weapons. Tell me about your dream."

When she scrunched her nose, he couldn't help but lean and kiss the tip. "You look so cute when you do that."

Shifting in his lap, she leaned against his arm and looked at him. "What do you want to know? The kind of weapons you and Mr. D used to hurt each other?"

"Among other things. You said that you were Princess Guinevere and that Arthur was your father. I assume that I was fighting the Doomer for your hand in marriage?"

She nodded. "You each had a sword in one hand and a shorter dagger in the other. He wasn't better than you, but he didn't fight fair, so he was managing to wound you worse than you were wounding him."

Julian stifled a smirk. The dream was proving his hypothesis. On a subconscious level, Ella knew that both he and Lokan were trying to seduce her, but while Julian's intentions were pure, Lokan's were sinister. And on top of that, the Doomer was fighting dirty by using compulsion on her.

But there was one part that caused him to frown. "I was losing?"

Ella nodded. "You were losing so much blood. Every time he made an illegal move, I screamed to warn you, and every time he cut you, I cried. I sobbed so hard that my head started hurting in the waking world. Maybe the headache was what saved me from seeing him deliver the death blow because I woke up just as he was about to chop off your head."

Well, that answered the question of who she'd been rooting for.

Tears pooling in the corners of her eyes, Ella cupped his cheek. "I don't know what the dream meant, but it might have been a warning that you shouldn't come anywhere near Mr. D. I'm not willing to chance your life."

As the tears started sliding down her cheeks, making dirty tracks with her dissolved makeup, Julian's heart melted.

Could it be that Ella loved him?

If she was crying over him getting hurt in a dream, she must have feelings for him.

That didn't mean, however, that he was going to abide by her wishes and stay behind while she and her mother walked into the lions' den.

Using his thumbs, he wiped her tears away and then leaned and softly kissed her trembling lips.

"Don't cry, Ella. It was just a dream, a vivid representation of your fears. Have you ever had prophetic dreams before?"

She shook her head. "What if this is the first one?"

"Nice try. But I happen to know someone who has those, and she's been having them since she was a little girl."

"Who is it?"

"Kian's wife, Syssi."

Wiping her cheeks with the back of her hands, Ella just made a greater mess of things. "That's so cool. Did any of her premonitions come true?"

"They did, but because her premonitions are vague, they are not actionable. The when and the how are usually missing. I wasn't here when she had them, so I only know what my mother has told me."

"Maybe I should talk to her?"

"What for?"

"So that she can tell me whether my dream was a premonition or not. She would know the difference, right?"

"I'm not sure, and there is no point in your bothering her. Your dream reflected your thoughts and fears, nothing more. Besides, I'm not letting you go without me regardless."

Crossing her arms over her chest, Ella pushed her chin out. "You can't tell me what to do."

"And I'm not going to. But by the same token, you can't prevent me from going."

She laughed. "Are we back to that again?"

"You started it."

"True, which means that I have to end it. You can come, but you have to do exactly what whoever leads the Guardians tells you. No heroics, please."

44

ELLA

"Good night, Julian. I'll call you tomorrow morning, okay?"

He held on to her hand. "Are you sure you don't want to spend the night at my place?"

"I can't. I need to dream." She looked away, not wanting to see the anger bubble up from him again.

Except, he surprised her with a smile. "Can I at least get a kiss goodnight?"

"I would love a kiss."

Swooping her up, he crushed her to him and fused their mouths in a kiss that was all about possession.

Holy Thor and all of Asgard, that was hot.

No gentle coaxing, and no tentative sweetness. His hands cupping her butt cheeks, Julian pressed her against his hardness while ravaging her mouth with his tongue.

Needing to take a breath, she was loath to stop the mother of all kisses, but Julian sensed her need and let her come up for air.

His eyes glowing like two blue neon lights, he rested his forehead against hers for a moment, and then let her down. "I'd better go. Good night, Ella."

Turning around, he jumped down the three steps separating the path from the front porch and broke into a jog.

Poor guy. Julian was probably suffering from the worst case of blue balls in the Northern Hemisphere.

The good news was that they had parted on a good note, so she knew they were okay as a couple and that Julian was no longer mad.

Which meant that she could go to sleep without worrying about that.

As much as she kept their relationship on a slow burner, Ella couldn't fathom not having Julian around. He'd become a vital part of her life.

Without him and his quiet and unwavering support, she wouldn't have been able to recover so quickly. Not that she was fully recovered, she would be deluding herself if she believed that, but she could function, and think, and come up with ideas, none of which would have been possible if she'd sunk into a depression.

It was still a daily struggle to keep it at bay, and from time to time disturbing thoughts managed to infiltrate the barricades she'd erected against them. But overall, she was doing better than she'd ever expected so soon after her rescue.

Julian was a godsend, and stubborn as a mule.

She didn't like that he'd refused to heed the dream's warning, or her asking him not to come. On the other hand, though, she liked that he'd stood his ground and didn't crumble under pressure.

Her guy was a fighter through and through.

Funny how her perspective had been completely changed by what had happened to her.

The old Ella had dreamt of marrying a nice guy who was fairly intelligent, motivated, and a hard worker, preferably tall because she was short and had a thing for tall men. Fighting skills hadn't been anywhere near the top of her list of desirable traits.

Quite the opposite.

She'd sworn that she would never marry a military man, no matter in what capacity he served. Her father had been a chopper mechanic, for God's sake, and he'd gotten killed, leaving a wife and two small kids to fend for themselves.

And the same went for cops, firemen, and any other dangerous profession.

But here she was, with a stepdad who was a combination cop and warrior, and a boyfriend who was a doctor, but a badass one who could fight.

Her mother would have scoffed at her, but Ella's priorities had shifted. She valued Julian's fighting ability more than his medical degree.

Knowing that he would defend her if necessary made her feel safe. Regrettably, though, he couldn't help her in her dreams, and she needed to make a mental shift in preparation for her encounter with Logan.

Which meant putting Julian out of her mind and filling it with information about colleges.

Getting inside, she tiptoed to her room, hoping Magnus and Parker wouldn't hear her through their soundproof doors.

It was late, and she still needed to spend a couple of hours on her laptop, researching colleges. Good thing tomorrow was Saturday, and she could sleep in.

Almost three hours later, Ella was still at it, but her eyes were getting tired, and although she was making notes of the information she was gathering, the details were all starting to blur together. She couldn't remember which of the colleges she'd checked out had a good nursing undergrad program and which had a good graduate program. Not to mention the different requirements each had for submitting an application.

Closing the laptop, she put it on the floor next to her bed and closed her eyes.

Sleep came almost instantaneously, and with it the dream.

"I've been waiting for you to start dreaming," Logan said. "I prepared this beautiful setting for you. And then you failed to show up."

They were lying on comfortable loungers on a sunny beach, the ocean in front of them lapping gently at the shore.

She was wearing a skimpy bikini, no doubt taken from Logan's imagination because she'd never owned anything like that. His muscular torso was bare, proudly displayed for her enjoyment, and he had on some sort of tight-fitting swimming trunks that left little to the imagination.

Did he think that was going to arouse her?

Well, it was quite impressive, and she took a quick glance before looking behind her to see where they were. Ella had been expecting a hotel, but the structure behind them was a private villa.

"Where are we?"

"In Hawaii." He motioned with his chin. "That's my house."

Was he telling her the truth?

This could have been the Doomers' island. It was hard to tell just by looking at the color of the sand and the ocean. Logan's house must sit on a big parcel of land because she couldn't see any other houses in either direction. Then again, this was dreamscape, and Logan could've created whatever he wanted.

"Very nice. I'm duly impressed."

Smirking, he flexed.

"I wasn't talking about you. I meant the house and the private beach."

"How disappointing." He looked at her stiff nipples that the bikini top was doing nothing to hide. "And untrue."

Ella crossed her arms over her chest. "I'm cold."

Leaning toward her, he whispered, "Liar."

"Think what you want."

Looking smug, he went back to reclining on his lounger. "Did you have trouble falling asleep?"

"No, I had trouble staying awake. I was researching colleges. My mother is pressuring me to get an education."

"Why? Don't you want one?"

"I do, of course. I'm just not ready to leave home. What if the Russian is still looking for me?"

"I don't think you have anything to worry about. Gorchenco's accepted that you are dead. Your mother's friends did a great job covering your tracks." He turned on his side and pinned her with his intense eyes. "I was wondering about that. How does a dental hygienist know people who can pull together an operation like that? Who are they?"

Crap, she should have known that he'd research her and her family.

Think fast, Ella!

"My father was in special forces. His old buddies helped my mother."

"Your father was a helicopter mechanic."

"For a special ops commando unit."

"I didn't find anything like that in his file."

Waving a dismissive hand, Ella snorted. "As if you would. Do you think information like that is accessible to just anyone?"

"I'm not just anyone."

"Right. You are a big-shot warlord. But guess what? This is the United States of America. I'm sure that if the military wants to keep some highly-classified information well protected, they can."

He smiled. "I'm actually glad to hear that. I was afraid that you and your mother were snatched by some secret organization that your government has for dealing with people like you, and that you were being kept locked in a research facility."

She arched a brow. "Why would you think that?"

"Governments love to get their hands on people with special abilities." His smile melted away. "Either to use them for secret missions or to experiment on them to find out what makes them special. I wouldn't want you suffering such a fate."

He sounded so sincere that Ella wondered if it was a superb act, or if he really did worry about her. Most likely, Logan was worried about someone else getting their hands on her and her mother first. It wasn't about her, but what he wanted from her.

"Yeah, I wouldn't want that either. But no one other than you knows about us. We were always very good at keeping our ability a secret."

"Very smart."

"Thank you. But it was actually my father who insisted on the secrecy."

"As I said, smart. The man protected his family."

"Yeah, he did. He was a good dad. I miss him."

Logan regarded her for a moment as if trying to decipher her meaning, but then he smiled and changed the subject. "So, Ella, what do you want to study?"

"Nursing. I've always wanted to be a nurse."

"Do you have a specific college you're interested in?"

"Not at the moment. I'm just collecting information and checking what the admissions requirements are, and how much it costs, and if they offer scholarships. I can't afford a fancy college."

Logan's eyes sparkled. "I have a friend in Georgetown. They have an excellent nursing program, and I can talk to him about arranging a scholarship for you."

Fortunately, Ella didn't need to stifle her excitement, just pretend that it was for a different reason. "That's awesome. Could you really do that for me?"

"I'll do my best. But if I get you an interview, can you get to Washington on your own?"

"Naturally, my mother would come with me."

"Of course." Logan smiled. "It's not safe for a beautiful young woman like you to travel alone. Big bad wolf might get you."

"Are you referring to yourself?"

He chuckled. "I'm big, and I'm bad, but I'm no wolf. A dragon maybe?"

Ella decided to play along. "I like dragons. But can you fly?"

"Regrettably, only on the wings of my imagination."

"That's a shame. I could have saved on airfare."

Crap, now she had given him an opening to ask where she was flying from. She needed to quickly redirect the conversation. "Joking aside, should I wait for you to talk to your friend or should I apply to Georgetown first?"

"I'll tell my friend to keep an eye open for your application. Fill it out as soon as you can. By the way, I assume you will not be using your real name, am I right?"

Crap, crappity, crap. What was she going to tell him?

She had no choice but to use the fake identity they'd given her and then make a new one.

What a mess.

Now she couldn't even buy an airplane ticket with that name because he would be able to find her before she reached the university. The clan would have to get her a new one.

"Tell your friend to look for an application from Kelly Rubinstein."

His eyes glowed demonic red as he smiled. "Oh, I will, lovely Ms. Kelly Rubinstein."

45

ELLA

Despite going to sleep as late as she had, Ella jumped out of bed and rushed to the bathroom as soon as she opened her eyes.

The net had been cast, and Logan had swallowed the bait, licking his lips and imagining how delicious it would taste. The red glow of his eyes had been so strong that Ella had had to bite her lip to stop herself from calling him a demon, or a devil.

Although knowing Logan, he would have loved it. Especially if she'd added sexy as a prefix.

In her closet, she reached for a pair of jeans, but then changed her mind. Something nicer was needed for when she delivered the news to Kian.

After all, she was a spy, a femme fatale so to speak, and this morning she felt like dressing the part. Maybe she should throw on the black wig and sunglasses for good measure?

Unfortunately, her closet offered a limited selection. Once she started earning some money, she could do something about it, but for now, she had to make do with what was there or borrow clothes from her mom.

A simple gray sweater matched her one long skirt, and the black monster boots didn't look too bad with that ensemble. A little mascara and lip gloss, and she was ready to conquer the world.

Or maybe just stomp over it with her boots.

In the kitchen, she found her mom making pancakes for breakfast, and Magnus sitting at the counter with a coffee mug in one hand and his phone in the other, no doubt reading the news as he did every day.

"Good morning, family." She kissed Magnus's cheek and then walked up to her mother and kissed her too.

"Good morning," Magnus stammered a little.

It was the first time she'd given him a good morning kiss, and he still looked stunned.

Vivian smiled. "You are in a good mood. Did you have a good night's sleep?"

"It was too short, but I had a dream visitor. Mr. D took the bait. When I told him that I want to study nursing, and that I'm checking which colleges I can get into on a scholarship, he offered to speak with his friend at Georgetown University. Do you know what that means?"

Her mother's hand flew to her chest. "That my baby is going to be in danger again."

Ella rolled her eyes. "No. It means that Mr. D is in Washington D.C."

"You need to tell Kian," Magnus said.

"I'm going to text him. I just wanted to tell you first. I had to give him my fake name, which means I'll have to choose another for later. I know it's a hassle, but I didn't have a choice. Mr. D said that he was going to tell his so-called friend to look out for my application. I had to tell him what name to look for."

Magnus rubbed his jaw. "I wonder if he really has a friend there, or if he's going to thrall or compel everyone on the admissions board."

"Yeah, I had the same thought. I'm just sorry to give up that name. I kind of liked Kelly Rubinstein, age twenty-one. I'm so excited."

Her mother braced a hand on the counter. "I'm feeling faint."

In a blink of an eye, Magnus was next to her. "Let me help you to a chair."

Her mother was such a drama queen.

"You should be happy, Mom, not hyperventilating. Things are moving along according to plan, and this is going to be over soon. I can't wait to get rid of my dream visitor."

Plopping down on a chair next to her mother, Ella took her clammy hand and warmed it between both of hers. "I want to start my new life, Mom, and I can't do that as long as that Doomer is part of it. Everything is on hold until this is resolved. My education, my relationship with Julian, it all waits until I'm free of him."

Vivian nodded. "I understand. But that doesn't make me any less afraid."

"We are going to have plenty of Guardians with us, and Magnus and Julian are coming too. We are going to be safer than the President."

Snorting, Vivian waved a hand. "All those Secret Service guys, and still some assassination attempts were successful. The President is not a good example."

"How about when he is in the Oval Office. I'm sure nothing can touch him there."

"Let's hope so," Magnus said. "I can imagine several scenarios in which not even the Oval Office is safe."

She cast him a hard stare. "You are not helping, Magnus."

"I'm sorry." He sat across from Vivian and reached for her other hand. "I can promise you this, though. The two of you are going to be even safer than the President."

"What's going on?" Parker asked, coming into the living room. "Why are you holding Mom's hands?"

"She needed a little reassurance," Magnus said. "Come give her a hug. I'm sure that will help."

Parker smirked. "I can do better than that. I can compel her not to worry over whatever she is worried about."

"Don't you dare." Vivian pulled her hands out of theirs. "Come give your mother a hug. That's all I need to feel better."

Ella got up and wrapped her arms around her mother from one side, and Parker did the same from the other. "Then a group hug should be even better." She looked up at Magnus. "Come on, big guy, don't be shy. Join the hug and share the love."

46

ELLA

Come to my office in half an hour. Ella read the text and put the phone in her purse.

"What did Kian say?" her mother asked.

"He wants to see me in his office in half an hour."

"Just you?" Vivian turned to Magnus. "Shouldn't we be there with her?"

Magnus shook his head. "If Kian thought we should accompany Ella, he would have said so."

"Can we just show up? He's not going to kick us out, is he?"

Wrapping his arm around Vivian, Magnus kissed her forehead. "Patience, love. Ella will tell us all about it when she comes back."

Deflating, Vivian rested her cheek against his chest. "It's good that at some point I'm going to turn immortal because this stress is taking years off my life."

"I hope that point comes sooner rather than later."

Feeling like she was intruding on their moment, Ella grabbed her purse and headed toward the door. "I'm going to stop by Julian's first."

It sounded like a good excuse for why she was leaving so early, but on second thought she decided it was a good idea. Julian had made such a big deal out of being involved that he would appreciate her keeping him in the loop.

She texted him while walking. *Put some pants on. I'm coming over.*

Ha, ha, was his answer.

Smiling, she dropped the phone back in her purse. The downside of wearing a skirt was having to schlep something extra just so she'd have somewhere to put her phone.

Perhaps after the talk with Kian, Julian could take her to the mall. She could get one of those cross-body wallets. That shouldn't cost too much, and she still had some cash left over from what Magnus had given her before.

Damn. She really needed to start earning some money.

Didn't spies get paid?

Julian opened the door wearing pants and a smirk and nothing else. "Good morning, beautiful."

Ella pretended to shield her eyes, admiring his muscular torso from between her spread fingers. "Cover it up. Your skin is so pale that it reflects the light and is shining it straight into my eyes. You are blinding me."

Looking down at his chest, he flexed, showing off impressive pectorals and abdominals. "I'm not that white."

She smiled. "I was joking, but really, Julian, cover it up." Walking by him to get into the house, Ella balled her hands to keep from reaching for that glorious chest and touching him all over.

"Am I distracting you?" He followed her inside.

"Terribly."

"Coffee?"

"Thanks, but I already had some, and I don't have time anyway. Kian wants me in his office in twenty minutes."

That got his attention. "Why?"

Ella smirked. "The dream-walker took the bait."

Reaching for her hand, Julian pulled her toward the couch. "Tell me everything."

She resisted. "Put on a shirt, and I'll tell you on the way. I want you to come with me to Kian's."

Heading to Julian's house she hadn't planned on asking him to accompany her, but now that she was here, it just seemed like the most natural thing to do.

"Thanks for asking me to join you."

"Yeah, I hope Kian doesn't mind. But since it involves filling in applications to universities, I can claim that I brought you along for your expert advice on the subject."

"That could work. Wait here. I'll be back in a minute."

He did it in less.

"I've just noticed that Ray isn't here," she said as Julian closed the front door. "Is he still sleeping?"

"Yeah. He partied until late last night."

"Oh, yeah? Where?"

Julian waved a dismissive hand. "Clubs, pubs, wherever the hunting grounds were good."

Right. She remembered Carol talking about it. Immortals prowled places like that for hookups. Did Julian?

She had no right demanding exclusivity from him, but she wanted it nonetheless.

"How come you didn't go with him?" she probed.

He cast her an incredulous look. "I haven't gone hunting since I saw your picture. Don't you get it? You are the one for me, and I don't want anyone else."

Ouch. He must have a really bad case of blue balls, and she couldn't help feeling a little guilty.

Taking his hand, she leaned against his bicep. "I'm sorry. It must be difficult for you."

He stopped and turned to her. "It's not your fault, so don't you dare blame yourself. It was my decision to wait. You were the one who was trying to rush things, remember?"

Ella felt her cheeks getting warm. She'd wanted to transition so badly that she'd convinced herself that she could go ahead with it, but Julian had seen right through her and had realized she wasn't ready.

With a sigh, she put her forehead on his chest. "I don't deserve you, Julian. How can you be so selfless?"

He kissed the top of her head. "I'm not selfless. I'm selfish. I want it to be perfect between us, and for that to happen, you need time to heal emotionally."

If only it were true.

Well, it was partially true. Just not entirely. But she couldn't tell Julian that she suspected Logan of compelling her attraction to him because then she would have to admit to what went on in their dream encounters.

Julian wasn't stupid, and he'd probably guessed it, but it wasn't the same as being told.

"Thank you. I appreciate it."

When they reached Kian's office, his door was open, and they walked right in.

"Good morning, Kian. I'm so sorry to drag you here on a Saturday."

He waved a dismissive hand. "I work on weekends anyway, and this is important. Tell me about your dream encounter and try not to skip over any details."

She nodded. "I'll do my best."

Neither Kian nor Julian interrupted her story, listening intently to every word until she was done.

"I'm sorry about the fake identity," she said preemptively. "I had no choice."

"Don't spare it another thought. We will get you another one. In fact, I don't want you leaving the village until you get it. From now until you leave for Georgetown, Kelly Rubinstein goes into hiding."

"I understand."

And just like that, gone were her plans to have Julian take her to the mall. Worse, Monday she was going to shoot a video, and Vanessa had already announced it to everyone.

"Don't worry about the plane tickets either," Kian said. "Kelly Rubinstein will buy airfare from Dallas to Washington, but she is going to miss her flight. Or something to that effect. We will fly you there in our private jet."

"I need to be in the sanctuary on Monday. Is there a chance those documents could be ready by then?"

"I will do my best, but I can't promise it."

"I have to be there. I have an event scheduled, and I would hate to postpone it."

For a long moment, Kian rapped his fingers on the table, but then he nodded. "As long as you are not driving and someone takes you to the sanctuary and back, I'll allow it even without the new papers. But nothing else. Don't use your credit card for anything."

He frowned. "Did you order anything online using it?"

Ella shook her head. "I didn't use it at all. The one time I went shopping I paid cash for everything."

"Excellent."

"Ella's travel arrangements to Georgetown should probably go through Turner," Julian said.

"Naturally, I just outlined the possibilities so she wouldn't worry needlessly. We will find a solution for everything." Kian turned to Ella. "Do you know what's involved in filling out a college application?"

"Not really. That's why I brought Julian along. To get into medical school, he must have submitted one hell of an application."

"My mother helped. But I know what's needed. What I don't know is how to get her fake transcripts. Unless the real Kelly Rubinstein had very good grades before dying prematurely, we will have to hack into her school records and do all kinds of illegal stuff."

"Roni will take care of that. All I need from you is a list of what's needed."

Julian chuckled. "Roni's mate is a perpetual student. I doubt he needs me to tell him what's involved in a college application."

"Nevertheless, I need you to prepare it. Sylvia didn't study nursing or anything related to it. I'm sure there is a difference and applying to study philosophy or some other nonsense like that is not the same as applying to medical or nursing school."

47

JULIAN

"I was hoping to go to the mall," Ella said as they left Kian's office. "But that is out now. I'm back to being stuck here until my new fake documents are ready."

Going down the stairs, he took her hand. "They might be ready by Monday. The forger is one of us."

"That would be awesome."

"How about I take you to the café instead?"

"Isn't it closed on Saturday?"

"It is, but Jackson keeps the vending machines stocked, and there are always people hanging out there on weekends. It's not like we have many options here." He opened the office building's front door for her.

Ella smiled up at him. "I could go for a pastry."

"Let's just hope we can find a table." He glanced in the café's direction. "Plenty to choose from."

"I see Wonder and Anandur, do you mind if we join them?"

"As long as they don't mind, I sure don't."

"Ella!" Wonder waved them over. "Come have coffee with us."

"Am I invited too?" Julian asked as he pulled out a chair for Ella.

Wonder rolled her eyes. "Would you care to join us, Doctor Ward?"

"Thank you, I would." He bowed his head. "But first I need to get nourishment for my lady. What would you like, Ella?"

"What Wonder is having. A cappuccino and a Danish."

"Your wish is my command."

"I'll come with you." Anandur pushed away from the table. "I'm ready for the second round."

As they headed for the row of vending machines, Julian cast Anandur a sidelong glance. "How are things going?"

"That's what I wanted to ask you. Why were you and Ella meeting Kian in the office on a Saturday morning?"

He should have known the guy wanted to fish for gossip. There was no harm in telling him, though. Soon enough all the Guardians would know what was brewing.

Except, it wasn't his story to tell. It was Ella's, and it was up to her how much or how little she wanted people to know.

"You're asking the wrong person."

Anandur arched a brow. "Should I ask Ella?"

"It's her story. I'm just the…"

What the hell was he?

The boyfriend?

The confidant?

"I'm just the escort."

The Guardian gave him an amused look from head to toe. "I can see how you would be, but I was under the impression that only older ladies required escort services."

Julian flicked his hair back and looked down his nose at Anandur. "I don't discriminate based on age or ethnicity. Just gender. So you're out of luck, buddy."

Laughing, Anandur slapped his back. "Let's get back to our ladies. I can't wait to find out what this is all about. Seems big to me."

Julian handed Anandur one of the cappuccino cups. "Can you hold it for me? I need to get the pastries."

"I'll take it to the table." Anandur turned to go.

"Hold on. Before you ask Ella anything, I want to check with Kian if it's okay for her to tell you about it. He didn't give us any instructions, and I don't want her to mess up."

Looking disappointed, Anandur nodded. "Personally, I believe in doing first and if needed apologizing later, but it's your call."

Worried that Ella had already told Wonder, Julian rushed back to the table, but when he and Anandur got there, Wonder and Ella were talking about the sanctuary.

Thank the merciful Fates.

Putting the coffee and pastries down, he pulled out his phone and texted his question to Kian.

The answer was, *Use your discretion.*

Great. What was that supposed to mean?

"Well?" Anandur was looking at him with his bushy brows raised in a question.

"He said to use my discretion."

Turning toward him, Ella asked. "About what?"

"Anandur wants to know what we were meeting Kian about. So, I texted the boss to ask if it was okay to talk about it, and that was his answer."

"Use our discretion?"

"Yes."

Pursing her lips, she shrugged. "If Parker knows, I don't see the harm in telling Anandur and Wonder. But please don't spread it around. I know that you trust each and every clan member, especially those living with you in the village, but I come from the human world where anything can happen, including family selling each other out or even killing each other."

Anandur patted her back. "Not all of us are good. I'm well aware of that. Whatever you tell Wonder and me will not leave this table."

When she was done, Anandur whistled. "This is huge. How come Kian didn't tell at least the head Guardians about it?"

"I guess because he didn't have a chance yet," Ella said. "Kian told me about his plan only yesterday, and I put it into action during the night. It worked like a charm. So, I texted him this morning to let him know, and he wanted to meet me. That's the whole story."

Pushing the fingers of both hands into his crinkly hair, Anandur stared at Ella with awe. "I can't believe it. I just can't. After all these years we finally have a chance to learn that bloody island's location, and it's thanks to an eighteen-year-old human girl. The Fates must be laughing their asses off."

Raising her palm in the air, Wonder grinned at Ella. "High five." They smacked hands. "And once again to girl power."

Smirking, Ella leveled her gaze at Anandur. "Speaking of girl power. I want to hear why and how Wonder kicked both your and your brother's asses. I told you mine, it's only fair that you tell me yours."

Anandur glanced at Wonder. "Do you want to tell the story?"

She blushed. "I should, shouldn't I? Ella was so honest about her dream encounters and the compulsion."

"Are you embarrassed about it?" Ella asked.

Wonder nodded. "I don't like flaunting my physical strength."

Taking her hand, Anandur brought it to his lips. "Your story is about much more than that. It's about courage, and about doing the right thing despite how difficult it was for you. You should be proud. And don't worry about my and Brundar's pride. I want everyone to know my mate is a hero and how proud I am of you."

48

ELLA

As Wonder told her story, Ella's eyes widened with each new detail. She'd known the girl from the study sessions with Parker, and she'd heard about her defeating the undefeated duo, but she'd never heard about the Doomers she'd singlehandedly captured and kept imprisoned for months, probably saving countless women's lives. And she'd done all that while living in a refugee shelter and working as a bouncer in a night club.

Providing meals for her captive Doomers had been a financial struggle, but she'd done it nonetheless, showing them compassion they hadn't deserved.

Ella wondered if in Wonder's shoes she would've been as kind to the monsters. Probably not, but could she have allowed them to starve?

Eventually, they would've gone into stasis, but Wonder had no way of knowing that at the time. Because of her amnesia, she hadn't known who she was or where she'd come from, let alone who and what the Doomers were.

"That's the most amazing story I've ever heard." Ella put her hand over Wonder's. "Anandur is right. You are a real hero."

The girl blushed again. "I did what I had to under the circumstances. The Fates had put the right person in the right place at the right time. I was just a cog in their grand plan."

Ella shook her head. "You're too modest. Next time I'm in my mother's bedazzling class, which is going to be this Monday, I'm going to make you a badass badge from rhinestones. And they are going to be all pink to symbolize girl power."

"I love it," Anandur said. "Can you make me one too?"

She arched a brow. "You want me to make you a badass badge from rhinestones? I don't think it's going to work for you."

He put his arm around Wonder's shoulders and leaned to kiss the top of her head. "Mine is going to say, my mate is a badass. And I'm going to wear it proudly. Make one for Brundar too. His will say, my brother's mate is a badass."

Wonder laughed. "I don't think Callie would appreciate it. I think his should say my mate is an awesome chef."

"Yeah, you're right. Can you add a chef's hat to your design?"

"Sure thing." Ella pulled a pen out of her purse, took a napkin, and drew a quick mock-up of the badge she could make for Brundar. "How about that?"

"I love it. Can I show it to him?"

She handed the napkin to him. "Don't forget to mention that it's going to be made from rhinestones."

Wonder glanced at Julian. "What would yours say?"

Poor Julian, it wasn't fair of Wonder to put him on the spot like that.

Ella came to his rescue. "How about my mate is a dreamcatcher?"

And wasn't that clever? She felt quite smug about coming up with that.

Wonder nodded. "I like it."

Julian didn't look happy, though, his brows dipping so low they formed an upside-down triangle between his eyes.

"I have a different idea. Ella's will say—Ella Takala, Director of Save the Girls. And mine will say Ella's deputy."

Was he the sweetest guy, or what? But way too modest.

She took his hand and gave it a little squeeze. "Let's wait with the badges until I actually accomplish something. I'm shooting the first video on Monday, and then Julian and I will probably have to edit the hell out of it before posting it on YouTube. Who knows if anything will come out of it? The idea seems good in theory, but there are no guarantees."

"Who did you convince to go first?" Wonder asked.

Ella grimaced. "Myself. I need to show the girls that I can walk the walk and not only talk the talk. That's the best way to encourage them to do it."

"That's very brave of you," Wonder said.

Anandur nodded in approval.

Julian shook his head. "I don't like it. That's too much exposure. Did you forget that you are hiding from Gorchenco and now also from a powerful Doomer?"

Crossing her arms over her chest, Ella lifted her chin. "I didn't forget a thing. We are shooting in silhouette, and we are going to distort my voice too. The whole point of me doing it is to show the girls that it's safe and that no one will be able to recognize them from the videos."

"What about the story itself? Gorchenco will recognize it. And once he has proof that you're not dead, he's going to hunt you down with every resource at his disposal. And those are vast."

She waved a dismissive hand. "I'm going to change the details. It's the gist of the story that counts, not the particulars. I want to emphasize that if it happened to me, it could happen to any girl."

From the corner of her eye, Ella could see Anandur and Wonder's heads turning as if they were watching a tennis match.

Julian's eyes were glowing when he pinned her with a hard look. "Write the script of what you're going to say. I want to go over it."

Oof, he was so annoying.

She liked that Julian was protective of her, but she didn't appreciate that he didn't trust her to know what she was doing.

"I'm not stupid, Julian. I know what to say and what not to. I'm not going to write a script because if my story sounds rehearsed, it will lose its emotional impact."

His tortured expression softened Ella a little, and she decided to give him a break. "Don't forget that we are going to edit it later. We can argue about what to leave in and what to cut out then."

He still didn't look happy. "Every clan member in this village, and probably those in Scotland too will watch it. Do you really want everyone to know what you've been through? Unlike the other girls, you are not going to be anonymous. People are going to know it's you."

Stubborn man. Apparently, he didn't know her as well as he thought he did.

"I'm not going to provide any sordid details, if that's what you're worried about. As I said before, I want my video to serve as a warning to other girls and to their parents. I'm going to emphasize the methods traffickers use to lure unsuspecting girls away from their families, and the extortion tactics they use to make them cooperate. But instead of delivering it as a lecture, I'm going to tell a personal story, which is much more impactful."

"Nevertheless, it's still incredibly brave of you," Wonder said. "I think you're doing the right thing." She cast an apologetic glance at Julian. "As Ella's mate, it is natural for you to want to cocoon her in bubble wrap and prevent her from exposure to any danger. But you need to fight that instinct. It's always hard on the partners. I worry every time Anandur goes on a mission, but I know that I have to let him go. Being a Guardian is more than a job for him. It's who he is."

Wow, that was a good speech. Ella would be surprised if Julian had anything to say after that.

"Anandur can take care of himself. He's a huge male immortal with centuries of fighting experience. Ella is a human girl. The comparison is irrelevant."

Ouch. That was insulting to Wonder.

But the girl was a badass even though she tried to deny it.

Smiling shyly at Julian, Wonder nodded. "You are right. Physically there is no comparison between Anandur and Ella. But her spirit is just as big, and her need to protect and to contribute is just as all-consuming as Anandur's. This is who she is, not what she does. Do you really want to try stifling that?"

Touché, Wonder.

49

JULIAN

Wonder's impassioned speech made Julian feel like an ogre who couldn't see further than the end of his nose. He had a feeling that if Ella didn't need him to show her how to fill out the applications, she would have gone home in a huff.

They walked in silence, with him brooding and feeling chastised, and her deep in thought about Fates knew what. Julian's sense of smell didn't detect anything overly troubling, but he'd learned that with Ella he could never be sure. The scents she emitted were so subtle that he often wondered whether she was a little like Turner, who didn't emit any at all.

The other option was that she wasn't letting herself feel, and since he knew she was adept at keeping up mental barriers, he speculated that it shouldn't be too difficult for her to block her emotions even from herself.

Surprising him, Ella threaded her arm through his and leaned her head on his bicep. "Don't mind what Wonder said. She got carried away. It's perfectly natural for you to want to keep me safe. I get it, because I feel the same about you. Remember our fight from yesterday? I didn't want you to accompany me to Georgetown because I was afraid for you."

He arched a brow. "That was a fight? I wasn't aware of it."

"You were angry at me, and I didn't like it. I call it a fight."

He patted her hand. "I'm sorry."

"We also promised each other not to apologize so much."

Damn, she was confusing him. "What should I say then?"

"We need to find code words to replace sorry. I wouldn't mind you admitting to behaving like an ass."

He chuckled. "So instead of saying I'm sorry, I should say I'm an ass?"

"Or I was an ass. That works too."

He leaned and kissed the top of her head. "I was an ass. Happy?"

"Yes, thank you. And I was an ass too. Now we are even, and we can erase that silly spat from our memories."

As they neared his house, they were greeted by the sounds of piano playing. "Ray is up."

"He plays so beautifully." Ella sighed. "But he's such a different person than what he lets out through his music. Hearing those sounds, I would have expected a shy, gentle, artist type. Instead, he acts like a juvenile delinquent. He reminds me of that guy I dated in high school who offered to buy my panties from me."

Julian growled. "What sort of perverted game was he playing?"

She laughed. "Despite his panty fetish, he was actually not a bad guy. Jim was harmless, so you can stop making that weird sound in your throat."

"What sound?"

"You were growling, Julian."

"Oh, that sound." He winked and opened the door.

Acknowledging them with a nod, Ray kept on playing.

Ella waved. "Hi, Ray. Don't mind us. We will be in Julian's room."

That hadn't been Julian's plan. If he wanted to keep his hands off her, the living room was a better choice.

"That's where your computer is, right?" She headed down the corridor.

"It's a laptop. I could've brought it out to the living room. The place doesn't belong to Ray."

She pushed the door open and got inside. "I don't want to interrupt his practice." She sat on his bed and grabbed one of the decorative pillows. "And your room is always so neat. I wanted to see if it was messy at least on the weekends."

Julian went over to his desk. "My mother programmed me to never leave my room without making the bed first. She says it helps start the day right."

"There is something to that. Your mom is a smart lady. Bossy as hell, but I like her. She has a spot on my badass girl team."

He took the laptop and brought it over to the bed. "So now it's a whole team? Who are the members?"

"Eva, Carol, Tessa, Amanda, Wonder, your mother. I'm sure that when I get to know more people, I will find others to add to my list."

"What about your mother?"

Ella waved a dismissive hand. "Vivian is a scaredy cat. I love her, but she is not a badass. She is too nice and sweet for that."

"You are nice too."

Ella made a face. "I'm working on it."

"On not being nice?"

Kicking off her boots, she pulled her legs up on top of the bed and lay on her side. "It's a real handicap. Like when someone is rude to me, and I can't force myself to say something nasty back. I keep thinking about it later and getting angry at myself for not being assertive enough."

Trying to ignore the way her sweater was stretched tight over her breasts, Julian opened his laptop and searched for a mock application they could fill in. "Next time someone is rude to you, tell me, and I'll beat him up."

She chuckled. "I believe you. After what happened in the halfway house, I know you would. But what if the offender is a girl?"

"Then you're on your own. I'm not going to beat up a woman."

"That's chauvinistic."

Was she teasing him? It was hard to tell. The imp kept her expression neutral.

He arched a brow. "So, let me get it straight. To prove that I am a feminist I have to beat up a girl? That's absurd."

Ella plopped to her back. "If you haven't noticed, we live in an absurd world."

He lifted his eyes from the laptop. "What do you mean? Not that I disagree, but I'm curious to hear your observations."

She waved a hand and closed her eyes. "I'm too tired to think of all the examples. There are just too many, and then people get their panties in a twist if you don't agree with their opinions even when they don't make any sense. Democracy and free speech are dying." She yawned. "Someone needs to tell Brandon to start pushing dystopian movies and stories about the end of democracy as we know it before it's too late and we turn into Soviet Russia."

A moment later she was snoring lightly.

Sliding off the bed, Julian pulled out a blanket from the closet and covered Ella's small sleeping form.

Her hands tucked under her cheek and her pink hair sticking out in all directions, she looked so tiny and so sweet. But Wonder was right. Inside that fragile, small body lived a tremendous spirit.

50

ELLA

"Hello, gorgeous." Blocking the sun, Logan leaned over Ella and planted a soft kiss on her lips.

The dream was so realistic that she could feel the heat coming off his bare chest and smell his enticing male musk. Both were intensely alluring. The guy was made for seduction, with everything about him a feast for the female senses.

Or was he making her think that? Compelling her?

Crap. Dreaming about Logan while sleeping in Julian's arms was so bad. She needed to make herself wake up pronto.

Except, what if he had new information for her?

Besides, she needed to make her exit elegant so he wouldn't suspect her reason for escaping the dream. After all, she was supposed to like him.

Ella shielded her eyes with her hand. "I must've fallen asleep while filling out applications. I didn't expect you."

"I was surprised too." He sat next to her on her lounger and put his hand on her thigh.

Ella didn't react, pretending she hadn't noticed. "Are you sleeping now? Or are you napping too?"

"It's night time where I am. But before I went to sleep, I called my friend at Georgetown. I have an instruction for you."

She smiled. "I like a man who takes immediate action. What are the instructions?"

Her answer must have confused him because he just stared at her for a moment. "You are a confusing young lady, Ella. Or is it Kelly?"

She put her hand on his back. "To you, it's Ella." Hopefully, she wasn't laying it on too thick.

He smiled. "I like Ella better. But back to my friend. He said you should go through the motions like every other candidate. Which means filling out the application, sending out all the transcripts, etc. You need to schedule an interview too, but don't feel discouraged if it's for months from now. He is going to try and push it through sooner. He also said that your GPA and SAT should be very high for him to be able to do anything at all."

"Don't worry. They are."

He arched a brow. "Ella's or Kelly's?"

"Mine. But I can get them under Kelly's name."

"How?"

"I can't tell you, mainly because I don't know. But it's going to be done." She leaned up and kissed his cheek. "Thank you for helping me. I need to go now, though. The applications aren't going to fill out themselves."

He frowned, his body temperature suddenly dropping. "Are you applying anywhere else?"

"Of course. I heard Columbia has an excellent nursing program, and I'm also checking several other places. But Georgetown is my first choice. I just hope it pans out."

His smile returned. "It will."

"Anyway, I have to go. I hear my mom calling me." She waved at him. "Until the next time."

Forcing herself to wake up always resulted in a headache, and this time was no different. It would've been nice to keep on sleeping a little longer, but Ella didn't want to spend time with Logan while snoozing on Julian's bed.

It was just wrong.

Where was he anyway?

"Julian? Are you in the bathroom?"

A moment later, he walked in with a mug of steaming coffee in each hand. "Hello, sleepyhead. Did you have a nice nap?"

Ella pushed up on the pillows and took the mug from him. "Yes and no. Thanks for the coffee."

Sitting on the bed next to her, he crossed his legs and propped his elbow on his knee. "You're welcome."

She took a sip, and then one more. "As soon as I slipped into dreamland, Mr. D was there. He informed me that he'd already spoken to his friend and that even with the inside help, I need an amazing grade point average. I also need to schedule an interview, which the friend is going to try expediting."

"The Doomer is tightening the noose. He is arranging it so you'll arrive at Georgetown on his schedule, not yours."

"Makes sense. He said that it was night time where he was, so I assumed he was on the island. It's supposed to be somewhere in the Indian Ocean, right?"

Julian nodded.

Ella took another sip of coffee. "He needs time to travel back to the States and organize the trap, so we probably have some time. And if not, I can stall by saying that my transcripts are not ready."

"Since he's not aware that you are onto him and that you have help, he doesn't need to do much preparation. I wouldn't be surprised if he doesn't know anyone at Georgetown and just arranges for you to get a fake invitation to an interview. Then all he has to do is show up and compel you and your mother to come with him."

Ella finished the rest of her coffee and put the mug on the nightstand. "That's true, but as I said, I can stall if needed. But we really need to take care of my nonexistent transcripts."

Julian reached for his phone. "Let me check if Roni is available to see us. This should be child's play for him."

"Wait, what time is it? How long was I asleep?"

By the empty feeling in her tummy, it should be dinner time. And just to prove it, her stomach made a gurgling sound.

"It's four-thirty. Why?"

"I don't want to intrude on Roni's dinner. It's Saturday, and he is probably having it with his fiancée, or girlfriend, or mate. I never know what to call the significant others."

Julian waved the hand with the phone. "You've just said it. Significant other covers all of the options."

"Nah, it sounds too formal. But anyway, how about we get something to eat before we invite ourselves to Roni's house?"

"You are too polite for your own good. What would you rather eat, another sandwich from the vending machine, or something fabulous that Ruth made?"

Ella scrunched her nose. "Isn't Roni's girlfriend's name Sylvia?"

Julian put his empty coffee mug next to hers on the nightstand. "Yeah, but Sylvia doesn't cook. Her mom does, and her name is Ruth."

"They live with her mom?"

"No, but they are very close, and Roni adores Ruth. Well, he probably adores her culinary skills, but in any case, she and her boyfriend, Nick, are always welcome at Roni and Sylvia's house."

"That's awesome." Ella put her hand over her chest. "It warms my heart to hear about a family that's so close. I hope we will be the same with my mom and Magnus, and Parker as well when he gets older and finds his love. I can imagine us all hanging out together, having Friday dinners and weekend barbecues at each other's houses."

Julian smirked. "That sounded like a proposal."

Embarrassed, she grabbed a pillow and tossed it at him. "I don't need to propose anything. It's you who keeps talking about us being fated for each other."

Naturally, Julian dodged the pillow.

"Do you object?" He lunged forward, trapping Ella under his big body.

She laughed and was about to tell him that his caveman antics were not going to wrestle an admission from her when he cupped the back of her head and smashed his lips over hers.

Holy Thor and all of Asgard, that was hot.

51

JULIAN

Julian hadn't meant to attack Ella and do precisely what he'd promised her never to do. It seemed as if a combination of several small triggers had snuck up on him and awakened the beast in him.

When she'd talked about them being a family, his heart soared on the wings of hope, and then when she'd teased him by making their relationship sound one-sided and tossing a pillow at him, his aggression got triggered. He'd felt an overwhelming need to prove to her that they were indeed fated for each other, and that she believed it too despite her protests.

His kiss wasn't the polite and tentative affair that he usually forced it to be, he was devouring her, and Ella was responding to it very differently than what he'd come to expect from her. Her arms wrapped around his neck and her legs parted to accommodate him between them, and she was holding him to her and moaning into his mouth.

Ella was aroused, and it wasn't the anemic, barely-there scent Julian had gotten from her up until now.

For the first time, her aroma held the richness of a woman's passion, and not that of a young girl who was still fearful and not ready for sex.

Emboldened by her response, he pushed a hand under her sweater and rested it on her soft belly, just below the swell of her breast.

Ella arched up, which he took to mean that she wanted him to touch her, but since it was the first time, he needed more explicit permission. Letting go of her mouth, he lifted his head and looked into her eyes as he inched his hand up in slow motion.

If she wanted to stop him, all she needed to do was to say it, or just put her hand over his to stop its ascent. But Ella did none of those things.

Gazing up at his face with hooded eyes and parted lips, she panted in anticipation.

He held her gaze as his hand cupped her breast gently over her bra, and when she closed her eyes and bit on her lower lip, he thumbed her stiff nipple and retook her mouth.

Her scent was doing all kinds of things to him, none of which encouraged the slow and patient. He wanted to tear her clothes off and sink his shaft into what he knew was wet and welcoming.

If it were up to him, Julian wouldn't let her out of this bed for days. He'd feed her and wash her and then make love to her over and over again, biting her so many times that her scent would change and every immortal male would know who she belonged to.

Somewhere in the back of his mind, he knew those thoughts were crazy, and that he couldn't take Ella from five to one hundred in a single swoop. But right now the part of him that thought logically wasn't working that well, and the primitive part that had overtaken most of his synapses was roaring for him to ignore everything and make her his.

Letting go of Ella's mouth, he leaned back and pushed her sweater up, exposing her bra-covered breasts.

It was a lacy thing that didn't leave much to the imagination, but it was in the way nonetheless, and he had no patience to fumble with a clasp.

Instead, he pushed the cups up, freeing her breasts.

Sweet merciful Fates, what a sight. His mouth salivated as he swooped down and took one between his lips while lightly pinching the other.

Delicious. He sucked on the ripe berry, pulling as much of her breast into his mouth as he could, then letting go and flicking it with his tongue. Then he switched, feasting on the other one.

Careful not to scrape her with his fangs, he licked and sucked like a man possessed, the growls coming out of his throat a sound he'd only made once before, and it was when those humans had threatened his mate.

Something wasn't right, though, and it took him a couple of seconds to realize what it was.

Ella wasn't moving, and she wasn't making any sounds either. The scent of her desire still permeated the air, but that could've been from before.

Letting go of her nipple, he looked up at her face.

Her eyes were closed tight, and given her expression, he was willing to bet that her hands were balled into fists at her sides.

Ella was enduring, not enjoying.

The realization cooled Julian down faster than if he'd dipped his dick in a bucket of ice.

Moving up, he cupped her cheeks. "What happened?"

"Why did you stop?" she whispered.

"Because you froze up on me."

"I'm sorry." A tear slid down her cheek.

"No apologies, remember? I just want to understand."

She shook her head. "It's like you said. I froze up. Maybe I'm not ready yet."

As another tear slid down her cheek, he dipped his head and kissed it away.

"There is no reason to be upset. It's my fault. I got carried away and broke my promise to you by pushing you into doing more than you were ready for."

The haunted expression on her face was killing him, and he didn't know what else to do to make it better.

The soft growl Ella's belly made, gave him the out he needed. "You're hungry. Let me text Roni and see if I can get us invited to dinner at his house."

As he moved over to the side, Ella pulled down her bra and sweater. Wiping her tears away with the sleeve, she chuckled. "I'm glad I didn't put any eye makeup on."

His text got an immediate response, just not the one he'd been hoping for.

"We are out of luck. Roni and Sylvia went out to a restaurant."

Ella let out a relieved breath. "I'm glad. I didn't feel like socializing. Do you have anything we can make dinner from?"

"I have frozen pizzas."

"That would do. Are there any veggies to make a salad from?"

"There might be some lettuce and tomatoes."

"And an onion too?"

"I think so."

"I can make a garden salad from that."

He pushed to his feet and offered her a hand up. "Come on. Let me feed you."

52

ELLA

*C*rap, crappity crap, and double crap.

Julian wouldn't be as understanding and sweet if he knew the real reason for her freeze-down.

Washing the lettuce leaf by leaf and then spending an inordinate amount of time chopping vegetables for the salad, Ella was buying herself a little time to sort out her thoughts and hide the maelstrom of confusing feelings away from Julian's attention.

One thing this episode had made abundantly clear was that Logan hadn't compelled her desire, and even if he had, he hadn't compelled the lack of it toward others.

As soon as Julian allowed his natural dominance to emerge, she'd responded.

Oh, boy, how she'd responded.

Ella had never been so aroused in her life. Up until now, the most intense cravings she'd experienced had been while reading some of the naughty romance novels she'd pilfered from her mother.

And that had been before her ordeal.

Since then, all she'd experienced were short-lived, anemic flares that had fizzled out almost as soon as they'd started, and she hadn't touched a romance novel since her rescue.

Fictional alpha males excited her. Real-life alphas, less so.

Not Logan, not Romeo, and certainly not the Russian. Only Julian had ever gotten her so hot and bothered.

So why had she freaked out?

Some of it had been her bad memories of lying under the Russian and trying to dissociate her mind from what was happening to her. Her eyes shut tightly, she'd pretended that she was one of the heroines in her mother's novels, and that the man with her was one of those sexy billionaires.

Sometimes it had worked, making things a bit easier, but not always. Some of it had been about enduring and counting the seconds until it was over.

So yeah, that would have been the most likely explanation for her freak-out, and what Julian believed had caused it.

Ella wished it was.

The truth, however, was that her freeze-up had been mostly the result of shame and guilt.

If Logan wasn't compelling her attraction, then it was coming from her, and that was troubling on so many levels. If she could feel that way toward a monster clad in a pretty skin, then she really didn't deserve Julian.

She'd felt so much better about herself when compulsion had been the most likely culprit.

Now, it was back to the darkness theory.

She was attracted to Logan because something inside her resonated with him. Carol thought that it was his dominance, but that wasn't likely. Forcing a kiss on her hadn't aroused her, it had repulsed her.

Still, she couldn't deny that his uber-alpha quality played a big part in it.

And what was the deal with not responding to Julian until he'd turned caveman on her?

She was damaged goods, that was the deal.

Leaning over her shoulder, Julian glanced at the cutting board. "Are you making salad or confetti?"

"Oh, I wasn't paying attention." She looked at the tiny pieces. "It looks like salsa."

He chuckled. "Don't worry about it. I like salsa. I wonder how it will taste on top of a pizza."

"Ugh, gross. What kind of pizza are we having?"

"Mushrooms and sausage."

She made a face. "Sounds yummy."

"Do you want something else? I can heat up a marinara pizza."

"No, that's fine. Where do you keep your oil and vinegar?"

He opened one of the top cabinets. "Everything is here. Do you want salt and pepper?"

"Sure."

When the oven beeped, Julian pulled the pizza out and put it on a cutting board. "Do you want a movie with your pizza?"

"I would love to."

That way she wouldn't have to talk to Julian and answer his probing questions.

Perfect.

It would take some intensive and creative thinking to come up with plausible answers that weren't lies, but at the same time didn't reveal the embarrassing truth.

Creativity was not restricted to artsy pursuits.

Pulling out two large plates, Julian loaded each with three slices of pizza and brought them over for Ella to add the salad. "Only a little for me. I'm not that fond of salads."

She cast him a sidelong glance. "Perhaps I'll change your mind about that."

"I doubt it." He lifted the two plates and carried them to the living room coffee table. "My mother is a vegetarian, and she tried her best to convert me."

Ella followed him with the cutlery. "Yeah, I can see that. You even like meat on your pizza."

Which Ella thought was gross, but she was in the minority. Judging by the supermarket frozen pizza aisle, pepperoni was the most popular.

"Don't most people?" Julian went back to the kitchen. "Can I get you a drink?"

"Do you have Diet Coke or Sprite?"

"I have the non-diet variety."

"That's fine."

She eyed the Snake Venom beer he'd brought for himself. "Magnus likes that one too. I don't know how you guys can drink it."

"Immortal metabolism. Regular beer is like piss water for us."

Popping the lid of a coke can, Ella wondered whether she would develop a taste for that super-potent beer after her transition.

She certainly had a taste for the super-potent immortals, except she was too much of a chicken to do anything about it.

"Okay." Julian reached for his tablet. "Let's see what's playing on Netflix."

Too hungry to care about what they were going to watch, Ella picked up a pizza slice, flicked off the pieces of sausage, and took a big bite. It was very good, although in her state of hunger anything even remotely edible would taste gourmet.

Julian turned to her. "Did you see that Fifty Shades movie everyone was talking about?"

Mouth full of pizza, she shook her head.

"Do you want to watch it?"

Why was he suggesting such an awful movie? For sure he didn't want to watch it. Did he think she would get aroused by it?

Finishing chewing, she shook her head again. "I read the book, and I didn't like it."

He arched a brow. "It was all the rage."

"I know. That was why I picked it up. I'm not some literary snob. I liked the love story and the way it was told, but I didn't like the premise."

"The rich guy, poor girl thing? Or was it the dominant-submissive interplay?"

Julian seemed surprised, which was understandable after her intense reaction to his mild show of aggression from before. Apparently, though, he had only a vague idea about what went on in that book.

"The Cinderella trope is very common in romance, and it's an overused one, but I have no problem with that if the story is good. And I also have no problem with the kind of games the guy in Fifty Shades liked to play. What bothered me about it, though, was that the girl wasn't into pain, and she didn't enjoy it. What's sexy about that? To me, it seemed abusive."

Shaking his head, he raked his fingers through his hair. "I didn't know that. The movie trailers were misleading."

Ella picked up another slice. "Maybe they changed it in the movie and had her getting off on the abuse. But even if they did, I still wouldn't want to watch that. Just not my cup of tea."

There was a big difference between dominance and sadism, even a mild one like in that book. The first one aroused her. The second one repulsed her.

53

JULIAN

If Julian was confused before, he was more so now. He needed time to piece together the crumbs of information Ella had revealed here and there, and from that to forge a key to unlock her secrets.

That she was keeping them, he was sure of. It was in her eyes when she averted them while answering his questions with half-truths, and it was in the sad expression that usually followed.

Whatever she wasn't telling him was eating her from the inside, and yet she was guarding it with fierce determination.

Scrolling through the selection, he chose a romantic comedy, something about a Valentine's Day mishap.

"Is that good?"

Ella nodded with a mouth full of pizza.

Feeding her made him feel as if he'd done at least one thing right by her, and wasn't that pathetic.

He was a twenty-six-year-old, well-educated guy who thought of himself as fairly intelligent and open-minded, and yet figuring out what made Ella tick was eluding him. Part of it was her great acting skill, and the other part was that he was predisposed to buying her badass, confident act because it was so much easier than digging deeper and discovering that she was suffering on the inside.

With a sigh, Julian clicked play and lifted his first slice, deciding to eat it slowly in case Ella was still hungry after finishing all three of hers. She hadn't been kidding about being hungry and was already on her second one.

Or maybe he should just put another one in the oven. Yeah, that was a better plan.

"I'll be right back. I want to heat up another pizza."

She smiled up at him. "Good idea. Ray will have some when he comes back."

A wave of jealousy washed over him. Why the hell was she concerned about fucking Ray?

Forcing a smile just until he turned around, Julian walked into the kitchen and pulled out a plain cheese pizza from the freezer.

Note to self. Stock up on meatless pizzas. And vegetables.

Back in the living room, he sat on the couch and lifted another slice. Pretending to watch the movie, he went over what he knew.

Up until today, Ella had responded to him with minimal excitement. The one time he'd momentarily lost control and had shown a little aggression, she'd lit up like a flare. But it hadn't lasted long, and she'd frozen up on him.

If her problem had been a troubling flashback, then how come she'd gotten into it in the first place?

Shouldn't any show of male aggression trigger her flight or fight response?

That had been the assumption he'd based his entire approach with her on, but apparently, he'd been completely off the mark.

Except, a girl who'd been forced into unwanted sex, who had her choices taken away from her, shouldn't respond to dominance, not unless it was something she'd enjoyed or rather craved before her abduction. Ella hadn't had any sexual experience prior to that, good or bad.

But evidently Ella had never been interested in those kinds of sex games. While every girl and her mother and grandmother had read the Fifty Shades book and enjoyed it, Ella hadn't.

It wasn't her thing.

Damn, he was so tired of guessing, tired of walking on eggshells, and tired of feeling like a martyr.

They had to have a frank talk, with Ella opening up and telling him what was going on with her. If she said she needed more time, he would wait patiently until she was ready. But he had to know where he stood.

Ella nudged his elbow. "Your pizza is ready."

The beeping hadn't registered because his mind had been somewhere else. "I'll get it." Julian rose to his feet.

Ella lifted her eyes to him. "Do you want me to pause the movie?"

"No. It's fine. I wasn't watching anyway."

In the kitchen, he pulled out the pizza, put it on the cutting board and sliced the hell out of it, dividing it into twelve tiny triangles just because he needed to keep his hands busy.

When he brought it to the living room, Ella clicked the television off. "Do you want to watch a different movie? I admit that this one is quite silly even for a chick flick."

"It's okay. You can keep on watching. I'm just not in the mood."

Ella put down the slice of pizza. "Is it because of me?"

His first instinct was to protect her fragile feelings and lie. But he was so done with that.

"You are confusing me, Ella."

She nodded. "I'm confusing myself."

As her despondent expression twisted his gut, he took her hand and entwined their fingers. "What's holding you back? Are you still fearful? Does intimacy with me scare you?"

Looking at their conjoined hands, she lifted them both to her lips and kissed his knuckles. "I'm not afraid of you, Julian. I never was."

The sweet gesture melted his heart, but he was adamant about getting to the bottom of this and going soft would be counterproductive. "So, what's the problem? Are you still getting flashbacks?"

"I do, but that's not the problem. At least not all of it. I'm stuck."

"What do you mean?"

She pulled her hand out of his and raked her fingers through her messy hair. "I'm stuck with the dream-walker. I need to pretend to like him, and I can't be intimate with you while I'm doing it. I just can't."

Why the hell not? He didn't like the idea of her playing nice with the Doomer, but it was unavoidable. And besides, it was only pretend.

Or maybe it wasn't?

What kind of liking was she talking about? Was she having dream sex with that son of a bitch?

Even though it was going to kill him if she was, Julian had to know. At least the guesswork would be over. Unless he got a straight answer, he was going to torment himself by imagining what went on in those dreams, and that was much worse.

Except, he wanted Ella to fess up without having to force the admission out of her. Instead, he cast a bait. "Why not? Being with me doesn't mean that you can't smile at other guys. I wouldn't like it, but that's my problem."

54

ELLA

"What if I have to do more than smile?" As soon as the words left her mouth, Ella's heart had plummeted to somewhere deep in her gut.

Why the hell had she let it out, committing herself to reveal what should've remained hidden?

And if her guilt and fear weren't enough, Julian's expression added another ton of bricks to the heavy load in her gut. He looked as if she'd plunged a dagger in his heart and then twisted it.

If only she could go back in time and stop herself from opening her big mouth.

"I'm sorry," she whispered.

"Define more."

Cringing, she averted her eyes so she wouldn't have to watch his anger flare up. "I had to kiss him."

Surprising her, he let out a breath. "That's all?"

Okay, maybe she was making a big deal out of nothing, torturing herself over something Julian considered insignificant. Perhaps his age and experience made him more tolerant. If Julian had told her that he kissed a girl in a dream, she would have been majorly pissed. Especially a dream that was not a fantasy but a real mind connection between two people.

"Isn't it enough? You have no idea how guilty it made me feel."

"Because of me?"

She nodded.

He clasped her hand. "I won't lie to you. I'm jealous. But knowing that you have no choice and that you're not enjoying it helps."

God, this was hard.

Should she tell him the truth?

To what end? She would be just hurting his feelings and souring their relationship.

Except, lying added another thick layer of sludge to her guilt, making her feel dirty and not worthy of someone as good and as pure as Julian.

He was so understanding, so mature about this, maybe he would be able to accept her misguided attraction to Logan too?

"The thing is..." She grimaced. "I would be lying if I said that he had to force me, or that I suffered terribly while doing it."

As Julian's face started turning red, she quickly added, "I was convinced that he was using compulsion on me, artificially making me feel attraction toward him and preventing me from feeling it toward anyone else."

Julian's eyes softened. "It might be true."

Crap, she was doing it again. Hiding behind an excuse she now knew wasn't true. "I wish it were," she murmured under her breath. "That would have explained so much." And transferred responsibility for her actions from her shoulders to Logan's, effectively eradicating most of the guilt.

Unfortunately, she could no longer use that to ease her conscience.

"How do you know he is not compelling you to feel things for him?" Hope shining in his soft, blue eyes, Julian scooted closer to her. "If he could so easily compel your silence, I don't see why he wouldn't do this. Doomers are not known for their high moral standards."

She should just let him believe that and shut up. It would save them both unnecessary heartache.

Except, Julian was a smart guy, and eventually he was going to realize the same thing she had less than an hour ago. If Logan's compulsion had been blocking her from feeling attraction toward other men, then she wouldn't have gotten so aroused by Julian's show of assertiveness, or anything else for that matter.

And once Julian figured that out, he would think that she was a liar in addition to being damaged goods who lusted after the worst possible guy.

With a sigh, she pulled her hand away and slumped against the sofa's plush pillows. "As I said, I wish it were true, but after reacting to you the way I did, I can no longer use this as an excuse. That's what really freaked me out, not some disturbing flashback. Not this time, anyway. I realized that the only reason I haven't been responding to you as strongly before was that apparently I've been craving intensity, while you've been walking on eggshells around me."

For some reason, Ella had trouble using the term dominance. Maybe because it suggested things that were further up the spectrum from what she craved. All she wanted was an alpha type male who was sexually assertive but not a caveman, and she was definitely not interested in the sort of games she'd read about in the Fifty Shades book.

It was so damn confusing. Was it like this for everyone?

She doubted it. Otherwise most would have not found compatible partners. In her case, it was like only one very particular shade could unlock her desires, and all the rest were ineffective.

In short, it was a recipe for disappointment.

He chuckled sadly. "The road to hell is paved with good intentions. I've been suppressing my caveman urges because I believed they would scare you. But now that we've figured it out, it should no longer be a problem."

If only the solution could be so simple. But nothing in Ella's life was.

"The thing is, you weren't wrong. Not entirely."

Shaking his head, Julian let go of her hand. "Now you've got me completely confused. One moment you say that you crave my inner caveman, and then you admit that he scares you. What am I supposed to do?"

Did he think that he was the only one who was frustrated by this?

"I can't help it, Julian. I crave something that scares the hell out of me, and I'm in a Catch 22 situation. For reasons I can't understand, I need to yield control to get aroused, but I'm terrified of letting anyone have that much power over me. It's not that I don't trust you, or that I'm afraid of you, but I just can't let go. I have to stay in control."

Hooking a finger under her chin, he lifted her head so she would look into his eyes. "Why do you need to stay in control? You are safe with me, and you are safe here in the village. I'm sure you realize it."

"I do. That's not the problem."

"Then what is?"

God, he was killing her. Forcing her to dig deep into what made her tick and look at what she didn't want to see.

"If I let go, I'll fall apart. The only thing holding me together is my control over what I allow myself to feel and what I don't. Numbness is my friend. Can you understand that?"

She was being unfair to him. Julian couldn't possibly know how it felt to be her. He'd never been humiliated, sold like a piece of property, and used. He hadn't felt helpless and hopeless, and he hadn't been touched by evil.

"I think I do." He scratched his short beard. "You keep everything bottled up inside and plow through by the sheer force of your will. That's your survival mechanism. But you are tired of pretending and of carrying this burden alone. It's like holding up a ton of bricks. They are too heavy for your arms, and you wish there was a way for you to put them down, but you can't stoop without breaking your back, and you are forced to keep trudging onward."

That was such an insightful analogy that she could actually visualize herself walking with a huge pile of bricks, not in her arms but tied to her back. If she crouched, her knees were going to buckle, and if she bent forward, the bricks were going to crash into her head and smash it.

There was no way out from under them.

Not now, and not ever. She was stuck with that impossibly heavy cargo weighing her down.

Unbidden, tears started pooling in the corners of her eyes, and a moment later they were streaming down her cheeks in twin salty rivulets.

"I can't see a way out, Julian. I'm stuck."

"Blast them, one at a time." He made a finger gun and aimed it at her invisible cargo.

Julian was trying to cheer her up, but once the dam had burst, there was no stopping the flood. The tears just kept coming.

Besides, she couldn't visualize his suggestion.

"How can I blast them when they are on my back? I can't aim." The words came out in a sob.

"What I mean by blasting is talking to me about them. As long as you keep them inside, they feed on you and gain substance. But putting them out there, not all at once, but one at a time, will suck that substance out of them and they will dissipate into thin air. Eventually, as the load gets lighter, you'll be able to stand up tall and shake the rest off."

Again, she could visualize that happening, but instead of the bricks falling off, they would just transfer onto Julian's back. His empathetic nature made working in a human hospital impossible because he couldn't take the suffering of strangers. Her suffering would be so much worse for him to carry.

"I wish I could. But I can't."

"Why not?"

"Because those bricks are not going to dissipate. They are going to land on your back. I don't want to do it to you."

Leaning, he kissed her tear-stained cheek. "My back is pretty sturdy, and my thigh muscles are strong. Once you transfer your bricks to me, I'll just crouch down and put them on the ground. Then we will take a big sledge-hammer and blast them all the way to hell where they belong."

55

JULIAN

*E*lla had reached a breaking point. Or perhaps it was a breakthrough? Trying to comfort her and stop the crying, Julian had been pulling nonsense out of his ass.

He'd never had to deal with an emotional meltdown before. His mother was a pillar of strength who he hadn't seen shed a single tear, and in the hospital, it hadn't been his job to provide comfort or counsel.

It was his fault.

If he hadn't pushed and probed, she wouldn't be sobbing right now like her world was ending.

Except, maybe it was good for her to let it all out, cathartic?

He just wished Ella would talk to him instead of sobbing. She'd been suppressing her feelings so well, probably from herself as well, because he hadn't sensed the turmoil in her.

Tears alone weren't going to purge the load she was carrying, and once the crying stopped, she would go back to showing strength she apparently didn't possess.

"I lost my virginity to a guy old enough to be my grandfather, and he wasn't an immortal with a perfect body. But that wasn't the worst of it." As another sob rocked her, Ella waved a hand and then bolted up.

Thinking she was running away from him, he reached for her hand.

"I need a tissue." She yanked her hand away and dashed to the powder room.

He was such an idiot. The girl was crying her eyes out, and it hadn't crossed his mind that she needed something to blow her nose into?

Idiot, he murmured under his breath.

The thing was, all he could offer her was a roll of toilet paper because he didn't have a box of tissues. But he could at least offer her water, or wine, or both.

In the kitchen, he suddenly remembered the stash of Godiva chocolates Ella had given him for safekeeping. If anything could lift her spirits, it was that.

Armed with his secret weapon, a bottle of wine, two bottles of water, and two glasses, Julian returned to the couch and organized everything on the coffee table.

As he waited for the nose blowing and sniffles to stop, he fought the urge to barge into the bathroom and take Ella into his arms.

Obviously, she was trying to get over her crying alone in there, and once she succeeded, she would come out and pretend like everything was alright.

It would be the end of their talk, and the weight of nasty she was carrying around would keep festering inside her.

Perhaps he should knock on the door and ask if she was okay?

Right. Talk about stupid.

She obviously was not.

When Ella finally opened the door, she was much more composed. Her eyes and nose were red, but she wasn't crying anymore.

"Sorry about that." She sat next to him on the couch. "I didn't mean to have a meltdown like that."

Wrapping his arm around her shoulders, Julian pulled Ella closer. "No apologies, remember? And besides, I want you to let it all out. No more keeping things from me and feeling guilty about it."

He leaned, opened the box of chocolates, and brought one to her mouth. "I can promise you this. No matter what you tell me, or how bad you think it is, nothing will make me walk away from you."

Chewing on the chocolate, she arched a brow. "What if I told you I had dream sex with Mr. D?"

His gut clenched with fury, but it wasn't directed at Ella. He was just going to kill Lokan. "Dream sex doesn't count. But I will have to kill him."

She chuckled. "Please don't. At least not until Turner and Kian finish interrogating him. And no, I didn't have dream sex with him. I would never go that far."

"How far did you go? I'm just asking, so this issue no longer creates a divide between us. I don't want you to carry guilt on top of that ton of bricks."

Reaching for another chocolate, she motioned at the wine. "Can you pour me a glass?"

"With pleasure."

Taking the wineglass, she sniffed it. "The Russian got me into wine drinking. I thought I wouldn't want to touch it because of the memories it brought, but I still like it." She chuckled. "I'm just glad he didn't feed me Godiva chocolates. If that put me off them, it would've been a disaster of epic proportions."

Ella was reverting to her old self, joking and making sarcastic comments, and Julian wondered whether she was doing it to change the subject and end confession time.

But she continued, "I let him kiss me, that was all. But it wasn't like with the Russian. With him, I was just enduring it."

She took another sip. "I feel so shallow and dirty, but I can't stay indifferent to the Doomer. Maybe it's because he's so handsome, and it's only physical. And maybe it's because he is intelligent in a cunning and evil way, and that makes him intriguing."

Looking into his wine glass, Julian's entire focus was on keeping his fangs from elongating, his eyes from glowing, and his throat from growling. He'd promised Ella he would keep his cool, and it was crucial that he didn't break that promise even in the slightest.

She was opening up to him, telling him things she'd feared were going to upset him, and he wanted her to keep talking.

Ella took another sip of wine, reached for another chocolate, but didn't pop it into her mouth. "I could've lived with that. None of it was too horrible for a human girl who didn't buy into the whole true-love mates thing immortals believe in." She took a little bite off the chocolate and chewed, probably buying herself some time to think.

Emptying the wine down his throat, Julian poured himself another glass.

This talk was illuminating on more than one level.

Apparently, the guilt she was feeling was his fault. After all, he'd been the one who'd pressed the issue of her being his true-love mate. No wonder she'd resisted accepting it.

When she finished chewing, Ella took another sip of wine and then continued in a near whisper. "What bothers me is that I might be attracted to his darkness because there is so much of it in me. I'm tainted, and so is he. Even when I was still terrified of him, I felt the pull. It felt to me as though like was recognizing like."

She chuckled without mirth. "I even called him Darth Sidious, and joked about him tempting me over to the dark side."

Julian's initial response was an intense need to get his hands on Lokan and tear his throat out. Luckily, not all of his brain had been taken over by the caveman, and some of the logic synapses were still operational.

"The pull you initially felt toward him had to be affinity. Amanda speculates that Dormants and immortals feel a special connection, and that is another indicator for identifying Dormants. That feeling of like recognizing like is exactly how she describes it. But because you didn't know what it was, you interpreted it as sexual attraction. And since the Doomer is, unfortunately, very good-looking, you had no reason to question that interpretation."

56

ELLA

*H*mm, could he be right?

It would be so nice if it were true.

Perhaps it was?

Amanda was a scientist, a neuroscience professor who was researching Dormants and ways to identify them. She must know what she was talking about.

Except, affinity had several meanings, and Amanda might have been referring to the sexual one.

"Affinity, eh? If I remember the definition correctly, it can also mean attraction."

"That's true, but what Amanda is referring to is the feeling of belonging to a group—the mutual origins that Dormants and immortals share. Most Dormants report a lifetime of feeling different than other humans, like they don't belong. But with immortals they experience that sensation you get when meeting someone for the first time and hitting it off right away. It's the like recognizing like you've talked about. That's what got me thinking about Amanda's affinity theory."

Feeling as if the boulder sitting inside her stomach had shrunk a little, Ella took in her first deep breath since this conversation had started.

"So, I'm off the hook? You're no longer jealous?"

"I didn't say that. Of course, I'm jealous. But I can live with that." He winked.

The boulder shrank by several more inches.

"You have no idea what a relief this is. You've just blasted half of those damn bricks, and I feel so much lighter. I was so sure something was really wrong with me. How could I feel a pull toward a despicable guy?"

She threw her hands in the air. "Even before I knew he was a Doomer, I knew that he was a warlord and that he was buying weapons from the Russian. He didn't even try to make himself look nice, admitting to being as bad as they come. Good looks shouldn't have been enough to blindside me, and neither should his smarts or his dubious charm. I saw through all of that down to the rotten core of him and still couldn't stop the bloody attraction."

"You know what your biggest problem is?" Julian refilled her empty wine glass.

The boulder started expanding again.

She should've known that Julian couldn't be as accepting as he'd seemed. After hearing her confession, any normal guy would've been foaming at the mouth or walking away, and as understanding and compassionate as Julian was, he wasn't a saint. Now he was going to tell her what he really thought.

Pretending nonchalance, she shrugged and lifted her feet onto the couch, tucking them under her long skirt. "There are so many of them that I wouldn't know which one you're referring to."

"You are stubborn."

That wasn't what she'd expected.

Ella lifted a brow. "How so?"

"If you'd talked to Vanessa when you'd just gotten here and told her what you've told me, she would have figured out immediately that what you felt for Lokan was affinity and would have explained it to you. You could've saved yourself weeks of needless fear and self-doubt."

That was a relief. She could live with Julian thinking that she was stubborn. It was much better than the other personality flaws he could have accused her of.

Grimacing, Ella took a long sip of wine. "I hate shrinks."

The box of chocolates was still mostly full, and she was tempted to reach for another. It had such a calming effect on her, but her stomach wouldn't appreciate it.

"You didn't give her a chance."

Ella waved a dismissive hand. "I knew she was going to suck the moment she tried to convince me that I was raped."

He arched a brow. "You weren't?"

"No. I was coerced. There is a big difference. I wasn't attacked, and I wasn't beaten up. I cooperated. I had no choice, but it was my decision to agree."

Julian shook his head. "I don't see the difference. What if you were at a club and someone slipped you a roofie or a similar date-rape drug? You wouldn't have resisted then either, but I'm sure that as soon as the drugging effect was over, you would've marched into the nearest police station to report it as rape."

"That's different.'"

"How so?"

"Because if I were drugged, I wouldn't have been able to make a conscious decision to cooperate."

"So, what you are saying is that your decision-making ability would have been taken away from you?"

In a shrink-like manner, he'd restated what she'd said in the form of a question, and that was no doubt leading somewhere.

Ella put her wine glass down and crossed her arms over her chest. "It would have been impaired by the drug."

"An impaired ability to make a choice."

He was starting to annoy her. "Where are you going with this, Julian? I hate the shrink-ish roundabout talk. Just say what you mean."

Raking his fingers through his hair, he sighed. "I was trying to lead you to the conclusion without having to say it myself, but you are more stubborn than a clan of badgers. So here it goes." He took a deep breath and pinned her with a hard look. "When your only choice is to cooperate, then it is like not having a choice at all. It is rape."

"I could have said no. I could've fought."

"Could you have really?"

Crap.

He was right.

She couldn't.

Not without risking her family, and not without sustaining significant injuries. And since it would have been utterly stupid to resist, the choice hadn't been really a choice.

It had been an illusion.

She'd been raped.

As the tears started falling anew, Julian wrapped his arms around her and lifted her onto his lap.

"I'm so sorry, love. I know it hurts, but I believe that the only way to put it behind you is to let it out."

She slapped his chest. "What would you know about it? Have you ever been humiliated? Violated? Treated like an object for sale? You know nothing, Julian."

It wasn't his fault, she knew that, but she hated that he was right, and she hated feeling like a victim, and he was the only one she could take out her frustration on.

"Shh, it's okay. You can hit me as many times as you want. Use me as your punching bag. I'll take anything if it helps you even a little bit."

Crap, why did he have to be so nice?

Now she couldn't hit him, and she needed to hit something.

"Stop it! I don't want you to be nice to me!"

"Why not?"

"Because I can't punch you when you're being so sweet."

"I can make you mad in a heartbeat."

"Oh, yeah? How?"

"I want you to promise me that you'll talk to Vanessa."

"She can't help me."

"I want you to give it a try. For me. Payment for turning me into your punching bag."

"The price is too high." She grabbed a throw pillow. "I'd rather punch this inanimate object and not talk to a freaking shrink."

He shook his head. "Then do it for love, for us."

Talk about playing dirty. "What do you mean?"

"It means that I love you, and that I want you, and that I want us to be a couple in all ways, and that I want you to transition so we can spend the rest of our immortal lives together. But first, you have to heal, and it would take much less time with Vanessa's help."

Ella felt a lump form in her throat.

Without saying the actual words, Julian had told her countless times and in so many ways that he loved her, but until now he had never said it explicitly, and hearing those three little words coming out of his mouth had made a world of difference.

There was no more guessing, or doubting, or disbelieving.

This was it, the real deal, and what she'd been waiting for without realizing that she had.

Suddenly, the boulder inside her gut felt as if it had shrunk to a size no larger than an apple, and after hauling such a huge weight around for so long, Ella felt buoyant.

"I love you too."

Crushing her to him, Julian kissed her as if he was trying to pour all of his love into that kiss. It wasn't gentle, and it wasn't elegant, and she was pretty sure her lips would be bruised from it, but it was so worth it.

When Julian finally let go of her mouth, she sucked in a long breath, filling her lungs with much-needed oxygen.

"If you keep kissing me like that, I'll heal in no time."

He nipped her lower lip. "Nice try. Are you going to see her?"

Ella still didn't believe in shrinks, and talking to Vanessa was as appealing as having a bikini wax one hair at a time. But it was important to Julian. And if there was even the slightest chance that the shrink could help her get her shit together faster, so she could be with Julian without dragging excess baggage into their nascent relationship, it was worth a try.

Any sacrifice was worth a clean start.

"I'm going to give her a chance. That's all I can promise."

"That's all I'm asking for."

DARK DREAM'S TRAP

1

JULIAN

"Good morning, my love." Julian walked into the bedroom with a tray.

The breakfast he'd prepared consisted of coffee and chocolates, because as far as food went all he'd found in the kitchen was a half-empty box of cereal and a couple of frozen pizzas. The chocolates were a lifesaver.

Even though Ella had feasted on them last night, he still had plenty left over in the box she'd given him for safekeeping. She loved those little treats, but it was a shame that this was all he could come up with the morning after the most monumental night of their relationship.

Not only had they confessed their love for each other, but Ella had promised to give the therapist a chance, and that was almost as big a deal as the I love you's.

"What time is it?" Ella mumbled, opening just one eye a crack.

"Around ten." He put the tray on the nightstand and leaned to kiss her soft lips.

She looked so adorable with her cheeks rosy from sleep, her pink hair sticking out in all directions, and her expression open and trusting and full of love.

For him.

"Would you like me to pour you some coffee?" He lifted the carafe.

"Breakfast in bed?" She stretched her arms over her head and yawned. "You're spoiling me, Julian. I might come to expect this every morning."

He dipped his head. "It would be my pleasure to serve."

"Aren't you sweet." Ella reached for his cheek. "I won the lottery with you." She planted a quick closed-mouthed kiss on his lips and then flung the comforter off. "I need to use the facilities, but in the meantime, I would love it if you poured me some coffee."

"It shall be done, my lady."

Chuckling, she rushed into the bathroom.

The sunlight from the open window made the plain white T-shirt he'd given her nearly see-through, outlining the contours of her curvy tight body as if she were wearing a sheer nightgown.

Sexy and adorable. What a killer combination.

As his shaft rose to attention, pressing painfully against his fly and accusing him of self-inflicted torture, Julian had no defense to offer his suffering member. He would be lying if he claimed that giving Ella his most worn-out T-shirt hadn't been a calculated move.

Shaking his head at his teenage antics, Julian was reminded of what his mother said about men. They were forever boys at heart, and that included immortals as old as Kian. There were exceptions, of course, like her mate.

Turner must have been born with an ancient brain. Julian could imagine him as a boy, somber and serious, dedicated to learning as much as possible and as quickly as his huge brain could absorb it. He probably had never taken part in the shenanigans ordinary boys amused themselves with.

Was that why Bridget had chosen him?

Every couple was different, and so was every relationship. There was something magical about that connection, though, something Julian hadn't expected.

Surprisingly, the incredible closeness and the feeling of being a unit had little to do with physical intimacy. It was more about the mental fusing, about the breaking down of barriers, and about laying one's soul bare for the other person and trusting that they wouldn't stomp all over it.

After Ella's meltdown last night, Julian felt closer than ever to her, and her confession about the attraction to Lokan hadn't diminished the effect in the least.

Her misguided feelings toward the Doomer mattered much less to him than the cleansing of her guilt over it and the obliteration of the wedge it had put between them.

There was a perfectly logical explanation for why Ella had reacted like that to Lokan. The affinity that Dormants and immortals felt toward each other had made her feel close to the Doomer, and because she had no way of knowing that he was an immortal and she was a Dormant, and what that meant, Ella had interpreted it as sexual attraction.

Or at least that had been the initial impetus.

Later, when he'd started intruding on her dreams, Navuh's son had used his good looks, his intelligence, and his charm to reinforce those feelings, and possibly compulsion as well.

As Julian had suspected from the moment he'd learned about Ella's dream visitor, Lokan was playing Ella and not the other way around. Despite all that had happened to her, she was still a naive eighteen-year-old, while the Doomer was an immortal with centuries of experience plotting and manipulating. She was no match for him.

Damn, she was so young and had gone through so much already.

It wasn't fair.

He wanted to hold Ella in the safety of his arms and shield her from the world twenty-four seven, but he would settle for the nights.

Having her curled against his body, his arms wrapped securely around her, had felt so right. It hadn't mattered to Julian that that was as far as it had gone. Well, the primitive side of him didn't like it one bit, but, fortunately, the savage occupied a very small part of his psyche and he'd beaten it into submission.

For now, he was satisfied with just being close. The rest would come later, after Ella had several sessions with Vanessa.

How did the saying go, "All good things come to those who wait"? It was a simple way to state a well-known fact. Those who were adept at delaying gratification got ahead of the crowd, and Julian was a master of that.

When Ella came out of the bathroom, he had the two cups of coffee ready, hers with cream and sugar and his with just sugar.

"I'm hopping right back." She crawled into the bed, stacked four pillows up against the headboard, got comfortable sitting up, and pulled the duvet up to her chest, covering everything up.

What a shame.

He handed her the mug. "Just as you like it. Cream and two sugars."

"Thank you." Cupping it between her hands, she took a sip and smacked her lips. "Perfect."

"Yes, you are." He bent and kissed the very tip of her nose. "I love you."

"I love you too." She shook her head. "Why does it feel so awkward to hear you say that?"

Because Ella still didn't believe that she deserved love, but that was going to change. Firstly, because she would be hearing him say it fifty times a day, and secondly, because Vanessa was going to clean up the trash that Ella had allowed to accumulate in her head.

All that nonsense about being tainted and about having some darkness inside her had to be disposed of as soon as possible. The longer it lingered, the more it festered, diminishing the brightness of Ella's incredible spirit.

"I'm going to say it a lot, so you'd better get used to it."

"Ditto."

"Nah-ah, young lady, ditto isn't going to cut it. I want to hear the words, preferably accompanied by a hot kiss." He was hoping for more than that, but for now it would do.

For some reason, Ella's smile turned into a grimace. "About that. I don't think we should hang out together until the mission is over."

Talk about driving a dagger into his unsuspecting heart. "What are you talking about?" Things were going so well, and now she was throwing this at him?

Grabbing another pillow from his side of the bed, she hugged it to her. "I don't want us to be apart either. But catching Mr. D is more important than us. We can wait a little longer, but every dream encounter I have with him, I'm running the risk of letting something slip, getting him suspicious, and sabotaging this opportunity for the clan."

"We've been hanging out together every day, and you did just fine."

She brought her knees up, curling her arms around the pillow as if it was a shield. "That was before we deciphered the combination to unlocking my passion. Now it will be so much harder to refrain from doing more. And I know it's going to rock my world, and then I won't be able to continue pretending with Mr. D."

Ella thought that making love to him was going to rock her world? At least he could take solace in that.

Julian let out a breath. "Do you trust me?"

Ella rolled her eyes. "Of course, I trust you. I don't trust myself."

"Until the mission of entrapping the Doomer is over, we will keep our relationship strictly platonic, and I'm going to be in charge of that, so you have nothing to worry about." He took her hand. "I might not look it, but I'm a stubborn guy. When I decide on something, it's very difficult to sway me away from that decision. I won't let you seduce me even if you try."

Smiling, she lifted a brow. "Are you sure about that? I'm stubborn too. You said so yourself."

"That you are. But remember, you made me a promise, and I expect you to keep it. I want you to make an appointment with Vanessa for Monday."

"I can't do it on Monday. I'm filming."

"So?"

"I can't get myself all worked up before it, and I scheduled the taping for after dinner."

"Fine. Then Tuesday."

Letting out a resigned breath, she nodded. "Okay, but just so we are clear on that. I'm going to have one session with her, and if I don't like it, I will not have another."

"Three. You can't decide if she's helpful or not based on one meeting." Remembering how Ella visualized everything, he added, "You can't clean all of your kitchen cabinets in one go, let alone your brain. All kinds of nasty things are lurking in there, and they need to get trashed. And after that is done, the interior needs a good scrubbing with soap. You can't start filling those cabinets with beautiful new china until all of this is done and they are sparkling clean."

2

ELLA

It was really clever of Julian to come up with something Ella could visualize. It worked. Those cabinets up in her brain definitely needed spring cleaning. She just wasn't sure that Vanessa was the right tool for the job. Talking to a shrink was like using a cloth to clean up caked-on grime. It just smeared it around but didn't get rid of it.

"I hope that Mr. D can expedite my interview. I want this over and done with, so I can focus on us and our relationship."

"You don't have to wait." When she opened her mouth to argue, Julian lifted his hand. "I'm not talking about sex. We can get closer in other ways."

"What do you mean?"

"We can be together, just not alone with each other. We can hang out with family and friends."

It was much better than not seeing him at all, which Ella wasn't sure she could actually do. Maybe with plenty of phone calls, but even those had the potential of sliding into sexual territory. For now, complete abstinence was best.

Hanging out with her mother, Magnus and Parker could actually be fun and bring the entire family closer. "You're always welcome in my house."

"I know. And I like your mother and brother, and Magnus too. When I come over, instead of going to your room or out for a walk, we can spend time with your family. And the same goes for you. So far, you've only gotten to know my mother and Turner in their professional capacity. I think it would be nice to meet for dinner as a family. My mom doesn't cook much, but Turner can bring takeout on his way back from the office, or we can all go out to a restaurant."

That sounded wonderful. Growing up in a tiny family, Ella had envied her friends who had uncles and aunts and cousins and grandparents. Their birthdays had seemed so much happier than hers. Secretly, she'd hoped to one day marry a guy with a large family or a clan.

"I love it, and not only because of the obvious. Hanging around a lot of people will fill my head with more than just you, which is good for the dream encounters."

He arched a brow. "What do you mean by obvious?"

"You know, we are kind of engaged, right? So, it makes sense for us to get close to each other's families and friends."

Embarrassed, Ella put her mug on the nightstand and popped a chocolate into her big mouth. She should've done that five seconds ago instead of blurting nonsense about a nonexistent engagement.

When Julian sighed, her gut clenched. Now he was going to give her a speech about rushing to conclusions and tell her that they were not getting married anytime soon.

Not that she wanted to, not yet anyway. She was too young, for one, and then there was the issue of her education. Ella hadn't given up on that. Couldn't even if she wanted to. Since she was a little girl, her mother had been drilling the importance of college education into her head. She couldn't disappoint Vivian like that.

Except, college and marriage were not mutually exclusive.

Kids were another thing, though. Getting pregnant with Ella was the reason her mother hadn't gotten the education she'd wanted.

Not that pregnancy had anything to do with marriage.

Because she and Julian couldn't use contraceptives while working on the activation of her immortal genes, there was a slight chance Ella could get pregnant during the process. But maybe the prohibition was only on condoms?

She needed to ask Bridget if oral contraceptives were okay.

Once she turned immortal, her fertility would drop to almost nothing, and that was regardless of whether she and Julian wanted to wait with starting a family or not.

At the thought, a wave of sadness washed over Ella. It wasn't that she wanted kids right away, but she didn't want to wait centuries to have them either.

Julian was going to make such a great father. He was warm, patient, smart...

Crap, way to get carried away. There was plenty of time before any of that became relevant, and she was pretty sure Julian was about to tell her precisely that.

Instead, he said, "This idea is growing on me, and the more I think of it, the more I like it."

Ella let out a breath and cast a sidelong glance at the three remaining chocolates on the little plate. She really shouldn't eat any more, but the thing about being addicted to the sweet goodness was that she treated it as a reward or a pick-me-up, whether she was stressed or relieved, happy or sad, celebrating or mourning. Right now it was stress.

Julian reached for one and handed it to her. "It's going to be like an old-fashioned courtship, when couples weren't allowed to be alone before the big day, and all their meetings were done with family members present. I think that when sex is not on the table, it eliminates a lot of pressure. It becomes a non-issue."

"Except for the blue balls," she murmured.

"Don't worry about that." He chuckled. "I'll survive."

Hopefully, not by using a substitute other than his own hand. Suddenly, it occurred to her that it was strange for Julian to be so understanding about her dream encounters with Logan, and about her other issues. Perhaps it was because he was slaking his needs elsewhere?

But as soon as the thought flitted through her head, she cast it aside. Julian was just an angel of a man. That was all. And, apparently, he liked a challenge, even if it was about withstanding torment. It hadn't escaped her notice that he was a highly competitive overachiever, and as such he must be very good at handling delayed gratification.

They had that in common.

Well, except for the freaking chocolates. She had no self-control with those.

Still, she had to ask, "How?"

"I'll buy a tool belt."

She arched a brow. "What does that have to do with anything?"

"Manual labor. I'll get Yamanu to teach me construction and work till I drop. It will be a double whammy. The halfway house will get done faster and for less money, and I'll come home too exhausted to think about anything other than getting in the shower and then bed."

He chuckled. "To sleep."

"Poor baby." She cupped his cheek.

"Not at all. I'm actually looking forward to it. It will keep me distracted while you clean your cabinets." He put his hand over hers on his cheek. "Going platonic will get rid of a source of tension between us and allow us to focus on getting to know each other instead."

Reaching for the coffee mug, Ella took a sip to wash down the chocolate and then put it aside and spread her arms. "Can I give you a hug? Because you are the best guy on the planet, and I'm the luckiest girl."

He leaned into her arms, put his cheek on her shoulder, and sighed. "You know, there is a medical explanation for why it feels so good to hug and cuddle."

"Go ahead. Geek out on me," she teased, but the truth was that she loved learning new things.

"Hugging stimulates the pressure receptors under the skin, which increases the activity of the vagus nerve, which in turn triggers an increase in oxytocin levels. Oxytocin can decrease heart rate and cause a drop in the stress hormones cortisol and norepinephrine. It can also improve immune function, promote faster healing from wounds and diseases. It also increases the levels of good hormones, like serotonin and dopamine, which in turn reduce anxiety and depression."

"Oh, wow. Doctors should prescribe hugs in addition to medication."

"I agree."

Stroking his soft hair, she chuckled. "I found the solution to your midlife crisis at twenty-six. You should become a proponent of hugs and cuddles as a cure-all. I can visualize you running a hugging clinic with volunteer huggers, preferably old grandmas with soft bosoms. Those are the best, but you wouldn't know since everyone here is young."

3

BRIDGET

"That's a beauty," Sandoval said as he took the ring from Turner. "But it pales in comparison to your lovely lady, my friend."

Bridget waved a dismissive hand. "You're such a charmer, Arturo."

His eyes twinkled as he spread his arms in an exaggerated gesture. "Please tell me that this marvelous, fiery red hair is done by a gifted stylist. I'll send my wife to him."

"Sorry to disappoint you, but this is my natural color."

"*Dios mio*! What a lucky man Turner is. I can just imagine the fire burning inside a natural red-head like you." He then shook his head. "But the temper, that must be very hot too."

It was good that Turner wasn't the jealous type, not overtly anyway, because Bridget was having fun flirting with the guy. It was harmless, he wasn't aroused, and it had been ages since she'd engaged in teasing banter like that.

The one downside of having a brainiac like Turner for a mate was the absence of easy, lighthearted banter. He was always serious, rarely smiled, and avoided nonsensical conversations like the plague.

"You have no idea. I go from zero to one hundred in a split second." She snapped her fingers.

"I believe that." Sandoval glanced at Turner. "But my friend here looks better than ever, so you must be good for him. All this new beautiful blond hair, and that unlined skin." He smoothed his hand over his thinning hair. "I want the name of that transplant place."

The story they had told him to explain Turner's youthful appearance was that he'd gotten a hair transplant and laser work on his face.

It always amazed Bridget how easy it was to sell people an unlikely story just because there was no other more reasonable explanation they could conceive of.

For most Dormants, the transformation didn't bring much change, but it had for Turner. He looked fifteen years younger and better than he had in his early twenties.

He'd also lost some of the hardness, the edginess she'd found so sexy when they'd first met. But even though it had been part of why she'd fallen for him, Bridget didn't miss it. He was happier now than he'd ever been, and knowing that she was the reason for it was priceless.

"When we get back to Los Angeles, I'll look for the brochure and email you the name of the place," Turner said. "The revolutionary technology was developed in Switzerland, and that's where their only location is. In a couple of years, they might open a branch in the States."

Sandoval grimaced. "Never mind. I'm not going to travel all the way there for a hair transplant. There are enough reputable establishments here."

Turner's expression remained as impassive as ever, but Bridget knew him well enough to imagine a ghost of a smirk lifting the corners of his lips. He must've known about Arturo's inability to visit Switzerland, and that was why he'd made up the story about the clinic being there.

Following a knock on the door, one of Sandoval's many security guards entered. "The appraiser is here."

Arturo waved a hand. "Let him in."

So that was what the flirting had been all about. While waiting for the expert to arrive, Arturo had been stalling.

"Is he trustworthy?" Turner asked. "I mean as far as spreading the rumor about the ring."

"You intend to sell it, yes?" Sandoval asked. "Then you need the word to spread."

"I was hoping you'd buy it from me and then sell it. I'm doing this as a favor for a friend, and it's already taking too much of my time."

Training his gaze on Bridget, Sandoval grinned. "I'm thankful to your friend. If not for the ring, I would not have the excuse to finally meet your beautiful wife and offer you both my hospitality."

As the guard escorted the appraiser into the room, Arturo got up and greeted the guy as if he were an old friend.

"Yasha, thank you for coming. Please meet my good friends, Victor and Bridget Turner."

As they shook hands, she exchanged glances with Turner. He'd asked Sandoval not to sell the ring in Russia, but he hadn't said anything about the nationality of the appraiser.

Not that Yasha was necessarily a Russian.

It was a common name, and he could've been from any country in the Eastern Bloc. Nevertheless, Bridget's good mood had taken a nosedive. Sandoval had just introduced an unknown variable.

It took Yasha five minutes to examine the ring. "Would you like me to email you the estimate?"

Arturo clapped him on the back. "Sure. But I need a ballpark figure. How much do you think it could bring on the black market?"

"Twenty-five to thirty."

"Millions, I assume?"

The guy snorted. "Dollars, not rubles."

Bridget's gut churned with unease. She had a feeling that the guy had not only recognized the ring, but that he also knew who'd originally bought it.

It was to be expected, though. Not many diamonds of this size changed hands in the world, and someone like Yasha would be familiar with each one of them.

After the appraiser collected his tools, Sandoval escorted him to the door. "Thank you. Can you do me a favor, my friend?"

"Anything, for you."

"Please don't tell anyone I have the ring." He leaned to whisper in Yasha's ear. "I'm considering buying it for my wife, and I want it to be a surprise."

"Of course." The guy dipped his head before leaving.

Obviously, Sandoval didn't intend to buy the ring for himself or his wife, but he liked to maintain the appearance of a legitimate businessman who didn't deal in anything illegal.

After closing the door, he walked back to his armchair and sat down. "I'll give you twenty for it."

Turner shook his head. "That's much less than its lowest appraised value."

Sandoval grinned. "Yes, but since you are doing this as a favor for a friend and want to be done with this as soon as possible, I'm offering to take it off your hands. Instead of waiting for me to find you a buyer, you can get the money to your friend right away."

"Twenty-three," Turner said.

Sandoval shook his head. "Twenty-one, and that's my final offer. Take it or leave it, my friend. And just so you know, I'm being very generous because of our friendship and because of what you have done for my family."

Reminded of what Sandoval's nephew had done to Turner, Bridget's temper flared hot, and before she could put a muzzle on it, she blurted, "Your relation, the one Turner spared and then convinced you not to kill, had ordered a hit on him. I think you can do better than twenty-one."

Sandoval laughed. "And here is that famous temper. But you are right, my dear Bridget. Twenty-two, and that's my final offer."

Bridget offered him her hand. "You're an honorable man, Arturo."

Twenty-two million was going to buy several halfway houses, not just one.

"Indeed, I am." He looked at Turner. "So, are we even now? My debt of honor to you is paid?"

"There was no debt, Arturo." Turner offered him his hand for a handshake. "Just old friends helping each other out."

4

LOSHAM

As his cell phone rang, the last name Losham expected to appear on the screen was his brother's.

He let it go to voicemail.

Lokan was a smart son of a bitch, and talking with him before he knew what the call was about was not a good strategy. The thing was, Losham's island sources hadn't reported any unusual activity or another shift of power among the half-brothers. Navuh liked to switch things around and reassign his sons to different leadership roles, so that none would get too comfortable or entrenched in their positions.

Another benefit of this system was that each knew the other's job.

Except for Losham, who until recently had been his father's right-hand man and advisor. Not anymore, though. He'd been demoted from his lofty position to leading the Brotherhood's drug dealing and pimping operations.

Except, Navuh hadn't replaced him with anyone else yet. Was that what Lokan wanted?

Was he sniffing around about the possibility of taking Losham's place?

It wasn't as if he would call to ask after his brother's wellbeing.

The half-brothers weren't close. To the contrary. The constant rivalry over leadership positions in the Brotherhood didn't encourage familial loyalty, and neither did their father's favoritism, which was a moving target.

The favorite son today could become the least favored tomorrow, and Losham was a prime example of that. He'd thought himself indispensable, his strategic mind and good advice vital to Navuh and the Brotherhood, but he'd been wrong.

He was still unsure what had brought it about. It could've been punishment for a series of minor blunders or the result of shifting priorities. But since he'd covered up his mishaps well, it was most likely the latter.

With major contributors leaving the Brotherhood's protective umbrella, funding had dried up, and a new source of income was needed.

Regrettably, hot spots around the world were cooling at a rapid rate, and there was little demand for the Brotherhood's army of mercenaries. Their entire business model was collapsing or, rather, leaning heavily on two spindly legs that at the moment couldn't carry its weight.

That was why Navuh had assigned his best man to the job of shoring them up.

What had been a fringe source of income that was used mostly to bribe and blackmail high-ranking public figures around the world had become the core that had to sustain them until a new source was found.

It was all about technology now, and the Brotherhood wasn't equipped to compete in this new world. At least not until Losham's new breeding program started bearing fruit, producing offspring with mighty brains rather than brawn.

When his phone announced that he had a new voicemail, Losham clicked on the recording and listened attentively, trying to pick up subtle nuances in his brother's tone.

"Hello, Losham. I'm in the Bay Area, and I thought it was a good opportunity for us to meet. How about dinner later today? I'm waiting to hear from you before making other plans, so please let me know as soon as you can."

Damn. Lokan hadn't hinted at what he wanted to talk about, and the way he'd phrased his request, Losham had no choice but to answer him promptly.

Any delay would be interpreted as fear, and that was even worse than meeting his half-brother unprepared.

On his laptop, Losham closed the news broadcast he hadn't been paying attention to anyway and straightened his shoulders.

The damn demotion must have eroded his self-confidence.

There was no real reason for him to be wary of Lokan.

The guy was younger, less experienced, and had done nothing overly daring in recent years, unless schmoozing with Washington's movers and shakers could be considered hazardous.

Well, for a human it could be, but not for Lokan.

The guy was charming, he had to give him that, and his ability to compel was nothing to sneer at. It was a rare and coveted talent, extremely handy when dealing with humans. But neither compulsion nor his brother's fake charm had any effect on Losham. It was absurd for him to get anxious over a friendly talk.

Instead of calling back, he shot a quick text with the name of a restaurant he wanted to hold the meeting at. At least he had the advantage of the home court. The location of the hotel he'd chosen was perfect for bringing in a team of warriors and stationing them all around the big place without Lokan being any the wiser.

As cunning and underhanded as his younger half-brother was, he was still no match for Losham.

5

ELLA

"Good morning, sweetheart," Vivian said as Ella came in, then looked her up and down and then up again. "You look happy. Good news?"

Ella knew precisely what her mother was asking, but she wasn't going to indulge her curiosity. Besides, there was nothing to tell on that front.

Instead, she opted to share her other good news.

"Mr. D is arranging an expedited interview for me at Georgetown. All I have to do is fill out the application and send them my transcripts, which is why I'm going to Roni. I don't know what kind of grades poor Kelly Rubinstein had before her premature death, and if he needs to give them a makeover."

Vivian's face fell. "Oh."

Remembering what Julian had told her about hugs, Ella pulled her mother into a tight embrace. "This is good news, Mom. The faster it happens, the faster it ends, right?"

Vivian sighed. "I know. What can I do that I'm such a scaredy-cat? Facing that Doomer terrifies me."

Ella let go of her mom. "He's actually not that bad once you get to know him. I bet most people think he is charming. But enough about him. I have to shower and change. Julian is picking me up in twenty minutes, and we are going to a barbecue at Roni's."

That brought the smile back to Vivian's face. "I'm so glad that you're making new friends. Roni is about your age, and his fiancée is very nice. You are going to have a good time."

Ella certainly hoped so. According to Julian, Roni wasn't the most charming of guys, but he was an amazing hacker and, more importantly, he was willing to help. She could handle some surly attitude as long as he helped her out.

As she stepped into the shower, Ella was thankful for the short haircut and the time it shaved off her bathroom routine. Most days she didn't even bother to blow dry it, letting it air dry instead. It seemed like the messier it was, the nicer it looked.

But today she was pressed for time, and two minutes with the blow dryer took care of that.

A little mascara, lip gloss, and she was ready with minutes to spare.

Julian was already waiting for her when she came out, chatting with her mother about the halfway house and how much easier it would be for her to run her classes there instead of schlepping all the way to the sanctuary and back.

"I would love not having to make that drive, but the girls in the sanctuary need me. Once they are in the halfway house, they are already on the road to recovery."

Ella leaned and kissed her cheek. "We'll talk about this later. Right now Julian and I have to skedaddle."

"Have fun, kids."

When they got to Roni's, the backyard party was already in full swing, with Roni flipping steaks over the weirdest looking barbecue Ella had ever seen.

It was egg-shaped.

"Let me introduce you to everyone," Julian said as he walked her over to Roni.

"Hi." Roni waved with a pair of tongs that were dripping steak juices. "Grab a plate. They're almost ready."

"Thank you. And thank you for helping me with the college application stuff."

"Pfft." He waved with the tongs again. "It's child's play for me."

"Nevertheless, I'm grateful."

He nodded, looking embarrassed.

That was cute. After Julian's warning, she'd expected the guy to be full of himself, and he kind of was, but he still felt awkward when thanked. She had a feeling that Roni's crusty attitude was a shield, and under it he was a nice guy.

"Hi, Ella." Sylvia came out into the backyard, holding a big salad bowl. "Come meet my mother." She put the bowl down and took Ella's hand. "She's in the kitchen."

Casting an apologetic glance at Julian, Ella let Sylvia drag her away.

"Tessa and Jackson are coming too, and so are Sharon and Robert. Do you know them?"

Ella shook her head. "I know Eva and Tessa, so naturally I've heard about Sharon and Robert, but I've never met them."

She was curious to meet Carol's ex and, also, the one he'd found true love with.

Sharon must be special to fill Carol's shoes, so to speak. Although small in size, Carol cast a big shadow.

In the kitchen, a short brunette was tossing a rice pilaf that smelled delicious.

"Mom, I want you to meet Ella."

She turned around, smiling shyly as she offered Ella her hand. "I'm Ruth, but I guess everyone knows me as Sylvia's mom."

There weren't many families in the village, and the only two with grown children that Ella had known about were Bridget and Eva, and now Ruth. But even though she should've been prepared, it was still hard to reconcile Ruth's youthful looks with her being Sylvia's mother.

In fact, the woman looked younger than her daughter. Perhaps because she was so shy while Sylvia was so outgoing, or maybe because the daughter was taller.

"Nice to meet you." Ella shook her hand. "Have you met my mother, Vivian?"

"I work outside the village and I come home late. So, I don't get to hang around much."

"Oh yeah? What do you do?"

"I run a café."

"Cool, so you're an independent businesswoman."

Ruth blushed. "I'm just the manager. The café belongs to Nathalie, Eva's daughter."

"Oh, right, the one Jackson manages..." Ella scratched her head. "I'm confused. Jackson manages the café here and Carol and Wonder work for him. You manage the one in the city, right? And both of you answer to Nathalie?"

"The original café where I work belongs to Nathalie, and this one and the one in the keep are partially hers as well. Jackson is in charge of the entire operation, and shares in the profits. I run the old café, and Carol runs the new one here. The keep has only vending machines."

"Are you talking about Jackson's sandwiches and pastries empire?" Tessa came into the kitchen.

Sylvia arched a brow. "I wouldn't call it an empire, but it's quite impressive for a guy his age. How old is he, nineteen?"

"Almost twenty."

"For someone so young to achieve so much is incredible," Ella said. "It gives me hope."

"Hope for what?" Sylvia asked.

"My charity. The idea is great, and I know it's going to work, but then I also have doubts because I'm thinking that an eighteen-year-old can't possibly know what she's doing. That's why hearing about Jackson's success is so inspiring."

Tessa wrapped her arm around Ella's shoulders. "It's going to work. I have a good feeling about it. And you, girl, have killer instincts."

Ella had no idea what Tessa was talking about. "What do you mean?"

"You know how to put the right spin on things. Like calling the filming tomorrow a presentation and not a lecture. It would've never crossed my mind that it might make a difference, but it would. And your decision to go first is not only brave but also smart. Your brain is just wired right for this. It's like you know what you're doing even though you've never done it before."

"What do you mean by going first?" Sylvia asked. "Doing what?"

"My story is going to be the first we tape, and I'm going to do it in front of all the girls currently residing in the sanctuary. Lead by example so to speak."

Sylvia whistled. "That takes guts. Doesn't it bother you that everyone will know your story?"

Ella shrugged. "We are filming in silhouette, and I'm thinking about manipulating the voice recording too. No one will know who did which video."

"Still, it takes immense courage to tell a crowd of people what happened to you, and then release it to the world," Tessa said.

"You know what Eva would say to that?" Ella put her arm around Tessa's tiny waist.

"What?"

"No guts, no glory."

6

LOSHAM

*L*osham arrived at the meeting place well ahead of time.
After verifying that his warriors were strategically stationed throughout the hotel's lobby and the restaurant itself, he ordered the most expensive bottle of whiskey the restaurant had to offer and an appetizer that was aromatic enough to mask any subtle scents he might emit.

As someone who had to hobnob with politicians, Lokan probably wasn't under the same monetary restrictions as the rest of the Brotherhood's leadership, and Losham planned on having him foot the bill.

After all, the meeting was Lokan's idea so he should pay for it.

What Losham wondered, though, was whether his brother would bring a team of warriors with him or flaunt his confidence by showing up by himself.

The only companion Losham was going to admit to was Rami, who was outside, waiting in the car.

As the host escorted Lokan to the private enclave Losham had reserved, Losham got up and opened his arms to embrace his brother. "It has been too long," he said as they slapped each other's backs.

"Indeed." Lokan smiled. "With both of us stationed in the States, we should make an effort to meet more often."

When the host left, Losham switched to their native tongue. "How have you been? Things going well for you?"

"As well as can be expected. I'm dealing and wheeling, but the thing about dirty politicians is that you can't trust their word. Not even with the hefty contribution we are making to their campaigns. Without the proper personal bribe and a nasty secret to threaten them with, nothing gets done. Which means even more time and money spent on digging out the skeletons buried in their backyards. I was lucky to find an excellent detective agency. If you ever have a need for that kind of work, I'll gladly share the contact information with you."

Was that an olive branch?

Losham chuckled. "With what I'm tasked with, I have no need for those types of services. But I'm surprised you do. With your compulsion ability it shouldn't be a problem for you. You could just force them to do your bidding."

"Regrettably, it doesn't work on everyone, and as I discovered, the more corrupt a human is, the harder it is to compel him or her. They are suspicious of everyone and everything and are not open to suggestion."

Losham was surprised at Lokan's admission. He was confessing to a weakness, which was like exposing his soft underbelly to an opponent armed with sharp teeth. Or fangs, as was the case.

Since Lokan was too smart to just let it slip, this must be his way of reaching out to Losham.

Interesting.

What did he have in mind?

Deciding to play along, Losham sighed. "Frankly, I envy your position. From my elevated station as our father's top advisor, I've been relegated to dealing with humanity's muck. I can't say that I enjoy what I'm doing." He smiled. "If you are willing to switch, I'll gladly take those corrupt politicians off your hands. In fact, you are much better suited for my job than I am. With your compulsion ability, you could order the girls to take themselves to the island. You could save us a lot of money and manpower."

Reaching for the whiskey, Lokan poured himself a shot and downed it. "I would love a change of pace, but I can't see myself doing what you do. The drugs I could manage. If stupid humans want to numb themselves and destroy their own brains, who am I to deny them that choice? But the women are a different story. I'm not a proponent of slavery, especially sexual slavery. There are enough women out there who would do it for the money."

That was a very odd sentiment for a Doomer. "Why do you care? Humans are like sheep, and they need an iron-fisted shepherd to guide them."

Lokan tilted his head and pinned Losham with a hard stare. "Do you really believe that, or are you parroting our father?"

Apparently, Lokan was not as smart as he seemed. He was talking treason and trusting Losham not to use that against him?

Perhaps it was a trap?

Yes, that made much more sense. Navuh had sent Lokan to check up on him, and his brother was goading him into admitting dissent.

This was bad. It meant that Losham was a suspect and everything he said was going to be used against him.

"Are you questioning my loyalty, Lokan? Because I can promise you that it is absolute. Our goal is to one day rule the entire world. If we leave it up to the humans, they are going to destroy themselves and this planet."

That was a line Navuh often used in his propaganda speeches to justify his world-domination ambitions. Whether it was true or not was irrelevant. The only thing that mattered was that the warriors believed in it and fought for the supposed cause.

Lokan regarded him for a long moment, as if trying to decide whether he was telling the truth, but Losham was careful to keep his expression impassive.

Next, his brother made a failed attempt at discreetly sniffing for emotions and grimaced. The Brussels sprouts in parmesan crust and garlic butter were delicious, but the same couldn't be said about their smell.

"I'm not here on behalf of our father, if that's what you're worried about."

Losham waved a dismissive hand. "Why should I be worried? I have nothing to hide."

Letting out an exasperated breath, Lokan poured himself another shot of whiskey and downed it. "So, you are happy with the status quo, you have no ambitions whatsoever, and you don't think it's time for a change?"

"What kind of change?"

"Our father's ideas are outdated, and he is too stubborn and set in his ways to change. If we don't do something, and by 'we' I mean the sons, the Brotherhood is doomed. It will become obsolete."

It was all true, but Losham couldn't decide whether Lokan was suggesting a revolt or just stating the facts as they were. In either case, he wasn't going to play into the cunning son of a bitch's hands.

"It is true that the world is changing around us and the Brotherhood cannot continue as it is, but our father is well aware of that. I suggested several changes to address the issue, and he accepted them all. We need to work with him, not against him."

Losham leaned closer to his brother. "You are still relatively young, Lokan, and somewhat naive despite your smarts. Navuh is irreplaceable, and his charisma is what holds the brotherhood together. Without him, infighting would have decimated our forces a long time ago, and we would have really become obsolete. We are strong just as long as we stick together and work as a team."

Lokan chuckled. "Only you would call a nearly one-thousand-year-old immortal young. Or naive." He poured himself and Losham another shot. "So, tell me, what are the changes that you suggested?"

"We need brains. That's the number one priority. Well, actually it's number two. First priority is to establish a reliable inflow of cash. We can't do anything about the level of intelligence of the Dormants we have, they are a given, but we can bring in smart humans to breed with them, which I've already started working on. The next generation of Doomers is going to be all about the brains and not the brawn, and the new generation of dormant females is going to be better quality too. We are going to keep improving the stock."

Lokan nodded. "That's a long-term plan."

"It is, but then we have time."

"Where are you getting the smart humans from?"

Spreading his arms, Losham snorted. "We are in San Francisco, the hub of new technology and the brains that come up with it. Most of these geeks can't get laid without paying for it, and they find a sex vacation to a mysterious island very appealing."

7

ELLA

*E*lla had been in dreamland for a while when the scenery suddenly changed.

"Logan? Is it you?" She looked around.

It wasn't the beach and it wasn't sunny. She was standing on a bridge with a canal passing under it, but it wasn't Venice. She'd seen enough pictures of it to know that.

"Where am I?" She crossed her arms over her chest to keep herself warm. Even though it was only a dream, the wet breeze was freezing cold and it was seeping through her clothes as if she was actually there.

Materializing behind her, Logan wrapped his arms around her and pulled her against his warm body. "We are in Hamburg. You wanted me to show you the world."

His hold was gentle, and his body was throwing off heat like a furnace. Leaning against him, Ella was thankful for the warmth.

"Did you bring me here on purpose because it's so bloody cold and I would have to let you hug me?"

Nuzzling her neck, he chuckled. "I did not. It's just a beautiful city, and you wanted me to show you the nicer places around the world. It's located in the northern part of Germany, so it gets really cold here even in the summer. But I can solve that problem for you."

With a snap of his fingers, she was encased in a long puffer coat. A bright pink coat that was the same color as her hair. Panicking, she reached for a strand and looked at it, but in the dream it was still shoulder length and light brown.

Thank God.

"Are you all warm and toasty now?" Logan asked.

"Yes, thank you. Can you also give me gloves?"

He snapped his fingers again. "Done."

"Thank you." She lifted her hands with the pink fingerless gloves. "They are cute."

He kissed the top of her head. "As are you. Do you want to go for a walk along the canal? There are fancy shops a few blocks away."

"I don't care about stores, but I would love a walk. I want to see more of this gorgeous city. It's like Venice, just in the north."

As they started walking and Logan wrapped his arm around her waist, she leaned her head against his arm. "Is Hamburg one of your favorite cities?"

He nodded. "I like the north. I come from a very hot place, so I appreciate cooler climates."

"I like warm weather. I don't like to be cold."

"I'll remember it for our next shared dream. I was thinking of taking you to Scotland. The Isle of Skye is one of the most beautiful places in the world."

"Then take me there. Just dress me up appropriately." She lifted her foot. "Can you give me warm boots too?"

He snapped his fingers. "Done."

"Thank you." Lifting her foot again to examine the boots he'd conjured for her, Ella admired Logan's taste. They looked like Eskimo moccasins, made from soft brown leather and with an intricate pattern in pinks and purples sewn on top. She wished she could take them with her into the real world, and wondered where he'd taken the idea from. Was he actually in Hamburg at the moment or some other northern country?

"You are visiting me more often lately. Are you less busy?"

He chuckled. "Not really. I just can't stay away. You've enchanted me, my Ella. I now understand Gorchenco's obsession with you. You're special."

Crap, why did he have to be so nice all of a sudden? Where was the devil she knew?

Except, he might be thinking of her telepathy and not her feminine charms.

Yeah, that was probably it.

"You're also not as wary of me as you were in the beginning," he added. "I enjoy spending time with you."

"You've learned to behave. And you should not be surprised that I was so scared of you after that kissing attack you launched. What the hell was that about?"

"I'm sorry about that. It's just that I'm not used to women refusing me. And sometimes a woman says no when she means yes. She just needs a little convincing. It's a very old game that males and females have been playing for ages."

Ella rolled her eyes. "That's such bullshit, Logan. Nowadays, if a girl wants to hook up with someone, she's not playing games and pretending that she needs convincing. That might have been true fifty years ago."

He cocked a brow. "Do you do that? Just hook up with some random guy and go for it?"

"Well, no. But that's because of what I've been through. I don't want to hook up with anyone. Not yet, anyway. But when I'm ready, I'm not going to pretend that I don't want to when I do. A no is a no. And a yes is a yes."

"That's because you are an American. Where I come from, women are not so progressive and things are very old fashioned."

"Why is that?"

He shrugged. "My country is very religious, and modesty is enforced."

Ella widened her eyes, affecting innocence. "Are you from Iran? I would never have guessed. You have no foreign accent."

Logan laughed. "Why Iran?"

"Hot climate, very religious, and bent on world domination. It all fits."

"I'm not from Iran."

"So where are you from? Pakistan? Afghanistan?"

He shook his head. "None of those. I come from a very small nation that you've never heard of, and I can't tell you which one it is."

Ella wondered if her eye trick would work on him. Probably not, and she didn't really need him to confess where he was from because she knew, but she was curious.

"Tell me something about yourself. I know that you like being mysterious and all that, and you think that it makes you sexy, but how can I develop feelings for you when I know nothing about you? Do you have brothers or sisters? Are you close to any of them?"

He sighed. "I have many brothers, but we are not close. We share a father, but each of us has a different mother."

She arched a brow. "Your father has a harem?"

Ella knew the answer to that, but she had to pretend surprise. Besides, she was curious to find out how Logan felt about it, and whether the focused gaze that had other people open up to her was working on him.

He nodded. "Yes."

Wow, it seemed that it did. Either that or Logan was in the right mood for revealing stuff about himself.

"Oh, boy. That's horrible. Is your mother okay with that?"

He grimaced. "I don't know."

"You never asked?"

"I couldn't."

Ella stopped and took his hand. "Did she die?"

"Probably. But I have no way of knowing because my father doesn't let his sons grow up in his harem. We were raised by caregivers."

"Why?"

He shook his head. "I don't want to talk about it. Let's move to more pleasant subjects. Did you email your application to Georgetown?"

It seemed that she'd discovered Logan's Achilles heel. The guy was angry at his father for getting rid of his mother or just separating them.

Why would Navuh do that, though? He was such a monster, even to his own children.

Taking his hand, she smiled at Logan in an effort to restore his good mood. He was scary when angry. "I'm waiting for my transcripts to arrive."

"The fake ones, I presume."

She nodded. "I don't like having to do a deceitful thing like that. My real grades were probably good enough to get in, but I can't use them because I'm supposed to be dead."

He gave her hand a little squeeze that reminded her of Julian.

Crap, don't think about him! Ella tried to visualize Jim, but it was no use.

Instead, she wrapped her other hand around Logan's wrist to enhance the contact.

He smiled down at her. "I'm glad you are alive. And don't worry about the fake grades. It happens all the time and in various ways. Those academic echelons are just as corrupt as any other organization where people can get bribed or blackmailed."

"How do you know that?"

He shrugged. "All of humanity is like that, even those who purport themselves as saints."

"I'm not like that. My mother is not like that. And I know a lot of good people who are not like that. You have a very warped perception of humanity."

He arched a brow. "Do I? Perhaps you can find good people among the common folks who are powerless. But once given power, people abuse it. It's just human nature."

"So what are you saying? That there is no hope for us?"

He sighed. "Don't mind me, Ella. I'm just an old, jaded warlord."

Her heart aching for him, Ella forced a snort. "Logan, are you having a midlife crisis at twenty-eight? Because you can't be a day older than that."

8

BRIDGET

"I'm glad to be rid of that ring,'" Bridget said as Sandoval's driver eased into traffic. "I didn't feel safe carrying it around."

Turner clasped her hand. "I don't know why. Okidu drove us to the airstrip, we took the clan's private jet, and Sandoval's men picked us up from the airport. At no time were we exposed to danger."

"I know. Still, I feel lighter without it."

"That's because it is no longer on your finger. That thing was massive."

For some reason, Turner had decided that the ring was safer on her finger than hidden within a purse. Bridget hadn't been happy about wearing it, and not for security concerns alone. The ring had a bad juju.

Shaking her head, she berated herself for believing in superstitious nonsense. She was supposed to be a scientist and stick to the facts. Nothing had happened on the way, and the trip was a success.

Both parties were happy with the deal they'd struck, and after Turner had verified that the twenty-two million had been wired into the clan's Swiss account, they had parted with hugs and kisses and promises of meeting again in Los Angeles for dinner.

Right. As if Bridget was going to allow that. The last time Turner had gone to a dinner meeting with Sandoval, it had been a trap set up by the guy's nephew who'd hired hitmen to assassinate her man.

"Are you sure that you want to waste the rest of the day at a quilting convention?" Turner asked. "Instead, we can play tourists in Miami, getting driven around in Sandoval's limo."

Knowing her mate, Bridget had come up with a productive twist for their sightseeing. She hadn't expected him to complain about it.

"There isn't much we can see in half a day. I'd rather check out the convention."

"I'm sure it's going to be a waste of time. What are the chances of Roni's grandmother being one of the finalists?"

Bridget shrugged. "Statistically, probably none. I know that you are going to scoff at this, but I've come to believe that the Fates play a much larger part in us finding suitable partners than anything we do intentionally. But if we sit around the village and do not get out there, they can't put us in their path. Like Julian and that psychic convention. If he hadn't gone there, he would've not met Vivian."

The partition was up, and the driver couldn't hear their conversation, but there was always a chance that Sandoval had listening devices in his limo, and it wasn't as if Turner could search the vehicle. Which meant that they had to communicate in code and not use terms like Dormants and immortals.

"There is a big difference between that and a quilting competition. It made sense to search for special people in a psychic convention."

She smirked. "And it makes sense to search for a talented quilter in a quilting competition."

"They have them all over. It's not like this is the only one."

"True." Bridget crossed her arms over her chest. "But this one is the biggest and most prestigious." She smiled. "Besides, I want to buy a quilt for Julian and Ella. I have a feeling she is going to move in with him soon, and his place needs a feminine touch. Nothing like a beautiful quilt to brighten up a bedroom."

Wrapping his arm around her shoulders, Turner kissed the top of her head. "Under that no-nonsense façade of yours, you are a closet romantic. Isn't it too soon for buying quilts?"

"I'm not going to give it to them until they move in together. I don't want to be the pushy mother who sticks her nose where it doesn't belong."

"Did Julian tell you about them having plans to do that?"

"No, but they are so in love. Everyone can see that. It's only a matter of time."

Turner shook his head. "She is too young. If I were her father, I would not be happy about this. She needs to go to college and experience life before committing to a life-long relationship."

"Right." Bridget snorted. "Would you have listened to anyone telling you to do that after you met me?"

"You can't compare us to them. We weren't kids when we met."

She leaned and kissed his cheek. "Consider them luckier. They don't have to spend years looking for that special someone. They've already found each other. And as I said many times before, eighteen is not too young. If she can be drafted into the army and trusted with a rifle, she can be trusted to know her heart and choose who she wants to spend the rest of her life with."

Pulling up to the building where the quilt competition was taking place, the driver stopped at the curb and lowered the partition. "Call me when you are ready to leave."

"Thank you," Bridget said.

"We won't be long," Turner added. "I have better things to do than spend the day looking at quilts," he murmured under his breath.

9

TURNER

As Turner and Bridget went from room to room, he scanned the audience while Bridget oohed and aahed at the quilts.

Come to think of it, there was no reason for them to be there. Most large venues like this convention center had surveillance cameras, and he doubted they were closed circuit. He should have Roni check on that. If the kid could hack into them and then run the recordings through William's facial recognition software, that would increase the chances of them catching Roni's grandmother.

Normally, Turner wouldn't have diverted resources to such a long-shot pursuit, but since Roni had a vested interest in it, he could do that in his spare time. If he had any.

The kid was suffering from the same affliction Turner and Kian had been cursed with. Not knowing when to quit. Luckily for the three of them, they had mates to force some time off on them.

"Look at this one," Bridget said. "Isn't it gorgeous?"

"It is. And so is the price. Five thousand dollars for a quilt?"

Not all the rooms were dedicated to competition pieces. Some had been rented by quilting artists to put their work up for sale.

The prices were extravagant. Not that they weren't justified. He could imagine how many work hours went into each quilt, but there were cheaper ways to produce them. An artist could make a computer rendering and have the quilt sewn in India or some other country with low wages. In fact, he was pretty sure some of them had done it. After all, even artists had to make a living.

She waved a dismissive hand. "It's a one of a kind work of art, not a quilt mass produced in China."

"Then it should hang on the wall instead of covering the bed."

"They can do with it whatever they please. I'm getting it."

He glanced at the other quilts hanging on the walls. All of them were beautiful, but the one Bridget had chosen was indeed unique.

"Fine with me."

As she whipped out her credit card and approached the artist, Turner was struck by a thought. What if Roni's grandmother was selling quilts as a way to support herself?

This was another avenue to investigate.

What if she'd done it in other venues like this one? There couldn't be too many quilting artists selling their creations in conventions, and they all probably knew each other. At least by sight.

Walking over to where Bridget was chatting with the woman, he pulled out his phone and showed her the grandmother's picture. "I was wondering if you've seen this quilter around."

She shook her head. "I'm sorry." She handed him the phone back.

"Are you sure?"

"I would've remembered a young woman like that because quilters tend to be much older. But you should ask Cheryl. She knows everyone."

"Who's Cheryl?"

"She's one of the organizers." The woman pushed to her feet. "Let me get her for you."

Before either of them had a chance to say anything, the quilter ran out of the room, leaving them alone with her creation.

"Isn't she afraid someone might steal one of her works?" Bridget asked.

"They probably have them tagged."

"True. But I can't see any."

A few moments later their quilter returned with a woman who he assumed was Cheryl. A ball of energy with a mountain of white hair piled up high on top of her head.

"I heard that you're looking for someone?" she asked.

"Yes." He pulled out his phone and brought up the picture again. "Have you seen her?"

As Cheryl took the phone, her pupils dilated momentarily, indicating recognition. "Why are you looking for her?"

"A good friend of mine is looking for his cousin who he has lost track of. He said she's a gifted quilter, and if I see her while I'm here to tell her to call him. Do you know where I can find her?"

She looked at the picture again. "I only met her once, and it was five years ago, I think. I'm not sure. I think her name is Melinda. Is that right?" She quirked a brow.

"The truth is that I don't know what name she uses." Turner went with the truth. "She's gotten in some trouble and changed her name. That's why my friend lost track of her."

Cheryl narrowed her eyes at him. "That friend of yours, is he really her cousin? And if he is, why is it so important for him to find her?"

"He is estranged from his parents, and she is the only other family he has."

The woman didn't look convinced. "I can't really tell you where you can find her, but I remember her talking about selling her quilts online. She told me the name of her website, and I even checked it out, but I can't remember the name of it for the life of me."

"What kind of quilts did she make?" Bridget asked.

"Mandalas. All of her quilts were gorgeous mandalas. But that's not uncommon. It's a popular motif."

"Did she win any prizes?"

"Not that I know of. If she did, it was probably in some small-town competition."

Bridget cast Turner a questioning look. "I think that's enough to go on."

"Perhaps."

10

ELLA

*E*lla adjusted the camera's angle and returned to the chair she'd put in front of the white backdrop.

"Try it now," she told Tessa.

"Looks good." The girl gave her a thumbs up.

The dining hall was getting transformed into a theater, with girls pushing tables aside and stacking them one on top of the other.

They were making room for the extra chairs that were being collected from all of the classrooms. Altogether, nearly a hundred girls resided currently in the sanctuary, and all of them were going to attend Ella's presentation.

The only speech she'd prepared was a warning about what she was about to do, so whoever was not up to hearing her story could leave. Newcomers were especially vulnerable, and it might be too much for them to be exposed to a retelling so soon after their rescue.

When her phone rang, she knew who it was before looking at the screen.

"Hi, Julian."

"How are you holding up?"

She got up and started pacing. "I'm nervous."

"I have good news for you that will cheer you up."

"Shoot. I need an infusion of positive before I plunge into the abyss."

"Turner called me. He sold the ring."

"For how much?"

"Are you sitting down? Twenty-two million."

That was a hell of a lot more than she'd expected. Ella let out a whistle. "How many halfway houses will that much money buy us?"

"Maybe two."

"Are you kidding me? That should be enough for thirty."

"Real estate prices in the Los Angeles area are insane, and then you need to factor in the cost of remodeling and furnishing and hiring staff and all that."

"What if we move the houses somewhere else? I'm sure we can buy double that in Nevada or Arizona. And if we go to places like Kentucky, we can build a small town for that much money."

He chuckled. "I'm not sure about that, but in principle you're right. The problem is that the clan is here."

She glanced around and whispered, "Kian should've built the village somewhere else."

"We need a large metropolis to hide in plain sight. And New York prices aren't any better."

"Right. Well, at least we can have two. Is it in addition to the one you're remodeling now?"

"I hope so. But I'm not an expert. I'll have to pay a visit to our accounting department and have a professional go over the numbers."

"I didn't know we had an accounting department."

"It's only four people. The rest is done by outside firms."

Ella still had so much to learn about the village and the business empire the clan owned, and how it was all managed. Heck, she'd learned that there was an entire rulebook of clan-specific laws. She wanted to take a look at that too. It should be fascinating to find out how the organization functioned, and she was sure it wasn't as difficult to understand as the medical research papers she'd tried to tackle for Merlin.

Perhaps she shouldn't pursue nursing as her profession. It seemed as if her natural talents were better suited for something else.

Ella Takala, Director of Save the Girls was a much more appealing title than Ella Takala, Nurse Practitioner.

"One day I want to sit down with you and have you explain how the entire thing works. But I have to go now."

"Good luck. I wish I could be there to support you."

"I know. I love you so much."

"I love you too."

The truth was that she preferred it that way and was thankful for the excuse of males not being allowed in the sanctuary. Regrettably, the same didn't apply to Vivian, and asking her not to come had been difficult. Her mother had shed a few tears, then nodded, saying that she understood.

Ella was going to bare her soul, but it was in front of others who'd gone through similar experiences.

There was no way she could have her mother or Julian present. Having them listening to her story would have influenced how she told it. Not because she wanted to hide things from them or make it less embarrassing for herself, but because she would have known how difficult it was for them to hear it, and instinctively she would have modified her story to make it more palatable.

That would have been counterproductive to say the least. The girls needed to hear her talk about her feelings and identify with her. Only then would they consider following her example and telling their own stories on camera.

Julian was still going to hear it when they worked on the editing, but maybe it wouldn't be as bad for him if she held his hand through it.

When the dining hall was full and everyone was seated, Ella addressed her audience.

"Many of you already know what this is about, but for those who don't I'm going to explain. Just like you, I was lured into a trap, sold, and violated. My story is not as horrific as some I've heard here. In fact, it's pretty mild in comparison."

She motioned to the camera and the white backdrop. "I'm going to talk about it on camera, and my friend Tessa is going to record it. The recording is going to be in silhouette, so no one can recognize me, and I'm even going to change my voice. Later, we are going to edit it so it's impactful enough to put on YouTube."

When murmurs started, she lifted a hand and waited until everyone hushed down. "It will serve two purposes. One is for the fundraiser that is going to provide money for more centers like this one and for transition places that are going to ease your re-entrance into society. The second purpose of these videos is to serve as a warning to all the unsuspecting girls out there and their families. We will tell them what to watch out for, and how to recognize the warning signs."

Ella paused, took in a breath, and then continued. "If any of you feel like this is too much for you, please don't feel bad about leaving. I know that I would not have been able to sit and listen to a story like mine right after being rescued. All I wanted to do was to forget. But then I realized that by hiding my head in the sand I was helping out the monsters. As long as this is swept under the rug of society, as long as people believe that this cannot happen to them, the monsters are going to keep winning."

She glanced at Vanessa, who nodded her approval. "We can make it harder for them. By telling our stories, we will warn others, raise public awareness to the atrocities being committed under their noses, and hopefully raise shitloads of money so we can help rescue and rehabilitate more girls."

When Ella was done, one of the queen bees started clapping, and a moment later the entire room erupted in applause.

Only one girl slunk out of the room.

Sucking in a long breath, Ella let it out through pursed lips. It was show time.

Raising her hands, she waited until the applause died out. "I need to ask you a favor. This is going to be as hard as chomping on broken glass, and I would hate to do it twice. Please try to be as quiet as possible until I'm done."

11

JULIAN

As Julian knocked on Ella's front door, he clutched the brand new box of Godiva chocolates he'd bought on the way home as if it were a precious miracle elixir for curing heavy hearts.

Not that he knew for a fact that her heart was heavy, but he assumed it was. It must've been so difficult for her to tell her story in front of a room full of people, despite all of them except for Vanessa being sisters in pain.

She'd sounded tired when he'd called her, not depressed, but Ella was very good at fronting strength she didn't possess. Hopefully, he knew her well enough by now to see through that façade.

Opening the door, she smiled at him, and then she saw the box. "Oh, Julian. This is exactly what I need." She reached for the chocolates. "Give it."

When he'd bought the box, he'd envisioned asking Ella for a kiss before handing them over, but her feral expression convinced him to reconsider. Ella didn't seem in the mood to tolerate teasing.

She was tearing the wrapping while closing the door behind him.

"Hi, Julian," Vivian said. "Would you like to eat something? I can warm up a plate for you."

"No, thanks. I've eaten."

"Coffee?"

"Yes, please."

"For me too," Ella mumbled around a chocolate.

Magnus chuckled. "That girl has a serious problem."

There was a moment of silence as everyone in the room stared at him.

Raising his hands in the air, Magnus shook his head. "I meant your addiction to chocolate. You're not an immortal yet, Ella. Those can't be good for you."

Julian cleared his throat. "Actually, chocolate has many health benefits if eaten in moderation. It has a positive influence on cognitive function, lowers bad cholesterol, and reduces the risk of irregular heartbeat."

"I just love it when you geek out like that." Ella wrapped her arm around his waist. "At least you say those things in a language people can understand."

"You didn't pay attention to the moderation clause," Magnus said.

Ella waved a dismissive hand. "Overindulgence is okay in emergencies."

That shut the Guardian up as if someone had stuck a shoe in his mouth. Turning on his heel, he beat feet after Vivian to the kitchen.

"Come on." Ella led Julian to the dining room table. "I brought my laptop out here so we'll have plenty of room." She winked at him.

He sat down and waited for her to join him. "How did the presentation go?" When he'd called earlier, she'd only said that it had gone fine without giving him any details.

"It was as good as can be expected from an unscripted and unrehearsed telling of a traumatic experience. It needs a lot of editing work, but it had the effect I anticipated. I have four volunteers for tomorrow. But I'll probably only manage two. I was surprised at how long it took me to tell my story. By the time I was done, my mouth was all dried out. I didn't think about bringing a water bottle with me. And I cried a few times and had to compose myself."

His heart felt like it was about to crack, but all he could do was clasp her hand. "You are so brave, baby."

She waved a hand. "The crying was good too. It made the whole thing more convincing."

Right, as if she'd done it on purpose.

"What did you do? Did you ask for volunteers after you were done?"

"Not right away. I could see the indecision on their faces, so I added that they will be able to edit their stories after the filming and cut out things they were uncomfortable with. And that after that we will edit them further. Naturally, I didn't elaborate that my editing assistant was a guy. Anyway, that seemed to reassure them, and that was when I asked for volunteers."

"Good thinking. What did Vanessa have to say?"

Ella grinned. "She was all over herself about how wonderful I did and how proud she was of me. She said I was an inspiration."

He narrowed his eyes at her. "I hope you didn't cancel your appointment with her tomorrow."

She huffed. "I did not. Only because of you, though. You should have seen Vanessa's face when I admitted to having been violated. She had tears in her eyes, and they weren't the sad kind. She looked so happy that I finally saw reason that I didn't want to spoil it for her and tell her that it was your doing."

Even though Ella was making it sound as if she was going to therapy just to please him, the vise around Julian's heart was starting to ease. Mainly because it seemed that telling her story had been therapeutic for her, and not traumatic like he'd feared.

As Vivian put the tray on the table, she seemed surprised that they were still there. "You can take the cups with you if you want."

Ella looked up at her mother. "We are going to work here, if you don't mind. I only have one chair in my room."

As Magnus and Vivian exchanged glances, the Guardian shrugged. "We can watch a movie in our bedroom so you can work in peace. Are you filling out the application for Georgetown?"

"Yes, and several other places in case Mr. D checks." Ella looked at Julian and smirked. "Roni gave me a stellar transcript. I feel so much smarter all of a sudden."

"You are smart," her mother said.

"I concur." Julian pulled out the folded printouts he'd brought along. "I saved my application essays. You can use them as a sample for yours."

"That's good. I had no idea where to start."

"Good night, kids," Vivian said. "And good luck with the applications."

"Thanks." Ella sent her an air kiss.

When they were alone, Julian chuckled. "So much for our plan. They couldn't get out of here fast enough."

"It's still a good plan. Parker comes out every twenty minutes or so to get a snack or something to drink."

Julian waggled his brows. "A lot of things can happen in twenty minutes."

"Yeah, we can fill out half of an application."

12

BRIDGET

After stowing the quilt in the overhead compartment, Bridget got comfy in her seat and glanced at the curtain separating the cabin from the bathroom area. She had fond memories from the last time she and Turner had flown first class.

"Not as nice as the clan's jet," Turner said. "I wish Charlie could have waited for us."

"I disagree. We needed the jet to deliver the artifact safely. The one we are taking back is not worth nearly as much, but it's dear to me and valuable in other ways."

The quilt was pricey, but the information they'd gotten while purchasing it was priceless. With Turner's resources, Bridget had no doubt he would locate Roni's grandmother, or Melinda as she'd been calling herself five years ago.

The only problem was that the information was old, and the woman might have changed her name again, or she might have stopped selling her mandala quilts online. The first was likely, the second not so much. First of all because it seemed to be a passion of hers, and secondly, she probably supported herself selling the quilts. The beauty of it was that she could do it from anywhere in the world, using the internet to promote her creations.

Unless something spooked her, she was going to keep on doing it.

"Would you like a drink, Ms?" the stewardess asked.

"Yes, I would. A Bloody Mary, please."

"And for you, sir?"

"Scotch, please."

"On the rocks?"

"Neat, thank you."

Leaning over the bulky armrests, Bridget whispered in Turner's ear. "There are advantages to flying first class commercial. Unlike the jet, you get a stewardess to serve you drinks and meals, and the facilities are roomier."

Her guy was bright, and it didn't take much for him to catch her drift.

With a sly smirk, his eyes darted to the half-closed curtain. "You have a point. Is that why you booked the redeye?"

"It didn't even cross my mind. I just wanted us to have the entire day to enjoy in Miami. The curtain brought back pleasant memories."

"Do you want me to perform reconnaissance?"

"Of course. Each model of aircraft is different."

Releasing his safety belt, Turner jumped up to his feet. "I'll be right back."

Bridget wondered how different it would be this time around. Turner was an immortal now, stronger and more nimble. Not that he hadn't been so as a human. He'd kept himself in excellent shape. Still, nothing could beat the fountain of youth that came with immortality.

Coming out, he smiled at the stewardess as he passed by her and then took his seat next to Bridget. "It's tight, but we can manage just as we did before."

"I can't wait," she whispered in his ear.

"Patience, love. We need to wait for the meal to be served and then for the lights to be turned down."

She was patient as a doctor, somewhat less as an administrator, and not at all as a woman. Especially when vivid memories of their initiation into the mile-high club were flashing through her mind. Just thinking about what they were about to do had her nipples contract painfully and her core tingle.

She used to hate moments like that, when her arousal flared in response to some trigger and she had to find a random hookup to sate her hunger. It had felt like a chore, like having to grab something to eat while pressed for time. She needed the sustenance, couldn't go on without it, but hated to take a break for it, and hadn't enjoyed it.

Now, with Turner in her life, she welcomed the random flares. Each one was an opportunity for something wonderful, and each time felt like they were connecting anew.

When the lights went down, Bridget walked over to the bathroom and cast a shroud around the immediate area, imbuing it with a light sense of dread. Whoever wanted to use the restroom wasn't going to stand right there and wait. They were either going to return to their seat and wait for the green light to come on or trudge to the crowded coach and use one of its bathrooms with the rest of the plebs.

A moment later the door pushed open and Turner squeezed in behind her, pulling it closed.

"Take off your dress, love."

He wanted her to get naked? Bridget had planned on pulling her skirt up and her panties down, not the full Monty.

But what the heck. It wasn't a hardship.

Her dress was the pull-on type, and it only took a second to yank it over her head, but trying to hang it on the hook was another story. Especially with Victor cupping her breasts from behind and his erection pressing into her ass as she was fumbling with the thing.

"I can't concentrate when you do that." She tried again.

Taking the garment from her hands, Turner reached over her and completed the task in a split second.

"Show-off."

"You like it." He pinched a nipple through her bra.

Yes, she did. Her mate was a one of a kind super brainiac who could do anything he put his mind to, and that wasn't limited to his genius. He'd also built a barbecue from scratch with his own two hands, which had impressed the heck out of her.

Standing in her high heels and her matching bra and panty set, she let her head fall back on his shoulder. "You'll have to take the rest off me."

Nuzzling and nipping her neck, he snapped the bra clasp and slid the straps down her arms. "Put your hands on the door and lean forward," he commanded.

Bridget liked where this was going.

With deft fingers, Turner hung the bra on the same hook that was barely holding the dress, but even the freaking inanimate object knew better than to try to best him.

In the end, Turner always won.

Crouching behind her, he hooked his thumbs in her panties and pulled them down. "Lift your foot. Now the other one."

She heard him stuffing them into his pocket. Was he saving them for her, or did he want her to spend the rest of the flight panty-less?

Kinky.

A moment later his warm hands cupped her ass, and he licked into her.

Her mate was talented in so many ways, and Bridget applauded his penchant for striving to be the best at everything he did, especially when it was pleasuring her into oblivion.

As she pushed back against his tongue, he circled his arm around her and pressed his finger to the top of her slit.

The dual sensations were like twin torpedoes, shooting her up toward an orgasm in seconds. Except, she needed a little more to break through the barrier, and Victor was taking his time, slowly licking and sucking and gently massaging that tight bundle of nerves.

Frustrated, she groaned and swiveled her hips, urging him to give her what she needed.

That earned her a hard slap on her ass-cheek.

The slight sting managed to help her stretch the barrier, but not break through it.

"I need to come now, Victor," she hissed through clenched teeth.

Obliging her, he retracted his tongue and replaced it with two thick fingers. Pumping in and out of her, he pressed the thumb of his other hand to her clit.

That was what she'd needed. Breaking through the barrier, Bridget rocketed into a climax that had her eyes roll back in her head and her legs turn into noodles.

Holding her up, Victor purred his approval and kissed her moist lips before pushing up.

As she heard him release his buckle and then lower his zipper, Bridget braced for the penetration that was coming, but after his gentle foreplay, the ferocity of that first thrust took her by surprise.

"Victor," she breathed.

Holding on to her hips, he pulled back and slammed into her again, and again. Oblivious to the door's rattling and to his own growls, Turner unleashed the beast living inside his immortal body.

Dimly, she was aware that her shroud might not hold up while her concentration was shot all to hell, and that the noise they were making would be overheard over the engines' noise.

Still, she somehow managed to maintain it almost to the very end. But when Victor bit into her and she was flooded with euphoria, there was no way she could hold on to it and she let it go.

Long moments passed until Bridget regained enough control to recast the shroud. Behind her, Victor was breathing heavily, his shaft still twitching inside her.

She chuckled. "Are you ready for round number two?"

"You know me. I'm always happy to rise to the challenge." He nuzzled her neck.

13

ELLA

"I'm so glad that you've decided to come to talk to me." Vanessa smiled and pointed to one of the two armchairs in her office, then sat in the other.

This time there was no desk between them, only a small side table with a box of tissue and a couple of water bottles on top of it.

Made sense. A lot of crying must go on in the therapist's office, and from experience Ella knew that confessions tended to dry out the throat.

Shifting in the wide armchair, she crossed one leg over the other. "To be frank, there are two reasons I'm here. One is that I promised Julian I'd talk to you, and the other one is the affinity thing that I want you to explain to me. Julian said something about immortals and Dormants feeling affinity for each other."

Vanessa nodded. "Amanda believes that, and there might be something to it, but we didn't have a large enough sample to test this hypothesis. Unfortunately, I don't think it's a good method for identifying Dormants. People feel an affinity for each other for a variety of reasons, and it's next to impossible to isolate one particular cause."

That wasn't what Ella wanted to hear. It sounded wishy-washy. "My mother says that she felt an immediate affinity for Magnus, but then he is a hunk, so it might have been infatuation and not affinity. But she also says that she feels at home in the village like she never felt anywhere else."

"What about you, Ella?"

"You mean if I feel at home here?"

Vanessa nodded.

"I do. But I didn't feel like I didn't belong in my old life." She waved a hand. "Naturally, there was some teenage angst, and this face made me feel different." She pointed. "But that was because people always stared at me. It wasn't like that with my friends, though, or even my classmates. After they got used to me, they kind of forgot about my looks and treated me like everyone else."

That wasn't entirely true. Ella remembered feeling like an alien from time to time, but talking with Maddie and her other friends, she'd realized that it was like that for almost everyone. They'd all been trying to find their place in the world.

"What about Julian? Did you feel an immediate affinity toward him? I understand that you guys are dating."

That was a mild way to put it, and Ella appreciated the therapist not jumping on that whole fated one and only wagon.

On the one hand, the promise of undying love and unbreakable commitment was alluring and hard to resist. But on the other hand there was too much pressure attached to that. Maybe that was something Vanessa could help her with.

"Julian is an amazing guy and so easy to love, but I still have trouble believing in the fated true-love mate thing. Any girl would have fallen for him, so it's not a big surprise that I did. But how do I know the difference between just loving him because he's great and accepting that he is my destined mate? Would I know for sure if I were an immortal?"

"Not really. Again, we don't have enough couples to base a theory on, and none of them came to talk to me, but from what I've heard, everyone had doubts at one point or another."

Letting out an exasperated breath, Ella slumped in the armchair. Expecting answers from Vanessa had been an act of pure optimism. Just like any other shrink, she had none to give, and only posed more questions.

"Eventually they know, though, right?"

"It would seem so."

"I have another question for you. Is it possible to confuse that affinity thing with sexual attraction?"

"What exactly are you asking?"

Ella rolled her eyes. "Let's say that an immortal guy meets a dormant girl and he feels an affinity for her but thinks that it's attraction, and vice versa. A dormant girl meets an immortal guy, feels an affinity, and mistakenly thinks that she's attracted to him."

"I think that affinity can reinforce attraction, but I don't think it can cause it or be mistaken for it. I might feel an affinity toward a dormant woman, but since I'm heterosexual it will not translate into desire. If I meet a dormant guy, without knowing what he is, I might or might not feel attracted to him. Other factors need to be present too."

"Like what?"

Vanessa smiled. "The obvious ones. We are each drawn to a particular type. And then there are pheromones, which may be a factor too, not a very significant one and not well understood yet, but we know they exist."

That was interesting. Ella didn't know much about pheromones, but since immortals had heightened senses, perhaps they were more sensitive to their effects than humans?

Running her fingers through her hair, Ella debated whether she should bring it up. Someone must have researched it or at least considered it.

Eh, what the heck. The worst that could happen was Vanessa smiling at her indulgently and explaining why it was total nonsense. Ella was not a scientist and therefore was allowed laypersons' stupid questions.

Not a big deal.

"What if the affinity immortals feel for Dormants is caused by pheromones? Immortal senses are sharper in every other way, so why not that?" When Vanessa didn't immediately dismiss it, Ella continued. "And the same can be true for the destined mates thing."

"There might be a connection. Testing in humans produced no definite results, but we haven't tested immortals. Except, it could explain why immortals feel affinity toward Dormants, but not the other way around."

Well, that was it for her theory. It had been worth a shot, though.

"That might explain why Julian is so sure that I'm his true-love mate, while I'm not. But on the other hand, he fell for my picture. We can't blame pheromones for that."

Damn, it was all so confusing. Like a puzzle made up of mismatched pieces.

Vanessa leaned back and sighed. "We are complicated creatures, Ella. It's impossible to reduce everything to hormones and pheromones, although some scientists love to do that. Many factors are at play. Julian might have been infatuated with your pretty face in the picture, but until he met you in person he couldn't have been sure that you're the one. It takes time, and with immortals it also takes sex."

That was an odd thing for a therapist to say. "Sex helps determine true-love, since when?"

"Immortals, when they are exclusive with each other, form an addiction. When bitten enough times by the same male, the female becomes addicted to him and repulsed by other males. Eventually, her scent changes in a way that affects the male in the same way. Even if they were originally not each other's true-love mates, they become that."

No one had told her that.

Did her mother know?

"That's one hell of a pill to swallow, and not as romantic as Julian made it sound. Addiction is not love."

Vanessa smiled exactly like Ella had imagined she would, with the indulgent expression reserved for the lay and the stupid.

"No, addiction is not love. But in our case love comes first. Immortals, like their godly ancestors, are lustful and promiscuous by nature. If they don't feel a special connection to their mate, they are not going to be faithful. As long as the female gets bitten by more than one immortal, the mixture of venoms will prevent her from getting addicted to just one, and her scent is not going to change, meaning that none of the males will become addicted to her either."

Ella groaned. "I think I feel a headache coming on. This is all so complicated. How come no one has told me about the addiction?"

"It's not well known and certainly not something that we discuss over coffee. Most of us don't have mates or even a prospect of one, so it's not an issue. Why does it bother you, though? Isn't fidelity something you would want from your mate?"

"Of course. But not because he is forced into it. I want it to be his choice, in the same way that I want it to be mine. Faithfulness is much more meaningful when it's observed despite outside temptations, and not because of their absence, especially when that absence is chemically induced. Talk about Stepford Wives."

Sighing, Vanessa leaned forward. "Give it some thought, and I'm sure you'll see the beauty of it. For most the addiction takes months to set in. If it's not the real thing, you'll have plenty of time to walk away and seek another partner."

"But I don't want another partner."

"We will talk about it in our next session." She smiled. "Perhaps we will actually get to discuss your experience. As I said before, I was very impressed by what you said in the recording. I think it was a breakthrough for you. But since I have another session scheduled right after yours, we will have to address this in our next one. How about tomorrow?"

"Same time?"

"Works for me."

Ella hesitated. "I know that you're busy, and there are girls here who need your help much more than I do. I hate taking up so much of your time."

And she wasn't even using that as an excuse.

"I'm not the only therapist here. We have plenty of volunteers who the other girls can go to. You, on the other hand, can talk only to me."

"That's true."

14

JULIAN

"Here is your swipe card." Julian handed it to Yamanu.

"Did anything get stolen?" the Guardian said as he regarded the new security measures at the construction site. "That's one hell of a fence."

Turner had recommended a site management service that provided tall fences that were wired to an alarm company. It was pricey, but with the proceeds from the ring, Julian no longer needed to count the pennies.

"Come inside, and I'll show you. Squatters used one of the bedrooms upstairs, and we need to get rid of everything in there."

Since Yamanu hadn't been there on Friday or Monday, he hadn't seen the fence getting installed or heard the story.

"That's strange." The Guardian followed Julian upstairs. "The building stood empty for months, and no one trashed the place."

"Yeah, well. They did now."

Grimacing, Yamanu pinched his nose even before Julian opened the door. "I can't believe they've stunk up the place so bad in one weekend. Did they piss on the floor?"

"Possibly. They were a couple of nasty druggies."

As they hauled the bed out of the room, Julian told the Guardian a shortened version of what had happened, omitting most of the drama.

"I'm so proud of you, kid. If I weren't carrying furniture, I would give you a good slap on the back. Correct me if I'm wrong, but I don't remember you attending any of the self-defense classes. How did you know what to do? Did you train elsewhere?"

Julian shook his head. "I let instinct take over. The beast knew what to do." He grimaced at the memory.

The thing was, he couldn't recall any actual thoughts, just the fury that had consumed him when those druggies threatened Ella. It had incinerated every civilized part of him and called up the inner caveman he hadn't even known was living inside him.

Grinning from ear to ear, Yamanu tossed the bed on top of the pile of construction debris outside. "Come here, my boy." He pulled Julian into a bro embrace, knocking the hell out of him as he slapped his back. "The beast is your friend. Embrace him."

When they were back in the room and away from human ears, Yamanu leaned against the wall and crossed his arms over his chest. "What did you do with the bodies?"

"I didn't kill them, only knocked them out. Ella wouldn't let me finish the job. I called Turner and he handled the cleanup. Those two are going to spend a lot of time in jail."

Looking disappointed, the Guardian nodded. "How much of the stuff did they have here?"

"Not enough to put them away for such a long time. I have a feeling Turner arranged for more to be delivered." Julian lifted the desk. "Grab the other end. We don't want the humans to start wondering."

"Sure thing."

As they took it out of the room and started down the stairs, Julian's phone rang in his back pocket.

"Damn, that's Ella."

Yamanu chuckled. "No kidding. With that ringtone, I didn't think it was your mother. Go ahead and answer it. I'll take the desk downstairs by myself. The guys think I'm a freak anyway."

The snippet from *My Girl* had seemed like a cool idea when he'd assigned it to Ella's contact, but maybe it wasn't. It was too obvious.

"Hi, sweetheart. How did it go with Vanessa?"

"Great. That's what I wanted to talk to you about."

Ella had said great about talking with a shrink? Something wasn't right.

Taking the steps two at a time, he went into one of the rooms upstairs and closed the door behind him. "Okay. I'm alone now. Shoot." He leaned against the wall.

"So, we started talking, and one thing led to another, and then Vanessa said something about pheromones influencing who we are attracted to."

As a therapist, Vanessa wasn't as well acquainted with human physiology as a medical doctor.

"Studies show that humans emit very little, and that their pheromones have no measurable influence on arousal."

"Yeah, Vanessa said that not much is known about pheromones. Did anyone test immortals for it?"

"Maybe, but if it was done no one has told me."

He heard her huff. "I can't believe that I'm the first one to think of it. What if immortals emit more pheromones than humans or more powerful ones? What if your enhanced senses pick up on some Dormant-specific pheromones, and that is what you interpret as affinity? I know from Vanessa that affinity can also be felt without sexual attraction attached to it, but I went on the internet and read that pheromones are not only for sex. Animals use them to communicate many other things. That could also explain the alarm immortal males feel when they meet a new one of their kind. You guys probably emit warning pheromones, and after you get used to them you don't sense them anymore. That's why immortal males don't feel alarm around male friends and relatives."

Ella sounded so excited, and what she'd said made a lot of sense, but he didn't think Amanda could have overlooked something as obvious as this. She'd probably investigated it and had realized it didn't work this way.

He felt bad about bursting her bubble. "I'm sure Amanda checked this out. Searching for Dormants is her thing."

"What about your mother? She said that before heading the rescue operations, she researched immortal genetics."

"She didn't find anything useful."

"Yeah, but did she investigate pheromones?"

"I don't know. I'll have to ask her."

"Please do. And one more thing. When were you going to tell me about the freaking addiction?"

Damn, it hadn't even crossed his mind. "We are not doing anything. So, I didn't think it was important to mention."

"But we are going to at some point. Don't you think I should have been given a warning?"

He raked his fingers through his hair. "When the time comes, sure. Frankly, I didn't think about it at all. My mind wasn't there yet."

"Does my mother know? Is it too late for her?"

Why was she so upset about it? The addiction wasn't a bad thing. It was just a side effect of the devotion between true-love mates.

"I don't know whether she does or not, that's between her and Magnus. And if she does, I'm sure she is not as upset about it as you seem to be."

Ella huffed again. "You want to tell me that it doesn't bother you to be ruled by some weird chemical reaction? Wouldn't you rather be faithful out of love and devotion to your partner than something you have no control over?"

"What if love and devotion are also chemical reactions? Have you thought of that? What if free will is an illusion and everything we do is determined by our genes and hormones and the inherited structure of our brains?"

As a long moment of silence stretched over the cellular connection, Julian wondered whether Ella was mulling over what he'd said or just taking time to rein in her anger.

"Do you really believe that?" she asked.

Did he?

"Not entirely, although I should. There is enough evidence to demonstrate that. A brain injury can change a personality, Alzheimer's robs people of their personality, and some drugs alter perception. So, if I were a purely logical creature like Turner, I would probably say that yes, that's all there is to us, and that nothing metaphysical or mysterious like a soul exists. But then I'm reminded of all the things that have no scientific explanation, like precognition and remote viewing."

Ella chuckled. "Why go that far? What about quantum physics? Does that make any sense? Or string theory? If that's real, I don't know why people having souls can't be."

At least she didn't sound angry anymore. "Does getting addicted to me really bother you that much? Because I have no problem being addicted to you for all eternity."

"That's so sweet and so creepy at the same time. I need to give it some thought. When are you getting home?"

"Six or six-thirty."

"Can I see you?"

"Of course. I need you. I'm already addicted to you without any chemicals involved."

"Oh, Julian, that's so sweet of you to say. Even though you're such a creepy geek sometimes, I love you so much."

He laughed. "Love you back."

15

ELLA

*I*n her mother's car, Ella dropped her head against the headrest and closed her eyes. "I hate disappointing Julian, but all I want to do when I get home is shower and sleep." Hopefully, without dreaming because she had no energy for Logan either.

Vivian patted her knee. "I'm sure he'll understand."

"Yeah, he will, but he will still be disappointed. I should call him right now so he can make other plans. It's not healthy for his psyche to spend time only with me. Julian needs guy buddies."

Vanessa would have been proud of her. She was spewing psychobabble like a pro. Not all of it was bullshit, though. As Ella could attest, mood certainly affected the body.

Yesterday, even though her presentation had been emotionally draining, she'd felt upbeat and motivated by the positive response. Today, on the other hand, she had listened passively to two horror stories, and to top it off, Tessa had a meltdown.

Ella had a feeling she would have to find a new filming assistant because Tessa wasn't coming back.

Maybe Julian could suggest a replacement?

Selecting his contact, she smiled at his picture. She should make it her screen saver, but then she'd be staring at it all day long, kind of like he had done with hers.

She wondered if he still did that.

"Ella, are you on your way back?"

"I am. I'm hitching a ride with my mom. Tessa had to leave early."

"Why? What happened?"

Ella sighed. "I shouldn't have asked her to do this. After I talked with you, we filmed two stories, and by the second one Tessa just fell apart. We had to call Jackson to come get her."

"Poor girl. She must be very sensitive."

Evidently, Julian didn't know about Tessa's past, and since Tessa preferred it that way, Ella honored her wishes. "Yeah, it's difficult to stomach. In fact, I'm afraid that when we work on the editing, you are going to have a meltdown as well."

"You don't give me enough credit."

"On the contrary, my love. I'm giving you all the credit. You're a sensitive and loving soul. It will be difficult for you."

"I can handle it. How are you holding up?"

"I'm drained. Emotionally and physically. All I want to do is take a quick shower and crawl in bed."

"Do you want me to come and tuck you in?"

"It sounds lovely, but I'm really beat. Can I take a rain check for tomorrow?"

"Sure."

"You're the best, Julian. I love you."

"Love you too, sweetheart. Sleep well."

"I hope so." Ella ended the call.

Next to her, Vivian was grinning like she'd won the lottery. "You didn't tell me that you were in the I-love-you stage. When did that happen?"

In the past, Ella would have run to her mother with every piece of exciting news, but those days were long over. And it wasn't the type of conversation she wanted to have over their mental link either.

"It's very recent. Saturday night."

Her mom arched a brow. "That's it? Saturday? That's all you're going to tell me?"

Ella dropped the phone into her purse. "There isn't much to tell. We talked, and Julian told me that he loved me, and then I told him that I loved him too. Not a big deal."

"Well, I think it is. Congratulations."

"Thank you. By the way, do you know about the addiction?"

"What addiction?"

Crap. Magnus hadn't told her. Should she?

Yeah, she should. Magnus might not be aware of it, but as a daughter, Ella couldn't and shouldn't keep such important information from her mother.

"Vanessa told me that over time the venom is addictive if a woman is exposed to the venom of only one male. The way it works is that you will want Magnus exclusively, and any other guy that you might have normally found attractive will repulse you. The only way not to get addicted is to have more than one immortal partner bite you."

Vivian frowned. "That's the first I've heard of it. Magnus hasn't said anything about it. I wonder if he knows."

Her mother didn't sound upset, but Ella felt like she should give Magnus the benefit of the doubt. The guy had been awesome to her mom and to Parker and her. He deserved some slack.

"Vanessa said that it's not something they talk about because it doesn't concern most of them, only those who find Dormant or immortal mates. And since that's so rare, Magnus might not be even aware of it."

Vivian shrugged. "It doesn't matter. Magnus is the one for me, and I don't want to feel anything for anyone else. And I certainly don't want any other immortal to bite me. It is what it is. It's not like he's doing it on purpose to get me addicted to him. It's just how it works for them."

"Well, the good news is that he's addicted to you, too, or will be. Vanessa said it takes time for the addiction to set in."

"At least it's fair."

"Yeah. And it gives one hell of a motivation to make up your mind early on if you want a guy or not. Dragging things out with someone you don't love is dangerous for immortals."

Ella wondered if that was why Carol had ended things with Robert. She hadn't mentioned anything about the addiction, so maybe she hadn't been aware of it either.

As tight as the immortal community was, it seemed like vital information wasn't getting communicated properly to its members. The village needed an adult sex education class immortal style.

"Did you and Julian get closer?" Vivian asked.

"Emotionally, yes. Physically, no."

"Are you concerned about the addiction?"

"That's not the reason, Mom. I have Mr. D to deal with, and my issues to overcome. When that is resolved, I can start thinking about intimacy with Julian."

"Perfectly understandable. I don't want you to feel pressured into anything. Take as long as you need. But if you love Julian, and he loves you back, the addiction thing shouldn't stand in your way. It's a small price to pay for love, and even a smaller one for immortality."

Her mother's attitude toward this was probably the right one. It was the way it was, and if Ella wanted Julian or any other immortal mate, she had to deal with it. It wasn't as if Julian intended to get her addicted to him on purpose, and wishing things worked differently for immortals was pointless.

16

ELLA

"Hello, my precious Ella." Logan pulled her into his arms gently and kissed the top of her head.

That was so out of character for him that for a moment Ella thought she was really dreaming, her own dream, and not dream-sharing with the Doomer.

"I have good news for you. Your interview is set for next Wednesday. You should be getting the email tomorrow, or rather Kelly Rubinstein is getting an email. That girl has some impressive grades, and her extracurriculars are even more so." He chuckled. "My friend was ecstatic about expediting your interview. I didn't need to put any pressure on him at all."

It was on the tip of her tongue or, rather, at the end of her synapsis to ask Logan if he'd used compulsion on the guy, but then she wasn't supposed to know that he could do that.

"Which extracurricular impressed him the most?"

"The charity you're supposedly running. The people helping you are real pros. I checked out Kelly Rubinstein, and she has a Facebook page with history and friends, including your pictures with a bunch of teenagers. How did they pull off a thorough job like this?"

Ella had no idea that Roni had gone to so much trouble for her. She needed to make him something special as a thank you.

"They are Special Ops. They can do anything. You know, access to government databases and things like that."

She had no idea what she was talking about, but that was fine. An eighteen-year-old wasn't supposed to know how those things worked. Playing dumb was her best defense.

"I wish I had access to your friends," Logan said. "I could use a good hacker."

Was he fishing for information, trying to find out who was helping her? She hoped it wasn't because he suspected his enemies were involved and still believed it was the government.

She shook her head and smiled up at him. "As I said, they are my mom's friends. I don't even know them."

He let go of her and then took her hand. "Let's take a walk. Look around you."

"Where are we?"

"Amsterdam. You liked the canals in Hamburg, so I thought you would like another city that had them."

"I do." She stretched up on her toes and kissed his cheek. "You're being very thoughtful. Thank you for everything you're doing for me. I'm so excited about this interview." Just not for the reason he thought she was.

Frowning, he stopped and turned toward her. "You don't sound excited. You sound tired. What happened?"

"I had a rough day, that's all. A friend of mine had a mini meltdown, and dealing with that was draining. I had to call her boyfriend to come pick her up because she couldn't even drive herself home."

"What triggered that?"

She had a feeling that he wasn't really interested, which made sense. He didn't know Tessa, and even if he did, he probably wouldn't care either. Logan was being really nice to her, but that was because he had an ulterior motive and not because he was a nice guy.

"She heard a very disturbing story that reminded her of bad things that had happened to her when she was younger. I feel guilty for dragging her into this. I knew she had issues."

Logan forced a smile. "I should let you get some real sleep then. I'm sure that in the morning everything will look brighter."

She nodded. "You are probably right. I feel tired even in the dream."

He kissed the top of her head. "Sleep well, my Ella. Good night."

When he was gone, Ella didn't continue sleeping. Opening her eyes, she looked out the window and watched the dark silhouettes of branches swaying in the wind. It had been a mistake to open the shutters after she'd turned the light off, but she wanted to let in fresh air. From her bed, the branches looked menacing, like gnarly arms and fingers tipped with claws.

With a voice command to the home system, she lowered the shutters and turned the light on in the bathroom. Huddling under the blanket, she thought about what Logan had told her.

Next Wednesday was only a week from now. Was it enough time to set up the trap?

This was actually happening. Up until tonight, it had felt like a game, but now reality was knocking on her window with dark, claw-tipped fingers.

For some reason, Ella didn't feel as excited as she thought she would be. Was it anxiety? Or maybe she was a little conflicted about entrapping Logan?

The thing she needed to remember was that he was planning the same thing for her, and if he was not, he wouldn't be there and nothing would happen. So, her guilt was utterly misplaced.

He'd been nice to her lately, which had softened her up toward him, but it had been only a convincing act. If he really cared for her, he wouldn't have evaporated when she was sad. It seemed that Logan didn't like dealing with her when she was in a bad mood.

Good to know for next time she needed to get rid of him fast. All she had to do was make a sad face, shed a few tears, and *poof*, he would be gone.

17

KIAN

"I have to go." Kian grabbed his laptop and headed out.

The text from Ella had arrived a little after two in the morning, but he'd only seen it when he'd checked his phone three hours later.

Syssi stopped him at the door. "Wait. I'll pour your coffee into a thermal mug. The guys can wait a minute longer."

After telling her the exciting news, he'd made a few phone calls and arranged a meeting.

"Thanks." Kian took the mug and kissed her cheek. "I'll make it up to you tonight."

Syssi smiled and waggled her brows. "A foot massage would do."

"It's a deal."

It had been a long time since he'd gone to work that early in the morning or scheduled a meeting before nine. He didn't like leaving the house without making love to his wife first, but as he'd promised, he would make it up to her later.

Smiling, he thought about the pleasure sounds she made when he kneaded her little toes. For some reason, that was her favorite part.

Thermos clasped in hand and a laptop tucked under his arm, Kian took the stairs up to his office two at a time.

One week wasn't long, and there was much to do. Surprisingly, Lokan had come through for Ella and expedited her interview for next Wednesday. Kian wondered whether the Doomer had collected favors owed or just compelled someone to push her up in the list. Not that it mattered one way or another, but he was curious. What business could the Brotherhood possibly have with the university that someone on its staff would owe Lokan a big favor like that?

As far as he knew, Navuh's sons didn't get to study abroad, but then his information about the Doomers' royal family was scant and unreliable.

"Good morning, boss." Onegus walked in with his own mug and took a seat at the conference table.

"Good morning, indeed. The rat has set the trap that he's going to get caught in."

Onegus rubbed his hands. "Who else is joining us at this ungodly hour?"

"Turner and Bridget, of course. And also Magnus and Julian because of their personal involvement. I'll leave it up to you to choose which Guardians you want to take to Washington."

Onegus arched a brow. "I'm going? I thought Turner was. This is his kind of operation."

"I am," Turner said as he and Bridget walked in. "You should stay here." He pulled out a chair for Bridget. "I want security around the village reinforced and put on high alert." He pulled out a chair for himself and sat down.

When Magnus and Julian entered next, Kian motioned for them to take their seats.

"Lokan might have shared more than Ella's dreams," Turner said. "If he has access to her mind and can read her thoughts from afar, he knows that she is with us, and he could have used bits and pieces of information she's subconsciously collected to deduce our location. He also might know that we are coming for him. This could all be an elaborate setup to lure Guardians away from the village so it would be open to attack. It's a remote possibility, but one we cannot ignore."

Turner was paranoid, but his advice was solid nonetheless. The village should be put on high alert.

"Do you think we should order a lockdown?" Kian asked.

In case of emergency, the entrance to the underground tunnel could be blocked by what looked like a rock formation, and no one could come or go until it was open again.

"That's an extreme measure," Turner said. "And probably over the top. If it were up to me, you know I would have done it. But it is your call."

Kian turned to Onegus. "What do you think?"

"Locking down the village should be reserved for real emergencies, and by that I mean an actual attack. I don't think it should be done as a precaution in case of a very remote probability of one."

Bridget nodded. "No offense, Victor, but I'm with Onegus on that."

Turner shrugged. "If later we have reason to suspect that one is coming, we can up the alert level and issue a lockdown command."

"What's the plan?" Magnus asked. "I assume you have one."

"I do." Turner opened his briefcase and handed everyone printouts. "When Kian called me this morning, I got in touch with my contacts in Washington. We have an entire hotel reserved to ourselves, so Ella and Vivian will be surrounded by Guardians. We will also have five taxis at our disposal. Each time the ladies have to travel, they will be using a different car."

"How are we getting them there?" Julian asked. "Are we taking the jet?"

"We are taking both. The Guardians and I are going to leave tomorrow and lay the groundwork. The ladies will go on Monday. I'll make decoy travel arrangements for them by train. And I'm also thinking of putting two female agents on it in case Lokan thinks to check on that. Now that he has Ella's fake name, it will be easy for him to find where she bought tickets. An internet connected world is one with no privacy."

He looked at Magnus and then at Julian. "You two can either leave with us tomorrow and join the preparations in Washington, or you can stay here and escort the ladies on the plane ride on Monday. But if you want to take part in capturing Lokan, you'll have to come earlier and participate in the prep."

Magnus and Julian exchanged glances.

"Tough choice." Magnus smoothed his hand over his goatee. "Naturally, I don't want to leave Vivian alone for nearly a week. But I want to be on the ground when shit is going down."

Turner nodded. "I'm counting you in for tomorrow's departure."

Magnus nodded.

"How about you, Julian?"

"I'm with Magnus. Who is going to escort Vivian and Ella?"

"Arwel and Bhathian. The two used to work together and they make a good team."

"That's what I thought when we originally paired them." Kian snorted. "But back then Bhathian didn't have Eva and was always grumpy as hell, and Arwel, well, we all know what bothers him. But I agree that they are the perfect escorts. Arwel because of his telepathy, and Bhathian because of his brawn."

"Is that enough, though?" Julian asked. "What if Lokan ambushes them in the terminal? If he can access Ella's brain, he would know she's coming on a private jet and where she is landing."

Turner's lips curved up in a rare smile. "We won't tell Ella the exact travel plans. All she will know is that she and Vivian are flying to some remote private airport in the area. It's better not to tell Vivian anything either, so she doesn't accidentally blurt something out."

"She won't," Magnus said. "But if that's how you want it, I have no problem with that."

"Good. Now let's move to organizing the Guardians. I'm going to take as many as can fit in the two jets." Turner handed Bridget another printout. "These missions will have to be postponed and the schedule reworked."

"I'm on it."

18

JULIAN

"Are Vivian and Ella going to the sanctuary today?" Julian asked as he and Magnus left Kian's office.

"Vivian doesn't have a class scheduled, and Ella was supposed to film, but she is without an assistant. I don't know if she can do it all by herself."

"Did Tessa quit for good?"

Magnus shrugged. "I don't know, but it makes sense that she would after the panic attack she experienced. Apparently, the girl is too sensitive for that kind of work. Ella is made from stronger stuff."

Even though Julian didn't agree with Magnus's assessment, he liked how proud of Ella the guy had sounded.

"Do you mind if I tag along? I want to talk to Ella."

The Guardian smiled and clapped him on the back. "You are always welcome in our home, Julian. You are part of the family, and that is regardless of what the future holds for you and Ella, although I'm sure you are going to get your happily ever after, as Vivian likes to say."

"Fates willing."

Magnus nodded. "I think they are."

When they neared the house, Vivian opened the door before they even made it to the front porch. She must've been waiting by the window, no doubt anxious to hear how the meeting went.

"Hi, Julian. Did you have breakfast?"

He rubbed his empty stomach. "After Kian called, I was too nervous to think about food."

The truth was that he still hadn't gone grocery shopping, and neither had Ray. His only option had been heating up a frozen pizza, which was gross for breakfast and took too long.

"Good, so you can join us. Ella and I made mountains of pancakes."

Julian sniffed. "I can tell. Lots of cinnamon."

Inside, Ella was setting the table, anxiety rolling off her in an atypical outpouring of emotion.

He walked up to her and pulled her into his arms. "It's going to be okay. You have nothing to be afraid of."

She pushed on his chest. "You think? Don't talk to me like I'm a baby."

"Ella," her mother warned. "Watch your temper. Julian is just trying to comfort you."

"It's okay," Julian said. "You can punch me if you want." He patted his chest. "Come on, right here. I can take it."

Fisting her hands, she gave him a couple of playful punches. "Thanks. It helped."

"Is that all you got?" He slapped his own chest. "Punch me harder."

"I don't want to. Sit down and eat your pancakes."

Parker came in with a bottle of syrup. "You want some?"

"No, thanks." Julian sat down and spread a napkin over his thighs. "I like mine with butter and honey."

"Your loss, dude. This is good maple."

After Magnus poured everyone coffee, Vivian lifted her mug and waited for him to sit down. "So, what's the plan?"

"The Guardians leave for Washington tomorrow, and that includes Julian and me. You and Ella will fly out Monday and meet us there."

"On the clan's private jet?" Ella asked.

"Yes."

"Kian said something about flying us to some remote airport and us taking a rented car from there. Is that still the plan?"

"I'm not sure what Turner is planning. He's the mastermind." He hated lying to Ella, but there was no way around it. Turner was right about that.

Vivian shook her head. "Why do you guys need to go with the other Guardians?"

Magnus put his fork down and wiped his mouth with a napkin. "We need to familiarize ourselves with the terrain and with the flow of foot traffic, find good spots for Guardians to hide around campus, and a thousand other details that go into planning and executing a successful operation. Simply put, if Julian and I are not part of the prep, we can't participate."

"How many Guardians are going?" Ella asked.

Julian glanced at Magnus. "About thirty, right?"

"More or less. Turner is taking as many as he can fit into the two aircraft."

Ella whistled. "That's a lot. Who is going to run the rescue missions if so many are going to Washington?"

"Bridget is going to reschedule or cancel them," Magnus said.

She shook her head. "I feel bad about it. There are only two of us, and we really don't need so much security. Those poor girls are suffering, and now their rescue is going to get postponed or canceled."

Julian reached for her hand. "It's not only about keeping Vivian and you safe. In the long run, catching Mr. D is more important than the missions that will get canceled. The information we can get out of him will save many more lives from ruin."

"How do you figure that?"

"If we know where the island is, we might be able to save the women who are held there against their will."

Magnus shook his head. "Sorry to disappoint you, Julian, but we won't be able to do that even if we know where it is. The Brotherhood has thousands of warriors. We can't attack their home base, and we certainly can't bomb it because of all the innocents who live there."

Ella threw her hands in the air. "So, what's the point of catching Mr. D if we can't do anything with the information we can extract from him?"

Magnus smirked. "I didn't say we can't do anything, just that we can't attack the island and free the women. There are other things we can do."

"Like what?" Vivian asked.

Magnus shrugged. "I'm sure Kian and Turner have a plan."

19

ELLA

With Magnus and her mother out on a walk with Scarlet, and Parker in his room, Ella and Julian were left alone in the living room with no chaperones, which for some reason filled Ella's head with naughty thoughts.

It was silly. She could be alone with Julian whenever she wanted. Magnus and her mother didn't even know that they were supposed to chaperone them.

A glance at Julian revealed that he either sensed her interest or had the same naughty thoughts. His eyes were glowing, and he seemed uncomfortable.

"Would you like to have coffee out on the front porch?"

That was as public as she could make it, but since their house was in the new part of the village, the only possible passerby was Merlin. Still, someone might decide to visit Merlin. But that was unlikely this early in the morning. She doubted the doctor was even up. From what she'd learned about him, Merlin was a night owl and liked to sleep in late.

"Good idea. I'll pour us what's left in the carafe."

Joining her on the loveseat swing outside, he handed her a full mug. "I fixed it the way you like it."

"Thank you." She took a sip. "I guess that with you and Yamanu gone, the work on the halfway house is going to stop."

"Yamanu is not coming. He is staying in the village to protect it if needed."

The wheels in her brain spinning fast, it didn't take her long to realize why the village needed extra protection. "Kian fears that Mr. D saw what's inside my head and figured out where the village is?"

"Turner, not Kian. He says it's a remote possibility, but he is a very careful guy."

Ella shook her head. "I wouldn't be able to find this village, so even if Mr. D could see what I did, there is no way he could find it. But that's irrelevant because he can't get into my head."

"You don't know that. When you met him, he'd not only peeked into your memories and found out about the telepathy you and your mother share, but he also made you forget whatever he talked with you about. As I said before, he is a very powerful immortal, and you should never underestimate him."

Ella smirked. "That may be true, but I found a way of getting rid of him really fast if I need to."

"How?"

"Last night when he entered my dream, I was sad over what happened with Tessa in the sanctuary. He didn't like dealing with my bad mood and poofed out as soon as he could. I figured anytime I don't want him to hang around my head, I can bring up sad memories. Until this is over, I plan to be sad often."

"Don't overdo it. What if Turner is wrong and he wants you for you and not the telepathy? He might change his mind if you keep acting depressed."

Ella chuckled. "Suddenly you don't mind me being nice to Mr. D? Should I up my game and pretend to seduce him?"

Julian's eyes blazed blue. "Just keep stringing him along. After centuries of having any woman he wants, the Doomer probably appreciates the chase more than the catch."

That soured her mood. "Do you think he thralls women into going to bed with him?"

"He doesn't need to. Or did you forget the giant brothel the Doomers have at their disposal on the island?"

"Right. I did. But he is stationed in the States, so he doesn't have access to it."

"There is no shortage of the paid variety here. Those who are voluntarily in it for the money, and those who are coerced by threats."

She wondered whether Logan frequented the kind of brothels the clan routinely raided to rescue girls who'd been sold into sexual slavery. He wasn't a good man, she had no such illusions, but he was also vain, and he appreciated luxury. Logan probably paid for the best escort girls money could buy, not some poor girls who'd been drugged and beaten into cooperation.

Unless he was perverted and enjoyed inflicting suffering.

She wouldn't put it past him. In fact, he would have made a much better choice as the lead for the *Fifty Shades* movie than the actor they'd chosen for that role. Still, if she were a casting director, she would have selected Logan to play Lucifer, and not some playboy billionaire with a kinky twist.

The king of the underworld suited him better.

"What are you smirking about?" Julian hooked his finger under her chin and turned her so she had to look at him.

"Nothing important. I was pretending to be a casting director in my head."

He lifted a brow. "Do you do that often?"

"Yeah, I do." She sighed. "I was having fun casting Mr. D as Lucifer, but I need to focus on casting someone new for the role of my filming assistant. I'm afraid Tessa is out. And now with you gone for the week, I also need someone to help me with editing. I want to put those videos up and start the fundraiser. I can't be the director of a charity that doesn't exist yet."

"Try Sylvia. She's not too busy, and she should be a quick learner after the many years she's spent studying."

"Isn't she dangerous to electronics, though?"

"Not unless she wills them to malfunction. At least that's my understanding.

Roni wouldn't have let her into his lair if she was going to damage his equipment."

"Do you have her number?"

"I have Roni's." He put his mug down on the floor and pulled out his phone. "I'll share the contact with you."

"Thanks."

Ella waited for him to put the phone back in his pocket before lifting her bottom and planting it in his lap. "If I'm not going to see you for almost a week, I need the kiss of all kisses to remember you by."

"Do you now?" He wrapped his large palm around the back of her neck, massaging the side with his thumb.

With his other arm wrapped around her waist, he had her trapped, but Ella didn't feel even a smidgen of panic. Only desire.

"Kiss me, Julian." She wound her arms around his neck.

His fingers gently rubbing the back of her head, he tilted his head and brushed his lips over hers. Soft and yet firm, cold and yet hot.

As the world spun around her, Ella moaned. When was the last time they'd kissed? Had it been Monday? Yeah, after they were done filling in the applications. But it felt as if he hadn't kissed her in ages.

He was going slow, drawing the kiss out and making her impatient for more, his tongue flicking over her lips, delving inside her mouth, and then retreating to lick her lips again.

As she arched into him, pressing her hardening nipples against his chest, his hand brushed lightly over the side of her breast, sending tiny bolts of lightning into her feminine core and igniting her desire.

"Touch me, Julian," she breathed into his mouth.

Without warning, he left her mouth and dipped his head, taking her nipple between his lips together with the bra and shirt covering it.

"Julian," she groaned.

Reaching for the hem of her shirt, she started lifting it up. But as suddenly as he'd taken her nipple, Julian let go of it, lifted her off his lap, and set her down beside him.

"Lean into me," he whispered. "Your shirt is wet."

A moment later Scarlet bounded onto the porch, her tail wagging and her tongue lolling.

Damn. Vivian and Magnus were back from their walk.

Chuckling, Ella murmured into Julian's shirt, "Saved by the dog."

20

VIVIAN

The walk had done little to alleviate Vivian's anxiety. Despite Kian and Magnus's reassurances, she had a bad feeling about them using Ella as bait to trap the Doomer prince, but she saw no way of backing out of it or convincing Ella to reconsider.

Not that at this stage of the game it was an option for either of them. Perhaps if Ella had been less enthusiastic and confident about her ability to lure Lokan, Vivian could've argued against it.

Probably not even then.

After all that the clan had done for her family, and how important catching Navuh's son was for them, refusing was not an option.

Talk about peer pressure.

If they backed down, living in the village would become intolerable. Everyone would pretend to understand, but on the inside, they would resent her and Ella, thinking of them as cowardly and ungrateful.

That was not how Vivian envisioned her and Ella's future in the village. Even Parker and Magnus would be affected.

As the door opened and Ella came in with Julian, Vivian plastered a pleasant smile on her face and took the empty mugs from his hands. "Would you like more coffee?"

"I need to change." Ella was holding her shirt away from her body. "I spilled coffee on myself." She darted into the hallway.

Looking after her retreating back, Julian sighed. "I would have loved to stay and have another cup with you, but I need to get moving. Yamanu is waiting for me at the halfway house. I need to make arrangements for the project to keep going while I'm gone."

"Can't you have someone else supervise the job?" Magnus asked.

"Not on such short notice, and Yamanu can't take my place because he needs to stay in the village during the heightened alert. When we started the project, I thought to save money by managing the job site and subcontracting the work. Now I regret not hiring a general contractor to handle everything."

"What about the pros Kian uses in the real estate development?"

Julian shook his head. "They don't do renovations." He turned to Vivian. "I guess the next time I'll see you will be in Washington."

Swallowing, she nodded.

"Good luck."

Listening to the guys talk about remodeling had been a momentary distraction, but Julian's reminder spiked her anxiety back up.

Vivian waited for the door to close behind him before walking up to Magnus and wrapping her arms around him. "I don't know what I'm going to do without you. You've become such a vital part of my days and my nights that I'm going to feel lost and lonely while you're gone."

He held her to him tightly, rocking her in place. "Are you having separation anxiety, lass?"

That wasn't the type of language Magnus used. Had he been consulting with Vanessa without telling her?

"Who have you been talking with?"

"Andrew. He says Phoenix cries every morning when he leaves for work, and it breaks his heart even though she stops the moment the door closes behind him."

"So, what are you saying, that I'm acting like a little girl?"

He shook his head. "No, love. It's just that this is the first time we are going to be apart since we met, and that's why it feels so uncomfortable. But it's not going to be the last. I'm a Guardian, and although most of the time I will be assigned to local missions, from time to time I will have to leave for several days. You'd better get used to that."

Resting her forehead on his chest, Vivian nodded. "I know. I'll have to keep myself super busy, that's all. Perhaps Vanessa can use my help with more things than just the sewing class. I just hope she'll be okay with me bringing Parker over. He's fine by himself for a few hours, but I don't want to leave him alone for entire days."

As she rambled on and on, Magnus rubbed slow circles on her back, waiting patiently for her to calm down. Even though they hadn't been together all that long, he knew her so well because he paid attention.

She lifted her head and kissed his lips. "I love you. You're the best."

Wearing a fresh shirt, Ella walked in and cast an amused glance at them. "Are we still going to the sanctuary today, Mom? Or do you want to spend every moment smooching with Magnus until he leaves?"

Kissing the top of Vivian's head, he gently disentangled himself from her arms. "I wish we could, but I have a briefing I need to attend."

"When?" Vivian asked.

"After lunch."

"Good, so we can eat together." She turned to Ella. "I called Vanessa and canceled for today. We need to go shopping."

"What for?"

"Clothes, shoes. You have nothing decent to wear for the interview. You can't go wearing your Frankenstein boots or sneakers."

Over her head, she felt Magnus nodding as if to encourage Ella to say yes. Sweet guy.

"Well, I need to add a few items to my wardrobe, and if it helps to take your mind off worrying, I'm all for it. But not today. After Julian comes back from the halfway house, I want to spend some time with him. Besides, we can go virtual shopping and order everything online."

"Things won't arrive on time."

"We can pay for expedited shipping."

Poor girl. She was still wary about leaving the safety of the village. "Are you afraid of going anywhere other than the sanctuary?"

Ella shrugged. "It hasn't even crossed my mind, but now that you mention it, I was reminded of what a hassle it was to put on my full disguise. I can't stand the contact lenses, and trying on clothes with sunglasses on will be too weird."

"Online shopping it is, then." Vivian headed to the kitchen and opened the fridge. "I'm just afraid of ordering shoes and then finding out that they don't fit. We don't have time to send them back and order another size." She pulled out lettuce and a wedge of parmesan cheese for a Caesar salad.

Ella followed her to the kitchen and leaned against the counter. "I need to go talk to Eva. I haven't thought about wearing the disguise while touring Georgetown, and the contacts are a pain in the derrière. I need to ask her if there are regular looking glasses that can fool facial recognition software."

Vivian frowned. "I hadn't thought of it either. Perhaps we both should go see her. We need better disguises."

Pulling out her phone, Ella glanced up. "I'll ask her if she can see us after lunch. Okay with you?"

"Perfect. We can do that while Magnus is at his meeting."

"Right. And I need to go visit Tessa too. Do you want to come with me?"

Vivian smiled. "I have a great idea. How about we make something special for lunch and bring it to her? I'm sure she is in no mood for cooking."

Ella waved a dismissive hand. "I don't know if she cooks at all. Jackson could be bringing stuff from the café. Besides, it isn't as if either of us is a great cook. I'm not going to take Tessa your meatloaf, if that's what you have in mind."

Vivian cast her a reproachful look. "I know more than one recipe, and besides, it's the thought that counts."

"I meant no offense, Mom. I love your meatloaf, but many people don't like that kind of food. If I bring Tessa something, I want to make sure she enjoys it. Like a box of Godiva chocolates."

"Do you have any left?"

Ella was a sucker for those. If she had any, they were most likely gone by now.

"I do. After I cleaned his kitchen, Merlin gave me a huge pack full of small boxes. I had Julian keep them so I wouldn't eat all of them at one sitting, but I have two boxes here. I can wrap one up and give it to Tessa."

"Perfect."

21

ELLA

"I have just what you need," Eva said. "Believe it or not, Roni printed them for me on a 3D-printer."

Vivian shook her head. "Technology is progressing at an amazing speed. I read that scientists at the Tel-Aviv university were able to 3-D print a small scale human heart using human cells. Pretty soon organ donations will no longer be needed. No more waiting in line for hearts and kidneys and the like. Each hospital will have a 3-D printer and replacement parts will be custom made for any patient that needs them."

Eva grinned. "I just love it. Yesterday's science fiction is today's reality. Like Jules Verne's stories. The inventions he wrote about were fantasy back then, but they became reality." She pushed to her feet. "Let me get my magic makeover case."

In his bassinet, Ethan was making cute little sucking noises, and Ella got up to get a better look. He was sound asleep, probably dreaming about nursing.

Such an adorable baby, and those pink cheeks were just asking to be kissed. Hopefully, he would wake up before they left so she could hold him for a little bit. Having the baby pressed against her chest felt like an infusion of good. It really was a bundle of joy.

Ella wondered if that feeling was produced by the same chemical reaction Julian had talked about, or if it was unique to babies. Hugging adults, or even Parker, had never flooded her with as many feel-good endorphins.

"Do babies have this effect only on women or on men too?"

"What do you mean?" Vivian asked.

"Whenever I've held Ethan, and I've only gotten to do it twice, I felt like I was high. It felt euphoric. So, I'm wondering if only females feel that because their bodies prepare them for motherhood, or do males feel that too?"

A sadness settled over Vivian's features. "Your father's eyes would roll back from pleasure every time he held you and later Parker." She chuckled. "But only until you started crying or made a stinky in your diaper. Then he would quickly give you back to me."

When Eva came back hefting a huge trunk, Ella rushed to help her. "This looks heavy."

Eva huffed. "Don't be silly. I'm at least twice as strong as you are." She put it down on the floor, crouched next to it, and sprung the coded locks. "Open sesame." The lid popped up.

Inside, several compartments of various sizes were separated by dividers. Eva pulled a makeup case out and opened it.

"I have three new pairs of those specialty glasses, but with clear lenses this time so they look like reading glasses. They are called adversarial, probably because they can fool your adversaries. They aren't the prettiest, and if you want, I can ask Roni if he can print something better looking." She handed one pair to Ella and the other to Vivian.

The frames were made from simple black plastic, but they weren't as hideous as Ella had feared something made with a 3-D printer would be.

"Can't we order nicer ones from a store?" Vivian asked.

"They are not commercially available yet. The instructions are not publicly available either, but you know Roni. When he wants to get his hands on something, he finds a way."

Ella took the glasses off and examined them closer. "Did he hack the instructions?"

"According to him, he did not. The inventors are sharing them with people in their close circle, and William knew a guy who knew another guy. That sort of thing." Lifting a handheld mirror from her case, Eva handed it to Ella. "Here, put them back on and take a look."

"They are not bad." Ella ran her fingers through her hair, spiking it. "Hipster style meets grunge punk. I like it." She handed the mirror to her mother who didn't look happy.

"Ugh, it's going to look awful with my black wig, but whatever. I'm not entering a beauty pageant."

"What else can you do for us?" Ella asked. "We need things that are not difficult to put on and keep on."

Eva looked her up and down. "You're fine. If you want, you can go to William's lab and have him run you through his program while you're wearing the glasses. If you pass the test, then there is no reason to go any further. And the same is true for your mom." She turned to Vivian. "But keep the wig on. Your hair is very distinctive, especially when combined with your tiny frame."

"I will."

"I have one here that might look better on you than the one Amanda gave you." She pulled out a shoulder-length wig. "It's not all black, so it looks more natural. Try it on."

The wig was dark chestnut, and it looked like it was real hair. Either that or it was made from better materials and didn't look as fake as the one Amanda gave Vivian. Except, Ella thought that it was kind of gross to wear someone else's hair.

"I love it. Thank you," Vivian said. "I don't look like a vampire in it. I'm normally pale, but when I'm stressed, I look like a ghost."

"Then I suggest you put on a lot of makeup." Eva smiled evilly. "You don't want to scare your prey off."

Vivian swallowed. "I need to buy more foundation."

Way to go, Eva. It was good that the woman wasn't a doctor because her bedside manner left a lot to be desired. She would've scared her patients to death.

Then again, her direct approach had worked for Tessa. After killing her tormentor, Eva had nursed the traumatized girl back to health, which meant that she wasn't as callous as she appeared. Or maybe Tessa responded better to tough love?

"How is Tessa doing?" Ella asked. "Did you talk with her since yesterday?"

"Jackson took her horseback riding. That boy is a genius. It would've never occurred to me that such an activity could have a therapeutic effect. But apparently, it's working for Tessa. When she called me earlier, she sounded fine."

"Well, his mother is a therapist. He must've asked Vanessa for advice."

Eva cocked an eyebrow. "Did you see any horses in the sanctuary? If that were Vanessa's idea, she would have a stable on the grounds."

"Horses are expensive and need a lot of care," Vivian said.

Eva waved a dismissive hand. "She could have made do with some cats or goats to pet."

Cats and goats were not in the same category as horses, but Ella wasn't going to point it out. No one liked a wiseass, and Eva was a bit scary. Pissing her off was not a good idea.

"Why not dogs?" Vivian asked. "Small ones, that is. I can see how some girls might be afraid of big dogs."

Ella took the glasses off and put them in her purse. "Dogs pee and poo where they are not supposed to. Scarlet still has accidents."

Vivian grimaced. "Tell me about it. I ordered half a dozen of those disinfecting spray bottles."

"Scarlet is so funny." Ella chuckled. "She always looks so guilty after doing something she knows is a no-no. As soon as she makes that face, we go looking for her mess right away."

As a sound of protest came from Ethan's bassinet, Eva walked over and picked him up. "Are you hungry, my sweet little boy?" She kissed his cheek.

The baby cooed and reached with his tiny fist, closing it around a strand of her hair.

"Don't pull on Mama's hair, precious." Eva smoothed a finger over his tiny ones but didn't attempt to pry them open.

Ella wondered if the baby would let go on his own. Perhaps when Eva started feeding him?

"We should go." Vivian pushed to her feet. "Thank you so much for all your help."

"My pleasure. And if I don't see you before you leave, good luck. I wish I could be there, but since my Bhathian is escorting you, I know that you are in good hands."

22

JULIAN

When Julian made it back to the village, it was after ten at night and he still needed to pack, but he had to see Ella before leaving. The flight was scheduled for early in the morning the next day, and he didn't think she would be awake to say goodbye.

Should he ask her to spend the night with him?

The yearning to hold her in his arms until the last moment was so intense that it made breathing difficult. A problem, since he was running.

Fifty feet or so away from her house, Julian slowed down to a walk and evened out his breath. There was no need for Ella to know how obsessed with her he was, and that he had run all the way from the pavilion.

Except, as soon as his foot touched the first of the three steps leading up to her front porch, Ella opened the door and stepped out. "Did you run all the way here?"

"What gave me away?" He climbed the stairs and took her into his arms.

"I timed it. You called me when you left the construction site. And I calculated the drive and the walk. You are seven minutes early."

It seemed that he was not the only one obsessed.

His heart felt lighter at the realization. "How are we going to survive these five days?"

She wrapped her arms around his neck. "We will have to talk on the phone a lot and video chat."

All kinds of visions crossed his mind, some naughtier than others.

"What's that smirk about?" Ella asked.

He kissed the tip of her nose. "You're not the only one with a vivid imagination. I entertained a few ideas for those phone calls."

Catching his meaning, she blushed. "We can't. Not yet."

He made a face. "It doesn't count when there is no touching involved."

"I'm sure that some touching was going on in your vivid fantasies."

"Guilty."

Ella sighed. "Just a little bit longer, Julian. By next Wednesday, I will be free. Hopefully. If everything works out as planned." She pushed out of his arms and took his hand. "It will be one hell of a disappointment if Mr. D doesn't show up, and all this careful preparation is for nothing. I will feel like such an idiot."

As they started walking down the pathway, Julian wrapped his arm around Ella's waist. "Do you know the phrase about the leopard and how he cannot change its spots? The same is true of the Doomer. It would be uncharacteristic for him to help you out of the goodness of his heart. He wants you. He admitted it."

"True." She shrugged. "Everything is set in motion, so there is no point in speculating. Whatever happens, happens. Just promise me to be extra super-duper careful. I won't survive it if anything happens to you." Her voice wobbled a little.

"Hey." He stopped and hooked a finger under her chin. "Look at me."

She had tears in her eyes.

"Nothing is going to happen to me. Thirty experienced Guardians can take on a platoon of Doomers. The most formidable warriors on the planet are going to guard you and your mom. I'm just tagging along because I'll expire from worry if I'm not there with you."

Wiping the tears with the back of her hand, she smiled. "And I thought that I was being melodramatic. Sorry for the mini-meltdown."

"Speaking of meltdowns, how is Tessa doing?"

Holding hands, they resumed their walk.

"Better. Jackson took her horseback riding. Except, I don't know what did the trick, him taking the day off to be with her or the horses."

"A little bit of both, I guess." He squeezed her hand. "I'm not going to bore you with a geeky explanation about why horseback riding releases endorphins."

"Why not? I love it when you tell me interesting facts. I can then use them in conversations and sound smart."

"You are smart." He leaned and kissed the top of her head. "But I'll save it for after we come back. Right now I want to hear about you and your day. Did you talk with Sylvia about assisting you in the sanctuary?"

"I did. She's going to help me film and also help edit the videos."

"Editing was supposed to be my job." On the one hand, Julian had been looking forward to spending long hours with Ella, but on the other hand, he hadn't been looking forward to the emotional pain of hearing horrible stories.

"It still is. I just want to edit the first three videos and put them up before I leave for Washington. I want to have this fundraiser up and running. Sylvia is going to help with those. When we come back, you'll help me with the ones I'm going to shoot tomorrow and the day after."

"Did you get more volunteers?"

"No, but I'm going to. Tomorrow I'm shooting the other two from the original four, and I hope more will sign up. We don't need all of them to do it, but the more the better."

"Good luck."

"Thank you." Ella looked down, found a small loose rock, and kicked it. "This project keeps me going. Whenever I feel scared or overwhelmed, or when bad thoughts intrude, all I need to do is think about the fundraiser to get excited and positive again."

It was a little disappointing that thinking of him was not enough to chase the gloom away, but he was happy that she had something to keep her upbeat.

Having a goal, especially a worthy one like that, was a powerful motivator.

Julian wished he had something like that to get him excited. Something he felt super passionate about. He could jump on the fundraiser wagon and help Ella or focus on remodeling the halfway house. Both were worthy endeavors, but they didn't get his juices flowing. He needed a challenge, something he was exceptionally good at, or believed he could be. Regrettably, he hadn't stumbled upon that one thing yet.

He was excited about catching the Doomer, though. Which brought back Ella's suggestion of him joining the Guardian force. Perhaps as a medic?

Nah, that wasn't it either.

Who did he want to be when he grew up?

Ella waved a hand in front of his face. "A penny for your thoughts."

"They are not worth even that. I was trying to figure out what would excite me as much as the fundraiser excites you."

"I don't think you can go looking for it. Fate has a way of putting the right person in the right place for the right job. The choice we have is either to step up to the plate or not. If you asked me a month ago if I was interested in fundraising, I would have said no way. I was convinced that I wanted to be a nurse. But one thing led to another and here I am, all consumed by this project that is way too big for me, but that I want to tackle anyway."

"You no longer want to be a nurse?"

"I'm not sure what I want."

"A doctor. You should study to become a doctor."

She shook her head. "I don't think so."

He chuckled. "That makes two of us. Neither of us know who we want to be when we grow up."

"Oh, I know who I want to be." Ella looked up at him and smiled. "I want to be Ella Takala, Director of Save the Girls."

23

ELLA

As they got back to her house, Julian swept Ella into his arms and sat with her on the loveseat swing.

"I need a kiss that will hold me through the next five days." He palmed the back of her head and took her lips.

Ella threw her arms around his neck and pulled him down to her, savoring the ferocity of his kiss. His mouth was hard on hers, taking, demanding, and beneath her his erection prodded her through his jeans.

God, she wanted him. She was ready, and even if it wasn't going to be perfect because of the baggage she was bringing along, she didn't want to wait any longer.

Except, that was a lot of empty bravado when she knew nothing could happen between them tonight.

With an effort, she pulled away and put a hand on his chest. "Next Wednesday, Julian, we are going to celebrate Mr. D's capture. The Guardians can bring him back here and we can stay in Washington for a few days. We will go to see all the monuments, eat in fancy restaurants, and spend our nights together."

Julian shook his head. "Don't."

"Don't what?"

"Make victory plans."

"Are you afraid to jinx it?"

"It's not about that. Don't rush things because you feel bad for me." He smirked. "When you're so ready that steam is coming out of your ears, then we will revisit your proposition."

Smiling, Ella clapped her hands over her earlobes. "I think it's happening already. I can feel the steam billowing out."

"Not yet, but it will. I guarantee it."

"I believe you, and I love you."

"I love you too, sweetheart." He lifted her off his lap and helped her stand. "I don't want to go, but I should."

Stretching up on her toes, she kissed his cheek, then the other one, and last she kissed his lips. "Good night, Julian. Call me when you get settled in Washington."

"I will."

She opened the door and went in, but before closing it, she stood there for a long moment and watched him walk away.

The next five days were going to be difficult but doable, with plenty of video calls and long talks into the night.

Yawning, Ella closed the door and tiptoed through the dark house to her room. Five minutes later she was in bed and hugging her pillow.

Showering could wait for the morning.

A soft kiss on her lips woke her up, and then a hard male body pressed against her, strong arms wrapping around her and pulling her closer. Smiling, she wrapped her arms around Julian's neck, her fingers stroking his hair.

Except, something didn't feel right. His hair was shorter, and coarser, and his body was leaner than she'd remembered. This didn't feel like Julian at all.

Gasping, she opened her eyes and leaned away.

"Did I scare you?" Logan asked. "You were smiling a moment ago. Did you expect someone else?"

Crap, she was in her room, in her own bed, and Logan was there with her, which meant that he was seeing into her mind. That was bad, really bad.

"I didn't expect to find you in my bed. Usually you take me somewhere nice."

"My apologies." He snapped his fingers, transporting them to a different room.

"Where are we?"

"My bedroom."

She looked over his shoulder, but it was too dark to see. "Can you turn on a light?"

"I can do better than that."

As the ceiling disappeared, revealing a starry night, Ella gasped with delight. It was magical. If only she knew more about the constellations, she could figure out where they were, but regrettably her knowledge was limited to their names. She couldn't discern the patterns in the sky.

Turning on her back, she crossed her arms over her chest. "This is beautiful, thank you. But you really shouldn't have taken such liberties. I told you that I'm not that kind of girl."

He leaned over her, caressing her cheek with his finger as he regarded her with his intense dark eyes. "I've done exactly what you've told me. I've taken you on walks in beautiful places, and I've behaved like the perfect gentleman. Then you explained to me how modern girls don't play games and hook up with anyone they want. I thought you were hinting at something."

"I also told you that I'm not ready to hook up with anyone."

"Don't you find me attractive?"

"I find you disturbingly so."

He arched a dark eyebrow. "What does that mean?"

"You're a dangerous man, Logan. You admitted as much. I should be afraid of you, not attracted to you."

Smirking like the devil he was, Logan rubbed his finger over her lips, the small touch sending goosebumps all over her arms. "Let me tell you a secret, little Ella. Women are attracted to dangerous men. Have you ever heard the phrase like a moth to a flame?"

"I have. And that's exactly how I feel." A slight exaggeration, but there was enough truth in it to sound believable.

His other hand smoothed over the curve of her hip. "It's a dream, Ella. You're in no danger from me or anyone else in here. You can have some harmless fun in dreamland."

She took his hand and moved it off her hip. "I'm not ready for fun. Not after what I've been through, which was not fun at all. In fact, I started seeing a therapist."

"And how is that working for you?"

"It's good. I only had one session so far, but I think I made some progress."

A grimace spreading over his handsome face, Logan turned on his back and crossed his arms under his head. "Americans and their shrinks. Do you really think some bobbing head knows better how to heal your mind than you do yourself?"

She couldn't agree more. "I'm giving it a try. If it helps, fine, and if it doesn't, I'll quit."

"You are a smart girl, Ella. You don't need the shrink or anyone else to tell you how to feel."

Damn. How did he know all the right things to say? Was he reading her mind after all?

"What if I feel sad?"

"It's okay to feel sad and angry and frustrated. This futile pursuit of feel-good and happy is a very Western sentiment. Suffering is part of the human experience."

She turned on her side and looked at him. "Are you suffering, Logan?"

"Every goddamned day of my life."

That was surprising. "You don't look like you do."

"Because I don't dwell on it. I plot and I scheme and I act. Instead of lying on a couch in a shrink's office and complaining about my troubles, I fix them."

"What if you can't fix something?"

"Then I put some work into searching for the right tool until I find it."

Reluctantly, she liked his attitude. A lot.

"I'm tired and I need to sleep, Logan. For real. Can we continue this conversation tomorrow?"

"On one condition. I want a kiss goodnight."

Oh, boy. This wasn't good.

"Not in bed. How about you take me to some romantic location and we kiss there?"

He didn't look happy about her request, but he did as she asked anyway. Snapping his fingers, he had them standing at the top of the Eiffel Tower.

"Is that romantic enough for you?"

"Oh, yeah. Thank you."

Wrapping his arm around her shoulders, he chuckled. "In reality, it's not as romantic as I made it for you."

"What's the difference?"

"I removed the metal grid and replaced it with glass panels." He glanced down at her. "You didn't notice the change in attire either. How do you like the gown?"

With the magnificent view all around her, Ella hadn't paid attention to anything else. Now that he called her attention to it, though, what she had on didn't feel like the nightshirt she'd gone to bed in.

He snapped his fingers again. "Here is a mirror."

The gown was indeed beautiful, and she appreciated Logan's good taste, but with him standing next to her, it was difficult to concentrate on her own reflection.

Regal was the word that came to mind. Right after dangerous and sexy as sin. Logan looked like the prince he was. Correction, the grandson of a god.

Lucifer had nothing on him.

24

AMANDA

"Master Parker." Amanda ruffled the kid's hair. "I came to check on your progress. Have you been practicing your powers?"

Vivian chuckled. "He's been tormenting Ella, and he even tried it on Scarlet."

"Did it work?"

"Nope." Parker shook his head. "She's cute, but she's stupid."

Amanda affected a scowl. "I hope you are referring to the dog and not your sister."

He grimaced. "Ella is not cute."

Exchanging glances, Vivian and Amanda burst out laughing.

"What?" Parker threw his hands in the air. "She might look cute, but she's not. Sometimes she's really nasty to me."

"She's not." Vivian motioned for Amanda to take a seat on the couch. "Can I offer you some coffee?"

"No, thank you. I've had too much already. But I'll take water. Do you have something cold and carbonated?"

"I'll get you a Perrier."

"Perfect. Thank you."

Amanda waited for Vivian to come back before turning to Parker. "Come sit with your auntie and tell me about your compulsion experiments." She put the Perrier bottle on the coffee table, crossed her legs, and rested her hands one on top of the other on her knee. Her teacher's pose.

"I figured out why sometimes it works and sometimes it doesn't." He sat on the other side of the couch.

The kid was still uncomfortable around her, but that would pass. She liked him, and hopefully in time he would feel the same about her.

"Do tell." Patting the spot next to her, Amanda motioned for him to get closer.

"There are several things I need to do at once, and it's not easy. First, I need to concentrate and visualize what I want the person to do, then I need to really want them to do it, and finally I have to use the voice."

Up until the comment about the voice, it sounded a lot like thralling.

"Can you demonstrate?"

He frowned. "You're an immortal. It's not going to work on you."

"I know. I just want to hear that special voice you use." She pulled out her phone and pressed record.

If this had to do with sound waves, William could analyze it. Although on second thought, it would be better if Parker came down to the lab and they recorded him using proper equipment.

Still frowning, Parker shook his head. "I can't think of anything I want from you. It can't be something I'm not really interested in."

Remembering his transition party demands, Amanda reached into her purse and pulled out her wallet. "If I detect something special in your voice, I'll give you a twenty." She pulled the note out of the wallet and waved it in front of Parker. "Do you want this?"

He nodded. "Then ask me for it."

Parker nodded, took in a deep breath, closed his eyes for a moment, opened them and leveled his gaze at Amanda. "Give me the twenty dollars, please."

"Here you go." She handed him the note.

Snatching it, he quickly put it in his pocket. "Did you hear anything in my voice?"

She hadn't, but it was important not to discourage him. The more confident Parker felt, the better he would do.

"I'm not sure." She glanced at Vivian. "Can he practice on you? I want to see him in action."

"Give me a moment." Vivian got up and rushed into the kitchen.

A moment later she came back with a small packet of roasted almonds. "These are like catnip for Parker."

The kid's eyes widened. "I didn't know we had any left."

"I hid them from you because you weren't eating anything else. Try to get me to give them to you." She dangled the small package from her fingers.

Amanda could almost feel the vibration of Parker summoning his powers, but then again, she wanted to feel something, so she could have been sensing what wasn't there.

Lifting his hand high in the air, he commanded, "Throw the almonds to me."

Vivian's hand shook as she tried to resist the command, but it was no use. The pack went flying straight into Parker's raised hand.

"What did you feel, Vivian?"

"It's the weirdest thing. It's like he took command of my arm and it did what he told it to do. My own body betrayed me." She looked up at Amanda. "What if it's a placebo effect?"

"Let's see how Ella reacts. Is she home?"

"She is in her room with Sylvia. They are working on editing the first two videos she shot at the sanctuary."

"Congratulations. I didn't know she'd already started. How is it going for her?"

Vivian sighed. "She lost Tessa. The girl couldn't stomach it. Sylvia volunteered to take her place."

"That bad, eh?"

"I don't know. Ella didn't let me see any of them. I'm afraid that I'll have to wait for her to upload them to YouTube first. She thinks I can't handle it."

Amanda lifted the Perrier and unscrewed the top. "Perhaps she's right. It's one thing to listen to a stranger's horror story, and another thing entirely to hear your own daughter recounting her nightmare."

Glancing at Parker, Vivian shook her head, indicating that they shouldn't talk in front of him. It was her prerogative as his mother, of course, but Amanda didn't believe that a teenager Parker's age couldn't handle some nasty.

"I'll call her," Vivian said.

For a moment, Amanda expected her to pull out a phone, but when Vivian just gazed at the direction of Ella's room, she was reminded that mother and daughter had a more direct way of communicating.

She heard the door open, and then Ella's light footsteps as she rushed into the living room. "Hi, Amanda. Mom said that you need me for something."

Amanda nodded. "I want Parker to show me how he compels you to do something that you don't want to do."

"Great." Ella rolled her eyes. "Just do it quickly and don't embarrass me. I want to be done with those three videos tonight."

Vivian didn't look happy. "I thought you were only working on the two you filmed on Tuesday."

"I also have mine from Monday."

"Please don't put it up. What if Gorchenco can recognize you? You were his wife, for God's sake. He can probably detect every inflection in your tone, and he knows your body language."

Ella waved a dismissive hand. "Once we are done with editing, I'll let you watch it and you'll tell me if I'm recognizable. After all, I was married to the Russian for only a few days, but I've been your daughter for eighteen years."

That seemed to mollify Vivian. "Promise?"

"Yeah. Now. Let's get on with the compulsion."

While they'd been talking, Parker had time to prepare, and he was ready with his demand. "Make me a sandwich exactly like the one you made me yesterday."

"Crap." Ella tried to shake it off, and then headed to the kitchen. "I don't understand how it works," she said as she pulled the ingredients out of the fridge. "I know he's about to do it, I brace to resist, and then I have to do it anyway. It's like he's taking control of my body. But when he did it unknowingly, it felt different."

"How so?" Amanda asked.

"Since I didn't resist, I didn't feel as if my body was obeying a command. I thought that I decided to humor him, that it was my decision."

Fascinating. Apparently, compulsion was undetectable unless the compelled knew it was coming. Amanda wondered what happened when the command went against the compelled one's moral code. Did they try to fight it, or did they convince themselves that they actually wanted to do what they were compelled to do?

It seemed that compulsion worked a lot like hypnosis, just with more muscle behind it. Resisting it was more difficult.

It could explain how otherwise sane people could be turned into a murderous mob by a charismatic leader. The question was whether those types of leaders used mass hypnosis or were gifted with the unique ability to compel.

It would be interesting to introduce Ella and Vivian to a powerful hypnotist and see if hypnosis affected them similarly to compulsion, and then ask them to compare the two.

25

JULIAN

"Is this also a clan-owned hotel?" Julian asked as their van pulled up to the building.

"Not this time." Turner slung the strap of his duffel bag over his shoulder and opened the sliding door. "I have many friends in Washington. Or rather acquaintances who owe me favors. This place is reserved for special operations. There are several of them scattered throughout the city. Different sizes and different levels of concealment."

Julian followed him inside. "Are we going straight to the campus? I wouldn't mind stopping somewhere for a bite to eat."

Turner smirked. "We are going to enjoy the cuisine of the student cafeteria."

"I don't miss that."

"We don't have time." Turner slapped his back. "The campus is sprawling and we need to get familiar with it while not attracting attention."

The clerk at the hotel's front desk was clearly not trained in the hospitality business. With a nod of acknowledgment, he handed Turner a bunch of plastic entry keys with sticky notes marking the room numbers attached to them.

Was he an agent? And if he was, which department did he work for?

"Thank you," Turner said as he took five and handed the remaining ones back. "The rest of my crew is arriving shortly."

The clerk nodded again.

"Are we sharing a room?"

Turner lifted a brow. "Do you want to room with someone else?"

"I was hoping to have one to myself. If everything goes well, Ella and I might stay over and do some sightseeing. We can come back on a commercial flight."

"No problem. We have rooms to spare." Turner turned around and went back to the front desk. "We will need one more room."

The clerk grimaced as he handed him the key. "I'll have the cleaning crew prepare it for you."

"Much appreciated."

The guy nodded.

Turner handed Julian a card. "We are on the ground floor. I'm number three and you are number five."

As he followed the guy down the corridor, Julian rubbed his jaw. "If Lokan has Ella followed to her hotel, he might notice that the majority of the guests are men. It could tip him off."

"I've thought of that. We will have female company."

Hopefully, he didn't mean the paid kind. Maybe the other guys would be happy about it, but Julian didn't think his mother would appreciate it if her mate arranged for it.

He stopped next to Turner as the guy opened the door to his room. "What kind of female company? Are we talking agents or call girls?"

"Neither." Turner got inside and motioned for Julian to join him. "Remember the women we rescued from the Doomers a while back?"

"What about them?" Julian closed the door and looked at the room.

Crappy, that was what Ella would've called it. Then again, it was probably what Vivian could have afforded on her own, so it fit the profile. Except, that was not how he wanted to spend a romantic weekend with Ella. Once the mission was done, he would get them a nice room in a luxury hotel.

"You were away at school, so I don't know how much of the story you've heard."

Julian sat on the bed. "Only that the Guardians rescued the girls and then torched the place. Also, something about taking them to a retreat in Hawaii."

"After the rescue, Amanda thralled them to forget that they had been held captive by the Doomers. She made them believe that they had spent the missing time training for a new job. Kian hired all of them to work in the clan's new hotel in Hawaii, and many of them stayed on."

"Cool. I'm glad that they were taken care of. But what does their story have to do with this?"

"I was getting there. We got them tickets to a hospitality convention in Washington D.C. and booked their stay right here in this hotel."

"Smart. Was it your idea or Kian's?"

"Actually, it was your mother's."

26

ELLA

"I have to go," Sylvia said after the rough edit on the first video was done. "I still have homework to do."

It seemed that Sylvia didn't like to work hard, or maybe she had a soft heart and the stories had disturbed her, but she was embarrassed to admit that. The result was the same, though. Ella was left to do the rest on her own.

"Thanks for your help. It would have taken me forever to figure out the editing software if you weren't here to show me how to use it."

Sylvia smiled. "I'm glad I was able to help at least a little. I'll come back tomorrow if I can."

That didn't sound promising. "Thanks. I really appreciate you doing this for me."

"No problem. Good night."

After she left, Ella sighed and went back to work. The truth was that without Sylvia it would have taken her the entire evening just to learn how to do the most basic things, and she would've gotten none of the editing done. Now, she might be able to finish the first two videos tonight.

When her phone rang long hours later, Ella snatched it off the charger and plopped on the bed. "Hi, Julian."

"You sound tired."

"I'm exhausted. I've been working on the recordings since morning and I only have one and a half done."

"Is Sylvia still there?"

Ella snorted. "She went home hours ago, saying she had homework to do. I think she either got bored or upset over the story we were working on."

There was a slight pause before he asked, "How are you holding up? It must be difficult for you."

Ella closed her eyes and sighed. "Maybe the first round was. But after that it became technical. I don't really listen anymore. I guess I'm like a surgeon, performing the operation on the organ without thinking about the patient. It's easier that way."

"Whatever works, sweetheart. I wish I could be there with you and help you out."

The truth was that Ella preferred not having Julian work on the editing with her. Spending time together could have been fun, but the subject matter was too difficult for him to stomach. It would have killed him to have to listen to those stories and be unable to do anything about it.

Ella hadn't realized that until she'd started the editing process, but the most potent emotion she'd experienced hadn't been pity for the girl. It was an intense hatred for the scum who'd hurt her and a powerful need to avenge her.

It would've been so much more difficult for a guy like Julian who had the soul of a Guardian.

"How are things in our nation's capital?" She changed the subject.

"All I've seen is the hotel and the Georgetown campus. We've spent most of the day scoping the place and getting acquainted with the grounds, which are sprawling. It's a beautiful place, though. Maybe we can tour it together after this is over."

Smiling, Ella lowered her voice. "Did you get a solo room?"

"I did, but it's not the kind of place I want to spend time with you."

"Why, is it dingy?"

"Kind of. It's old and moldy."

"My mom and I are going to stay there too, right?"

"Yeah. But that's different. This hotel is part of the setup. It's close enough to the campus without being too pricey, so it fits the profile of students coming in for a tour. In fact, Turner arranged for us to pose as potential football recruits. We even had a fake meeting with the coach who is a friend of Turner's from his military days."

Ella could only imagine what the guy had thought when he'd seen Turner. "How did he explain his youthful looks?"

Julian chuckled. "With his usual lack of expression, Turner told the guy that he'd gone for a hair transplant and a laser resurfacing on his skin because he'd married a much younger woman and didn't want to look like her father. He even showed him my mother's picture."

"Bridget is beautiful."

"The coach thought so too. It's good that Turner is not the jealous type because there were a few hubba hubba's and whistles thrown in."

"You like Turner, don't you?"

"He's okay. And he is a perfect match for my mother. Not to mention a real asset for the clan. Even before Turner's transition, Kian relied on him to organize complicated missions. But back to us. I think I like your idea of staying over the weekend. Not here, of course. Somewhere nicer. If you're still game, I should make reservations before there are no decent rooms left."

That was different from just staying a little longer in the same place. A romantic weekend in a nice hotel was a much bigger deal. She would be obsessing about it and imagining what was going to happen, which could be a problem when Logan entered her dreams. Until he was captured, she needed to keep coasting on neutral with Julian.

"I don't want to jinx it. Let's wait until this is over."

"It was your idea."

He was right. It had been momentary bravado. Or perhaps it had been just a good moment. She had those occasionally, feeling like her old upbeat self, but they didn't last long. That was the downside of the project she'd undertaken. It was a daily reminder of what she'd been through.

"I know, but making reservations in a different hotel takes it to another level. Besides, my head is full of organizing the fundraiser. I can't concentrate on anything else." Hopefully, that was enough said for Julian to understand. "I have one video ready, and I need to figure out how to put it on YouTube, and then how to upload it to the fundraising site. It's all new to me, and I'm freaking out a little. I think I bit off more than I can chew."

She was talking a mile a minute to hide her discomfort, but that didn't mean that she was making it up. Up until now, she'd talked a big game without having the knowledge to back it up. Not that she couldn't figure it out, eventually she would, but it was stressful.

"I was lucky that Sylvia was familiar with the editing software and showed me how to use it. If not for her, I would still be struggling with it. But I don't have anyone to help me with the other things. Do you know anyone who puts up videos on YouTube? Because I've never done it before."

"You could ask Roni or William. Not that they post anything there, but I'm sure it will be easier for them to figure it out than it will be for you."

"That's an awesome idea, but how do I get to them? Do I just ask someone where the lab is and go there?"

"First of all, yes, you can do that. But you can also call Roni. By the way, you should ask him what to do to get more views. I don't know much about it, but there are keywords and phrases you can include that will make it come up in more searches and suggestions."

"Good idea. I'll do that. I didn't even think about search engine optimization because I don't know anything about it. Do you think Roni or William do? They are not into marketing or promoting stuff."

"Don't worry about it. Those two can figure anything out."

"Yeah, but do they have time? I'm sure they have better things to do."

Julian chuckled. "You're tired, Ella. Go to sleep and tomorrow everything will look less daunting."

"Yeah, you're right. I should."

27

ELLA

Before getting in bed, Ella browsed the internet, looking up information about Georgetown. If Logan entered her dream tonight, and she had a strong feeling he would, her head would be filled with tidbits about the university, the grounds, the dorms, the cafeterias, and all the other things a prospective student would be interested in.

It was what Logan would expect from someone who was excited about actually going to a prestigious place like that.

As Ella drifted off, images of the various academic halls were playing like a slide show in her head, and when the dream began, she was strolling along a path on Healy Lawn, with Logan at her side.

"Do you like it here?" he asked.

"It's beautiful. I can't wait to actually see it with my own eyes instead of on a computer screen."

"You are seeing it."

She turned to him and smiled. "Are you creating the scenery, or am I?"

"It's coming from my memory. I've been to the campus recently, and I walked down this path."

"Oh, yeah? What were you doing there?"

He wrapped his arm around her waist. "Talking with my friend about a certain young lady I wanted him to admit to the undergrad program."

He was tipping his hand, revealing that he was in Washington. The question was whether it had been a slip, or had he done it on purpose, hoping she would suggest a meeting?

"I can't thank you enough for arranging this for me. I've never dreamed of getting into such a prestigious university. President Clinton went there, Justice Scalia, the CIA Director, several congressmen and Wall Street moguls. I will probably feel like the country mouse visiting the city. Royalty from around the world send their kids to Georgetown for heaven's sake."

He laughed. "Don't worry about it. Ordinary people go there too. Not that you're ordinary, far from it. You're more extraordinary than all those snobs whose parents are famous politicians, which makes them American royalty, or those who are royal by birth. And if you are concerned about not having money to flaunt, I'll take care of this for you as well."

Crap. She needed to think fast because that could be a test. If any of this were real, she would not accept money from him, but if she said so, she might blow the whole thing up.

What to do?

"I can't take money from you, Logan. A favor is all I can accept."

"It's not going to be my money. My friend will arrange a full scholarship for you, and whatever you planned on spending on tuition and living expenses, you'll be able to spend on things to impress your new snobby friends with."

Was this another trick? Was Logan a compulsive liar?

Because if he was planning to snatch her and her mother, there was no reason for him to arrange a scholarship for her. Why make it up? She was coming for the interview anyway.

"That's awesome, but I feel guilty about accepting this. I'm sure there are more deserving students than me for a full-ride scholarship."

He hugged her closer to him. "You are more deserving than most. You're smart, resourceful, and you are willing to work hard. Besides, you need it. I'm sure that with no father to support the family, finances are tight. Last I checked, dental hygienists don't make much."

Why didn't it surprise her that he'd investigated her?

Did he think that she was desperate for money and he could use it to his advantage?

But then if she never got to actually study at Georgetown, she would have no need for it.

She sighed. "Thank you. I really need a scholarship because I can't afford a place like that. I can take out student loans and work part-time while I'm studying, but I'm afraid that as a nurse I will not make enough to repay the loans in a reasonable time. The financial burden would be suffocating."

Logan seemed so pleased with himself, so genuinely happy to be able to help her, that Ella was starting to seriously doubt his motives.

Perhaps Julian and Kian and the others were wrong about Logan, and he wasn't rotten to the core. What if he was helping her just to gain her approval and get her to date him?

Have sex with him?

Seemed like a lot of trouble to seduce a girl, when it was obvious that Logan could have anyone he wanted. Not only was he incredibly handsome and rich, but he could also compel or thrall compliance.

Still, it might be an ego thing. Even a Doomer might want to seduce a girl the old fashioned way, by courting her and making himself indispensable to her, and her falling for him because she thought he was wonderful.

Especially someone like Logan who wasn't an ordinary Doomer. He was the son of their leader, which made him Doomer royalty.

Curiosity burning hot in her gut, she had to find out even though asking point-blank was risky. "Are you going to be in Washington when I'm there?"

A sly smirk lifting one corner of his lips, he looked into her eyes. "I might. Do you want to see me?"

She shrugged. "You still scare me a little, but after all that you have done for me, I should at least invite you to dinner. My mother would have to come along, of course, but given your traditional upbringing, you shouldn't be a stranger to the concept of a chaperone."

Pausing their stroll, Logan turned to her and put his hand on her shoulder. "You must realize that if I want to abscond with you, your mother is not going to be an obstacle for me."

"Do you still want to kidnap me? Or would you rather I came willingly?"

She was playing with fire, but the game demanded that she act as if it was real. Anything else would seem suspicious to Logan. He was smart, and he didn't trust anyone. A man not easily fooled.

"Would you come willingly to me?"

Stretching on her toes, she kissed his lips lightly. "That depends on you. I expect to be treated like a lady and courted properly. If you ask me on a date and don't try anything shady, then I'll gladly agree to another one, and then the next, and the one after that."

The sly smirk was back. "I was under the impression that you are a modern, liberated woman, and that you feel free to hook up with whomever you choose."

"I am all that, but I also have standards. A guy has to work hard to get me to open up to him, and he has to prove that he's worthy of me." She grimaced. "I thought like that before the degrading experience I went through, and even more so after."

His expression somber, he hooked his finger under her chin and tilted her head up. "I'll treat you like you are my princess and I'm your knight." He kissed her softly, his arms wrapping around her tenderly.

A lover's kiss.

The guy was either the best actor on the planet, or she'd misjudged him completely.

28

VIVIAN

"Ready to go home?" Vivian glanced around the makeshift studio Ella had organized in the classroom.

She was impressed. Ella was making this happen without much help and with no prior training. Maybe it was the advantage of youth because Vivian couldn't imagine undertaking such a huge project. Heck, organizing the sewing class had seemed like a big deal to her.

Ella still believed that she could conquer the world, and Vivian had a feeling she could. Her daughter was incredible.

"Yeah. I'm done. Let me just stow the camera away." She put it back into its case. "The lights can stay where they are. It took me over an hour to get them positioned just right, and Vanessa said that I can leave everything like it is for the next shoot."

"How did it go?"

"I only did one today. With the hours it takes to edit them, I'm in no rush to tape more. Besides, I didn't have an assistant. Sylvia couldn't come."

"Did you talk with Tessa?"

Ella slung the camera bag over her shoulder. "I did. She said she'll be good to go by Monday, but I told her we were leaving for Washington, and she'd have a longer break. I don't think she should come back though. No reason to make herself miserable."

They walked out of the classroom and headed out to the parking lot.

"You'll need someone to drive you. I'm not here every day."

"I don't plan on being here every day either. And besides, after we are back from Washington, I'm asking Kian for a car. I'll take it as payment for entrapment services rendered."

"Every clan member gets a car. It's not a payment since it doesn't really belong to them. The cars are owned by the clan."

Ella put the bag in the trunk. "I know. But it's cool to think that I'm getting paid." She grimaced. "Although perhaps it is better that I'm not. I dream-shared with Mr. D again, and he was so super nice that I'm really starting to doubt that he has nefarious intentions. He said he's going to arrange a full-ride scholarship for me. Why would he do that if he knew I would never use it? And there wasn't even a reason for him to lie about it. It's not as if I'll cancel my trip to Washington because I'll suddenly realize that I can't afford Georgetown."

Vivian added her own bags to the pile and then walked over to the driver's side. "Maybe he wants to make sure that you arrive as planned. Just as we are preparing and laying a careful net for him, I'm sure he's doing the same for us. The scholarship was just extra honey to make the bait more appetizing."

"I hope you're right. I would hate to get everyone's hopes up for nothing. Not to mention the resources. If this is all for nothing, I'll have to compensate the clan for their expenses and not the other way around."

Vivian waved a dismissive hand. "It's just nervous jitters. Besides, the trap is Kian and Turner's idea, not yours, so they bear responsibility for it. What you're doing for the clan is priceless. Meaning that I would have never agreed for you to risk yourself for monetary compensation."

As she turned the engine on, Ella pulled out the new glasses Eva had given them and put them on. "I don't know if there is a saying like this, but you can't live on good deeds, lofty ideals, or even satisfaction. I need money."

That was true. Ella was working her butt off and not getting a penny for her efforts. "Did you upload the video you finished editing to YouTube?'

"Not yet. I talked to Julian last night, and he suggested I ask Roni for help with that. I'm just thinking of a nice way to do it. I can't offer him anything in return, and I hate asking for a favor I can't repay."

"You're not asking anything for yourself. The entire clan is involved in this humanitarian effort. I'm sure he will be glad to help. But if you like, we can invite him and Sylvia to dinner. It's going to be easier to ask for a favor in an informal setting."

Pulling out her phone, Ella glanced at the time. "We can stop at the supermarket and get stuff. But let me check with Sylvia first. They might have plans for tonight. What time should I tell her?"

"Let's make it seven so we'll have plenty of time to cook."

Ella's fingers flew over the screen as she typed up the message.

When Sylvia didn't respond, Ella shrugged. "Do you want to stop on the way for takeout? Parker wouldn't mind a hamburger, and neither would I."

"Sounds good to me. But let's get groceries just in case."

The return message came while they were waiting in line in the drive-through.

"She says they would love to and apologizes for not answering before. She was in class and her phone was turned off."

Vivian was glad. Friday dinner without Magnus and Julian would have been a sad affair. In fact, maybe they should invite more guests to make it even merrier?

"What do you think, should we invite Ruth and Nick too?"

Ella scrunched her nose. "Ruth is a really good cook. We are not in her league."

"We don't have to be. Let's make something simple that is impossible to mess up. How about fettuccini with mushrooms and a couple of your specialty salads?"

"Parker will want meat, and so will Roni. I don't know about Nick, but he probably is a meat eater too."

"What about fish? I can make salmon. That always comes out good."

"That could work. I like it, and so does Parker, probably because it's soft and doesn't irritate his gums. I hope the others will like it too."

"Salmon it is, then." Vivian smiled at Ella. "Having dinner with friends is more about the company than the food. It doesn't have to come out perfect."

"No, but it should be tasty and plentiful. Otherwise they won't come again."

29

ELLA

"I'm stuffed." Roni pushed his plate away and reached for the pitcher of water. "Everything was excellent."

Ella wondered if this was a good time to ask for his help.

"Thank you for inviting us," Sylvia said. "I feel so bad about not helping Ella today, but I had an important class I couldn't miss."

Smiling, Ella waved a dismissive hand. Sylvia had just provided her with the opening she needed. "Don't worry about it. I shot only one video, but there is no rush. I have four already, two of them edited and ready for upload to YouTube, but I don't know how to do that. I'm sure it's not a big deal, but with everything new there is a learning curve. And once that's done, I need to actually set up the fundraiser, again not something I've done before."

Nick put his fork down. "I can help you out with YouTube. It's so easy that I can do it right now. Just bring me your laptop."

That was unexpected. Ella hadn't thought of Nick, but she should have. Eva had told her that the guy was a whiz with electronics and surveillance equipment.

"Thank you. But would you mind showing me how to do it? I'd rather not have to run for help anytime I need to upload a new video."

"Sure thing."

As Ella pushed to her feet, her mother cleared her throat. "Can this wait until everyone is done eating? And we also have dessert."

Glancing at Ruth who was still picking at her salmon, Ella sat back down. "I'm sorry. You're right. It's just that I'm so excited and eager for the fundraiser to start."

Across the table, Parker looked at her as if she'd offended him.

"What's your problem?"

"You could've asked me. I know how to do it. But no one ever thinks I can do stuff because I'm just a kid."

He wasn't wrong. She should've thought about him, but to admit it would be like throwing more fuel into his fire.

"Do you know anything about search engine optimization?"

He shook his head.

"Well, that's what I need the most help with. It's not enough to upload the videos. If I want anyone to see them, they need to be discoverable."

"I can help with that," Roni said. "I can have these videos suggested to tons of people. What I need from you is a list of things your target audience is interested in, so I can have your videos suggested to them."

"Who is the target audience?" Ruth asked.

Ella thought that everyone should watch it, but perhaps certain segments of the population would react more strongly to the message. "Teenage girls and their mothers, I guess. Which I should have thought of before. Damn."

"Why? Is that a problem?" Vivian asked.

"If I want them shown to teenagers, I need to make sure that the videos don't contain anything inappropriate for a younger audience, but that's almost impossible given the subject. And what's more, girls under eighteen should be aware of the risk. Traffickers don't shy away from taking minors."

"Not in the States, I would think," Sylvia said. "If a minor goes missing, the police get involved. It's easier and less risky for the traffickers to go after legal adults."

Roni put his glass down. "You can make two kinds of videos. One aimed at the over-eighteen crowd that will show the videos you are shooting at the sanctuary, and another one for minors that's more of a general warning and has no details. I would even make two separate channels so there is no confusion between the two."

It was a good idea, but it meant doubling the work. In fact, Ella wasn't sure she could edit the recordings so much. She would need to shoot new ones with teenagers in mind.

"Yay, more work for me."

"You can hire someone to doodle cartoons for you," Parker said. "Like they do in infomercials. You'll need to write a script, though."

That shouldn't be too hard. She could write highly modified versions of the stories the girls told. Except, it was more work and she was already overwhelmed.

"I need to find someone to do that. I don't have time to write scripts in addition to everything else I'm doing. And where am I going to find a doodler?"

"Many clan members are creative," Sylvia said. "You can post a note on the virtual bulletin board."

"I don't have money to pay them."

Next to her, Ella saw Vivian's shoulders start to shake. "What's the matter, Mom? Are you crying?"

Vivian let out a snort and then started laughing. Strange woman. Was missing Magnus making her crazy?

"What's so funny?" Parker asked.

Waving a hand, Vivian caught her breath. "It's funny what the brain can come up with. When Parker suggested making doodle presentations, I thought that it was a cool idea and that there could be a whole series of simple cartoons showing different dangerous scenarios a girl can find herself in. But then I thought that someone would need to write scripts for the narrator to read."

She reached for her glass, took a long sip, and then put it down. "Naturally, the first person that came to my mind was Eva because she wrote a book and has some experience with creating stories. But since she somehow managed to turn her romance novel into a detective story full of gore and blood, she would probably do the same with the cartoons, writing terrifying stories that were way worse than the ones the girls recorded."

Nick joined in the laughter. "I can imagine that. My boss trying to write a romance is a joke. But she can write killer detective and spy novels." He laughed even harder. "Killer stories about killers."

If he only knew the half of it.

Nick and Sharon didn't know about Eva's vigilante days, and she'd told Tessa only recently. Surprisingly, she'd told Ella too.

But that was because of Ella's weird effect on people. Come to think of it, if she really had a unique ability to have people open up to her and tell her things they didn't tell anyone else, it might be a special talent she had in addition to the telepathy she shared with her mother.

And if it was indeed a talent, and not a case of having the kind of personality that invited confessions, it would grow stronger after her transition just as Parker's compulsion ability had.

In a way, what she did was sort of unintended compulsion. It was as if people felt compelled to tell her their secrets. The difference was that she didn't do anything to force the confessions, and later people didn't regret opening up to her.

Or perhaps they did?

Ella wondered if Eva had had second thoughts about sharing her dark past with her and Tessa.

The answer could shed light on whether Ella had done anything to actively compel the confession. Maybe she'd just been at the right place at the right time and armed with the right attitude.

30

JULIAN

As he came out of the bathroom, Julian checked his phone for a new message from Ella. It was getting late and he was tired after a full day of preparations.

She'd said she would call or text as soon as she was done with Nick and Roni, but it seemed the three of them were still working on uploading the YouTube videos.

It shouldn't take that long, unless Roni started working on the search engine optimization. Why would he do it on a Friday night while his mate was waiting, though?

The guy didn't need Ella to do his hacking magic or whatever it was he planned to do. He could do it from his house or on Monday from the lab.

Except, Ella might have wanted to see how it was done.

Julian smiled. The girl was like a sponge for information, her brain going a hundred miles per hour all hours of the day. And she wasn't just absorbing it, she was turning it into a fountain of creative ideas.

His mate was awesome.

He couldn't have asked for a more perfect match. The more he got to know her, the more the age difference that had bothered him in the beginning was becoming irrelevant. Ella was bright and confident in her own way, and she didn't treat him like the older guy she should defer to.

Heck, she didn't give him an inch, and he loved that she wasn't a pushover. A lot of it was bravado, and on the inside she hid insecurities, but those were the result of her captivity, and in time they would fade away.

He would make sure of that.

His mate shouldn't feel tainted, or undeserving, and he was going to reassure her day in and day out that she was pure and kind and selfless, and that she deserved every bit of happiness that life with him would bring.

When his phone finally pinged, Julian let out a relieved breath, read Ella's short message, and called her.

"It's about time, I was about to hit the sack. It's after three o'clock in the morning here."

"I'm sorry about that. But it didn't feel right to leave Roni and Nick to do the work while I went chatting with my boyfriend."

"What took so long? Is it complicated?"

"No, not really, but they also helped me with establishing the fundraiser. We are up and running. Or rather crawling, but we are up."

"Congratulations."

"I'm crossing my fingers. Do you have a clan member who's a witch? Because I could totally use some good luck charms or incantations."

He chuckled. "The closest we have is Merlin. But he's all about potions. I don't think he does charms."

"A potion is not going to do it, but enough about me. How was your day?"

"Grueling. Turner is having us check out every corner of the campus and memorize it. After today, I can find any place here blindfolded. Tomorrow, he's going to assign positions. He must really be concerned with Mr. D. I think he takes him more seriously than he took Gorchenco."

"He should, and he shouldn't."

"What do you mean?"

"As you've pointed out, Mr. D is a god's grandson. He is smart and has powerful abilities. So that's a good reason to take every precaution Turner can think of. But on the other hand, he might have no nefarious intentions other than to win me over."

Julian shook his head. "He's playing you. Did he invade your dreams again?"

"He did. He said he's arranging a full-ride scholarship for me. Why would he do that if he knows I'm not going to go? But that's just a side note. He's acting as if he's really happy to help me get a great education. He is either an amazing actor, or I am clueless because I'm inclined to believe him."

"The guy is old. He's had centuries to hone his acting skills. Doomers are not into charity and doing good deeds, they regard humans as only a little better than sheep, and getting an education is not high on their priority list even for themselves."

Ella sighed. "You can't generalize. Look at Dalhu and Robert. Not all Doomers are evil."

Julian was getting annoyed. It was good that this was coming to a head because Lokan was messing with Ella and little by little pulling her over to his side.

"Your own impression from him was that the guy was bad."

"True, but then when you're the son of a despot, you can't act like a nice guy even if you are one on the inside. Every dream we share, he sheds more of his thorns."

Pushing up to his feet, Julian started pacing the small room. "Don't tell me you're falling for his lies, Ella."

What he actually wanted to ask was if she was falling for the Doomer. But that would have been stupid. Ella would've denied it, probably because she hadn't even realized that it was happening. Lokan was messing with her head big time.

"I'm not sure. But all this guessing is futile. We will know in a few days. I can't wait to see the campus and go touring the city with you. How is the weather? Is it cold?"

"It's very pleasant here. After all of this is over you might consider going here for real. You don't need any charity from the Doomer. The clan will pay for your tuition and your living expenses."

There was a moment of silence, and then she sighed. "It sounds lovely, but I don't want to leave the village. I decided to go to a local college."

It should've been good news, and he should've been happy about her decision, but Julian didn't want Ella giving up on her dreams or even compromising them on his account.

"Is it because of me?"

"Yes, but not exclusively, so don't let it go to your head. I just found a new home and an extended family. Leaving it to go to college and hang around a bunch of humans I have nothing in common with doesn't appeal to me at all. I'd rather stay in the village and commute to a local college every day. That way I can have it all."

"It's a compromise."

"Why would you say that? It's not like there is a shortage of great universities in Los Angeles, and with my fake transcripts and list of achievements I can get into any of them. I don't see it as a compromise at all. On the contrary, I think I'm being very smart about it. Besides, I don't like being away from you. It's been only two days and it feels like you've been gone for weeks."

The vice that had squeezed his heart when Ella had waxed poetic about Lokan not only loosened but fell off completely.

Ella loved him.

"Same here. It's tough being away from you."

"You see? And you want me to go away to college?"

"I would've gone with you."

That stunned her for about three seconds. "Really? And what would you have done? Studied for another degree?"

"Maybe. Or I would have found a job wherever you went to school. There's no way I can live without you. I love you."

"Oh, Julian. I can't live without you either. I love you so much. You're the best guy on the planet."

31

ELLA

*E*lla was about done packing her suitcase when her phone rang. Expecting Julian, she snatched it off the nightstand, but it wasn't Julian's handsome face on the screen.

"Hi, Tessa."

"Are you very busy? I wanted to stop at your house and give you a good luck charm."

"Oh, thanks. I was telling Julian how I needed one to make the fundraiser successful."

"How is it going so far?"

"The first day it was nothing but crickets, the second we got a trickle of donations, mostly from clan members, and today it's too early to tell."

"It's going to pick up. Those things take time."

"That's what Roni is telling me. I'm crossing my fingers."

"The good luck charm is for the trip, not for the fundraiser. But I'll get you another one for that."

"Thanks. That's so thoughtful of you. I'm almost done packing, but my mother and I need to be at Kian's office in about an hour. So, hurry up."

"I'm walking toward the door as we speak."

"I'll turn on the coffeemaker."

In the kitchen, Ella found her mother scrubbing the counter. Again.

"You're going to rub it down to nothing and we will have to order a new counter."

Vivian gave her an evil look when she pulled the coffeemaker out. "Don't make a mess. I want to leave the house clean."

As if it was going to stay that way. Parker and Scarlet were supposed to stay with Merlin, but Ella doubted he would be spending the entire time there, and for sure he wouldn't want to sleep there. Her brother was going to want some quiet time to himself, and he was going to make a mess in the kitchen.

"I promise to clean up. Tessa is coming over. What do you want me to serve her? Water?"

Vivian waved a hand at the fridge. "We have soft drinks."

"We should leave them for Parker. Merlin is a fun guy, but he forgets to go grocery shopping. I'm glad we cooked enough to feed both of them while we are gone."

Provided everything went according to plan, Vivian would come back home Wednesday night. Ella planned on spending the weekend with Julian, but nothing had been decided yet.

"Wonder invited Parker to come to stay with her and Anandur."

"I didn't know that. Should we take the food to her place?"

That could be a good solution. Their house was not a disaster zone like Merlin's. On the other hand, she wasn't sure they would be okay with hosting Scarlet.

Vivian shook her head. "Parker prefers staying at home by himself and hanging out with Merlin when he gets lonely."

"What's the matter? Is he over his crush on Wonder?"

Her mother snorted. "He's not, but that's exactly why he doesn't want to spend so much time in her house. It's stressful for him."

That was true. Ella had forgotten how nerve-wracking crushes could be. She'd had one when she was Parker's age, and it was on the UPS guy of all people. She remembered how excited she would get whenever they were expecting a delivery, but she also remembered how sweaty her palms would get whenever he smiled at her, cute twin dimples forming in his cheeks.

With perfect timing, Tessa rang the bell at the same time the coffeemaker finished brewing.

Opening the door, Ella glanced at the small package Tessa was holding. "What's in there? Can I open it now?"

"Sure." Tessa handed her the package.

"Come on in. Coffee is ready."

"It smells clean in here," Tessa said as she followed Ella to the kitchen. "Hi, Vivian. I wanted to come and wish you luck before you left for Washington."

Her mother smiled. "Thank you. That's very thoughtful."

Ella poured the coffee into three mugs and put them on the counter. "Didn't you notice that the marble top is missing a quarter of an inch?"

Tessa examined the counter and then looked up with a puzzled expression on her face. "Did you do something to it?"

"My mother went into a cleaning frenzy over the weekend, which is what she always does when she's stressed. This counter got scrubbed at least five times."

"Don't mess it up." Vivian wagged her finger at them. "Besides, I did more than clean. We went grocery shopping, and then we cooked so Parker would have food while we were gone, and then we cleaned."

"I stand corrected." Ella leaned toward her mother and kissed her cheek. "I'm just teasing. You are right about cleaning being calming."

"For me it's arts and crafts," Tessa said. "Making this thing gave me hours of calm." She motioned to the package. "Open it."

Ella tore through the wrapping paper and pulled out a dream catcher. "It's so pretty. Do you think it will protect me from the dream walker?"

Tessa shrugged. "It's worth a try."

"It's gorgeous. Thank you. Although right now I'm more concerned about him not showing up in my dreams. Do you think the dream catcher can help me lure him back? He didn't come Saturday or Sunday night, and I'm starting to worry."

Tessa arched a brow. "Why, do you think that something happened to him?"

"No, I'm worried that he is busy doing whatever he does for Navuh and that he won't come to Washington. I don't know what I'm scared of more. Mr. D trying to snatch me or not showing up at all."

As the doorbell rang again, Ella and Vivian exchanged glances.

"Did you invite anyone else?" Vivian asked.

"I didn't. Let me see who it is."

Maybe it was Merlin with a good luck potion, or perhaps just a relaxing tonic. Both she and Vivian needed it.

"Ray, what a pleasant surprise." Ella forced a smile.

If he thought to start something while Julian was away, she would promptly show him how wrong he was.

"I came to wish you luck, and I brought you invitations to a concert I'm giving next week." He handed her an envelope. "I included tickets for your brother and Magnus as well. I hope you all can come."

That was innocent enough.

"Thank you. I would love to come, and I'm sure my mother and Magnus would love to as well. But Parker, not so much." She opened the door wider. "Please, come in. Would you like some coffee?"

"Thank you. I would love some."

Half an hour later, Vivian started getting antsy. "We need to go. I don't want to be late for the debriefing."

Ray got the hint and rose to his feet. "Thank you for the coffee, and again, good luck. I'll keep my fingers crossed when I'm not playing."

Tessa hugged Vivian briefly and then crushed Ella to her chest. "Be careful."

"I will."

32

KIAN

Hands tucked into his back pockets, Kian stood next to his office window and gazed at the village square below. It wasn't as if he had nothing to do, but with the nervous energy coursing through him since morning, he had been too distracted to concentrate on work, and the foot-tall stack of files on his desk remained untouched.

In less than fifteen minutes, Vivian and Ella were scheduled to arrive for the debriefing, which gave him just enough time to grab a quick smoke. He wasn't supposed to do that during his workdays. The deal Kian had made with himself was that he was only going to indulge while relaxing outside in his garden, but here and there he snuck one in.

Especially when he felt tense and frustrated like he was now.

Grabbing a pack of cigarillos and a lighter from his desk drawer, he headed out into the corridor and opened the door to the emergency escape stairs leading to the roof.

His not so secret hideout.

Bridget, whose office was a couple doors down from his, knew he was sneaking out there, but she was cool about it, keeping it to herself and refraining from making comments.

When Kian needed a few moments alone, the last thing he wanted was for people to know they could find him on the roof.

He lit up as soon as the roof door closed behind him.

Staying in the office while Turner led a mission that Kian would have loved to be a part of was frustrating as hell.

Since when had he become a glorified pencil pusher?

He used to lead missions like that.

Catching Lokan was going to be the biggest coup the clan had ever scored against the Doomers, and he was going to miss out on that because Turner had declared him a security liability.

Fucking Turner.

Kian was still the American clan's leader, and until bloody Turner had shown up and taken over operations, Kian had been in charge of defending the clan and heading missions.

So what if Turner was better at it? It didn't make Kian a fucking liability or obsolete.

Taking a long puff, he blew out the smoke and looked up at the sky. He was damn good at it too. The rescue he'd headed in what was now the sanctuary had been a complicated operation, and he'd pulled it off without losing a single Guardian. And that had been despite several glitches.

The operation before that, however, was a different story.

Amanda's so-called rescue had been a joke. Not his fault, though. How could he have known that his sister had not only fallen for the Doomer but had him wrapped around her little finger?

Fates, what an embarrassment that had been.

Perception had a way of warping reality into what was expected. Mistakenly interpreting Amanda's scream as resulting from torture and not a climax, Kian had rushed headlong into danger. He would've never made such a mistake if it was any other female. But he'd found it inconceivable that Amanda could be having sex with a Doomer.

Back then he'd thought of them as worse than worms and couldn't forgive her.

A lot had changed since then, and Dalhu as well as Robert had managed to overcome Kian's centuries of deep-seated hatred that put every member of the Brotherhood in the same dirty basket.

Grudgingly, he had to concede that not all Doomers were pure evil, and as in any society, some were better than others.

Perhaps Turner was right, and Kian was too hotheaded and emotional to lead this particular mission. He'd been lucky with Dalhu because the guy had operated solo and had had no malevolent intentions toward Amanda.

It could easily have been a trap, one Kian had run headlong into without thinking.

True, capturing Navuh's son didn't carry the same emotional intensity as rushing to save his sister, who he'd thought was being tortured, but it was tantalizing enough to cause him to make a move just as stupid.

Turner, cold fish that he was, had no such problems. With him it was always mind first, heart second. Besides, the two organs differed disproportionately not only in influence but also in size. Turner's brain was huge, and his heart was tiny.

With Kian, it worked the other way around. Not that his brain was small, just that his heart was so much bigger.

Stubbing the cigarillo out, he threw it into the metal trash can and headed back to his office.

When he got there, he found William waiting for him by the door. "I'm not late, am I?" he asked as he opened the door.

The guy pushed his glasses up his nose. "No, I'm early."

He'd been wondering for years why William needed glasses and had learned the reason only recently. There was nothing wrong with William's vision, but his eyes were sensitive to the computer glare and the glasses had a special filter for that. Still, William never took them off. He might have just forgotten to do so when he left the lab, which didn't happen often, or maybe he thought of them as an accessory.

"Did you bring the trackers?"

"I have them here." William followed him inside and pulled out a small box from one pocket and a second one from the other side. "The miniaturizing is amazing. Each of these boxes contains ten trackers."

He joined Kian at the conference table and opened one.

"There is a tracker in there?" Kian lifted an earring that was just a small stud. "Where is it?" He turned the thing around.

"This is it. You're not going to find anything. There is a tiny transmitter embedded in the gold." William lifted a hairpin. "I like this one the most. No one would suspect a plain thing like this to be anything out of the ordinary. Ella and Vivian can put several in their hair."

"Which reminds me that their passports were delivered earlier. Kian got up and walked over to his desk. "One for Mrs. Victoria MacBain and the other for Ms. Kelly Rubinstein." He took the envelope out of the drawer and brought it over to the conference table.

"They should start practicing the fake names right away," William said. "By the way, you didn't say anything about getting them earpieces."

"Unless you can get something as tiny and inconspicuous as these trackers, they can't use them. If Lokan is setting a trap for them, he would be watching them closely. But that's not a problem. Ella and Vivian will never be out of sight or earshot. Thirty Guardians should have no problem keeping a close eye and ear on our two ladies."

33

JULIAN

*J*ulian loaded a tortilla with steak strips and bell peppers. "This is really good." He rolled it up.

"Not bad," Liam said after biting into his taco. "I'm not crazy about Mexican, but as fast food goes there is nothing better. You can tell that the ingredients are fresh. They don't pull it out of the freezer and stick it in the microwave."

The Guardians had split up for dinner, checking out eateries surrounding the campus. There were many of them, which meant going solo, or in his case being paired with Liam. Which rankled, but Julian wasn't technically a Guardian.

Still, Turner could have entrusted him with such a simple assignment as keeping his eyes open for Lokan.

Hacking into every available surveillance camera on campus and the area around it, William and Roni were scanning for the Doomer, but not every place was equipped with them, and Turner believed in boots and eyes on the ground.

"When are the ladies arriving?" the Guardian asked.

"I'm waiting to hear from her. She said she's going to call me once they're up in the air."

When he'd called earlier, Ella said that Tessa and Ray were there, which had pissed him off big time. What had Ray been doing at Ella's house? Had the sly bastard waited for Julian to be gone before making his move?

If he had, the guy was either an obtuse idiot or a sucker for pain.

Ella hadn't shown any interest in him, and after his stupid comments, she'd barely acknowledged his presence. Once this was over and they got back, Julian was either going to get a new house or ask Ray to move. His bachelor days of living with roommates were over. He had a mate now, and she was the only one he was going to share a house with. Except, of course, for the children they would one day have, Fates willing.

Since Ella had told him about her decision to stay in the village and commute to college, he'd been thinking about it a lot, but he hadn't said anything to her yet. Not only was it premature, but it also might fill her head with stuff that shouldn't be there while she was dealing with Lokan.

As his phone rang, Julian quickly wiped his sticky hands with a napkin and accepted the call.

"Hi, sweetheart. Are you in the air?"

"Yes."

"I can't wait to see you."

"About that." She sighed. "My mother and I were instructed by Kian not to interact with any of you. We are to act as if we don't know any of the hotel guests."

Julian's heart sank. He'd been counting the minutes until he got to see Ella again, and now she was going to be within reach, but contact was disallowed.

"It's probably Turner's doing. The guy is paranoid."

"I think he is right. If Mr. D finds a way to follow us, it will look suspicious if we mingle with the other guests at the hotel. We are not supposed to know anyone."

Curiously, Lokan hadn't visited Ella for the past two nights. Had he been busy setting the trap?

If he had, the guy was incredibly sneaky because none of the Guardians had reported noticing anything suspicious. Not only that, none of the cameras around campus, and there were many, had caught him hanging around.

Perhaps he was using a disguise? Or maybe in addition to his other talents he could also do what Sylvia did and manipulate electronics?

Except, if Julian believed in the Occam's razor principle that the most straightforward and simple solution was most likely the correct one, then Ella's hunch was right, and Lokan wasn't coming.

Or, maybe he'd been busy and was going to arrive tomorrow, or on the day of the interview, and wing it. With his power of compulsion, Lokan didn't need much of a setup.

"Julian? Are you there?"

"Yeah. Sorry for zoning out on you. I've been thinking about what you've said regarding Mr. D not coming. There is no trace of him."

He glanced around the restaurant, checking that the clientele was still comprised of humans, and switched to a whisper just in case. "William and Roni have been running the camera feed from all around town through William's facial recognition software, and they got nothing so far. He didn't check into any of the hotels and hasn't been to any restaurants with cameras. He either isn't here, or he's staying in a private house and ordering meals delivered to him."

"That's possible. I have a feeling that he is stationed in Washington, so it makes sense he has a permanent place here. You should tell Roni to check older feeds and see if he shows up in any of the restaurants. Friday, he told me that he'd been to the campus recently. There must be footage of him."

"I'll tell Turner."

"You know, there could be another possibility. He could be using the same kind of glasses Eva gave my mother and me. If William is running the feed through his software, it's not going to pick him up."

"Why would he do that? Unless he suspects something, there is no reason for him to avoid detection."

"Not necessarily. He might be doing it as a precaution. He is still an immortal who needs to hide the fact that he doesn't age. Besides, he might have other enemies. He is a warlord, after all."

"True, but we don't have the personnel to check that much feed by eye, so that's a moot point. We just need to assume that he is here and keep our eyes open."

Ella sighed. "It's going to be torture to know that you are in the same building and not be able to go to you, but it is for the best. I need to keep my head in the game, so to speak."

"We can still talk on the phone."

"Thank God for that. I was afraid Turner would prohibit it as well. But I guess he trusts the clan's phones are secure against hacking."

"They are. We use our own satellite and the signal is encrypted."

She chuckled. "I don't even know what that means, but it sounds impressive. Listening to Nick and Roni when they were helping me with the charity setup, I felt like an uneducated schlump. I didn't know half the terms they used."

Smiling, Julian switched the phone to his other ear. "Don't tell me that you've decided to study computer engineering instead of nursing."

"No way. But I'm no longer sure that I want to study nursing either."

"Have you given some thought to what you want to study instead?

"I'm still thinking it over. Physician's assistant sounds cool, but I need to get an undergrad degree first, the same as nursing." She laughed. "We could open a hug clinic together. You'll be the physician, and I'll be the assistant."

"Sounds awesome, but we will hire professional huggers. I'm not letting you hug any guys older than twelve or younger than seventy."

"Deal."

34

ELLA

As the jet started its descent, Ella pulled out her makeup case and went to work on her face. Next to her, Vivian put on the chestnut wig Eva had given her and pulled out her own case.

"Should we put in the trackers now?" Ella asked Bhathian.

The Guardian nodded. "From now on, always have at least a few on you. The Doomers could strike at any point."

Ella swallowed.

It was show time, and she was ready, but that didn't mean she wasn't scared. Getting captured by Logan and his henchmen was a remote possibility, but it was still there. As someone who'd just recently gotten free, that was a terrifying prospect, and she got nauseous every time she thought about it.

Which meant that she did everything to avoid those thoughts and switched to something else. Contemplating her future in college and what she wanted to study usually did the trick or thinking about the fundraiser and all the things she still had to do.

Like finding a doodler and a scriptwriter. Her post on the clan's bulletin board had yielded no results so far.

"They are so tiny," her mother said. "And surprisingly pretty."

The case containing the ten trackers was no bigger than a bracelet's jewelry box, and as she opened it, Ella once more marveled at the miniaturization. The question was whether Logan was aware that such tiny trackers existed. If he was, he would search for them, and as small as the devices were, they weren't invisible.

After putting on the earrings and the pendant, and sticking four pins into her hair, Ella was still left with three little studs she could attach to her clothes. But to do that, she needed to go to the bathroom.

With Arwel and Bhathian in the small cabin, it wasn't as if she could attach a stud to her panties.

When the jet touched down, Ella unbuckled and pushed to her feet.

"Is it okay to take the seatbelt off?" Vivian asked.

Arwel nodded.

"I'm going to attach the remaining studs to my clothes. I suggest that you do the same, Mom."

Vivian waved a dismissive hand. "I have the earrings on and two pins in my hair. I think that's enough for now. I'll put the rest on when we go to the interview."

"We might never get to the interview, Mom. As Bhathian pointed out, the enemy may strike at any time. Besides, it could very well be that there is no interview, and that Mr. D was lying the entire time."

On their private channel, she sent, *I'm going to put one in my panties. You should do the same.*

Isn't that going too far?

Maybe, but I'd rather be safe than sorry. One captivity in a lifetime is enough.

You're right. I'll wait until you're done.

Ella nodded and ducked into the bathroom. Unlike the dim light in the cabin, the one in the tiny compartment was bright, and as she looked into the mirror, Ella realized that she'd put on too much makeup.

Then again, it had been a while since she'd gone all out with it, so maybe that was just right.

The nearly black purple lipstick was a cool addition to her disguise. It was so strong that she'd been able to draw a new lip line with it, changing the shape of her mouth.

Between the makeup, the glasses, and the hair, she looked nothing like the old Ella. If she ever got to that interview, however, that grungy look was going to get her rejected for sure. It was a good thing that she had no intention of going to Georgetown.

With the rest of the studs attached to her clothes, Ella pushed the door open and stepped out. "Your turn, Mom."

"You went a little too heavy with the makeup."

"I know. I'll fix it when we get to the hotel. On the way, it's better to have more than less."

Vivian grimaced. "We will have to do something about your looks for the interview. This makeup and this hair don't go with the nice outfit we got for that."

"I'm not really going to Georgetown, Mom, so it doesn't matter if I make a good impression on the interviewer or not. Once this is over, Kelly Rubinstein will cease to exist."

"I don't see why. With the Doomer out of the picture, you don't need to abandon this identity, and if you get accepted, you should go. With the clan paying for your education, you can go for the best there is, and it doesn't get much better than Georgetown."

"I decided that I want to stay home and go to a local college. There is no shortage of them in Los Angeles. And with my fabulous grades and the clan's financing, I can pick the best." She winked.

Her mother smiled. "Is it because of Julian?"

"Yes, but not only. I found a home in the village, and the extended family I always wanted to have. I don't want to leave that and go room with strangers in some dingy dorms."

35

JULIAN

First-floor hotel rooms that faced the street were usually the least desirable, but Julian was very happy to have one. Standing by the window, he waited for the taxi to arrive. The driver was one of the Guardians whose name he'd forgotten. Another Guardian driven taxi had picked up Arwel and Bhathian, and it was trailing Ella and Vivian's in case they encountered trouble on the way.

When the cab finally stopped in the front, Julian let out a relieved breath. He'd had no reason to anticipate anything happening to them en route, but then he didn't know what to expect and when.

There was still no sign of Lokan or any other Doomers, and it worried him. Julian vacillated between thinking that Ella's hunch was right and that Lokan wasn't going to show up, to imagining crazy scenarios with a bunch of Doomers arriving at the time of the interview and taking the entire admissions office hostage.

It could happen.

Except, they had enough Guardians stationed around the building to deal with that. Lokan and his cronies wouldn't get anywhere near that office. Especially since he wouldn't suspect anyone lying in wait for him.

Julian smiled when Ella got out of the taxi. Despite the glasses she had on, he could see the heavy purple makeup around her eyes, and her lush lips were painted with lipstick so dark that it looked black. But she was adorable even in her full Goth costume.

He missed his little pixie girl with her spiky pink hair and monster boots.

Rubbing his aching heart, he tried to imagine how he was going to survive having her so near and not going to her. Perhaps he should ask one of the Guardians for a reinforced pair of handcuffs. He should cuff himself to the bed because he was bound to sleepwalk to her room.

As she and Vivian entered the hotel, he contemplated going out to the lobby so he could at least look at her and smell her.

A text from her surprised him.

Hi, we are here at the hotel, safe and sound. I thought we had the entire place to ourselves, but I see women in the lobby. Who are they?

Julian chuckled, regretting not having the ability to read Ella's mind. Who did she imagine the women were?

He texted her back. *I will tell you only after you try to guess.*

I heard them talking about a hospitality convention they were attending. Are they working for Turner's friend?

Not as exciting as he hoped. Usually, Ella's imagination was more inventive, and he expected her to suggest that they were secret agents, or call girls, or secret agents impersonating call girls.

He texted back. *I was expecting some wild speculations from you. But your guess was half right. They work in one of the clan's hotels in Hawaii. Turner thought it would look strange if there were only guys staying here with the two of you, so he arranged for them to attend the convention.*

Smart guy. He thinks of everything.

It would seem that way. Text me again when you're settled in your room. I have instructions for you and your mom for tomorrow.

She sent him the thumbs up emoji.

His phone rang a moment later with the tune he'd assigned to Turner.

"Ella and Vivian are here. Come to my room."

"On my way."

Since the door was slightly ajar, Julian knocked and walked right in.

"Close the door behind you," Turner said. "And put some music on."

Julian walked over to the nightstand and found a classical station on the radio. "Is that good?"

"A little louder." Turner walked over to the door connecting his room to the next and knocked.

When Vivian opened it and peeked in, Julian cast him a murderous glare.

The sly bastard had arranged connecting rooms for himself and the ladies, while feeding Julian crap about not having contact with them until after the mission.

"Give us a moment," she whispered. "We need to freshen up, and then we'll be right there."

Turner waved a hand. "Take your time." He looked at Julian. "I should have waited a little longer before knocking. I forgot that ladies need more bathroom breaks than guys do."

"You planned this all along while feeding me bullshit about not seeing Ella."

Turner shrugged. "You chose to have a separate room."

"Let's switch."

"You can move back with me if you wish. That's the best I can offer."

"Why?"

"Because this is not a honeymoon, and this room is the headquarters. If you stay here, Magnus would want to stay here too, and you can imagine the rest."

As always, Turner was right, but he should've mentioned the adjacent rooms instead of pulling Julian's leg about not seeing Ella until Lokan was captured.

When mother and daughter entered a few moments later, Ella's face was clean of makeup, her natural beauty even more breathtaking than Julian had remembered.

Ignoring Turner and Vivian, he pulled her in for a quick embrace. "I missed you."

She clung to him. "I missed you too. This is such a surprise. I thought we wouldn't be allowed to see each other until this is done."

"Me too." He cast another angry glare at Turner. "Apparently, this was Turner's idea of a joke. Not a good one."

"Is Magnus coming?" Vivian asked.

"He is bringing takeout. I figured you'd be hungry after your trip."

Ella waved a dismissive hand. "Who can eat? My stomach is tied in knots."

"Same here," Vivian said.

"Take a seat, ladies." Turner motioned to one of the queen beds. "We have things to go over."

"Shouldn't we wait for Magnus?" Vivian asked.

"It doesn't concern him directly."

Ella took Julian's hand and pulled him to sit with her on the bed.

"Tomorrow you are going on a campus tour," Turner started. "Four Guardians are going to make the tour with you, pretending to be prospective students, but you shouldn't acknowledge them."

Julian squeezed Ella's hand. "I wanted to do the tour with you, but Turner didn't allow it."

"Why not?" Ella looked up at Turner.

"Because you two would not have been able to keep from casting loving glances at each other, and you're supposed to pretend that everyone on the tour is a complete stranger. Also, don't forget to use your fake names. Kelly and Victoria. I suggest that from now on, you use them exclusively."

Ella nodded. "Not a problem for me, since I call my mother Mom most of the time."

"I'll have to practice," Vivian said.

"Did the dream walker visit you lately?" Turner asked.

"The last time was Friday night, and nothing since. Maybe I'm too nervous to dream-share?"

Turner tilted his head. "Was that your experience? Have you been nervous or anxious on the night he didn't come?"

Ella sighed. "I don't know. I'm just throwing ideas around. It bothers me that he didn't come so close to the interview. I expected him to visit me nightly to make sure that I'm coming."

Turner didn't look worried. "There could be many reasons for his absence, the main one that he can't sleep at the same time you do. If he's on the island and busy, he can't take naps in the middle of the day to visit you."

36

ELLA

As Ella stood on the lawn with the rest of the students and their parents, waiting for the tour guide to arrive, she stole quick glances at their faces, trying to find the Guardians. She'd recognized Kri as soon as they'd gotten there, but not the others. Evidently, she hadn't met any of the three, which made it easy not to acknowledge them.

Stop looking, her mother sent.

It's normal to check out people in your group. I can even start talking to Kri, pretending that I want to make friends.

Turner said not to, so don't.

Fine.

As the tour guide arrived and introduced herself, Ella hardly paid any attention to the girl, scanning the vicinity for Logan instead.

"Please, follow me," the guide said, and the group started walking.

It was probably her overactive imagination, but Ella could feel Logan's eyes on her. He was watching her from somewhere. Ella had read that people could feel it when they are being watched, even if it was through a camera lens. The roofs were too steep for him to hide there, but he could be at one of the windows, or he could be flying a drone.

Those usually made a buzzing noise, but if it was high up she wouldn't hear it.

Damn, she felt as if ants were crawling up her arms. If he got near her, he could thrall her, get into her mind, and see the plan. The entire operation was hinged on the Guardians catching him before he could do that.

Not to mention his ability to compel her and any other human. God only knew what he could do with that. On the one hand she was scared shitless, but on the other hand, she had a morbid curiosity to see him in action.

The waiting and guessing were the worst part.

You're doing it again, her mother sent.

I can't help it. I feel as if he is watching me. We shouldn't have come for the tour.

That would have been suspicious. All prospective students and their parents go on one. That's part of the experience.

How would you know? You've never gone to college.

I've read about it.

About an hour later, when the tour was over, Ella was exhausted, not from walking but from the constant state of vigilance and stress.

Her phone pinged with an incoming message from Turner. *Follow Kri. She and the other Guardians are going to a restaurant named Matchbox for lunch. Try to choose a table close to them.*

Ella sent the message to her mother.

Turner had decided against earpieces because they were hard to hide, so all communication was done through the phones. But at least she and her mother had the trackers all over them.

Oddly, those reassured her more than the presence of Guardians did. If anything happened and Logan managed to somehow snatch them, they could be rescued in no time.

"Hi." A girl walked up to Ella. "I'm Kristen." She offered her hand. "I heard you mention that you're interested in the nursing program. So am I."

"I'm Kelly." Ella shook the girl's hand. "And this is my mother, Victoria."

The girl gasped. "You are her mother? I thought you were another student. You look so young. People probably mistake you for sisters all the time."

"Thank you." Vivian offered Kristen her hand. "We are heading to a place called Matchbox for lunch. Would you like to join us?"

"I would love to. I was there yesterday, and the food is really good."

"Great, so you can lead the way. I was about to ask someone for directions."

"Follow me."

As Kristen chatted with Vivian, Ella resumed her scanning. The girl was a good cover, and she wondered whether Turner had sent her.

Or could she be a spy for Logan?

She glanced at the girl out of the corner of her eye. Kristen seemed genuine enough, but that didn't mean anything. Logan could compel any human to do his bidding.

"Where are you staying?" Kristen asked, raising Ella's suspicions.

"At the Hilton," her mother deadpanned.

Good for you, Mother.

Vivian smirked.

"Which one?" Kristen kept pushing.

"The one on 22nd Street. The Hilton Garden Inn."

Ella was impressed. *Where did you get that from?*

It was in the instructions Kian gave us. I actually read and memorized them.

That's why I didn't. I knew you would.

Vivian smiled indulgently. *Glad to be of service.*

Unaware of the conversation going over her head, Kristen kept talking, telling them about the hotel she was staying in and why her parents couldn't join her for the tour.

Ella sent to her mother. *Do you think she's working for Mr. D?*

Anything is possible.

37

VIVIAN

As they got back into their hotel room, Vivian kicked her shoes off and plopped on the bed. "I need to start exercising. I'm so out of shape it's ridiculous."

They'd been walking all day, and after a while even her most comfortable shoes had started to chafe.

Thank God for the taxi and the Guardian who'd driven them back to the hotel. Or rather thank Turner for arranging it.

According to their driver, Guardians had been following the two of them around, hoping to flush the Doomer out, but he was still a no show.

Kristen and her questions had seemed suspicious at first, but they'd learned pretty soon that she was asking everyone where they were staying and what they thought about their accommodations because she was collecting information for her blog. It could've been a great cover story, but Vivian believed that it was true.

She and Ella were just jumpy and seeing shadows where there were none.

Lying on the other bed, Ella turned on her side and propped herself on her forearm. "You won't have to do anything special once you transition. I don't see Bridget or Amanda exercising."

"Amanda runs on the treadmill. I don't know about Bridget."

"You're avoiding the subject, and by that I mean your transition, not your exercise routine."

"I'm not. Once this is over, I'm going for it. I promised Magnus."

"Finally." Ella got up and pulled out a coke from the mini fridge.

"I miss Magnus." Vivian sighed. "Maybe I can ask Turner to invite him to his room so we could be together for at least a little while."

"Do it. I'm sure he wouldn't mind. And I want to see Julian too."

Vivian wasn't sure at all. "Should we open the connecting door to Turner's room?"

"I don't think they are there. I can't hear anything, and these walls are not soundproof."

Vivian got up and pulled out a water bottle from the fridge. "I sleep better knowing that Turner is next door. It's funny how I don't feel safe with all the Guardians surrounding us, but I do with him, even though he's not a warrior."

"He was. But I know what you mean. It's like he has the answers for everything and always knows what to do. The Guardians follow his orders."

Pulling her phone out of her purse, Ella checked her messages. "Nothing from Julian. I'm going to text him." She typed a quick message.

"I should text Magnus too. He's supposed to be wherever I am, so he should be here in the hotel."

"He was probably following us all day long." Ella snorted. "If I couldn't detect him or any of the other Guardians watching over us, it was silly of me to think that I could spot Mr. D."

When Ella's phone pinged with a return message, she read it out loud. "Turner and I are on our way back. What do you want for dinner? We can bring takeout."

Vivian waved a hand. "I don't care. Whatever they bring is fine. I just want to see Magnus."

"I'll ask Julian to ask Turner if it's okay."

For a moment, Vivian thought to tell Ella not to bother him, but then reconsidered. Seeing Magnus was worth the little embarrassment. Everyone knew that mates were inseparable. Poor Bhathian hadn't stopped scowling since they'd boarded the plane.

Only Turner seemed indifferent, but that was because the guy didn't show emotions. Vivian was sure he missed Bridget as well and was talking on the phone with her whenever he could.

"He says Magnus can join us for dinner."

"Wonderful. Thank you. And thank Turner too."

"I already did." Ella sat on the bed and crossed her legs. "Georgetown is so beautiful. I wish the campus were in Los Angeles."

"You can still decide to go here."

Ella shook her head. "I made up my mind. I want to stay home, with you and Magnus and Parker, and, of course, Julian. I'm also not sure about nursing anymore. The village doesn't need more nurses. I don't know how I feel about working in the outside world. I kind of like living in this secret universe, surrounded by my people. I would like to find something I can do that would be beneficial for the clan."

Vivian had a feeling she knew where this was going. "You want to head that charity, don't you?"

Ella smiled. "Passionately. I'm much more excited about that than I ever was about nursing."

"What does one need to study to manage a charity?"

Ella tossed the empty coke can in the wastebasket. "Some kind of management, I guess. I would assume a Master in Business Administration degree is good for that, but maybe there is something more specific."

Vivian scooted back against the pillows and patted the spot next to her. "We can find answers on the internet. Bring your laptop."

This could have waited for later, but they were both anxious about the interview tomorrow, and this was an excellent topic to take their minds off it.

As Ella joined her on the bed, Vivian wrapped her arm around her shoulders. "Just like old times. Remember how you and Parker would come to snuggle in bed with me and have me read you a story?"

Leaning, Ella kissed her cheek. "Yeah, I loved doing that even though the stories Parker wanted you to read were lame." She opened the laptop. "Let's ask Oracle Google what should I be when I grow up."

"It's amazing how you can find everything online these days."

"Here is one." Ella clicked on a link. "Online bachelor's degree in nonprofit management." She read the description out loud. "I don't even have to go anywhere. I can study at home." She turned to Vivian. "Isn't that awesome? I can do homeschooling like Parker, but for college."

"Let me see."

It looked legitimate and it was accredited, but Vivian had always imagined Ella getting to do what she couldn't, and that included going away to college and experiencing youth to the fullest.

But it seemed that her daughter had found love at a young age, and same as her mother was willing to skip all that to be with her guy. Unlike Vivian, though, Ella was making a conscious choice and wasn't forced into it by circumstances.

Or maybe she was?

Vivian had no doubt that part of the decision to stay in the village had to do with Ella's captivity and her fear of the outside world. Or more specifically the Russian mobster who was probably still searching for her. And then there was the evil Doomer who was planning to kidnap her.

"I have to check how the fundraiser is going," Ella said. "Maybe I'm flapping my wings in the wrong direction, and this entire project is a flop."

"I'm crossing my fingers."

As Ella looked at the figures, her eyes widened. "Oh, wow. It's doing much better than I thought it would. We've collected seven thousand three hundred and seventeen dollars."

"Is that a lot?"

"I think it is. We only uploaded the video on Friday night, and Roni said he was going to work on the algorithm on Saturday. I think this is pretty amazing."

38

ELLA

When Logan entered her dream, Ella felt a weight lift off her chest. And when he wrapped his arm around her, she sighed and leaned her head against his solid chest. "I've missed you the last couple of nights. Where were you?"

"I've been busy."

"Doing what?"

He smirked. "Warlord stuff. I didn't have time for naps."

So, Turner had been right and Logan was on the island, or he had been.

"Which is what? Are there any wars going on that I'm not aware of?"

"There are always conflicts somewhere on the globe. Many don't make the news in the States, or anywhere else in the western world."

"Why is that?"

He shrugged. "Politics, I guess. Some conflicts are more newsworthy than others even though they might be insignificant in comparison."

She'd learned as much from Gorchenco. It was interesting how the bad guys had a better grasp on global affairs than the good guys, or maybe just the misinformed masses. Naturally, it wasn't because the warlords and mobsters cared more, but because they profited from conflicts large and small and, therefore, made it their business to know.

Unlike other warlords, though, Logan didn't live in the war zone. His island was probably the safest stronghold on the globe because no one knew of its existence.

"Are you back home, wherever that is? I assume that night and day are flipped over there."

He chuckled. "They are flipped over where you are. Are you home? Or are you at Georgetown already?"

Boy, was he a good actor and an expert deflector. She couldn't detect a note of falsehood in his tone. He must have known she was there already, even if all he'd done was to hack into university computers and check the tour's roster.

"My mother and I arrived Monday night. We did the tour today and tomorrow is the interview."

He squeezed her shoulder. "Are you excited?"

Ella hoped she was as good an actor as Logan and could fake as flawlessly. Then again, she was excited, just not for the reason he thought.

"I'm nervous. What do you think I should wear? My mom bought me a pantsuit, but I think it's too formal. I usually wear jeans, but jeans are too casual. Maybe I should wear a skirt? But I don't know which one. A short one to show off my legs, or a long one that will make me look modest and romantic. Help!"

That's how teenage girls talked when they were excited, right?

Not too long ago she'd been one too, but she could barely remember herself from the days before Romeo. Had she talked like that?

Logan laughed. "Just be yourself and wear whatever makes you feel confident. If you put on something that you don't normally wear it will make you even more nervous."

"That's good advice."

It really was. That's what she would've told Maddie or any other friend going for an interview. Except, Logan wasn't her friend, or was he?

"You're welcome. Anything else I can help you with?"

"How should I talk? Should I use a lot of fancy words to show off my vocabulary, or should I talk like I normally do?"

He stopped walking and turned her toward him. "You know that it doesn't matter, right? My friend is going to recommend your acceptance even if you come in wearing a bikini." He chuckled. "He might get a stroke seeing you in one, so I don't recommend it. Since I don't know anyone else on the board of admissions, we need to make sure my friend lives to conduct another interview."

Logan had a sense of humor? That was new. He was like a chameleon, changing his colors according to who he needed to charm, and it was working.

"I can't thank you enough for making this happen for me."

"I know how you can thank me." He waggled his brows. "I want a kiss. I want much more than that, but I'll settle for a good and long thank-you one. Or two, or three."

Ella wanted to ask about his plans to take her out on a date, and whether he wouldn't prefer a real kiss to a virtual one, but she was too much of a chicken to do that.

Except, chicken or not, she needed to find out what his plans were. Or at least get an inkling.

Wrapping her arms around his neck, she smiled. "What about the real-life date you've promised me? Wouldn't you like your thank-you kiss to be real?"

He arched a brow. "In front of your mother? I don't think so. I may be an evil warlord, but I do have some basic manners."

This wasn't the answer she needed.

"Is that why you decided not to meet me after all? Was it because I told you that my mother would have to come along?"

Instead of answering her question, he asked one of his own. "When are you going back home?"

Ella did some quick thinking. If he'd been held up and couldn't make it, she could salvage the situation by waiting for him.

"We are staying for the weekend. I want to absorb the atmosphere, and my mother wants to visit the monuments."

"That's good. I have a few loose ends I need to tie up before I can leave here, but I think I can be done by Friday. We can meet on Saturday." A sly smirk lifted the corner of his lips. "Are you going to make it worth my while?"

"You just said that you're not going to kiss me in front of my mother."

"I can come to your hotel at night and throw pebbles at your window."

Ella laughed. "Where are you getting these crazy ideas from? Old movies?"

For the first time since she'd known him, Logan seemed uncomfortable. "Where I come from, I'm like royalty, and I don't have much contact with ordinary people. What I know is from watching movies and reading books."

Knowing that what he was telling her was the truth, Ella felt touched and a little sad for him. As Navuh's son, Logan's life was probably all about the Brotherhood and taking care of its various interests. Even if it allowed him to live in the lap of luxury, it didn't allow for experiencing most of what she considered worth living for.

Family and friends.

No wonder he liked sharing her dreams and getting exposed to the ordinary in a very extraordinary way.

Or, he was playing her.

Yeah, that was more likely. Julian had told her not to underestimate the Doomer. Logan had had hundreds of years to perfect his manipulating technique. He was appealing to her softer side.

He wasn't the only one with tricks up his sleeve though. By now she'd gotten to know Logan a little. The Doomer had an enormous ego and a soft spot for pretty girls.

Smirking, Ella rubbed his neck with her thumbs. "I'm sure that doesn't apply to kisses. You've probably kissed many girls." She'd almost blurted thousands, catching herself at the last moment. She wasn't supposed to know that he was much older than he looked.

"I'm an exceptional lover, and all of my vast experience is hands on."

Yep. An overinflated ego and then some.

He dipped his head until their lips were almost touching. "Enough stalling. Am I going to get my thank-you kiss or not?"

Looking into Logan's dark eyes and the red flakes of light sparkling in them, Ella realized that this was most likely the last time they were going to kiss. Heck, it was the last time she was going to kiss any guy other than Julian.

She'd better make it count.

39

TURNER

Turner parted the drapes and looked out the window, scanning the street for any suspicious activity. It was superfluous, he'd assigned Guardians to do that in shifts throughout the night, but it was a habit and a healthy one at that.

He had a knack for spotting things that others didn't and for seeing patterns in seemingly random occurrences.

Not this time, though. He was either pitted against a superior opponent who was even more paranoid than he was, or their underlying assumptions were all wrong and they were wasting their time because the Doomer wasn't coming.

A light knock on the connecting door preceded the thing opening a crack, and then Ella's head peeked inside. "Is it too early for the briefing? I heard the door open and close several times, so I knew you and Julian were awake."

They were supposed to meet at seven, but given Ella's troubled eyes, she was anxious to start. Or maybe she wanted to see Julian, who'd moved in with him to be closer to her.

"Come on in. Julian and Magnus are bringing breakfast. They should be back soon."

She walked in and sat on Julian's bed. "Mr. D came into my dream last night."

Turner perked up. "That's great news. What did he tell you?"

"That he's been busy, and that he might get here on Saturday. And that was only after I dangled a date in front of his nose."

"Did you believe him?"

The girl shrugged. "I don't know. If he were a regular human, I would have been sure that he was telling the truth. But Julian and you warned me that I shouldn't do that."

"And you are very smart for heeding that warning."

"Thank you. Just in case he wasn't lying, though, I told him that my mom and I planned on staying in Washington over the weekend. He might have been detained by his father, or by some emergency, and it would be a shame to miss this opportunity by giving up too early."

"Excellent. Did he ask you where you were staying?"

Ella shook her head. "Nope. Does it mean that he knows?"

"We should assume that he does. He could've sent people to follow you back here. That's why we went to all the trouble of staging things, including bringing in the ladies from Hawaii. They have no clue why they are really here, so they can't divulge any information if asked."

"But you don't know that for sure."

"No, I don't, and we have loads of monitoring equipment in addition to the Guardians. If anyone followed you, we would've known."

Roni and William hadn't come up with anything either, but Lokan might have achieved that by wearing specialty glasses. Still, none of the Guardians had spotted him either, and they'd been searching relentlessly.

On the face of things, everything pointed to Ella's conclusion being right. The Doomer wasn't coming. Not yet, anyway. But every instinct in Turner's body screamed that Lokan was there and that he was setting up his trap.

Pushing up to her feet, Ella walked over to the window and peered outside. "Where did Magnus and Julian go for food?"

"The corner deli."

"I think I can see them coming, but with my human eyes I can't be sure."

Turner walked up to her and stood behind her. "It's them. Is your mother coming?"

"Yes, I am." Vivian walked in through the connecting door. "Good morning. Was the meeting pushed forward earlier and no one told me?"

Ella shook her head. "I wanted to tell Turner about the dream visit and I didn't want to wait. Julian and Magnus are bringing breakfast."

Vivian regarded Ella's sweatpants and T-shirt. "After we are done, you need to get ready. Did you decide what you want to wear for the interview?"

"Not yet. I'm too nervous to think about outfits."

As the door opened, and the men walked in, the mood in the room changed markedly.

"Yay, coffee." Ella rushed up to Julian and wrapped her arms around his neck, ignoring the cardboard tray he was holding. "Good morning," she whispered and kissed his cheek.

Vivian was a little more circumspect about her excitement to see her mate, but not by much.

Regrettably, it wasn't the time or place for a love fest.

"Let's go over everything one more time while we eat." Turner motioned to the two beds, and pulled out the only chair in the room for himself.

Grabbing a coffee off one of the trays, he focused on the ladies. "I know that all of you are concerned with Lokan's compulsion ability, but let's not forget that his men can thrall too. Fortunately, you can prevent them from getting into your head. All it takes is keeping your mind closed off."

"How am I supposed to do that?" Vivian asked.

"A suspicious and contrary attitude. Thralling is easy when the victim is unaware. When a person suspects the thraller, it is much more difficult and requires a stronger thralling ability." He turned to Julian. "I can't thrall well yet, so you'll have to do that. Try to get into Vivian's head."

She lifted a hand. "Wait a minute. Maybe Magnus should do that?"

"You trust Magnus, so you are not going to fight it as hard."

"I trust Julian too, but I'm more comfortable with Magnus."

"That's who we got, so that's what we have to work with. I want you to think of something you wouldn't want Julian to find out. Like a birthday present that you bought for him and want to keep it a surprise."

"Got it." She smiled at Julian. "Go for it."

The guy frowned. "I can't get in. She's blocking me."

Vivian's eyes widened. "I am? I don't know how I'm doing it."

"I told you that it's easy. Once you are aware of it, you can deny entry. Doesn't always work, but just as with hypnosis, if the subjects are reasonably intelligent and resist the hypnotist, it can't be forced on them."

"I wish it worked the same with compulsion," Ella said. "But I know for a fact that it doesn't. As hard as I try, I can't resist Parker's commands."

"We should have brought him along," Julian said. "He could command Ella not to succumb to Lokan's compulsion."

Turner shook his head. "I don't think it would work if Lokan uses his full power up close."

"It's worth a try," Vivian said. "Let's call Parker and ask him to command both of us to resist the Doomer's compulsion."

"Does it work over the phone?" Julian asked.

Vivian pulled the phone out. "We didn't try it, but if it can be done in a shared dream, I'm sure it can be done over a cellular signal."

"Mom, what's up?" Parker answered.

"I want you to command Ella and me to resist Mr. D's compulsion."

There was a long moment of silence before he answered. "I can give it a try. I'm imagining how much I hate him, and how I don't want him to get anywhere near you or Ella. I hope it will help."

"Just do your best, sweetheart."

40

ELLA

*A*s Ella came out of the bathroom, her mother looked her up and down and then nodded her approval. "You look lovely."

"Thank you." Ella stifled the impulse to roll her eyes.

No matter how many times she'd told her mother that the interview was irrelevant, Vivian insisted on treating it as if it was for real. Perhaps it was easier for her to focus on that than on what this was really about.

Humoring her, Ella had put on a long flowing skirt that wasn't new, and a matching blouse that was. The shoes were also a new purchase, comfortable and old-fashioned, with a low chunky heel and a strap across the top.

Only after she was fully dressed, standing in front of the mirror and examining her reflection, had Ella realized that she'd followed Logan's advice. She felt comfortable and confident in her own style of clothing. Pant and skirt suits were a reminder of her captivity, of dressing up to please the whims of her owner and not her own taste and preferences.

She'd smoothed her pink hair back instead of spiking it, had gone easy with the makeup, and had donned the pretend reading glasses Eva had given her. They weren't stylish and made her look bookish, but she actually liked them.

The most important part of her attire, though, were the trackers. A matching set of earrings and pendant, four hairpins, and three tiny dots that were attached to the inside of her clothing.

It was a little early, but Ella was too nervous to wait. "Ready to go, Mom?"

"Yes." Vivian picked up her purse. "Let's text our taxi driver."

When the Guardian picked them up from in front of the hotel, they did their best to act as if he was just a driver, and when they arrived at campus, Vivian pretended to pay him.

He returned her credit card and smiled. "Good luck."

Knowing that Magnus and Julian had been following them in another cab, Ella tried not to look over her shoulder.

Instead, she looked at her mother. *Do you think it will be okay if I pull out a mirror and pretend to check my hair?*

Vivian shook her head. *Save it for when we actually need it. I'm sure the guys are behind us.*

As they walked to the admissions office, Ella barely breathed, expecting an ambush at every corner. It was so damn nerve-wracking that she let out a sigh of relief when they got there.

"Please take a seat," the receptionist said. "These gentlemen are ahead of you, and then it's your turn."

"Thank you."

Ella eyed the two, but they seemed precisely who they were supposed to be. One was a guy about her age, although he looked much younger, and the other was obviously his father and looked to be in his mid-fifties.

No immortals posing as humans here, she sent to her mom as she took a seat.

When Vivian started chatting with the father, Ella smiled at the son and then pulled out her phone, pretending to read. She was in no mood for small talk, and besides, her throat was dry. She'd forgotten to get a water bottle and wondered if it was okay to go get one.

A quick text to Julian solved her dilemma.

There was a vending machine out in the corridor, and a couple of Guardians were hanging around in its vicinity. Kri was across from it in the ladies bathroom, stationed there in case Ella or Vivian needed to use the facilities.

She tapped her mother's shoulder. "I'm going to get a bottle of water Do you want anything from the vending machine?"

"Water would be lovely, thank you."

Ella pushed to her feet and looked at the father and son. "Would you like me to get you anything?"

"I'll come with you." The son started to get up.

His father stopped him. "You can't leave. That door may open at any moment and it will be your turn."

Deflated, the guy sat back down. "I guess I'm stuck. Can you please get me a coke?" He handed her two bucks.

"Sure. Diet or regular?"

"Regular. Thank you."

The trip to the vending machine and back was uneventful, but at least she got to see the two Guardians monitoring the corridor.

On the way back, she saw a girl and her father leave the waiting room, and when she entered it, the son wasn't there.

Ella handed the father the coke and the change. "Sorry I was too late."

"He'll have it when he gets out. Thank you for buying it for him."

"You're welcome."

She wondered if the father had stayed behind because it had been his choice or because parents weren't allowed inside.

Not that she cared one way or another, but Vivian seemed so excited about the interview that she would probably be disappointed if she was left out. Besides, it wasn't a good idea for them to separate.

Walking up to the secretary, Ella waited for her to get off the phone and asked, "Can my mother come in with me, or does she have to stay outside?"

The woman smiled indulgently. "It's up to you. Professor Perry is not going to kick your mom out." She leaned closer. "On the contrary, he'll be mad if she doesn't come in. Students are off limits. But mothers are not." She winked.

Ella glanced at Vivian. She was indeed beautiful, and the boy's father was practically drooling over her. Was that the reason he'd stayed behind?

It never ceased to amaze her how stupid some men got over pretty women.

"My mom is taken."

"Pfft." The woman waved a dismissive hand. "As if that has ever stopped him."

Time dragged on, and with it the stress buildup. Despite the Guardians Ella had seen with her own eyes, and the many others hiding in various places, she watched the door, expecting Logan to saunter in at any moment.

In the movie she'd created in her head, he would walk in, order everyone to keep quiet, compelling their silence so no one could sound the alarm, smile at her evilly, and crook his finger, beckoning her to him.

She would try to resist, but it would be no use. He would compel her and her mother to follow him, maybe stealing a kiss before ushering them out of the waiting room.

Outside, there would be a horde of Doomers, holding the Guardians in chains, but just as all hope was lost, Magnus and Julian would come and save the day.

How?

Her imagination had no answer for that.

So yeah, she was an optimist at heart. In her imagination, even the worst case scenario had a happy ending.

41

JULIAN

The men's room was the last place Julian would've chosen as headquarters for their stakeout, but Turner had convinced him that it was perfect.

A Guardian named Edan was shrouding the place in such a heavy cloak of dread that human males chose to bypass it and continue to the next bathroom down the hall. And if an immortal happened to wander in, there would be one less Doomer for them to worry about.

Not that there were any.

The small surveillance cameras they'd installed around campus revealed nothing suspicious, and a whole lot of nothing was happening in the interviewer's waiting room, except for some guy flirting with Vivian.

Magnus was probably going out of his mind. The feed from the room was broadcasting on the private channel all the Guardians had access to through their phones. Julian had no doubt that Magnus was watching it as avidly as he was.

Turner, on the other hand, was watching the feed from the interviewer's room.

Not that anything interesting was going on there either. The tiny portable transmitter was mounted on the wall across from the interviewer, so all that was visible was the professor's pudgy face and the young guy's back. There was no sound, or maybe Turner was just keeping the volume off.

For the first fifteen minutes or so the two had talked, and then the professor had turned around to the monitor mounted on the wall behind him and had started playing a documentary about the university's history. It was running for over twenty minutes already and didn't seem to be nearing the end.

"Do you think he shows that to every student?" Julian whispered.

They were supposed to keep silent in case of immortals overhearing them, but since none were around except their own people, it didn't matter.

Turner shrugged. "It's an easy way to make the interview seem longer than it is and justify more hours," Turner whispered back.

Minimizing the window, Turner brought the rest of the feeds up on his tablet and scanned them quickly. There was even one transmitting from Ella and Vivian's room in the hotel.

Where a whole lot of nothing was going on as well.

"He's not coming," Julian whispered.

Turner shook his head. "My brain agrees with you, but my intuition doesn't. Which is a first for me. I never rely on feelings."

Intuition was not a feeling. It was a collection of clues too small for the conscious mind to notice, but not for the subconscious that collected everything.

The problem was that Julian's intuition was saying the exact opposite, and, since getting to Washington, he and Turner had been exposed to the same input. The only difference was Turner's experience, which allowed his subconscious to make more connections and see more patterns than Julian's.

Trusting Turner's gut more than he did his own, Julian tensed. Something was about to happen. The question was when, where, and how.

42

ELLA

A whole freaking hour had passed since the guy had gone into the interviewer's office. Ella had finished her water and needed to pee, but she was afraid to leave in case the guy finally got out.

On the other hand, it was a bad idea to keep holding it in throughout the interview, especially if it was going to last so long.

She tapped her mother's shoulder. "I'm going to the bathroom."

Vivian gave her a pained look. "I need to go, too." She rolled her eyes at the guy's father.

"So, come with me. We can tell the receptionist that we are going and will be right back."

"Good idea."

After a quick stop at the secretary's desk, they rushed out and headed to the bathroom, passing two Guardians posing as students on the way.

"I don't really need to go," Vivian said. "But that guy was getting overly friendly. Can we hide out in the bathroom until he leaves?"

"Sure." Ella smiled and switched to a silent mode of communication. *We can ask Turner to let us know when it's safe to come back.*

It could've been beneficial to keep the channel to her mother open, but Ella was afraid that by doing so she was going to open her mind to attack. Her best bet was to keep her shields up and reinforce them as much as she could.

In the bathroom, they found Kri, dressed in a custodian's coveralls and polishing the counters.

"Good afternoon, ladies," she greeted them.

Ella stifled a giggle. "Good afternoon to you, too."

With her height and broad shoulders, Kri wasn't a very believable custodian, and besides, she'd joined them on the tour of the campus as a student. Then again, some students took on jobs like that to help with their living expenses.

Once Ella was done, she double checked that the transmitters were still attached to her clothing before getting out. A moment later her mother joined her at the sink. "We should go back. I just hope that Larry and his son are gone already."

No such luck.

When they got back, the father was still sitting in the waiting room. Not for long, though. A couple minutes later the son got out.

"What took so long?" Larry asked.

The guy glanced at a receptionist before answering. "A long documentary about the university's history and every important person who ever attended it or donated big bucks to it." He rolled his eyes. "There were a lot of both." He turned to Ella. "Good luck. Professor Perry is a nice guy. The hardest part of the interview was watching that movie."

"Thanks."

"You can go in," the receptionist said. "Professor Perry is ready for you."

The guy must have a bathroom in there. Otherwise he would have needed a pee break, Ella sent to her mother.

Vivian smiled. "Let's not keep the professor waiting."

The interviewer's office was made to impress, with fancy bookcases lining both its sides, and heavy furniture that looked as old as the university.

"Welcome." Professor Perry got up and headed straight for Vivian. "Ms. Kelly Rubinstein and her lovely mother, Mrs. Victoria MacBain." He shook Vivian's hand first and then Ella's.

"Second marriage?" he asked as he pulled out a visitor chair for her mother and then for Ella.

"I've remarried after Kelly's father passed away."

"My condolences," he said as he took his seat behind the desk.

Finally looking at Ella, the professor gave her a quick once over. "My friend spoke very highly of you, but he failed to mention how pretty you are."

Ella affected a polite expression. "Thank you for the compliment, but I'm very glad that he didn't. I would like to be judged based on merit and not looks."

"You are a wise young woman." He lifted his notepad and took a look. "Very impressive grades. And you also organized a charity?"

"Yes, I did."

"Tell me about it."

Ella had that part prepared. It was a variation on the one she was actually working on, but instead of helping girls who'd been lured away from their families and violated, her invented charity was about helping victims of child abuse. A much less controversial subject.

Once she was done, he asked some more questions about the charity, and after she answered those, he asked why she'd chosen Georgetown.

"That's an easy answer. Georgetown is one of the most prestigious universities in the country, and the campus is beautiful. Also, its nursing program is extremely well regarded."

Her answer seemed to please him. "I think you are a very good fit for us. And it has nothing to do with my friend putting in a word for you. You're an excellent candidate, Kelly." He turned around and clicked the monitor on. "But if you are still not sure that this is the place for you, this documentary is going to convince you."

As the movie started playing, Professor Perry rolled his chair sideways and out of the way, taking the notepad and pen with him.

Now the movie made sense. Instead of summarizing the interview after the student was gone, he was doing it while the movie was playing and saving himself working after hours.

What else seemed clear was that Logan hadn't planned a trap and everything he'd told her was aboveboard.

She owed him a big apology. Except, she could never tell him what she'd suspected and why.

About ten minutes into the movie, the professor got up, walked over to one of the bookcases, and pulled out a book.

Evidently, he was done summarizing the interview and was going to spend the rest of the time reading.

43

MAGNUS

*A*rwel clapped Magnus's back. "Relax. It's only harmless flirting." Sitting on a bench in front of the admissions office, they were supposed to be watching the entry, with Arwel monitoring moods and intentions for any disturbances.

But since nothing was happening, Magnus busied himself with watching the feed from the waiting room.

"The asshole is drooling all over Vivian. He's been slowly inching closer to her, and now he's practically sitting in her lap. I want to get in there and teach him some manners."

"Patience, my friend. His son is going to come out soon, and they are going to leave. The worst that could happen is Vivian having to stop by the ladies room to clean his drool off her shoes."

As worst case scenarios went, that was, of course, a joke. Magnus had bigger worries on his mind. But it seemed that this operation was a bust, and that the Doomer really wasn't going to show up.

Not today anyway.

The question was whether he'd told Ella the truth and would arrive on Saturday.

Magnus wasn't sure which outcome he was hoping for. On the one hand, catching Lokan was important to the clan, but on the other hand, he would have preferred to keep Vivian and Ella as far away from danger as possible.

Next to him, Arwel was doing his thing, with his eyes closed and his head tilted back, tuning into the vibes coursing through the campus.

"Are you getting anything?"

Arwel shook his head. "I'm getting plenty, just not anything that is interesting to us."

"Let me guess. The asshole in the waiting room is thinking dirty thoughts about my mate, and his kid is anxious."

"The kid was anxious, and now he is bored, and you're right about the horny bastard." Arwel scratched his head. "There is something else too, but it's faint and it's subtle. Like a low-level excitement." He waved a dismissive hand. "It's probably nothing. Someone looking forward to a hookup."

Magnus snorted. "This place is packed with young humans. All of them are thinking about hookups twenty-four seven."

Turning back to his phone screen, he focused on the door to the interviewer's room. Instead of looking at the human male making advances toward his mate, he should be watching that door, which was the only way into the inner office. They had checked the room the night before last, verifying that there was no back exit.

About ten minutes later, it opened and the young human stepped out, smiled at Ella and said something to her.

"Hallelujah, the kid is out, and he's taking his father with him."

Arwel nodded. "I can feel his relief, and also the older man's disappointment."

"Ella and Vivian are going in. Do you feel them?"

"I can feel Vivian, and she is excited, but Ella's shields are up, and she emits next to nothing. I can't get a reading on her emotions."

"That's good, isn't it? She is less vulnerable."

"It's very good, and I need to ask her how she does it. Maybe she can teach me how to protect my mind. I would love some peace and quiet in there."

Magnus felt an unreasonable wave of pride wash over him. Even though she wasn't his flesh and blood, he couldn't help thinking of Ella as his daughter. When an old and experienced Guardian like Arwel believed he could learn something from such a young girl, Magnus couldn't help but feel pride in her achievements.

"I doubt she can help me, though," Arwel added. "Ella learned how to block her mother when she was very young, and she probably does it without thinking. Besides, she needs to block only one person. I'm not that lucky."

"There shouldn't be a difference between blocking one and many. You should talk to her. If she can help you, great, and if she can't, at least you tried, right?"

Arwel nodded. "When we get back, I'll stop by your place."

"I'm not sure you'll find her there. Once this is over, I have a feeling she's going to move in with Julian."

Arwel arched a brow. "It's getting serious between them, eh?"

"Very. They are obviously destined for one another."

44

ELLA

*E*lla watched the professor from the corner of her eye, expecting him to take the book and go back to his chair. Instead, he put it on another shelf and remained standing with his hands clasped behind his back and his face turned toward the movie.

Maybe he got tired of sitting?

But then she heard a noise that didn't come from the loudspeakers playing the movie's soundtrack. Something creaked, then whined, like a very old door being pushed on squeaky hinges.

Did you hear that? Ella sent to her mother.

What are you talking about?

Never mind.

The small hairs on the back of her neck prickling, she turned her head in the direction of the noise and saw the professor just standing there. He either hadn't heard it or was ignoring it.

It was probably nothing. The admissions office was located in an old building, and it made all kinds of weird noises, which everyone who worked there was most likely used to.

She was just jumpy, that's all.

Turning back to the movie, Ella tried to ignore the creaking, but then Vivian's back stiffened, indicating that she was probably hearing the weird noises too.

They both turned their heads at the same time.

"Not a sound, ladies." Logan stepped out from behind the bookcase that had been somehow pushed forward. "And don't move a muscle either," he said as calmly as if he was saying hello.

The professor dipped his head in greeting and said nothing.

The power behind Logan's compulsion made Parker's seem like child's play.

What Logan had done in her dream hadn't been even a minuscule fraction of what he was doing now.

Ella was paralyzed, stuck in the same pose and mute. She couldn't even look at her mother because her head had been turned toward the noise when Logan issued the command. Hell, she couldn't even move her eyes.

The one thing he couldn't control, though, was her mind.

As Logan instructed the professor to go through the opening, Ella sent to her mother, *Shields up, Mom. And don't worry. The Guardians are going to be here any second.* She then slammed her own shields into place.

When the professor had gone through the secret opening, Logan walked over to them, leaned, and kissed Ella's forehead. "I'm sorry about this, Ella, but I need you and your mother for a special mission. Once that is done, I will let you both go. I promise."

Where were the freaking Guardians?

"Please get up, ladies, and follow the professor. Take your purses with you."

Ella fought the compulsion with all she had. If she could only stall for a couple of minutes, the Guardians would burst through the door and end this.

She was too damn weak, and the only thing that seemed to be working was her tear ducts that started leaking. She couldn't even raise her hand to wipe them away.

Like a couple of zombies, she and her mother did as they were told, got up and headed toward the protruding bookcase.

Walking through the opening, they entered a tunnel that would've been completely dark if not for the professor holding up his phone with the flashlight activated. Logan entered behind them and closed the way.

"Keep walking," he told the three of them.

Was the professor under Logan's control too?

Had Logan somehow tampered with the camera inside the room? But how?

And what was that mission he'd talked about?

Damn, she couldn't open her mouth to ask, and she could barely see because the tears were blurring her eyesight and she couldn't wipe them off.

They must've walked about a third of a mile when they met up with one of Logan's men.

"Stop," he issued the command from behind them.

As the man, or rather immortal, handed Logan a duffle bag, Ella's panic intensified. What was in there? Gags? Blindfolds? Handcuffs?

Turning toward the professor, who was standing just as motionless as Ella and Vivian, Logan pointed at another tunnel forking away from the one they were walking in. "You are free to leave, Perry. Once you get out, you will remember nothing of what happened from the moment you saw me earlier today. Am I clear?"

The professor nodded.

"You can start walking, Perry. Ladies, you stay right where you are."

As the professor walked away, Logan turned to them, his forehead creasing as he took in Ella's tear-stricken face.

"There is no reason to cry, Ella." He wiped her tears with his thumbs. "No one is going to touch you or your mother without your permission, and that includes me. This is not about sex, like it was with Gorchenco. I need your minds, not your bodies."

As if she was going to believe the liar. But that was neither here nor there. Soon, the Guardians would come and rescue them.

Why hadn't they already?

As Logan unzipped the bag, the last thing she'd expected him to pull out were two string bikinis.

"Please hand me your purses." He took them and gave them to his guy. "When I say now, I want you to take off all of your clothes, toss them in front of you, and put these on." He looked at his man. "Turn your back to the ladies."

When the guy did as he was told, Logan pulled two sets of exercise clothes and two pairs of flip-flops out of the bag and put them on the floor at Ella and Vivian's feet.

"I'm going to turn around. When you have the bikinis on, stop, and wait for further instructions." He turned his back to them. "Now, strip. You have thirty seconds before I turn around."

Obviously, he was concerned about trackers. But how had he known to suspect them?

As Ella stripped and tossed her clothes on the floor, she was thankful for the jewelry and the pins in her hair. Next to her, Vivian did the same. Then they both put the bikinis on.

Turning back, Logan nodded his approval, and then walked in a circle around them.

The freaking bikini was nothing more than three tiny triangles held together with a bunch of strings. All it covered were her nipples and her mons. Everything else was on full display.

If he wanted to ensure that they had no trackers on their bodies, he had achieved his goal. Even the one she'd attached to her panties was gone, and she'd thought it would be the hardest to discover.

Except, he didn't know about the miniature ones in their jewelry and hairpins.

"Toss your shoes on top of the pile, and after that take off your earrings and your necklaces and toss them too." He glanced at Vivian's hair and smirked. "The wig has to go too. And these funky glasses you are both wearing. Now."

Crap, Ella hoped he wouldn't notice the pins in her hair. She also hoped that no camera was going to pick them up on the way. Logan wasn't the only one she had to worry about. There was more than one wolf after her.

When that was done, he pointed at the folded exercise clothes and the flip-flops. "Put these on."

To his man he said, "Collect all their belongings, put them in the duffel bag, and go. You know what to do."

"Yes, sir."

45

VIVIAN

The Doomer was acting like the classic evil mastermind, polite and gentlemanly to a fault, and yet scary as hell.

Vivian had always found the intelligent, soft-spoken villains more frightening than the bully types, and Lokan was the scariest of them all.

The fact that Ella had thought to take someone like him on proved how naive she still was. Her daughter was no match for that devil, and a devil he was, despite his false reassurances and his concern for their dignity.

Frankly, Viv hadn't expected him to turn around and let them keep their modesty. It gave some credence to his claim that he needed them for a mission and not as sex slaves for the Doomer's island, or for his own perverted needs.

She could imagine that there were some psychos out there who entertained fantasies about having sex with both mother and daughter. Hopefully, Lokan wasn't one of those.

"Follow me," he said after they were dressed.

Lokan's man had gone in the same direction as the professor, and he was probably going to lead the Guardians on a wild goose chase around town. She wouldn't be surprised if the plan was to distribute the trackers between several Doomers and have them drive in different directions.

What she couldn't understand was how come the Guardians weren't already there. The feed from the camera inside the interview office should have alerted them to what was going on, and if the thing had malfunctioned, someone would have come in to investigate.

As they walked down the tunnel, she listened for hurried footsteps coming from behind, but the only sound echoing from the walls was the flapping of her and Ella's flip-flops.

The tunnel looked ancient, like something that had been built together with the university in the 1700s. Someone must have thought that escape tunnels were needed in case of an emergency or an invasion.

How come Turner hadn't thought to check for that?

She'd been reassured that the interview room had been thoroughly searched and that the only way in and out of it was the door to the waiting room. Had no one bothered to take a look at the building's blueprints?

Then again, the originals might have been lost, and no one knew the tunnels existed. Lokan, on the other hand, was old enough to have seen the original structure built.

Vivian wished she could share her thoughts with Ella, but her daughter was keeping the channel closed. Which was smart of her. She needed to keep her shields up against the Doomer.

Hopefully, the fear and hatred Vivian felt for Lokan was enough to block him from entering her mind as well. If the Doomer got even a glimpse, he could compel them to tell him whatever he wanted.

"You are probably wondering how I knew to avoid the trap you were setting for me," he said out of the blue, sending panic surging into Vivian's throat.

"Don't worry, I don't blame you for that. I know you had no choice but to do as you were told. I figured that you've been aided by your government in exchange for letting them use your special talents."

What the hell was he talking about?

As he glanced back at them to gauge their responses, Vivian hoped her wide peeled eyes were conveying her fear and surprise, and that he would assume they were the result of his brilliant, yet erroneous, deduction.

Satisfied with her and Ella's appropriately shocked expressions, he smirked. "I'm well aware of their secret program to collect people with paranormal abilities and use their talents in warfare. Unfortunately, I wasn't able to get close to anyone on the inside, or I would have raided their facilities a long time ago. I'm very curious about what else is out there, and if they found another dream walker. As far as I know, I'm the only one."

So, Josh had been right about the government snatching people with special abilities and keeping them locked up somewhere. God only knew what was being done to them.

Lokan cast a glance at Ella over his shoulder. "I must conclude that my compulsion doesn't work as well in dream world. Either that, or they have people who can break through it. Otherwise, you wouldn't have been able to tell them about my dream-walking ability. You were pretty convincing, but I knew that you were trying to play me when you started acting all nice and flirty. I figured out that the people holding you wanted to put their hands on me too."

As Turner and Julian had warned, Lokan had suspected Ella all along, but he had reached the wrong conclusion. The results were still the same, though. He'd managed to avoid capture and abscond with them.

At least he didn't know who was after him, which gave the Guardians an advantage. Lokan was confident in his ability to compel humans to do his bidding, but his reliance on it was his Achilles heel.

He was in for a big surprise.

"Three things confirmed my suspicions," he kept on bragging. "The first was the excellent fake identity you were supplied with. Only the government has access to such resources. The second was the hotel that you were staying at, which is a government-owned facility. And the third was the camera your people installed in the interview office. I sent my men through the tunnels to check out the room last night, and when they found it, I had the final proof that what I suspected was right." He chuckled. "Your people are probably still watching the loop my guy is feeding them. I just wonder when they are going to notice your slight body movements are repeating. By the time they figure it out, we will be up in the air and out of their reach. My idea to put on the movie was brilliant, if I say so myself."

Quite full of himself, isn't he? Ella sent.

Vivian shook her head, signaling Ella that she shouldn't talk.

Her daughter was strong enough to send thoughts directly into Vivian's head, but Vivian's ability was much more limited, and she was afraid that her response could be picked up by the Doomer.

He looked at them over his shoulder. "I apologize for keeping you silent and conducting a one-sided conversation. As soon as we are safely away, I'm going to remove the silencing compulsion and you'll be able to ask me questions."

Hopefully, by then they would get rescued.

Both she and Ella still had the hairpins in, which meant that as soon as Turner realized that he was watching a loop, the Guardians would come after them.

The problem was that the Guardians would be chasing after more than one signal, following the trackers Lokan's man had taken and most likely distributed among several of his comrades. Which meant that they would have to split up.

Vivian's gut clenched. What if Lokan had a large force with him and each tracker led the Guardians into a trap?

Supposedly, they were better trained and stronger than the Doomers, but that wouldn't help them if they found themselves vastly outnumbered.

46

ELLA

*E*lla felt like an idiot. She'd been naive and full of herself, and Julian had been right about her being no match for Logan. The only secret she'd managed to keep from him was the real identity of her rescuers.

So far.

She prayed that they would get rescued before he had the chance to figure that one out too.

Supposedly, Doomers weren't aware of the fact that Dormants possessed special ability in a much higher percentage than the general human population. That was what Dalhu claimed. But Logan wasn't an ordinary Doomer, and he was probably privy to information kept from the simple soldiers.

He was smart and seemed well-educated, which also differentiated him from the average Doomer. He could've figured out stuff on his own, and once he discovered that Ella and Vivian were Dormants, all his gentlemanly promises would be forgotten. He would either throw them into the Doomers' breeding program or keep them for himself. His own little harem of mother and daughter.

Talk about gross.

"You should actually thank me for freeing you from your government's clutches," Logan continued his villainous mastermind monologue. "Once you complete the mission that I need your help with, I'll set you free with new identities and enough money to last you for the rest of your life."

Right, it was just as true as the scholarship he'd promised her. Once again, he was blowing smoke up her ass, but this time she wasn't buying it.

"Naturally, it would be best if you don't return to the States and opt for settling somewhere in South America. You'll be much harder to find, and your money will buy you a more luxurious living."

As if he was ever letting them go. All his promises had one goal. To ensure their cooperation. What she wondered, though, was if he'd be satisfied with dangling the carrot in front of them or was he going to also introduce the stick?

Which would be extremely easy for him. All he would have to do is threaten to hurt one of them for the other to agree to whatever he wanted. Come to think of it, he wouldn't even need to do that. He could just compel them to do what he told them. They would be like puppets on his strings.

Glancing at Ella, Logan smirked. "Except for me, of course. I might need you to perform more services for me from time to time. You have no idea how valuable your mind-to-mind communication is. It's completely undetectable."

Damn, the guy knew how to sound convincing. She could visualize herself lazing on a beach somewhere in South America, only having to do favors for Logan from time to time to keep the money coming. From his point of view, and given what he believed Ella and Vivian's situation to be, Logan's plan seemed like a win-win.

"You are going to live like queens, and I probably won't need your special services for more than several days a year." He smiled. "That's one hell of a compensation package for very little work."

Was he playing her again, just from a different angle?

This new Logan seemed like a completely different person from the one who'd shared her dreams, and he was treating her as if she was a tool to be used in his schemes and not someone he desired.

Evidently, Turner had been right about that too, and Logan had faked his infatuation with her the same way she'd faked hers with him.

All along, they'd been playing each other.

What she wanted to find out more than anything else, though, was whether he'd compelled her attraction to him. Would he admit to it if she asked?

They'd been walking for at least twenty minutes when they reached another fork in the tunnel.

"This way, ladies." Logan motioned for them to go ahead of him.

The short offshoot terminated in a brick wall, but as Logan grabbed one of the bricks that was sticking out and pulled, some kind of a pulley mechanism was activated and the wall started moving back.

On the other side was nothing but a staircase leading up, and Logan motioned for them to take it. Four stories later, they exited through another door and onto the roof of a parking structure.

Except, instead of a car, there was a helicopter waiting for them.

Crap. Where was he taking them? What was the helicopter's range? And more importantly, was it shorter than the trackers'?

47

MAGNUS

Magnus switched from watching the feed coming from the waiting room to the one coming from the interviewer's office. "It's taking too long."

Arwel stretched his legs in front of him. "Are they still watching the documentary?"

"The thing drags on and on. I don't know how they are not falling asleep."

"I think they already did because I'm not picking up anything. There was a brief moment when Vivian tensed, but after that nothing. The professor must have said something to upset her."

"What about Ella?"

Arwel shook his head. "I told you. She's blocking everything. I can't sense her at all."

"Is there a timer on the feed? Because the movie seems longer this time around."

"There should be. Tell Turner to check. He has the full display."

Taking a quick glance around to make sure no one was listening, Magnus tapped his earpiece. "Turner. I have a feeling that the movie has been running longer this time than during the previous interview. Can you check the timer?"

"It's just your perception," Arwel said. "What do you think could be happening in there? We are watching all the entry and exit points, and the interview room has only one door that opens to the reception area."

In his ear, Turner said, "You're right. It has been running for about two minutes longer. It might be a different version of the documentary."

"Something doesn't feel right. I'm going in."

"Stay where you are. I need the entrance to the building guarded. I'm sending Julian in."

"Okay."

The doctor wasn't a Guardian, and therefore hadn't been assigned any guard duties. He was the more logical choice.

Magnus was still watching the feed and waiting for Julian to enter when he heard him in his earpiece.

"There is no one here! The fucking movie is playing and they are not here!"

Magnus leaped up and started running. "Where the fuck are they? Who is watching the door to the reception room?"

Behind him, he heard Arwel's boots pounding on the pavement.

"I'm activating the tracking," Turner said in his ear.

Inside, all mayhem broke loose, with Guardians piling into the waiting room, and the receptionist watching them with wide, terrified eyes.

"I got this," Arwel said and walked up to her.

Rushing into the interviewer's office, Magnus joined Julian and Turner in their search for a hidden exit.

"We are wasting time. Let's follow the trackers," Julian said. "It doesn't matter how they were taken. Only that we find them before he takes them beyond the trackers' range."

"I've already dispatched the Guardians stationed closest to the parking lot. The trackers are moving in four different directions."

"Fuck." Magnus kicked a chair, sending it toppling to the floor. "He was on to us the entire time."

"It would seem so." Turner removed a bunch of books off a shelf and peered inside the space he'd made. "I just hope he didn't find all of the trackers and that some are still on Ella and Vivian."

"Let's go, Turner," Julian insisted. "I know you want to find out how the bastard did it, but it's not important right now."

Ignoring Julian's suggestion, Turner kept moving books. "There is no point in us going after them until we know which direction is the right one."

Throwing his hands in the air, Julian headed for the door. "We are not going to find that out by staying in this room. I'm going to pick a direction and follow it."

"Don't be an idiot, Julian," Turner barked in a rare show of irritation. "We will get moving once it is clear which of the trackers are on Ella and Vivian. Guardians are already in pursuit and there is nothing more we can do at this point."

Groaning, Julian turned away from the door.

The damn movie was still playing in the background, and with the sound on, it was clear that it was on a loop. Except, Magnus wasn't sure he would've noticed that even if he'd been watching the feed and listening to the monotonous, droning narration.

It all sounded the same and was annoying the hell out of him, but he didn't want to waste time looking for the remote to shut it up while the Doomer was getting away with Ella and Vivian.

Magnus was losing his ever-loving shit.

Vivian had told him about putting a tracker in her underwear. If the bastard had stripped her naked, he was going to tear out the Doomer's throat with his bare fangs and watch him bleed out.

"I found it," Turner said.

Reaching into a gap he'd made between books, he pressed or pulled something. There was a subtle click of a mechanism engaging, and the bookcase started moving.

"That's how he got them out. We were watching a loop of a recording taken in the first minutes of the documentary playing, and none of us paid attention to the screen."

Magnus would have felt like a total idiot, but the fucking Doomer had outsmarted even Turner.

48

ELLA

The helicopter wasn't big, and aside from the pilot, there was only enough space for the three of them. Hopefully, that meant that its range wasn't long.

Without much preamble, Logan lifted Vivian into the chopper and then reached for Ella. There was nothing sexual in the way he handled her. Just a quick and efficient lift.

After he had them both seated inside, he got in and sat next to the pilot. Turning the chair around, he locked it in place and handed them each headphones. He then donned a pair himself. "You can talk now."

Whoop dee doo. Should she tell him how much she despised him?

Not a good idea to antagonize the enemy, especially if she wanted him to clarify some things.

As the chopper took off, Ella's stomach rose up into her throat. The feeling passed when it reached its cruising altitude.

"Can the pilot hear us?" Vivian asked.

Logan motioned for the guy to remove his headphones. "Now he can't. So what do you want to ask me?"

Before her mother had a chance to say anything, Ella blurted the question that had been troubling her for so long. "Did you compel me to feel attracted to you?"

He smirked. "It didn't require much effort. All I had to do was to eliminate your fear of me, and the rest was all you."

Did she believe him? Ella wasn't sure. "What about compelling me to ignore other guys?"

He chuckled. "You have a poor memory, my dear Ella. Remember when I told you that you'd be sorry if you let anyone else touch you?"

Crap, he had said that.

"What did you think I meant by that?"

"I thought it was an empty threat."

"It was a simple compulsion. Every time you tried to get close to another man, you would be assailed by guilt."

Wow, that explained so much.

"I also told you that we were meant for each other, and that no one could give you what I could, making it clear that I meant sexual fulfillment. If you tried to get intimate with someone, male or female, I'm sure that it wasn't very satisfying."

Ella felt tears of relief pooling in the corners of her eyes.

This was huge. If despite Logan's compulsion she'd managed a few moments of strong desire toward Julian, it meant that her attraction to him was so powerful that it had overridden the Doomer's command. It would've been off the charts without it. They were indeed each other's true-love mates, with everything that implied.

Logan reached to wipe her tears away. "I'm sorry. I know that you hate being manipulated like this."

It was the second or third time he'd apologized, but Ella doubted Logan felt any real remorse. He was just being polite.

"But you're guilty of the same, Ella. You were pretending to warm to me, so I wouldn't suspect anything. Before you came up with the college idea, and I realized that you were orchestrating a trap for me, I had to find a way to ensure that you would want to meet me face to face."

It was a poor excuse for what he had done, but she wasn't looking for a real apology from him. However, his misinterpretation of her tears of relief for tears of frustration had given her an opening for the most important request.

"Can you please remove the compulsion? I can't stand having my mind under your control. It's a horrible feeling."

"I'm sorry to disappoint you, my dear Ella." He shook his head.

Ella's heart sank.

"We were not meant for each other," he continued. "Not that you're lacking in any way. Despite the pink, messy hair, you're still a beautiful young girl, and I even find you surprisingly intriguing, but I like my women a little more seasoned." He glanced at Vivian. "And more voluptuous."

"Thanks," her mom said. "You're not my type either. I like my men honest and law-abiding."

Logan laughed. "Touché."

At first, Ella had panicked, thinking that he wasn't going to grant her request, but then she realized that this had been his way of releasing her from that particular compulsion. Except, there were two more parts to it that he'd conveniently forgotten to address.

"What about being sorry if I let anyone touch me, and the other thing about no other man being able to give me what you can?"

"Very good, Ella." He nodded his approval. "It's important to be precise with compulsion. I still don't think anyone can give you what I can, but since I'm not going to seduce you, you are free to fornicate with whomever you please."

"Do you really need to be so rude?" Vivian asked. "What you are putting us through isn't bad enough?"

"My apologies." He bowed his head. "English is not my native tongue, and sometimes my choice of words could be better."

He was so full of shit. Logan was very eloquent, and if Ella didn't know who he was and where he came from, she would've never suspected he wasn't a native speaker.

"Let me rephrase." He looked her straight in the eyes. "Ella, you are free to feel anything you want toward whomever you choose and enjoy it to your fullest capacity." He turned to Vivian. "Better?"

"Much. Thank you."

Ella wasn't sure. Had he really released her? She'd expected a major change, an unfurling of her metaphysical wings that would lift her up on clouds of desire, soaring toward Julian.

But none of that happened.

She still found Logan devastatingly handsome.

Except, when she imagined kissing him, nothing happened either. There was no tingling of excitement and no butterflies in her stomach. If anything, she felt slight nausea. Then she thought about kissing Julian, and everything inside her ignited as if she'd thrown a match into a puddle of gasoline.

It worked! It freaking worked! She was free!

Except, she wasn't.

As the chopper started its descent, she looked out the window and all of her excitement vanished. They were landing in an airport.

Which meant that their final destination could be as far as the Doomers' island, and there was no way the trackers would work once they reached jet plane altitude.

We are royally screwed.

The irony was that Ella recognized the place. It was the same private airport they'd arrived in.

49

TURNER

*J*ulian's pacing and seething were getting on Turner's nerves, and if that wasn't enough of a distraction, the waves of anxious energy he and Magnus were emitting definitely was.

"Magnus, can you take Julian out of here? I need to concentrate."

Julian plopped into a chair. "I'm not moving from here until you're ready to go after them."

For the past ten minutes, Turner had been monitoring the four different tracker groupings as they spread out and away from the city in four different directions. He was trying to figure out which of them was the odd one out. They were all moving very fast. Using the freeways, the vehicles were all exceeding the speed limit by at least thirty percent.

At some point, they would have the police stop them, which would slow them down only for as long as it took to thrall the officer and keep going, but in the meantime, they were making sure that those chasing them couldn't close the gap.

The Doomers had at least half an hour head start and were pushing the pedal to the metal.

One grouping was moving slightly faster than the others, though, and he was willing to bet this was the escape vehicle. It was either a fast sports car or maybe even a chopper. His bet was on a helicopter. It seemed to be following the freeway, but that along with the moderate speed was most likely done to make it inconspicuous.

Lokan was a smart and careful bastard, and he wasn't taking any chances.

"It's this one." He pointed at the screen. "And I think I know where it's heading."

As Magnus and Julian got behind him, Turner zoomed out and pointed at the airport they'd arrived at. "That's where he's heading. Which means that he has a plane waiting for him and he's going to take off as soon as they get there."

532

Julian groaned. "We are never going to make it on time."

"Not necessarily." Turner pulled out his phone. "As I've mentioned before, I have many friends in Washington who owe me favors."

"Cops can't stop a helicopter," Magnus said. "What are you going to do, call the air force base and have them send fighter jets after him?"

Turner shook his head and waited for his friend to pick up.

"Hello?"

"Hi, Fred. It's Turner. I need a favor."

50

ELLA

Logan's private jet was very similar to the one they'd arrived on. Apparently, Navuh's son didn't enjoy the kind of luxury Gorchenco did. Was there more money in selling weapons than using them?

It seemed so.

Still, Gorchenco's legitimate business was an executive plane service, and he used the fleet's jets for his own needs.

"Are you comfortable?" Logan asked as they were seated with the safety belts on.

As usual, Ella's tongue ran faster than her brain. "What if we are not?"

He smiled. "It doesn't matter. Unless there is an emergency, and I mean the plane is on fire, don't move. If you need to use the bathroom, let my men know and they will call me. Understood?"

The two Doomers guarding them wore twin impassive expressions as they nodded their understanding, even though Logan hadn't been talking to them.

Experimentally, Ella tried to lift her hand, but the compulsion held her immobilized. "It's not comfortable to sit like that. Can you modify your command and just tell us not to get out of our seats?"

"I can do that." He smiled indulgently. "I want you to be as comfortable as possible. Don't get out of your seats. Otherwise, you are allowed to move."

"Thank you. Where are you taking us? Are we going to your homeland?"

Logan liked to talk about his brilliant plans. Maybe if she managed to engage him in a conversation, she could buy them some time.

"No, not right away. For now, I just want to get out of this country and away from your government's reach."

"What if they send fighter jets after you?"

He smirked. "You are so naive, Ella. That's not how governments work. It's not like one big machine with all the cogs working in sync. Each department is its own machine, and they don't cooperate with each other unless they are forced to by the higher-ups, and then it takes a lot of red tape. The organization in charge of paranormal abilities research is highly classified and not rich in resources. They are not going to involve other agencies in the chase."

"How do you know so much?"

"I've been hanging around Washington for a long time. I can tell you so many stories, but it will have to wait for after takeoff. We are in a bit of a rush." He winked and ducked into the cockpit, leaving them in the company of the two somber Doomers.

Ella wondered if he was going to pilot the plane himself.

Probably not.

But who knew? It didn't look like he had limitless resources at his disposal. Not that it mattered one way or another. Hopefully, he wasn't going to take off anytime soon, and the Guardians were going to catch up to them.

Except, her hopes took a nosedive when the dual jet engines roared to life. She tried to remember how long it had taken the clan's jet to warm up its engines, but she hadn't been paying attention. Bhathian had explained something about the pilot going through a pre-flight checklist, but she had no idea how long that took.

Next to her, Vivian sniffled. "You were right. We are so screwed."

Reaching over the armrests, Ella took her mother's hand and gave it a squeeze. "At least we are together."

Now that it seemed like they were not getting rescued, Ella was even more afraid to open a channel to her mother. She would have to be extra careful not to leave even the tiniest opening for Logan to dive inside her head, and she would have to keep doing that indefinitely.

Could she even maintain her reinforced shields for so long?

"Parker is going to be all alone." Tears started flowing down her mother's cheeks. "I was afraid to move forward because I didn't want to leave him. And you. You might think that you're all grown up, but you still need me."

"Of course, I need you. And I always will."

Vivian nodded. "I wish I could be as brave as you."

Fighting her own tears, Ella snorted. "I'm not brave. I'm terrified. I'm just good at fronting confidence I don't have."

Was she ever going to have the wonderful future she'd imagined with Julian? Was she ever going to experience the passion that now flowed freely from her and yearned for him?

Fate couldn't be so cruel, dangling the best life had to offer in front of her nose and then yanking it out of her reach.

"You know what I think?"

Vivian wiped her eyes with her sleeve. "What?"

"I think that Loki is real and that he is the one in charge, playing tricks on us mortals. Do you think I should pray to him? Or maybe I should flip him the finger? What would make him stop toying with us like this?"

That got a sad smile out of her mother. "Praying is a safer bet. But since we don't know who's in charge, let's just address it to whoever is listening."

"Good plan."

Ella glanced at the two Doomers, but they were acting as if they were deaf and mute. If she didn't know better, she would've suspected Logan of compelling their silence as well. But according to Dalhu, he couldn't compel other immortals.

She really hoped Dalhu was right about that. If he wasn't, she and her mother were doomed for sure.

As the plane started moving, Ella squeezed her mother's hand harder and fought to keep her tears from spilling. But as it slowed down and then stopped, it wasn't in preparation for takeoff because the engines didn't rev up. Instead, they revved down, and a moment later Logan stepped out of the cockpit.

"There is a slight delay. A foreign dignitary's jet is about to land, and there has been a terror attack warning. No one is allowed to take off or land until he's out of the airport."

It was Turner's doing. She was sure of that.

How the hell had he pulled off shutting down the entire airport?

Glancing at her mother, Ella saw the same hope she felt reflected in Vivian's eyes.

51

TURNER

With Magnus driving like a maniac, Turner had to remind himself that he was an immortal now, and that a car accident was not going to kill him. But it was damn hard to concentrate on making phone calls when the car was taking such sharp turns and tilting this way and that. He was clutching the phone so hard the thing was about to break even though it was clan issue and had been built with immortals in mind.

"Charlie, what do you have for me?"

He had one man at the airport, and that was the pilot. Luckily, Charlie had decided to sleep on the plane. Regrettably, he was not a Guardian, but a civilian pilot.

Except, that was what he had to work with and it was better than nothing.

"I found the Doomer's jet. After the shutdown order your guy issued, they opened the door, and I saw Lokan leave the plane and head inside the terminal. He left Vivian and Ella inside the cabin, guarded by two men. There is also the pilot, who we have to assume is a Doomer as well. Other than that I didn't see anyone else. I think that's all he has with him."

"He has other men driving away from the city with the trackers he removed from Ella and Vivian. He might have compelled humans to do this for him, but we can't assume that. Stay at a safe distance and let me know the moment anything changes. The team that was following the right tracker should be there any moment. We are about fifteen minutes behind them."

"Got it."

Frank was preparing a hangar for their use, and he was supposed to supply them with airport security uniforms and vehicles. It was a lot to ask on such short notice, but Turner had served with Frank in Special Ops, and he knew that the guy could pull it off.

"How much longer?" Julian asked for the hundredth time.

"Five minutes or less," Magnus bit out.

Turner's phone rang again. This time it was Frank with the same question. "How much longer do you need? I'm going to eat shit for this."

"You're not. If anyone asks, direct them to me. No one wants an international incident because we allowed a foreign dignitary's wife and daughter to get kidnapped. For obvious reasons, the husband wants to keep it quiet, but if we fail to retrieve them, he's going to raise hell."

Fortunately, it wasn't the first time he'd been charged with taking care of a diplomatic mess like that, and his reputation as a private operator who dealt with such situations was well known. The story he'd told Frank was believable enough, and if his friend got in trouble for that, Turner had other friends in high places who could clear this for him.

The downside was that he would be cashing in a lot of owed favors, which meant he would have to work hard to earn more.

"You didn't answer how much longer you need me to keep the place on lockdown," Frank said.

"Give me an hour. But don't do anything until you hear from me."

"Roger that."

"We are turning into the airport right now. Do you have the airport security vehicles I asked for ready?"

"They are waiting for you by the storage hangar. Do you know where that is?"

"I do."

"Use entrance C. The guards are expecting a taxi with a bald guy sitting up front."

"I had a hair transplant."

"No kidding? I need to call them with the update."

"There are three other vehicles following behind me, and later on I expect three more. The drivers all have the code you gave me."

"I know. I was just kidding about the bald head."

"Thanks, Frank."

"Yeah, yeah. You owe me."

"I know."

Disconnecting the call, he pointed. "Turn here and then take a left."

"I can see the signs," Magnus said.

Turner tapped his earpiece. "When you reach the airport, follow the signs to entrance C." He waited for the other drivers to acknowledge the instructions. When they were done, he asked, "What's your ETA?"

52

ELLA

Logan returned to the plane looking pissed as hell and barking orders at his men. "Airport security is looking for terrorists, and they plan on boarding every aircraft on the field. Try to look more friendly and less menacing."

Confused, the two Doomers looked at him as if he asked them to grow horns. Nevertheless, each nodded in turn and offered a yes sir.

Shaking his head, Logan waved a dismissive hand. "If anyone asks, you are my bodyguards. That will fit your expressions."

He turned to Ella. "You will say that you're my fiancée and use your fake name. I have your passports here. Vivian, you are Victoria MacBain, Kelly's mother. You will tell whoever asks that you are coming with us to meet my family in the Maldives. Understood?"

Ella nodded. "What if they ask where we met?"

It wasn't that she expected anyone to do that. Most likely the terror threat had been fabricated by Turner, and he and the Guardians were impersonating airport security personnel. But now that her mood was up, she felt like messing with Logan.

He smirked. "You can tell them that we met on the beach in San Diego, and that I swept you off your feet. You just couldn't resist my charm and good looks. You agreed to marry me on our third date. I took you with me to Washington because I had business to conduct here, and I invited your mother as a chaperone." He winked. "I'm old-fashioned and come from a traditional family who doesn't believe in premarital sex."

"Good story."

He looked smug as he took his seat across from them. "I know."

An exceptional liar, Logan was good at coming up with plausible stories. The one he invented about his whirlwind courtship would explain why she knew next to nothing about him.

Why had he bothered with it, though? If the airport security people were human, he could just compel them to walk away and say that they'd checked the plane and found nothing suspicious.

Maybe not everyone was susceptible to compulsion?

Just as not all humans could be hypnotized or thralled, some must be immune to compulsion too. Logan couldn't take the risk that he might fail to control one or more of the security people.

Therefore, he had to invent a convincing story and compel those he knew were susceptible to repeat it.

He thought he had it covered.

Ella couldn't wait to see that smug expression of his melt away when he realized who he was dealing with, and how completely wrong he'd been about the people aiding her. He thought he was so smart figuring out that the government had her. It would be one hell of a blow to his ego when he learned his mistake.

Except, that would be the least of his concerns. Logan was about to get taken, and he was never going to be free again.

Crap, as much as she resented him for kidnapping her and her mother, the thought of him losing his freedom and living the rest of his immortal life in captivity bothered her.

It shouldn't have, but it did.

She wondered when exactly he was going to realize what was really going on. Was it going to happen as soon as the Guardians climbed the stairs?

Julian had told her about the tingling alarm all immortal males were equipped with to detect the presence of unfamiliar males of their kind, but she didn't know how close they needed to be to each other for it to activate.

What would Logan do when his alarm went off?

Would he try to slam the plane's door shut and take off?

Or, would he grab her and put a knife at her throat, threatening to kill her if the Guardians didn't back off?

Damn, if she could only move, she could duck for cover as soon as it started, but she was literally a sitting duck. Heck, he could command her to put a knife to her own throat, or to her mother's.

53

TURNER

"Don't do this to me, Turner. I have to come with you," Julian said while buttoning up the uniform's shirt.

"You need to tuck your hair under the hat. Airport security personnel don't look like hippies."

To say that Julian didn't like getting assigned to backup was an understatement. But he was a civilian, and Turner needed to keep his mate's son safe. Besides, the kid was going to understand why Turner had to go in alone once he explained the plan to everyone.

Including Julian and Magnus, Turner had twenty Guardians with him inside the warehouse, all of them busy getting into the uniforms Fred had kindly provided for them. The others were still chasing after the decoy trackers. Those Doomers had to be captured as well. And if the drivers were compelled humans, they would have to be brought back, and Turner would have no choice but to ask Parker to release them from the compulsion.

Twenty Guardians made up a formidable force, unfortunately though, useless for what he needed them to do.

"There is a good reason for why you're coming in the second vehicle, and Magnus is going to be there with you. I'm the only one who does not trigger the immortal alarm, and that's why I have to get inside that plane by myself. I can't even have the humans accompany me because they are too vulnerable to both thralling and compulsion. They are going to stay in the Jeep."

Julian shook his head. "You can't take on three Doomers all by yourself and at the same time ensure that Ella and Vivian don't get hurt. Worse, he can use them as hostages and take off."

"Don't worry. I have it covered."

Turner hated going in with a half-assed plan that he'd hatched on the way, but it was the best he could do.

Turning around, he clapped his hands. "Okay, people, gather around."

When he had their attention, he signaled for Arwel to cast a shroud around the group. Per his request, Frank had ordered all the employees out of the warehouse, but Turner preferred to play it safe.

"Here is how we are going to do this. We have five vehicles. I'm taking the bulletproof one, and the rest of you will have to squeeze into the remaining four."

He pulled out his iPad and showed them an aerial picture of the airport with all the grounded planes waiting for takeoff.

"This is Lokan's plane." He pointed. "And those are ours." He pointed at the two clan jets. "We don't start with him. We start with those closest to the terminal. You go in, ask the pilot, crew, and passengers to come down two at the time, check their passports, pretend to double check with headquarters, and then let them back up and ask for the next two to come down. That's what Lokan is going to observe and that's what he's going to expect."

He glanced at Julian before continuing. "When I go up, I'll ask the pilot and Lokan to come down first, check their papers and then let them back up."

"He's going to try to compel you," Magnus said.

"I was immune as a human, and there are more like me out there. He would assume I'm one of the anomalies."

"I hope he doesn't do something stupid once he realizes that you are immune."

"He's not. After I'm done with him and the pilot, I'm going to do the same with the two Doomers, and lastly with Ella and Vivian."

Understanding dawning, Julian nodded in agreement. "He will not be alarmed because he is going to expect them to get the same treatment."

"Precisely. Except, I'm going to pretend there is a problem with their papers and ask them to come with me."

"He's not going to allow it," Magnus said.

"Not much he can do other than attacking me, but it's not going to get to that point. By the time Ella and Vivian are inside the bulletproof vehicle with the doors closed, the rest of you will have enough time to sneak into position. I'm going to go back up to explain the situation with the papers and reassure them that it's only a formality. That will solve two problems. He and his men will have no time to pull out weapons, and since I'm going to stand in the doorway, I will block the view. When their immortal alarm goes off, it's going to be too late for them to do anything but surrender."

"That's not true," Julian said. "They could kill you before anyone else makes it up there."

Smirking, Turner pulled out the gun from its holster. "I'm armed, and they are not. That gives me all the advantage I need."

54

JULIAN

As Julian watched Turner climb up the stairs to the Doomers' plane, Magnus shook his head. "I don't like him going in alone. He is not a trained Guardian. But it's not as if we have any other choice."

"I trust Turner. He's the best man for the job." Julian meant every word.

Not only that, he was infinitely thankful for Turner and the huge ego that was allowing him to take on Navuh's son with his typical fearlessness and nerves of steel. No one could've pulled off this job better than Turner. Lokan wasn't going to suspect a damn thing because Turner didn't emit any scents that would've given anyone else away.

The Doomer might wonder about the strange guy he was going to mistake for a human, but he would probably assume that he was dealing with a sociopath.

They were all wearing earpieces, but, unfortunately, not the sophisticated ones that William had equipped them with. Impersonating airport security meant using their equipment, and they had those clunky old things that were at least a decade-old technology.

Still, the earpiece was functioning just fine, and they could hear Turner talking to the Doomer.

"Good afternoon, ladies and gentlemen. I apologize for the delay, but a terror threat has been made, and we take those very seriously, even though this one is probably a hoax. Are you the owner of this plane, sir?"

"Yes."

"I need you and the pilot to come down with me. And bring your passports with you. If you are not American citizens, please bring your visas as well. The rest of you please remain seated until I come back for you."

"I'm sure it is not necessary. Our papers are all in order."

That was no doubt Lokan's attempt at compelling Turner to leave.

"I'm sure they are. But I have my orders, sir. This is the standard procedure in case of a terrorist threat. Please follow me down so I can run your documents through the scanner and verify your identity."

After watching them perform the same procedure with the other planes, Lokan didn't press the issue and did as Turner asked.

Turner made a big deal out of examining the paperwork, went inside the vehicle and checked things on the attached laptop, then came out and handed the documents back.

"Everything seems fine. Thank you for your cooperation, gentlemen."

He escorted them up, and then came down with the two Doomers, repeating the same procedure.

Hopefully, Ella and Vivian were playing it cool and not doing anything to give him away. Julian trusted Ella's acting ability, but he wasn't sure about Vivian.

Waiting for the two of them to come down was nerve-wracking.

Like the pro that he was, Turner didn't act hurried, taking his time with the two Doomers as if there was no urgency, his expression as stoic as usual and his tone bored and even. An Oscar-worthy performance.

"Balls of titanium," Magnus murmured.

As soon as he escorted the two back up, the four airport security vehicles started moving toward Lokan's jet.

"Ladies, please follow me down," Turner said.

Apparently, nothing happened because he said, "Is there a problem?"

"No, not a problem," Lokan said. "My fiancée is just a little timid. It's okay, darling. You can go with the officer. He's only going to check your papers. You too, Mom."

Magnus cursed under his breath, probably because of the mom address, but Julian let out a relieved breath. Lokan had just removed his compulsion, allowing Ella and Vivian to move.

Once on the ground, Turner repeated the same act, taking the paperwork into the Jeep and pretending to check it on his laptop. A moment later he came out.

"I'm afraid there was a problem with your papers. You need to come with me." He opened the Jeep's back door and helped Vivian in and then Ella.

Lokan appeared at the top of the stairs. "What seems to be the problem, officer?"

"Their passports don't check out. I'm sure it's just a technicality. Please step inside the plane, sir."

Ignoring Turner's order, Lokan started down.

Several things happened at once.

The Jeep sped away leaving Turner to face the Doomer alone, Turner whipped out his gun and pointed it at Lokan's head, the laser beam point blank between his eyes, and all four vehicles screeched to a stop with Guardians piling out.

"Game over, Lokan. You don't want me to splatter your brains all over your nice jet. I have perfect aim."

The Doomer leaped back.

His reflexes were fast, but not faster than a bullet. Turner nailed him in the leg, and then immediately shot the other, sending Lokan toppling down the stairs.

55

ELLA

Turner was putting on the act of a lifetime. Lucky for Ella and Vivian their nervousness could be attributed to other causes. Like the compulsion not to say anything about being taken against their will or disclose any information that could be harmful to Lokan in any way.

If asked about him, Ella had been instructed to say that he was a wonderful fiancé and that she was madly in love with him.

"Ladies, please follow me down." Turner motioned for them to get up.

Except, Lokan had forgotten to remove the compulsion not to move from their seats.

Turner arched a brow. "Is there a problem?"

"No, not a problem," Lokan said. "My fiancée is just a little timid. It's okay, darling. You can go with the officer. He's only going to check your papers. You too, Mom."

If looks could kill, Lokan would be dead now.

Ella's legs shook as she followed Turner down, and she felt faint as she stood by the Jeep and waited for the pretend inspection of their passports, which Lokan had handed to him.

She'd thought that the Doomer who'd taken their stuff had been driving around town with the duffel bag and leading the Guardians on a fake trail, but apparently, he'd pulled out their passports and driver licenses first and had given them to one of Lokan's bodyguards.

"I'm afraid there was a problem with your papers. You need to come with me." Turner opened the Jeep's back door and taking her mother's elbow, helped her to get inside. Ella was next.

Exchanging glances with her mother, she gave her a discreet thumbs up.

They were free.

"What seems to be the problem, officer?" Lokan asked and started getting out.

Turner shut the door behind them and blocked Ella's view of Lokan with his back. "Their passports don't check out. I'm sure it's just a technicality. Please step inside the plane, sir."

She didn't hear the answer, because the jeep's driver peeled out and sped away.

He and the other officer sitting in the back weren't Guardians. She had a feeling that they were ordinary humans. "Where are you taking us?"

"To the warehouse. Turner said to keep you there until he comes for you."

The guy sitting next to them in the back smiled reassuringly. "Everything is going to be okay, ma'am. The scumbag who was trying to kidnap you is going to be apprehended, and after you give a statement, you'll be safely returned to your father." He looked at Vivian. "Your husband must be anxious to hear from you. Would you like to call him?" He handed her his cellphone.

What kind of a story had Turner told the human authorities?

Vivian gave the phone back. "Maybe in a little while, after my heart stops racing. I'm too shaken up to talk."

"Naturally. What did the scum do to you?" He looked at Vivian and then at Ella.

Ella shook her head. "I'd rather not talk about it." All that would come out of her mouth would be that Lokan was a wonderful fiancé and that she was madly in love with him.

The guy looked disappointed, but he nodded. "I understand."

Once they reached the warehouse, the officers escorted them inside and stayed to watch over them.

Regular conversation was not possible, but with Lokan neutralized, Ella could open a channel to her mother.

I hope everyone is okay.

Her mother patted her knee. *I'm sure they are. Thirty Guardians, one Turner, and one Julian can handle three Doomers no matter how powerful.*

Stupidly, Ella hoped they didn't hurt Lokan too badly either. He wasn't a good guy, but he wasn't as bad as she initially believed him to be.

She'd seen real evil, and it had been all human. Romeo, Stefano, the two druggies in the hotel that Julian was turning into a halfway house, and all of those men who'd violated and abused the girls in the sanctuary. Those people had no redeeming qualities, or rather nothing that could redeem the evil they'd perpetrated.

Gorchenco and Lokan were different than that scum. They weren't good people, but they both had redeeming qualities. Or at least she believed they had.

Less than fifteen minutes later, Turner entered the warehouse alone.

"Thank you for your help, gentleman," he addressed the officers. "My associate is waiting for you outside for debriefing."

Which probably meant thralling. After their talk with the *associate*, they were not going to remember any details from the rescue operation.

"Glad to be of assistance. Is the airport cleared for takeoffs and landings?"

"Yes, it is."

When the men left, Turner lifted his hand to stop Ella and Vivian's barrage of questions. "No one got hurt, except for Lokan and his men, but nothing fatal. Their injuries are going to heal in no time."

"Thank God. Or rather, thank Turner." Ella ran up to him and wrapped her arms around his neck. "Thank you." She kissed his cheek. "Thank you so much. You were amazing. You should get an Oscar for that performance, and I mean it. Totally believable."

"Let the man be." Her mother tapped her shoulder. "You're smothering him."

"Sorry." Ella let go, realizing too late that Turner had been like a stiff broom in her arms, waiting for her assault to be over.

She needed to remember that her future father-in-law was not a hugger.

56

JULIAN

*J*ulian couldn't wait to hold Ella in his arms, but there was a lot of cleanup work to do.

His job was to patch up Lokan and the other two Doomers, while the Guardians conducted *interviews* with everyone on the field, erasing memories and planting a story that Turner had prepared.

Reluctantly, Julian headed toward the bigger of the two clan's jets, where the injured Doomers had been stowed.

There was only one Guardian with them, but it seemed the three were neutralized.

"I already knocked them out with sedative shots," Liam said.

"If he were awake I would have knocked him out with a punch to his smug face." Even injured and knocked out, that expression was still there. "I'm going to wash my hands."

After scrubbing up the best he could in the small bathroom, Julian wiped his hands with a paper towel because that was all there was.

Immortal bodies would not get infected, but washing before touching a wound was so ingrained in him that he hadn't stopped to think that he didn't need to scrub so hard.

When he came out, he looked for the med kit, finding it in one of the overhead compartments. "Did he ask any questions before you put him to sleep?"

"I knocked him out before he regained consciousness after hitting his head falling down the jet's stairs."

"That's a shame." Julian opened the kit and pulled out a pair of scissors. "I would've paid to see the expression on his face." He started cutting the pants off to expose the wound.

Seeing the defeat in the Doomer's eyes would have been so satisfying.

He wasn't a vindictive kind of guy, but that scumbag had almost gotten away with stealing Ella, the most important person in Julian's life, and that was unforgivable.

After tearing the rest of that pant leg off, Julian went to work on the other one.

The wounds weren't serious. Apparently, in addition to all his other talents, Turner was also an excellent sharpshooter. Somehow he managed not to hit any major artery or shatter a bone. Was it a fluke? Or had he been careful not to damage the important Doomer?

They needed to interrogate the son of a bitch, but that didn't mean that he had to be delivered in pristine condition. The types of injuries he'd sustained were going to heal by the time they returned to Los Angeles.

"Was he disbelieving, raging, anything?"

Liam shook his head. "Sorry to disappoint you, mate, but the dude was as cool as a cucumber. The only emotions I picked up from him were sadness and resignation. He probably expects us to kill him or torture him."

"The second one is going to happen for sure. Kian wants to get information out of him, and he's not going to volunteer it."

"Who knows?" Liam shrugged. "I wouldn't be surprised if he has daddy issues. Can you imagine being Navuh's son?"

"Could be worse. The bastard is not a loving father, that's for sure, but he puts his sons in positions of power. That's a better fate than that of the other Doomers."

After digging out the first bullet, Julian sutured the wound closed and bandaged the leg.

"We don't know that. Sometimes it's better to be an invisible speck than a diamond under the microscope of evil."

Shaking his head, Julian started on the other leg. "Where did you hear that saying?"

"I made it up."

Ignoring his hatred for the Doomer and treating him as he would any other patient, Julian did a good job. That was what decent doctors did. He could always beat Lokan up later when they got home.

The guy wasn't going anywhere.

Once Julian was done with the other two Doomers as well, he went to the bathroom and washed his hands again.

"I'm heading out. Are you okay here by yourself with the three of them?"

Liam smiled and lifted a case full of syringes. "No one wakes up without me allowing it."

"I'll see you back in the village."

"Say hello to Ella and Vivian for me and tell them welcome back."

"I will."

Now that he was done with his duties, Julian was going to take Ella into his arms and never let her go.

Turner had said that he was going to keep her and Vivian in the warehouse until the cleanup was done. That was about a mile and a half away, and the vehicles had been returned already, which meant that Julian was going on a run.

57

ELLA

When Turner left Ella and Vivian alone in the warehouse, it was somewhat anticlimactic, especially after the movie Ella had created in her mind.

In that scene, Julian was running up to her in slow motion like the hero of a romantic movie, sweeping her into his arms and swinging her around.

In real life, she was sitting on a dusty crate beside her mother, both of them waiting for their men to be done.

Julian had been tasked with tending to the wounded Doomers, while Magnus and other Guardians were busy thralling memories out of the minds of humans.

Still, it was so much better than the alternative.

"What do you think they are going to do with Lokan's jet?" Vivian asked. "They can't just leave it like that. Someone has to take it away."

"I don't know, but I'm sure Turner has a plan. He thinks of everything."

"I wonder what Navuh will think? Is he going to worry about his son? Does he care about him?"

"What I wonder about is whether Turner is going to make it look like Lokan had deserted."

Vivian chuckled. "I'm glad that it's no longer our concern. We did our parts and are now free to live our lives. The only thorn in that beautiful future is Gorchenco."

It wasn't the only one. Her mother still had to transition without incident, and so did Ella.

As she thought about Julian ushering her on that journey, a flutter of excitement started in her belly. There was no more reason for waiting. No more worrying about Lokan, and no more compulsion preventing her desire for Julian from manifesting in its full intensity. Ella wanted him with every fiber of her body and soul.

Was he in for a big surprise.

As the warehouse doors screeched and started to open, the butterflies in Ella's stomach took flight, their wings flapping in a mad frenzy. And when Julian entered and started running toward her, Ella jumped off the crate and ran into his waiting arms.

It was just as she'd imagined.

With a face-splitting grin, his arms closed around her, and he swung her up and around.

"Ella," he whispered her name like a prayer. "My sweet, beautiful Ella."

Despite her mother watching, Ella tightened her arms around Julian's neck and pulled his head down for a kiss.

He groaned as she licked inside his mouth, finding his tongue and caressing it with hers. In no time, she felt his fangs grow longer, and knowing what it did to him, she licked around one and then the other.

They were so absorbed in the kiss that they didn't notice Magnus come in until he cleared his throat. "I hate to interrupt the reunion, but we need to return the uniforms and clear the premises."

As he spoke, more Guardians entered the warehouse, all wearing airport security uniforms.

"Later," Julian whispered in her ear as he put her down.

"You bet," she whispered back.

Climbing to stand on the crate, Vivian clapped her hands to get everyone's attention. "Thank you all for coming to our rescue, and I think Turner deserves a big round of applause for orchestrating yet another flawless mission."

Without hesitation, everyone clapped, making Turner visibly uncomfortable. His expression didn't change much, the only thing giving him away was a slight thinning of his lips.

"That's not necessary, people. I was just doing my job. But thank you. Go change out of the uniforms so we can all get out of here."

"Shouldn't we give them some privacy?" Vivian asked.

Magnus kissed her cheek. "It doesn't bother them, love. But if you're uncomfortable, I can take you to the plane."

Her mother grimaced. "I don't want to be alone with the Doomers."

Magnus tightened his arm around her and kissed the top of her head. "You won't be. They were taken to the big jet, and you're going in the small one. Besides, they are all sedated."

Julian growled. "Tell me what they did to you."

Crap. He'd interpreted her mother's grimace to mean that they'd been mistreated.

"Nothing. Logan is a wonderful fiancé and I'm madly in love with him." Ella slapped a hand over her mouth and shook her head.

Julian's eyes were blazing as he asked, "Did he compel you to say that?"

She nodded.

He turned to Magnus. "We need to call Parker."

Magnus looked at Vivian. "Did Lokan compel you too?"

"Yes. What Ella said is the only thing I can say about him."

Pulling out his phone, Magnus made the call. "Parker. Your mother and sister are safe, but we need your help to override the Doomer's compulsion again. He ordered Ella and Vivian to say only nice things about him. I'm putting you on speakerphone."

Ella shook her head. "I don't think hearing his voice alone will work, but let's give it a try."

Over the speaker, Parker commanded, "Ella, say something nasty about Lokan."

"Lokan is a wonderful…crap. It didn't work."

Turner handed Magnus his tablet. "Try putting him on a video chat."

"Give me a moment," Parker said. "I'm going to my computer. You'll be able to see me better."

When he was ready, Magnus handed Ella the tablet. "Good luck."

On the screen, Parker smirked at her. "I told you that you should've taken me. I bet you're sorry now."

"Terribly. Get on with it, Parker. I hate having no control over my mouth."

"You never do."

"Parker!"

"Fine. Ella, tell me something nasty about Lokan."

"He's a liar." Ella jumped up and down. "It worked! Parker, you are a lifesaver. I love you. I'm going to give the tablet to Mom now. You need to tell her to do the same thing."

When Parker was done with Vivian, she had a few more choice words to say about the Doomer.

Taking Ella's hand, Julian turned her toward him. "I'm surprised that all you have to say about him is that he's a liar."

"A liar, a manipulator, a kidnapper, and probably many other things. But other than compelling us to say nice things about him and not to talk or to move, he treated us with respect." She looked at Vivian. "Right, Mom?"

Her mother waved a dismissive hand. "He was manipulating us, that's all. It was all fake. I'm sure all of his lofty promises were lies."

"What did he promise you?" Julian asked.

"Later." Turner clapped his back. "We will go through a full debriefing on the plane home. Right now I want you to change out of the uniform and then escort Ella to the smaller jet." He looked at Magnus. "You too."

"What about our things?" Ella asked. "We have stuff in the hotel."

"Kri is on her way with your things. She packed up for everyone who's going home today."

"That's good. I would like to change out of this freaking bikini."

Julian frowned. "What bikini?"

"I'll tell you on the plane."

58

JULIAN

"There goes our romantic weekend in Washington," Ella said as they entered the smaller of the two clan jets.

"I'm just thankful that everything ended well and that none of ours got hurt." Julian motioned for Ella to take the window seat and then sat next to her. "So far."

She frowned. "What do you mean, so far? Isn't it all over?"

"Did you forget about the Doomers with the trackers? The idiots are still driving away like maniacs. We have Guardians chasing them."

"How many were there?"

"Three cars are being followed. We don't know how many Doomers are in each."

"Don't worry about it," Magnus said as he helped Vivian into a seat. "That's child's play compared to what we pulled off here. We all owe Turner big time. If not for his friend grounding Lokan's plane, we would have never made it on time."

Following Magnus's statement, there was a long moment of silence, as each of them imagined the ramifications.

"I vote for throwing him a party," Ella said. "What does he like to eat?"

Julian scratched his head. "I will have to ask my mother. Which reminds me."

He pulled out his phone and texted Turner. *A friendly reminder. If you didn't do so already, please call Bridget asap. She's mad that you didn't yet.*

"Is he coming home with us?" Ella asked.

"He's waiting for the other Doomers to get captured and delivered to the larger jet. He will fly home with them."

"I see." She turned to the window.

Reaching for her hand, he clasped it between his. "Talk to me."

"I can't." She slanted her eyes toward Magnus. "When we get back home, there are a lot of things I need to tell you."

Julian tensed. "Good or bad?"

Her smile was sly. "Very good." She waggled her eyebrows.

And if that was not enough to grab his shaft's attention, her feminine scent suddenly intensified, causing it to punch out against his zipper in an instant.

"Whose home are we going back to?"

Ella cast a quick glance at Vivian, who smiled and nodded.

"Yours. I'm moving in with you. If you don't mind, that is."

"Mind? Are you nuts? I love you. I never want to be apart from you again."

He pulled out his phone, hesitated, leaned to kiss her cheek, then went back to the phone. "I'm texting Ray. He needs to find someone else to share a house with."

"He can move in with my former roommates," Magnus said. "They still didn't find anyone to take my place."

"I'll suggest it."

He tried to phrase the text to Ray as politely as possible, but it was still offensive. There was no nice way to boot someone out of his house within a five-hour notice.

I'm coming back with Ella, and she is moving in with me. I would very much appreciate it if you could find another place to stay before we arrive. Magnus suggests that you check with his former roommates.

A few minutes passed before Ray replied.

Congratulations. I'll find someplace to crash tonight, but I'll have to come back for my things tomorrow. Also, you'll need to help me move the piano.

Julian didn't want Ray to come back the next day. He wanted Ella all to himself.

How about you pack up your stuff and leave it by the front door. Once you find a place, I'll bring your things over, including the piano.

This time Ray responded right away. *I appreciate the free of charge moving service, but you have to be extra careful with my baby. She's irreplaceable.*

Julian smiled. *I'll wear white gloves and treat her as if she's made from eggshells.*

You'd better. One scratch on her and I'll make you pay.

The guy was such an asshole, but so was Julian for throwing him out. *I promise there will be no new scratches on her.* Before moving the fucking grand piano, he was going to take pictures from all angles and document all the existing scratches.

Pocketing the phone, he smiled at Ella. "All done."

"When is he moving out?"

"Before we get back."

Her eyes widened. "You told him to just pack up and leave tonight? That's terrible."

"Don't worry about him. Once he finds a permanent place, he's getting a free moving service from me, and that includes his piano."

"It's still rude. But I have an idea how you can make it up to him."

Julian arched a brow. He didn't owe Ray a thing, and if the situation were reversed, Ray would have had no qualms about booting Julian out.

"He invited my mother and me to a concert he's giving. How about you come with us? It will mean a lot to Ray."

"Of course, I'll come." Not as a gesture of goodwill toward his ex-roommate, but to make sure that the guy didn't flirt with Ella, which was most likely the reason he'd given her the invitations in the first place.

Ella smiled happily. "We can all go together. Magnus? Will you come too?"

"Sure. I like classical music."

Footsteps on the stairs announced someone coming up, and a moment later Kri appeared at the door with duffel bags slung over each shoulder and a suitcase in each hand. "Hello, everyone."

Magnus jumped up to take the luggage from her. "Why didn't you give me a shout? I could've carried all of this up."

She waved a dismissive hand. "I told you to stop treating me like a girl. I'm a Guardian, and a goddamned good one even if I'm relegated to the least exciting jobs. Like packing stuff." She grinned at Ella and then Vivian. "You can't imagine how glad I am to see you two. I had a few moments of panic there, and I didn't like it at all."

"Thank you for bringing our things," Ella said. "Are you coming with us?"

"I'm going on the other plane." She winked. "It's much more interesting over there. See you back at the village, people." She saluted them and turned around.

Magnus closed the door behind her and then knocked on the pilot's door. "Morris, we are ready to go."

They all buckled up, but it took another ten minutes or so until the plane started moving.

Ella looked up at the overhead compartment. "If I remember right, there is a blanket and a pillow up there."

"I'll get it for you." Julian released the buckle and got up. "Anyone else want a blanket?"

"Is there another one?" Vivian asked.

"There are plenty."

"Then sure." She cuddled closer to Magnus. "There is nothing I like better than snuggling with my guy."

"Same here," Ella murmured.

Magnus opened the fridge compartment and pulled out four bottles of Snake's Venom. "Champagne would have been better, but since this is the only alcohol here, we will have to make a toast with beer." He popped the caps off the bottles and handed them out.

"To mission accomplished and a long and happy future for us all." Magnus raised his bottle, clinked it with the other three, and then took a long swig.

"Amen," Vivian said and took a small sip. "God, this stuff is potent."

"Julian? Do you want to make a toast?" Ella asked.

He raised his bottle and clinked it with hers. "To us."

"To us," she repeated.

59

VIVIAN

"I'm going to carry Ella home," Julian whispered as the limo stopped at the village's underground parking.

Vivian looked at her daughter's peaceful sleeping face and smiled. Ella hadn't looked so relaxed since before her ordeal.

She'd fallen asleep on the plane, then had woken up when they'd landed, and fallen asleep again in the car. Julian had been holding her the entire time as if afraid to let go of her even for a moment.

Love was in the air, and it smelled fantastic.

Vivian patted his bicep and whispered, "When you wake up tomorrow, come by our house. We can have a late breakfast or early lunch together."

"Will do." Julian maneuvered himself and his precious cargo out of the car. "Good night."

"You too."

The chances of them actually showing up for breakfast or lunch were slim. Maybe they would come for dinner.

Listening to the conversation between Lokan and Ella during the helicopter ride had explained so much.

Ella's attraction to Julian had been suppressed by Lokan's compulsion, which had caused her to doubt their relationship.

Fated mates were supposed to crave each other with overwhelming intensity, and Vivian could attest to the veracity of that claim.

Her craving for Magnus had been so intense and so immediate that it had overpowered her feeling of anxiety and despair. In the midst of a crisis, with her daughter taken by traffickers and sold to a Russian mobster, she couldn't keep her hands off him.

It was still just as powerful, and tonight, for the first time since the very beginning of their relationship, she was going to enjoy him without any barriers between them.

It was going to be epic.

Magnus slung his duffle bag over his shoulder and reached for Vivian's suitcase which Okidu was holding on to. "Thank you for getting us home, Okidu."

The butler bowed. "It was my pleasure, master. But my service is not done. I will carry the luggage to your home."

"That won't be necessary." Magnus took the suitcase from his hand. "Good night, Okidu."

Looking offended, the butler bowed again. "Good night, master." He bowed to Vivian. "Good night, madam."

She still found it hard to believe that Okidu was a sophisticated robot. Maybe that's what he had been originally, but in her opinion, he had everyone fooled. At some point he had become a sentient being. After all, he was supposed to be ancient, like in tens of thousands of years old. The amount of information he'd accumulated over the years should have been enough to facilitate self-awareness.

But she wasn't a scientist, and her information came mainly from watching and reading science fiction. If the butler was sentient, William would have known that.

Outside the pavilion, they parted ways with Okidu, and Magnus transferred her suitcase to his other hand. "What's that sly smile about?" He wrapped his arm around her shoulders.

"You know what is happening tonight, right?"

He smirked. "I've been entertaining a few ideas. If you're not tired, that is. You didn't sleep on the plane."

"I wonder why?"

As soon as Ella and Julian had fallen asleep in each other's arms, Magnus and Vivian had started kissing and hadn't stopped until the young couple woke up.

"No regrets here."

"Nor here, and I'm not tired. Well, not too tired. But other than that, what else is happening tonight?"

"A foot massage?"

"Hmm, why not. I would love one. But aside from that too."

He shook his head. "Just tell me, or I'll keep guessing all the way home."

Should she?

Now she was considering surprising him. But was it too late to back off?

"I think I'll wait until we get home to tell you."

"Why is that?"

She looked at the heavy suitcase he was schlepping. "You might drop the luggage on your foot, and then I'll feel guilty for causing you injury."

"Easily solved." He stopped walking, put the suitcase down, and the duffel bag on top of it.

"Come here." He pulled her into his arms. "Now tell me what you're planning, or I'll have to kiss it out of you."

"That's not a threat, silly. But fine." She stretched on her toes and whispered in his ear. "Tonight, we are throwing away the condoms."

Magnus lifted his face to the sky. "Thank the merciful Fates."

Cupping his cheeks, she brought his face down and kissed his lips. "Let's go home, my love."

60

ELLA

Snuggled against Julian's chest, Ella was warm and cozy despite how chilly the village got at night. "What about our luggage?" she murmured into his neck.

"I got it."

Her eyes popped open. "You are carrying me and the luggage? Put me down!"

He nuzzled her cheek. "We are almost there. Besides, how else am I going to prove that I'm a worthy mate for you? Strong and capable?"

"I can think of a much more pleasant way you can prove it to me."

He looked puzzled. "Are you uncomfortable? Am I squeezing you too hard?"

She laughed. "No, silly. I'm very comfortable. I was just thinking how nice and warm I am in your arms, despite how cold it is here at night."

He climbed the stairs to the front porch and dropped her suitcase to open the door. "Is there something I'm supposed to say as I carry you over the threshold?"

"Welcome home?"

"That works. Welcome home, my love." He entered the dark house and continued straight to the bedroom. "Do you want to grab a shower? Or do you want to go straight to bed?"

"Shower first."

"I'll bring in the luggage."

Should she suggest that they shower together?

Until now they'd only kissed, except for that one time that Julian had gotten carried away, but that had been so brief, and she'd reacted so badly to it, that it didn't count.

Ella didn't know how to initiate, or how to tell him that she was ready. Heck, should she just tell him about the compulsion and be done with it?

Let him figure the rest out?

In any case, it was better that she shower alone. It would give her time to come up with a plan. Their first time together should be special. She didn't want to half-ass it.

Sexy lingerie would have been helpful, but she had none. The closest thing was the string bikini Lokan had forced her to put on, but nothing of his was going to taint her time with Julian.

As he returned with her suitcase, Julian laid it on top of the dresser. "I'll shower in Ray's room and then make us coffee. You said that there are things you need to tell me when we get home."

"Yeah." She'd forgotten about her promise.

So that's how this was going to happen.

She was going to tell Julian about the compulsion and its removal. Then she was going to tell him that the moment it had been lifted, her desire for him ignited like an inferno.

Or, she could hurry up with the shower, be done with it before he was back, and wait for him naked in bed.

That should do it.

Because frankly, she didn't want to talk. What she wanted was to join with the man she loved and become one in every possible way.

Which included a venom bite.

God, she didn't know if she craved it or feared it. A little bit of both, probably. Oh, heck, she was such a liar. She definitely craved it, and the little fear that came with it only added to the excitement.

So, she was a little weird that way. Or maybe not. Maybe it was natural for a Dormant to crave her immortal lover's bite.

Yeah, that totally made sense. Survival of the species and all that.

As she stepped under the spray, Ella chuckled to herself. She was nervous, which usually made her ramble on and on, and now she was doing it inside her own head.

Except, what reason did she have to be anxious?

She and Julian were in love, and they wanted each other passionately. These were just wedding-night type jitters.

She'd never had voluntary sex before.

Was she going to be any good at it?

Lockstep with her desire was fear, entwined together with performance anxiety. A combustible mixture, that was for sure.

61

JULIAN

*J*ulian moved with immortal speed as he set up the coffeemaker and then rushed into the shower. The plan was to be done before Ella finished her shower and wait for her in bed.

Something had changed after her second rescue. Ella seemed different. Perhaps the prospect of never seeing him again had been so traumatic that it had burned away the last vestiges of her previous ordeal?

Given her subtle clues and the not so subtle scent of her desire, he had a feeling she was ready to be his, but as he had promised, she was in the driver seat and he wasn't going to assume anything.

She'd had this done to her enough times.

The first time they made love, it would be entirely by her choice and without any pressure or even coaxing from him.

That didn't mean, though, that he couldn't tempt her, and waiting for her in bed with his naked torso on display was fair play. In case he'd misinterpreted, the boxer shorts had to stay on. Besides, he didn't want to appear presumptuous.

Ella might interpret it as him pressuring her into sex before she was absolutely sure she was ready.

Still slightly damp from his quick shower, Julian poured them both coffee and sped to the bedroom. The water was still running in the bathroom, so he had a few moments to prepare.

After putting down the mugs on the nightstands, he went into the closet and pulled on a pair of boxer shorts, then opened a new bottle of cologne and sprayed himself with it.

Hopping in bed, he sat propped against a pile of pillows, pulled the comforter over his lower half, and reached for the coffee mug. When Ella got out of the bathroom, she was going to find him sipping coffee in bed, looking as nonchalant as could be. Lucky for him, she wasn't an immortal, so she wouldn't smell the scent of his excitement and arousal.

Except, his pretend nonchalance was blown away as soon as Ella stepped out of the bathroom with nothing but a towel wrapped around her delectable body.

His fangs didn't elongate gradually, they just punched out over his lower lip.

Holding the towel clutched in her fist, she looked at him with hooded eyes, the scent of her arousal perfuming the air.

"Hi," she whispered.

"Hi to you too, gorgeous."

But even though his words came out sounding like a cross between a hiss and a growl, Ella didn't seem frightened. Just shy and hesitant.

Perhaps she needed a little encouragement?

"I wish I had X-ray vision. I can't wait to see your stunning body."

She chuckled. "You don't? With that glow, I was sure you could see right through this towel. But since you can't…" She let it drop.

"Dear sweet Fates." He hissed in a breath. "Gorgeous."

Her breasts were perfectly shaped, round and yet upturned, with small rosy nipples that were hardening right before his eyes. Her narrow waist flared into generous hips, not too large, just rounded and feminine, and her legs were long and shapely.

She was perfection, all creamy paleness and feminine softness, rendering him thunderstruck.

Blushing, she lifted her arms, but instead of shyly covering her breasts like he'd expected, she spread her palms over her belly. "I could lose a few pounds."

That was it, he couldn't stay in bed a second longer. Leaping out, Julian was in front of her before she had a chance to suck in a breath.

"You are perfect." He peeled her hands away from her beautiful belly. "I love it that you're soft all over."

She lifted her face to him and smiled. "I'm not perfect, but you are. You would make any mortal insecure with that six pack of yours and everything else." She waved a hand over his mostly bare body.

"To me, you are a goddess. Always and forever." He wrapped his arms around her and lifted her to him. "Can I take you to bed?"

Ella lifted her hands and threaded her finger into his hair. "Yes."

62

ELLA

Julian's voice must have dropped a full octave, making him sound different. If Ella hadn't known him as well as she did, that would have been enough to scare her, let alone the inch and a half long fangs and glowing eyes.

Except, she'd had plenty of time to mentally prepare for this. At first the idea of getting bitten had seemed so foreign and frightening, but after spending weeks with immortals she was more intrigued than scared. Besides, this was Julian, the man she loved and trusted with her very life. Which meant that before they took this major step, he should be aware of all the facts.

As he laid her on the bed, she took his hand and kissed it. "I have to tell you something."

"What is it?"

While in the shower, she'd prepared what she wanted to say to him and how, but for fear of spoiling the mood, she'd planned on doing it after and not before they made love. Except, it didn't feel right to hold off. Julian deserved to know that he'd been right about them being fated for each other from the very start.

"Lokan admitted to compelling my attraction to him and to blocking me from feeling it for anyone else. He also made me feel guilty whenever I was getting close to you. I interpreted that feeling of guilt as not being worthy of you, and of having darkness in me, but it was all artificial. Once he removed the compulsion, it was like a smothering blanket was lifted off me, and I felt an intense desire for you. I knew then that I was not only ready but eager to make love, and that we were fated for each other. My desire for you has been muted by his compulsion, but even as strong as his hold over me was, he couldn't kill it completely because my need for you managed to overpower it."

Throughout her monologue, Julian gazed at her, his glowing eyes not straying for a moment from hers. "I'm going to kill him," he said when she was done.

He'd get over it. Once they made love, Julian would find it in his heart to forgive Lokan. Especially since he couldn't kill him even if he really meant it.

Reaching for him, she smiled. "You'll have to wait for Kian and Turner to be done with him first. Now I want you to make love to me, and I don't want you to hold anything back. I want to experience the real Julian, not a watered down version of you."

A sly smirk lifted one corner of his mouth, which looked really funny because of his fangs. "Are you sure? I can get pretty intense."

God, hearing him say that ignited her libido as if he'd flipped the override switch, cranking the dial all the way into the red zone.

"No holds barred," she husked.

Talk about a switch.

If he'd looked feral before, it had been because of the fangs, but now his entire expression was changed. Gone was the softness in his eyes, replaced by a burning desire.

Ella was in for the ride of a lifetime and she couldn't wait.

In a heartbeat, he covered her body with his and pulled her arms over her head, threading their fingers.

"Am I too heavy for you?"

"You are perfect." She loved feeling his weight, the hard contours of his chest pressed against her breasts.

Her man was magnificent.

He took her lips, kissing her softly at first, and then possessing her mouth. His tongue went dueling with hers, then retreated and thrust again in an unmistakable imitation of what he intended to do to her next.

She was panting by the time he let go.

Lifting his head, he looked into her eyes. "Still okay?"

"Perfect."

"Your skin is so soft all over." He nuzzled her ear, his hot breath sending shivers through her body.

Her nipples tightened.

"You like this, don't you?" He nipped her earlobe, then sucked it into his mouth.

She arched up. "Yes."

Unthreading their fingers, he left her hands over her head and propped himself on his forearm. Looking at her with those intense glowing eyes of his, he cupped her breast, then swirled a finger around her areola. "Lovely, soft and hard." He lightly pinched her nipple.

Biting down on her lower lip, she stifled a moan as he did the same with the other one. If he kept this up, she was going to climax just from that.

As he pinched her nipple harder, a bolt of lightning shot straight to her throbbing center. "Your moans belong to me. Don't hide them. I'm greedy for every sound you make."

Bossy Julian was sexy, she just needed to make sure that this new facet of him didn't leave the bedroom or wherever else they were making love. He could boss her around all he wanted in bed, but not anywhere else.

Skimming his hand down her belly, he looked into her eyes, gauging her response.

Touch me, she said in her head, hoping he could hear her, and as his fingers brushed over her mons, she thought he had. But then he stopped, and returned them to her nipple, pinching it lightly again.

His gaze rapt on her breasts, he murmured, "I love how responsive your nipples are." Then he dipped his head and sucked one into his mouth.

"Yes." She arched up. "More."

His fingers skimmed over her belly again, but this time, he didn't stop, and as they reached her throbbing clit, Ella almost jumped out of her skin.

Two seconds of this and she was going to come all over those magic fingers. Spreading her legs lewdly, she invited more. Could he bring his other hand into play and push two inside her? She was aching to be filled, but still too embarrassed to ask for what she needed.

Maybe next time she would, but not their first. She just couldn't.

"You're so wet," he murmured against her nipple.

"I need you," she whimpered, hoping it would be enough.

"Need me to do what, this?" He swirled his finger around her clitoris without touching it directly.

"Yes. More."

Without warning, his finger left the top of her slit and pushed inside her.

Ella hadn't expected to climax so soon, and as the orgasm exploded out of her, she arched her back like a bow, impaling herself on that magic finger as deep as it could go.

63

JULIAN

As Ella climaxed, Julian had to call on every bit of restraint he could muster not to mount her and take her right there and then. After nearly two months of abstinence, it was mission impossible.

Except, he would make it possible because he wasn't done preparing her. She was small and he was a big guy, and unless she was sopping wet as he entered her, it would be painful.

Not acceptable. The only pain she would suffer tonight would be the momentary one of his fangs piercing her flesh.

The orgasm was a fluke. Ella hadn't been supposed to climax after so little foreplay, but it seemed that she hadn't been exaggerating when she'd claimed her desire for him was intense.

Planting a soft kiss on her parted lips, he stroked the damp hair off her forehead. "That was just the appetizer to the appetizer."

"You're going to kill me with too much pleasure."

"Not a chance. There could never be too much pleasure for my mate." Sliding down on the bed, he pressed his engorged erection to the mattress and implored it to hold off for just a few minutes longer. As turned on as Ella was, it wouldn't take long to bring her up again and have her explode all over his tongue.

She didn't protest, which meant that she wasn't a stranger to oral pleasuring. On the one hand it enraged him that the Russian had stolen even that from them, but on the other hand he was glad that the bastard had given some consideration to her pleasure.

Lifting his head, he looked into her eyes. "I hope I don't come in my shorts the instant I get your taste on my tongue."

Smirking, she reached down and cupped his cheek. "I've heard that immortal males need no recovery time, so that shouldn't be a problem."

He pretended to frown. "Who told you that?"

"Carol. Why, isn't it true?"

She seemed worried, which made him chuckle. "I can go all night long, but you're not ready for that. Once you are immortal, though…"

"Oh, God. I can't wait."

Applying gentle pressure to her thighs, he coaxed them to part a little wider. Her little clit was swollen, and she was slick from her earlier release, her lower lips plumped and parted, exposing her inner sheath.

And yet, Ella didn't shy away from his touch or his eyes, which was the best indication of how ready she was. Or maybe of how much she loved him.

Or both.

Fates, it was so inviting. He could extend his tongue and thrust it into that welcoming heat, but there was more to making love than going straight for the target, and the longer the buildup the better it was going to be for her.

He was going to die in the process, but it was a worthy sacrifice. Trailing his lips up one thigh, he resisted the urge to hurry, kissing his way up and stopping just before the gates of heaven to kiss the inside of her other thigh.

"Julian," she hissed. "Don't tease me."

He lifted his head. "Are you in a hurry to go somewhere?"

Cranking her neck, she looked at where his head was and smirked. "I have all night. But do you?"

"Imp." He nipped her thigh.

She was right, though. He wanted to believe that his will was invincible and that he could carry on for as long as he pleased, but the reality was a painfully hard shaft that he was subduing into obedience by pressing it as hard as he could into the mattress. Except, the thing was too soft to provide enough pressure. A granite altar would have worked much better.

It would have been appropriate too.

After all, he was about to worship his goddess with his tongue, which required an altar.

She rocked her hips. "Kiss me, Julian."

He liked that she asked for what she wanted. It was the best proof that she was more than ready to make love for the first time. What had been done to her before didn't count as such.

Pressing a soft kiss to her puffy lips, he inhaled her sweet scent, his eyes rolling back in his head from pleasure. "I think I'm already addicted to your scent. From now on, I'm going to do this every night." He flicked his tongue over her engorged bud.

Ella's hips jerked and she hissed. "Good, because I'll never get enough of this."

Unable to wait any longer, he speared his tongue into her drenched sheath, scooping her juices and groaning as they coated his mouth.

She let out a moan. "Oh, Julian. I'm getting close again."

"Not yet." He nipped her thigh. "Try to hold it off for a little bit longer."

"I can't. I need to come."

Lusty imp. He'd never expected her to be so orgasmic. Was he a lucky guy or what?

Next time, he was going to prolong her pleasure. But this time he was going to give her what she wanted. After all, he'd promised her that she would have all the control. And even though she'd given it back to him, he wasn't going to push her just yet. Not on their first time.

With a growl, he cupped her ass cheeks and pushed his tongue inside her again, going as deep as he could and nuzzling her clitoris at the same time. Not the most elegant cunnilingus, but it seemed to please her nonetheless.

"Yes!" Her sheath tightened around his tongue, and her fingers threaded into his hair, pulling hard. "Yes!" She threw her head back and uttered the most delectable sound. A moan that had started as a whimper and ended as a groan.

He'd never heard a woman make a sound like that. It was the sexiest thing ever. Snarling, he lapped up her copious juices, the taste and smell and her gyrating hips finally snapping his resolve.

Practically tearing his shorts off, he pushed up and settled between her thighs, aligning his loaded gun with her entrance.

64

ELLA

As Ella gazed into Julian's lust-infused eyes, her heart swelled with love for him.

"My mate," she whispered. "Make us one."

Grasping his shaft, he ran the tip up and down her wet folds, coating it in her juices, then nudged her entrance.

She arched up, encouraging him to press forward. "I'm ready, Julian. Don't make me wait any longer."

But he didn't ram into her as she'd expected. Instead, he eased inside her an inch at a time, stretching her impossibly wide but painlessly. Watching his beautiful face straining with the effort to go slow, she followed a drop of sweat as it detached from his forehead and landed on her chest.

"I love you," he whispered and took her mouth before she could say it back.

Sweet, sweet Julian, so considerate, so selfless, but she was done waiting, and she wasn't as fragile as he thought her to be. Wrapping her arms around him, she reached as far as she could, dug her fingers into the tight muscles of his buttocks, and pushed up, impaling herself on his length.

For a brief moment it stung, but not enough to take away from the intense pleasure of being filled by him.

Joined at last.

With a groan, Julian rested his damp forehead against hers. "Impatient girl."

"Very." She arched up again, getting him even deeper inside.

It was on the tip of her tongue to ask him to fuck her hard, but that kind of language didn't belong between them. It was what she'd heard in movies and read in books, but it wasn't how she wanted to communicate with her mate.

"Make love to me, Julian," she said instead.

And the words felt right, settling between them like a soft cloud, contrasting with the hard length pulsating within her. But the beauty of it was that both were about passion and love.

As he pulled out and surged inside her again, her inner walls clamped around him, wresting a strangled groan from his throat.

As Julian's thrusts got harder and faster, she knew he wasn't going to last, but that was fine. They were in no hurry, and the night was still young.

Well, not really, it was probably two in the morning, but time was irrelevant. She'd had a good rest and he was an immortal. They could keep going for hours.

Letting go of his ass cheeks, she lifted her hands to his back and wrapped her legs around the back of his thighs, clinging to him and readying for the wild ride he was about to give her.

Muscles tight, he rammed into her, hitting the end of her channel, again and again, the glow in his eyes so bright that she could feel the heat of it on her skin.

Or was she imagining it?

It was hard to tell with all the sensations bombarding her at once. And yet, she could feel him swelling impossibly big inside her, and as his ragged breaths turned into growls, she instinctively turned her head and offered him her neck.

As his hands clamped on her head, immobilizing it, she experienced a moment of fear, but instead of the bite she'd braced for, she felt his tongue laving the soft spot where her neck met her shoulder.

Even as wild as he was, Julian retained the presence of mind to prepare her, and as his fangs sank into her flesh, it was more erotic than painful. Her sheath convulsing around him, Ella's eyes rolled back in her head as she orgasmed again.

It was too much.

And yet when his shaft kicked inside her, filling her with his semen, another climax rocked through her.

Then his venom hit her system and she floated away on a cloud of euphoria.

65

JULIAN

As Ella drifted off, Julian retracted his fangs, licked the puncture wounds closed, and buried his face in the hollow of her neck, still slowly thrusting inside her and riding out his orgasm.

He wasn't nearly done, and if Ella were an immortal he would have waited a moment for her to float down and started over again. But she was still human, and as it was, this had been the best sex of his life, and he shouldn't be greedy for more. Instead, he breathed in her scent, feeling grateful beyond measure for the gift of her.

Fates, the intensity with which he loved this incredible girl was overwhelming. She'd blown his mind, changed him from the inside out, and he was never going to be the same again. But it was all good. She'd made him a better man. She'd given him purpose, and he was going to spend the rest of his immortal life worshiping at her feet.

Right now, though, he needed to clean her up and tuck her under the blanket because she was wiped out and was probably going to keep sleeping till morning.

Sliding out of her as gently as he could, he winced as their combined issue spilled onto the sheets. There was nothing he could do about it without waking Ella up, other than maybe pushing a towel under her.

With that in mind, he tiptoed to the bathroom, grabbed a clean towel and several washcloths and tiptoed back, only to realize that he should probably soak the washcloths in warm water.

He was a novice at this, but he was going to learn and be the best mate possible to Ella. A gold medalist at taking care of his girl.

He chuckled softly as he headed back to the bathroom. His competitive streak had kicked in, and as with everything else, he needed to be the best at being a mate too.

It was a worthy goal, though. Probably more important than all the others combined.

Padding back with the wet washcloths in hand, he sat on the bed and cleaned his beauty as best he could, then gently pushed a dry towel under her tush, and covered her with the blanket.

After disposing of the washcloths, he lifted the comforter and joined his love in bed. Snuggling up to her, he kissed her temple. "Good night, my precious," he murmured.

Lying on his side, he watched her gorgeous face. She looked happy, relaxed, and a small smile was lifting the corners of her lush lips. A wave of pure satisfaction washed over him because he was responsible for that expression.

A happy wife meant a happy life. He'd read or heard it somewhere. And if that was true for humans, it was even truer for immortals.

A happy true-love mate meant an eternity of bliss.

66

KIAN

"And I thought Turner was paranoid," William said as he finished preparing the third cuff. "I understand that he is Navuh's son, but he's not Houdini. And if he can open one cuff, he can open all four. But he can't. I guarantee it."

"It's for the psychological effect." Pushing away from the desk he'd been leaning against, Kian dusted off the back of his pants.

Even though William still used his old lab from time to time, it looked like it hadn't been cleaned since he'd moved to the new one in the village. He hadn't used it for cuff making, though. The last one William had made had been for Robert. That was why he hadn't brought the components to the new location.

Nevertheless, he'd been working on a new design, and Lokan would be the first one to have the displeasure of being a test subject.

Waving with the caliper, William huffed. "If you want a psychological effect, you shouldn't put him in the nice cell apartment. Stick him in the smallest one and have him ponder the torture he's about to suffer."

He clamped the tool on the completed cuff and compared the measurement to the one Turner had provided. It was important that the cuffs fit snugly but not so tightly as to cause injury.

"Turner's plan to extract information from Lokan consists of several stages, and in the first one he's going to be treated as well as a guest would."

"I don't see how that would work." William buffed the cuff with a cloth and then placed it next to the other two.

"Neither do I." Impatient for the Doomer prince's arrival, Kian started pacing. "But I trust Turner. He hasn't failed us yet. The guy is a fucking genius, and I'm not saying it lightly. Sometimes I feel as if he's taken over my job as the clan's strategist."

"If you ask me, that's a good thing. You can focus on drumming up more business." William removed his glasses, replaced them with protective goggles, and then reached for his earphones. "I'm about to use the whiny power sander."

The thing should have been called a head drill because that was what Kian felt every time William turned it on.

"I'm going to be out in the corridor."

William nodded, waiting for Kian to leave the lab before turning the tool on.

Glancing at his watch, Kian checked the time. Turner's plane should be landing soon, and since traffic was not a problem this late at night, the Doomers should be arriving within an hour. Not that he was interested in Lokan's men, they were already in stasis and heading for storage in the catacombs, just in their leader.

He still couldn't believe how lucky they'd gotten. It seemed like the Fates had been working overtime to bring this about. So many things had to happen to bring Lokan into his hands.

If Julian hadn't gone to the psychic convention, he wouldn't have met Vivian and fallen for her daughter's picture. But if he had acted upon it right away and started dating the girl, she wouldn't have fallen victim to traffickers, wouldn't have been sold to the Russian mobster, and would have never met Lokan, who'd become obsessed with her too.

Then there was Turner. If not for him and his connections in Washington, Lokan would have absconded with Vivian and Ella and they would have been lost forever to the clan.

The question that occupied his mind now was what he wished Navuh to believe happened to his son.

One option was to rig the plane to explode somewhere in the middle of the ocean and have Navuh believe that Lokan was dead.

The other option was to hide the plane somewhere and make him think that Lokan had deserted.

Kian preferred the first choice, but in case Navuh actually cared for his son, Lokan could be used as a future bargaining chip.

Until that was decided, though, they had to make sure that Navuh didn't suspect the clan's involvement in Lokan's disappearance. Even if he cared nothing for his son, it would be a matter of pride for him to retaliate against the clan and he would go to great lengths to do that, including hurting humans who he suspected of association with them.

That's why they were going to hide Lokan's executive jet in Mexico. Once again, a friend of Turner's was taking care of that. Evidently, making planes disappear was a service that the private operator was providing for governments as well as individuals.

It would buy them time to interrogate Lokan.

What they would learn from him would influence which option was best.

67

ELLA

Ella woke up with a smile on her face, which hadn't happened in a long time. Being snuggled in Julian's arms might have something to do with that, as well as a good night's sleep without expecting a visitor.

Julian had assured her that with the strong sedative Lokan had been given, he couldn't dream actively. Which meant no dream sharing.

The question was what would happen later. Once Lokan was locked up in a cell, Kian wasn't going to keep him sedated. Could they threaten him with bodily harm if he dared to intrude on her dreams again?

She would have to suggest it to Kian. After what she'd gone through to help him capture Navuh's son, he owed her at least that. But that was all the mind bandwidth she was going to dedicate to the Doomer.

This was a new day and a new beginning for her, and Ella didn't want to dwell on the past if she could avoid it.

"Good morning, gorgeous." Julian nuzzled her neck. "Did you sleep well?"

"Fantastic." In fact, she'd never felt better.

Was it the effect of the incredible lovemaking? Or had it been the venom? She felt vital, invigorated, happy.

"That's good to hear." He kissed her lips.

She kept them tightly closed. "I need to brush. And pee."

"Then go." He lifted the blanket, exposing her nude body.

Her first instinct was to snatch it from him and cover up, but she didn't.

She was starting this new day with a bang, and that meant confidence in her body, which Julian was practically devouring with a pair of hungry, glowing eyes.

"You'd better hurry, love, or you won't make it to the bathroom."

As she swung her legs over the side of the bed, Julian held on to her with his arm around her middle.

She glanced at the towel he must have put under her last night. "That won't help much if you don't let me go, and I pee on your bed."

"Our bed." He removed his arm from her waist. "I need to go too." He flung the comforter off him.

Oh, boy. Ella stopped and gawked. He was fully erect, his shaft standing up like a mast. "Is that your morning wood or is it for me?"

"Both." Smiling, he slapped her bottom. "Go. Before I change my mind."

If she didn't need to pee so bad, she would've stayed and taunted him some more. He wasn't the only one ready for round two.

Julian allowed her about a minute of privacy before coming in, and then he joined her in the shower.

She ended up very clean and very satisfied, and then he toweled her dry and carried her back to bed.

"I could get used to that," Ella said as he put her down.

"Me too." He leaned and kissed her nose. "I'm going to make coffee."

Hey, she could get used to that too, especially since Julian hadn't bothered to put anything on, and she delighted in the sight of his beautifully muscled backside as he headed for the kitchen.

When he returned holding a tray with two coffee mugs and a plate of chocolates, she also got an eyeful of his glorious front.

"These will have to do for breakfast. We are out of everything else." He put the tray on the nightstand.

"We could go grocery shopping." She grinned. "This will be my first time buying stuff for my own kitchen."

"Do you have your special glasses with you?"

Her smile wilted. "No, Lokan took them from us, together with the trackers and everything else we had on. We were lucky that he didn't think that the hairpins could have trackers in them."

"Thank the merciful Fates." Julian rubbed a hand over his face. "I don't know what I would have done if I had lost you. I would have spent every moment of my life searching for that fucking island."

"Don't." She reached for his hand and brought it to her cheek. "It doesn't make sense to get angry over what ifs. I'm here, and we are together, and Lokan is locked in a cell."

"What if he enters your dreams again?"

"I give you permission to beat him up if he does."

That got an evil smile out of him. "I'm looking forward to it. I don't want him anywhere near you ever again. That evil son of a bitch is handsome. Takes after his monster of a father."

Ella leaned and kissed Julian's lips. "He can't hold a candle to you. You are a god even among immortals."

The smile got even wider. "I think I just grew an inch."

She glanced down. "I'd say."

"Lusty wench." He picked up a chocolate and put it in her mouth. "I would happily join you in bed for round three, but I need to feed you something healthier than chocolates, and the house is empty of food. We have to either go shopping or hit the café."

She grimaced. "I don't want to go to the café. We won't have a moment's peace there, with everyone wanting details of what went down. But I can't go grocery shopping without my glasses. I think we have no choice but to go to my parents' house."

"Your mom invited us for brunch."

"I know. I heard her. I just didn't want to open my eyes." She sighed. "I wish I were truly free, and that includes the Russian giving up on finding me."

"You should have let the Guardians kill him."

She waved a dismissive hand. "I'm glad I didn't. The roadblock operation was much safer for everyone than the fake fire Turner planned to set on the Russian's estate. No one got hurt, and I'm grateful for that. Besides, it's not a big deal. I don't plan on leaving the village often."

"What about college? You said you were going to find one in the area and commute."

"I found an even better solution. An online university."

He arched a brow. "Since when do they teach nursing online? It's a hands-on occupation."

"I decided to study something else. I wanted to be a nurse to help people, but I can help more by organizing charity. My mom and I checked, and we found an accredited online bachelor's degree in nonprofit management. I can do that while running the charity. Which reminds me." She jumped out of bed. "I want to check how it's doing."

She opened the suitcase, which was still on the floor where Julian had put it last night, pulled out her laptop, and hopped back in bed.

Sitting cross-legged even though she was nude, which was a testament to how comfortable she was with Julian, Ella booted it up. Hopefully, it had enough charge left for a short session.

"Oh, wow. It keeps on growing. No major donations, but tons of small ones. We've collected close to thirty thousand."

"That's great news." Julian didn't sound overly enthusiastic.

"I know it's a drop in the bucket, but we've just started. It will grow exponentially, you'll see."

"Fates willing."

"Oh, they are."

As his phone started buzzing, Ella remembered that hers was gone. "I hope the Guardians captured the Doomers who had our purses. The clan phones are in there. If they fall into the wrong hands, they can be reverse-engineered."

Julian snatched the phone. "Hi, Vivian." A long pause. "Sure. I'll tell Ella. See you later."

"Was it about lunch? Because I'm starting to feel hungry."

"Yes, and also about a party. Callie and Wonder are organizing a barbecue on Sunday to celebrate your safe return."

"Awesome. I'm glad they are doing it on the weekend and not right away. Now let's get dressed and go to my parents to eat. I also need to give Parker a big hug for his help."

As she said the words, it dawned on her that she'd been referring to Magnus as her parent, and that it hadn't been the first time she'd done it.

In part, it was because saying she was going to her mother's house didn't sound right, and neither did going to her mother and Magnus's house. But the truth was that she was starting to think of him as a father figure, mainly because in every way that counted he was.

Her real father would always be in her heart, she was never going to forget him, not even for one day, but she had room in there for Magnus too. He'd certainly earned the right.

The heart was a funny thing.

Its capacity had no limit, and there was always room for more people to love.

Dear reader,

Thank you for joining me on the continuing adventures of the **Children of the Gods**.

As an independent author, I rely on your support to spread the word. So if you enjoyed the story, please share your experience, and if it isn't too much trouble, I would greatly appreciate a brief **review**.

Love & happy reading,
Isabell

COMING UP NEXT
Dark Prince Trilogy

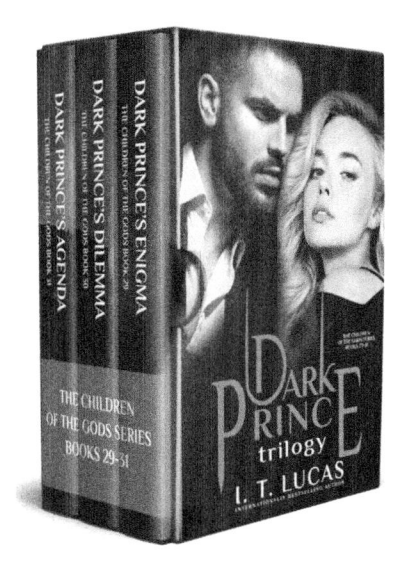

Read the enclosed excerpt

INCLUDES
29: Dark Prince's Enigma
30: Dark Prince's Dilemma
31: Dark Prince's Agenda

FOR EXCLUSIVE PEEKS AT UPCOMING RELEASES
Join my VIP Club and gain access to the VIP portal at itlucas.com
CLICK HERE TO JOIN

(If you're already a subscriber and forgot the password to the VIP portal, you can find it at the bottom of each of my emails. Or click **HERE** to retrieve it. You can also email me at isabell@itlucas.com)

Don't miss out on
THE CHILDREN OF THE GODS ORIGINS SERIES
1: Goddess's Choice
2: Goddess's Hope
THE PERFECT MATCH SERIES
Perfect Match 1: Vampire's Consort
Perfect Match 2: King's Chosen
Perfect Match 3: Captain's Conquest

DARK PRINCE EXCERPT

LOKAN

As Lokan's awareness returned, it was accompanied by a throbbing headache, nausea, and disorientation.

Drugs.

He must've been pumped with shitloads of them. Other than a severe injury, drugs were the only thing he could think of that could cause an immortal to experience such symptoms.

And if that wasn't bad enough, Lokan couldn't open his eyes more than a crack without it feeling as if someone was sticking needles in them.

With a groan, he let his lids drop. The room was steeped in such complete darkness that there was no point in forcing it. He couldn't see anything anyway.

If Lokan had ever wondered what being drunk and drugged felt like, he knew now and was doubly glad for never allowing himself to drink excessively or touch drugs.

Why people would want to deliberately impair their faculties baffled him. Getting shit-faced was the prerogative of plebs, not leaders. Lokan couldn't allow himself to partake in excess even if he was ever tempted to. His very survival depended on him always being sharp and alert.

The ever-present competition for positions of power and influence in the Brotherhood was demanding and subject to the whims of a despot. The fact that his competitors were his half-brothers and the despot was his father only raised the stakes and made the game more dangerous.

Was one of his brothers responsible for this?

And what exactly was 'this'?

The bed he was lying on was superbly comfortable, like what he would expect to find in a luxury hotel, and the sheets smelled freshly laundered.

Was he in a hotel room?

Why couldn't he remember what had happened to him, or how he'd gotten there?

Was he suffering from drug-induced amnesia?

Fighting the mental fog, Lokan went back to the last thing he remembered, which had been calling his pilot and telling him to have the jet ready for takeoff.

Why had he done that, though?

He had just returned to Washington from his mandatory visit to the island, and his next scheduled report wasn't until next month. He had work to do, meetings with politicians and lobbyists to attend, and a couple of powerful telepaths to snatch from their government's clutches...

Fuck! Suddenly it all came rushing back.

He'd failed.

The mighty son of Navuh had been outmaneuvered by fucking humans. For that failure alone, his father was likely to execute him. And if Navuh was merciful enough to spare his life, he would definitely demote him like he'd demoted Losham.

Except, whatever his brother had done to prompt his fall from grace couldn't have been nearly as bad as what Lokan had gotten himself into.

Which meant that Navuh could never find out about this fiasco.

And that wasn't even the main reason why his father could never know about this. It would be difficult to explain why Lokan had invested so much effort and had taken such unreasonable risks to capture two telepaths who could only communicate with each other.

No one was supposed to find out about this personal acquisition of his.

First of all, because the mission he needed them for was top secret, and if discovered would cost him his head for sure. And secondly, because the dream-sharing ability that had allowed him to set the trap for the telepaths needed to stay forever hidden from the Brotherhood and especially from his father.

Navuh wouldn't tolerate anyone in his organization having an advantage over him, not even his own son, and not even if the talent was pretty useless.

Until meeting Ella, Lokan hadn't found any practical purpose for the dream-sharing. Provided that it was used wisely, however, it was an asset nonetheless, and as far as Lokan knew, he was the only one on the entire planet who possessed it.

Much good it had done him, though.

Where had he gone wrong?

After weeks of dream-sharing with Ella and charming her into trusting him, he had realized that she'd been attempting to use her meager feminine wiles to lure him into a trap of her own. But since the girl was too young and inexperienced to devise a plan like this, and he didn't think she had any real motive for trying to entrap him, he had concluded that she'd been doing it on behalf of the agency holding her and her mother captive.

Most likely under duress.

Lokan still believed that his plan to snatch both telepaths from under their handlers' noses had been ingenious. He was sure that it had failed not because of any mistake on his part, but because of the unprecedented level of military support the agency responsible for collecting paranormal talents evidently had access to.

He hadn't expected such an obscure and highly classified department to get Special Forces backup.

It had been clear to him that Ella's rescue from the Russian mafioso and the faking of her death had been orchestrated and executed by highly trained professionals, but what he knew about government agencies and how they operated had led him to believe that it had been a one-time collaboration.

Lokan thought it probable that Vivian had revealed the truth about her and Ella's telepathic connection in a desperate attempt to get the government to rescue her daughter.

It seemed that she had succeeded in that, but the price was her and Ella's freedom, as well as that of Ella's younger brother. As far as Lokan was concerned, Vivian might have saved her daughter from sexual slavery, but to do so, she'd sold her soul and the souls of her children to the devil.

Evidently, the agency had been willing to put just as much effort into getting their hands on a dream walker as they had into securing the telepaths. After all, his talent was just as rare as the mother and daughter's ability to talk to each other in their heads.

That agency must have other exceptional talents as well.

As more and more details of what had happened were coming back to him, Lokan remembered that the guy who'd shot him knew his real name.

"Game over, Lokan," he'd said.

Since Ella had only known him as Logan, and so had all of his Washington contacts, Lokan figured that the only way the guy could've known his real name was by entering his mind, and that was the most alarming development of all.

Because he could've learned much more than Lokan's name.

Humans were not supposed to know about the existence of immortals or the secret island that served as their base. But that was only the tip of the iceberg. It was basic information that could've been obtained from any captured member of the Brotherhood.

What they could learn from Navuh's son, however, was much more damming than that.

Humans possessing such strong paranormal abilities was something neither Lokan nor his father had anticipated.

Nor had he expected to ever get caught by them.

The plan he'd constructed had seemed foolproof. No one born in this century knew about the secret tunnels running under the university and, given the wild goose chase he'd sent Ella and Vivian's handlers on, there should have been no way for them to stop him.

They had outmaneuvered him with the airport shutdown, something only a powerful government agency could have pulled off.

There was no point in dwelling on his failure, though. What he needed to focus on was devising a new plan of action before they came in to question him, especially if they brought the mind reader along.

He decided he would have to kill that human first and then deal with the others.

The problem was that they seemed to be aware of his ability to compel and would no doubt bring in immunes to deal with him, which meant that thralling was out as well.

Those who couldn't be compelled couldn't be thralled.

Lokan would have to rely on his basic immortal super traits of strength and speed, which the humans wouldn't be expecting.

First, though, he should try to dream-share with Ella and find out as much as he could from her. After more than a month in the place, she should be familiar with its personnel and safety procedures.

Ella might be still angry at him, but there was no reason for her to hide what was going on and what he was up against, and perhaps she would even use the opportunity to gloat.

It was most likely that she was somewhere nearby, perhaps even in the same facility. Not that distance played a factor in his ability to dream-share with her.

He had done it from the other side of the world.

It had been early afternoon when he'd been captured, and unless the room was devoid of light because the shutters were closed, Lokan assumed it was night, so she should be sleeping.

Drifting into dreamland while his head was throbbing was a challenge, but he'd practiced doing so at will. Taking a deep breath, he imagined what he wanted to dream about and then counted back from ten.

CAROL

"You're bouncier than usual." Wonder handed Carol a plate of sandwiches. "These are for table six. What's going on?"

"I'm excited."

"About what?"

"Let me finish with that order first."

Lifting the tray with the cappuccinos and sandwiches Wonder had made, Carol headed toward her waiting customers with a spring in her step and a big smile on her face.

Navuh's son had been captured, and she couldn't wait to talk about it with someone. Was she allowed, though? Or was it a secret?

Wonder probably knew because Anandur had told her, and the same was true for the other Guardians' mates.

Thank the merciful Fates for the earpiece Brundar had given her and had never asked her to return. That little device was keeping her in the loop. Listening to the communications between the Guardians, Carol was getting the latest news before everyone else.

She wasn't supposed to share what she'd learned, but this was big news, and Carol was sure it was going to spread throughout the village like wildfire. After all, there was no point in keeping it a secret. It wasn't as if the information could be shared with outsiders.

Humans didn't know immortals existed, and keeping it that way meant that none could be told about the capture of one of the most prominent figures of the Devout Order of Mortdh Brotherhood, the son of their evil leader no less, or how incredible it was for the clan.

Bottom line, even if everyone in the village knew about Lokan's capture, there was no way the news could get back to his father.

From what she'd heard over the earpiece, the idea was to make it look as if

Lokan had deserted. If Navuh discovered that the clan had his son, the consequences would be disastrous.

Unable to retaliate against them directly, he would strike at humans, knowing how much it would hurt the clan.

It would be a matter of ego for the despot.

She wouldn't be surprised if Navuh tried to blackmail the clan into releasing his son by threatening to nuke a large city. Not because he loved Lokan, but because his son probably knew things about the Brotherhood that Navuh couldn't afford his enemy to discover.

It was better to let him think that Lokan had deserted, or even gotten killed by having his private jet explode in the middle of the ocean.

In her opinion, the second option was better. With no one searching for Lokan, they would have all the time they needed to milk him for information. Finally, they were going to learn the location of that freaking island the Doomers called home, which meant that Kian could finally approve her mission.

Well, there was one small detail that might still prevent it, but she planned on taking care of it as soon as possible.

Returning with the empty tray, Carol put it on the counter and wiped it with a rag. "Is Anandur going to stop by this morning?"

From her spot next to the cappuccino machine, Wonder glanced at Carol over her shoulder. "Maybe in the afternoon. Kian is on his way to pay a visit to you-know-who, and he took Anandur and Brundar with him."

Carol leaned closer and whispered, "Is the one you're referring to supposed to stay a secret?"

"I'm not sure. Until I'm told it's okay to talk about it in public, I'm going to assume that it should."

Tucking a curl behind her ear, Carol leaned against the counter and crossed her arms over her chest. "A spy in our midst would be the only reason to keep it a secret. But if there was one, discussing you-know-who would be the least of our worries. Our location would've been compromised, and we would have been attacked by Doomers a long time ago."

"Not necessarily." Wonder turned to stand next to Carol and glanced around, making sure no one was close enough to eavesdrop. "With the self-driving cars and the hidden tunnels, the village's residents don't know where it is. So even if there is a spy amongst us, he or she can't disclose our location."

"That's true. But what are the chances of a clan member spying for the Brotherhood? Unless you suspect the ex-Doomers." Carol huffed. "I can assure you that Robert is not a spy, and neither is Dalhu. Both are happily mated and would never betray their mates."

"I don't suspect them or anyone else. I'm just saying that it's possible."

"Perhaps, but it's highly unlikely." Carol pushed away from the counter. "I'm going to call Anandur about the hunting lesson he's supposed to give me."

"Didn't you say that you were not going to do it?"

"I changed my mind. No guts, no glory, eh?"

"I guess." Wonder grimaced. "But it's gross."

"Can't argue with that. It's just that I've realized that eating meat but not being willing to hunt for it is hypocritical. It's time for me to woman up." She could have lived with the hypocrisy, but she had to do it if she wanted Anandur to approve her for the mission.

"Good luck."

"I'll call Anandur from the playground so I can have some privacy while I grovel. Are you going to be okay here by yourself for a little bit?"

Wonder waved a hand at the tables. "All the customers have been served, and there are no new ones in line."

"It won't take long."

The playground was about a minute's walk from the café, and as usual, there was no one there. Kian had built the place with hope for the future, but in the meantime, there were only two kids in the entire village. Phoenix was a toddler and Nathalie brought her to the playground from time to time, but Ethan was still too small to play.

Hopefully, Merlin's fertility treatments were going to work, and the clan would be blessed with many more babies.

Not that Carol was interested in having kids herself, but there was nothing like the happy squeals of playing children to boost morale and hope for the future.

Sitting on one of the swings, she placed the call.

"What's up?" Anandur answered on the second ring.

"Are you stopping by the café anytime today?"

"Maybe later. Why?"

"I want you to take me hunting. I'm ready."

"Oh, really. What made you change your mind?"

"I decided that I have no problem killing freaking coyotes. When I hear their howling at night, I'm ready to get my shotgun."

Anandur laughed. "They howl to mark their territory and to court mates. They are not as bad as people think they are."

"Oof. Don't tell me that. You wanted me to hunt to prove that I'm capable of killing. And now that I'm finally ready, you make even coyotes sound innocent?"

"Of course, they are innocent. They are animals fighting for survival. They don't harbor sinister plans to conquer the world or kill for the fun of it."

"Like the Doomers."

"Precisely."

"Can I practice on them?" She waved a hand even though he couldn't see her. "I'm just joking. Can we skip the hunting thing, though? I'm sure that I can kill in self-defense or to protect others."

A long moment passed before he answered. "What prompted your reawakened interest? Does it have anything to do with Lokan's capture?"

She rolled her eyes. "Of course, it does. When we extract the island's location from Lokan, Kian might finally approve my mission. I'm ready to go and start planting the seeds of revolt in the hearts of Doomers."

"I bet you are. But we don't have the location yet, and it might be a while until we get it out of him. Then we need to figure out how to get you there, how to communicate with you, and how to extract you if needed."

"You are not telling me anything new. Knowing where the freaking island is will make all of this doable, while before it wasn't. So, I figured that the only thing still preventing me from going is your stupid condition that I kill an animal and take out its heart."

"How about we cross that bridge when we get to it?"

"We are practically there, Anandur."

KIAN

"You shouldn't hold the phone while driving," Kian said as Anandur ended the call with Carol. "Why didn't you link it with the car's system?"

"Carol called me. Not you, Andrew, or Brundar."

In the back seat, Andrew chuckled. "We all heard her anyway."

Anandur shrugged. "I know, but it's a matter of decorum."

Kian cast him a sidelong glance. "If you were concerned with propriety, you should've told her that you were in the car with us before letting her talk."

"Maybe, but then all of you would've thought that Carol and I were keeping secrets. Besides, it saves me the trouble of repeating what she said." He glanced at Kian. "Are we still considering that crazy plan?"

"That depends on what we learn from Lokan."

"Is he even awake yet?" Andrew asked.

"Arwel said that he woke up and then dozed off again." Kian removed his sunglasses and put them in his pocket. "Probably because of all the sedatives we've pumped into him."

"I'm surprised you didn't demand that Lokan be awakened last night when they brought him."

"I wasn't ready to talk to him yet. I wanted to talk with Turner first and get his opinion. I also wanted to hear Ella and Vivian's versions about what went on while Lokan had them. Their insight into his personality was very helpful. According to them, he seems smart, educated, well-mannered, and full of himself."

"Wasn't pumping him with shitloads of sedatives dangerous to his brain?" Anandur asked.

"It's not. Bridget approved it. She said that keeping him asleep will allow his body to repair the damage he sustained."

"I thought that Turner shot him in the legs." Anandur frowned. "Did he shatter his kneecaps?"

"No, but after getting shot, Lokan fell back down the jet's stairs and hit his head on the last rung."

"That's not a big deal either."

"We needed to keep him sedated until he was locked down in the keep's dungeon. A few more shots to keep him asleep throughout the night weren't going to make a difference."

"Do you think he realizes who has him?" Andrew asked.

"Unless he figured it out when Turner shot him, I don't see how he could. It was lights out for him seconds later."

Andrew chuckled. "I wish I could peek into his head and see what he imagines happened to him. That should be interesting."

"He's a Doomer," Brundar said. "He probably thinks one of his brothers set him up. Dalhu says they are constantly competing for positions and for their father's approval."

Kian didn't want to speculate. What he'd been itching to do since Lokan's capture was to start the interrogation.

Last night, it had been too late to question Ella and Vivian about their interactions with Lokan and what they had learned from him. Ella had gone home with Julian straight from the plane, and Kian had no doubt the two had been busy celebrating her safe return.

The same was true of Vivian and Magnus.

This morning, Kian had waited for as long as he possibly could before calling them up to ask a few questions. The rest would have to wait for Monday after all the celebrating was done.

The main thing Ella had warned him against was how good of a liar Lokan was. That was why Kian had called Andrew and asked him to come along. His brother-in-law's lie-detecting services were needed.

The second thing Ella had warned him about was Lokan's chameleonic adaptive ability. Apparently, the guy knew how to make himself likable when he wanted.

Not that it was going to work on Kian.

As someone who'd witnessed the atrocities committed by Doomers, Kian's hatred for them ran deep. The only reason he'd accepted Dalhu and Robert into the clan was the sacrifice each of them had made to prove themselves worthy.

But it hadn't been easy to do. It had taken him a long time to accept that not all Doomers were evil, and that some managed to escape their leader's relentless brainwashing and maintain some basic decency.

That, however, could not be true of Navuh's sons. They were privy to the backstage of their father's propaganda, and they were the ones in charge of executing his evil plans.

No one would ever convince him that they had any decency left in them at all. Except perhaps for the one who had gotten away.

Kalugal.

What Kian had managed to piece together was that Kalugal had faked his own death during the Second World War and escaped to the States. Sometime later, he'd had a chance encounter with Eva, activating her dormant genes and turning her immortal without either of them realizing it.

Even a skeptic like Kian had to concede that the Fates had something to do with that. The chain of events was just too fantastic for it all to have happened by chance.

As Kian's phone rang, he accepted the call, and Arwel's voice came through the car's speakers. "He is getting out of bed. Any instructions?"

"Get him breakfast," Anandur said.

"I'm not his servant."

"The dude needs to eat."

"So, you get it," Arwel said.

Anandur huffed. "Fine, I will. I'll get him stuff from the vending machines."

"Bring some for me too."

"I'm not your servant, buddy."

As humorous as the exchange was, the truth was that Kian would have to make arrangements for the Doomer and his keepers to have their meals delivered.

Last night, Arwel had volunteered to stay down in the dungeon in the cell adjacent to Lokan's and head the team of Guardians assigned to him. Evidently, deep underground or high in the sky were the only places Arwel could escape the bombardment of emotions normally assailing him. This assignment was perfect for him, and he'd jumped at the opportunity.

The problem was that they hadn't figured out the logistics yet. Until they did, the Guardians on rotation in the keep would have to take turns bringing in meals for Lokan and those in charge of keeping an eye on him

Kian's other option was to bring Okidu to prepare meals for them, but then he would be giving up his butler for the fucking Doomer.

Wasn't going to happen.

Whatever the solution, he was going to address it later when he got back to the office. Right now, he was too jazzed up about interrogating his prisoner and getting game-changing intel out of him.

Was Lokan going to be a hard nut to crack?

The Doomer was old and experienced, a seasoned soldier, but the question was how loyal was he to his father? If they were lucky, Lokan hated Navuh and would cooperate freely, but Kian didn't like to indulge in wishful thinking.

"I'm curious to see how different Lokan is from the other Doomers," Andrew said. "Even Dalhu, who was a unit commander, and Robert, who was Sharim's right-hand man, knew very little of use to us. I think Navuh keeps information highly compartmentalized. Lokan might know more than Dalhu and Robert, but not much."

Anandur shrugged. "We will soon find out. I bet it's going to be interesting, though. From what Ella and Vivian said about him, Lokan is charming and smart. His plan to kidnap them was brilliant. If not for Turner's connections and quick thinking, the Doomer would have succeeded in snatching them from under our noses despite all the men we had in place. Not only that, he would have done it with significantly fewer resources at his disposal. I can despise what he attempted to do, but I have to respect his smarts."

Dark Prince Trilogy
INCLUDES
29: DARK PRINCE'S ENIGMA
30: DARK PRINCE'S DILEMMA
31: DARK PRINCE'S AGENDA

THE CHILDREN OF THE GODS SERIES

THE CHILDREN OF THE GODS ORIGINS

1: Goddess's Choice

When gods and immortals still ruled the ancient world, one young goddess risked everything for love.

2: Goddess's Hope

Hungry for power and infatuated with the beautiful Areana, Navuh plots his father's demise. After all, by getting rid of the insane god he would be doing the world a favor. Except, when gods and immortals conspire against each other, humanity pays the price.

But things are not what they seem, and prophecies should not to be trusted...

THE CHILDREN OF THE GODS

1: Dark Stranger The Dream

Syssi's paranormal foresight lands her a job at Dr. Amanda Dokani's neuroscience lab, but it fails to predict the thrilling yet terrifying turn her life will take. Syssi has no clue that her boss is an immortal who'll drag her into a secret, millennia-old battle over humanity's future. Nor does she realize that the professor's imposing brother is the mysterious stranger who's been starring in her dreams.

Since the dawn of human civilization, two warring factions of immortals—the descendants of the gods of old—have been secretly shaping its destiny. Leading the clandestine battle from his luxurious Los Angeles high-rise, Kian is surrounded by his clan, yet alone. Descending from a single goddess, clan members are forbidden to each other. And as the only other immortals are their hated enemies, Kian and his kin have been long resigned to a lonely existence of fleeting trysts with human partners. That is, until his sister makes a game-changing discovery—a mortal seeress who she believes is a dormant carrier of their genes. Ever the realist, Kian is skeptical and refuses Amanda's plea to attempt Syssi's activation. But when his enemies learn of the Dormant's existence, he's forced to rush her to the safety of his keep. Inexorably drawn to Syssi, Kian wrestles with his conscience as he is tempted to explore her budding interest in the darker shades of sensuality.

2: Dark Stranger Revealed

While sheltered in the clan's stronghold, Syssi is unaware that Kian and Amanda are not human, and neither are the supposedly religious fanatics that are after her. She feels a powerful connection to Kian, and as he introduces her to a world of pleasure she never dared imagine, his dominant sexuality is a revelation. Considering that she's completely out of her element, Syssi feels comfortable and safe letting go with him. That is, until she begins to suspect that all is not as it seems. Piecing the puzzle together, she draws a scary, yet wrong conclusion...

3: Dark Stranger Immortal

When Kian confesses his true nature, Syssi is not as much shocked by the revelation as she is wounded by what she perceives as his callous plans for her.

If she doesn't turn, he'll be forced to erase her memories and let her go. His family's safety demands secrecy – no one in the mortal world is allowed to know that immortals exist.

Resigned to the cruel reality that even if she stays on to never again leave the keep, she'll get old while Kian won't, Syssi is determined to enjoy what little time she has with him, one day at a time.

Can Kian let go of the mortal woman he loves? Will Syssi turn? And if she does, will she survive the dangerous transition?

4: Dark Enemy Taken

Dalhu can't believe his luck when he stumbles upon the beautiful immortal professor. Presented with a once in a lifetime opportunity to grab an immortal female for himself, he kidnaps her and runs. If he ever gets caught, either by her people or his, his life is forfeit.

But for a chance of a loving mate and a family of his own, Dalhu is prepared to do everything in his power to win Amanda's heart, and that includes leaving the Doom brotherhood and his old life behind.

Amanda soon discovers that there is more to the handsome Doomer than his dark past and a hulking, sexy body. But succumbing to her enemy's seduction, or worse, developing feelings for a ruthless killer is out of the question. No man is worth life on the run, not even the one and only immortal male she could claim as her own…

Her clan and her research must come first…

5: Dark Enemy Captive

When the rescue team returns with Amanda and the chained Dalhu to the keep, Amanda is not as thrilled to be back as she thought she'd be. Between Kian's contempt for her and Dalhu's imprisonment, Amanda's budding relationship with Dalhu seems doomed. Things start to look up when Annani offers her help, and together with Syssi they resolve to find a way for Amanda to be with Dalhu. But will she still want him when she realizes that he is responsible for her nephew's murder? Could she? Will she take the easy way out and choose Andrew instead?

6: Dark Enemy Redeemed

Amanda suspects that something fishy is going on onboard the Anna. But when her investigation of the peculiar all-female Russian crew fails to uncover anything other than more speculation, she decides it's time to stop playing detective and face her real problem —a man she shouldn't want but can't live without.

6.5: My Dark Amazon

When Michael and Kri fight off a gang of humans, Michael gets stabbed. The injury to his immortal body recovers fast, but the one to his ego takes longer, putting a strain on his relationship with Kri.

7: Dark Warrior Mine

When Andrew is forced to retire from active duty, he believes that all he has to look forward to is a boring desk job. His glory days in special ops are over. But as it turns out, his thrill ride has just begun. Andrew discovers not only that immortals exist and have been manipulating global affairs since antiquity, but that he and his sister are rare possessors of the immortal genes.

Problem is, Andrew might be too old to attempt the activation process. His sister, who is fourteen years his junior, barely made it through the transition, so the odds of him coming out of it alive, let alone immortal, are slim.

But fate may force his hand.

Helping a friend find his long-lost daughter, Andrew finds a woman who's worth taking the risk for. Nathalie might be a Dormant, but the only way to find out for sure requires fangs and venom.

8: Dark Warrior's Promise

Andrew and Nathalie's love flourishes, but the secrets they keep from each other taint their relationship with doubts and suspicions. In the meantime, Sebastian and his men are getting bolder, and the storm that's brewing will shift the balance of power in the millennia-old conflict between Annani's clan and its enemies.

9: Dark Warrior's Destiny

The new ghost in Nathalie's head remembers who he was in life, providing Andrew and her with indisputable proof that he is real and not a figment of her imagination.

Convinced that she is a Dormant, Andrew decides to go forward with his transition immediately after the rescue mission at the Doomers' HQ.

Fearing for his life, Nathalie pleads with him to reconsider. She'd rather spend the rest of her mortal days with Andrew than risk what they have for the fickle promise of immortality.

While the clan gets ready for battle, Carol gets help from an unlikely ally. Sebastian's second-in-command can no longer ignore the torment she suffers at the hands of his commander and offers to help her, but only if she agrees to his terms.

10: Dark Warrior's Legacy

Andrew's acclimation to his post-transition body isn't easy. His senses are sharper, he's bigger, stronger, and hungrier. Nathalie fears that the changes in the man she loves are more than physical. Measuring up to this new version of him is going to be a challenge.

Carol and Robert are disillusioned with each other. They are not destined mates, and love is not on the horizon. When Robert's three months are up, he might be left with nothing to show for his sacrifice.

Lana contacts Anandur with disturbing news; the yacht and its human cargo are in Mexico. Kian must find a way to apprehend Alex and rescue the women on board without causing an international incident.

11: Dark Guardian Found

What would you do if you stopped aging?

Eva runs. The ex-DEA agent doesn't know what caused her strange mutation, only that if discovered, she'll be dissected like a lab rat. What Eva doesn't know, though, is that she's a descendant of the gods, and that she is not alone. The man who rocked her world in one life-changing encounter over thirty years ago is an immortal as well.

To keep his people's existence secret, Bhathian was forced to turn his back on the only woman who ever captured his heart, but he's never forgotten and never stopped looking for her.

12: Dark Guardian Craved

Cautious after a lifetime of disappointments, Eva is mistrustful of Bhathian's professed feelings of love. She accepts him as a lover and a confidant but not as a life partner.

Jackson suspects that Tessa is his true love mate, but unless she overcomes her fears, he might never find out.

Carol gets an offer she can't refuse—a chance to prove that there is more to her than meets the eye. Robert believes she's about to commit a deadly mistake, but when he tries to dissuade her, she tells him to leave.

13: Dark Guardian's Mate

Prepare for the heart-warming culmination of Eva and Bhathian's story!

14: Dark Angel's Obsession

The cold and stoic warrior is an enigma even to those closest to him. His secrets are about to unravel...

15: Dark Angel's Seduction

Brundar is fighting a losing battle. Calypso is slowly chipping away his icy armor from the outside, while his need for her is melting it from the inside.

He can't allow it to happen. Calypso is a human with none of the Dormant indicators. There is no way he can keep her for more than a few weeks.

16: Dark Angel's Surrender

Get ready for the heart pounding conclusion to Brundar and Calypso's story.

Callie still couldn't wrap her head around it, nor could she summon even a smidgen of sorrow or regret. After all, she had some memories with him that weren't horrible. She should've felt something. But there was nothing, not even shock. Not even horror at what had transpired over the last couple of hours.

Maybe it was a typical response for survivors--feeling euphoric for the simple reason that they were alive. Especially when that survival was nothing short of miraculous.

Brundar's cold hand closed around hers, reminding her that they weren't out of the woods yet. Her injuries were superficial, and the most she had to worry about was some scarring. But, despite his and Anandur's reassurances, Brundar might never walk again.

If he ended up crippled because of her, she would never forgive herself for getting him involved in her crap.

"Are you okay, sweetling? Are you in pain?" Brundar asked.

Her injuries were nothing compared to his, and yet he was concerned about her. God, she loved this man. The thing was, if she told him that, he would run off, or crawl away as was the case.

Hey, maybe this was the perfect opportunity to spring it on him.

17: Dark Operative: A Shadow of Death

As a brilliant strategist and the only human entrusted with the secret of immortals' existence, Turner is both an asset and a liability to the clan. His request to attempt transition into immortality as an alternative to cancer treatments cannot be denied without risking the clan's exposure. On the other hand, approving it means risking his premature death. In both scenarios, the clan will lose a valuable ally.

When the decision is left to the clan's physician, Turner makes plans to manipulate her by taking advantage of her interest in him.

Will Bridget fall for the cold, calculated operative? Or will Turner fall into his own trap?

18: Dark Operative: A Glimmer of Hope

As Turner and Bridget's relationship deepens, living together seems like the right move, but to make it work both need to make concessions.

Bridget is realistic and keeps her expectations low. Turner could never be the truelove mate she yearns for, but he is as good as she's going to get. Other than his emotional limitations, he's perfect in every way.

Turner's hard shell is starting to show cracks. He wants immortality, he wants to be part of the clan, and he wants Bridget, but he doesn't want to cause her pain.

His options are either abandon his quest for immortality and give Bridget his few remaining decades, or abandon Bridget by going for the transition and most likely dying. His rational mind dictates that he chooses the former, but his gut pulls him toward the latter. Which one is he going to trust?

19: Dark Operative: The Dawn of Love

Get ready for the exciting finale of Bridget and Turner's story!

20: Dark Survivor Awakened

This was a strange new world she had awakened to.

Her memory loss must have been catastrophic because almost nothing was familiar. The language was foreign to her, with only a few words bearing some similarity to the language she thought in. Still, a full moon cycle had passed since her awakening, and little by little she was gaining basic understanding of it--only a few words and phrases, but she was learning more each day.

A week or so ago, a little girl on the street had tugged on her mother's sleeve and pointed at her. "Look, Mama, Wonder Woman!"

The mother smiled apologetically, saying something in the language these people spoke, then scurried away with the child looking behind her shoulder and grinning.

When it happened again with another child on the same day, it was settled.

Wonder Woman must have been the name of someone important in this strange world she had awoken to, and since both times it had been said with a smile it must have been a good one.

Wonder had a nice ring to it.

She just wished she knew what it meant.

21: Dark Survivor Echoes of Love

Wonder's journey continues in *Dark Survivor Echoes of Love*.

22: Dark Survivor Reunited

The exciting finale of Wonder and Anandur's story.

23: Dark Widow's Secret

Vivian and her daughter share a powerful telepathic connection, so when Ella can't be reached by conventional or psychic means, her mother fears the worst.

Help arrives from an unexpected source when Vivian gets a call from the young doctor she met at a psychic convention. Turns out Julian belongs to a private organization specializing in retrieving missing girls.

As Julian's clan mobilizes its considerable resources to rescue the daughter, Magnus is charged with keeping the gorgeous young mother safe.

Worry for Ella and the secrets Vivian and Magnus keep from each other should be enough to prevent the sparks of attraction from kindling a blaze of desire. Except, these pesky sparks have a mind of their own.

24: Dark Widow's Curse

A simple rescue operation turns into mission impossible when the Russian mafia gets involved. Bad things are supposed to come in threes, but in Vivian's case, it seems like there is no limit to bad luck. Her family and everyone who gets close to her is affected by her curse.

Will Magnus and his people prove her wrong?

25: Dark Widow's Blessing
The thrilling finale of the Dark Widow trilogy!

26: Dark Dream's Temptation
Julian has known Ella is the one for him from the moment he saw her picture, but when he finally frees her from captivity, she seems indifferent to him. Could he have been mistaken?

Ella's rescue should've ended that chapter in her life, but it seems like the road back to normalcy has just begun and it's full of obstacles. Between the pitying looks she gets and her mother's attempts to get her into therapy, Ella feels like she's typecast as a victim, when nothing could be further from the truth. She's a tough survivor, and she's going to prove it.

Strangely, the only one who seems to understand is Logan, who keeps popping up in her dreams. But then, he's a figment of her imagination—or is he?

27: Dark Dream's Unraveling
While trying to figure out a way around Logan's silencing compulsion, Ella concocts an ambitious plan. What if instead of trying to keep him out of her dreams, she could pretend to like him and lure him into a trap?

Catching Navuh's son would be a major boon for the clan, as well as for Ella. She will have her revenge, turning the tables on another scumbag out to get her.

28: Dark Dream's Trap
The trap is set, but who is the hunter and who is the prey? Find out in this heart-pounding conclusion to the *Dark Dream* trilogy.

29: Dark Prince's Enigma
As the son of the most dangerous male on the planet, Lokan lives by three rules:

Don't trust a soul.

Don't show emotions.

And don't get attached.

Will one extraordinary woman make him break all three?

30: Dark Prince's Dilemma
Will Kian decide that the benefits of trusting Lokan outweigh the risks?

Will Lokan betray his father and brothers for the greater good of his people?

Are Carol and Lokan true-love mates, or is one of them playing the other?

So many questions, the path ahead is anything but clear.

31: Dark Prince's Agenda
While Turner and Kian work out the details of Areana's rescue plan, Carol and Lokan's tumultuous relationship hits another snag. Is it a sign of things to come?

32 : Dark Queen's Quest
A former beauty queen, a retired undercover agent, and a successful model, Mey is not the typical damsel in distress. But when her sister drops off the radar and then someone starts following her around, she panics.

Following a vague clue that Kalugal might be in New York, Kian sends a team headed by Yamanu to search for him.

As Mey and Yamanu's paths cross, he offers her his help and protection, but will that be all?

33: Dark Queen's Knight

As the only member of his clan with a godlike power over human minds, Yamanu has been shielding his people for centuries, but that power comes at a steep price. When Mey enters his life, he's faced with the most difficult choice.

The safety of his clan or a future with his fated mate.

34: Dark Queen's Army

As Mey anxiously waits for her transition to begin and for Yamanu to test whether his godlike powers are gone, the clan sets out to solve two mysteries:

Where is Jin, and is she there voluntarily?

Where is Kalugal, and what is he up to?

35: Dark Spy Conscripted

Jin possesses a unique paranormal ability. Just by touching someone, she can insert a mental hook into their psyche and tie a string of her consciousness to it, creating a tether. That doesn't make her a spy, though, not unless her talent is discovered by those seeking to exploit it.

36: Dark Spy's Mission

Jin's first spying mission is supposed to be easy. Walk into the club, touch Kalugal to tether her consciousness to him, and walk out.

Except, they should have known better.

37: Dark Spy's Resolution

The best-laid plans often go awry...

38: Dark Overlord New Horizon

Jacki has two talents that set her apart from the rest of the human race.

She has unpredictable glimpses of other people's futures, and she is immune to mind manipulation.

Unfortunately, both talents are pretty useless for finding a job other than the one she had in the government's paranormal division.

It seemed like a sweet deal, until she found out that the director planned on producing super babies by compelling the recruits into pairing up. When an opportunity to escape the program presented itself, she took it, only to find out that humans are not at the top of the food chain.

Immortals are real, and at the very top of the hierarchy is Kalugal, the most powerful, arrogant, and sexiest male she has ever met.

With one look, he sets her blood on fire, but Jacki is not a fool. A man like him will never think of her as anything more than a tasty snack, while she will never settle for anything less than his heart.

39: Dark Overlord's Wife

Jacki is still clinging to her all-or-nothing policy, but Kalugal is chipping away at her resistance. Perhaps it's time to ease up on her convictions. A little less than all is still much better than nothing, and a couple of decades with a demigod is probably worth more than a lifetime with a mere mortal.

40: Dark Overlord's Clan

As Jacki and Kalugal prepare to celebrate their union, Kian takes every precaution to safeguard his people. Except, Kalugal and his men are not his only potential adversaries, and compulsion is not the only power he should fear.

41: Dark Choices The Quandary

When Rufsur and Edna meet, the attraction is as unexpected as it is undeniable. Except, she's the clan's judge and councilwoman, and he's Kalugal's second-in-command. Will loyalty and duty to their people keep them apart?

42: Dark Choices Paradigm Shift

Edna and Rufsur are miserable without each other, and their two-week separation seems like an eternity. Long-distance relationships are difficult, but for immortal couples they are impossible. Unless one of them is willing to leave everything behind for the other, things are just going to get worse. Except, the cost of compromise is far greater than giving up their comfortable lives and hard-earned positions. The future of their people is on the line.

43: Dark Choices The Accord

The winds of change blowing over the village demand hard choices. For better or worse, Kian's decisions will alter the trajectory of the clan's future, and he is not ready to take the plunge. But as Edna and Rufsur's plight gains widespread support, his resistance slowly begins to erode.

44: Dark Secrets Resurgence

On a sabbatical from his Stanford teaching position, Professor David Levinson finally has time to write the sci-fi novel he's been thinking about for years.

The phenomena of past life memories and near-death experiences are too controversial to include in his formal psychiatric research, while fiction is the perfect outlet for his esoteric ideas.

Hoping that a change of pace will provide the inspiration he needs, David accepts a friend's invitation to an old Scottish castle.

45: Dark Secrets Unveiled

When Professor David Levinson accepts a friend's invitation to an old Scottish castle, what he finds there is more fantastical than his most outlandish theories. The castle is home to a clan of immortals, their leader is a stunning demigoddess, and even more shockingly, it might be precisely where he belongs.

Except, the clan founder is hiding a secret that might cast a dark shadow on David's relationship with her daughter.

Nevertheless, when offered a chance at immortality, he agrees to undergo the dangerous induction process.

Will David survive his transition into immortality? And if he does, will his relationship with Sari survive the unveiling of her mother's secret?

46: Dark Secrets Absolved

Absolution.

David had given and received it.

The few short hours since he'd emerged from the coma had felt incredible. He'd finally been free of the guilt and pain, and for the first time since Jonah's death, he had felt truly happy and optimistic about the future.

He'd survived the transition into immortality, had been accepted into the clan, and was about to marry the best woman on the face of the planet, his true love mate, his salvation, his everything.

What could have possibly gone wrong?

Just about everything.

47: Dark Haven Illusion

Welcome to Safe Haven, where not everything is what it seems.

On a quest to process personal pain, Anastasia joins the Safe Haven Spiritual Retreat.

Through meditation, self-reflection, and hard work, she hopes to make peace with the voices in her head.

This is where she belongs.

Except, membership comes with a hefty price, doubts are sacrilege, and leaving is not as easy as walking out the front gate.

Is living in utopia worth the sacrifice?

Anastasia believes so until the arrival of a new acolyte changes everything.

Apparently, the gods of old were not a myth, their immortal descendants share the planet with humans, and she might be a carrier of their genes.

48: Dark Haven Unmasked

As Anastasia leaves Safe Haven for a week-long romantic vacation with Leon, she hopes to explore her newly discovered passionate side, their budding relationship, and perhaps also solve the mystery of the voices in her head. What she discovers exceeds her wildest expectations.

In the meantime, Eleanor and Peter hope to solve another mystery. Who is Emmett Haderech, and what is he up to?

For a **FREE** Audiobook, Preview chapters, And other goodies offered only to my **VIP**s,

JOIN THE VIP CLUB AT ITLUCAS.COM

TRY THE SERIES ON

AUDIBLE

2 FREE audiobooks with your new Audible subscription!

THE PERFECT MATCH SERIES

Perfect Match 1: Vampire's Consort

When Gabriel's company is ready to start beta testing, he invites his old crush to inspect its medical safety protocol.

Curious about the revolutionary technology of the *Perfect Match Virtual Fantasy-Fulfillment studios*, Brenna agrees.

Neither expects to end up partnering for its first fully immersive test run.

Perfect Match 2: King's Chosen

When Lisa's nutty friends get her a gift certificate to *Perfect Match Virtual Fantasy Studios*, she has no intentions of using it. But since the only way to get a refund is if no partner can be found for her, she makes sure to request a fantasy so girly and over the top that no sane guy will pick it up.

Except, someone does.

Warning: This fantasy contains a hot, domineering crown prince, sweet insta-love, steamy love scenes painted with light shades of gray, a wedding, and a HEA in both the virtual and real worlds.

Intended for mature audience.

Perfect Match 3: Captain's Conquest

Working as a Starbucks barista, Alicia fends off flirting all day long, but none of the guys are as charming and sexy as Gregg. His frequent visits are the highlight of her day, but since he's never asked her out, she assumes he's taken. Besides, between a day job and a budding music career, she has no time to start a new relationship.

That is until Gregg makes her an offer she can't refuse—a gift certificate to the virtual fantasy fulfillment service everyone is talking about. As a huge Star Trek fan, Alicia has a perfect match in mind—the captain of the Starship Enterprise.

Also by I. T. Lucas

THE CHILDREN OF THE GODS ORIGINS
1: GODDESS'S CHOICE
2: GODDESS'S HOPE

THE CHILDREN OF THE GODS

DARK STRANGER
1: DARK STRANGER THE DREAM
2: DARK STRANGER REVEALED
3: DARK STRANGER IMMORTAL

DARK ENEMY
4: DARK ENEMY TAKEN
5: DARK ENEMY CAPTIVE
6: DARK ENEMY REDEEMED

KRI & MICHAEL'S STORY
6.5: MY DARK AMAZON

DARK WARRIOR
7: DARK WARRIOR MINE
8: DARK WARRIOR'S PROMISE
9: DARK WARRIOR'S DESTINY
10: DARK WARRIOR'S LEGACY

DARK GUARDIAN
11: DARK GUARDIAN FOUND
12: DARK GUARDIAN CRAVED
13: DARK GUARDIAN'S MATE

DARK ANGEL
14: DARK ANGEL'S OBSESSION
15: DARK ANGEL'S SEDUCTION
16: DARK ANGEL'S SURRENDER

DARK OPERATIVE
17: DARK OPERATIVE: A SHADOW OF DEATH
18: DARK OPERATIVE: A GLIMMER OF HOPE
19: DARK OPERATIVE: THE DAWN OF LOVE

DARK SURVIVOR
20: DARK SURVIVOR AWAKENED
21: DARK SURVIVOR ECHOES OF LOVE
22: DARK SURVIVOR REUNITED

DARK WIDOW
23: DARK WIDOW'S SECRET
24: DARK WIDOW'S CURSE
25: DARK WIDOW'S BLESSING

DARK DREAM
26: DARK DREAM'S TEMPTATION
27: DARK DREAM'S UNRAVELING
28: DARK DREAM'S TRAP

DARK PRINCE
29: DARK PRINCE'S ENIGMA

ALSO BY I. T. LUCAS

30: Dark Prince's Dilemma
31: Dark Prince's Agenda
Dark Queen
32: Dark Queen's Quest
33: Dark Queen's Knight
34: Dark Queen's Army
Dark Spy
35: Dark Spy Conscripted
36: Dark Spy's Mission
37: Dark Spy's Resolution
Dark Overlord
38: Dark Overlord New Horizon
39: Dark Overlord's Wife
40: Dark Overlord's Clan
Dark Choices
41: Dark Choices The Quandary
42: Dark Choices Paradigm Shift
43: Dark Choices The Accord
Dark Secrets
44: Dark Secrets Resurgence
45: Dark Secrets Unveiled
46: Dark Secrets Absolved
Dark Haven
47: Dark haven Illusion
48: Dark Haven Unmasked

PERFECT MATCH
Perfect Match 1: Vampire's Consort
Perfect Match 2: King's Chosen
Perfect Match 3: Captain's Conquest

The Children of the Gods Series Sets

Books 1-3: Dark Stranger trilogy—Includes a bonus short story: The Fates take a Vacation
　Books 4-6: Dark Enemy Trilogy —Includes a bonus short story —The Fates' Post-Wedding Celebration
　Books 7-10: Dark Warrior Tetralogy
　Books 11-13: Dark Guardian Trilogy
　Books 14-16: Dark Angel Trilogy
　Books 17-19: Dark Operative Trilogy
　Books 20-22: Dark Survivor Trilogy
　Books 23-25: Dark Widow Trilogy
　Books 26-28: Dark Dream Trilogy

ALSO BY I. T. LUCAS

Books 29-31: Dark Prince Trilogy
Books 32-34: Dark Queen Trilogy
Books 35-37: Dark Spy Trilogy
Books 38-40: Dark Overlord Trilogy
Books 41-43: Dark Choices Trilogy
Books 44-46: Dark Secrets Trilogy

MEGA SETS

The Children of the Gods: Books 1-6—includes character lists

The Children of the Gods: Books 6.5-10—includes character lists

**TRY THE CHILDREN OF THE GODS SERIES ON
AUDIBLE**
2 FREE audiobooks with your new Audible subscription!

FOR EXCLUSIVE PEEKS AT UPCOMING RELEASES & A FREE COMPANION BOOK

Join my *VIP Club* and gain access to the VIP portal at itlucas.com
CLICK HERE TO JOIN
(http://eepurl.com/blMTpD)

INCLUDED IN YOUR FREE MEMBERSHIP:

- FREE Children of the Gods companion book 1
- FREE narration of Goddess's Choice—Book 1 in The Children of the Gods Origins series.
- Preview chapters of upcoming releases.
- And other exclusive content offered only to my VIPs.

If you're already a subscriber, you can find **your VIP password** at the bottom of each of my new release emails. If you are not getting them, your email provider is sending them to your junk folder, and you are missing out on **important updates, side characters' portraits, additional content, and other goodies.** To fix that, add isabell@itlucas.com to your email contacts or to your email VIP list.

Printed in Great Britain
by Amazon